I0772347

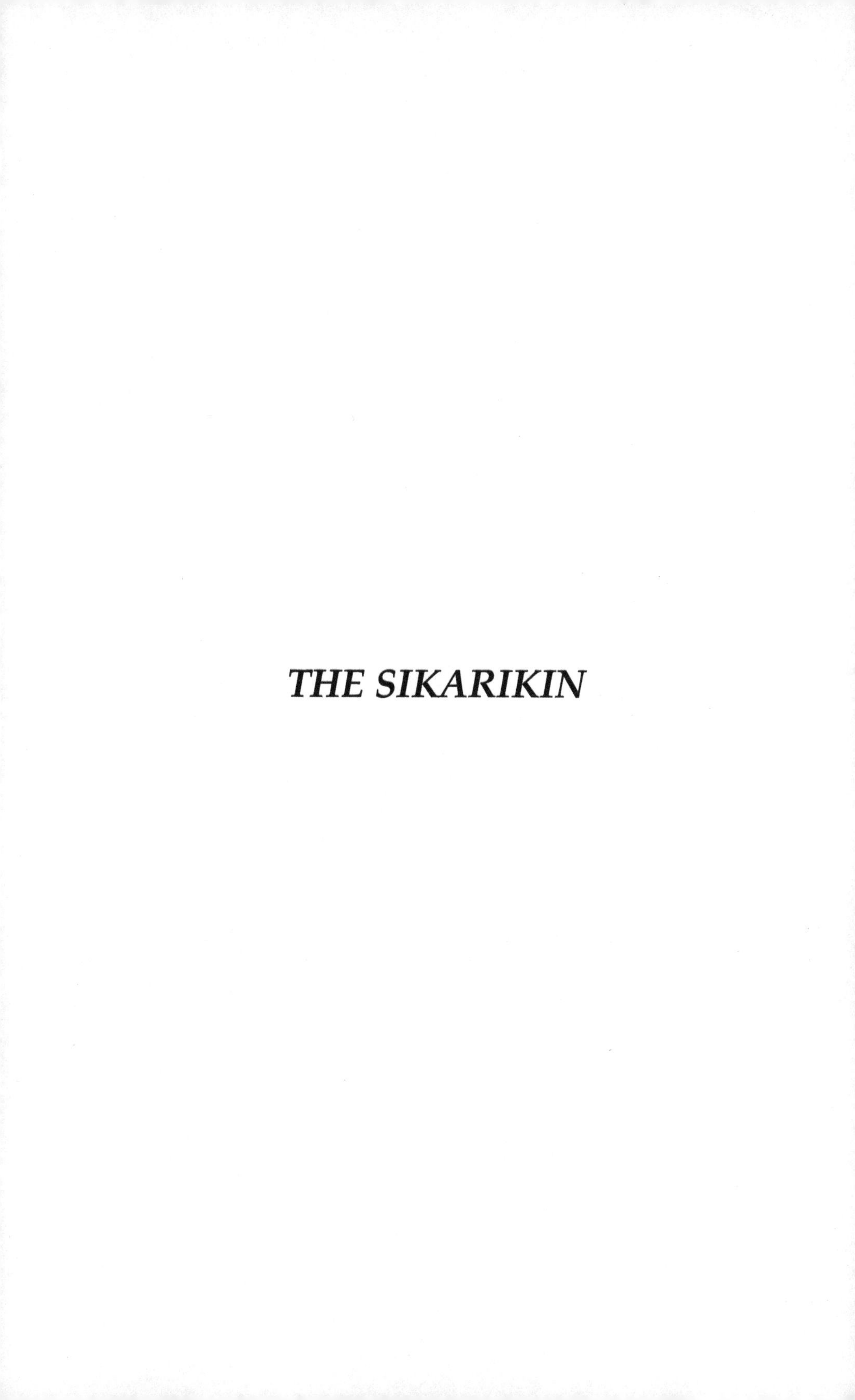

THE SIKARIKIN

The Sikarikin

Fight for Freedom or Road to Destruction?

Harry Steven Lazerus

A Copan Books Publication
ISBN: 979-8-9911463-3-3
The Sikarikin

Copyright 2023 by Harry Steven Lazerus
All Rights Reserved
Cover concept by the author
Cover by Shadab Shadman

Acknowledgements

I would like to thank Lee Slonimsky, the author of *Pythagoras in Love*, for his advice and encouragement throughout the years, and in particular, for reading the manuscript and making numerous corrections and suggestions.

Contents

Then and Now

"… another type of bandit sprang up in Jerusalem, known as 'Sicarii'.

These men committed numerous murders in broad daylight and in the middle of the City. Their favourite trick was to mingle with festival crowds, concealing under their garments small daggers with which they stabbed their opponents. When their victims fell, the assassins melted into the indignant crowd, and through their plausibility entirely defied detection. The first to have his throat cut by them was Jonathan the high priest…"

The Jewish War by Josephus translated by G. A. Williamson. Page 153 (Barnes and Noble NOOK version of the Penguin Books edition)

"It was not surprising that…suspicion for the murder of Arlosoroff fell on this group. Achimeir…had written an ideological pamphlet for his group (*Megilat Hasikarikin*) which maintained that the judgment of a political crime was a subjective affair. Referring to the actions of the *Sikarikin* (a radical sect during the Jewish war against the Romans who… kill[ed] their political enemies during mass meetings…)…The *Sikarikin* as he described them were unknown heroes who chose as victims central figures of the established order. They were not murderers, since they were not out for personal gain. What mattered was not the action itself but the purpose behind it."

The History of Zionism by Walter Laqueur Page 362

Dramatis Personae (in order of appearance)

Judah ben Ezra: Former bandit in the Galilee, now a revolutionary leader in Jerusalem agitating for war with Rome.

Shaul ben Yitzchak: A follower of Judah ben Ezra.

Reuven: Rabbi Aaron's younger son.

Rabbi Aaron ben Avraham: Brother of Rabbi Moshe ben Avraham, member of the Peace Party. A brilliant scholar.

Rabbi Moshe ben Avraham: One of the leaders of the Peace Party. A brilliant speaker.

Eleazar ben Ananias: Captain of the Temple ministers, son of the high priest, a member of the War Party.

Rabbi Hania ben Avel-Mayim: Reluctant member of the War Party.

Rabbi Zechariah ben Abkulas: Member of the War Party who provides religious justification for the war.

Ananias: High priest, member of the Peace Party, father of Eleazar ben Ananias.

Bruria: Wife of Rabbi Moshe ben Avraham.

Metilius: Roman commander of the garrison stationed in Antonia fortress.

Benjamin: Rabbi Aaron's older son.

Ruth: Wife of Rabbi Aaron.

John ben Dorcas: A member of Judah ben Ezra's group. A cut-throat.

Drusilla: Metilius' servant girl from north of Italy.

Ananus ben Ananus: High-ranking priest with an important role in strengthening Jerusalem's defenses.

Amram ben Gedalyahu: Guide.

Albus: Roman soldier in Gamla, fortress town in the Golan.

Gnaeus: Roman soldier in Gamla, fortress town in the Golan.

Dvorah: Girl in Gamla; engaged to Shaul ben Yitzchak.

&

Jerusalem: Capital City of the Jews.

Gamla: Mountain town in the Golan holding out against Rome.

Book I: The Lamb Shakes Off the Eagle?

"Ha-Shem is my shepherd…through the valley of the Shadow of
Death"
Tehilim #23

"The eagle… the head of every legion... king of birds… most
fearless of all"
The Jewish War by Flavius Josephus, G. A. Williamson translation.

Part One: Assassination, Rebellion, Massacre

June – October 66 CE

Chapter One

12 Jun 66 CE / 1 Tammuz 3826

Judah ben Ezra's right hand drew closer and closer to the haft of his knife as he stalked his prey. His body pressed against the jumble of rough two-story gray stone houses that lined the narrow street of the Lower City of Jerusalem. Across that street, a tall young man, Shaul ben Yitzchak, matched Judah's motion.

Two Syrian auxiliaries, soldiers of the procurator Florus, their faces shaved like their Roman overlords, marched down the middle of the street. Each held tightly the arm of the man in the middle. Yosef ben Mavet, a wealthy Jewish businessman, walked reluctantly, his black and white beard stained red by the blood running down his forehead from the cut just above his left eye.

Yosef's only crime was having money that Florus could extort. And while Judah hated the rich of Jerusalem, he hated the occupying Romans more. Besides the satisfaction of striking at Roman power, freeing Yosef was a moral obligation. The merchant had been paying Judah and his band for protection, though Judah had never made clear if the protection was from Romans or Judah himself.

Now it was simply a matter of picking the right moment to strike.

And then Judah saw something that made the hair on his arms

stand up.

A young boy, no older than 14, stepped into the middle of the street, as if to block the soldiers and their captive. The boy challenged the soldiers, calling out, in a strong voice:

"Why have you arrested this man?"

The procession stopped. The Syrian on the left released Yosef and strode toward the boy. He glared down at the youth, who did not flinch. Without saying a word, the soldier raised his right arm and struck the lad on the side of head, sending him flying to the ground.

Judah saw the Syrian raise his sandaled foot above the boy's head. As the foot came down the youth rolled out of its way. The foot stamped on the ground and raised again.

Judah could see the look of terror on the boy's face.

Before the Syrian could bring his foot down once more Judah leaped into action, followed by Shaul. Judah was on the Syrian who had struck the boy, Shaul upon the other. Blades flashed in the sunlight, slashing the throats of the auxiliaries.

As they lay dying, writhing on the street, Judah helped the stunned boy to his feet.

"That was a brave thing you did," Judah said. "You'll make a fine revolutionary one day. Now run along home."

The boy did not move. He stared at Judah, transfixed.

Judah smiled. There was a gap in his front teeth. He had a wild beard and intense dark eyes.

The boy's eyes widened. He remained transfixed.

Does he know who I am? Judah wondered.

"I said run along home," Judah repeated, gently, but firmly. "We have to remove the bodies."

"Thank you," the boy whispered, in a tiny voice, a sharp contrast to the one that challenged the auxiliaries of the Roman procurator.

Then the boy turned and ran. Yosef ben Mavet had already fled and was nowhere to be seen.

Chapter Two

12 Jun 66 CE / 1 Tammuz 3826

Two men, deep in conversation, sat on low wooden benches at a rough-hewn wooden table. An oil lamp threw a shaky light over the room and dancing shadows on the bare walls. Fourteen-year-old Reuven ben Aaron was waiting until his father, Rabbi Aaron ben Avraham, and uncle, Rabbi Moshe ben Avraham, noticed him.

"You must continue speaking," Aaron urged his brother. "We must also get the people on our side."

Moshe sighed.

"I don't think the high priest Ananias is strong enough to resist if the Eighteen Decrees are passed," he said, shaking his head. "It will lead to war with Rome."

"That's just what the revolutionaries want, to start a war. The fools think we can win. That is why you must continue giving speeches," Aaron insisted.

"What are the Eighteen Decrees?" Reuven blurted out, his patience exhausted.

Both men turned toward Reuven.

"There is a minority of rabbis who support the revolutionaries," Reuven's uncle Moshe said gently. "They want to call a rabbinical council to pass decrees that will keep us separate from the Gentiles around us. We'll be forbidden their food, their gifts..." Moshe fell silent.

"Why will that start a war with Rome?" Reuven asked.

"If those decrees are passed," Moshe sighed, "the priests in charge of the Temple will have to refuse the Roman emperor's offering. It will be a grave insult; who knows how Nero will react? He's a madman."

"You said those rabbis were in the minority. How can they pass any decrees?" Reuven insisted.

"There's no telling what those rabbis and their revolutionary friends will do to get them passed, what kind of skullduggery they will engage in," Reuven's father, Aaron, explained. Then, his voice harsh and demanding, "What happened to you? There's blood on your face."

Reuven felt his cheek. In the excitement of what happened he didn't realize the Syrian's blow had cut his face.

Reuven hung his head sheepishly.

"I saw two Syrians had arrested Yosef ben Mavet. I demanded to know why they arrested him."

"You demanded, you demanded?" Aaron exploded. "Are you crazy? They could have killed you!"

Reuven shrugged.

"What happened then?" Moshe asked gently.

"One of the Syrians knocked me down and tried to stomp on my face."

"I'm surprised they didn't kill you!" shouted Aaron. "Blessed be the Name of the Lord; you are still alive."

"They probably would have killed me, if someone hadn't killed them instead," Reuven said.

"Who?" father and uncle cried out in unison.

Reuven hung his head again.

"Judah ben Ezra."

Both men gasped.

"That brigand!"

Reuven wasn't sure which one said that now, but he had heard his father and uncle describe Judah ben Ezra that way many times before.

"That's what you both say about him, but he saved my life," Reuven said defiantly. "What's so terrible about him?"

Before Reuven's father could reply, his uncle, Moshe, said gently:

"Because, when he was in the north, he was a leader of a group of bandits that extorted money from rich townspeople. They killed Syrian and Roman soldiers. And then he fled here. He wants to start a war with Rome. He is, as Rabbi Johanan ben Zakkai described him, a robber. He is a dangerous man."

"Has he killed Jews?" Reuven asked.

"Not yet," his uncle replied. "Not yet, but he will, Reuven, he will."

"Don't even think about joining them," his father shouted, "or you will wind up killing Jews, also."

"I'll never kill another Jew," Reuven insisted.

"Oh, you will, you will son, if you join them. You will kill Jews before you kill Romans."

Reuven did not respond.

"I want you to promise me that you will have nothing to do with the revolutionaries," Rabbi Aaron demanded.

Reuven said nothing. He respected his father and uncle, he admired them, he loved them, but how could he promise when he himself was not sure of the best way of dealing with the Roman occupation.

"Reuven!" his father commanded. "Promise!"

Reuven would not lie. And he would not openly defy his father. He simply bowed his head, muttered something inaudible under his breath, and left the room before any of the adults could say anything.

Chapter Three

15 Jun 66 CE / 4 Tammuz 3826

Judah ben Ezra slowly opened the chipped and smoke-stained wooden door and stepped outside. His eyes went to the right and then to the left, closely examining the jumble of rough houses that clutched both edges of the narrow street in the Lower City of Jerusalem. Even the roofs did not escape his careful gaze. He did this inspection twice and then stepped back inside and closed the door.

"There are Roman spies everywhere," he said.

"Is it the Roman ones who worry you, or the Jewish ones?" Eleazar ben Ananias, captain of the Temple ministers asked, a half-smile on his face.

Judah smiled in return. There was a gap where one of his front teeth had been knocked out from a beating by a Syrian auxiliary. That gap, combined with his wild beard and intense dark eyes, made his grins more frightening than his glares.

That's the way he wanted it.

Fear was a great ally.

"You are correct, my friend," Judah responded.

Though he lived in the shadows, Judah's reputation was well-known. It took three years for Judah to pay back that Syrian auxiliary. On a bright sunny day, without a cloud in the sky, Judah had followed the Syrian into a narrow alley. Before the soldier could turn to see the presence sensed behind him, Judah had leaped on him, grasping his face with his left hand. With the knife in his right hand, Judah slit the Syrian auxiliary's throat.

Judah fled his home village in the north and hid out in the hills of Galilee and the Golan, gathering followers who made hit and run attacks on the occupation forces and enemy villages, until a Roman legion, sent to put a stop to his depredations, forced him to flee to Jerusalem.

"The Romans do what they do because that is what powerful nations have always done: Conquer weaker ones," Judah said. "Their Syrian allies do what they do because they hate us." He paused and added solemnly: "And as my grandfather taught us, we Jews should only do what is right in the eyes of God and bend the knee to no one but Him." Then Judah's voice became bitter as he concluded: "But a Jew who betrays another Jew for money is lower than the worms in the mud."

"Not all who oppose us do it for money!" exclaimed Rabbi Hania ben Avel-Mayim. "There is an honest difference of opinion among scholars."

To Judah's ears Rabbi Hania's voice was like the squeaking of a mouse. He didn't understand why Hania was even at this meeting, apart from the fact that it was his house. True, Hania was Rabbi Zechariah ben Abkulas' assistant, and Rabbi Zechariah provided the religious justification for the planned revolt, but why Rabbi Zechariah had chosen Hania was something Judah did not understand. Judah was about to respond when Eleazar spoke.

"You are wrong, Rabbi Hania," Eleazar said gently. "It is for the money and the houses and the food and the clothing and the status that they counsel submission. They have grown fat and comfortable under Roman rule and do not want to risk everything for freedom. Believe me, Rabbi Hania, I know."

Judah looked intently at Eleazar. The captain of the Temple ministers was dressed in fine clothes, unlike the shabby garments of everyone else in the room. Judah's gray cloak was threadbare, as was his tunic hanging below it, blue fringes fading. The belt holding his cloak was rough cotton, as was the not-quite white *cova* that draped his head. Judah could see that Eleazar was uncomfortable sitting on the simple chair in this plain house; he was used to more luxurious surroundings. Yet he was willing to risk everything for freedom! Though Judah hated men of Eleazar's class, he deeply admired the young Temple captain, son of the high priest. Eleazar was a true patriot!

Judah's admiration must have shown on his face, because Eleazar said:

"You are wrong, Judah. I risk nothing. My father, the high priest, and the other priests, and the appeasing rabbis who counsel patience, and the other men of wealth and status, they are all wrong. As long as we are not free their fine homes and good lives are not secure. They can bow to the Romans all they want, but their masters can take it away from us at any time. See what their procurator Albinus did to us. And now Florus is even worse. He steals openly from us, and even scourges Jews who are Roman citizens!"

"But one week is such a short time to issue these Eighteen Decrees! Can't we postpone the rabbinical assembly that is to decide on them?" Hania protested. "It will give us time to convince the others."

"No, Rabbi Hania. That extra time will not help us. Do you know who Demosthenes was?"

No one replied.

"He was a great Greek orator," Eleazar explained. "He lived in their city of Athens. Demosthenes roused his people to oppose the Macedonians who wanted to take over all the Greek cities. He was a small, puny man but he had a powerful voice and a skill with words that convinced leaders and common people alike."

Judah immediately grasped Eleazar's point.

"Like Rabbi Moshe ben Avraham!" Judah exclaimed. "He's a little slip of a man with the voice of a giant and a tongue of gold! Only Rabbi Moshe counsels surrender!"

"Yes," Eleazar said. "Rabbi Hania, if we wait too long Rabbi Moshe will turn the people against us."

"But we are in the minority!" Hania objected. "The vote will go against us if the assembly is in only a week!"

Judah laughed.

"It will not go against us," he said, pointing to Shaul ben Yitzchak, a tall, young man standing silently in the corner. Shaul held a short, thick wooden stave in his right hand. His face was expressionless. "Why even if it was just the two of us," Judah continued laughing, "we would be enough to silence the opposition and ensure their compliance. But there will be more there than just the two of us. There will be no problem from the Hillelites. If any one of them dare oppose us," he pointed to Shaul again, now striking the palm of his left hand harshly with the wood, "a few whacks will teach him silence."

"You! You!" Hania cried. "You and your gang have no right to be there! You are no Torah scholar. Why, even Eleazar does not have the right to be there!"

"Who's going to stop us? You?" Judah challenged.

"We don't do things that way!" Hania's exclamation was directed at Rabbi Zechariah, who was sitting next to him.

Rabbi Zechariah laid a hand lightly on Hania's shoulder. It was Rabbi Zechariah, one of the senior Torah scholars with the standing to do so, who had called for the rabbinical assembly to gather next week to decide on the Eighteen Decrees.

"Hania," he said softly. "If these were normal times I would agree with you. We could debate and vote on each decree, one by one. And the majority would determine which passed and which failed.

"But these are not normal times," Zechariah went on. "Even the judgment of the scholars is corrupted by what they receive from the Romans. No, these Eighteen Decrees are needed to restore Torah law and free the nation."

There was silence for a moment. Then Eleazar spoke again.

"Rabbi Zechariah, once they are passed I'll have a religious justification for refusing Nero's offer at the Temple."

"That will mean war with Rome!" Hania exploded.

Judah wanted to say, "Yes, you fool. That's the point. Now keep your mouth shut, you worm!" Instead, Judah said nothing. Zechariah would handle Hania.

But Hania was not finished.

"We cannot defeat Rome!" he cried. "They have the most powerful army in the world!"

"We defeated Antiochus," Rabbi Zechariah said calmly. "We will defeat the Romans. These Eighteen Decrees will restore Torah law to the nation and then God will defeat the Romans as He defeated all our enemies."

Zechariah turned to Eleazar.

"Will your father cause a problem?"

"No," Eleazar replied. "He's an old man now. He doesn't have the strength, neither he, nor his brother, nor the other senior priests. The daily sacrifices to Rome will stop once the decrees are issued."

"So it is decided," Judah said. "We'll leave now and go our separate ways."

Shaul followed Judah out. They had gone some distance when Eleazar rushed up to them, almost out of breath. Judah kept walking with Eleazar by his side, Shaul several steps behind them.

"I'm concerned about Hania," Eleazar puffed.

"I am, too," Judah agreed.

"It's clear he's not with us," Eleazar went on, his breathing returning to normal. "I'm afraid he may warn others, despite what Rabbi Zechariah will tell him. Hania may even go to Rabbi Moshe directly."

Judah stopped walking. His face became hard.

"You are right, Eleazar. Shaul and I will make sure Rabbi Hania understands that he is to keep silent."

And without waiting for Eleazar's reply he turned and signaled to Shaul to follow him as he ran back to Hania's house.

But Judah was too late. Rabbi Hania had already gone.

Chapter Four

16 Jun 66 CE / 5 Tammuz 3826

Judah ben Ezra glared down at the short, squat figure of Naomi, Rabbi Hania ben Avel-Mayim's wife.

"Where is Rabbi Hania?" Judah demanded.

"I told you I don't know!" the woman replied, trying to sound brave.

"You're lying!"

Just before dawn Judah and Shaul ben Yitzchak had burst into Rabbi Hania's house, rousing the startled Naomi from sleep. It was their fourth visit before finding someone home. Judah and Naomi stood in the center of the room. Shaul ben Yitzchak loomed in the doorway, blocking entrance or exit.

"What do you want with him?" Naomi asked, her voice starting to quiver.

"To warn him to keep his mouth shut and not go blabbing to people about things that are none of their business."

"Rabbi Hania is not a blabber!" Naomi protested, shaking her fist at Judah. "He's a very discreet man. He only says what is necessary!"

"Where is he?"

"I don't know," she replied firmly, looking straight into Judah's eyes.

"If I were one of Herod's men, or a Roman, I could make you talk!"

"Some freedom fighter," Naomi sneered. "Deep down you're a tyrant like them. Herod, that filthy pagan, and those uncircumcised Romans. Secretly you admire them. Those are your heroes, not Torah scholars like my husband!"

Judah was taken aback.

"No," he said sighing and shaking his head. "No, I don't want to be like them. I don't torture old women to get them to tell the truth." But the thought arose in his mind: *Their methods are effective.*

"I am telling the truth," Naomi insisted. "I don't know where he is. He never came home. I'm worried about him." A sob escaped her.

Judah's gaze probed the expression on her face. He gauged that she was telling the truth.

"You weren't home when we came looking for him. Where were you?"

"I was with my sister Rivka in the afternoon. She was watching her granddaughter. Rabbi Hania wasn't here when I got back. I prepared supper. When he didn't come home, I took his supper to his workshop. He wasn't there. I went looking for him at the market. I went to Rabbi Zechariah. No one had seen him. I started to worry. I went back home and he still hadn't returned. Now I was really worried. I went back to Rivka. Her husband Amos helped me look for him. We looked everywhere. By the time we gave up it was late. I went home to wait for him. He never came home.

"Oh!" she suddenly wailed, "I know something happened to him." A look of confusion crossed her faced, soon replaced by anger. Her small eyes narrowed as she pointed a finger at Judah. "You killed him! I know it! You killed him. You're only pretending to look for him!"

The accusation startled Judah.

"What? You're crazy." Judah regained his composure. "I kill Romans and Greeks and Syrians and the other Gentiles we have to share the Land with, and maybe even Jewish traitors, but I'd never kill a Torah scholar, not even a fool like your husband."

"Rabbi Hania is no fool!"

"For both your sakes I hope so. Tell your husband to keep his mouth shut about yesterday's meeting. To everyone, including you." He looked at Shaul.

"Let's go," he said.

Before he stepped out of Rabbi Hania's home he turned back to Naomi and made a warning gesture with his hand.

When the door closed Naomi collapsed, weeping.

"Oh, what have you done now, Hania?" she cried.

Chapter Five

16 Jun 66 CE / 5 Tammuz 3826

Rabbi Moshe ben Avraham firmly grasped Rabbi Hania ben Avel-Mayim's arm, trying to steady him as they walked. Despite all Moshe's efforts he could not calm the older rabbi. Hania kept repeating the same things over and over again, demanding the same reassurances.

"You did the right thing by coming to me," Moshe gently insisted. "You know that. What they are planning will lead to war. That's what they want. We can't win that war. You know that, too."

They were on the broad lanes of the Upper City, heading to the house of Ananias, father of Eleazar, captain of the Temple ministers. The mid-morning sun was bright, the blue sky was feathered with an occasional cloud. Moshe had sheltered Hania at his own home the previous night.

"I could have tried to convince Rabbi Zechariah!" Hania wailed. "I shouldn't have come to you!"

"Rabbi Hania, there is no way you could convince Rabbi Zechariah. He has been set on this course for a long time.

"And it's all right that you came to me even though you belong to the School of Shammai and I belong to the School of Hillel," Moshe went on. "Our Houses may disagree on some interpretations. We say a married woman in her monthly period of seclusion can adorn herself before she has gone to the ritual bath. You say no. We disagree under what conditions a husband can divorce his wife. But on the fundamentals of the Torah there are no divergences of opinion. This question of what to do about the Romans is political. The scholars of your House urge confrontation; those of mine accommodation, but even you, Rabbi Hania, see the folly of rebellion. And you know that the majority of the scholars are against a hopeless war."

"But I didn't try hard enough to convince Rabbi Zechariah!" Hania's voice had turned into a whine.

Moshe sighed. There was no way of reassuring Hania. Moshe was starting to wonder if bringing Hania along was the right thing to do. He could have reported Hania's information directly to Ananias. On the other hand, Ananias had the means to offer the shaken-up Hania protection.

Moshe saw from Hania's expression that despite his agitation he was reacting to the luxuriousness of the Upper City.

"Have you ever been here before, Rabbi Hania?"

Hania shook his head, confirming Moshe's suspicion.

"Yes, it is pretty fancy here," Moshe said. "I'm impressed every time I come. Wait until you see Ananias' home."

"It's strange that we're going to a Sadducee for help," Hania responded.

"Not at all. Ananias can't stop the Eighteen Decrees but he can make sure the Roman sacrifices still get accepted. If there is war, and especially if the extremists start it, it will be ugly and vicious. We won't just lose; the Romans will certainly burn the City and destroy the Temple. Ananias and the Sadducees will not only lose their lives; their whole vision of the Torah and the Law will disappear."

"We will *all* lose if the Temple is destroyed!" Hania exclaimed. "The whole Jewish nation will lose. It is the center of our worship."

Hania looked at Moshe with reproach.

"Even if the Temple is destroyed, we will still have the Torah," Moshe replied. He stopped walking. His face took on a rapturous glow, his gaze went far into the distance; he saw a world not yet born. "The Torah is the center of our religion. We will always have that, and the words of the sages, and the interpretations of the rabbis, with or without a physical temple."

Rabbi Moshe returned Rabbi Hania's reproachful look with one of certainty and determination.

"The Temple was destroyed once and rebuilt," Hania said, nodding his head up and down as he spoke. "It could be rebuilt again."

Moshe shrugged and resumed walking.

"Perhaps," he said, without any real feeling. Then, more brightly: "But why all these dark and gloomy thoughts? We are on our way to Ananias precisely to prevent this from happening!"

Moshe pointed to Ananias' home. Hania's eyes grew wide.

"It's not a house. It's a palace!" he said.

"You are right," Moshe agreed.

Two large brass doors swung slowly outward in response to Rabbi Moshe's knock. A servant, dressed in finer clothes than either rabbi was wearing, led them to a central courtyard that was surrounded by the four wings of the two-story house. One wing was an open walkway with marble columns that supported the second story. In the middle of the courtyard was a small pool with a fountain that gushed clear water. Fruit trees stood like heavily laden sentinels around the pool and its fountain. Brightly colored birds sang from a cage that was suspended from one of the trees.

Hania gasped at the sight.

The servant brought them to a stone table with an inlaid mosaic in the center. The mosaic depicted the courtyard with its pool and fountain and trees. The chairs were large and of polished wood. Both rabbis sat down. The servant left.

"Is this what they have in Rome?" Hania asked in amazement.

"I've never been outside the Land," Moshe replied. "I do not know."

The servant returned a few moments later with a tray carrying three glasses tinted green filled with cool water and a bowl of fresh figs. Then he retired for the last time.

Moshe and Hania waited in silence. They did not touch the water or the figs.

Ananias appeared wearing his ceremonial robes. Moshe saw scarlet and blue and deep green in the threads. He marveled at the workmanship and wondered about the cost.

Ananias nodded at Moshe and sat down at the table.

"I'm listening," Ananias said. His head was tilted slightly backwards as if his nose were in the air and he was looking down at them along his narrow cheekbones.

"Your son Eleazar is planning to refuse Nero's offering for the health and well-being of Rome."

Ananias raised his eyebrows and waved his right hand as if instructing Moshe to continue. But Moshe turned to his companion.

"Tell Ananias what you told me."

At first, trembling with nerves, Hania spoke in a shaky voice, but as his telling went on his delivery became stronger, especially when he related his own reactions to Judah ben Ezra's scheme.

When Hania finished Ananias let out a long sigh. It was clear from the expression on his face that he believed Hania.

"My son is hard to control," Ananias said sadly. "But I will not allow this to happen."

"I fear for Rabbi Hania's safety," Rabbi Moshe said. "It is clear that they are ready to use violence against their opponents."

"He can stay here, in my house. I have many guest rooms. He will be safe. No one will touch him."

"What about my wife? I'm worried about her!" Hania asked anxiously.

"They won't harm a woman," Moshe said. "They have not descended to that level." He wanted to add the word "yet" but thought better of it.

Ananias stroked his white beard. He seemed to be contemplating something.

"You have a metal workshop, don't you Rabbi Hania?"

Hania nodded.

"You won't be able to work. We will replace your income so your wife doesn't starve."

"I'm not doing this for money!" Hania said with heat.

"I know," Ananias said. "You're a patriot. You have saved your country from the madmen who would destroy it."

Ananias turned to Moshe.

"Will you be able to stop them from issuing the decrees?"

"If Judah and his men attend—against all protocol—there will not be an open discussion or a free vote. It is clear he plans to intimidate any opposition into silence and compliance. Therefore, I will not go. I will counsel my brother, and all the others, to stay away. Rabbi Zechariah does not have enough allies and students to issue decrees on their own. Without a majority of the Torah scholars any decree that they do issue will have no authority."

Ananias nodded and said:

"At any rate, the Romans don't care about decrees issued by rabbis. But they will care if we refuse their offerings. I will make sure that does not happen."

He brought his fist sharply down on the table.

Then he took a sip of water and a fig. The two rabbis followed suit.

Rabbi Moshe walked back to the Lower City alone. He was tired and troubled. Even if a set of decrees issued by a rump group of dissident rabbis had no religious authority, that hothead Eleazar could still use them as justification for refusing to accept Nero's offerings to the Temple. And despite Ananias' apparent confidence, Moshe had strong doubts about his ability to stop his son.

Moshe's house was not far from Hania's, and not any finer. Moshe sat down at the kitchen table. The weariness showed on his face.

"Where were you?" his wife, Bruria, demanded.

"I had business with Ananias."

"What business?"

"Not women's business."

"Humph!"

Moshe sighed.

"I'm tired, Bruria. Worn out. Could you please fix me some food? I'm hungry."

"I'm tired of living in a house not fit for a Syrian's pig," she said sharply. "That's what I'm tired of. Most of your rabbi friends live in nice houses in the Upper City. They have money and servants. What do I have? Nothing. Not even children."

"It's not my fault that you're barren, Bruria."

"Maybe if you were a real man, with ambition, you would be able to give me children," Bruria said spitefully.

Moshe covered his face with his hands.

"I could divorce you for being barren," he said dejectedly.

"Divorce me then! I can do better!"

Moshe looked at her.

She's beautiful, he thought, even with all her bitterness.

He did not want to divorce her, despite all her nagging, despite her giving him no children. He still desired her.

"Make me some food, Bruria. It will give me the strength to make love to you."

"Give me a nice house, decent clothes, and some money and I'll let you have me again."

There was a loud knock and the door flew open. Judah entered.

"What are you doing here?" Moshe demanded.

For a moment Judah said nothing. He stared at Bruria.

Then he looked at Moshe.

"Where is Rabbi Hania?"

"Get out of my house!"

"Where is Hania?"

"Are you threatening me?"

Judah looked around the house as if he were expecting to find Hania there, but his gaze kept going back to Bruria.

"You can't stop us, Moshe. We will be free. I will fulfill my grandfather's dream."

"I won't debate an ignorant cutthroat. Get out of my house or I will bring you up on charges."

"Just like a traitor to go to the Romans."

"I don't have to go to the Romans. We have our own courts. Do violence here and even Rabbi Zechariah and Eleazar will have nothing to do with you."

"I'll see you in Gehinom," Judah sneered.

"You will bring Gehinom from the world to come to this world. You will bring it on your own people. One day your name will be cursed along with the names of all our enemies."

"You won't stop us. Remember my words."

Before Judah left he gave one last glance at Bruria.

She was trembling. Moshe looked downcast but not frightened.

Bruria wanted to rush to him. She wanted to take him in her arms, tell him that he was better than all the others and deserved to live as well they did. She wanted to tell him that she believed in him, that she loved him, and then lead him to their marriage bed.

She could not. Her bitterness stopped her where she stood.

"I'm not hungry anymore," Moshe said. "Or filled with lust." He took a deep breath and looked at her long and intently. "Scripture tells us of a time when the living will envy the dead. Judah will soon bring that curse upon us."

Bruria shivered. Moshe's words frightened her more than Judah's threats.

Rabbi Moshe looked down at the table. Then got up and walked out of the house without saying a word.

Chapter Six

17 Jun 66 CE / 6 Tammuz 3826

Judah ben Ezra's arms stretched wide. His hands grasped a large gray dress of plain wool. Shaul ben Yitzchak stood expectantly in front of him. They were in the basement of the rundown house in the Lower City where Judah lodged.

"It wasn't easy getting this done so quickly," Judah said. "I had to guess your size. Here. Try it on."

"Did Rabbi Zechariah approve?" Shaul asked.

"I haven't told him yet. Try it on."

Shaul struggled to get the dress onto his large frame. It fit, badly.

"Hmm," Judah murmured. "You won't get any marriage proposals but it will do." He reached for a shawl resting on a nearby table. He wrapped it around his hair and the lower part of his face. "Like this," he said, and handed the cloth over to Shaul.

It took Shaul several attempts until Judah nodded approval.

"Let me see if you can keep your hands hidden in the sleeves," Judah said, and waited for Shaul to comply. "Good, very good. Just don't open your mouth and say anything!" And Judah laughed heartily after giving this admonishment.

Shaul did not smile.

"What if Rabbi Zechariah says no?" he asked.

"He won't."

"But if he does?"

"We go ahead anyway."

"Without rabbinical approval?"

Judah gave Shaul a long look. The incongruity between Shaul's appearance in the ill-fitting woman's clothing and what he wanted to say made Judah pause.

"Take those things off," he said to Shaul.

Judah waited until everything was folded and back on the table.

"Shaul, listen to me," Judah began, his tone serious. "There are times when you have to take history into your own hands and act decisively. There are times that call for an elite to step forward and push the course of events in the only direction they must go. In times of crisis, such as these, the common people are often wrong in their understanding. The rich are often wrong. Even the wise men can be wrong. We alone understand what is unfolding and that understanding gives us the responsibility to act. That is what we are going to do. That is what you are going to do.

"Do you understand, Shaul?" Judah concluded.

"Yes, Judah, I do."

"I know it's hard, Shaul. The mind rebels against it because of everything we've been taught. To stand alone—against family, friends, neighbors, leaders, the whole of society—to do what is right takes courage and strength. You will be cursed and reviled for it. You will be abandoned and isolated. But there will come a time, in the arc of history, when your brave and noble deed will be remembered, when it will be understood that you alone grasped the truth and had the strength and the courage to do what is needed; and though no one will know your name, your deed will be known and therefore you will be praised for eternity, not just here on earth but also in heaven. When you go out on your mission listen closely to that band of heavenly angels singing your praise."

"I will, Judah, I will. I promise."

"Good. Until then I want you to keep out of sight. I'm going to speak to Rabbi Zechariah."

Judah climbed the steps from the basement and walked out into the narrow alley. He walked briskly through streets and alleys of the Lower City, past the one and two-story cramped houses of the lower and working classes, past the occasional stalls selling bread and meat and fruit and wine, past other people—men, women, and children—none of whom had any idea of the great mission he was about to embark on, a mission that would change their lives forever.

Rabbi Zechariah's two-story house had a separate entrance for the large room that was used as a study hall. Rabbi Zechariah was lecturing to five students.

"I'm sorry to interrupt, Rabbi," Judah said as soon as he entered, "but I must speak to you immediately. We have a problem."

Rabbi Zechariah ushered out his students, each giving Judah many curious glances as he left. When the last had gone, before Judah could say anything, Zechariah spoke:

"I haven't seen Rabbi Hania for two days. He's vanished." His voice was heavy with what sounded to Judah like a feeling of betrayal.

"There is a rumor he's gone to Ananias," Judah said sharply.

"A rumor, a rumor, must we believe rumors?"

"There's something more than rumor here."

"I know, I know," Zechariah said, shaking his head sadly. "Two of my students came to me and said they would not support the Eighteen Decrees or the refusal of Roman offerings. How could they know of this if Rabbi Hania hadn't been spreading the word about our meeting? How could he have betrayed me, betrayed us, the cause, the nation?"

"The problem is not just Rabbi Hania."

"I know that, too, Judah. When I asked them what had changed their minds they gave me arguments I'd never heard from them, arguments straight from the tongue of Rabbi Moshe ben Avraham. And this morning Rabbi Oniah, an ally of mine, told me he would not stand with me on this. He told me that Rabbi Moshe convinced him of its folly." Zechariah sighed heavily. "If this goes on…" His voice trailed away. His gaze fell to the floor.

"If this goes on we are doomed," Judah finished for him. "The problem isn't Hania. He doesn't matter anymore. The problem isn't even Ananias; he won't be able to stop his own son from rejecting Roman offerings. No, the problem is Rabbi Moshe."

"What can we do?" Rabbi Zechariah asked plaintively, his hands rising from his lap in a gesture of helplessness. "I'm truly at a loss."

"Rabbi Moshe must be silenced," Judah said firmly.

"But how?" Rabbi Zechariah asked, a puzzled look on his face.

Judah said nothing. He stood straight as a statue, his eyes fixed on Zechariah. He wanted the implied, unspoken thought to enter Rabbi Zechariah's mind on its own.

"How?" Rabbi Zechariah repeated. "We could kidnap him and hold him until Eleazar has stopped the offerings, but where would we hold him?"

"There is only one way to silence Rabbi Moshe," Judah said coldly.

"I don't understand."

"Yes you do," Judah said harshly, unwilling to let Zechariah avoid facing the truth.

Judah drew his right forefinger in a slicing motion across his own throat.

"I cannot allow that!" Zechariah cried.

"You must!"

Zechariah's head hung down.

"I cannot allow the murder of a Torah scholar."

"He's a traitor!"

"He's not a traitor. This is an intellectual dispute, a difference of opinion. Rabbi Moshe loves the Torah and the Jewish people and the Land as much as I do."

"Rabbi Moshe is the only one who can stop us. He will peel away your allies. He will turn those scholars who are still on our side. He will even turn the common people against us. He has been giving speeches in the Xystus Plaza and is swaying crowds who at first came to jeer him."

"I cannot do this," Zechariah said weakly, shaking his still-lowered head.

"You have to do nothing!" Judah declared. "I will handle everything!"

"No. I cannot countenance this. I cannot give my assent." His voice had dropped so low Judah could barely hear.

"Do you forbid it?" Judah asked loudly.

Rabbi Zechariah did not reply. His head remained down. Tears dripped from his eyes.

"Do you forbid it?" Judah asked again, his voice filling the room.

Judah waited and waited but Rabbi Zechariah remained silent.

Judah had his answer. He left the room without saying a word.

Chapter Seven

19 Jun 66 CE / 8 Tammuz 3826

Reuven was swallowed up by the crowd still forming in the Xystus Plaza. A smell of sweat emanated from the men around him, men who were murmuring angrily, some of whom carried weapons. Tension swept in waves over the crowd, like the motion of water in a large pond disturbed by the random throwing of stones.

Reuven felt the tension in his gut. He was angry, too, but he tried to push that anger away and keep his mind clear. He wanted to give his uncle, Rabbi Moshe ben Avraham, an objective hearing. He knew basically what his uncle was going to say but he wanted to hear how he would handle the hecklers.

The truth was, Reuven was not sure what to believe. He felt like he was on a high, thin ledge, and the slightest breeze could push him to the right or left, into one kind of abyss or another. Reuven admitted that his father and uncle's arguments for avoiding rebellion were reasonable and perhaps correct, but deep down he felt something had to be done to stop Roman depredations. And today's speech would clarify; only yesterday the Roman procurator Florus had committed a new provocation. His uncle Moshe would be asked about that from someone in the crowd.

Reuven raised his head and looked around him. He noticed a strange looking woman on the outskirts of the crowd. She was very tall, perhaps as tall as his father, perhaps taller, and moved almost like a man. She wore a large gray dress and seemed to be edging deeper into the crowd.

Rabbi Moshe ben Avraham arrived. Reuven turned his attention from the strange woman to his uncle.

Chapter Eight

19 Jun 66 CE / 8 Tammuz 3826

As he ascended the fifteen short steps of the platform that faced the Xystus Plaza Rabbi Moshe ben Avraham felt his excitement dimmed by anxiety. He had enjoyed the challenge of the last several days turning hostile crowds friendly with his rhetoric and his commanding voice. Today, though, the stakes were higher; he was caught between two opposing forces that had the same goal: to provoke a war. No longer was it just Rabbi Zechariah ben Abkulas and Judah ben Ezra, revolutionaries who wanted to goad the people to rebel against the Romans. The Roman procurator Florus only yesterday had committed a fresh outrage by removing seventeen talents from the Temple treasury, on the pretext that the emperor needed the money. Without doubt Florus also wanted to goad the people to rebel to cover up the crimes for which one day he was sure to be charged before Caesar.

Moshe wished now that his brother Aaron was with him. Aaron had offered to go but Moshe, knowing how much his brother hated crowds, told him it was not necessary. Indeed, any gathering of more than a few people made Aaron uncomfortable.

It would be hard to take the two for brothers, much less the twins that they were, though they had similar features and the same deep voice. Aaron was born first, and he was big and strong. Aaron spoke slowly, sometimes hesitantly, and if he was speaking to more than two or three people his voice would become so soft it was almost inaudible. Often during the rabbinical discussions Aaron talked at such a low volume that he would be interrupted by another who didn't realize Aaron was speaking. The interrupter would be shushed by those sitting near Aaron for what he had to say was valued by all the other rabbis. And while Moshe was considered a great speaker, perhaps the greatest among them, Aaron was considered the greater Torah scholar of the two.

The differences between the brothers did not stir envy; they only drew Moshe and Aaron closer together.

"Ah, Aaron," Moshe thought. "I should have told you to come. Your presence would have given me strength."

The plaza was beginning to fill with people. The mood was angry. Some carried clubs, a few spears or swords. Two rows of Syrian auxiliaries commanded by a Roman officer were arrayed in the portico behind him and the one to his left. They were there to keep order and prevent any disturbances from breaking out.

Moshe was facing the massive wall of the Temple complex that stood high above the Xystus Plaza. The wall consisted of large rectangular gray blocks of Jerusalem stone. To his left, beyond the white portico with its carved colonnades, was the northern portion of the first wall that defended Jerusalem. Time and kings had added two more protective walls to guard the City. West of the portico behind him was the Palace of the Hasmonean kings, the descendants of the Maccabees and their non-Maccabee spouses. King Agrippa II, whose realm was to the north and east of Judea, and his sister Berenice, stayed at the palace when they came to Jerusalem. The palace sat at the eastern edge of the Upper City with its broad streets and luxurious houses of the rich. To Moshe's right, spreading south, was the warren of small houses of the Lower City.

The crowd had grown so large that it spilled out beyond the plaza, onto the walkway before the Temple walls, and even onto the short stairway that led to the wide bridge that connected the Temple Mount with the Upper City.

Jerusalem's morning cool was rapidly giving way to an early summer heat under a clear sky and bright sun. Rabbi Moshe wiped the sweat from his forehead with the sleeve of his cloak.

"Hear me citizens of Jerusalem and those who have come from throughout the land to our holy city, hear me my fellow Jews, hear me out, for these are dangerous times and we are at a perilous crossroad!"

Rabbi Moshe's words boomed over the crowd and seized its attention.

"There are those who counsel rebellion against Rome. That way lies folly!" Moshe cried.

"Enough is enough," someone near the front of the crowd shouted.

Moshe pointed to the heckler.

"My friend here shouts 'Enough is enough'," Moshe repeated, for the benefit of those who could not hear the heckler's words.

"Indeed," Rabbi Moshe went on, "when is enough too much? Surely Florus provokes us. Is it enough to risk a ruinous war with Rome, a war we cannot win?

"The Romans rule everywhere. Their legions are undefeated. They have conquered lands larger than ours, nations more numerous than ours, and kingdoms with more wealth and resources than we have in Judea. From beyond the Euphrates to the east, to Libya and the deserts to the south, to Cadiz to the west, and even as far as Britain—"

"We defeated Antiochus and his armies," someone interrupted from the crowd. "We'll defeat these uncircumcised Romans."

Moshe raised both hands, palms out.

"Another fellow here reminds me that we defeated Antiochus and the Syrians, and says we can do the same to the Romans. Ah, my friends, I see no Judah Maccabee here! But perhaps you say, one will rise when the need comes. Perhaps. But consider. Judah Maccabee had the support of the Torah sages in the days of Antiochus. Do the Torah sages of to-day support war against the Romans?"

Moshe lowered his hands and leaned forward. His eyes scanned the crowd, gauging their reactions. Then he noticed something peculiar. There were mostly men in the crowd, and a few women, but one woman in particular caught his attention. She was tall, taller than all the men, maybe even bigger and taller than his brother Aaron. He had never seen a Jewish woman so large. Perhaps she was a convert? She was ungainly, too, for she had a most unfeminine way of walking. And that was the other strange thing about her. While everyone else in the crowd was staying in place, this odd woman was constantly moving, making her way along the outskirts of the assembled throng.

Moshe realized that he had been distracted and silent for too long and was in danger of losing his audience.

"No!" he thundered. "There is a very important difference between Antiochus and Caesar. Antiochus wanted to stamp out the Jewish reli-gion. He forbade the study of the Torah. He forbade circumcision. The Romans do not interfere with us. Indeed they make offerings to our Temple. And yet there are those who would insult Rome and Caesar by refusing their offerings!"

"Nero is a madman!" someone bellowed.

Rabbi Moshe did not repeat those words for the benefit of those who had not heard.

"When Emperor Nero, not knowing our laws, wanted to set up an idol in our Temple, he relented when we petitioned him," Moshe said.

"We don't need Nero's permission to keep our Temple pure," came a shout from the man who had called out against Nero. "Shut up, you coward, and go back to your mansion in the Upper City with the other traitors."

Rabbi Moshe responded immediately.

"Now here's another fellow that had something to say. He called me a coward and a traitor. He told me to go back to my mansion in the Upper City." Rabbi Moshe smiled broadly. "I wish I had a mansion in the Upper City. I live there," he said, pointing to the southeast, "with the rest of you. I'll tell you a secret. My wife is constantly nagging me to get her a better house. The one we have isn't good enough for her. She says it's not fit for a Syrian's pig!"

Laughter swept through the crowd.

Moshe saw the strange woman again. She was no longer on the outskirts of the crowd but was moving through it, getting closer to the speaker's platform. Moshe felt his attention being pulled away from his task at hand, and stopped following the woman with his eyes.

"My friends, let me share another secret. A few days ago my wife told me that she was not going to accept my advances until I get her that bigger house."

"Divorce her!" someone shouted.

"Someone said 'Divorce her'," Moshe repeated. "I'll tell her you suggested that."

Again there was laughter.

"I tell you this, my friends, if I thought war with Rome would get me that mansion in the Upper City, as small and puny as I am, I would take up a sword and fight Rome!"

Gales of laughter greeted Moshe.

The strange woman in the gray dress was now at the front edge of the crowd. She was staring straight up at him.

Rabbi Moshe deliberately looked over her head.

"But the truth is," he went on, "if there is war with Rome it will be long and bitter, and at its end there will be no Upper City mansions, no Lower City houses, and no Temple! Why make war with Caesar and Rome when our quarrel is wi—"

A disturbance in the middle of the crowd cut Moshe off. Two men had started fighting, and like ripples in a pond, a disorganized wave of pushing and shoving, of men tripping over each other, moved outward. In response, the auxiliaries came pouring from the porticoes and moved forcefully into the undulating mass of people.

"Calm down, my friends, calm down!" Rabbi Moshe pleaded over the rising din.

And then Rabbi Moshe saw, out of the corner of his eye, that woman rushing up the steps, rushing toward him.

What could she possibly want?

He turned to face her.

She sprung like a leopard upon a hapless gazelle, a mother leopard eager to feed her hungry brood. She spun Rabbi Moshe ben Avraham around and clamped a strong hand over his mouth.

Rabbi Moshe struggled valiantly. In vain.

A sharp blade sliced deep into his throat.

Chapter Nine

19 Jun 66 CE / 8 Tammuz 3826

They were alone together, brother and brother, but the living was more alone than the dead.

Aaron could not imagine life without his brother. No Jacob and Esau were they, but brothers together from the womb through life; not rivals but the closest companions. And now Moshe was gone. Aaron could barely comprehend it.

He gazed down at his brother's body wrapped in its linen winding sheet. He had no more tears left. He was floating in a vast emptiness, its darkness broken only by occasional sparks of rage.

I will find the murderer, he thought, and there will be justice.

Aaron and his two teenage sons had washed Moshe's body. They combed his hair and beard. They dressed him in a robe of light blue, for while white was the preferred color, Moshe had agreed strongly with Aaron's words for his own burial one day: "Not in black, lest I appear as a mourner among the righteous who are clad in white in paradise, nor in white, lest I be clad in festive garments when I should bewail my sad lot."

The men of the burial society had come bringing the funeral bier, the spices of myrrh and aloe, and the linen winding sheet. They had placed the spices in the folds of Rabbi Moshe ben Avraham's clothes, and they had wrapped the body in the sheet and laid it on the bier.

Mourners came to pay their respects. Moshe's house had been full; now it was empty, save for Aaron and Bruria. Moshe's widow was in the bedroom, weeping. Aaron could hear her sobs interspersed with blood-curdling wails.

It was too late in the day to bear the body to the family tomb that had been cut into the rock on a hill outside Jerusalem, a hill that over-looked the holy Temple. In the morning would be the funeral proces-sion, with hired women mourners chanting in the lead, with flute players, and with men bearing the bier holding Moshe's body on their shoulders, taking turns with the other mourners as they marched from the City to the hills beyond.

The circular stone that closed the tomb would be rolled away and the body placed inside. In three days the stone would be rolled back to close the cave, three days in case Moshe was somehow still alive. A year from now Aaron would go back to the tomb to collect the bones and place them in an ossuary.

The sobbing and wailing ceased. Aaron heard Bruria shuffle into the room.

"Aaron," she stammered. "I have sinned. I was a bad wife to Moshe."

Aaron did not respond. He did not turn to her. He continued looking down at his brother as he thought:

What do you want? Absolution? Leave me alone with my grief. I will miss him more than you will.

"Aaron, I made his life miserable. I nagged him constantly. I wanted a bigger house and finer clothes. I made him so unhappy!"

I know that, you witch, Aaron thought.

A shriek escaped from Bruria.

"Oh my darling Moshe, I would gladly live naked in a cave if I could have you back!"

If only you would have gotten wisdom while my brother was still alive, you she-devil, Aaron thought.

"Aaron, I even denied him happiness during his last days on earth. I told him I would not sleep with him again until he got me a house in the Upper City."

Aaron turned to Bruria.

"I cannot give you absolution, Bruria. Learn to live with your guilt."

Her hair was disheveled, her face dirty and tear-streaked, and her clothes in disarray.

Aaron silently cursed himself; he could feel desire well-up in him.

He turned back to his brother, his cheeks burning.

What a strange creature a man is, he mused. Driven by hunger and lust, wanting food and sex, no better than an animal. And yet, if men did not eat they would die of hunger, and if they did not lie with women there would be no humans to replace them when they died. But a man was more than just an animal; he could follow God's commandments and ascend from the physical to the spiritual level. It could be done.

Oh, how hard it is. The animal always pulls us back!

Rabbi Aaron ben Avraham often pondered this irony, this contradiction, this conundrum without a solution.

Oh, why has God made us this way, giving us bodies and souls, causing us to suffer so?

He looked at Bruria again. In ninety-two days he would have to decide whether to enter a levirate marriage with her and try to produce a son who would carry on his dead brother's name.

Rabbi Aaron closed his eyes. Again he could feel stabbings of lust as he wondered what it would be like to take Bruria to bed.

Of course he could not marry her, especially after those thoughts. Besides, his own wife Ruth would never accept it. No, he would choose the chalitzah ceremony. They would go before a rabbinical court, Bruria would remove the shoe from his right foot, and she would spit on the ground before him. And that would be that. He and Bruria would go their separate ways.

Rabbi Aaron opened his eyes. Bruria had gone to sit on a low wooden bench in a corner of the room. Rabbi Aaron looked down and resumed gazing at his brother.

Memories stretching back to childhood flooded through him, of games they had played with each other, of studies together, even of childhood mischief they had gotten into.

Rabbi Aaron's reverie was interrupted by the door opening hesitantly.

Judah ben Ezra stepped into the house.

"What are you doing here?" Rabbi Aaron demanded.

"I've come to pay my respects."

"Pay your respects or gloat?" retorted Rabbi Aaron. "I imagine you'd be out celebrating."

"Rabbi Aaron ben Avraham, you do me a great injustice," Judah said, his face registering astonishment. "Not only are you wrong about the Romans, you are wrong about me.

"Why would I want Rabbi Moshe dead?" he went on. "Because he opposed resisting the Romans and counseled submission? My dear rabbi, war is inevitable. They gave us Albinus, who was bad. Now we have Florus, who is a hundred times worse. The next procurator may be worse still, perhaps he will demand that pigs be sacrificed in the Temple. But it won't come to a next procurator. Florus is bent on provoking a war. His outrages will only continue. It is better for us to challenge Rome while we are still strong, before Florus weakens us further. And when war comes all of the House of Hillel will join us. Even you."

Rabbi Aaron noticed that Bruria was staring fixedly at Judah, and that Judah gave occasional glances in her direction while he spoke. The looks they exchanged were not the same; Judah, from the expression on his face, did not seem aware of the hatred in her eyes.

"You are very sure of yourself, Judah ben Ezra," Rabbi Aaron said with contempt.

"Not of myself but of the truth, and the rightness of the cause," Judah responded. "You will see, Rabbi Aaron, you will see. And if your brother were still alive he would join us, too. His death is a loss; his voice would have been a weapon in our struggle against Rome. No, rabbi, I do not rejoice in your brother's death."

"And of course," Rabbi Aaron said, "you know the truth better than the Torah scholars."

"Rabbi Zechariah ben Abkulas is not a Torah scholar?"

"On this matter his views are in the minority," Rabbi Aaron said

"It never happens that the minority position later becomes the official ruling?" Judah asked, satisfaction in his voice.

Before Rabbi Aaron could respond Bruria stood up. She pointed a finger at Judah.

"You killed him!" she cried.

The skin on Judah's cheekbones turned white. He trembled. Even Rabbi Aaron was surprised at her outburst.

"How can you say that, poor woman?" Judah exclaimed. "Rabbi Zechariah is my spiritual guide. Do you think he would countenance the murder of another Torah scholar? If he had only a hint that such a thought was in my mind don't you think he would have told me it was forbidden? And if I did have such a thought, don't you think I would have gone to Rabbi Zechariah for guidance?"

"Sit down, Bruria, and be silent!" Rabbi Aaron admonished her.

Judah held out his arms to Bruria in supplication and said:

"I do not know who was behind your husband's murder or why it was carried out, but if there was a conspiracy it is very likely that Florus wanted to silence a voice for peace."

To Rabbi Aaron he sounded sincere but Bruria's expression did not change.

Judah turned to Rabbi Aaron.

"I am sorry for your loss," he said. "I am sorry for the loss of a great scholar. May Rabbi Moshe ben Avraham's name and memory be a blessing to the people of Israel."

Judah delivered these words and left without waiting for a response.

When the door had closed Bruria said:

"I know he killed Moshe!"

"How can you say such a thing, woman?"

"I know. I know. He came to our house and threatened Moshe."

"How?"

"He wanted to know where Rabbi Hania was. Moshe refused to talk to him. He told Moshe he would see him in Gehinom."

Rabbi Aaron's breath came in sharply. Which was the real Judah ben Ezra? The one he had just seen, the one who was conciliatory, or the one who had uttered a threatening sacrilege to his brother? Could he even trust the accuracy of Bruria's account?

"Bruria, we need proof before we can accuse him of such a thing."

Bruria rose again and walked over to the body of her husband.

"I will avenge your death, my love," she cried, her voice breaking. And then, as calm as a grave and as sharp as a knife, she said:

"I will avenge your death even if I have to go to Satan to do it!"

Bruria's words and icy visage burned into Rabbi Aaron's brain and eyes, and he shivered as the hair on his arms and the back of his neck stood erect.

Chapter Ten

20 Jun 66 CE / 9 Tammuz 3826

A long and unhappy day was coming to a close, and though the Sabbath was quickly approaching with the setting of the sun Rabbi Aaron ben Avraham felt no joy in welcoming it. Would it always be thus, even after the period of mourning? It wasn't only his brother he buried earlier in the family tomb; a piece of himself remained in that Jerusalem hillside. The empty space left behind was so real it was palpable; Rabbi Aaron was certain that if he could somehow put his hand inside his heart he could touch that emptiness.

He sat at the table in his brother Moshe's house, waiting for the sounds of the shofar. The door to the outside was locked to prevent uninvited visitors from entering.

Bruria, his wife Ruth, and his two sons looked at him across the table, which was set with the meal the two women had prepared. There was wine and olive oil and two kinds of bread, a thick loaf and several thin, flat loaves. There was a plate with rice and a large bowl of soup made with lentils, chickpeas, and onions. One plate held slices of goat cheese, another grapes and figs. Near each person was an empty plate and a small cloth towel. Large wooden serving spoons lay next to the soup and rice.

Oil lamps on the table provided light, illuminating the entire room. If any of them went out, it would not be relit until the Sabbath was over.

All were silent, waiting. Then three blasts of the shofar sounded from far away and the two women rose, walked over to another table and lit the Sabbath candles. A few moments later there were three more shofar blasts. The Sabbath had begun.

Bruria came with the ceramic pitcher filled with water for the ritual hand washing. Ruth carried the bowl into which the water would be spilled. Rabbi Aaron and his two sons stood.

"We are ready to begin," Rabbi Aaron said.

A sharp knock shook the door; it was met with an equally sharp intake of breath from Rabbi Aaron. He did not move.

The knock was followed by incessant pounding. Rabbi Aaron sighed and went to the door.

A Roman officer flanked by two auxiliary soldiers stood outside.

The officer's helmet and breastplate gleamed in the light that came from inside the house. On one hip was a long sword, on the other a knife that was less than a foot long. On his feet were the caligae made of several layers of leather studded with hobnails; the caligae were laced firmly around his foot and ankle. The officer, shorter than Rabbi Aaron, had a shaved face and clear blue eyes.

Rabbi Aaron recognized him.

"Greetings, Commander Metilius," Rabbi Aaron said. "Shabbat shalom to you. To what do I owe this honor?" Rabbi Aaron spoke in Greek, the lingua franca of the region. Metilius was the commander of the garrison stationed in Antonia, the fortress that stood at the northwest corner of the Temple.

The hint of a smile softened Metilius' features.

"I want to ask you about your brother," he said.

"Since when does the murder of a Jew concern an officer of Rome?"

Metilius looked straight into Rabbi Aaron's eyes. It seemed to Rabbi Aaron that the Roman squared his shoulders even straighter.

"Rome wants peace and order in her provinces, Rabbi Aaron," Metilius declared. "And Jerusalem is a jewel of the empire. We do not want it torn apart by strife and war."

"Ah, commander, our Sabbath has just begun, as you no doubt heard from the blasts of the shofar. We are about to start our meal. You are welcome to join us. Your men, too."

"My men will remain outside. I have no need to eat. I will just ask you a few questions and then you can go back to your Sabbath."

Metilius entered the house of the murdered rabbi. He looked at the food on the table, at the two women, and at the two boys. The younger, fourteen year old Reuven, stared at the Roman officer with open-mouthed wonder. The boy's hands moved down both cheeks and the sides of his neck, following the flow of the side extensions of Metilius' helmet.

"They are to protect my face and neck in combat," Metilius explained, smiling at the boy. He turned to Rabbi Aaron and asked, "Does he understand Greek?"

The older boy, sixteen year old Benjamin, answered for his father:

"We speak Greek, Hebrew, and Aramaic!"

"Some Latin, too," cried Reuven. "*Salve, domine!*"

Metilius' smile broke into hearty laughter.

"I will join you!" he declared.

"Benjamin, bring a chair for the commander," Rabbi Aaron said.

A chair was brought, and a plate and a towel. Rabbi Aaron introduced his family to Metilius.

"Well," Metilius said, eying the food, "no need for you to stand on ceremony on my account. Sit and eat and I will join you."

Rabbi Aaron smiled at Metilius and said:

"Commander, the table is set with food and we are hungry. But we do not just sit and eat. First we pray. When all the proper rituals are completed we sit and eat. Thus God, by requiring us to follow His laws, teaches us self-discipline."

"A Roman soldier learns discipline, too." Metilius said, looking at Reuven.

"To make war and conquer," Rabbi Aaron appended softly and with resignation.

"One either conquers or is conquered," Metilius replied. He took off his helmet. "But I will not argue for Roman arms on your Sabbath. I have heard that your prophets promise peace. There will be enough unpleasant things to discuss after the meal."

Rabbi Aaron took the ceremonial wine cup in his hand, said the blessing in Hebrew, waited for the response of "Amen" from his family, and took a sip. He walked around the table and handed the cup to Metilius, who took a sip and handed it back to Rabbi Aaron. Rabbi Aaron brought the cup in turn to each member of the family: the oldest boy, the youngest, Ruth, and Bruria. Then the rabbi took the pitcher of water and poured some over each hand into the bowl as he said a prayer. He dried his hands with his towel and passed the pitcher and bowl around. By the time it reached Metilius the Roman commander copied what he had seen. When all had done the ceremonial washing Rabbi Aaron picked up one of the thin loaves of bread, said the blessing, waited for the response, and broke off pieces and handed them around to everyone at the table.

"Now we can eat!" Rabbi Aaron announced and sat down for the meal.

As they began Rabbi Aaron said to Metilius:

"At the Sabbath meal I usually question the boys about their lessons during the week. We discuss what they learned and what is implied beyond what they have learned. We speak in Hebrew and Aramaic. Today the boys will have a special challenge, in your honor. We will do it all in Greek."

Rabbi Aaron noted that Metilius followed the ensuing discussion with interest. At one point the conversation reached a pause and Metilius jumped in.

"You and your sons argue about everyday matters with such enthusiasm and intensity. Two men find a tunic in a field. Who owns it? Can a man carry a key to his house on the Sabbath? And I know that Jews are forbidden to eat pork, a tasty meat by the way." Metilius grinned as he said this. "But what is you Jews really believe, fundamentally?"

Rabbi Aaron nodded gravely.

"A good question. Its full answer would take longer than we have at this meal. But a great sage of ours named Hillel was once asked by a pagan to explain Judaism while standing on one foot. Hillel replied: 'Do not do unto others what is hateful unto you. All the rest is commentary. Now study Torah.'"

Metilius grunted.

"It would certainly be a more peaceful and just world if everyone followed that advice," he said.

"Rabbi Hillel is the founder of the school of Torah interpretation that I belong to," Rabbi Aaron said. He laughed gently. "If you are really interested, I would be happy to teach you more."

Metilius picked up a piece of bread from his plate and appeared to examine it. His fingers pushed and prodded at the bread, changing its shape as he did so.

"What does your god look like?" he asked.

"He has no shape or form," Rabbi Aaron answered. "Unlike the Greek and Roman gods. He does not have human foibles or weaknesses; He does not carouse and fornicate and quarrel the way your gods do."

Metilius leaned back in his chair and seemed to sigh.

"Our gods are simply men, just bigger and stronger and more corrupt. They are legends, stories we tell each other, subject matter for poetry and plays. No man of understanding can truly believe they are real, real like the chair I sit in or the table before me. But if our gods are absurd there is something slippery about yours. You cannot tell me what he looks like or anything about him."

"God is beyond our understanding," Rabbi Aaron responded. "Do you know why the stars shine or the rain falls? Why the dew is upon the ground or the sun gives heat and light? All these are His handiwork. He created the universe and all that is in it.

"He gave us the Torah to guide our lives," Rabbi Aaron continued. "Every Jew, from the simple farmer to the most learned sage, is commanded to study it. And He gave us the Sabbath, a most precious gift, a day on which we do no work, neither we, nor our servants, nor our beasts. A day of rest for all! You Romans, and the Greeks before you, call the Jews lazy. No, the Sabbath is a holy day of prayer and contemplation; six days we live in the mundane, on the seventh we experience a divine gift. Imagine if the whole world, even slaves and beasts, had one day of rest! Imagine!" Rabbi Aaron concluded triumphantly.

Rabbi Aaron noticed his wife looking at him quizzically. He grinned at her sheepishly.

"Moshe's spirit must have entered you," she said. "I have never seen you so eloquent or forthright before a stranger."

"My wife is right," Rabbi Aaron said thoughtfully to Metilius. "I almost cannot believe it myself. Perhaps his spirit has entered me."

"The time has come to talk about your brother," Metilius said. "Do you have any idea who might have wanted to kill Rabbi Moshe?"

Before Rabbi Aaron could answer Bruria cried:

"Judah ben Ezra! He murdered my husband!"

"Hush woman!" Aaron admonished. "You have no proof."

Bruria ignored him.

"He came to my house. They quarreled. Judah threatened him. I'll swear it before any court!"

"Where can I find this Judah ben Ezra?"

"He lives in this quarter," Rabbi Aaron answered. "I don't know where exactly."

"Who would?"

Rabbi Aaron was silent. He hesitated before giving Rabbi Zechariah ben Abkulas' name.

"You know something," Metilius said, noticing the expression on Rabbi Aaron's face. "Rabbi Aaron, listen to me. The peace and stability of this province are vital to Rome. Your brother was an advocate for peace. He was murdered. We want to find the killer and his accomplices and bring them to justice."

"Accomplices? How do you know there were any?" Rabbi Aaron asked.

"There was a disturbance while your brother was speaking. Two men started fighting. Men from my garrison moved into the crowd to restore order. Everyone was distracted. That's when your brother was killed. That fight was planned precisely to allow the killer to strike without witnesses.

"And we couldn't find any. We questioned many people. No one admits to seeing anything. Rabbi Aaron, please ask your people to come forward if they know anything. That includes you," Metilius concluded earnestly.

Rabbi Aaron covered his face with his hands and sighed deeply. He let his hands fall to his lap and told Metilius that Rabbi Zechariah ben Abkulas would know where Judah was.

"Thank you, Rabbi Aaron."

Reuven, who had been fidgeting in his seat, spoke up.

"I saw someone who might be a witness." Surprise greeted Reuven's statement. "I went to hear my uncle speak, and I saw this strange woman who was first on the outskirts of the crowd. She was very tall, maybe as tall, or taller, than you, Father. She wore a gray dress. She didn't stay where she was. I saw her move slowly toward the center of the crowd. Just before the disturbance started she was very close to where Uncle Moshe was speaking."

When the astonishment around the table died down, Metilius said, enthusiastically:

"Very good, young man! That is very helpful!"

"Commander Metilius, did the procurator tell you to investigate this murder?" Aaron asked.

A look of disgust crossed Metilius' face.

"He has left Jerusalem, as you probably know," the Roman said.

"There is another possibility," Rabbi Aaron began. "You know that Gessius Florus is doing everything he can to provoke the Jews to revolt. It would not be beyond—"

Metilius cut him short. He stood and put on his helmet.

"I will leave you to enjoy the rest of your meal," he said curtly. Then, with the hint of a smile, he added, "If you don't mind, though, I will take some grapes and figs to share with the men." He strode to the door.

"Commander, may I ask you something?"

Metilius paused.

"Yes? What is it?"

"Do you have children?"

"Yes. A boy and a girl of roughly your children's ages." Rabbi Aaron heard sadness and longing in his voice. "I haven't seen them for three years."

"You experienced our Sabbath meal," Rabbi Aaron said. "Compare it your Roman banquets: Discussions, yes, but accompanied by gluttony and drunkenness and sexual promiscuity. Which would you rather have for your children?"

Metilius glanced around the table at the family gathered there.

"Only a fool would choose our way over yours," he said wistfully.

"Come to me when you are able," Rabbi Aaron urged. "I will teach you our ways. When you go back to Italy you can teach them to your children."

Commander Metilius put his hand on the door.

"I may just do that, Rabbi Aaron. I may just do that."

After the Roman had left, Rabbi Aaron wondered: *Will he? Will he?*

Chapter Eleven

21 Jun 66 CE / 10 Tammuz 3826

Judah ben Ezra watched sourly as the door opened.

"Who is it now?" he wondered.

Rabbi Yoel ben Jotham entered the room.

Yoel was one of Rabbi Zechariah's students. He was even more radical than his teacher; Yoel was a young firebrand, someone who Judah was sure would take up a sword or a knife if he knew how.

Judah liked Yoel.

"A message from Rabbi Zechariah," Yoel said, dispensing with a greeting and getting right to the point. "It's a warning. A Roman officer is coming to question you about Rabbi Moshe's murder."

"You're a little late," Judah replied drily, "he was already here. With two guards and a translator. That Roman officer doesn't speak Aramaic, and I hardly know Greek."

"Is anything wrong?" Yoel asked anxiously.

"No, no. Someone—I think I know who—accused me of killing Moshe. But Shaul here," Judah pointed to the corner where Shaul sat, staring at the floor, apparently oblivious of the visitor, "backed me up that I was nowhere near the Xystus Plaza. That Roman is the commander of the Antonia garrison. I figured Shaul and me were more than a match for the four of them, and thought of sending them all to their Hades, including the Jew who translated for them, but it didn't seem worth the effort."

"Good. Good," Yoel responded. "Rabbi Zechariah said he wanted to speak to you after the Roman left."

"About what?"

Yoel shrugged.

"He didn't say. I have the feeling he wants to postpone the rabbinical assembly to discuss the Eighteen Decrees. If that's what it is, I hope you can convince him otherwise."

Judah grinned.

"I'll do my best, Rabbi Yoel."

"Well, come along then."

"Give me a moment, Rabbi Yoel. I want to talk to Shaul. Do you mind waiting outside?"

Without a word Yoel turned on his heels and left the room.

"Shaul? Shaul?" Judah asked. "Are you going to be all right?"

Shaul shivered.

"I heard them, Judah, I heard them, just like you said. I heard the angels singing. It was like I was there but not there, in the plaza but also among the angels. It was the most incredible experience. The angels were singing to me, just like you said." Shaul sounded full of wonder and exhilaration. Then he stifled a sob and said, his voice flat, without any emotion, as if something inside him had died, "I don't hear them anymore, Judah, I don't hear them anymore."

Judah shook his head, worried about what was happening to Shaul.

"Maybe you need to kill someone else, Shaul," Judah said sharply.

Shaul had been acting strangely ever since he returned from the mission. He just sat in the corner, muttering over and over, "I don't hear them anymore, I don't hear them anymore." At night Shaul tossed and turned. Sometimes he cried out. Judah heard him calling a woman's name. "Dvorah!" Who was this Dvorah? A girl he left behind in Gamla?

Judah sighed. Maybe I should be more understanding, he thought. Rabbi Moshe wasn't some Syrian auxiliary; he was a Jew, and a Torah sage, no less.

Judah walked over to Shaul and stroked his head gently.

"Listen, Shaul, my friend. You're going to be fine. It will just take a little time. Meanwhile, get a grip on yourself. I have to go and talk to Rabbi Zechariah. I'll come right back when I'm done. All right? All right? Answer me, Shaul!"

"All right, Judah. All right. I'll wait for you here."

Judah blinked as he passed from the dimly lit room into the bright sunlight. Rabbi Yoel started walking briskly. That was another thing Judah liked about him.

"The rabbinical assembly is supposed to take place tomorrow," Yoel said. "I do hope Rabbi Zechariah does not postpone it. At this juncture time is not on our side. The House of Hillel grows stronger every day; we grow weaker."

"The death of Rabbi Moshe weakens our opponents."

"True," Rabbi Yoel agreed. "Nevertheless, the death of a Torah scholar is to be mourned." He smiled. "Yet I would thank whoever carried out the deed, for in truth he struck a blow for the freedom of the people and the Land."

If Zechariah ever loses his nerve, Judah thought, Rabbi Yoel will be a worthy successor to the cause.

Rabbi Zechariah's study hall was serving as a synagogue; he and his students were engaged in prayer. Rabbi Yoel beckoned Judah to join him inside. Judah declined. He was not a praying man.

Judah waited until services were over and Rabbi Zechariah was alone. When he entered the rabbi was sitting on a bench. Zechariah looked up at him plaintively.

"I had to tell that Roman where to find you, otherwise it would have seemed suspicious." Zechariah had a note of apology in his voice.

"I understand," Judah said.

"I tried to warn you in time."

Judah nodded.

"I know," Judah said. "Everything's fine. Shaul confirmed that I was with him the whole time. I'm cleared."

"Who denounced you?" Zechariah asked anxiously. "Do you know? Was it Rabbi Aaron?"

"More likely the widow."

Zechariah looked down. He took a deep breath before starting to speak.

"I've decided to postpone the rabbinical assembly. Out of respect for Rabbi Moshe. Until the mourning period is over."

"That's a bad decision," Judah said firmly. "The thrust of events is on our side. We lose that advantage if we postpone."

"It's the loss of Rabbi Moshe ben Avraham that concerns me. It was a terrible tragedy. We must take that into account in deciding how we proceed."

"We did take that into account," Judah retorted. "That is why we silenced him."

"We? We?" Zechariah looked up, his dark eyes flashing with anger. Judah saw the rings that had formed under them in the last few days. "How dare you say we! I had nothing to do with his murder."

"Come now, Rabbi. You knew what was being planned."

"I knew no such thing. I never gave you permission."

"I asked you to forbid me. More than once. You said nothing. Any rabbinical court would hold you complicit in the crime. Any Roman court, too."

"Are you threatening me?" Rabbi Zechariah thundered. He started to rise but slumped back down into the bench. The mask of anger that had been on his face was replaced by resignation.

"No, Rabbi Zechariah," Judah said gently, "I'm not threatening you.

I don't even know why you're accusing me of threatening you. All I'm saying is that as things now stand events are in our favor: Tomorrow you will head the rabbinical assembly where the Eighteen Decrees will be passed. The people will return to the Torah, Eleazar will refuse the Roman offerings, and we will expel the Romans from Jerusalem and all the Land of Israel. That is the way it must be."

Zechariah said nothing.

"Agreed?" Judah prompted.

There was no reply.

"The assembly will be held tomorrow as planned?" Judah's voice was forceful. It demanded an answer.

"Yes," Rabbi Zechariah said weakly.

"Good. Shabbat Shalom, Rabbi Zechariah."

Judah was relieved to get out of his presence, out of the stuffy study hall, and into the fresh air. He took a deep breath and let it out slowly between pursed lips.

Though he had promised Shaul that he would return immediately, there was one more person Judah wanted to see. He could not say exactly what he expected of her.

Chapter Twelve

21 Jun 66 CE / 10 Tammuz 3826

Judah ben Ezra stood on the threshold, the door still open. She did not tell him to enter, she did not tell him to leave. An awkward silence ensued. He was not sure what to do next.

Bruria did not look like a widow in mourning. She wore a bright red dress that more than hinted at the curves of her body; subtly applied makeup highlighted her perfect features.

The future queen Esther presenting herself before the king of Persia could not have been more lovely, he thought.

Bruria held his gaze without flinching. Judah began to imagine she had prepared herself thus because she knew he was coming to her.

Is it possible, he wondered, even if she denounced me to the Romans?

Judah stepped inside and closed the door.

"Bruria," he said. "I know you believe that I killed your husband. That's what you told the Romans, isn't it?"

Not a flicker in her eyes, not a word from her lips. Judah could not read her expression.

"A Roman officer came to question me. I am cleared of any suspicion. I've been with my companion, Shaul ben Yitzchak, these last few days; that officer, the commander of the garrison of Antonia, determined that to be the truth. He knows I am innocent of Rabbi Moshe's murder; do you know that now? I did not kill your husband!"

There was no response. Bruria could have been sculpted from stone she was so still.

"Bruria, believe me. I would have been taken in for questioning if there were any grounds for suspicion. Bruria, I did not kill Moshe!" Judah's strong voice was filled with pleading.

Several moments went by. At last Bruria spoke.

"My husband's thoughts were not mine. He counseled patience with Rome. He counseled surrender to Rome. I wanted to fight them!

"My husband was a mouse. You are a man. You will fight the Romans. You will lead our people to freedom. You will be king of Israel!" she shouted triumphantly.

Judah could hardly believe what he was hearing. Questions flew wildly around his head: She sees me as king of Israel? A woman who denounced me? Are both possible? Who can know what goes on in a woman's mind?

From the first moment Judah saw her desire consumed him; since that day he had been unable to get her out of his thoughts. And now, and now, she was proclaiming him king of Israel! That look she gave him then, that strange look, there must have been sparks and flames from the very beginning for her, also.

"When a Roman dishonored me," Bruria continued, her rising voice interrupting his thoughts, "my husband did nothing. He counseled patience, forbearance. He told me to forget what happened, that he would forget, too. What a mouse! Whoever killed him in the Xystus Plaza freed me from a marriage to a half-man."

Judah's eyes widened with amazement. Did she know the truth? That he, Judah, had freed her? Did that throw fuel on her fire for him?

"You, Judah, you are a real man," she said. "You would have avenged my dishonor. You would have found that Roman and cut his throat with all the ferocity of a Syrian slaughtering a pig. You are a man of Israel, Judah, but one day you will be its king!"

Judah was trembling. Was there anything stopping him from taking her in his arms?

Bruria smiled. It was a seductive smile, a beckoning smile.

"I know you are a man among men, Judah," she said, her voice teasing. "Are you also a man among women?"

Chapter Thirteen

22 Jun 66 CE / 11 Tammuz 3826

Like a caged lion, Shaul ben Yitzchak paced anxiously around the dim and constricted pale to which he had been confined.

"Where are you?" he cried to the empty room.

Judah said he would return right after going to Rabbi Zechariah. He never did. Evening had come, bringing with it the end of the Sabbath and the start of the first day of the new week. Evening passed into night, night into morning, and still no Judah.

What happened to him?

Important work was to be done today. Preparations had to be made. The rabbinical assembly was to adopt the Eighteen Decrees, and he, Shaul, was going to help Judah and the others make it happen.

Were they excluding him because he had fallen into that low and confused state after killing Rabbi Moshe? Did they no longer trust him?

In truth, he had only gotten out of his corner because of concern over Judah's absence. Instead of asking where were the angelic voices he was now asking where was Judah.

The thought made him smile with its irony.

"From angels to Judah," he muttered.

Have I finally recovered? Am I back to myself?

This uncertainty led him to the conclusion that he should take some decisive action to reassure himself.

He weighed whether he should go out and look for his leader. Judah had told him to remain out of sight. Shaul didn't understand why this was still necessary. They were no longer under suspicion and the blood-stained dress was safely hidden away at the bottom of the large wooden box in the opposite corner of the room.

Where to look?

Rabbi Zechariah ben Abkulas would know!

It was resolved; he would ignore Judah's admonition and start searching for him.

Shaul stepped outside and began walking in the direction of Rabbi Zechariah's house. He had taken less than a dozen steps when a familiar voice called out to him.

He turned, and there coming down the narrow street toward the house he had just left was Judah!

Someone bent and limping was walking beside him. Judah's companion was completely covered with clothing so that even when they got closer Shaul could not see who it was.

Shaul was already at the door when the two reached it. He still could not make out the person with Judah.

"Where were you going?" Judah asked curtly as soon as they were inside.

"Looking for you! Where have you been?"

Shaul peered closely at Judah's companion, He could only see eyes and a hint of forehead.

"Never mind that," replied Judah, flicking his right hand in the air as if brushing away the question. "We have business to take care of today."

"Who's that with you?" Shaul asked.

The eyes look like they could belong to a woman, Shaul thought. A young one. Yet she is bent and crippled like an old man.

"Someone who needs a place to stay, a place where no one will see him," Judah answered, frowning. "There's not enough room for the three of us. Rabbi Yoel agreed to put you up until we sort this all out."

"Sort what out? What's going on?"

Shaul kept looking at the mysterious stranger, who gave him an intense and startled stare before turning away from him.

"I've got to hide him for a while. Important for our mission." Judah's tone was peremptory, brooking no questioning. "Come, gather your things. I'll take you to Rabbi Yoel and then we'll meet the others."

As curious as Shaul was, he knew better than to ask any further. He obediently collected his few possessions, put them into a beat-up leather satchel, and left the room with Judah.

But not before giving one last glance at the stranger who was replacing him.

Chapter Fourteen

22 Jun 66 CE / 11 Tammuz 3826

Rabbi Aaron ben Avraham scanned the half-empty loft and wondered: Is this where the end begins, from this rabbinical assembly to the destruction of the Temple?

Members of the rabbinical Sanhedrin were still arriving and taking their places at the long wooden table that took up much of the center of the loft. Along the table were low benches, also of wood. The walls of the loft were dark brown and bare. An array of oil lamps rescued the room from gloom and darkness.

At one end of the table were the students of the House of Shammai. There sat Rabbi Zechariah ben Abkulas, who would be presenting his eighteen proposals. He was leaning forward, looking around the loft, his glance occasionally catching the eyes of Rabbi Aaron. To Zechariah's right sat Rabbi Hanania ben Hezekiah ben Geron who owned the house where the assembly was taking place. On Zechariah's left was Rabbi Yoel ben Jotham.

At the other end of the table were the students of the House of Hillel. There sat Rabbi Simeon ben Gamliel, the president of the rabbinical Sanhedrin. To Rabbi Simeon's right sat Rabbi Johanan ben Zakkai, who had been the great Hillel's youngest student and was expected to succeed Rabbi Simeon as president one day. Rabbi Aaron had managed to sit on Rabbi Johanan's right for this meeting.

The rabbinical Sanhedrin was composed of seventy rabbis. With the murder of Rabbi Moshe ben Avraham they were down to sixty-nine; it would take time to find someone with equal stature to replace him.

Fifty members were required as a quorum for any discussion that would result in a ruling. While a simple majority of those present was required for a ruling to be passed, attempts were usually made to produce rulings that had as broad support as possible.

The majority of the rabbinical Sanhedrin's members belonged to the House of Hillel. Rulings often went according to their views.

May it go that way today, prayed Rabbi Aaron silently.

His brother Moshe had warned him that Rabbi Zechariah might bring thugs to intimidate the Hillelites, and even suggested that members of their House avoid today's assembly, thus denying Zechariah and his allies a quorum. So far, though, only rabbis who were allowed to attend had entered.

No robbers here, as Rabbi Johanan would say, thought Rabbi Aaron.

More rabbis had entered. Rabbi Aaron counted fifty-three men, enough for a quorum. By his estimate thirty-two were students of the House of Hillel, a comfortable majority.

Rabbi Simeon, as president, began the proceedings. When he rose from his seat the rest of the assembly followed.

"Blessed be the Name of the Lord," Rabbi Simeon intoned, "who has given man wisdom to discern right from wrong and good from evil. May He grant us wisdom this day so that our deliberations will arrive at just and righteous conclusions."

He sat down and when everyone else was seated he continued:

"We are gathered today to consider eighteen measures proposed by Rabbi Zechariah ben Abkulas. He will present these measures, we will discuss them, and then we will vote on each measure, one by one. Rabbi Zechariah, you may begin."

Zechariah stood. He cleared his throat.

"The Land of Israel is under occupation by a pagan empire. The men they send to enforce their rule rob and murder us. They favor the gentiles who live in the Land, the gentiles who hate us, the gentiles who wait for the day to slaughter us all, farmer and townsman, poor and rich, Sadducee and Pharisee, the House of Shammai and the House of Hillel!"

Rabbi Zechariah's voice grew louder and more forceful as he spoke; it filled the loft.

"Rome's procurators get worse; each does more evil than his predecessor. Albinus was bad. Now we have Gessius Florus, who stole seventeen talents from the Temple Treasury. He did not stop there; when he took insult from the protests against his thievery he set Roman soldiers and their gentile allies upon the Upper Market. They sacked it and killed all whom they encountered. We still hear the wails of the mourners!"

Zechariah's shout rang in the ears of those assembled around the table. Rabbi Aaron saw anger on the faces of those swept up by Zechariah's rhetoric, even among members of the House of Hillel. Indeed, he himself felt rage rising inside him at the injustice of the Romans.

"I have asked myself why this is happening," Zechariah went on. "Why has God abandoned us? I have found only one answer. It is because we have abandoned God!" he thundered.

"Do any of you have another explanation?" he demanded. "We are supposed to be a holy people, separate from the other nations. During the time of Antiochus the pious fought not only against the Seleucid armies but also against those Jews who wished to ape the ways of the Greeks. We purified ourselves, we purified the people, just as we purified the holy oil used in the lamp of the Temple. And because we purified ourselves God gave us a great victory over the heathens!"

Jewish faces were glowing now, Rabbi Aaron noted; only Rabbi Simeon and Rabbi Johanan had stolid expressions.

"Since that time," Zechariah continued, "starting with the successors to the Maccabees, we, and the people, have been backsliding. Once again we begin to ape the ways of the gentiles." He paused and looked at the other rabbis, whose eyes were fixed on him. "Are we not a holy people? Is that not our mission?" he cried.

There was stirring around the table. The rabbis leaned forward, hanging on Rabbi Zechariah's every word. Rabbi Aaron saw no skepticism on their faces, except again, for the two rabbis on his left.

"If we look back to the time of the Maccabees," Zechariah said, his tone calmer now, as if he were merely giving a lecture to eager students, "is there any doubt that if they had not arisen all of our people would have fallen under the spell of Hellenist civilization, and both the people and Torah would have disappeared? It is only because a determined minority, armed only with the truth, took the fate of the people and the Land into their own hands that we are here today!"

Members of the House of Shammai nodded in agreement; even some Hillelites joined them.

"Oh yes, we have been backsliding," Zechariah said sadly. "We have been imitating the ways of the heathen Romans. One can see it in the behavior of the people and the elites and even of the rabbis." Zechariah turned his gaze on Rabbi Johanan. "Rabbi Johanan ben Zakkai, our esteemed scholar of the school of Hillel, left the Galilee and came to Jerusalem because he said the people of Galilee hate the Torah and will thus fall into the hands of the robbers! And so, in all humility, I propose eighteen measures that will compel the people to separate themselves from the gentiles and thus return to the Torah."

Rabbi Zechariah looked at Rabbi Simeon and tilted his head.

"You may proceed," Simeon said.

Zechariah nodded, looked around the table, and again addressed the assembly.

"It is necessary to separate ourselves from the gentiles," he said. "These eighteen decrees will accomplish that. These are forbidden: their bread, their cheese, their wine, their vinegar," Zechariah spoke the list with rhythmic precision, "their sauces, their cooking salts, their pickled food, their boiled foods, their salts, their spelt, their grinded foods, their fish, their language, their testimony, their gifts, their sons, their daughters, their first born."

When Zechariah finished the loft fell so silent that the heavy breathing of each rabbi could be heard, until a commotion broke out as the students of the House of Shammai shouted their assent and most of the students of the House of Hillel hissed their disapproval.

Rabbi Simeon raised his hand. The hubbub ceased. Zechariah sat.

"I am sure there are those in this room who would speak in opposition to your decrees," Rabbi Simeon said.

"If only Rabbi Moshe were here!" someone from the House of Hillel cried.

Rabbi Aaron took a deep breath. He gave a quick look at rabbis Simeon and Johanan, saw their nods of approval, and slowly rose from the bench, hesitantly at first; by the time his full height was above the table he was standing tall and straight.

"I will speak for my brother," he said, so loudly everyone could hear him.

"Well, well, the man who whispers has finally found a voice," Rabbi Yoel called out mockingly.

"My brother's spirit has entered me," Rabbi Aaron responded.

"I would have thought you would have remained at home to mourn your brother!"

"I have come so I will not have to mourn the Temple!" retorted Rabbi Aaron.

Yoel did not respond. He gave a sly smile, stood up, and left the room without even giving a glance at his teacher, Rabbi Zechariah, closing the door so quietly that it did not make a sound.

"I have much to say about these decrees," Rabbi Aaron began. "For the moment I will not discuss how refusing their gifts means refusing the Roman emperor's Temple offerings, which will lead to war. And I will not discuss how these decrees will cut off all dealings with our neighbors. And I will not discuss how we already have restrictions on some of these; wine, for example. No, I want to point out to our colleagues in the House of Shammai that these decrees will fall most heavily on the poor and those who work the land, on those very people and classes that you of the School of Shammai care so strongly about. Is a Jew forbidden to buy bread or spelt or fish from a gentile? That will mean that in some places the only supplier will be a Jew. He will have a monopoly and be able to charge whatever he likes. The common people will suffer, suffer more severely than if the Romans—"

The door to the loft burst open with a loud bang. Rabbi Aaron stopped speaking in mid-sentence, and with everyone else, looked toward the entrance of the loft.

Rabbi Yoel entered, followed by Judah ben Ezra and seven of his men. Except for the rabbi, they were all armed. Each had a knife in his belt. Rabbi Aaron recognized one of the seven, Shaul ben Yitzchak. Shaul held a thick wooden stave. The other six, none of whom were known to Rabbi Aaron, carried lances or swords. All, including the rabbi, had threatening looks on their faces.

"This is an outrage!" shouted one of the Hillelite rabbis. "Rabbi Zechariah, tell Rabbi Yoel to get these hooligans out of here!" Cries of agreement accompanied his demand and echoed through the loft.

"As the Maccabees did, so we do," Zechariah said gravely.

"You are not the Maccabees," declared Rabbi Johanan ben Zakkai. "And Nero is not Antiochus. Furthermore, your student Yoel has brought the very robbers I feared would rule the godless people of Galilee."

"There were those among the Jews who called the Maccabees robbers," replied Zechariah.

"Not the Torah scholars!" insisted Rabbi Johanan.

"I, too, am a Torah scholar, Rabbi Johanan," said Zechariah. "And I see what the students of your school, blinded by the privileges they receive from the Romans, cannot or will not see. And I know what needs to be done!"

"Your arrogance will destroy a nation!" cried Rabbi Johanan.

"One of these men, whom you call robbers," said Zechariah heatedly, "is the grandson of the great rabbi Judas of the Galilee. Judas taught us that only God should be our master. When Quirinius, legate of Syria, wanted to conduct a census to tax our people Judas urged opposition. His revolt failed; he was killed. Now the time has come to fulfill his dream and free ourselves. And the time has come to vote on these measures."

"I'm leaving," Rabbi Tarfon ben Zadok called out. He stood up at once. "I suggest we all leave. Without a quorum this gathering has no standing."

Rabbi Tarfon was a short, bent man in his sixties who walked with a pronounced limp. As he neared the door Shaul ben Yitzchak blocked the exit.

"Out of my way!" Rabbi Tarfon demanded.

Shaul raised the stave high in the air and brought it down forcefully against the cheek and jaw of Rabbi Tarfon.

The rabbi fell to the ground, crying out in pain, blood gushing from his face.

There were gasps and shrieks from around the table coming from the Hillelites.

"Get him to a physician!" someone shouted.

"We will," said Judah ben Ezra. "Once a vote is taken."

Rabbi Aaron watched and listened with disbelief.

"This is a house of Torah scholars?" he roared in anger. "This is not a rabbinical assembly; this is a house invaded by highwaymen and robbers! You are worse than Florus. Even he would never dare such a thing!"

Zechariah ignored him.

"We will proceed with the vote," he declared emphatically. "On all the measures, not just one by one."

The rabbis from the school of Hillel were in such shock that they sat numbly without protesting as all twenty-one rabbis from the school of Shammai voted to approve the eighteen decrees. When their votes had been taken there was silence in the loft, except for the moans coming from Rabbi Tarfon, who lay writhing on the floor where he had fallen.

Rabbi Zechariah broke that silence.

Turning to Rabbi Shlomo ben Uzziel, the Hillelite rabbi sitting closest to those who just voted, he asked, "How do you vote, Rabbi Shlomo ben Uzziel?"

Rabbi Shlomo ben Uzziel was thirty-two years old, tall and thin. He stood resolutely and declared:

"I vote no to all!"

Judah ben Ezra walked over to the table and faced Rabbi Shlomo. Judah smiled sardonically.

"Perhaps you'd like to reconsider," he said. "My friend here with the stick has a very convincing argument."

"I'm not afraid of you, Judah ben Ezra," retorted Rabbi Shlomo.

"I'm not afraid to die. Kill me if you must. I vote no!" he shouted.

One of Judah's men, John ben Dorcas, who carried a lance, stepped toward the table. Before anyone could say or do anything John ben Dorcas thrust his lance into Rabbi Shlomo's chest. The rabbi stumbled backwards and forwards, falling onto the table where the lance kept his lifeless body propped up as blood dripped from it.

Screams of terror filled the room. Fear rooted the Hillel rabbis to their seats; any one of them might be killed next.

Even Judah ben Ezra looked shocked; his eyes widened momentarily before he glared angrily at John ben Dorcas.

Rabbi Zechariah rose, trembling.

"Let us proceed with the vote!" Zechariah said, his voice breaking, its power gone.

Rabbi Aaron stood up.

"How dare you call for a vote now!" he cried. "You have turned this rabbinical assembly into a desecration of God's name! And now you are an accessory to murder!"

Zechariah grew pale, he had to lean on the table for support. But John ben Dorcas calmly pulled the lance from Rabbi Shlomo's body, allowing it to flop onto the table, and sauntered over to where Rabbi Aaron stood.

"You next?" he asked, readying his bloody lance.

"No!" cried Zechariah.

Judah laid a hand on Dorcas' shoulder. Dorcas shook it off.

"I think we should finish the voting before anyone else meets an untimely end!" Dorcas declared. "And I think you," he added, pointing at Rabbi Aaron with the lance, "had better sit down and shut up."

The eyes of the rabbis went from Dorcas to Rabbi Aaron and back to Dorcas again. Rabbi Aaron sat down.

All opposition had been cowed. The vote was unanimous.

"You have what you want," snapped Rabbi Simeon ben Gamliel. "Now let us leave and get help for Rabbi Tarfon. It is too late for Rabbi Shlomo."

"I will bring Rabbi Tarfon to a physician," Zechariah said, his voice shaking. "One of Judah's men will help me. I will also take Rabbi Phineas ben Cathla of the House of Hillel with me." He paused, caught hold of himself, and continued calmly, "I am going to announce the results of this assembly to the Temple ministers and the priests and the people. Rabbi Phineas will confirm what I say. When I return you all can leave and say and do whatever you please."

"What? Are you holding us captive?" asked Rabbi Simeon ben Gamliel.

"Call it what you will," Zechariah replied. He was back in command of himself now; he spoke with the same authority that he had before Dorcas killed Rabbi Shlomo. "Rabbi Yoel ben Jotham is in charge. Judah ben Ezra will keep order. If anyone needs to use the privy one of Judah's men will accompany him to make sure he returns. If anyone is hungry food will be provided from Rabbi Hanania's house below. Remember, you must remain here until I return," Zechariah said with finality.

Judah pointed to Shaul and to the floor where Rabbi Tarfon lay. Shaul walked over to Rabbi Tarfon and picked him up. As Rabbi Zechariah was about to leave with the dragooned Rabbi Phineas and Shaul ben Yitzchak carrying the still moaning Rabbi Tarfon, Rabbi Johanan called out:

"Rabbi Zechariah!" Zechariah turned back to look at Johanan. "Today the robbers lay siege to the rabbinical Sanhedrin. Tomorrow the Romans will lay siege to all of Israel. We will not eat your food, we will go hungry instead, so we will know what lies ahead, for when the Romans come Jerusalem will suffer the agony of starvation!" Rabbi Aaron shivered; Rabbi Johanan said in words what he could see before his own eyes. Rabbi Johanan pointed an accusing finger at Rabbi Zechariah and in the fierce voice of a prophet proclaimed: "This day will be recorded as hard for Israel as the day on which the golden calf was made!"

Rabbi Zechariah shuddered in the face of Johanan's charge. He turned away from him, his head bowed, and left without saying a word.

Chapter Fifteen

22 Jun 66 CE / 12 Tammuz 3826

Judah ben Ezra was hungry, he sorely wanted to go downstairs and get some food, but when even the rabbis from the School of Shammai were refusing to eat in the presence of Rabbi Johanan ben Zakkai, Judah decided it would be too arrogant to walk around smacking his lips over bread soaked in olive oil. Prudence dictated that he wait like everyone else.

Rabbi Shlomo ben Uzziel's body had been covered and laid in a corner. Several of the rabbis were escorted to the privy but apart from that they sat without talking as the hours passed slowly.

Unbelievable, Judah mused; these rabbis who constantly chatter are now silent as a grave in the presence of a corpse.

The thought made Judah laugh out loud. He returned the angry glares with a frightening smile of his own.

When at last the door to the loft opened and Rabbi Zechariah ben Abkulas stepped inside with Rabbi Phineas ben Cathla and Shaul ben Yitzchak, life again stirred around the table. Men spoke again, some loudly, some in quick whispers. Others stood. A few pointed at the body of Rabbi Shlomo and wailed.

"We are done," Rabbi Zechariah announced. "Let us attend to Rabbi Shlomo ben Uzziel's body. Then we can all go our separate ways."

Zechariah nodded at Judah.

"You and your men are no longer needed," Zechariah said, adding solemnly, in a voice strong enough for all the room to hear, "The burden you have taken on will be remembered with gratitude by future generations of Israel, even if your names remain unknown."

Judah looked at Rabbi Zechariah, smiled, raised his right fist and called out to his men. "Fellow freedom fighters, our mission here is accomplished. Let us leave the rabbis to their own affairs." Then he strode to the door of the loft, trailed by his seven followers.

After descending the stairs and exiting the house of Rabbi Hanania ben Hezekiah ben Geron, Judah realized how much time had actually passed. It was night, the sky was filled with stars. His hunger sharpened. He wanted food even more than before.

Shaul walked by his side. The other six scattered in different directions.

"I'm glad to get out," Judah said, taking a deep breath. "Ah, fresh air! It stank in there! Besides, I'm starving! But first tell me, what happened with Rabbi Zechariah?"

"First we found someone to take care of Tarfon," Shaul related. "He was crying like a baby but he was all right. Then we went to Eleazar." Shaul grew excited. "Eleazar and the young Temple ministers around him listened as Rabbi Zechariah listed the Eighteen Decrees one by one. Eleazar asked if that meant they should refuse the offerings from Rome." Shaul stopped walking, spread his arms wide, and cried, "Of course! Eleazar and his men cheered!" Shaul grinned broadly and resumed walking. "Then Rabbi Zechariah went to Ananias and the other old priests and spoke to them. They were mad!" Shaul laughed. "They sputtered and shouted they would nullify the decrees."

"Let them scream all they want. What can they do?" Shaul went on. "Later Rabbi Zechariah gathered a group of prominent citizens. I didn't know any of those people. When he told them about the decrees, they were as mad as the priests!" Shaul laughed again. "I bet the priests and those rich folks are going to get together and try to reverse the decrees. Anyway, after that, Rabbi Zechariah went to the Upper Market and announced the Eighteen Decrees. Some of the folks there cheered, others were quiet. He went to the Sheep Market and the Wood Market, too. He went everywhere!" Shaul concluded.

"You're in a fine mood," Judah noted. "Your funk is gone. Hearing the angels again?"

"It's not that," Shaul explained. "When I saw John ben Dorcas kill Rabbi Shlomo I felt a weight lifted from me."

"That fool!" spat Judah.

Shaul stopped walking again and looked at Judah quizzically.

"What's the difference between the first and the second?" Shaul asked.

"It was necessary to silence Rabbi Moshe," Judah explained. "We had no other choice. Shlomo was another matter. Killing was not needed. Why, a few whacks of your stave and he would have come around. And if that didn't work, I would have changed his mind." Judah laughed bitterly, then added, "No, there was no need to kill Shlomo. You see, Shaul, you only kill when necessary. Violence is a means, not an end. I'm afraid John Dorcas enjoys killing for its own sake. He's dangerous. He'll cause problems if he's not watched."

Judah put his arm on Shaul's shoulder and nudged him to begin walking.

"Oh well," Judah said, "I guess we won't have any Roman officers looking into Rabbi Shlomo's death. Pretty soon they'll have bigger things to worry about."

They reached the cross-street where they were to go in separate directions, Judah to the left and Shaul to the right. Judah glanced over at Shaul.

"All right," Judah said, "something's bothering you. Tell me what it is."

Shaul lowered his left foot to the ground and spun on his instep to face Judah.

"Who did you bring to your room?"

The question caught Judah by surprise.

Yes, he wondered. Who is that person? Do I even know her?

Judah slipped into a reverie as Shaul, puzzled at the sudden change, waited for an answer.

Yes, who is Bruria, Judah asked himself. A remorseless whore who could sleep with an intriguing stranger two days after her husband was murdered? A fiery patriot—forced to hide her views—finally freed to join the cause and truly believing that he, Judah, would drive out the Romans and become king of Israel? Or was she simply a woman who had become unbalanced by her husband's death?

Judah never had a woman give herself to him so completely, so ferociously. Yet when he asked her if she had denounced him to the Romans she stared at him with icy eyes and lips held tight, saying nothing.

Perhaps she is all three, he reasoned. Whore, patriot, mad woman.

Judah did not know; he was not sure she knew, either. It did not matter. He was eager to get back to her.

She's waiting for me, he thought with assurance, waiting for me to tell her of my triumph.

"Judah, who did you bring to your room?" Shaul asked again.

Judah didn't bother answering. He turned away and continued on alone. Shaul's curiosity was of no concern to him.

Chapter Sixteen

22 Jun 66 CE / 12 Tammuz 3826

As he set forth into the night, Rabbi Aaron ben Avraham's tall frame bent under his double burden of mourning. Several paces behind him walked Rabbi Johanan ben Zakkai. Rabbi Aaron slowed his stride.

"May I walk with you a while?" Rabbi Aaron asked Rabbi Johanan. Rabbi Johanan nodded.

"I mourn my brother," Rabbi Aaron said. "And I mourn the coming catastrophe. Torah scholars are murdered without justice, illegitimate decrees are passed by a Sanhedrin under duress, and learned men countenance vile acts in order to start an unwinnable war. It can only lead to the Temple in flames, the Land abandoned, and the people bereft of hope. I don't know what to do. I can't bring my brother back to life. Can I, can we, stop the destruction about to engulf us?"

In the faint starlight Rabbi Aaron saw a smile light the face of Rabbi Johanan.

"Look up at the heavens, Rabbi Aaron," Johanan replied. "See its multitude of stars. Can we count them? Would a lifetime be enough? Perhaps. But the Holy One, Blessed be He, is like the counting of stars that has no beginning and no end, even if we had thousands upon thousands of lives in which to count. God is the *ein sof*, the Infinite. This is beyond the understanding of men, even the wisest of them. Despite our limitations we can bring the infinity of God, the Creator of the world, nearer to our own conception by imagining the space of the cosmos extended to unthinkable distances."

Rabbi Aaron raised his head and gazed upward, trying to grasp the meaning of Rabbi Johanan's words as the world around him was descending into chaos.

"God exists in all the vastness of the universe," Rabbi Johanan continued. "And He exists outside the universe. He is not limited to the Holy of Holies in the Temple in Jerusalem. Even if the Holy of Holies, and the Temple, and the City itself is destroyed, even if all the people are exiled from the Land, we can still find the Holy One, Blessed be He, as long as we do not lose Torah love and Torah learning. At all costs these must be preserved!"

Rabbi Aaron looked sharply at Johanan and said:

"Then you think war is inevitable."

"I do not know, Rabbi Aaron. I truly do not know. Gessius Florus is doing everything he can to oppress the people and spark a revolt to cover up his crimes. Rabbi Zechariah and the robbers will do all they can to fan those sparks into flames of war."

"Why is Rabbi Zechariah involved with men like Judah ben Ezra?" Rabbi Aaron asked.

"I do not know that, either. Rabbi Zechariah is a true Torah scholar. He must believe that he is acting with righteousness. Perhaps he will realize his error one day. By then it will be too late, for the robbers he has unleashed believe in nothing. They love violence for its own sake. They will struggle with each other for dominance and the worst among them will succeed. Did you see Judah ben Ezra's face when one of the robbers killed Rabbi Shlomo? Beating Rabbi Tarfon was fine with Judah; killing Rabbi Shlomo was not. In the end, men like that robber will rule even the leaders like Judah ben Ezra. Shammai rabbis will never control them. Rabbi Zechariah shook when Rabbi Shlomo was murdered; he was as horrified as the rest of us. Soon the robbers will swallow the Shammai rabbis as big fish gulp down little fish. Then they will destroy Israel as surely as the Romans will."

It was too much for Rabbi Aaron. He stopped walking and gasped for air.

"Ah, my dear Rabbi Aaron," Rabbi Johanan comforted, "we must do everything we can in the struggle for peace. Rabbi Simeon will issue a statement declaring that the vote was coerced and therefore meaningless." Johanan paused for a moment. A sigh escaped him. "Unfortunately, we can't call another assembly to revoke the Eighteen Decrees. We don't have enough rabbis on our side for a quorum." He sighed again. "At least we will make clear to the people and the Romans that the House of Hillel is against these decrees."

"Are we that helpless?" Rabbi Aaron exclaimed. "Is that all we can do?"

"No," Rabbi Johanan responded quickly. "There are ways we can act strategically. We must understand the Romans, know how they think, and know the best way to approach them so we can surrender with reasonable terms if there is war. To receive reasonable terms from them any war must be limited. Jerusalem is a jewel of the Roman Empire, they will not destroy it unless we force them to. But Rome will not let Judea go. If Judea revolts, they will send their best general against us; our success would lead other provinces in the empire to revolt. The Romans will not allow that.

"They say Nero is cruel and a madman. A man can be cruel and keep a throne; if he is also mad he will lose it. Herod, like Nero, murdered his family. But Herod was cunning; Nero is not. Herod's rule lasted many years; Nero's days are numbered. One of his generals will overthrow him, perhaps the one who subdues Judea."

Rabbi Johanan shuddered; it was contagious, for Rabbi Aaron shuddered, too.

"What is it?" cried Rabbi Aaron, alarmed.

"Herod, Herod," Rabbi Johanan muttered with distaste. Rabbi Aaron thought that another man would have spat the way Johanan said the name.

"What, Rabbi Johanan? What is it?"

"Herod, that evildoer, may his name be erased, created the Temple as we see it today. It was he who embellished it, made it outwardly magnificent, turning it into one of the wonders of the world. Herod was a cruel and godless man. Perhaps his touch laid a curse upon—"

Rabbi Johanan ben Zakkai could not go on, he could not finish his thought. Rabbi Aaron saw Johanan's whole body shake uncontrollably. Rabbi Aaron was not sure what to do; he wanted to grab Rabbi Johanan and steady him.

The shaking stopped.

"Good night, Rabbi Aaron," Johanan said curtly. "It is time for us to part. Your brother was a great scholar and one of the peacemakers; may Rabbi Moshe ben Avraham's memory live forever in the minds and hearts of the Jewish people, may it serve as an inspiration and a blessing to them."

Rabbi Johanan ben Zakkai did not wait for a reply. He walked out into the night, leaving Rabbi Aaron more burdened than before.

Chapter Seventeen

22 Jun 66 CE / 12 Tammuz 3826

The moment Judah went out of the room with his tall young friend, Bruria felt one weight lift and another descend. She had sullied herself with Judah, on the Sabbath, no less; she was glad to be out of his presence. But now that she was alone she began to be plagued by doubt.

She took off her concealing cloak and shawl and tossed them on the table. She glanced around the room

What if she were wrong? What if Judah hadn't killed Moshe? That Roman officer seemed a competent and serious fellow. He told Rabbi Aaron that Judah had been cleared of Moshe's murder. He had interrogated Judah himself; Judah had been with a companion nowhere near the Xystus Plaza at the time of Moshe's death. Judah's companion confirmed Judah's story.

That companion? Was he the tall young man she replaced in Judah's room?

As Judah was leaving Bruria's house this morning to "take care of business", as he put it, he told her he would be back later. "No!" she insisted. It was not safe for him to visit her. Someone might see him. Her reputation would be ruined and there would be consequences. He would have to take her to his place in secret. She gathered her things, took a few silver denari to have money, and covered herself from head to toe. She accompanied him affecting a limp and walking bent. She was sure no one would recognize her.

Judah's room made the home Moshe gave her seem like one of the mansions in the Upper City. No matter. Her life was not of concern anymore. Only vengeance for Moshe!

That companion! Was he involved? What about that big, tall woman in the gray dress? She must have seen something! Should she have searched for this mysterious woman before embarking on this dangerous plan?

The doubts buzzed about her head more thickly. She felt dizzy. What if she were wrong? To the sin of whoring would she be adding murder?

Bruria found herself standing in the center of the room, her head turning slowly on her neck, her eyes scanning the wall, the table, the wooden box, the bed, everything she could see, as if searching for guidance.

How ironic, she thought. If only Moshe were here to guide me.

How she had made his life miserable! What a harpy she had been, constantly nagging him. Her home was not good enough. Nothing was good enough. Yet he always treated her with kindness and understanding. Oh Moshe, you died without knowing how much I loved you!

Tears sprang to her eyes, distorting her vision.

She knew, in her bones, that Judah was responsible for Moshe's death. She had heard the threat. She could not bring Moshe back to life. She could not make up for what she never gave him. But she could get justice for her husband and revenge for herself.

Justice? The word flew around in her head, eluding capture. There was no evidence and no witnesses. And the civil authorities had cleared him. Who was she to take the law into her own hands? Only the Romans and the rabbis were responsible for such things.

She wiped her eyes and looked around the room again. Perhaps there was something, anything…

Though it seemed like such a weak possibility, and she felt foolish for even thinking it, she resolved to search the room. There might be something that proved Judah's guilt.

She searched everywhere, looking under the bed, in the simple cupboard, even the underside of the table and into cups and empty jars. As time passed, the feeling of being foolish increased.

Then she came to the wooden box in the corner. It was the last thing left to examine.

She stared down at the box. The hair on the back of her neck stood up.

Bruria went down on her knees and opened the box. She slowly removed items one by one and examined each. At the very bottom was a carelessly folded thick cloth of gray wool. She took it out and stood.

She held it by one end and allowed it to shake loose. A very large gray woolen dress unfolded gracefully to the floor. A gray woolen dress with bloodstains.

Bruria shivered.

Moshe's blood!

Her hands shook and her mind reeled at the obscene juxtaposition of Moshe's precious blood and the murderer's cruel disguise.

It took her several moments to regain her composure and fight the urge to put the dress down.

She held the dress up, trying to ignore the blood so she could concentrate and gauge the size of the dress. Too large for Judah, she concluded. The right size for the tall young man she had seen in this room.

Bruria laid the dress down gently along the top of the box.

She saw everything clearly now. That big, tall woman in the gray dress was not a woman at all. It was Judah's companion, the one she had seen here, and he wasn't simply a witness. He was the one, during the disturbance the Roman commander described, who had gone up and delivered the actual blow that killed Moshe. The plan, though, was Judah's. He was the brains behind it all. The young man was only a follower.

I'll deal with Judah first, Bruria thought. Then I'll take care of his young man.

Her decision satisfied her, until another doubt crept into Bruria's mind.

Should I take this dress to the Roman commander? Show it to Rabbi Aaron? Let them handle it?

As she pondered this option she ran her hand casually through her hair. The motion reminded her of the way Judah had stroked her hair before she had put on the cloak and shawl to conceal herself.

She felt physically sick.

I have turned myself into a whore, she thought. I will have vengeance by my own hand.

Bruria carefully put the dress, and everything else, back into the box and closed it. She took her money and went out into the street, to the shops, to prepare a feast, as Queen Esther prepared one for Haman, only she, Bruria, would be Jael to Sisera. Not a pale beautiful queen who ran to men for protection; she would be a warrior woman of the tents who slew an enemy of Israel with her own hand.

Bruria was ecstatic as she went from shop to shop, buying fresh bread, olive oil, figs and dates. She bought goat meat and wine, lots of wine. She knew what business Judah had referred to. She knew about the rabbinical assembly with its Eighteen Decrees. She was sure Judah would return triumphant. She would offer him a feast and wine, and then herself. More wine would follow. He would sleep. She would have her revenge.

When she came back to Judah's room she set the table. She made up her face and put on a dress that she wore only on festive occasions. And then she waited. And waited.

Afternoon passed into evening. Judah entered with a smile.

"Bruria!" he cried.

She pointed to the set table.

"A feast for my king!" she declared.

Judah looked at the food greedily. He sat and ate, sometimes wolfing down the food, sometimes savoring it. He drank the wine, at first with slow sips and then gulping it.

When he finished the meal, when his stomach was sated, she offered herself. When he came to take her she responded with such intensity it surprised him. *He thinks it is passion,* she thought, looking into his eyes; *he sees lust; his own lust clouds his eyes; he cannot see the revenge in mine.*

Afterwards, she poured him more wine. He drank where he lay, his head unsteady, his eyes glazed. He fell back on the bed. Soon the sound of his even breathing filled the room as he slept.

Bruria went to the clothes Judah had discarded on the floor and took the knife from his belt. She had never held one so long and so heavy before. Her hand trembled for an instant before steadying. She crept silently toward him.

Bruria stood over Judah and looked down.

His neck, she thought, *his neck. I will slice through it as he did to my Moshe.*

She grasped the knife firmly in both hands, raised it, took a deep breath, and with all her strength drove it downward as fast as she could toward the neck of the sleeping Judah.

It never reached its mark.

Strong hands grasped her forearms. Dark eyes filled with sadness stared up at her.

"Why, Bruria, why?" Judah asked in anguish.

"You fooled the Romans, you fooled his brother." Bruria's voice was hard, her eyes shone with hate. "But I knew, I knew from the very beginning! No, even before that. When you threatened him! I knew!" The confusion on Judah's face was slowly replaced by understanding.

"You know," he said, his voice heavy with regret. "I could not decide whether you were the whore of Israel or you truly believed in me and our cause. Revenge never occurred to me." His brow furrowed for an instant. "That story about the Roman dishonoring you was made up to trick me, wasn't it?"

Bruria could dissemble no longer. Rage overcame her fear.

"You conceited son of a pig! So cunning. You'd believe anything a woman told you. Moshe will live on in the memory of the Jewish people. You will die forgotten at the hand of one of your own cutthroats."

Anger replaced understanding on Judah's face.

"My dear Bruria," he said, "your problem is that I am not Sisera and you are not Jael. I am a freedom fighter for the people and Land of Israel. You are just a poor misguided fool who has wasted your courage. Ah, yes, what a waste, you and your husband. He could have been the voice of freedom, instead of the voice of treason. He could have swayed all the doubters among the rabbis and the people, instead of having to die for betraying them. You could have been a woman of valor, pouring boiling oil on the Romans when they came to our walls to scale them, attacking with your knife any who managed to get through. You could have inspired other women with your bravery, instead of having to die for betraying me.

"Ah, Bruria, it is all such a shame. Nevertheless I salute you, for despite everything you are a woman of valor. How sad your husband never knew what you were willing to do for him."

Judah shook his head and smiled his ghastly smile.

"I will miss you, Bruria."

Powerful fingers twisted Bruria's wrists. She screamed in pain; Judah's knife clattered to the floor, useless. Those same fingers circled her neck; she gasped, trying to recite a final prayer. She closed her eyes and saw Moshe's face. Then all went dark.

Chapter Eighteen

22 Jun 66 CE / 12 Tammuz 3826

Reuven remained silent throughout his father's diatribe. In truth, Reuven was horrified by what happened yesterday at the rabbinical assembly. And yet...

His father finished speaking. Reuven knew a response was expected. Reuven wished he knew what to say, or even what to think.

"It was terrible," Reuven agreed with his father. "And the murder of Rabbi Shlomo was unforgivable. But you yourself said that Judah ben Ezra was surprised by it. A leader can't always control his followers."

"A leader is responsible for what his followers do!" Rabbi Aaron thundered.

Yes, Reuven thought, but I can't condemn Judah. He saved my life. And he is fighting for the freedom of the Jewish people.

"And what about the passing of the Eighteen Decrees?" his father demanded. "Down our throats? With violence?"

That was wrong, Reuven thought. There had to be a better way. As for the decrees themselves, Reuven was not sure. Perhaps they were a good thing. Perhaps they were needed. As for the method used to pass them, distasteful, surely, but what if they were necessary to achieve the needed results?

"And they will lead to war with Rome!" his father shouted.

"Perhaps war is inevitable, Father," Reuven said softly. "Perhaps we should be preparing for it."

"What? What did you say? Are you crazy? Do you know what the result will be?"

Reuven let his father rage on. He lowered his head and remained silent, the way an obedient son should.

Then he raised his head and looked his father straight in the eyes.

Am I an obedient son? he asked himself. Do I want to be?

He lowered his head again, but stood up and walked out of the room while his father was still in mid-sentence.

Chapter Nineteen

23 Jun 66 CE / 12 Tammuz 3826

Shaul ben Yitzchak watched and listened as Ananias, the high priest of the Temple, harshly scolded his son Eleazar, the captain of the Temple ministers, at the public meeting in front of the Bronze Gate of the Temple. Shaul wondered: Does Eleazar feel the way I did when my father warned me against joining Judah's men?

"This is insanity!" Ananias shouted. "A bunch of rabbis issue decrees and you follow them without consulting me? They were issued under duress. They have no validity. Rabbi Simeon here can testify that they only passed because the revolutionaries threatened to kill everyone if they didn't."

Ananias stood at the foot of the fourteen curved steps that led up to the Bronze Gate. From the top of those steps, in front of the gate, Eleazar looked down at his father.

Eleazar had a smirk on his face.

Gathered around Ananias were the senior priests, many of the most prominent citizens of the Upper City, and a few rabbis from the House of Hillel. Behind the elite was a curious crowd of mostly ordinary citizens. Shaul had positioned himself at the outermost edge of this group.

The entire assemblage was located in the easternmost section of the inner court of the Temple. Behind Shaul was a wall that surrounded the inner Temple complex and enclosed the Temple itself. Further back the massive wall that protected Jerusalem and the Temple from the east towered over the steep drop to the Kidron Valley below.

"This is an outrage!" Ananias cried, shaking his fist. "Yesterday some rabbi I never heard of comes to you with a bunch of decrees and you stop accepting the sacrifices from Rome? This is unheard of! We've always accepted gifts for the Temple and sacrifices from foreigners. And you refuse an offering from the emperor of Rome? The emperor of Rome! Are you mad? When he finds out he might order all sacrifices to cease. What then? You want a war? This is insanity! You must resume the Roman sacrifices immediately!"

The smirk on Eleazar's face widened.

No, Shaul thought, Eleazar is not like me. He's supremely confident. I did not give my father that kind of look.

Shaul remembered his father's admonition. "I hate the Romans as much as you do, Shaul," his father had said, "but this Judah is up to no good. There's no way he can fight the Romans and win. He'll get himself killed and you along with him. The only way we'll have deliverance is to pray for the Messiah to come. There are signs that that time may be soon." When Shaul tried to argue his father wouldn't listen and said harshly: "I forbid you to leave!" Then, in a softer tone: "Stay here with me. Take over the farm when I get too old. Why don't you marry Dvorah, that nice girl from Gamla?"

Gamla was a town in the Golan, on the far side of the Sea of Galilee. Shaul and his father were poor farmers who lived outside the town. Shaul, unwilling to openly defy his father, snuck away at night, though not without misgivings.

No, Shaul thought, Eleazar is not afraid to defy his father.

There were two buildings forty feet high in the court, one on the north side and one on the south side. Each building had a chamber at its east and west end with a narrow section in the middle. Thus, there were four chambers in the court; the southeast was for those who made special vows, the southwest held oil, the northwest was for the purification of those with skin diseases, and the northeast was the wood store. Stone pillars supported the overhanging roofs with short parapets. On those roofs, the young Temple ministers, followers of Eleazar, kept careful watch on the proceedings below. Shaul saw that they were armed with swords and spears.

Shaul nodded with appreciation. There is no way Ananias can force Eleazar to accept the Roman sacrifices, he thought.

The Bronze Gate, made of Corinthian bronze, gleamed in the morning sun. It had double doors, each forty-five feet high and almost twenty-three feet wide. On either side was a pillar that supported a lintel over the entrance to the gate. Past each pillar was a gate room forty-five feet square. The whole structure was over sixty feet high. The Bronze Gate led to the Court of the Israelites, the altar, and the Temple itself.

No, Shaul thought. There is nothing they can do. The Temple itself is in the hands of the rebels.

Shaul was disappointed that Judah wasn't there. None of Judah's band were, neither those who had been with him at the rabbinical assembly the day before nor the fifty-two others who had followed him down from the north to Jerusalem. Rabbi Zechariah and Rabbi Joel were also nowhere to be seen.

Shaul scratched his head. Rabbi Aaron stood among the rabbis but not Rabbi Johanan ben Zakkai, the one who had laid a curse on Rabbi Zechariah. Why wasn't he there? Shaul had heard there was bad blood between Rabbi Johanan and Ananias. The rabbi once made a ruling about the way Ananias was carrying out some ritual in the Temple. The substance of the issue was beyond Shaul's ken, but it was common knowledge that Ananias had been enraged at Johanan's interference, and had grown even angrier when he had to yield to the rabbi.

Shaul smiled with satisfaction; any split in the party of the traitors was good for the rebellion.

He was so lost in his thoughts that he did not hear Ananias conclude his speech. By the time he started paying attention again another man was addressing Eleazar and his supporters, Nakdimon ben Gorion, one of the richest men of the City.

"We cannot allow this to continue!" Nakdimon declared. "If you do not stand down we will be forced to take over the Temple so that the sacrifices for Rome can resume!"

Shaul looked up at the armed Temple ministers.

If there's going to be a fight, he thought, Judah and our gang should be here.

Shaul spun around, ran through the open back gate, through the outer courts, and into the magnificent Basilica with its two stories of porticos supported by pillars topped with gilded Corinthian capitals, pillars so thick three men with arms outstretched could barely encircle one. Then down the stairs, jumping two at a time, out through the Huldah gate, past the monument to the prophetess Huldah, past the part of the city known as Ophel, and into the narrow streets of the Lower City. By the time he reached Judah's dwelling Shaul was panting heavily.

Shaul flung open the unlocked door. Judah was sitting at the table, swaying slightly side to side. He glanced up at Shaul but did not seem to recognize him. Judah was drunk, very drunk.

Shaul looked around the room. Judah's guest lay on the bed, asleep. He was covered head to toe with a sheet. Shaul looked more closely. The dress he had used to disguise himself when he killed Rabbi Moshe lay on top of the sleeping form. Shaul was startled.

He had to lean against the doorpost. His labored breath, that dress draped over the guest, and Judah drunk—Judah whom he had never even seen take a sip of wine—were all too much for Shaul. It took several moments for Shaul to recover.

"Judah!" Shaul shouted at last. "Judah!" he shouted again.

Shaul saw recognition in Judah's eyes.

"Shaul, Shaul," Judah muttered.

"Judah, sober up. There's a meeting at the Bronze Gate. Eleazar refused the Roman sacrifices. The traitors may try to force him to resume. We should all be there to help Eleazar!"

"What?" Judah rubbed his face with his hands. "So what?"

"So what? Ah, you're still drunk!"

Who is that sleeping through all this noise, Shaul wondered. He resolved to satisfy his curiosity. After he had taken a few steps toward the bed, Judah called out:

"Don't go there!"

Shaul stopped. Two conflicting impulses fought for control; on the one hand he wanted to see the unmoving sleeper but on the other Judah had become like a father to him and he was loathe to defy Judah.

I couldn't openly disobey my father, he thought. Eleazar did! Can I disobey Judah?

"Who is it?" Shaul demanded. "Why isn't he moving?"

Judah didn't answer.

Shaul looked from the bed to the back of Judah's head. Ah, he realized, there's probably a good reason his guest is not moving.

"Is he dead?" Shaul asked, in a tone that indicated he knew the answer.

Judah nodded.

"How?"

"I killed him," Judah said heavily.

"Why?"

"He tried to kill me."

"Who was it?" Shaul really wanted to know now.

"It doesn't matter!"

It does to me, Shaul thought, and strode over to the bed.

He pulled the sheet slightly away from the head of the corpse. Though it was only the briefest glance Shaul was sure that he recognized a familiar face. Shaul shuddered and put the sheet back over the head as quickly as he had tugged it away.

He pulled the knife from his belt and turned toward Judah.

"You bastard!" Shaul hissed. "You killed her!"

For a moment he stared at Judah, hate shining from his eyes. It gave Judah enough time to react to the charge and turn around to face Shaul. When Judah saw the knife in Shaul's right hand, its blade at right angles to Shaul's arm, Judah's face moved from the fog of wine to the sharpness of survival.

Shaul leapt at Judah as he shouted, "You killed my Dvorah!"

Judah jumped up from his seat and caught Shaul's forearm. But the younger man was taller and had leverage, Shaul's right arm was stronger than both of Judah's, and, though Judah was alert now, his reflexes were still slowed by the wine.

"Are you crazy?" Judah cried as the knife moved closer. "Who in Gehinom is Dvorah? The dead women is Bruria, wife of Moshe!"

Shaul's mouth fell open. He stopped the downward drive of his arm. Pulling his forearm free of Judah's hands, he stepped backward.

"Look, you lunatic, look!" screamed Judah. "Look and see it's not your Dvorah!"

Shaul's glare at Judah slowly changed to an expression of confusion. He stepped back to the corpse and pulled away the sheet. He stared at the face for a long time.

"It's not her, it's not her," he murmured softly. "They look so much alike…"

He turned back to Judah.

"I'm sorry," he said. "I thought it was Dvorah…"

"The girl you left behind?"

"Yes."

"Damn you, boy, maybe you should have stayed home and married her. You almost killed me." Judah made a face as if he had just bitten into a sour fruit.

"I'm sorry, Judah."

Judah shook his head with resignation.

"Forget it," he said, shrugging. "Just help me dispose of the body."

"Were you sleeping with her, Judah?"

"Yes."

"That wasn't too smart."

"I know. It's a good thing she didn't manage to kill me. You would have been next, Shaul."

"She wouldn't have gotten to me, Judah. She wouldn't have been able to entice me. She wasn't my Dvorah. Why did she try to kill you?"

"She knew, Shaul. She knew."

Shaul nodded.

"I understand," he said. "That's why you should have never let her get close to you. There was always the chance she would suspect."

Judah grinned and sat down.

"I made a mistake, Shaul," he said, raising his hands, palms up, in gesture of helplessness. "Just like you almost did. It doesn't matter now. We have to get rid of the body."

"How?"

"I want you to hire a donkey. We'll wrap her body really well, take it outside the City walls, and dump it somewhere."

"We can't do that, Judah. We have to bury her."

"I don't know where Moshe's grave is. Shall we ask his brother?" Judah replied sarcastically.

"We can't just dump the body, Judah. The Torah requires we bury her. Even executed criminals are entitled to that."

"Yes, yes," Judah responded, waving his hand dismissively. "We'll bury her." He got up and walked over to a pouch hanging on a hook. He plunged his hand inside and retrieved some silver coins.

"Here," he said to Shaul. "Take these and hurry back."

"What about the goings-on at the Temple?" Shaul asked.

"That will have to wait. Hurry, Shaul!"

Shaul took the coins and went to the door. He looked back at Judah with cool appraisal. Gone was the hero worship in his gaze.

"What can I say, Shaul? You killed the husband. I killed the wife."

Chapter Twenty

23 Jun 66 CE / 12 Tammuz 3826

Metilius marveled that he, a Roman officer in an occupied Jewish city on the brink of rebellion, without the guards he normally would have posted outside the door, could sit comfortably at the table of a Jew and not be concerned for his own safety.

"Do you always treat your guests to such a banquet?" he asked, smiling, looking down at his now empty plate.

Rabbi Aaron ben Avraham smiled in return.

"I am sure you are merely being polite and this humble meal is nothing compared to the banquets you have experienced, Commander Metilius."

"Those banquets never had the sense of peace and serenity that I experienced in your house during that Sabbath meal," Metilius responded. "And in your house you can just call me Metilius."

The smile left Rabbi Aaron's face.

"Well, I guess it's time to get to the purpose of your visit," he said. "It's not hard to figure out why you're here."

Metilius placed his hands flat on the table and looked squarely at Rabbi Aaron.

"Refusing the offering of Rome was an act of rebellion," Metilius said. "It was an insult to Nero and Rome. If it isn't reversed I can't say what the consequences will be, but they will be severe. I don't have authority to intervene in your religious affairs but once Rome hears about this—"

"I know, I know," Rabbi Aaron interrupted, throwing his hands up. "Believe me, I understand the implications of what was done, and the hopelessness of any attempt to revolt against Rome."

"I'm trying to understand what's going on," Metilius said. "I want to help you avoid a calamity, for all of us. Why did the rabbinical assembly pass those measures? They were passed unanimously!"

"We had no choice. We would have been killed otherwise."

"What?" Metilius was truly surprised. "Killed? By whom?"

"The rabbis who wanted to pass those measures were in the minority. They knew that. So they brought some thugs to threaten us if we didn't go along."

"Would they really have killed anyone?"

"They did," Rabbi Aaron replied shaking his head sadly. "Rabbi Shlomo ben Uzziel was murdered in front of our eyes as a warning."

Metilius shot up from his seat.

"Why didn't you come to me?" he demanded.

"Did you find my brother's murderer?"

"He was killed four days ago. What do you expect? We're still searching for that woman witness."

"Look, look, I'm sorry." Rabbi Aaron bowed his head and covered his face. He took several deep breaths before looking up at Metilius again. "We're still trying to figure out what to do," Rabbi Aaron went on, "about Rabbi Shlomo's murder, my brother's murder, and how to stop the coming conflagration. If we don't resume the sacrifices…" He shrugged. "The first two won't matter. We're all doomed."

Metilius sat down and leaned across the table.

"I want to help you," he said earnestly. "I'm trying to understand the situation. That's why I came to you before filing my report."

"We sent a delegation to Florus asking for help," Rabbi Aaron said.

Metilius saw Rabbi Aaron's sardonic smile; it was in reaction to the involuntary expression on his own face at the mention of the procurator's name.

"I know you can't agree with me," Rabbi Aaron said. "I don't expect any help from him. I'm sure Florus wants to see a rebellion; he's doing everything he can to provoke one. But we also sent a delegation to King Agrippa for help, and I'm sure he'll send some. His kingdom is not that far away, and he is a Jew; a war between the Jews and Rome will do him no good. With help from Agrippa we can retake the Temple from the revolutionaries and the sacrifices can resume."

"Who killed the rabbi during the meeting?" Metilius asked.

"I don't know. I never saw him before. He was with Judah ben Ezra."

"Judah ben Ezra!" Metilius exclaimed. He still had unanswered questions about the man.

"In fairness," Rabbi Aaron explained, "I don't think Judah planned for anyone to be killed. He was as surprised as everyone else. It looked like the murderer acted on his own." After a moment he added, disgust in his voice, "Of course, that didn't stop any of them from using it to force us to go along with them."

"Judah would know who killed the rabbi?" Metilius said this more as a statement of fact than a question.

"Undoubtedly."

"Did you tell your sister-in-law that Judah was cleared of her husband's murder?"

"As soon as you told me," Rabbi Aaron answered.

"Does she believe it?"

"No!" Rabbi Aaron replied emphatically. "And I'm worried about her because of that. I'm afraid of what she might do. What she might be doing…"

"I want to talk to her," Metilius said thoughtfully, leaning back.

He saw the troubled expression on Rabbi Aaron's face deepen.

"What's wrong?"

Rabbi Aaron shook his head.

"We haven't seen her in two days. I keep sending my wife to look after her, to make sure she's all right. She's never home. It's like she vanished."

"When you do see her, please let me know. I want to ask her why she's so sure Judah killed her husband. And I'm going to question Judah about the murder during the rabbinical assembly. I want to arrest the man who killed Rabbi Shlomo." Metilius started to get up as if he was leaving then abruptly sat down again.

"Rabbi, I want to ask you a question," he said, his voice gentle. "Why don't you Jews eat pork?"

Metilius smiled; he saw the look of surprise on Rabbi Aaron's face at the question that seemed to come out of nowhere.

"You seem stuck on that one," Rabbi Aaron replied.

"It's because it is delicious. Why deprive yourself of something that tastes good? Have you ever tasted it?"

"No."

"Why not try it? Just to see what you're missing?"

"Let me ask you some questions," Rabbi Aaron countered. "Do you know why the dew coats the grass at dawn or why the stars shine at night? These are the simplest of questions. The minds of men cannot comprehend all that the Creator of the Universe knows. But He has not left us in darkness. He has given us the Torah to guide our lives, to elevate us, to make us holy.

"I do not know why he has allowed some foods and forbidden others. The reasons may be beyond our understanding. Or it may be as simple as teaching us discipline. I do not know. But if you are interested I can teach you those rules and how we apply them, and explain how they bring us closer to living the good life, as we understand it, and as the Greeks might say."

"I am interested, Rabbi Aaron," Metilius responded.

"Then come over when you can and I will teach you."

"I will. Thank you, Rabbi Aaron. I must be going now."

Out in the street Metilius paused and looked at Rabbi Aaron's house.

I will come back, he thought. There is something worthwhile in what Rabbi Aaron believes.

The door opened and Rabbi Aaron's younger son, Reuven, stepped out and closed the door. He stared at Metilius for a moment and then called out: "*Salve, domine!*"

Metilius smiled and nodded in response.

The boy continued staring at him. Metilius stepped closer.

"Yes?" Metilius asked. "What is it?"

"I want to be like you," Reuven said. "I want to carry a sword and a knife and to walk down the street unafraid. To not bow down before anyone. To be my own master."

"Do you want to become a soldier of Rome?"

Reuven did not reply to the question.

"I am not my own master, Reuven. I must follow the orders of my officer, and he his, all the way up to the emperor, before whom we all bow. Your father only bows before God. Sometimes I think I would like to be like your father."

"They're all afraid. All of them," Reuven retorted sharply. "They're cowards. I want to be like you. I want to walk down the street standing tall, unafraid, like you do."

As soon as he finished speaking Reuven turned and ran down the street. Metilius watched him run until Reuven disappeared into an alley.

It occurred to Metilius that he should be flattered by Reuven's admiration.

He wasn't. There was something in the last look Reuven gave him that deeply troubled Metilius.

Chapter Twenty-One

24 Jun 66 CE / 13 Tammuz 3826

The Roman commander's face was stern, his tone harsh, his question sharp; the Jew in detention looked back with a half-grin that revealed a missing tooth. Neither man was having the desired effect on the other.

Judah was detained in a gray room with a single window in Antonia, the fortress built up by Herod on the northwest corner of the Temple. The room was bare, without even a bench on which to sit. There was just enough space in the square chamber for a man to step four paces from one wall to the other. Metilius, bareheaded, was interrogating Judah with the assistance of the translator, a short Jew who nervously tugged at his beard while he worked, his eyes darting about, sometimes looking up, sometimes at Metilius, never at Judah. Metilius was flanked by two Syrian auxiliaries in full battle dress, with helmets, breastplates, and round shields.

"Did you order the killing of Rabbi Shlomo ben Uzziel?" Metilius demanded.

"Once again prefect—that is your rank, isn't it?—the answer is no!" Judah could see that even before the translator spoke Metilius understood that last word, which he had shouted vigorously.

"Then who did order the killing if not you?" pressed Metilius.

"No one. The killer acted on his own."

"And his name?"

"John ben Dorcas." Judah had no problem giving the name; Rabbi Shlomo's murder was committed in front of witnesses. Everyone in Judah's group knew who carried it out, and there might be one or more rabbis who could identify the killer. But Dorcas was safe from the Romans; Judah had stashed him away in one of the many safe houses the group had in the Lower City.

"Where can I find him?" asked Metilius.

"I have no idea. If I had known where he was there would be nothing left for you to find anymore."

The skeptical look on Metilius' face was met with Judah's narrowed eyes.

Judah thought: This dumb Roman thinks he's craftier than a Jew? A tale that's almost true will be accepted quicker than an outright lie.

Judah said: "I'll be honest. We were going to strong-arm some of those rabbis to get them to go along. Slap them around a bit. You know what I mean? But kill them? Never! You slap a man, after the bruise goes away, he forgets about it. You kill a man, his mother and father, his sisters and brothers, his wife and children, his family, his friends, his community, they never forget. You've created a whole world of enemies. No, if I could get my hands on Dorcas, I'd turn him over to you or the Sanhedrin."

"I don't believe you," Metilius responded.

Judah shrugged.

"We Jews are not united the way you Romans are," he said. "That's why you can rule us. We're divided into sects and subsects. We're constantly fighting and disagreeing with each other. There are the Sadducees, the priests of the Temple, and those who adhere to their ideas of the Law. There are the Pharisees, the rabbis, the ones who are most learned in expounding the Law. Among the Pharisees there are disputes between those who hold strictly to the old ways of interpreting the Law and those who are trying to conform to the world of the Greeks and the Romans. There is even a sect of the Jews called the Essenes who are monastic and live apart from the rest of us."

Judah waited until the translator had finished before concluding with a flourish:

"All this disunity! No, commander, I would turn Dorcas over to you because what he did only increased that disunity!"

Judah thought: I'm almost convincing myself here!

But Judah wasn't sure if he had convinced the Roman interrogating him.

"I should keep you locked up," Metilius said.

"What good would that do?" Judah countered. "Don't you have enough to worry about? Florus left you with only one cohort. That's less than 500 men. Why stir up more trouble by arresting me?" Then, seeing that the Jewish translator was hesitating at conveying the threat, Judah growled, "Translate what I said!"

"Are you threatening me?" Metilius asked. "You?"

"No, commander, just asking you to be reasonable. I've done nothing wrong that Rome should be concerned about. On what charge would you arrest me?"

Metilius stared at Judah for several moments. Judah tensed, waiting for what would come next. Freedom or imprisonment?

"When was the last time you saw Bruria, the widow of Rabbi

Moshe?" Metilius suddenly shouted at him.

Judah flinched and fought to gain control of himself. He could feel the color drain from his cheeks beneath the beard. He already questioned me about Moshe's death, Judah thought. He cleared me. Why is he asking about it now?

"At Rabbi Aaron's house," answered Judah, hoping his voice remained calm. "I came to pay my respects after Rabbi Moshe's death."

"Murder," Metilius corrected.

"Murder," Judah agreed, nodding his head, wondering if the Greek had the same nuanced difference the Aramaic did.

"Did she accuse you of killing her husband?"

Keep to the truth as much as possible, Judah thought frantically. He's looking for more details. What has roused his suspicion?

"Yes, she did," Judah replied. "I had gone to Rabbi Moshe's house exactly a week ago. He and I quarreled."

"About what?"

"As I explained, there are two different schools of rabbinical thought." Judah could feel his calm returning. "I follow the rabbis of the older school. Rabbi Moshe belonged to those who wanted to accommodate the Greek and Roman way. I told him that in the end we would win the dispute."

"Did you threaten him?" Metilius asked sharply.

Judah felt Metilius' eyes boring through him. Judah smiled in response.

"Only in a very abstract, theological way. I told him I'd see him in what you would call Hades," Judah said, using the Greek word for the underworld.

Metilius looked at Judah for a long time, as if he were weighing something in his mind. Finally, he said:

"All right you can go now."

Metilius abruptly left the room without waiting for the translator to finish.

The two auxiliaries escorted Judah out of Antonia, the translator trailing behind them.

As Judah walked back to the Lower City, he stopped and turned to gaze at the fortress.

You think I'm stupid, don't you, prefect, he thought. I know you're going to have me watched by some Jewish spy.

Judah smiled and waved gaily at Antonia as if saying goodbye to a friend he would see again soon.

"I'll be back," he whispered. "Don't worry, Antonia, I'll be back, and when I come it will be with enough freedom fighters to kill every Roman and Syrian auxiliary inside of you!"

Chapter Twenty-Two

24 Jun 66 CE / 13 Tammuz 3826

Still raging from his encounter with the Roman commander, Judah ben Ezra rushed through the streets of the Lower City, ostensibly to check on John ben Dorcas and let him know that the authorities were looking for him, but in the back of his mind to make sure that the out-of-control assassin was staying out of trouble.

Ah, maybe not, he thought with disgust. Maybe I could send him on a mission to kill that Metilius.

Judah was boiling with anger because the Roman had confiscated his knife. Of course, Judah owned more than one knife, and never to be without one, had stopped off at his room to get another blade before proceeding to Dorcas' safe house.

Damn Roman thieves, he thought.

The knife Metilius had taken was his favorite.

Judah stopped, turned, and scanned the street. Satisfied that he was not being followed, but still cautious, his eyes on the road he had just traveled, Judah stepped sideways into an alley.

An unexpected blow to his left shoulder rocked him. He had collided with a man trying to leave the alley. Judah made a quarter turn and jumped back two steps.

"Fool!" Judah hissed, before getting a good look at the fellow. "Why don't you watch where you're going?"

Judah immediately regretted his words. The man, dressed in worn-out clothes that seemed about to fray into shreds, was Judah's height but built like a bull, with huge arms and fists, one of which he raised as he shouted, "You're the fool! Why don't you watch where you're going?"

Judah pulled out his knife.

"Coward!" the man sneered. "You need a weapon to fight."

"Fool!" Judah retorted. "Fighting without a weapon!"

They glared at each other. Then the leader of revolutionary brigands put his knife away with a flourish and flashed his opponent a huge grin. The other fellow laughed and Judah clapped him on the shoulder.

"Brother," Judah said jovially, "what's eating you?"

The question produced an instant effect on the man's expression, which had gone from anger to mirth and now registered profound dejection.

"It's hard being poor in Jerusalem," the man replied sadly. "The rich, the priests, the rabbis, and the Romans grind you into dust."

Judah put his arm around the fellow and said, "Come, let me buy you a drink and you can tell me your troubles." He led him out of the alley and onto the street.

His soon-to-be drinking partner looked at Judah dubiously. Judah looked back at him and thought: He's even stronger than Shaul! Dorcas can wait. This fellow surely has an interesting story. He could be useful.

They walked north, perpendicular to the slope of the hill, occasionally passing food stalls jutting out from the buildings lining the streets, forcing the two of them to squeeze past shoppers and other pedestrians. Judah noticed his companion gazing longingly at the meat and bread and fruit in the stalls.

He must be hungry, Judah thought. I'll soon fix that.

They reached a wide cross-street with a stairway that went up and down the hill. Judah turned left and strode up the steps. They passed one street and as they approached another Judah pointed to its far corner on which a three-story building stood.

"That," he said, "is a great place with excellent food." The two hurried toward it.

The ground floor held a large dining area; wooden tables with benches along the sides were positioned throughout the room. A series of tall windows, reaching almost to the ceiling from two feet off the floor, with straight bottoms and curved tops, were evenly spaced along the street side and east side of the building, flooding the area with light from the day outside. On the tables and the windowsills were unlit oil lamps. Opposite the entrance narrow doorways led to the rooms where food was prepared.

Two of the tables had customers eating and drinking. Judah led his companion to a table in the corner out of earshot of the other patrons. A waiter came over.

"Two bowls of barley soup," Judah said. "And wine and a plate of figs." He pulled out a silver denarius and laid it on the table.

Judah saw his companion's eyes widen with surprise at the way he nonchalantly threw down the money. The man made no comment about this, however. Instead, he asked Judah:

"You're not from Jerusalem, are you? From your accent I'd guess you're from the north."

It was Judah's turn to be surprised. He slapped the table lightly with his open palm and said, "Very good! You're not just strong as a bull, but smart, too!"

"My name is David ben Ephraim," came the reply. "To what do I owe your kindness?"

"I am Judah. I am starting a war to drive the Romans out. I could use a brave, strong, and smart fellow like you."

David laughed as if he had been told a joke. Then, seeing the serious expression on Judah's face he said:

"You're not kidding!"

"No," Judah replied solemnly. "I'm not."

"You're going to do this all by yourself?"

Judah laughed.

"No, of course not. You're going to help me. The two of us together will expel the Romans. My knife and your fists."

Judah laughed again and David joined in.

"For a moment I thought you were serious!" David said amused. Then, the smile gone, he added:

"Let me tell you something, Judah. It's not just the Romans. Oh sure, maybe they're the cause of it all, they certainly don't help things, but the priests and the rabbis are just as responsible for making our lives miserable. Why, they say the rabbis just passed a ruling forbidding us to buy food from the gentiles. Do you know what that will do to the price of bread and fish and cheese?"

Judah's expression grew pensive as he remembered what Rabbi Aaron said at the rabbinical assembly: the Eighteen Decrees would immiserate the poor. So he had been right, Judah thought. This is not good; we want to free the people, not make their lives harder. Is it possible that by helping men like David we can speed our national liberation?

David saw the changed look on Judah's face. He frowned and shook his head.

"I guess you wouldn't know about such things, with the money you have," David concluded bitterly, interrupting the beginning of Judah's speculation.

"My friend," Judah replied quickly, "any money I have has been provided, willingly or unwillingly, by rich patrons. Mostly unwillingly."

The waiter arrived with the food and drink. He placed some bronze coins on the table as change for Judah's silver denarius.

"Tell me your story now, friend," Judah said. "I want to hear it."

David was married and had a young child. He inherited a small farm not far from Jerusalem. A bad year left him without enough money and crops to pay his taxes to the Romans and his tithes to the priests. He had to take out a loan using his land as collateral. Another bad year left him desperate. He was told they needed strong, unskilled laborers in Jerusalem. He went, hoping to make some money and get out of debt.

"I did find work," he said. "Saved a little money. Then the work started drying up. Hardly anything now. And you're competing against the next fellow who wants it as badly as you and is willing to underbid you. If you do get a job you're not paid enough to buy food and lodging for yourself, forget about saving anything."

Judah nodded sagely when David finished.

"Tell me," Judah said. "Are there others in your situation?"

"Many," came the reply. "Many."

"Men with nothing to lose, such as yourself?"

"I have much to lose," David corrected. "My farm. The bondholder will come and take it away if I cannot pay off my debt."

Judah's eyes fixed on David's face to gauge his reaction when he asked the next question:

"David, if the fight to free us from Rome also meant changing the conditions for men like you, would you join that fight?"

David thought for a moment.

"Yes!" he answered emphatically.

"And do you think the others would join, also?"

"Many probably would," David replied.

"Could you convince them to join?"

"What, your movement of one?" David asked sharply.

"I lead a band of sixty men," Judah answered. "We came down from the north when things got too hot for us. We fought Romans and their auxiliaries in the Galilee and the Golan. We raided their Jewish and Syrian collaborators. There are others who fight also. And there are rabbis and Temple ministers who want to join the fight. A great upheaval is coming. Soon the whole nation will join in the struggle. The Land and the people will be free of the Romans and oppression."

"Rabbis and priests? They are part of the problem!"

"That is why we need you and men like you!" Judah's voice was intense with new-found discovery. "So your voices can be heard, so your concerns can be addressed. For now the calls for freedom come from men like me, fighters, from rabbis who know that the Law demands we bend the knee to no one but God, and from priests who know that

Roman overlordship profanes the holy Temple. This is your chance to be part of the vanguard that overthrows this whole rotten and corrupt system!"

David looked doubtful.

"What have you got to lose?" Judah demanded. "Could things be worse for you?" He reached into a pocket and pulled out five silver denari. He put the money on the table in front of David.

"This should tide you over for a few days," Judah explained. "Give you time to think, a chance to try to convince some of your fellow workers who are struggling."

David picked up the money.

"I know many men in my situation," David said. "Barely working or unemployed. Many of them in debt. They can be convinced to join an uprising. By someone who knows how to speak. By someone who knows how to explain the causes of today's troubles and can also paint a picture of a happier tomorrow. That person is you, Judah, not me. You're eloquent. I'm not. I'll only do it if you come with me. I'll introduce you to the men I know. I'll vouch for you. But you will do the talking."

"Agreed!" Judah responded enthusiastically.

They finished their food. The wine was left untouched. Pointing to it, David said:

"It's best for what lies ahead to remain sober."

"Wise words," Judah said, rising from his seat. "David, it's time for me to take you to the Temple and introduce you to Eleazar ben Ananias, the captain of the Temple ministers."

Chapter Twenty-Three

24 Jun 66 CE / 13 Tammuz 3826

The Bronze Gate behind Shaul ben Yitzchak gleamed in the sun; the multi-colored mosaic of small stones of aqua, green, dark blue, and red at his feet sparkled in the bright light; on the roofs of the buildings that flanked the north and south sides of the court Temple ministers stood watch, now armed with large stones in addition to swords and spears; on the ground guards patrolled the area to make sure there was no interference with Eleazar's rebellion; while in front of Shaul stood a boy barely into adolescence who looked up at Shaul with earnest, dark eyes.

"Beat it, squirt!" Shaul said, trying to suppress a smile. "Your mother's looking for you."

The boy did not move.

"How old are you kid? Ten?"

"I'm fourteen!" the boy retorted defiantly.

"You have no business here. Scram! I don't know how you got past all the guards."

The boy continued staring up at Shaul.

"Alright, kid, what do you really want?" Shaul asked with exasperation.

"I already told you. I want to be a freedom fighter."

"You're too small. Grow up first." Seeing no response from the boy, Shaul asked:

"Why you bothering me, kid?"

"They told me to look for Shaul ben Yitzchak or Judah ben Ezra."

"What's that got to do with me?"

"Shaul is a big, tall guy. Very tall."

"They told you wrong, kid. Shaul's a short, skinny guy. Like you."

"Then I'm not too small to be a freedom fighter!" the boy countered.

Shaul laughed.

"All right, kid. What's your name?"

"Reuven, Reuven ben Aaron."

Shaul's mouth fell open. Was this the Hillel rabbi's son?

"Is your father Rabbi Aaron ben Avraham?" Shaul asked in amazement.

"Yes."

Shaul shook his head.

"You don't belong here, kid. Go back home. Your father won't be happy to find out you came here."

"You do everything your father tells you?" Reuven asked.

The question rocked Shaul back on his heels. The smile disappeared from his face.

"No, kid, I don't."

"The Romans walk around Jerusalem tall and unafraid," Reuven explained. "We Jews slink through our streets, trembling at our own shadows. Except for the freedom fighters like you."

Shaul's eyebrows went up in surprise at the clarity of Reuven's reply. He scratched at the side of his beard.

I understand how he feels, Shaul thought. It's why I joined Judah in the north, against my own father's wishes. He seems sincere, but…

"Let me ask you something, kid." Shaul's voice was hard. "How do I know you're not a spy for your father's side?"

"Huh?" Reuven was taken aback. "Gee. I don't know. Even if I say I'm not, well, if I was a spy, I'd still say I wasn't." Reuven looked crestfallen. "Gee, I don't know…" Reuven's voice trailed off.

Shaul thought Reuven was about to break into tears. The boy turned and started walking away, his head hung low.

Shaul let him walk several paces before calling out:

"Hey, kid, come back!"

Reuven turned, a puzzled expression on his face.

"Kid," Shaul said, as Reuven came up to him, "if you were a spy you wouldn't have walked away like that. They would have coached you how to answer my question."

A hopeful look spread over Reuven's face.

Shaul rubbed his chin, pondering what to do with Reuven.

"I've got to talk to my leader," he said at last.

Shaul glanced past Reuven at two men who had just entered the back gate.

"Hey, look!" Shaul exclaimed with excitement. "There he is! Wait here, kid!"

Shaul ran to greet Judah, who was accompanied by a stranger.

"Shaul!" Judah cried, as Shaul approached, "Shaul ben Yitzchak, I want you to meet David ben Ephraim here. He's joining us, and he's going to bring many more fellows like him!"

Shaul grinned at David, who was staring at the Bronze Gate with wide-eyed wonder and mumbling something to himself under his breath.

"Great!" Shaul said enthusiastically. "We need more men!"

Without waiting for a reply, he turned to Judah, and in a quieter voice, added, "Judah, I have to speak with you." He pulled Judah aside, threw his right arm around Judah's left shoulder, and began to whisper conspiratorially.

"See that boy over there?" Shaul asked, pointing with his left hand. "That's Rabbi Aaron's son."

"What?" Judah's tone told Shaul that his friend was as amazed as he had been when he learned who the boy was. "Rabbi Aaron's son? What's he doing here?"

"He wants to become a freedom fighter."

Judah laughed.

"Are you kidding me?"

"No, Judah, I'm not."

"Why? Why would the son of Rabbi Aaron want to join us?"

Shaul replied immediately, his voice full of conviction.

"For the same reason I followed you, Judah. For the same reason we all fight."

Judah looked at Shaul. A slight grin creased his mouth.

"I understand," Judah said, nodding gravely.

He was silent for a moment.

"How do you know he's not a spy?"

"He's not, Judah. I accused him of that. He didn't know what to say. He looked so sad. He almost started crying. Then he slunk away like a beaten dog. If he was a spy they would have coached him how to answer that charge, Judah."

Judah nodded again and put his right hand on Shaul's shoulder.

"Very good," he said. "We can use him. I have to decide how. Tell him to return tomorrow. Then come back to us. We're taking David to meet Eleazar." Judah took another look at Reuven ben Avraham, his eyes squinting. A loud laugh erupted from deep inside Judah.

"Wait," he said to Shaul. "Do you know who that kid is?"

"Yeah, I told you. Rabbi Aaron's son."

"No, Shaul," Judah replied. "He's more than that. I've seen him before, and so have you, only I got a close-up look at him back then."

Shaul looked puzzled.

"Shaul!" Judah roared. "That's the kid who tried to stop those Syrian auxiliaries from taking Yoseph ben Mavet!"

Now it was Shaul's turn to laugh.

"You're right!" he exclaimed.

Shaul hurried back to Reuven.

"Hey, kid, you've already proved yourself. Judah recognized you; I didn't. You tried to stop those Syrian auxiliaries from taking Yosef ben Mavet! I was with Judah that day."

"Both of you saved my life." Reuven's voice was solemn.

"Well," Shaul said, "won't be the last time, and the time will come when you will probably save ours. Come back tomorrow. I have to go now." The words were no sooner out of Shaul's mouth when he ran back to Judah and David.

The three men ascended the curved steps in front of the Bronze Gate. When they reached the top two guards came out of each gate room.

"Who is that?" a guard on the right shouted to Judah, as he pointed at David.

"A friend," Judah called back. "I need to speak to Eleazar. It's important."

The guard disappeared back into the gate room. Judah, David, and Shaul waited.

Though David still gaped at the gate above him with fascination, he began to grow visibly restless as time passed.

"Don't worry," Judah reassured him. "Eleazar will come if I tell him it's important."

David looked at Judah and shook his head in disbelief.

"We'll see, Judah, we'll see."

Shaul, his eyebrows raised, gave Judah a questioning look. He, too, was beginning to wonder if Eleazar would show.

"Patience!" barked Judah. "Patience!"

It took a while longer for Judah's patience to be rewarded. Two guards came out of the gate room carrying a large chair which they set down in front of the center of the Bronze Gate. The chair, with carved wooden arms, had an embroidered seat and back. The embroidery was green with bright blue and red threads running through the green in a fantastic variety of patterns.

Eleazar emerged from the gate room on the right and walked regally to the chair and sat down.

Eleazar wore a white linen tunic that extended from his neck to his feet. Around the tunic a belt of fine twisted linen was tied in the middle, both ends hanging down in front of him. The linen belt was embroidered with sky-blue, dark-red and crimson dyed wools, a combination of materials forbidden to ordinary men. On his head was a turban of white linen wrapped around his head in a conical shape. Underneath his tunic were white breeches that went from his waist to his knees.

"My, you look fancy," Judah observed drily.

Eleazar laughed.

"Well, Judah," Eleazar said. "What's so important? And who is this new fellow you brought along?"

Judah introduced David to Eleazar and prompted David to tell his story. Eleazar leaned forward and listened intently. He showed no anger when David concluded with his opinion of the priests and the rabbis. Then Judah spoke, and Eleazar leaned back, his face relaxed, as Judah explained his plan for David.

"Excellent," exclaimed Eleazar, clapping his hands when Judah finished.

"David comes to us at a crucial time," said Eleazar. "My father and his associates have sent emissaries to Florus and Agrippa asking for help in retaking the Temple. I'm sure Agrippa will send soldiers. Judah, while you go with David to collect men to defend the Temple, could you send Shaul north to rouse the freedom fighters there to come to Jerusalem to help us? Your name must still carry weight in the Galilee and the Golan. I will provide horses and supplies for Shaul. By the time Agrippa's forces arrive, we will be ready for them."

Back to the north! Shaul thought with excitement.

Eleazar leaned forward again and fixed David in his gaze.

"You spoke of the priests," Eleazar said. "Well, David ben Ephraim, let me tell you something. There are priests and there are priests. There are priests as rich as me and priests as poor as you. We higher ranking priests are as corrupt as Florus and the Romans. Tithes are supposed to be distributed fairly. They are not. The higher ranks have been stealing—there is no other word for it—the tithes due to the lower ranks, and have made themselves rich from that thievery. And so there are many poor and impoverished priests who are no better off than you are. I know; I benefit from my own father's corruption. You may wonder why I am willing to bring down this whole rotten system since I am a beneficiary of it. I'll tell you why. Roman sacrifices profane the Temple of God. Roman rule profanes the Temple of God. This man's grandfather," here

Eleazar pointed to Judah, "was a great rabbi who taught us that we must bend the knee to no one but God. I am no Pharisee, no follower of Shammai or Hillel, my vision of Judaism is different than that of the rabbis, but Judah's grandfather, Judah the Galilean, taught us a great lesson."

Eleazar leaned back and folded his arms. He looked at the three men standing before him.

"Let me ask you something, David ben Ephraim. The bond which pledges your farm for the loan, is it stored in the Record Office here in Jerusalem?"

"Yes."

"I thought so," Eleazar said. He stood up and pointed behind him, toward the west. "The Record Office is not far from here; it is quite near the Temple. No doubt, once the forces of Agrippa arrive there will be fighting as they try to retake the Temple." A sly smile appeared on Eleazar's face. He looked straight at Judah. "What a shame if during one of those struggles the Record Office were to go up in flames. How would the moneylenders collect their debts?"

Judah laughed and slapped his thigh.

"Brilliant!" he exclaimed.

Eleazar turned to David.

"You understand that this great upheaval, in which you are about to take part, will benefit you and your fellow workers as well."

"Yes!" David responded with conviction. "The workers, and the farmers, the artisans, the tradesmen; all the common people!"

Eleazar looked hard at each man standing before him. His face gloomy, his voice joyless and solemn, he intoned the following words slowly, as if he were relaying a prophecy whose truth he was reluctant to acknowledge:

"Know that the day is coming when the whole nation, united, will fight the Romans. Know also that before that day comes, we will have to fight each other."

Chapter Twenty-Four

24 Jun 66 CE / 14 Tammuz 3826

The street was crowded, more crowded than Judah ben Ezra had ever seen a Jerusalem street, so crowded he could not move side to side, only forward at the pace of the mass of humanity around him. That pace was slow, measured; they didn't dawdle, they didn't hurry. It frustrated Judah; he wanted, no needed, to move faster. He had to get to the Wood Market in the New City. Why he had to get there he did not know.

Some people were singing. Some people were angrily shouting nonsense syllables, others were shouting them joyfully. There were people looking down at the ground and people looking upward towards the sky with their mouths open. On the roofs of the buildings that flanked the street people waved and shouted in unison. Judah could not make out the words over the din.

He noticed that the street was wide, wider than any Jerusalem street he had ever seen, so wide it held more disorganized columns of marchers than Judah could have imagined possible.

Judah looked down. He saw the same kind of multi-colored stones that covered parts of the Temple complex. They didn't belong on an ordinary street. Judah was puzzled. What were they doing here? Ah, but they were smudged from the passage of so many people, not clean like the ones in the Temple courts.

And now he was passing the magnificent Temple complex. It dominated the view on the right. As his gaze moved downward he realized that the man marching alongside him was his childhood teacher.

His teacher turned to him and snapped:

"Have you been studying? You know you're being tested tomorrow!"

Judah hadn't studied. No wait, he had. No, now he wasn't sure. Maybe he had just imagined that he had.

A woman several rows ahead turned and waved at him. She smiled.

It was Bruria! Bruria!

Judah struggled to move ahead of the people in front of him. All his pushing and shoving accomplished nothing. Judah kept his eyes fixed on the back of Bruria's head.

He had to catch up to her!

She moved sideways, to the right, and entered one of the buildings.

It seemed as if it was taking forever for Judah's section of the crowd to reach it. Instead of pushing forward Judah slithered to the right and managed to get to the edge of the street.

At last Judah reached the gray stone structure Bruria had entered. He looked up and saw her waving at him from an open window on the second floor.

Judah stepped to the entrance.

The Syrian auxiliary who had knocked out his tooth blocked the way.

One of the soldier's hands held a shield. The other was on the hilt of his sword. He glared at Judah, his eyes filled with hate.

I'll kill you again, Judah thought.

Judah's hand went to his knife as he prepared to spring at the auxiliary soldier.

The knife would not budge. Judah could not pull it out, no matter how hard he tried.

The Syrian soldier sneered. He drew his sword and raised it high above his head.

Judah tugged and tugged and tugged at the unmoving knife as the sword descended.

Judah screamed. The Syrian, his sword, the crowd, the city, everything vanished.

Shaul stirred in the corner and cried out, "What happened?", then went back to sleep.

There was no going back to sleep for Judah.

He was covered in sweat and trembling.

Judah got up and began pacing the room.

What did that dream mean? What caused it?

Ah, he thought. Seeing that boy, Rabbi Aaron's son. Like a chain: From son to father to uncle to aunt. Bruria! That's it!

But it wasn't just about Bruria. There was that Syrian soldier, the one who had knocked out his teeth and whom he had killed, as he had killed Bruria who had tried to kill him, and there was his teacher, and that crowd marching through a changed Jerusalem.

What did it all mean?

He thought of Rabbi Zechariah. Zechariah did not believe in dreams. Neither did Judah, but perhaps the rabbi could explain the meaning.

Judah hadn't seen Rabbi Zechariah since the rabbinical assembly had passed the Eighteen Decrees, more than two days ago.

"Rabbi Zechariah isn't available." Judah was told, when he went to see the rabbi after meeting with Eleazar in front of the Bronze Gate. From the way the young rabbi delivered the message Judah suspected that Rabbi Zechariah was deliberately avoiding him.

Is it because of Rabbi Shlomo's death? Judah wondered. Not death, he corrected himself, murder. But Zechariah knows I had nothing to do with that!

At any rate, he can't avoid me forever.

Judah shivered. The dream, nonsensical as it was, wouldn't leave him.

He pushed the image of Bruria from his mind and turned to practical concerns.

What to do with that boy, Rabbi Aaron's son? Use him as a spy? Turn him over to Shaul?

Judah sighed and stopped pacing. This was not the time to solve problems. It was the middle of the night. He needed sleep.

There was important work to begin when the sun rose.

Chapter Twenty-Five

4 Jul 66 CE / 23 Tammuz 3826

Another mournful Sabbath was approaching, the third in a row, with calamity piled upon calamity, leaving Rabbi Aaron ben Avraham wondering if The Master of the Universe had turned him into a modern-day Job. He hugged the stone that closed his brother's grave and wept.

"Brother, oh brother," he cried, "why aren't you here with me?"

Rabbi Aaron laid his head on the stone. It was cool, and soothed him. The sun was still high; it was early afternoon, Yom Shishi, the Sixth Day of the week. When the sun set and evening came the day would slide into Yom Shabbat, the Seventh Day.

Once again the Sabbath could not be welcomed with joy.

First there had been his brother's murder. Then Bruria vanished without a trace. And now his youngest son had run away.

The trouble began on Yom Shani, the Second Day of the week, right after Metilius came to warn him about the consequences of refusing the sacrifices for Rome. Reuven left home immediately after that visit and did not return until evening. He was also gone for most of the following two days.

Rabbi Aaron grew suspicious. Was Reuven engaging in some immoral activity and hiding it from the family?

Rabbi Aaron remembered the painful confrontation with his son when Reuven came home that final evening.

"Where have you been?" Rabbi Aaron demanded. "What have you been doing? And why are you neglecting your studies?"

Reuven stared back at his father, his jaw tight, and said nothing.

"Answer me, Reuven!"

The boy glared back at him as if daring his father to force him to answer.

Rabbi Aaron was shocked. Reuven had never been defiant before.

Then Rabbi Aaron did something he had never done before.

He slapped Reuven. Hard. A large red welt appeared on the face that was only beginning to grow a beard.

That was the last time he saw his youngest son. Reuven stole away in the night.

The next Shabbat meal, without his youngest son, was funereal.

There was silence, with no thought of the usual discussion. As the meal was ending Rabbi Aaron asked Benjamin if he knew what was going on with his younger brother.

At first Benjamin gave only evasive answers. Finally, under his father's intense questioning he admitted he knew what his brother was doing.

"He's joined the biryonim," Benjamin said.

Rabbi Aaron almost choked on the fig he was eating.

The biryonim! The robbers, as Rabbi Johanan ben Zakkai called them. The gangs of cutthroats who attacked Romans, Syrians, and even Jews, pretending to be fighting for freedom but often only out to steal and loot.

Judah's group was one of these biryonim. There were other groups, too, all just as bad.

"Whose did he join?" Rabbi Aaron had demanded of Benjamin.

"He didn't tell me," replied Benjamin.

Rabbi Aaron did not know whether Benjamin was telling the truth or not. He did not want to press the matter. He did not want to lose another son.

But Rabbi Aaron was unwilling to give up; he had another avenue to find out where his youngest son was: Metilius. The commander of the Roman garrison of Antonia had begun coming to him for instruction in the Jewish religion.

Rabbi Aaron went to Metilius to ask for his help.

"I'll do what I can, Rabbi," Metilius said. "But I can't promise quick results. Jerusalem is so big someone can easily disappear if he doesn't want to be found. And I don't have enough troops—or the authority—to bring in every troublemaker in the hope that one of them can be forced to reveal Reuven's whereabouts."

The disappointment on Rabbi Aaron's face must have shown because Metilius quickly added:

"Don't worry." Metilius spoke gently, trying to reassure the skeptical Rabbi Aaron. "Your scholarly son will come to his senses soon enough and realize he doesn't belong with those brigands, that his place is at home with you."

Metilius didn't sounded very convincing.

A large cloud drifted across the sun, shielding Rabbi Aaron.

Like the gourd that God raised over Jonah outside Nineveh, Rabbi Aaron thought.

In truth, Rabbi Aaron reasoned, the calamities are not only personal. Moshe's murder robbed the nation of a strong voice for peace. There was the brazen murder of Rabbi Shlomo in front of other Torah scholars designed to frighten them. And the passing almost two weeks ago of the Eighteen Decrees was sure to set the country on an inevitable course of war with Rome.

And now there was a new curse: Groups of large and beefy men, unemployed workers, had taken over the Lower City. They roamed the streets armed with clubs and lances, threatening supporters of the senior priests who wanted to resume the sacrifices to Rome, threatening Hillel rabbis they saw in the streets, threatening anyone they heard talking of peace. There had been no violence from these men yet, but the threat was always there.

This interweaving of his own private tragedies with that of the public's only added to his burden. He felt helpless.

Rabbi Aaron stood up and stepped away from the rock that guarded his brother's tomb. He stared at it for a long time, as if trying to see through it. Then he cried, to the emptiness of the hill and to God above:

"Moshe, I swear to you that I will find your killer and bring him to justice!"

With head bowed and heavy step, he started on the journey back to the City that he feared was fated to become a tomb of its own.

Chapter Twenty-Six

17 Jul 66 CE / 7 Av 3826

Looking down from a height of fifty feet at the human heads below, poised to drop the large stone in his hands on one of those heads, Reuven ben Aaron was scared. He had never seen fighting before, much less killing. Violence, except for some tussling with his older brother and that recent slap from his father, was unknown to him.

"It's alright, kid," Shaul ben Yitzchak said, laying a reassuring hand on Reuven's shoulder. "We're all scared the first time. But you're safe up here. They can't reach you, not with their swords or spears. This height gives you a real advantage. From up here, what you're holding in your hands is as deadly as a sword or a knife is at close range. Besides, they're attacking and we're defending, which gives us an advantage in our position."

"They're fellow Jews," Reuven said wistfully.

"Yeah, well, some of them are, that's just the way things turned out. You can't get wool without shearing the sheep."

Reuven and Shaul stood on the rampart of the western wall of the Temple complex, above the bridge that led to the Upper City. An undifferentiated mass of soldiers and civilians was storming the gate at the end of the bridge. Other points of entry to the Temple Mount, on the west and south walls, were also under assault. Only the east, facing the steep Kidron Valley, and the north, protected by Antonia, whose soldiers were staying out of the internecine fight, were quiet.

Agrippa II had sent help: 2,000 soldiers under the command of two officers. They were his own troops, not Romans or auxiliaries commanded by Romans. Thus encouraged, the Peace Party, citizens who were opposed to those bent on inciting war, took over the Upper City and the New City on the northern outskirts of Jerusalem. The Lower City and the Temple Mount had already been taken over by the Temple rebels, the biryonim partisans, and unemployed workers, all of whom opposed Rome and the ruling elite. Strengthened by the addition of Agrippa's men, the Peace Party was now making a coordinated assault in an attempt to retake the Temple from the rebels.

"The guy there," Shaul pointed. "Not the one in front of the gate, the one behind him. Aim at him!"

Reuven did as instructed. He lifted both hands, and threw the stone down as hard as he could. His eyes widened as he watched his missile's descent.

Reuven's target was struck on the shoulder. He rocked to his side and fell, knocking down the man next to him.

Shaul gave a victorious shout; Reuven stared in shock at the violence he had committed.

"Good job, kid!" Shaul cried, grabbing a rock from the pile and sending it flying down on the man who was attending to his injured comrade. Shaul's shot landed right on the back of the head; Shaul's target collapsed on the man he was trying to help.

"Come on!" Shaul whooped. "Keep throwing."

One stone after another stone flew from Shaul's hand, crashing down on the crush of men below who were trying to force their way in.

Reuven still didn't move.

"Help me, Reuven!" screamed Shaul.

Hearing his name roused Reuven from his torpor. He joined Shaul in unleashing a barrage on the attackers below.

The soldiers and civilians attempting to besiege the Temple Mount began to retreat under the hail of rocks, dragging their fallen comrades with them.

As they fled the gate was flung open and men with swords, lances, and clubs streamed out, pursuing those fleeing.

"Cease!" shouted Shaul.

Reuven let the stone in his hand fall to the floor.

"Come on! Let's join the fun!" Shaul cried, picking up a club from the floor and rushing down the steep internal steps from the rampart to the level of the Temple courts and then down the broad stairway to the lower level of the complex and out the gate. Reuven, unsure what to do, simply followed on the heels of his new mentor.

By the time they joined the rebel pursuers they were at the rear of the pack. Reuven found himself caught up in the excitement; Shaul was disappointed he was not at the center of the action.

And then, just as the Peace Party reached the end of the bridge, they were joined by reinforcements from the Upper City. They quickly whirled around to face their pursuers, and the newly enlarged force charged the rebels who were coming from the Temple Mount.

Two mighty waves crashed into each other, swirling currents of men swinging clubs, slashing swords, and thrusting spears. As the men in each group who were further back pushed their way forward, jostling those in front ever deeper into enemy lines, the two opposing camps became so intermixed that a man fighting a foe in front of him could be back-to-back with an enemy who was facing that first man's friend.

Shaul waded into the fray with glee, swinging his club with all his strength, a broad smile on his face, as men fell before him. Reuven, both terrified and exhilarated at the same time, incautiously stayed right behind Shaul, his eyes moving this way and that, watching the men around him fight.

He never saw the man who came up behind him. Strong hands grabbed his neck, twisting it harshly, stifling Reuven's scream for help. The boy struggled to turn and face his attacker. He could not.

Sweat poured from Reuven's head, dripped down his neck, and slid between the fingers tightening around him. Reaching backwards, grabbing the man's body for leverage, and with the fingers around his neck now slippery from the sweat, Reuven finally succeeded in turning around and facing his attacker.

Reuven looked straight into fierce dark eyes that held a determined look to kill.

Reuven raised his hands, grabbed the man's face, and with all his might jabbed his thumbs into the man's eyes, digging them in as deeply as he could.

The man screamed in pain.

The scream alerted Shaul, who turned, moved the club from his right hand to his left and drew out his knife with his free hand. Before he could do anything, Reuven, who was digging his thumbs ever deeper into the man's eyes, was suddenly released as the man continued howling with pain.

Shaul stepped forward and slashed the man's neck. His knife still dripping blood, Shaul returned it to his belt and lifted the fallen Reuven with his right arm.

"You alright, kid?" Shaul asked.

"Yes," the boy gasped.

"You did good kid, real good. I'm proud of you." He put Reuven down. "Watch yourself, kid." Then Shaul returned to the fight.

Reuven, still shaking, terrified by almost getting killed, wanted to run away and hide somewhere, but it was impossible to get through the thick throng of men still fighting. He had no choice but to remain behind Shaul.

It seemed to Reuven that the fighting went on forever. But as more men were injured, as more men fell, and as others grew tired, the pace of the fighting slowed. Men gradually moved backward to their respective strongpoints and the clusters of combatants slowly separated.

Neither side had gained a victory: The Peace Party was unable to take the Temple Mount; the rebels were unable to penetrate the Upper City.

A short barrel-chested man with a gray beard and dark gray eyes came up to Shaul.

"Call out for a truce," he declared, much to Shaul's surprise, who didn't understand why he had been chosen for this task. "So we can collect the dead and wounded," the man added.

Shaul shrugged.

"Truce! Truce!" he cried. "Let us gather our dead and wounded."

Shouts of agreement echoed from both sides. Men, in pairs, lifted casualties; the wounded crying out in pain, the dead silent.

The task done, the Peace Party and the rebels faced each other across the broad and long expanse of bridge that was streaked with blood.

Shaul called out: "Until tomorrow!"

Both sides withdrew from the bridge, the Peace Party and Agrippa's soldiers to the Upper City and the rebels to the Temple Mount.

Shaul took Reuven by the arm.

"Let's go back up, kid. I want to talk to you."

Reuven dutifully followed Shaul back up the same way they had come down.

When they got to the rampart Shaul walked over to the parapet and looked down. Nodding with satisfaction, he turned to Reuven.

"You alright, kid?"

"Yes," Reuven replied, in barely a whisper.

"Look, you should be very proud of yourself. You showed courage and quick-thinking. You'll make a great fighter someday. No, you're already a great fighter!"

"Shaul, I was scared. I still am."

Reuven shivered.

Shaul laughed.

"Of course you are, kid! That's to be expected. Why, I bet you were scared out of your wits when that man was choking you. But you didn't freeze. You did what you had to do. That's what makes a great fighter!"

Reuven looked at Shaul hopefully.

"Thanks, Shaul."

"I'm proud of you, kid. You're the little brother I never had." He punched Reuven affectionately on the shoulder. "Now I hope you're continuing your studies with Rabbi Yoel. Make sure you don't neglect them."

Reuven had been staying with Rabbi Yoel ben Jotham since he had run away from home.

Reuven shrugged.

"No, no, you really should take your studies seriously. You don't want to wind up like me, do you?" Then Shaul laughed again, and added, "I understand if you find what happened today more exciting."

He paused and grew thoughtful.

"I've got to find a weapon for you," Shaul continued. "You're too small for a sword or spear or club, and you won't always be up high where you can toss rocks down on the enemy. Well, you saw what happened today. I'll get you a knife and teach you how to use it. You'll need something else, too. Ever use a sling?"

Reuven shook his head.

Shaul looked disappointed.

"Well," he said, "up north all us farm boys learn how to use one. I'll get one for you and teach you how to use that, too. Remember, King David, when he was a shepherd boy around your age, brought down Goliath with one small stone from a sling."

Shaul smiled, evidently pleased with the way things were going.

Reuven had a serious look on his face.

"Shaul, can I ask you something?" Reuven asked hesitantly.

"Sure, kid. Anything."

"When you went up north three weeks ago, did you go to see your girl?"

The smile on Shaul's face instantly disappeared. His face became so sad it seemed he was about to cry.

"No, Reuven, I did not," Shaul replied, his voice about to break. "No, I did not," he repeated, his face drawn and his eyes empty.

"Why not?"

Without a moment's hesitation Shaul answered.

"Because I would not have come back to Jerusalem if I had. I would have stayed in Gamla. I would have married her and taken over my father's farm, as he wanted me to."

"What's her name?"

"Dvorah."

"What will you do if she marries someone else?"

Shaul sighed.

"What can I do, Reuven? That's life."

"Does she understand why you left her?"

"Yes, Reuven, she does. She believes in what I'm doing. If she were a man she'd be fighting alongside me."

"If she were a man," Reuven said, smiling, "then she wouldn't be your girl."

Shaul laughed. Reuven could see that his little joke had lifted Shaul's spirits.

"Come kid, I want to show you something."

As they looked out over the City, Shaul swept his arm around in a wide semi-circle.

"It's a big city, Reuven. There are a lot of people in it. Right now we have the Temple and the Lower City. They have the rest. We'll have to have all of Jerusalem, and its people, before we can take on the Romans."

He took a deep breath and turned to Reuven, who was still looking out at the City.

"Reuven, today was the first battle for Jerusalem. There will be many more. Many more. And with each one, more blood will be shed."

Reuven turned away from the City and looked into Shaul's eyes.

What he saw in them frightened him as much as Shaul's words.

Chapter Twenty-Seven

24 July 66 CE / Av 14 3826

"Battles and bloodshed, battles and bloodshed; thus Shaul prophesied, and thus it has come to pass," Reuven whispered rhythmically, standing on the rampart of the western wall of the Temple complex.

Seven days of mutual slaughter. Neither side dislodged from its original position. All that had been accomplished by this week-long war between Jews—fierce fighting unbroken even by the intervening Sabbath—was more dead and injured.

Reuven was certain the standoff was about to end. He looked down at the deserted bridge that led to the Upper City; he listened to the hubbub of the thousands of armed men in the Temple complex who had just entered the City to join the fight on the side of the rebels.

Beyond the bridge, rows of Agrippa's soldiers, with a mass of ordinary citizens behind them, waited for the next onslaught. The peace party had managed to figure out the trick that had been played on them.

Earlier, at dawn, Eleazar—now de facto head of the rebellion—had gathered the leaders of the partisan bands in the court in front of the Bronze Gate. Shaul had gone with Judah and Reuven had gone with Shaul.

The cold blue sky and prickly chilly air were counterpointed by Eleazar's warm and expansive smile.

"You wonder why I smile," Eleazar began.

Eleazar pointed to Shaul with a sweeping gesture.

"Shaul's mission has borne fruit. Thousands of freedom fighters are coming from Galilee and the Golan. They arrive today, the Festival of Wood-carrying. Our enemies will not bar them from entering Jerusalem; their weapons will be hidden and their arms will be laden with wood. It will seem they have simply come to bring fuel for the Temple, as is the custom. With these reinforcements we will take the rest of Jerusalem."

Eleazar gave a satisfied chuckle when he finished.

He nodded at Shaul and then noticed the smaller figure standing beside him.

"Who is this?" Eleazar asked, again pointing.

"Shaul's tail," answered Judah, producing gales of laughter. "He may be young," Judah went on, "but according to Shaul he's already a fighter. He gouged the eyes of someone who tried to strangle him. Shaul taught him to use a sling. We'll see how he does in the next battle."

The flush of pride Reuven felt at Judah's words was mixed with fear and uncertainty.

For six days Shaul had worked with Reuven, teaching him how to use the sling, with its leather pouch in the middle and two cords attached to opposite sides, each cord ending in a loop. Shaul took Reuven down to the Kidron valley where they collected the smooth, round stones that would be the sling's arsenal. They spent hours together each day, with breaks for Reuven to rest his arm and for Shaul to join whatever battle that was taking place.

At first Reuven was terrible, unable to release the loop from his thumb at the correct moment when swinging the sling through the air. Once he almost hit Shaul with a stone.

Reuven had stared at Shaul, frightened at the near-mishap, but Shaul only laughed.

"You'll get it, Reuven. You'll get it. Don't worry," Shaul reassured him.

"It really can be a devastating weapon," Shaul went on to explain. "It's not just David bringing down Goliath; the Romans use slingers with their legions. An experienced one can send stones as far as a bowman shoots an arrow. Of course, they've been practicing since they were little children, and spend their whole lives doing it. We'll never get that good. Even so, it's still an effective weapon in our hands."

Shaul proved to be correct. Reuven did improve. On the twentieth practice try Reuven released the loop correctly. Thereafter, his accuracy grew slowly with each set of throws.

"You're a natural!" Shaul cried with delight. "Your hand and eye work beautifully together."

But practice was one thing and combat was another. Reuven still had not gotten over his first exposure to violence and the fear it had raised in him. Now he stood ready for his first real test with the loops of the sling around two fingers of his right hand and a collection of round stones in a pouch around his waist.

The blast of a shofar cut through the background noise.

Eleazar's men began lining up to stream out of the gate. The enemy across the bridge, both Agrippa's men and the citizens behind them, stirred; the soldiers straightened their ranks.

Reuven placed a stone in the sling, swung his arm round, and released the stone.

It sailed harmlessly off to the side.

Gritting his teeth, he tried again.

The second stone clattered onto the empty bridge.

Reuven took a deep breath, relaxed, and swung his arm. This stone flew through the air and struck one of Agrippa's men in the cheek. It wasn't the one Reuven had aimed at, he was two men off to the right, but no matter, the unintended target clutched his cheek and doubled over.

The next stone hit precisely where aimed, at the top of the head of a man three rows behind the front. There was no clutching at the stone's impact point this time; the target collapsed to the ground.

Conflicting emotions ran through Reuven: a rush of victory and a seeping horror that seemed to spread out from somewhere inside him that he may have killed a man.

Reuven's reverie was broken by two blasts of a shofar. In response men came streaming out of the gate, over the bridge and towards the waiting lines of the peace party. The men from the Temple emerged without formation, without order, as a disorganized mob, and were thrown back by Agrippa's men who held their orderly ranks.

Reuven, who had refrained from casting stones while the two groups collided to avoid hitting his own side, let loose with more round missiles. Three more men across the bridge fell from his barrage.

Again there were two more blasts of the shofar, and again the rebels charged. Even more men streamed out of the gate this time.

The disciplined array of Agrippa's soldiers, overwhelmed by the wild mob thrusting, slashing, and stabbing at them, began an orderly retreat. Reuven saw soldiers and civilians tripping over the four men he had brought down as they backed away from this fresh onslaught.

The rebels, infused with confidence at this initial success, attacked more fiercely. More men poured out from the Temple gate. The orderly retreat by Agrippa's men and the people supporting them became a rout. Soldiers and civilians alike turned and fled into the Upper City, followed by their howling pursuers.

Men with torches brought up the rear of the rebels.

Reuven stared at the flames, hypnotized by the dancing lights. Then he shoved the sling into his pouch and hurried down to the bridge leading to the Upper City, anxious to see what would go up in smoke.

Chapter Twenty-Eight

24 July 66 CE / Av 14 3826

The flames at the end of the torch danced as if they had a life of their own, danced as if they were celebrating their soon-to-be savored victory, danced as if they were about to quench their thirst for destruction.

Reuven, wide-eyed, stared at the raging gods waiting to be released from their confinement. They await the sacrifice due them, he thought.

Then Reuven shuddered at his blasphemy.

The Record Office was a two-story building four streets from the end of the bridge that led from the Temple. Agrippa's forces were nowhere to be seen; the citizens who supported them had laid down their arms and fearfully disappeared into their homes. So far, it seemed, the City belonged to the rebels.

Armed men had entered the Record Office and now frightened clerks were streaming out. Judah, Shaul, and David ben Ephraim watched from the street.

David held the torch that fascinated Reuven. David's face glowed with anticipation.

A man with a red beard and sharp features exited the building. He clutched a sheaf of papers protectively. He had a foxlike expression and eyes that darted anxiously around him. He did not look like a clerk.

He saw the three men and the boy. He saw the torch.

The man with the papers swallowed nervously.

There was fear in his eyes, and greed. He looked slyly from one face to another.

"Where are you going with those bonds, my friend?" Judah asked jovially.

"They're mine!" he hissed.

"Only for the moment," replied Judah.

The man's eyes went to the flames. He trembled.

"Hand them over, friend," Judah said gently.

"No!" The owner of the bonds was trying to sound brave, but he could not hide his terror.

"Friend, there's been enough killing. Just give them to me and you can go home," Judah said. The gentleness in his voice was tinged with steel.

"I'll sign over half to you if you let me keep the rest. You'll be rich!"

Judah laughed. It was a gay laugh, without a hint of malice.

"Friend," he asked, "do you think I'm here to get rich?"

Then Judah laughed again. He smiled broadly, showing the gap between his teeth. The man shivered in response to the smile.

The bond-holder's eyes swiveled from one face to another and to the spaces between their bodies. He rose slightly on his toes, preparing to flee, but before he could move Shaul was upon him, his strong hands around the bond-holder's neck.

The man screamed and dropped his papers. Shaul released him and he ran howling into the depths of the Upper City.

The three men laughed. Reuven gathered up the papers and handed them to Judah who handed them to David.

David entered the building, his torch burning brightly.

Is this right, Reuven asked himself?

He did not know the answer.

The armed men who had seized the building came out. Only David remained.

When he finally emerged, the torch was no longer in his hands. Smoke had begun seeping out of the building.

"The Jubilee Year has been declared!" David cried.

"Slaves are free, land is returned to its original owner!" Judah proclaimed.

Goosebumps rose along Reuven's arms.

Then fire leaped wildly from the windows, from the door. It burst through the ceiling. Smoke and ashes and dust flew everywhere as the gods of the flames consumed the Record Office.

Reuven's doubts vanished with the columns of smoke that rose to the heavens.

"The Land is free, its people are free!" he exclaimed.

A crowd gathered, watching in awe as a hated building went up in smoke and flames.

Reuven pointed at another rising column of smoke in the distance, further into the Upper City.

"What's that?" he asked.

"Let's go see," Judah replied.

The four of them made their way through the broad lanes of the Upper City to the source of the smoke.

The two large brass doors that were the entranceway to a once-luxurious home were flung open. The men fleeing the compound were better dressed than those who had fled the Record Office. They were obviously the servants of some rich man.

"I know this place," Reuven said. "My father took me here once. It is the home of the high priest, Ananias."

"His son leads the rebellion," Judah said.

"It was beautiful inside," Reuven protested. "Beautiful! Why is it being destroyed? I understand the Record Office, that was necessary, but this? Why? Just for the sake of destruction?" Reuven's voice was plaintive.

Judah shook his head.

"I don't know, Reuven, I don't know. This mansion served no purpose; neither does destroying it. Perhaps to prevent another would-be ruler from occupying it?"

Judah shook his head again.

"It was not my decision," he said. "I don't know whose decision it was, but I will not cry over it. You shouldn't either."

A grinning man came out through the open doors. He carried a knife stained with blood and wore a triumphant expression on his face.

It was John Dorcas.

"Greetings, comrades!" he cried. "What a victorious day!"

No sooner had he spoken then another servant came running through the doors, tears flowing down his face.

"Why? Why did you do this?" he shouted, his eyes going from one partisan to another. "Why would you do such a thing?"

Judah was about to reply but before he could get a word out Dorcas leaped at the servant and thrust his knife into the man's chest.

As the servant fell to the ground writhing in death throes Judah called out:

"Why in God's name did you do that? He was no threat! Why did you kill him? Are you mad?"

Reuven's eyes went in shocked horror to the body twitching on the ground, to Judah's angry face, to the look of contempt on Dorcas.

"Weakling," Dorcas sneered. "You don't have the strength to fight the Romans."

"You fool!" shouted Judah. "I've killed more Romans and Greeks than you ever will." His hand went to the knife on his belt.

Something was about to happen. What, Reuven did not know. He saw Shaul move to Judah's side and David shift uncomfortably, obviously not understanding what was going on.

Reuven did not understand, either.

Reuven looked through the open doors and to his surprise saw the short figure of Rabbi Hania running toward them.

"Look!" Reuven shouted. All eyes turned toward the direction of his hand. The tension was broken for the moment.

Rabbi Hania came through the entrance of Ananias' house, breathing heavily.

He pointed an accusing finger at Judah.

"You! You! You caused this, you and your robbers and murderers. See the smoke here? Soon all of Jerusalem will be burning. You murdered Rabbi Moshe, you murdered Rabbi Shlomo, you will murder us all!"

He turned to Reuven.

"What are you doing with these criminals? That man," here he pointed at Judah again, "murdered your uncle, your father's brother, the great rabbi Moshe ben Avraham!"

"That's a lie!" retorted Judah immediately. "I was so accused, but the Romans investigated and cleared me!"

"Ah," replied Hania, "perhaps you did not wield the knife. Perhaps one of your henchmen did. It does not matter. You are all murderers."

"Traitor!" spat Dorcas. He strode toward Rabbi Hania and grabbed the top of the rabbi's cloak. "I will silence you for good!"

Reuven's body shook. He did not know if it was from fear or anger or disgust but he was certain that he had to do something to stop Dorcas from murdering Hania. And he had to do it soon.

But what?

Reuven did not know.

"What can I do?" echoed inside his head like a scream as Dorcas raised the knife above the helpless Hania.

Chapter Twenty-Nine

24 July 66 CE / Av 14 3826

Standing at the edge of a precipice, staring down into the endless void, grasped at the back of his neck by a strong Hand, Rabbi Aaron wondered if the Hand would pull him back to safety or shove him into the abyss.

He felt neither hope nor fear, only an ineffable sadness.

"Why are you crying, Father?" Benjamin asked.

Rabbi Aaron wiped his tears and shook his head. He sat, his elbows on the table, and looked up at his eldest son who was standing across from him.

"These calamities, small and large, private into public, would not be happening unless God allowed it," he answered. "Why? Why?" Rabbi Aaron's voice rose. "Why has God turned His face away while we destroy ourselves? First my brother murdered, then his wife vanishes, then Rabbi Shlomo is murdered during a rabbinical assembly, and now the biryonim are taking over the whole City. Where will it all end?"

"In victory and freedom, or death and destruction?" Benjamin responded. He spoke rapidly. "If you don't know, Father, how can I? How can anyone? Only God knows the answer to your question."

Rabbi Aaron knitted his brows, leaned forward, and reaching across the table seized his son's left forearm with his right hand. Looking into his eldest son's eyes he cried:

"Even my youngest, my Reuven, ran away to join the robbers!"

Benjamin bent down and placed his free hand on his father's shoulder.

"Reuven is well, Father."

"Well?" Rabbi Aaron laughed sardonically. "My son joins a band of cutthroats and his brother tells me he is well?"

"Reuven is doing what he thinks is right," Benjamin replied. "Just as you are."

"And you, you, do you think Reuven is doing right?" Rabbi Aaron asked, his voice quivering.

"Father," Benjamin replied gently, "I do not know who is right: The rabbis who counsel patience or those who urge war against Rome. But I understand why Reuven made the choice he did."

"Why, Benjamin, why did he run away?"

Benjamin removed his right hand from his father's shoulder and freed his left forearm. He straightened up and took a small step backward as he met his father's gaze.

"Reuven told me that when he saw that Roman officer with his sword and shield, standing tall, unafraid, he was sickened by how we Jews go around trembling before the Romans, slaves in our own country, the Land God gave us."

Rabbi Aaron took a deep breath, shook his head once more, and said:

"That Roman officer, Metilius, has been coming to study with me."

"I know that, Father. I also know that he still commands the Roman garrison, and even if he became a Jew tomorrow it would change nothing."

"Do you think the war is winnable, Benjamin?"

Benjamin shrugged his shoulders.

"No, probably not. But we did defeat Antiochus when he oppressed us."

"Ach, not that again!" Rabbi Aaron exclaimed. "Antiochus tried to wipe out our religion. He forbade studying the Torah, he forbade observing the Sabbath, he forbade circumcision. The Romans do none of that. They respect the Temple; they even offer sacrifices, which we have now rejected."

Rabbi Aaron gave his son a sharp look.

"Who do you think killed Uncle Moshe?"

"I do not know, Father. Perhaps one of the biryonim, perhaps someone paid by Florus to stir up trouble. But I am sure it was not Judah ben Ezra; your own Metilius cleared him."

Rabbi Aaron's eyes narrowed into almost a squint, as if he was trying to see something that was hidden in the distance.

"I'm not so sure anymore," he replied. "Bruria was convinced he was guilty. Perhaps she had some special intuition. We can't ask her, though. She has vanished. It's hard to believe her disappearance has nothing to do with Rabbi Moshe's murder. It may be that she discovered her husband's murderer and they killed her for that."

Rabbi Aaron fell silent for several moments. Benjamin stirred uncomfortably.

"I want to speak to Reuven," Rabbi Aaron said suddenly.

"So you can slap him again?"

"No, no!" Rabbi Aaron declared, holding his hands up. "That was wrong of me. I admit it. No. I just want to talk to him, about your uncle's murder. He may have heard something, and even if he hasn't, he can help me find the murderer."

Benjamin looked at his father quizzically.

"I may not be able to do anything to save the City from its coming destruction," Rabbi Aaron said, "but I want to find my brother's assassin before the end comes. And I do not believe Florus was responsible. Why would he even choose Moshe? What does he know about the internal struggle of the Jews? Ananias would have been a more likely target.

"No," Rabbi Aaron went on emphatically. "It must be one of the biryonim. Perhaps Judah himself did not strike the blow, but he may have planned it. And if not this group, then one of the other gangs carried out the murder. Whatever the truth is, Reuven is uniquely positioned to learn it."

"I'm not so sure," Benjamin responded.

"You must tell him to come speak with me!" Rabbi Aaron roared "It is terribly important. I need your help, Reuven!"

A slight smile crossed Benjamin's face.

"I am Benjamin, Father, not Reuven" Benjamin replied. "And yes, I will help you. I will speak to Reuven."

Chapter Thirty

24 July 66 CE / Av 14 3826

Reuven shouted as loud as he could and charged at Dorcas. The knifeman, startled, released Hania and turned toward the oncoming boy. Reuven tackled Dorcas and the two went sprawling to the ground. Reuven grabbed Dorcas' knife-hand by the wrist with both of his own hands and tried to wrestle the knife away. In the background Reuven heard the sounds of laughter, two distinct voices.

The struggle lasted only a moment. Shaul and Judah separated the two combatants and pulled them to their feet. Both Shaul and Judah could not stop laughing.

"You are something, aren't you?" Judah exclaimed, slapping his thigh. "A regular lion cub!"

Even Dorcas began to laugh.

"All right, you," Judah said, addressing Hania, "get out of here. Go back home."

Hania had a look of incomprehension on his face. It was obvious he was trying to understand what was going on. Then he gathered his wits and made a movement to flee.

"Stop!" cried Reuven.

Hania froze and looked fearfully at Reuven.

"We need him!" exclaimed Reuven.

"Hania? Are you joking? What do we need Hania for?" asked Judah in amazement.

"Rabbi Hania," Reuven said, "if it comes to war with Rome will you sit idly by at home or will you help your people and your country?" Before Hania could give an answer Reuven turned to Judah and said:

"Rabbi Hania has a metal workshop. He is a master craftsman. We will need to produce weapons. Rabbi Hania can oversee the effort."

Judah stroked his beard as he considered Reuven's advice.

"Well, it seems you're not only a brave little cub, but a wise one, too. Well, Hania, what about it? Seems the whole City is in our hands now. Are you with us, or should I let John here finish what he started?"

Hania was shaking.

"Rabbi Hania," Reuven said gently, "if you need to, you can ask Rabbi Zechariah for his guidance before you decide."

Tears filled Rabbi Hania's eyes. He shivered.

"I don't need to ask. I've decided. I will help."

"Good," Reuven said. "Go home in peace now. War is coming. We will send for you soon."

The five of them—Reuven, Judah, Shaul, Dorcas, and David ben Ephraim—watched as Hania hurried toward the Lower City.

Judah turned to Dorcas.

"Watch that knife of yours!" he demanded. "We can't kill everyone on the other side."

"We'll be better off when all the traitors are eliminated," Dorcas retorted.

"There will be no one left to fight the Romans," Judah said.

"We'll be stronger when only the steadfast remain," insisted Dorcas. "There will be no one left to weaken us from the inside."

Judah pointed his right index finger at Dorcas.

"I told you to lay low," he said.

Dorcas laughed.

"Who do I have to fear now? The Romans? They're shut up in Antonia. It won't be long before we take care of them, too. The peace rabbis, the ones who saw me kill Shlomo? Without the Romans they are nothing. No, I am free, free to come and go as I please!"

Judah shook his finger at Dorcas.

"You come back with me to the Temple now. I want you where I can see you or I'll send you back north!"

Reuven saw defiance and fear on Dorcas' face.

"I don't have to answer to you, Judah!" Dorcas exclaimed. His voice quavered, but his eyes had narrowed and he held Judah's gaze without flinching. "I'm getting my own followers. I don't need you."

Dorcas spun on his heels and ran, west along the broad street, then disappearing as he turned south around a corner.

"He still fears your authority," Reuven observed. "He's running, not walking away from you."

"I'm not so sure," Judah replied. "That one has turned into a monster."

"Judah," Reuven began thoughtfully, "do you think he killed my uncle Moshe?"

"What? No!" Judah appeared flustered. "No. I'm sure that was Florus' doing." There was a brief pause. "Why did you ask me that?"

"Because of what Rabbi Hania said. He accused you. I know you had nothing to do with it. Maybe it was Dorcas, acting on his own."

"I don't think so, Reuven," Judah replied. "I'm sure Florus arranged your uncle's murder to stir up trouble. But I'll look into it. If it was Dorcas, I promise I will make him pay for it."

Reuven saw Judah wipe new-formed sweat away from his forehead.

"Thank you," Reuven said.

The four exchanged quick glances with each other. Then the three turned to Judah as if waiting further instructions.

"What happens now?" David asked.

Judah shrugged.

"I don't know. I'm not in charge. Eleazar is. Let's go back to the Temple. I want to talk to him."

They walked in silence. The streets were deserted save for scattered bands of armed men roaming through the Upper City, prowling for any remaining opposition.

There was none to be seen. Smoke drifted skyward from a few torched buildings but most of the houses of the rich were left alone, their occupants cowering inside.

Reuven tried to make sense of the day, the good and the bad. He could not. Burning the Record Office he understood, but not the destruction of Ananias' home. Fighting Agrippa's troops and the citizens who supported them for control of the City he also understood, but not the cold-blooded killing of a harmless servant. Was all of it, the good and the bad, necessary, or had forces been set in motion that would lead to more senseless acts of violence?

In times past Reuven would have gone to his father or Uncle Moshe for guidance; now he was estranged from his father and his uncle was dead.

And if Dorcas, a supposed ally, had killed his beloved uncle? If so, what was his own duty to his dead uncle and his family? Did Judah's promise relieve him of that responsibility?

Reuven lowered his head with weariness and stared at the ground as he walked. Confused thoughts flew through his head. He did not like the uncertainty.

As they neared the Temple David said goodbye and made his way into the Lower City. At the Temple Judah went looking for Eleazar. Reuven and Shaul went to their perch on the rampart overlooking the City.

Benjamin was waiting for them.

"Brother!" Reuven cried with delight.

Shaul looked at Benjamin with curiosity.

"Have you come to join us?" Shaul asked. "If you're half the man your little brother is, we can use you." Then he laughed.

Benjamin ignored Shaul's taunt. Before he could say anything to his brother Reuven cried:

"We are victorious today! The City is ours!"

Benjamin pointed down into the Upper City, at the palace of Agrippa and Berenice. Thick swirls of smoke roses from several places in the palace.

"From the looks of it, you're not waiting for the Romans. You'll burn Jerusalem yourselves first," replied Benjamin drily.

Reuven followed Benjamin's hand. His eyes widened with surprise.

Why are they torching that? he wondered.

He scratched at the scraggly beard sprouting on his face as he tried to think of a response.

"Much good, some bad," was all he could say.

Benjamin came close.

"I must talk to you alone," he said, taking Reuven's arm and leading him away from Shaul. He walked north along the east rampart, until they were in front of the Temple. "It's about Father."

"What's wrong?" Reuven asked, alarmed.

"I found him crying. He thinks God has abandoned us. He feels helpless. He wants to talk to you--"

"So he can slap me in the face again?" Reuven interrupted.

"No!" Benjamin said. "He's sorry about that. There's only one thing he thinks he can do, and that is find Uncle Moshe's murderer—"

"What's that got to do with me?" Reuven interrupted again. "It was obviously someone sent by Florus."

"Father doesn't think so. I don't either."

"Who then?" asked Reuven.

"One of the biryonim. He thinks you can find out who."

"Me? Why me?" Reuven's voice was shaking.

Benjamin looked at the top of the Temple behind them and then at his brother.

"Because you are one of the biryonim now," he said solemnly, as if pronouncing sentence upon his brother.

Reuven looked down at the ground. A loose pebble lay there, on a surface that once would have been swept clean. He kicked at it, sending the small stone flying into the distance. Two different streams of thought were running through his head, both flowing from the same man.

"Tell me, brother, does Metilius still study with Father?" he asked Benjamin.

"Yes. Almost every day."

"Do you think he could be persuaded to join the revolt?"

Benjamin laughed.

"Metilius studies with Rabbi Aaron, not Rabbi Zechariah."

Reuven nodded.

"Yes, you are right," he said. "It's a shame, though. I don't know anything for sure, but my guess is that Antonia will be attacked next. It would be a loss if something happened to him. If he could be persuaded to send his troops out of Jerusalem and remain behind himself, he could teach us much about Roman strategy and tactics."

Reuven glanced up at the Temple, at the golden spikes on top that gleamed in the sun.

They're beautiful, he thought. And they also keep the birds off.

He turned back to his brother. His eyes focused on Benjamin's face, his voice several tones deeper, and said, slowly and emphatically:

"Benjamin, remember when I spoke about a possible witness to Uncle Moshe's murder? A very tall and large woman in a gray dress. How many Jewish women have you seen that fit that description? Doesn't that sound more like a Gaul or a German, a woman from one of the barbarian races north of Rome? A Gaul or a German would be connected to the Romans, not the biryonim. And in that case she wouldn't just be a witness; she was part of Florus' plot."

Benjamin's look of surprise at his suggestion was gratifying. Reuven smiled.

"Perhaps," Benjamin replied after a moment's reflection. "Perhaps. But how many Jewish men are as tall as Father? Or your friend over there? Are they Gauls or Germans?"

Reuven turned to look at his friend and mentor. And then a strange thought entered his mind: If Shaul were a woman, he would fit the description of the witness to his uncle's murder.

And that thought made Reuven shudder.

Chapter Thirty-One

Sat 26 July 66 CE / Av 16 3826

Rabbi Aaron showed him one face of what it meant to be a Jew; the enraged mob assaulting Antonia showed him another.

Metilius drummed his fingers on the map that lay unrolled in front of him. He sat in a chair hunched over a table in his austere headquarters. The large rectangular table had six chairs, three on each long side. A bin against the wall held maps and documents; a stand supported a long pole with a golden eagle at its top.

The morning after the rebels burned the Record Office and took over the City attacks began on Antonia. This was the second day of waves of assaults on the fortress. The attackers were disorganized partisans and civilians, clearly not military men under the command of an experienced, battle-tested leader. The Jews threw themselves helter-skelter against Metilius' forces, without order and discipline, though with as much courage as his own men possessed. Their numbers gave them brief advantage; several of his men were wounded and a few were killed. But the Jews made no progress in their attempt to capture Antonia; at the end of each battle the Jewish forces were thrown back with many casualties. This did not stop them from trying again and again. Metilius knew that it would not be long before the sheer weight of the numbers of the frenzied insurgents would overwhelm his garrison of less than 500 men.

While there were small, cramped entrances to Antonia on the north and east, the real points of entry that had to be defended were on the west, and on the south, where the fortress joined the Temple. Luckily, the Jews themselves had eliminated that last during a previous disturbance instigated by Florus.

Florus had sent troops to sack the Upper Market and then made moves on the Temple itself from the Antonia fortress. To prevent Florus from occupying the Temple and stealing its treasures the Jews cut the colonnades linking the Temple to Antonia.

Ah, Florus, Metilius thought. You didn't bother to hide your avarice and thievery! Can I blame the Jews for revolting? You used the might of Rome to murder ordinary men and even scourged and crucified Jews of equestrian rank! And you did not have the cunning to keep order after committing your crimes. You had to leave the City with most of your forces to prevent further outbreaks, leaving only me and my men, whom the Jews accepted because we had not taken part in your outrages.

When Agrippa II came after Florus' departure to calm the population, and urged the Jews to repair the colonnades to demonstrate that they were not in rebellion against Rome, those inclined toward peace began the repair work. But once Agrippa left Jerusalem the work ceased. Now, instead of stopping Romans from occupying the Temple from Antonia, the cut colonnades prevented the Jews in the Temple from occupying Antonia.

Thus it was from the west that they made their main assaults.

Two broad doors at the top of a wide stairway led into Antonia from the area west of the fortress where there were markets and store-houses, between the first and second wall of Jerusalem. Metilius had placed the bulk of his men at those doors, but he could not risk putting all his forces there to defend the western entrance; the other points of entry could be infiltrated by small groups who could make suicidal but effective attacks from with Antonia itself.

Sooner or later, he thought, they will overwhelm us if we remain in Antonia.

Metilius sighed loudly. He rubbed his eyes.

"Can I get you something, sir?" a soft feminine voice called from the corner of the room.

Metilius turned in his seat to look at the servant. She was young, with smooth fair skin, golden hair, and blue eyes. He was aware of her beauty. No doubt she was from one of the lands north of Italy. He barely knew her name.

Drusilla, he thought. I could drag her into another room and take her. She couldn't stop me and I would answer to no one.

Metilius laughed. It sounded bitter to his own ears.

I've been with no other women since I married Aurelia and I've never taken a woman by force. Am I more Jew than Roman soldier?

Ah, the Jews. There's Rabbi Aaron, who talks of peace. And that guttersnipe Judah, who practically threatened me.

"No," he said to the girl.

Metilius gave one last look at the map and stood up.

He walked out of the room and along a wide corridor that opened to chambers much more luxurious than his Spartan headquarters: dining rooms, living quarters, bathrooms. In other parts of the fortress there were colonnades and expansive courtyards with fountains. Antonia was as much palace as fortress.

What a builder Herod was! thought Metilius. But the Jews hated him, and it did not matter to which school of thought they belonged.

He was a cruel ruler, Rabbi Aaron had explained. He murdered members of his own family, including sons and a wife who was a descendant of the Maccabees. He killed others, too, and was feared for his cruelty. On his deathbed he arrested many prominent citizens with orders to execute them when he died. Herod wanted to ensure that his passing would bring mourning and not joy to the Land of Israel. It was only luck that prevented Herod's posthumous plans from being carried out.

Metilius had nodded after Rabbi Aaron's recitation but countered with:

"King Herod kept the peace, he turned the cities of Israel into jewels of the East, and he even beautified and expanded the Temple. Is that not worth something?"

"Not at the price he exacted," Rabbi Aaron replied.

At a stairway to his right Metilius rapidly ascended its many steps and stepped outside onto the southeast tower of Antonia.

Antonia had four towers, one at each corner. The tower Metilius had entered was the highest, at 105 feet. From its vantage point the whole Temple could be viewed.

The Temple courtyards were filled with men. Some were armed, some were robed-priests carrying out rituals, and some were ordinary citizens who had come to bring sacrifices.

Metilius watched the activity for a while. It was an ironic turn of events. His mission, to keep order in the Temple and prevent rebellion, was impossible to carry out now. Instead, he kept watch on the Temple to secure the survival of his own men.

Metilius turned from the Temple and looked north. If he wanted to abandon his post to flee Jerusalem with his troops—the sanest course to take—the best route would be to steal out from Antonia's exit on the east, then move through Bezetha, the newer, northern section of Jerusalem between the second and third walls, and then go out through the third wall.

Would he be charged with deserting his post?

Would he be exposing his men to attack in the open areas of Bezetha by an overwhelming number of Jews?

Metilius turned back to the Temple.

That damn Florus, he thought. Sitting in Caesarea. He starts a fire and does nothing to put it out.

Metilius' one hope was Cestius Gallus, legate of Syria, who had ultimate responsibility for the province of Judea and Jerusalem. If Metilius could buy some time, hold out a little longer, Cestius would come from Antioch and with the Twelfth Legion put an end to the rebellion.

A Roman legion, with real Roman soldiers!

Metilius smiled with anticipation. For a moment his anxiety dissipated.

Enough men and equipment to subdue the rebels!

There were Jews who did not want war who managed to inform Metilius that they had sent word to Cestius. They also informed Metilius of the goings on in the rest of the City. The rebels had control of it all, except for Herod's Palace, located at the far western end of the Upper City. Herod had spared no expense in building it, and it was also both palace and fortress. Agrippa's soldiers had retreated to it after the takeover of the City. They were joined by citizens who actively opposed the revolt.

How many of Agrippa's men were left after the losing battles?

That, Metilius did not know. The force had started out with 2,000 men.

If we can join them, Metilius thought, we may be able to hold out until Cestius comes with the Twelfth Legion. I must wait for an answer.

Metilius had sent his Jewish translator to negotiate with Eleazar, the apparent leader of the rebellion. Metilius had offered to surrender Antonia in return for safe passage to Herod's Palace.

Metilius could think of no reason why Eleazar would refuse the offer. He would get Antonia without losing any more men and the hated Roman presence would be removed from the Temple area.

But Metilius also realized that he could never be sure how these unpredictable Jews would respond to a reasonable offer.

He gave one last look around and descended the stairs.

The short Jewish translator was waiting for him. He was pulling nervously at his beard and shifting uncomfortably from one foot to the other. He looked anxiously at Metilius.

"Well, did you speak to Eleazar? What does he say?" Metilius asked impatiently.

"Eleazar agrees to give you safe passage to Herod's Palace on one condition." The translator spoke quickly. He took a big gulp of air, looked down at the floor and then up at Metilius. He was obviously frightened. "You and your men have to surrender your arms. And he wants an answer by tomorrow morning or the attacks will resume with even greater force than before." When he finished speaking he began trembling, waiting for Metilius' reaction.

Metilius nodded.

He looked closely at his translator. His name was Noah. Metilius understood Rabbi Aaron. He even understood Judah. But this man was a mystery. Could he be trusted?

"Noah," he said gently, watching the translator closely, "I have an important mission for you. I want you to go to Herod's Palace and tell them to expect the arrival of the Roman garrison from Antonia."

"Will you be coming with your arms?" Noah avoided Metilius' eyes when he asked.

Metilius gave Noah a cold stare.

"You will go with one of my men," Metilius said, his voice as hard as a Roman shield. "You will be escorted to the palace and then straight back here. Do you understand?"

Noah's head bobbed up and down, as if attached to a string.

Tonight, Metilius thought, I will lead my men to Herod's Palace under cover of darkness.

With their arms.

Chapter Thirty-Two

Thu 14 Aug 66 CE / 5 Elul 3826

The air in the Upper Market was infected with an anticipation of victory. A mass of revolutionaries was clustered in front of the tower in the wall that protected Herod's Palace.

The partisans were waiting for the tower to collapse.

"They'll think it's the hand of God," Shaul declared, smiling, referring to the defenders on the other side.

"It will be, if it succeeds," Reuven responded.

"It will succeed," Judah said. "But only the Jews will think it's the hand of God; the others will think it is magic. They don't know the God of Israel."

Shaul looked at Judah and then at Reuven. Judah's expression proclaimed his certainty; Reuven's that he would believe it when he saw it. While Shaul shared Judah's certainty he understood Reuven's skepticism.

On the other side of the wall were citizens who opposed the revolt, what remained of Agrippa's soldiers, and the hated Romans and their auxiliaries who had abandoned Antonia almost three weeks ago.

Once the partisans were in possession of Antonia they put their full attention on Herod's Palace. Their attempts got nowhere. The defenders refused to leave the palace grounds to do battle face-to-face and the attackers could not approach the walls, from whose heights the defenders were able to hurl missiles on the attackers.

Things are about to change in our favor, Shaul thought.

"Was the tunnel your idea, Judah?" Reuven asked.

"Only partially," came the reply. "I said to Eleazar, in a purely offhand way, that if we dug a tunnel under the walls we could get into the palace. He liked the idea and came up with a better one."

Herod's Palace, at the western edge of the Upper City, was surrounded by walls. On the west was a section of Jerusalem's first, and oldest, wall. That wall was impregnable because it overlooked the steep Hinnom Valley. The other walls, forty-five feet high, separated the palace and its grounds from the rest of the Upper City. Though stout, they could possibly be breached, if attackers could get close enough.

Eleazar had devised a stratagem based on Judah's idea. They dug a mine to the tower that faced the Upper Market. The digging started inside a stall so that the watchmen on the tower couldn't see what they were doing. When the mine reached the tower, the weight of the tower was transferred to wooden props. When the full invasion force was ready, the props would be set on fire. When the tower collapsed, bringing that section of the wall with it, the rebels would storm Herod's Palace.

"It was your idea," Reuven said, "and Eleazar's implementation, but now Menahem is in charge of the City."

A man named Menahem, a leader of his own band, had gone to Masada, a desert fortress built by Herod, and broke open King Herod's armory. Thus armed, and with a fresh supply of recruits, he arrived in Jerusalem. He put himself at the head of the rebellion and took over the siege of Herod's Palace.

Judah nodded.

"How does Eleazar feel about that?" Reuven asked.

"He's not happy," Judah replied. "There's not much he can do about it at the moment. Many of the rebel bands prefer being under an outlaw like themselves rather than under a Temple minister."

"You, Judah?"

Judah shook his head.

"I prefer Eleazar," Judah said.

Shaul nodded in agreement. He, too, preferred Eleazar.

"Is this a good turn of events?" Reuven asked.

Shaul smiled at his friend's earnestness.

Judah shrugged.

"I don't know anymore," he said.

"He claims to be a grandson of Judas the Galilean," Reuven went on. "Is he really your cousin?"

Judah laughed.

"Anyone can claim anything," he said. "I never heard of him. From what I see, while my grandfather said we should bend the knee to no one but God this Menahem says we should bend the knee to no one but him."

"Judah, what about John Dorcas?" Reuven asked.

"He's gone," Judah replied. "Joined Menahem's outfit."

"So you were never able to find out if he killed my uncle."

"No. I never saw him again after that day. Be patient, Reuven. If the killer is one of us, I'll find him and you'll have your justice."

Shaul could not suppress a shiver. He was glad Reuven's eyes were on Judah.

What would happen if Reuven learned the truth? Shaul wondered.

Would he understand that Rabbi Moshe's death was necessary to protect the revolution? Or would he demand vengeance for the death of his father's brother?

For Shaul, Reuven was more than a comrade-in-arms or a friend. He was the little brother he never had. The thought of Reuven turning against him pained Shaul.

And if the roles were reversed, how would I react? he asked himself. Shaul did not know.

There was another question Shaul could not answer, and it threatened to throw in doubt his own commitment to the revolt: Would he still have killed Rabbi Moshe if he had known Reuven then?

Shaul's eyes fell to the ground as these thoughts flew through his head. His reverie was broken by a shout from Reuven.

"Look!" the boy called out. "The watchmen on the tower have gone!"

Shaul's head went up.

It was true. As if a signal had been given, the men in the tower who had been watching the Upper Market had deserted their posts.

"Not just the ones on the tower!" Shaul cried. "The ones on that section of the wall are also gone. What does it mean, Judah?"

The expression on Judah's face turned gloomy.

"Not good, I'm afraid," he said. "Did someone warn them? Is there a spy among us?" After a moment he added: "Oh well, it doesn't matter. Once that tower collapses we're inside and there is nothing they can do about it."

And he shrugged his shoulders and threw out his hands.

Shaul breathed a sigh of relief.

A thrum of voices spread out from the stall where the mine began. Everyone's eyes moved to the tower, everyone's hand moved to his weapon. The partisans were ready for the assault.

They did not have long to wait. The tower began to sway, gently at first, then more vigorously, until the bottom collapsed, bringing down the whole structure with a loud crash, along with the adjoining portions of the wall.

The partisans began their charge with the ear-splitting roars of wild beasts.

Then they stopped cold. Shouts of combat turned to groans. Mouths flew open in amazement.

The siege of three weeks was not over.

The defenders had put up another wall.

Chapter Thirty-Three

Fri 15 Aug 66 CE / 6 Elul 3826

Regret coursed through his mind like a foul river of poison.

I should never have left Antonia, Metilius thought. I should have stayed and fought, or else taken my men out the east exit, through Bezetha, and then out of Jerusalem and on to Caesarea.

Metilius watched in dismay as the soldiers of King Agrippa II and the Jews of Jerusalem who had supported them prepared to abandon Herod's Palace, leaving him and his men to fight on alone.

It was Metilius who realized what the partisans were planning and who warned the officers in charge of Agrippa's soldiers. But there was nothing they could do to stop the revolutionaries from building the mine to the tower. The defenders were too weak to carry out sorties to stop the underground work. They would have been overwhelmed by the greater numbers of the partisans.

In desperation the defenders built a second wall as a stop-gap measure. It was not as well-constructed as the first. Thus, when the original wall fell, exposing the second wall, consternation was not confined to the attackers. The men inside Herod's Palace knew that it was only a matter of time before this second wall was breached.

The citizens and Agrippa's officers sued for peace and asked for safe passage from the palace.

It was granted, but not to the Romans.

Metilius' position was now totally untenable.

Without the others, Metilius thought, Herod's Palace is less defensible than Antonia. It has to be abandoned. We must fight our way out and make it to Phasael Tower.

Not far from Metilius' position were three strong towers built by Herod. Like Antonia and Herod's Palace itself, these towers were part fortress and part palace. One of the towers was named after Herod's beloved wife Mariamme, descendent of the Maccabees, whom Herod murdered in a jealous rage. Another was named Hippicus, after a friend. The third, Phasael, was named after Herod's brother who died in battle.

Phasael was the tallest and the strongest. The bottom section was sixty feet deep, sixty feet wide, and sixty feet high. Running around its top was a colonnade fifty feet high which was protected by breastworks and bulwarks. In the middle of this section rose another tower topped by ramparts and turrets. This second tower was divided into luxurious apartments that even included bathrooms. The entire structure was 135 feet high and solidly built. It was strong enough to withstand any attack that could be mounted by the rebels and well-enough equipped to hold out during a siege of reasonable length.

Metilius watched his previous allies prepare to depart. The citizens of Jerusalem were to exit through a gate in the south wall on the palace grounds, Agrippa's troops through a gate in the north wall. The soldiers' journey to Agrippa's kingdom would lead them past Phasael Tower, out a gate in the first wall of Jerusalem, through Bezetha as they skirted the second city wall, until they finally left Jerusalem through the Women's Gate in the third wall that protected Jerusalem from the north.

Metilius gathered his officers and gave them instructions. They were to abandon Herod's Palace as Agrippa's men left, charging through their lines, and then fight their way past the rebels, making an orderly retreat to Phasael Tower. Under no conditions were they to allow the Jews to penetrate their ranks. If that happened, all would be lost. Furthermore, they were not to stop to gather any dead; it was a luxury they could not afford in their present circumstances. Once in the tower they would be safe and could hold out until Cestius arrived with the Twelfth Legion.

When Agrippa's soldiers began to walk out of the gate, Metilius' men were already arrayed for battle.

One of Agrippa's officers came up to Metilius and eyed the orderly Roman formation suspiciously.

"I'm sorry," he said. "We had no choice."

Metilius did not reply. He stared stonily ahead. The man left and returned to his own troops. Metilius cursed under his breath. The king's soldiers who had been sent to aid the Peace Party continued their withdrawal.

When half of Agrippa's soldiers had passed through the gate Metilius raised his sword and cried: "Now!"

The Romans and their auxiliaries moved forward at a half run, three men abreast. Without breaking formation they crashed into the backs of their former allies.

Startled, some turned to face the Romans, weapons still undrawn. Others started running toward the open gate. Their confused response allowed Metilius and the front lines of his men to force their way through the king's troops without engaging in combat.

The area outside the gate was crowded with the fleeing soldiers of the king and the armed partisans who were keeping watch on them. The former were not sure what to do. They were not expecting a fight and indeed the Romans were not attacking them. But the partisans, surprised to see armed Romans also emerging from the palace, assumed they had been tricked and that everyone coming through the gate was now an enemy. And so the revolutionaries fell upon armed Romans and the hapless king's troops alike, as they swung their swords, thrust their lances, and wielded their clubs.

Agrippa's soldiers, weapons still sheathed, fell to the onslaught of the partisans as well as to the Roman troops who inadvertently killed them while defending themselves from the attackers. In the wild melee that ensued, some of the revolutionaries even hacked away at each other.

But the Romans never broke ranks as they pushed inexorably forward.

Metilius reached the door on the southern face of Phasael Tower. The four men guarding it stared at Metilius in amazement before they roused themselves to respond. It was too late. Metilius and the men behind him quickly cut them down and gained control of the entrance to Phasael.

Metilius forced the door open. He assigned the first five rows of men to stand guard on the open door to allow those following safe entry to the tower.

He watched as his soldiers kept their formation of three men to a row as they marched. The man on each flank turned to the side to fight off the partisan attackers. The man in the middle turned one way and another to help whichever man at his side was in trouble. Sometimes the row behind would join in to fight off a fresh group of attackers.

Metilius' men never stopped their forward movement, chanting rhythmically as they marched. Some of his soldiers did fall, but many more partisans and king's soldiers lay dead or dying. Metilius felt pity for his fallen men and grudging admiration for the Jews who continued to fight despite their losses; for the allies who had abandoned him and his men he felt nothing but contempt.

Of the Jews he thought: They are fierce and undisciplined, like wild animals. With training and a good commander they would make formidable soldiers. Cestius will not have an easy time subduing them.

That realization made him uneasy as he watched the last of his troops reach the tower.

They entered, followed by those who had guarded the open door.

When the last man had gone inside, Metilius himself entered and barred the door, to the howls of the revolutionaries outside who kept charging forward.

What remained of the Roman garrison that had once kept watch over the Temple was safe.

For now.

Chapter Thirty-Four

16 Aug 66 CE / 7 Elul 3826

His home burned, his place of refuge overrun, Ananias stepped out of the dry canal where he and his brother Hezekiah had been hiding and sleeping. His clothes were dirty and torn, his life was in danger, but what brought tears to his eyes was the destruction he saw around him.

Herod's Palace had been magnificent, Ananias thought bitterly. Herod spared no expense building it. Its grounds and structures were beyond compare. Green lawns and walkways flanked by colonnades, with stands of trees of every kind, and beds of flowers whose brilliant colors—red, blue, pink, orange—mimicked the hues of the rare stones brought from all over the world to decorate the grounds. Artificial streams and ponds and canals, with cotes of tame pigeons and songbirds, and bronze statues pouring forth water. The structures on the palace grounds were no less wonderful. Banquet halls and guestrooms with 100 beds, and rooms without number, each different, filled with objects of gold and silver! The dream of a master builder fulfilled! And now? A smoking ruins. Look what my son has brought about! It would have been better if he had never been born!

Ananias roused his brother.

"It is not safe here," Ananias said.

"Where shall we go?" Hezekiah lamented. "They have the whole City now."

"They cannot have killed everyone," Ananias replied. "There must be some homes in the Upper City that have been left unscathed. We can find shelter in one until we are able to leave Jerusalem."

"To go where?"

Ananias did not respond to his brother's question. A man of medium height, with a lithe body, was taking light, quick steps toward them. He was dressed like a commoner.

In his right hand he held a knife, the hand held level with the ground, the knife pointing downward. The man had a grin on his face.

A cruel grin Ananias surmised, as the man came closer.

"Ho!" the fellow cried. "What do we have here? Two high priests? Traitors to the nation?"

Ananias trembled, with anger as much as fear.

"Look what you have done!" he cried. "You and your band of cutthroats. Are you proud of yourself?"

"This palace was built by that pagan king Herod, that lackey of the Romans," the man replied. "A place of delight for Romans and Jewish traitors, a heathen place filled with statues that are forbidden in this holy city! It is just that this place of idolatry was destroyed."

"Who are you to decide that?" Ananias retorted. "And what do you know of holiness, you who are holding a weapon of war in your hand on the Sabbath?"

The man came closer. He raised his knife.

"This will answer for me," he said.

"I am a high priest, as is my brother. How dare you threaten us!"

The man sneered.

"I killed a rabbinical scholar at the rabbinical assembly that passed the Eighteen Decrees," he said. "What are one or two priests compared to that?"

Ananias saw his brother Hezekiah turn away and start running.

Ananias calmly faced the assassin.

"*Sh'ma Yisra'eil Adonai Eloheinu Adonai echad,*" he chanted as a last prayer. Hear, O Israel, the Lord is our God, the Lord is One.

Chapter Thirty-Five

16 Aug 66 CE / 7 Elul 3826

Rage, rage like he had never felt before, consumed Eleazar like a great fire.

"Who did this terrible thing?" he roared.

Eleazar's voice echoed among the ruins of Herod's Palace.

There was no one among his retinue who could answer.

Eleazar stared down at the body of his father.

"I will have vengeance!" he shouted. "For him and my uncle!"

Hezekiah's body had been found fifty yards away.

"Who did this?" he cried, again to no answer.

It would not have been one of the Jerusalem citizens taking refuge from us in Herod's Palace, Eleazar thought. They would never kill a high priest. Agrippa's soldiers? They had come to restore the previous order of my father. Why would they kill him? The Romans! The Romans who fled to the tower! Yes, the Romans! Most of them aren't even Romans, but Syrian auxiliaries who hate us Jews in their very bones!

For a moment Eleazar felt a kind of satisfaction; it would not be long before he would have vengeance on the Romans and their auxiliaries who had taken their last stand in Phasael Tower.

Then another thought came to Eleazar.

There were other killings of Peace Party adherents after his men had taken over buildings and sections of the City. There were the servants killed in his father's house when it was burned to the ground, and from which his father had fled to Herod's Palace. There were no Romans in those places. Or Agrippa's soldiers, for that matter.

Slowly, reluctantly, it dawned on him that it had to be one of the revolutionaries, someone on his own side.

"Bring me Judah ben Ezra!!" he cried.

As Eleazar continued staring down at his dead father, he began to weep. He blinked away the tears that distorted his vision; he wanted to see his father clearly for the last time. He had never meant for the revolution he began to lead to the death of his father.

Eleazar lost track of time as he stood there, mumbling prayers for his father, for the dead, for Jerusalem, even for himself.

"Eleazar, what is it?" he heard Judah ask. And then, "Oh no!"

Eleazar whirled to face Judah.

"Did you do this?" he demanded.

"What?" Judah responded. "Me? No! Why would I kill a helpless old man? What threat was he?"

"Who did it then?" Eleazar asked, as if he expected Judah to know.

"Why would I kill him?" Judah went on. "Jerusalem is ours now, except for the Romans holed up in Phasael Tower. Killing other Jews only weakens ourselves. They'll all come around to our side eventually. Even your father would have."

"Who then?" Eleazar's face was contorted with rage.

"I don't know, Eleazar. This was madness." After a moment, Judah added: "We don't run the City anymore. Menahem does. Ask him."

"It was Menahem, wasn't it?" Eleazar stared at Judah, seeking confirmation on his face. Judah raised his eyebrows before replying.

"He took over the siege of this palace," Judah said slowly. "He is responsible for your father's death."

"I will put a stop to this," Eleazar said with finality. "I will rid Jerusalem of this mad upstart."

Chapter Thirty-Six

18 Aug 66 CE / 9 Elul 3826

Drusilla looked at him anxiously, as if she could read his thoughts.

"Is something wrong, sir?" she asked.

Metilius sighed. He shook his head no. Then he debated whether to share his thoughts.

He needed to talk to someone now. It was a weakness, he knew, but better this servant girl than one of his men. A commander must always be optimistic.

Drusilla waited as if she saw he was about to speak.

Metilius sighed again.

"The march to Phasael tower did not go as well as I originally thought," he said. "We did an accounting of our losses. Almost a fifth of our forces were killed in the retreat; less than 400 men are left in the cohort."

"But we are safe here, now, aren't we? Cestius Gallus will come with his legion and rescue us, will he not?"

Metilius did not know how to answer. The march from Antonia to Herod's Palace had taken place without incurring any casualties. Drusilla had gone with them. But when they had to abandon Herod's Palace he realized that there would be fierce fighting and that Drusilla would not be safe. He found a secure place for her to hide on the grounds and provided her with food.

She had begged him to take her with them.

"I know no one here. I do not speak the language," she said. "What will I do when the food runs out? Where will I go? If I am going to die, let it be during a battle, among those I know, and not alone, with strangers surrounding me, aiming their swords and spears at only me and cheering my death."

Metilius had put her in the middle of the marchers and assigned men to protect her. Drusilla had come through safely, as had her guards. And now she was here in Phasael Tower, sharing his and what was left of his cohort's fate.

How much should he tell her?

"Yes, we are safe here," Metilius said, trying to answer Drusilla's plaintive question as hopefully as he could. "And Cestius Gallus will come with the Twelfth Legion."

"When?" Drusilla's blue eyes were large and frightened.

"I do not know. In Antonia, and Herod's Palace, word reached us of the goings-on in Jerusalem and beyond. Here we are shut away. Menahem has invested the tower. Nothing can come in, not even news from the outside. But the watchers on the towers will know when Cestius has arrived at the gates of Jerusalem. And no doubt, when that happens, the Jews will surrender."

"Do we have enough food to last a siege?" she asked.

What do I tell her? he wondered. There are fewer supplies than I thought. With almost 400 men food will run out in a few weeks. We'll be facing starvation.

Drusilla took a deep breath. She had read his face. The fear left hers. She stood straight and said:

"It is no matter. There are Roman masters and barbarian slaves. In the end we all die. May I die as bravely as you, domine."

Metilius inclined his head as in a salute.

"Do not be afraid, Drusilla, whatever the outcome. You were meant for Elysium." Then, seeing the look on her face, he added, "So you do not believe in the Fields of Elysium, or the Plain of Asphodel, or Tartarus?"

Drusilla laughed.

"Stories to frighten children," she said.

Metilius smiled, more to himself than to her.

"I must say, I agree, Drusilla."

"What do the Jews believe, sir?"

"In truth, I'm not sure. The priestly sect does not seem to believe in an afterlife. The rabbis do. But what it is or under what conditions one gets there is still not clear to me." Metilius smiled again, this time at Drusilla. "At any rate, we are both still alive. I will do what I can to make sure you come through this, Drusilla. In the meantime, stay close to these quarters. Do not go roaming around the tower. Discipline has not broken down yet, but as time goes on..." His voice trailed off. "I don't want any of the men touching you against your will," he concluded firmly.

Without waiting for a response Metilius turned away from the girl and walked out of the luxurious room that now served as his headquarters, with its large soft bed and exquisite furniture that would have stood just as proudly in any Roman nobleman's bedroom, so different than his spare headquarters in Antonia.

Metilius made his way to the top of Phasael Tower, and there, 135 feet above Jerusalem, he looked to the north, from whence he hoped help would eventually come.

"Where are you, Cestius?" he whispered under his breath, quietly so that the men watching from the rampart would not hear the fear in his voice.

Chapter Thirty-Seven

29 Aug 66 CE / 20 Elul 3826

Like a supremely confident king blissfully unaware of his subjects' murderous dissatisfaction, Menahem, clad in royal robes, entered the Temple grounds followed by fifty of his most trusted men, all with their weapons prominently displayed. As he made his way across the outer court the crowd parted like the surface of the sea before an oncoming vessel.

The Temple itself stood in the center of an inner, walled court and a larger outer court that had two main wings, one on the north and one on the south.

It was through the south wing that Menahem was moving toward the inner court. A large audience watched his progress. On top of and against the wall of the inner court stood the young priests, followers of Eleazar, with Eleazar himself at their center. In the walkway of the western colonnade and on the western ramparts were the men David ben Ephraim had organized, at the behest of Eleazar. On both levels of the Basilica at the south end of the Temple complex were the older priests, those who opposed both Eleazar and Menahem and who only wanted peace with Rome. They were joined by men from the upper classes. In the walkway of the eastern colonnade, on the eastern ramparts, and throughout the open court were the common people.

All were also armed. There were swords, lances, spears, and clubs. Many of the commoners and older priests carried stones.

Menahem, however, was not alone with his fifty-man retinue; some of his followers were scattered around the south court, others were concentrated in the north wing, while the rest of his forces were just outside the Temple complex.

Reuven stood on the west rampart. Below him were Shaul, Judah, and what remained of Judah's band.

Reuven clutched the now-useless sling in his right hand as his mind raced with questions, their speed in counterpoint to the slow procession he was watching.

What does it mean that the Temple looks like it is about to become a battlefield?

Are we fighting the Romans, or ourselves?

Are the common people rebelling against Menahem to reinstall

Eleazar as leader or in hopes of ending a war before it begins in earnest?

Reuven knew he would only be a spectator in what was about to ensue; he was still not adept enough with the sling to use it in the close quarters of the Temple grounds, and the knife he carried was purely for self-defense. Reuven put the sling into the pouch with the stones and waited.

Menahem neared the inner court. Eleazar raised his hand and shouted "Now!"

Young priests, old priests, rich men, poor men, partisans opposed to the newcomer, all fell upon the startled Menahem and his fifty men.

They formed a tight knot and fought back bravely but were no match for the furious crowd. They were about to be overwhelmed when their cries for help were answered by a stream of Menahem's supporters coming from the north court and from outside the Temple complex.

Soon they were countered by other men streaming in from the outside, these armed with clubs and stones, ordinary citizens wishing to be rid of Menahem.

The wild fray of slashing swords, thrusting lances, and swinging clubs was accompanied by a rain of stones and spears from above. Blood spurted from wounds, bones cracked from blows, injured men staggered, dying men fell, bodies jerked spasmodically on the ground. To Reuven the carnage seemed both random and purposeful. He could not tell which side was gaining advantage.

He focused on Shaul, swinging his stave with wild abandon as men collapsed to the ground around him.

One of Menahem's men, his lance held out straight before him, charged at Shaul, whose attention was elsewhere.

"Shaul! To your right!" Reuven shouted as loudly as he could, not knowing whether Shaul could hear him above the din.

Shaul did turn. He deftly sidestepped the charge, seizing the shaft of the lance with his left hand and bringing down the stave in his right on the hands of Menahem's man. Shaul was about to strike another blow when a second attacker coming from Shaul's left slashed at his arm with a knife. It must have struck its target because Shaul wavered and a third man came at Shaul with a club, striking Shaul so hard that he dropped his stave.

Without hesitation Reuven rushed down the steep internal steps that led from the rampart to the court below. Reuven dashed through clumps of combatants, managing to avoid getting struck or stabbed, until he reached Shaul, who was still struggling with the three men.

Shaul was fending off the attacker with the knife while receiving blows from the man with the club and kicks from the one with damaged hands.

Without regard to his own safety Reuven leaped on the back of the attacker with the knife, grabbing his face with his left hand and thrusting his own knife deep into neck below. The man gave a cry, stumbled backwards, and fell on top of Reuven, who kept stabbing as the man writhed above him, his blood seeping out over Reuven.

The struggle seemed to go on forever.

Suddenly the body on top of him was pulled off and flung to the side.

Shaul was grinning down at him.

"You saved my life, kid," Shaul said. "I can handle two, but three is a bit much for me."

"Are you all right Shaul?" Reuven asked anxiously, alarmed at the blood trickling down Shaul's left arm.

"It's just a surface wound," Shaul reassured him. "It'll patch up fine. At worst there will be a scar."

Reuven looked up at Shaul wide-eyed. The rush of combat was beginning to fade. He could feel and smell the dying man's blood on himself. He glanced over to where the body twitched and became still, a man who was once alive and was now dead, a man he had just killed in hand-to-hand fighting, and who just as easily could have killed him.

Reuven trembled. He started crying and could not stop. Shaking all over, he turned to the side and threw up.

"It's all right, kid. Look around you. Menahem's gone. We won."

Reuven sat up. He looked around. The battle was over, it was won, yet he still felt sick inside. He wanted to take off his wet clothes and bathe. He wanted to go back to his home, his father's house, and his mother's embrace. He didn't want to fight anymore. He just wanted peace for himself, but he knew it was too late for that. Once more he turned to the side and threw up.

Then Reuven remembered what his father had said about personal and public tragedy.

The sacred Temple grounds were covered with blood.

Chapter Thirty-Eight

31 Aug 66 CE / 22 Elul 3826

Melancholy had become a slow-cooked stew of disappointment and anger, with a bit of loss of faith thrown into the pot. It simmered inside Rabbi Aaron's soul and fed his spirit. As he sat at the table staring at the closed door to the outside world he wondered if he was beginning to enjoy what had started out as an unpalatable meal. Could there be wisdom in this, the wisdom of Kohelet?

Melancholy turned to astonishment when the door suddenly opened and there stood his renegade son Reuven and the robber Judah ben Ezra.

No, he corrected himself. The murderer Judah ben Ezra.

Judah started to enter. Reuven raised his left arm in front of Judah's chest to stop him.

"May we enter, Father?" Reuven asked gently.

"So you finally visit me," Rabbi Aaron replied, "and bring with you that murderer." He tugged at his beard until at last he said, "All right. Come in."

The two stopped at the edge of the table and looked down at him.

"Why did you bring that murderer with you?" Rabbi Aaron asked, looking up at his son.

"Rabbi Aaron, why do you keep accusing me of that?" Judah replied in a tone of exasperation. "Your own Roman-becoming-a-Jew already exonerated me."

"Perhaps Metilius was becoming a Jew," Rabbi Aaron retorted, "but you've already become a pagan! Get out of my house!"

Judah raised his hands palms forward and stepped back.

"I'm here as an emissary of Eleazar."

"Did you kill his father, too?"

Judah shook his head.

"No. I fought against the man responsible for Ananias' death. Reuven is here to talk to you about Metilius. I am here to tell you that Eleazar has given Reuven the power to negotiate with Metilius the terms of the garrison's surrender."

"Reuven? A fourteen-year-old boy?" Rabbi Aaron laughed. "Why didn't Eleazar come himself?"

"He has many things to attend to," Judah answered. "And, well, he's also…" Judah hesitated. "He's still recovering from his father's death."

Judah's expression showed his unease with the subject. "And well, well, he prefers only dealing with those he knows."

"How do I know you're not lying?"

"I wouldn't lie to you, Father," Reuven said quietly. "Eleazar told me I have the authority. All that Judah says is true."

"Get out of my house, Judah ben Ezra," Rabbi Aaron said. "I will talk to my son alone."

Judah took another step back.

"All right, Rabbi Aaron. Sooner or later you'll come around to our side. It's inevitable, once we are free of the last Roman."

He turned to go and then stopped himself. Turning back to Rabbi Aaron he said:

"I want you to know that your fourteen-year-old son is not only a brave fighter; his counsel is taken seriously by those who make decisions, including Eleazar."

When Judah left, Rabbi Aaron said:

"So, robbers and rebels take your counsel. Do you still study Torah?"

Reuven sighed.

"No, Father, there will be time for that when the war is over and we are free. I will become a scholar and make you proud of me."

"So now you are a fighter?"

Reuven looked down at the floor. He did not answer.

"Do you enjoy fighting and killing?"

"No, Father, I hate it!" Reuven trembled. He looked back up at his father. "It's horrible!" he exclaimed heatedly.

Rabbi Aaron thought he saw the beginning of tears forming in his son's eyes.

"Your mother misses you," Rabbi Aaron said.

"I miss her, too." Reuven stifled a sob. "Where is she?"

"At the market. She's worried sick about you."

"Doesn't Benjamin tell her that I'm all right?"

"It's not the same as seeing her son in front of her," Rabbi Aaron said. "You must come and visit her."

"I will. Where is Benjamin?"

"At the study hall, where you should be. Come home, Reuven, come home. Disentangle yourself from this madness."

"I can't."

"If you hate fighting so much why do you do it?" Rabbi Aaron asked.

"For our freedom." Reuven's voice was flat, the energy sucked out of it.

For several moments neither spoke. Reuven sat down opposite his father. He rested his elbows on the table and laid his head on his hands. A look of utter dejection was on his face.

"What's this about Metilius?" Rabbi Aaron asked.

Instantly Reuven's expression changed. He raised his head. His eyes came alive. Despite himself Rabbi Aaron felt a touch of pride that his son was able to put his own feelings aside and deal with the business at hand.

"I know that Metilius has been coming to you for instruction," Reuven began.

"I haven't seen him in more than forty days," Rabbi Aaron quickly interrupted. "Once they abandoned Antonia for Herod's Palace I lost all contact with him. And now they're under siege in Phasael Tower by that cutthroat Menahem."

"Menahem has been overthrown," Reuven said. "Two days ago."

Rabbi Aaron, surprised by the news, asked, "By whom? The people?"

Reuven leaned back slightly.

"By Eleazar. He's been organizing opposition to Menachem. We attacked him when he came to the Temple."

"The Temple? A battle on the Temple grounds?" Rabbi Aaron was horrified.

Reuven nodded, reluctantly.

"Blood in the sacred precincts?" Rabbi Aaron said, more a statement than a question.

Reuven sighed.

"Is that what this has come to?" Rabbi Aaron demanded. "What happened to Menahem?"

"He was found yesterday, hiding in Ophel. He was put to death, by torture, so the word has come back to us."

"Torture?" Rabbi Aaron asked in disbelief. "Is that what your side has descended to?"

"We don't know who did it," responded Reuven. "It could have been anyone. Eleazar managed to put together a large coalition to overthrow Menahem; it took him two weeks to bring everyone together. There were young and old priests, the workers who supported the rebellion, and even other partisans. And the rich, joined by many, many common people. Eleazar claims he did it because Menahem was becoming a dictator and acting like a king. However, I think it was also because Eleazar didn't like being under someone like Menahem's thumb and also because he holds Menahem responsible for his father's murder."

Rabbi Aaron barely listened to all of Reuven's recitation; he seized on one part of it.

"All the priests, the rich, and the common people?" he asked, feeling hope for the first time. "Does that mean the siege of Phasael Tower will be lifted?"

Reuven smiled grimly.

"Eleazar has taken over the siege," he said. "That is why I am here. Eleazar wants the siege to end without bloodshed, but he wants the Romans out of Jerusalem. He is offering terms."

"What terms?"

"The garrison has safe conduct to leave Jerusalem. They surrender their arms before they leave. Metilius remains as a hostage."

"A hostage?" Rabbi Aaron asked sharply.

"That's what we'll call it, for Metilius' sake," Reuven explained. "In fact, we'll treat him like a guest. You will have complete access to him, perhaps be in charge of him. We need Metilius, Father, we need his knowledge of Roman tactics and strategy. We need his knowledge of the political situation in Rome. I know we have our own contacts there but he can give us an insider's view that they can't."

Rabbi Aaron placed his elbows on the table, interlaced the fingers of his hands, and laid his head on them. He thought for a few moments.

"Very wise. That makes sense." Then he added, "If he agrees to help you."

"Keeping Metilius was my idea," Reuven said, smiling.

Rabbi Aaron smiled also.

"Why would he help you?" he asked.

"Us, Father," Reuven corrected. "Why would he help us? Perhaps because he has developed some sympathy for the Jews thanks to you."

"It's possible. I don't know. Tell me, why do you think he would agree to surrender?"

"How long can he hold out? If he is counting on Cestius and the Twelfth Legion to rescue him it's a false hope. They have made no moves yet and once they do it will take time for them to organize an expedition. If they come, taking Jerusalem will be no easy matter, and there is no guarantee of success. By that time, Metilius' garrison will have starved to death. We have been informed by those who were in Phasael Tower before the Roman takeover that the supplies there were low."

"And what have I to do with all this?"

"I want you to convince him, or at least, convince him to talk to me," Reuven answered.

"Why should I?" Rabbi Aaron asked, leaning forward and glaring at his son.

"Because it will avoid the death by starvation of the Roman garrison. Or their slaughter in battle," Reuven replied calmly.

Rabbi Aaron did not respond for many moments as he considered his son's request.

"All right," he said at last. "I'll take you to Metilius and ask him to listen to you and your offer. Whether he will or not is another matter. But I will only do my part on one condition."

"What is that, Father?" Reuven asked meekly.

In a firm voice Rabbi Aaron replied:

"That you promise to do everything you can to find your uncle's murderer."

Chapter Thirty-Nine

2 Sep 66 CE / 24 Elul 3826

The lions, trapped in their den, were no doubt hungry for the blood of a defenseless lamb. Waiting to step into that den, it occurred to Reuven for the first time that he should be afraid.

He was not.

I've killed Jews and soldiers of that so-called Jewish king Agrippa, he thought, but no Romans. No, no Romans. Reuven realized, though, that the men with Metilius did not know this. Still, he was confident that his father's status with the Roman commander would keep them safe. What really worried him was not living up to his mission.

Reuven stood next to his father in front of the forbidding tower of Phasael that Herod had built. As Reuven let his gaze move along its solid surface from bottom to top, the men investing the tower, now under Eleazar's command, made a big show of withdrawing some distance away. Then he and his father stepped forward, closer to the door on the southern face of Phasael.

His father lifted his head, cupped his hands and shouted:

"I am Rabbi Aaron ben Avraham. I request safe conduct to speak to Commander Metilius."

There was no immediate response.

Rabbi Aaron repeated his cry.

Father and son waited.

"Are you afraid, Father?" Reuven asked, taking his father's hand.

"No."

"Once more, Father," Reuven said. "Perhaps they have not heard."

Rabbi Aaron took a deep breath and raised his voice even louder.

"I am Rabbi Aaron ben Avraham. I request permission to speak to Commander Metilius."

His voice echoed back from the tower.

Again they waited.

The door to the tower opened and a phalanx of armed soldiers emerged. Their forward officer held his shield out and looked around suspiciously.

"You may enter," he said in Greek.

Reuven and Rabbi Aaron walked toward the door as the officer moved to the side and the troops parted. Once they stepped inside the narrow, arched entrance chamber the soldiers followed. The door to the outside slammed shut.

A cold gust of air struck Reuven. He shivered. It seemed as if he was now entombed in a solid block of stone. For a moment he felt trapped.

A corridor that led to a stairway lay before him. Metilius stood halfway down the corridor. He walked slowly toward them. He stopped several paces away and regarded the two of them with curiosity.

"It's been a long time, Rabbi," Metilius said.

"Too long," Rabbi Aaron responded.

"Yes," Metilius agreed, and came closer.

The two men briefly embraced.

Metilius looked quizzically at Reuven.

"What's this?" the Roman asked.

"*Salve, domine!*" Reuven said, raising his right hand, trying to imitate the Roman salute.

Metilius smiled.

"This must be more than a social visit," he said.

"Yes. My son has a message from Eleazar ben Ananias, captain of the Temple ministers, who is now in charge of the City," Rabbi Aaron responded.

"Your son?" Metilius laughed. "Why didn't Eleazar come himself if he has a message for me? Why did he send a boy instead? And your Eleazar is not in charge of Jerusalem; Gessius Florus is, acting in the name of Emperor Nero."

Reuven lowered his hand and took a step backward.

"Gessius Florus fled Jerusalem because his crimes were so great he feared a popular uprising," Reuven countered. "He acted in no one's name but his own, certainly not in the name of the emperor of Rome."

Metilius raised his eyebrows. He looked at Rabbi Aaron. Then he laughed.

"You have a bold boy here," he said. "Come to my headquarters. Both of you. It's good to see you, Rabbi Aaron. I'll listen to what your son has to say."

They followed the Roman commander as he led them down the corridor and up the stairway. It was a long climb. Reuven guessed it would have been like going up a building with six or seven floors.

They emerged into the first level of the second tower. Everything changed. They walked down a broad hallway. Father and son gasped as they passed luxurious bedrooms and bathrooms and even a banquet hall. It was their first time in Phasael.

Metilius entered one of the bedrooms. Reuven had fallen a few steps behind his father. Reuven suddenly stopped just outside the small room adjacent to Metilius' headquarters.

He could not move. He stood there, transfixed. A shaft of light fell on a sight he had never seen before.

His mind immediately leapt to the tales he had heard about the false gods of the Greeks and Romans.

This must be what their goddesses looked like, Reuven thought.

She had golden hair and fair skin. Her eyes were as blue as the sky. She was taller than him, and a few years older.

Reuven had never seen such a beautiful woman.

His head swam.

The girl saw the expression on his face and laughed gaily.

Reuven felt faint.

A strong hand grasped his arm and shook him roughly.

"Metilius is waiting! You have business to attend to!"

Reuven saw his father glare angrily at the girl. She laughed again, mockingly, at the both of them, shrugged, and returned to her work. Rabbi Aaron dragged Reuven to the next room.

The young man seemingly recovered his composure and as he looked around he said:

"What magnificent headquarters you have, *domine*. It must be good to be a Roman commander." There was sarcasm in his voice.

"Commander Metilius' headquarters in Antonia was much more austere," Rabbi Aaron said. "It was you crazy revolutionaries who caused him to leave." He shook his son angrily. "Is this any way to behave? You have business to attend to!"

Reuven blushed with shame.

"My apologies, *domine*. I did not mean to be rude."

"That's all right, boy. I'm guessing my pretty servant girl in the next room threw you off and disoriented you." He laughed and Reuven blushed even deeper. "Let me tell you something, Reuven. I'd rather be home with my wife and children on my simple farm in Italy than here in your accursed country!"

"Then why are you here, commander?" Reuven asked earnestly. "Why are you Romans in another peoples' country?"

"We spread civilization," Metilius answered gravely. "And we keep the peace throughout the world. Pax Romana. Here we keep the peace between the Jews and their neighbors, and between the Jews themselves."

"Pax Romana?" retorted Reuven. "You fight wars for conquest. What peace is there in that? And do you keep peace among the Jews? Well, that is certainly not your fault, but the strife between the Jews and the gentiles in the Land of Israel is only exacerbated by your presence."

Metilius nodded.

"It's true," he said, "that Florus has sided with the Gentiles and has instigated problems between them and your people to cover his own crimes. But Florus is not Rome."

Reuven held Metilius' steady gaze and said:

"He is to us."

"What is your message from Eleazar?"

"Eleazar wants every Roman out of Jerusalem. He also wishes to avoid any more bloodshed with your men. He is offering you safe passage out of Jerusalem."

Metilius nodded.

"Your men will leave the tower and march through Bezetha. When they get to the gate in the north wall, just before they leave the City, they are to abandon their weapons."

"Abandon our weapons? Never!"

"Commander, you cannot expect us to let an armed cohort of Roman soldiers march through our towns at a time like this."

"And you cannot expect us to put ourselves at the mercy of a hostile population without arms to defend ourselves!" Metilius turned to Rabbi Aaron. "Is this some kind of joke? Why did they send a pipsqueak to negotiate with me? Why didn't Eleazar come himself? Is he a coward that he sends a young boy and a peaceful rabbi in his stead?"

"Commander, I requested this mission."

"Why would he give it to you?"

"Because of your connection to my father. And my status as an advisor."

Metilius laughed merrily.

"So now the Jewish revolutionaries take advice from a pipsqueak?"

"Make fun of me if you like, but I've tasted battle. I've killed Jews and soldiers from Agrippa's army. And Eleazar and other leaders have already accepted counsel I have given."

Reuven's reply took Metilius by surprise. It took a moment for him to respond.

"That still doesn't explain why Eleazar himself is not here to give the guarantees."

Reuven sighed.

"This is kind of difficult, and perhaps I should not say this; since his father's murder Eleazar has not quite been himself."

"Then how can I trust him?"

"I will have Eleazar give them a safe passage letter in Greek and Hebrew," Reuven said.

In the center of the room was a large table with elegant chairs around it. Metilius walked over to the table, sat in a chair, and beckoned the two to follow suit.

Metilius breathed deeply, leaned across the table, and said:

"Tell me, Reuven, why should I surrender? Why shouldn't I hold out until Cestius Gallus comes and puts down your rebellion?"

He leaned back and looked at son and father in turn.

"Commander," Reuven began, "are you sure Cestius is coming, and if he does will he get here in time? Today we just got news that only now is he starting to gather his forces. How long will that take? And how long will it take before he gets here and subdues the City, if he is able to put down the rebellion at all? Weeks? No. More likely a month or even two.

"We know how much food was here when you arrived. You've already been here for nineteen days. With the number of men you have you'll run out of food in a few weeks."

Metilius looked at Rabbi Aaron.

"If Cestius arrives at the gates of Jerusalem with the Twelfth Legion do you think the rebellion will continue?"

"I wish I could say no," Rabbi Aaron said with resignation. "The majority of the people want peace. They don't want war with Rome. But Jerusalem is in the grip of violent revolutionaries who have imposed their will on the rest of us. They will not allow us to open the gates to Cestius and restore the rule of Rome."

Metilius turned back to Reuven.

"Why do you think that you and your fellow revolutionaries have the right to impose your will on the rest of the people? Why does your desire for independence take precedence over the desire of the common people to live their lives undisturbed? Why do you think you are wiser than learned men like your father who only want peace?"

"Sometimes," replied Reuven, "it is necessary for a dedicated and enlightened minority, seeing what the masses and elites do not, to take action on its own."

"Dedicated and enlightened?" countered Metilius. "Or ruthless?"

"I hope not," said Reuven softly.

"When does Eleazar want an answer?" asked Metilius.

"Immediately," responded Reuven. "However, I am willing to give you three days."

"You have the authority to do that?"

"Yes."

Metilius glanced over at Rabbi Aaron.

"Does he really?"

"I can't say for sure," Rabbi Aaron answered. "I think he does." He looked at Reuven. "I'm pretty sure he does."

"There's one more condition," Reuven said.

"What's that?" asked Metilius.

"You remain behind as a hostage."

"A hostage?"

"That's what we're calling it, for your men and superiors in Rome. In truth you'll be our guest and not a prisoner," Reuven explained. "Keeping you behind was my idea," he added.

"I don't understand why you'd want to keep me here."

Reuven brought his hands together and looked at the Roman intently.

"We need you, Commander Metilius. We need your knowledge of Rome and Roman ways. We need your knowledge of military tactics and strategy, so we can put up a successful defense with a minimum loss of life, Jewish and Roman. We need your knowledge of the political situation in Rome, so we know how to get the best possible agreement with Rome."

"An agreement with Rome? I thought the revolutionaries wanted total independence."

"They do. But the people will settle for peace with fair terms, and a way to remedy the grievances against a corrupt procurator. If that is a possibility, the revolutionaries will not be able to press for further war. The people helped Eleazar overthrow Menahem and regain power. He will not be able to ignore them if a fair peace is offered by Rome."

"Why should I help you with this?" Metilius asked.

"I saw you at our Sabbath table," Reuven replied. "I remember what you told me outside my father's house. I do not believe that you prefer the false gods of Rome over the true God of the Jews. I also think you have some sympathy for us because you know how evil Florus was. And your help might forestall a terrible war that will do no good for the Jews or Rome."

Metilius drummed the table with his fingers for a long time. Rabbi Aaron began to stir uncomfortably. Reuven remained calm.

I did what I came to do, he thought. The rest is up to Metilius.

At last Metilius spoke.

"I will consider Eleazar's offer. And think about what you said you need from me."

"Thank you, *domine*."

The three rose. Metilius led the way, followed by Rabbi Aaron, with Reuven at the rear.

I will not look into that room, Reuven thought as he stepped into the hallway, I will not look into that room.

But he did.

The girl was not there.

Chapter Forty

6 Sep 66 CE / 28 Elul 3826

Alexander, Metilius' first officer, led his troops in tight formation through Bezetha. The road was lined on either side with what must have been thousands of armed Jews with murder in their eyes.

The day after that rabbi and his son had come to Phasael, Metilius agreed to the Jews' terms. Alexander and the men begged Metilius not to remain behind.

"Who knows what those Jews will do to you once you are alone," Alexander said.

Metilius assured them that he would be fine.

The next day the rabbi's son brought the safe passage document, in Hebrew and Greek, signed by Eleazar, the captain of the Temple ministers. It was this that Alexander clutched in his right hand as he marched. In his left was his shield.

Would the Jews keep their end of the bargain?

Alexander had expressed his concern to Metilius.

"That's why I picked a Sabbath day for you to leave," Metilius said. "It is forbidden for Jews to break an oath and it is especially forbidden to violate the law on a Sabbath."

If the Jews watching them decided to attack his men would be slaughtered, but they would go down fighting, taking many of the enemy with them.

Alexander shivered.

He felt safer in Phasael Tower and wished they could have stayed until Cestius arrived, but as Metilius explained by that time food would run out and they would die of starvation, a death worse than falling in combat. As for Cestius and the Twelfth Legion, Metilius said:

"They would have been here already if Cestius were planning on coming soon to rescue us. Antonia was abandoned and Jerusalem taken over by the rebels more than forty days ago; without doubt word reached the legate of Syria not long after it happened."

Now Metilius was staying behind facing who-knows-what and he, Alexander, and the men were leaving. How he wished Metilius, a brave and wise soldier, was with them.

That servant girl, Drusilla, was also staying behind.

Alexander licked his lips.

Ah, what a comely wench! he thought.

He had asked Metilius about her once, to find out if he was enjoying her charms and therefore off-limits to everyone else.

"You are not to touch her!" Metilius warned sternly. "No one is, including me." Then, in a softer tone, "I have a wife. The Gods hate immorality."

Had Metilius said "The Gods" or "God"?

Alexander was not sure.

He had teased Metilius about turning Jew after learning of his visits to that rabbi. Had Metilius done so?

Ah, if Drusilla had come with us. Without Metilius' protection…

Thoughts of the young, desirable girl were a welcome relief to Alexander from the reality that confronted him on both sides and what lay ahead on the road from Jerusalem to Antioch.

The men carried food rations on their backs but Alexander was not sure if they would last the journey. If the supplies did not last, they would have to live off the land and raid for food. How could they raid without weapons? Ah, there were friendly Greek villages along the way that would no doubt give them provisions.

Alexander and his men were almost at the north gate. He noticed a tall young man with a stave in his hand and an older man standing next him. The older man smiled, a smile full of bile and hate, revealing a gap in his teeth. Alexander shuddered. The man shouted something, a curse no doubt.

The gate was closed. A large group of armed men were guarding it. At their head stood Eleazar, captain of the Temple ministers, whom Alexander recognized from his time in Antonia.

The moment had arrived for his men to begin laying down their weapons, as had been agreed upon.

When all his men had been disarmed Eleazar spoke in a loud, clear voice in the native language, which Alexander did not understand.

Suddenly a strange thing happened. The tall man and the one with the gap in his teeth started shouting angrily. A group of Eleazar's men grabbed them and started pulling them away. The tall one broke free and ran toward Alexander. There was no bad intent in the man's face or eyes. When he reached Alexander the young man grabbed the arm holding the safe passage document and yanked it high in the air, waving it around and shouting something as loud as he could. Another group of men seized that young man and dragged him away, still shouting.

The Jews on both sides of the road and in front of the gate advanced with their weapons drawn toward Alexander's cohort.

Alexander finally understood what was happening.

"We have an agreement!" he cried, waving the document in the air.

Eleazar answered, in perfect Greek:

"Cestius has gathered his forces and is on the march. He has been burning and looting Jewish villages, killing the inhabitants. You will pay for their crimes."

"We are the one cohort that did you no harm!" Alexander protested. "That is why we were allowed to stay."

Eleazar gave no reply.

"The agreement, the agreement! It is the Sabbath!" Alexander cried, to no avail.

The Jews closed in on his men. Swords, spears, and lances did their deadly work against the helpless soldiers who served Rome.

Alexander was the last to fall.

The lance that went through his throat stopped him from bringing down a curse upon his enemies.

Part Two: Victory and Suicide

October – November 66 CE

Chapter Forty-One

6 Sep 66 CE / 28 Elul 3826

Was he an important, high-ranking guest escorted by a military procession or a prisoner marching with armed guards to a luxurious jail cell? Had he cravenly given up freedom and honor in return for his life and the life of his men or had he made the best decision given the circumstances, thus ensuring the optimum outcome for himself, his men, Jerusalem, and Rome?

Metilius did not know.

There were stories of men who wrestled powerful opponents. Rabbi Aaron told one of a man who wrestled an angel. A Greek writer told another of the leader of a Jewish sect who wrestled a demon. Metilius was sure he had grappled with a tougher and wilier opponent than either man had: he had struggled with his own mind. And he had faced this opponent more than once because he was forced to make a host of decisions without the information needed to be sure he was deciding rightly. Now, as he made his way from Phasael Tower to a new place in the Upper City, Metilius questioned each of those decisions, starting with the one to leave Antonia for Herod's Palace.

Several paces ahead of Metilius marched four men; two carried swords, two carried lances. Slightly ahead and to his left walked Reuven;

slightly behind and to his right was Drusilla. Taking up the rear several paces back were another four armed men.

They are not marching in disciplined order, Metilius thought. They are strolling, like civilians. Reuven says they're from Judah ben Ezra's group. No matter which revolutionaries they are, none of these Jews have military training. They will be no match for Cestius Gallus and the Twelfth Legion.

Metilius did march, with measured step. He wore his helmet and breastplate and carried his shield in his left hand. On one hip was his sword, on the other his long knife. Reuven had looked at him in surprise when he saw him thus arrayed, but said nothing. On Metilius' back was his pack with his soldier's equipment and personal belongings, and the few things that Drusilla owned.

I had no good options, he thought. Cestius would never have gotten to Jerusalem in time. I had no choice except to withdraw our forces from the City. But I could have insisted on leaving with my men who are probably by now departing through the north gate. Why didn't I? Was it sympathy for the Jews? Was it hope that I could one day serve as an intermediary between the Jews and Rome?

Why didn't I leave? If I had insisted Eleazar would have acceded, if he really wanted to get the Roman presence out of Jerusalem without a fight. Reuven can't have enough influence to force the issue.

Metilius looked at Reuven. He noticed a curious interplay between Reuven and Drusilla. Her eyes often went to Reuven. He occasionally, and surreptitiously, turned to glance at her; every time he did so she quickly turned away from him.

Drusilla had asked about Reuven after the first visit of father and son to Phasael Tower; she had masked her real interest by first asking about the father.

Metilius smiled at the thought of the two of them; it was his first worry-free smile in a long time. He liked Rabbi Aaron, and was growing to respect and like the son, despite his present circumstances of being under an armed guard. As for Drusilla, once he knew he would not make demands on her he began to feel paternal towards the young woman.

They were walking south on a broad avenue in the Upper City. They passed the Upper Market on the right and large two-story homes on the left. Not many people were on the avenue to view the procession but anxious residents could be seen peering from windows and half-open doors as Metilius and his entourage went by. At the fourth cross-street they turned right. Another block to the west and Reuven called a halt in front of one of the houses.

"This used to belong to a rich Jew who supported Rome," Reuven explained. "When Antonia was taken over he fled to a second home he owned in Caesarea. The revolution confiscated his property in Jerusalem. I'm sure you'll find the accommodations here comfortable."

"The guards?" Metilius asked.

"They will remain," Reuven said. "Both to protect you and to keep up the appearance that you really are a hostage so you won't have any problems when you return to Rome. You are not a prisoner, Commander Metilius, you are free to come and go as you please, however, guards will accompany you wherever you go."

The one-story house was surrounded by a stone fence. Reuven led Metilius and Drusilla through the gate. The eight guards remained outside.

A central courtyard had a pool, rows of fruit trees, and flower beds. Despite having been taken over by the rebels, Metilius thought that the courtyard had been well maintained.

Metilius and Drusilla followed Reuven inside. The ground floor enclosed living quarters and reception rooms. The basement held ritual baths, bathrooms, cisterns, and store rooms.

"The whole house is yours," Reuven said, moving his arm in a sweeping motion after giving them a tour of the premises. "The guards will not come into the house or the courtyard."

"This place makes my home in Italy look like a hut," Metilius said drily.

"It's a palace compared to mine," Reuven replied.

"It could belong to a well-to-do Roman," Metilius added. "Except for the absence of statues."

Metilius chose a bedroom next to a living room; beyond that was a kitchen. The bedroom and living room walls had colorful frescoes of geometrical shapes and stylized flowers and plants. The living room floor had a mosaic tile of red, blue, and yellow, intricate shapes of lines and angles and curves. A large stone table with carved wooden legs stood at one end of the room. Both the living room and the kitchen had stands on which were placed jars, bowls, plates, and cups.

Metilius turned to Drusilla.

"Well," he said, "here is your chance to live like a patrician for a while. Pick any other bedroom for yourself."

Metilius noticed a change in Reuven's expression, as if a look of relief flitted across his features.

"Don't worry, Reuven," he said. "She's not my mistress. I'm not sleeping with her." Then he laughed as both of them turned red.

Reuven recovered quickly.

"Eleazar has chosen five men, along with himself, to learn about Roman tactics and strategy from you," he said.

Metilius laid down his pack. He stared at it for a moment and then looked straight at Reuven.

"I won't speak to anyone except you and your father," he said firmly.

"Eleazar said—"

"I don't care what Eleazar says," Metilius interrupted. "They'll get what they need to know through you. I will not deal with them and there is no way to force me to," he concluded, glaring at Reuven.

Reuven swallowed hard and nodded.

"I will tell Eleazar," he said.

Metilius sighed and shook his head in disgust.

"I should have been with my men on the road to Antioch."

Then he sat down on the bed and buried his face in his hands.

Chapter Forty-Two

6 Sep 66 CE / 29 Elul 3826

The dying light of the setting sun behind the Temple, the flames of the torches, the glow of the lamps; all combined to throw grotesque shadows against the walls and floor of the court in front of the Bronze Gate, shadows of the mass of men gathered there. Darkness and shadow never frightened Judah ben Ezra, but a cold chill enveloped him now.

At the top of the stairs to the gate a man was about to speak. He was bent and thin and he trembled. Next to him a larger man stood.

"My name is Amos ben Yoseph. I come from Caesarea."

The bent man spoke in a voice that shook, so weak it could hardly be heard. The large man beside him repeated what he said in a stentorian voice, so all could hear.

"There were 20,000 of us Jews in Caesarea. They killed us all." Amos ben Yoseph gave an anguished shriek.

Without thinking about it, Judah reached out and clutched Shaul's arm for support.

The man next to the bent man dutifully repeated his words, though everyone had heard.

"The troubles started when news reached the rest of the country that Antonia had been taken over by the Jews," Amos ben Yoseph went on. "Syrian villages started attacking Jewish ones, and they retaliated by attacking Syrian villages. Cestius Gallus, when he heard about Antonia, and the fighting between the Jews and Syrians, gathered his forces, and blaming the Jews for the troubles, started sacking Jewish villages."

Amos ben Yoseph began to tremble violently and would have collapsed if the man beside him had not grabbed him and held him up.

"Two nights ago they came for the Jews in Caesarea," Amos ben Yoseph said. "Bands of local Syrians with swords and knives and spears and clubs. Many of them were our friends and neighbors. We had no warning. We were unable to prepare so we could defend ourselves."

There was absolute silence among the crowd. No one stirred.

"We awoke in the middle of the night to the sounds of screaming; the roars of the Syrians and the cries of the Jews. They entered my home shortly after the screaming started," Amos ben Yoseph went on. "They grabbed my wife. She fought back. I went to her rescue but someone hit me with a club and I fell. I heard screams, hers and our children. I blacked out. When I woke all was quiet. The dead body of my wife was on top of me. I was covered with her blood. My children, too, were dead, run through with swords. One had his head chopped off…"

A shudder ran through the crowd. Amos ben Yoseph fainted. Shouts of revenge filled the court of the Bronze Gate. The large man then added:

"Amos ben Yoseph snuck out of Caesarea. He said all the Jews in Caesarea were killed. It took him two days to walk here. He arrived this morning."

The shouts of revenge grew louder. Eleazar stepped up to the top of the stairs. He raised his right hand. It took several moments for the crowd to quiet, and then he cried:

"It is war! War between us and the Romans! War between us and the Syrians!"

A giant shout issued from the crowd.

Shaul tugged at Judah's arm.

"Let's go," he said, a troubled look on his face. Judah allowed himself to be pulled away. They pushed through the buzzing crowd and left the Temple complex, Judah vaguely aware that something major was bothering Shaul and that he wanted to speak about it.

He'll tell me when he's ready, Judah thought.

They walked through the darkened streets of Jerusalem.

Suddenly Shaul said:

"Judah, I'm confused. I'm still troubled by what Eleazar did today. Does what I heard from Amos ben Yoseph justify massacring the Roman garrison after they surrendered and gave up their weapons?"

"No!" Judah replied sharply. He stopped walking and turned to Shaul. "Look, I want to kill Romans and Syrians as much as anyone, but there are some things you don't do. That's why you and I tried to stop Eleazar today. Even in war there have to be rules. If a man surrenders on terms and drops his weapons, you do not kill him. If Eleazar wanted to wipe out the Roman garrison he could have let them starve to death or he could have killed them one by one if they tried to flee the tower. But he should not have offered terms and then massacred them after they gave up and disarmed. There are some rules you just don't break, even in war."

"What do we do now, Judah?"

Judah snorted with disgust.

"What can we do, Shaul? Join the Peace Party? There's a war now.

We have no choice. We must fight and put what happened today behind us."

"Judah, I'm worried about how Reuven will react when he learns about the killing of Metilius' men. He gave Metilius his word that his men would be safe."

"We all gave our word," Judah replied hotly. "How were we to know what Eleazar had planned, if it was planned and not done on the spur-of-the-moment. Are you afraid he'll tell Metilius?"

Shaul did not answer directly. "We'll have to prepare Reuven," he said. "We must tell him ourselves so he doesn't hear it from anyone else. You'll have to explain to him why we have to go on fighting, the way you just explained to me."

Judah reached up and grabbed Shaul's shoulder as he tried to peer into his eyes through the darkness.

"I was with Eleazar late this afternoon. Neither he nor the men around him spoke of the massacre. Reuven came and informed him that Metilius would not speak to him or anyone else, only to Reuven himself," Judah said. "Eleazar did not take it well. Said he'd have to think about it. Listen, Shaul, do you think you could convince Reuven to remain with Metilius? There's enough room in that house. It will serve two purposes. First, it will speed up Reuven's getting information from the Roman. That will convince Eleazar there's no problem with Reuven being the go-between. Second, it postpones Reuven finding out what happened today at the north gate. He'll be more isolated from the rest of the City and it will take longer for the news to reach him. Yes, we'll have to tell him, and soon, but I want a little time, no telling how he'll react. I think the deeper he gets into gaining and transmitting Metilius' knowledge the more likely he'll continue, no matter how he feels about the massacre of Metilius' men."

"Sure," Shaul responded. "I think I can do that. What about Rabbi Aaron?"

"Yes, what about Rabbi Aaron. He will be a problem," said Judah. "As soon as he hears about the massacre of the garrison he'll go running to Metilius. We must keep him away from that Roman. Inform the guards at the house that under no circumstances is Rabbi Aaron to enter or to approach Metilius." Judah sighed. "We can't very well kill the rabbi, can we?"

Chapter Forty-Three

Sun 7 Sep 66 CE / 29 Elul 3826

"What are you staring at little boy?" the young woman asked peremptorily, shaking her head and sending the waves of her golden hair undulating.

The most beautiful being I've ever seen, Reuven wanted to say, but the words stuck in his throat.

"Well?" she demanded.

"I-I was looking for Metilius," he stammered.

Reuven stood at the entrance to the living room next to Metilius' bedroom. The night before Shaul had convinced him to stay permanently in the house where Metilius resided. Reuven came in the morning with his personal possessions and chose a room at the far end of the house.

"He's in the bath," the young woman replied. "Would you like to join him?" Her voice was mocking.

Reuven breathed heavily. He did not reply to her mockery. He kept staring; he could not look away.

"Why are you staring at me?"

"You're beautiful," he finally managed to say.

She laughed, at him, no doubt. He did not care.

"How old are you, little boy?"

"Fourteen. I'll be fifteen soon."

Once again she laughed.

"Well, I'm nineteen. So stop looking at me and go away."

Reuven did not move. All he could do was keep gazing on this magical creature.

"Well, don't just stand there like a fool. Do something useful!"

Reuven noticed she was holding a brush in her hand. On the stone table near where she stood was a pan filled with water.

She held out the brush.

"Take it," she said.

He stepped into the room and came close to her. He was shaking. He could see the amusement in her eyes. They were startlingly blue, like the color of the sky, or what he had heard the Middle Sea looked like. He took the brush from her with trembling hands.

"You put the brush in the water and you scrub the table," the young woman said, as if she were talking to a little child.

Confused, he did what she said. He began scrubbing the table, all the while giving her sidelong glances. He saw the look of amazement on her face, knew he shouldn't be doing this; he could not help himself.

Reuven felt a tightening in his midsection, followed by a hint of dampness.

No, he thought, not the emission that comes at night! Not now!

The thought that were he on the Temple grounds he would have to leave, and would be impure until he bathed in the evening and the sun went down, entered his mind.

And this evening is the first day of Tishrei, Yom Teruah, the first of the ten Days of Awe.

Reuven stopped scrubbing for a moment as he pondered this. The young woman cluck-clucked her annoyance and he resumed his cleaning.

She patted him on the head.

"Good boy," she said.

Overwhelmed, he dropped the brush and it fell off the table. As he bent down to pick it up, his knife clattered to the floor.

Quick as a flash of lightning she jumped and snatched the knife, dancing away from him, a triumphant smile on her face.

"What are you doing with a knife, little boy? Aren't you afraid you'll hurt yourself?"

"Give it back to me," Reuven said in a weak voice.

"No!"

She waved it around in the air.

"Give it back to me!"

"Take from me!" she challenged.

He shook his head no.

"Take it from me!" she repeated.

"I can't."

"You're afraid, you're afraid of me, aren't you, Reuven?"

She knows my name, he thought.

"What's your name?" he asked.

"None of your business."

Reuven was at a loss. He did not want to wrestle the knife away from her for that would mean touching her. That was forbidden. What if it was the time of her impurity?

He made no move to approach her.

"You are afraid of me, Reuven!"

Though he was its object, her laughter was beautiful music.

King David's *kinor* was not sweeter, he thought.

"Metilius says you're a soldier, that you've killed. He says elders heed your counsel. He says if you were Roman you would grow up to be a great general and senator. I think he was teasing me. I think he was joking. You're just a scared little boy." She held up the knife. "Tell me little boy, did you ever kill anyone with this knife?"

His mood of euphoria vanished.

"Yes," he said. "I have. And probably will again. It is not pleasant."

He looked down at the floor.

When he looked up again he saw that her face had grown serious. As soon as she saw him looking at her, it took on a mask of gaiety.

"Come here," she said.

Reuven moved closer and the awe her presence produced returned. She put both hands behind her and said:

"Come here and kiss me. Then I'll give you back your knife."

Reuven's eyes grew wide.

He couldn't possibly do that!

She crooked her finger at him.

"Come," she said.

His heart pounding wildly, wondering if he should run away, the knife forgotten, he came to her. She lowered her head next to his and pressed her lips against his lips.

His head swam, his consciousness floated in rapture; a physical release forced itself upon him and he quivered.

She seemed to hold him in the kiss forever, and yet when it ended, it seemed to have lasted only for the blink of an eye.

She leaned back. Her breath bathed his face. She said gently, "My name is Drusilla." She looked into his eyes. "Drusilla," she repeated.

"Drusilla," he said.

He murmured it to himself, over and over, a whisper and a shout in his own ears.

She put her hands on his shoulders.

Her voice not mocking now, she asked:

"Reuven, am I going to die?"

Reuven shuddered.

"We're all going to die one day, Drusilla," he said. "No one lives forever."

"I mean now," she responded. "In the war between the Jews and the Romans. I don't want to die young, Reuven. I want to die when I'm old. I want to live until then. I want to marry, have children, and die surrounded by my grandchildren."

Reuven had to look away. What could he possibly tell her?

He looked at her again and took her hands in his own and squeezed them.

"We will win our freedom," he said with a certainty he did not feel. "And then there will be peace with Rome and you will be able to return home."

"I have no home," Drusilla said softly.

As Reuven looked at her, to everything else he was feeling, a profound sadness was added.

Poor girl, he thought. And then: Mine may be destroyed with the coming of Cestius. No sense frightening her, though.

"Drusilla," he said in a firm voice, "Commander Metilius will protect you. I will protect you. And I have enough influence to make certain that none of my people will harm you."

She smiled, leaned up toward him, and kissed him again.

He melted into her lips as the world melted away. He could have stayed in this state forever.

The world did not let him. It intruded in the form of hearty laughter. To Reuven's dismay Metilius stood in the doorway.

"You work fast, Reuven!"

Reuven's cheeks flushed with embarrassment.

"Don't worry, I won't tell your father!"

Again, the hearty laughter.

Reuven saw Drusilla's cheeks now red, and could feel rising anger that Metilius was making her uncomfortable, too, when the Roman said:

"Don't worry, Drusilla. It's all right. Terrible situation we're all in. Might as well find happiness where we can. Come, young fellow, don't we have work to do?"

Drusilla handed Reuven the knife. The blush had faded. He looked into her eyes. He wanted to say something, but could not find the words. He turned from her and walked stiffly towards Metilius.

The Roman commander watched him with curiosity.

"Something happen, boy?"

Does he know? Reuven wondered, and turned red again.

Metilius leaned his head back and roared with laughter.

Reuven followed Metilius into his bedroom, where Metilius took a seat behind a smooth wooden table. He motioned Reuven to join him.

Reuven approached with the same stiff walk. He did not sit down. Metilius smiled knowingly.

"Have you ever been with a woman, Reuven?"

Reuven shook his head.

"So your father never took you to a prostitute?"

"Oh no!" Reuven responded with horror.

"Of course not! I should have realized that. Well, there are baths in the basement. I guess you want to clean yourself up and change clothes. Then we can get started."

Reuven nodded. He turned to leave.

"Wait!" called Metilius.

Reuven turned back to face Metilius.

"She's a good girl, Drusilla," Metilius said. "And a clever one. She not only speaks her native barbarian language; she's fluent in Latin and Greek. She reads Greek, too. I've seen her reading some of the books I had in Antonia. You could do a lot worse than Drusilla. But you took a chance. You do not know her, and when she kissed you she still had your knife in her hands. She could have easily plunged it into your back."

Reuven looked surprised. He never considered that.

"Remember, Reuven, a woman can easily unman you; she can be more dangerous than a battlefield opponent. Drusilla could have killed you."

Reuven nodded.

"You are right, Commander Metilius. She could have killed me. It would have been better if she had. Dying in her kiss would be preferable to what awaits me: violent death at the hands of a Roman or a hated Syrian auxiliary." He paused, before adding, "Or a fellow Jew."

Reuven turned and left the room, his own last words ringing in his ears, haunting him as he crossed the threshold.

Chapter Forty-Four

11 Sep 66 CE / 4 Tishrei 3827

Now I'm a prisoner, too, Reuven thought. And I can't tell Metilius. Besides, I don't even know why I'm a prisoner.

Reuven shifted uncomfortably in his seat. Metilius was speaking, droning on, but Reuven was not paying attention.

Why is Eleazar keeping me confined to this house and its grounds? Where are Shaul and Judah? Do they know about this?

And Metilius, can I believe him or has he just been trying to scare me with the invincibility of the Roman legions?

Can I trust anyone?

Besides my father?

This morning, when he went out to greet the guards outside the walls of the grounds, as he had done since he moved in, Reuven did not recognize any of the men there. Previously, they had all been members of Judah's band. These were complete strangers.

"What's going on?" Reuven had demanded. "Where's the regular crew?"

"We replaced them. Eleazar's orders," came the reply from a short man with a pockmarked face.

"Why?"

No one answered.

Reuven started to leave to find Eleazar and question him when the heavy hand of the largest man there was placed on his chest, preventing him from moving.

"You can't leave the grounds!" the pockmarked man said.

"What?"

"Eleazar's orders again. You can't leave until Eleazar calls for you."

"Why?"

Again no answer.

Now, Reuven absent-mindedly drummed his fingers on the table in front of him. What's going on, Reuven wondered. Why is this—

"Reuven, are you listening to me?" Metilius asked sharply.

"I'm sorry, Commander. My mind was wandering."

"That's all right," Metilius said gently. "I'm amazed how you've been concentrating for the last four days."

"The training from my religious studies," Reuven responded with a grim smile. "It's like a counterpart of the training you Roman soldiers go through."

Metilius smiled in response.

"Speaking of your religious studies," he asked, "why hasn't your father visited me? I miss his lessons. I'm not under siege in Herod's Palace or Phasael Tower anymore."

"It's only been a few days," Reuven replied. "When I go home again I'll tell Father to come."

How will I do that? Reuven thought. I can't leave this place.

"Something is disturbing you," Metilius asserted, his eyes narrowed.

Reuven shrugged.

"Perhaps I'm frightening you with my tales of Roman military might," Metilius said. "I'm only telling you the truth, Reuven. The smartest thing is to surrender at the right time to get the best conditions from Rome. You don't have a chance of defeating Rome on the battlefield. You can avoid a fight by withdrawing into the City. The walls defending Jerusalem are very strong and you will be able to withstand a siege, but only for a while. Eventually Cestius will break through Jerusalem's walls; he has the tools and the men to do so. The best time to sue for peace is after the siege has started but before he begins to undermine the walls. Do not wait too long. This is when you will get the best terms.

"Perhaps you think you can defeat Cestius on the battlefield," Metilius continued. "It may be possible. He's not the best general. The only place you can hope to do so is in the pass of Beth Horon if you control the hills and the Roman forces are pinned down in the pass. But that will only give you a temporary victory. Nero will simply replace Cestius with someone like Vespasian, a truly great general who has won many victories. You will never be able to defeat him.

"Reuven, Jerusalem is one of the jewels of the Roman Empire; losing her would be a humiliating defeat. And if Judea threw off Roman rule the rest of the empire would grow restless. Other provinces would see the Jews as an example and also revolt. Rome cannot afford to let you go," Metilius concluded.

"You make our chances seem bleak," Reuven said glumly.

There was a momentary silence. The two became aware of a silent third presence in the room.

"Forgive me, Commander," Drusilla said. "I wanted to wait until you had finished speaking. There is someone outside who keeps asking for Reuven. I do not understand what he's saying."

"What does he look like?" Reuven asked.

"He's a very tall young man."

Reuven nodded.

"Excuse me, Commander. I know who it is. It's probably important that I speak to him."

"Go. We can continue later, or tomorrow," Metilius said.

Before leaving the room Reuven gave a long glance at Drusilla. She met his gaze boldly, as if they had a secret understanding between them. Since that kiss they had not spoken a word and had seen each other only a few times.

Outside Reuven found Shaul waiting for him. Further back, inside the gate, stood Judah, who quickly came up to him.

"Eleazar wants to speak with you," Judah said, before Reuven could utter a word. "But first, we have to talk to you."

"Please do!" Reuven responded. "What's going on here? Why did they change the guards? Why aren't I allowed to leave?"

"Nice place you have here," Judah said smiling. He pointed to a row of trees and a bench underneath them. "Let's go there and talk."

Reuven had heard that Judah's smile was frightening. It never frightened him. Now he found the gap-toothed smile annoying.

"All right," Reuven said. "Just get to the point quickly. I feel like everyone is playing games with me."

They walked to the bench and sat down, Reuven at one end, Judah at the other, and Shaul in the middle.

"Why am I being held prisoner here?" Reuven demanded.

"We don't know," Judah answered in a flat voice. "We also don't know why Eleazar changed the guard."

"Very helpful," Reuven said sarcastically.

"I'm being honest."

"I believe you. Why does Eleazar want to speak to me?"

Shaul laughed bitterly.

"We don't know that, either," Shaul said. "We're here to let you know what's been going on before you go to Eleazar. At least, let you know what we know. When I spoke to you a few nights ago I should have told you what happened in Caesarea. I could tell you hadn't gone to the meeting at the Bronze Gate."

"What meeting? What about Caesarea?" Reuven asked anxiously.

"So you still haven't heard?" Shaul asked.

"Since I moved in I haven't left the grounds," Reuven said. "Except for the people who brought us some new food, and the guards, I haven't seen anyone. Or heard anything. What happened in Caesarea?"

"A Jewish refugee from Caesarea addressed the people in the court of the Bronze Gate that night," Shaul said. "His Syrian friends and neighbors slaughtered the whole Jewish population of the city."

"What?" Reuven gasped. "Why? There must have been ten or fifteen thousand Jews there."

"Twenty thousand," Judah said. "Twenty thousand."

"Why?"

"Ever since we took over Antonia there's been fighting between the Jewish and Syrian villages," Judah explained. "It spread to the city of Caesarea. There's a war going on now, Reuven. We either defend ourselves or we die."

Reuven took a deep breath. He looked from Judah, to Shaul, and back to the house.

"I wonder if Metilius is right," he said softly, looking down at the ground. "He told me yesterday that Pax Romana keeps the peace, that it stops the local people from fighting each other where the Romans rule."

"What peace?" Judah asked heatedly. "Did the Roman procurator stop that Caesarean pagan from sacrificing a bird on top of an upside-down chamber pot in front of a synagogue on a Sabbath? Did he punish the perpetrator, or did he punish the Jews for what followed from it?

"Peace!" added Judah with disgust. "Are you going soft, Reuven? Losing your stomach to fight? Want to go back to being a toady to the Romans?"

"No, Judah, I'm not going soft," Reuven retorted. "When a Jew asks questions it does not mean he is going soft. And another Jew should not think so."

"Fair enough, Reuven" Judah replied, obviously taken aback by Reuven's response. "There's something else—"

Shaul reached out and touched Judah's arm, stopping him.

"Reuven," Shaul said earnestly, "you must believe us. We had nothing to do with it. We both tried to stop it. They had men pull us away."

"What are you talking about? What happened?" There was alarm and fear in Reuven's voice.

"This isn't general knowledge yet. After the garrison disarmed at the north gate," Judah said heavily, "Eleazar had them slaughtered."

"What?" Reuven was horrified. He could hardly believe his ears. He stood up and looked at both Judah and Shaul accusingly.

"Did you know this was going to happen?" he demanded.

"I swear to you, Reuven, we had no idea," said Shaul.

"I gave my word to Metilius!" Reuven shouted.

"And I gave mine to your father. We tried to stop it," insisted Judah. "We couldn't. It was wrong, Reuven. No question about it. It was terrible. Even in war there are rules. You don't break an agreement of that kind."

"What do we do about it?" Reuven asked angrily.

"What can we do?" answered Judah. "There's war now, between us and the Syrians and us and the Romans. There's no going back. Sometimes even your own side does something terrible and there's nothing you can do about it. You just soldier on."

"So our side does something wrong, something terrible and we do nothing?"

"This isn't Torah class," Judah said gently. "This is the real world. This is war."

"What do you think Metilius is going to do when he finds out?" Reuven asked. He was breathing heavily.

"Metilius is not going to find out," Judah said sternly. "And you're not going to tell him."

"My father will," Reuven said. "Once he finds out."

"The guards will not let your father anywhere near Metilius," replied Judah. "Come," he said, standing up. "It's time we went to Eleazar."

Reuven pulled out his knife.

"If I see Eleazar I'll kill him"

Judah and Shaul laughed.

"You're a wild little cub aren't you?" Judah said.

"I mean it, Judah."

"What do I tell him?" Judah asked.

"Tell him whatever you want. Tell him I'm impure by reason of a night emission and I can't go to the Temple complex."

Both men laughed again.

"Is that true, Reuven?" Shaul asked.

"Yes," answered Reuven sheepishly. "Almost every night." He did not tell them it happened during dreams of Drusilla. "Although it didn't stop me from trying to go to Eleazar this morning to find out what's going on…" His voice trailed off. "Or, tell him that I'm deep in talks with Metilius and don't want to interrupt them. Tell him whatever you want.

I don't care."

He started to leave and head back to the house.

"You going to be alright, kid?" Shaul asked solicitously.

Reuven stopped.

"Yeah," he said with resignation. "Yeah. I just need some time to digest all this."

"Don't say anything to—" Judah started to warn.

"He won't," Shaul interrupted. "Don't worry, Judah, he won't," Shaul said reassuringly.

Reuven continued on his way to the house.

Drusilla was waiting for him at the doorway.

"Are you all right?" she asked, a worried look on her face.

"No."

"What's wrong, Reuven?"

He shook his head and walked past her, continuing on to his room, where he threw himself on the bed. His body trembled and tears filled his eyes. Thoughts flew wildly around in his head, so fast he could not catch them.

He felt the bed shift slightly. His head was lifted up and placed on a soft lap. Drusilla's sweet voice entered his ears, driving away the demon thoughts that tormented him.

"My poor boy, my poor sweet boy," she said. "What burdens you must have on your young shoulders." Then she began to sing in the strange language of her childhood, a language neither Latin nor Greek, a language wholly unknown to Reuven. It must have been a lullaby because soon Reuven felt himself drifting off into a peaceful sleep.

Chapter Forty-Five

15 Sep 66 CE / 8 Tishrei 3827

Shaul watched the unfolding tense scene with admiration. The kid did not flinch in the face of the older and more powerful man's opposition.

On either side of the long, dark hall in which they stood chambers were cut out from the stone. The nearest room was brightly lit by oil lamps on stands, with a large, rectangular table at which seven men sat, all facing the open door. In one direction the hall led to the bridge to the Upper City; in the other to the rest of the Temple complex.

"I will not speak with you in the room," Reuven insisted.

Even the ears of Eleazar ben Ananias turned red with anger.

"How dare you talk to me like that!" he hissed. "Who do you think you are?"

"I'm the one who has the Roman commander's knowledge," Reuven retorted. "You're the one who broke a written promise and committed an atrocity on the Sabbath."

"You…" Eleazar started to say, raising his hand and sweeping it toward Reuven's face to slap him. The captain of the Temple ministers was not able to complete the motion; Reuven grabbed Eleazar's wrist with his left hand and with his right pulled out his knife.

"Try that again and I'll kill you," Reuven warned.

The kid has balls! Shaul thought with amazement.

Eleazar ben Ananias pulled his hand free and stepped back. A scrum of young priests surrounded him and made a move toward Reuven. Shaul and Judah stepped on each side of Reuven and the priests halted.

"They're waiting for me," Reuven said and entered the room, motioning for Shaul and Judah to follow.

"They are not on the list!" shouted Eleazar ben Ananias.

"They're on mine," countered Reuven calmly.

In truth, Shaul had no idea who had made up the list of those who were to hear Reuven. With the Romans gone from the City various factions had formed committees that were trying to work together. Shaul assumed some combination of these decided who would attend. It was clear that despite having sparked the rebellion with his refusal to accept Roman sacrifices at the Temple, Eleazar was losing power, and he was not happy about it.

It was a disparate group in the room. There was Ananus ben Ananus, one of the high priests. Shaul had doubts about his commitment to the revolution. At the other end of the spectrum, there was another Eleazar, Eleazar ben Simon, the leader of a group of partisans that called themselves Zealots. They were no less anxious to fight the Romans, and even fellow Jews, than Judah's band. There was also Simon ben Gioras, a hothead from Gerasa. Shaul had heard him speak once and would not be surprised if he joined forces with men like David ben Ephraim. The other four men there Shaul knew nothing about: Joseph ben Gorion, Jeshua ben Sapphas, Niger the Peraean, and John the Essene.

Shaul and Judah took seats at the end of the table.

"Gentlemen," Reuven began, "Metilius, the Roman commander of Antonia has transmitted much information to me. More is to come. To-day I will give you an overview; on future days there will be more detail. I know that you are all familiar with the Romans one way or another, but Commander Metilius can give us an insider's view of what we face."

"Why didn't he come himself?" Ananus ben Ananus asked. "Why are we getting this from a mere boy?"

"I do not know," replied Reuven, shrugging his shoulders. "He insisted he would only talk to me. May I continue, sir?"

Shaul thought: He's not intimidated by any of them!

"We face a formidable enemy," Reuven went on. "From their training, their discipline, their weapons, their numbers, and their experience, they will not be defeated easily."

"Are you trying to scare us?" cried Eleazar ben Simon.

"In truth, yes," answered Reuven. "If we have any hope of defeating the Romans we must be united. And we must try to understand as much as we can about them. It is no accident that their legions rule the world. To start with, the training regimen of the legions. Metilius explained it in detail. It is," here Reuven threw his hands up, "overwhelming. The best way for me to describe it is as the physical equivalent of Torah study. Roman troops never rest. Even during peacetime they are constantly training; Metilius says their battle drills are no different than the real thing; he describes it as 'our drills are bloodless battles; our battles bloody drills.'"

Shaul looked at the faces of the seven at the table. They did not seem impressed. Reuven noticed their lack of reaction and shook his head with resignation.

"Gentlemen," Reuven said, "you do not seem to appreciate the importance of their training. In a debate between a Torah scholar and a common man, who do you think will win?" He shrugged again and continued.

"Here is a brief picture of their personal weapons. The infantry are protected by a breastplate and a helmet. They carry a blade on each side; the shorter is slightly longer than the span of a man's hand. The regular troops have a javelin and a long shield; the general's bodyguards a lance and a small, round shield. The cavalryman has a long sword on his hip, an enormous pike in his hand, and a shield slanted across the horse's flank. He also has a quiver with three or more light, broad-pointed spears. He, too, wears a helmet and breast-plate. And then there are their war machines: catapults, ballistae, and spear-throwers. They have battering rams, which they will certainly bring against our walls. Their engineers build ramps and towers and platforms—"

"You *are* trying to scare us!" shouted Eleazar ben Simon.

"Let him finish!" cried Ananus ben Ananus, obviously annoyed.

"We can't fight effectively if we don't know what we're up against," Reuven responded, unruffled. "Now, listen carefully. This is how the Roman army advances. In the vanguard are lightly-armed auxiliaries and bowmen. Their purpose is to fight off any sudden attacks and to act as scouts to make sure there are no ambushes lying-in-wait, in woods, for example."

"Does that mean," interrupted Simon ben Gioras, "they're vulnerable to hand-to-hand combat, because they're lightly armed?"

"I'll leave that to those with more military experience to decide," Reuven said. "There are several points of possible Roman vulnerability that I will bring up later.

"To continue with their marching order. Right behind this advance guard are heavily-armed Roman troops, mounted and on foot. After these are ten men from every century acting as surveyors, carrying equipment to mark out their future campsite. These are followed by the road engineers, who straighten out curves and level rough surfaces in the road to make it easier for the rest of the army to march. They'll also cut down any vegetation that obstructs the way."

"Are they also armed?" asked Niger the Peraean.

"Yes, both the surveyors and road engineers are carrying their regular gear," answered Reuven. "Next comes a strong cavalry force protecting the personal baggage of the commander and his senior officers. The commander himself, with a select force of infantry, cavalry, and spear-men, follows. Then ride the legionary cavalry; each legion has 120 horse-men. Behind them are the mules and wagons bearing the Roman war engines. Following them are the generals, the prefects of the cohorts, and the tribunes, protected by a bodyguard of specially chosen troops."

Reuven paused, looked around him, and smiled.

"Remember," he said, "these Romans, for all their sophistication, are still pagans. They need their objects of worship, the legionary stan-dards and eagles, one for each legion. Capture one of these and you disgrace the legion. The Romans will die to protect them. These idols, if I may call them that, are carried behind the generals, prefects, and tribunes, and are followed by the trumpeters. Next come the main body of troops, marching six abreast, accompanied by centurions to maintain the formation. After the infantry are the servants of every legion; they take care of the solders' baggage carried by the mules and other animals. Behind the legions are the bulk of the auxiliaries. The rear of this mas-sive military column is protected by light and heavy infantry and a strong detachment of cavalry."

Reuven paused and gazed down at the men looking back up at him.

"Any questions, so far, questions I can answer? No? Then I'll con-tinue. I want to describe how they set up camp because it's important if—"

A tall, thin man, sweating heavily, his face and clothes dirty, burst into the room.

"I've come to warn you about troubling events," he gasped. He looked around the room anxiously.

"Fighting between the Jews and the Syrians in the Land has in-tensified," he began, breathing heavily. "In Ascalon, 2,500 Jews were killed, in Ptolemais, 2,000, in Scythopolis 13,000. The unrest has even reached Egypt. In Alexandria, the apostate governor, Tiberius Alexan-der, let loose two Roman legions on the Delta quarter of the Jews. They destroyed the houses and murdered tens of thousands of our people."

Cries of anguish filled the room.

"The bad news does not stop there," the tall, thin man continued. "Cestius Gallus left Antioch at the head of the Twelfth Legion. He add-ed 2,000 men from each of the other three legions stationed in Syria. He also added auxiliaries of six infantry cohorts and four troops of cavalry. Local kings also sent forces: Antiochus IV of Commagene 2,000 horse and 3,000 foot, all bowmen; Soemus 4,000 men, of whom a third were mounted and a majority bowmen; and that traitor to his people, Agrippa II, sent 3,000 foot and nearly 2,000 horse. Agrippa rides with Cestius and advises him.

"There are 35,000 to 40,000 arrayed against us. They destroyed Zebulon. They killed 8,400 in Joppa. They ravaged the toparchy of Narbata. They are in Caesarea now, preparing to march against us."

Judah stood up.

"Well, gentlemen," he said drily, "we should be having visitors to our noble City within several days." Then he smiled sardonically.

The seven men picked to hear Reuven muttered to themselves, spoke hasty words to their neighbors, and rose to leave. Shaul saw some with eager and excited smiles, others with frowns of worry and fear. Reuven, however, looked supremely annoyed.

"I'm not finished!" he cried.

The seven ignored him as they hurried from the room.

Reuven sighed with exasperation, shook his head, and looked questioningly at Judah and Shaul.

"How can we organize an intelligent defense if the people responsible for our security run around like scared chickens or else like mad dogs just looking for a fight?"

Judah did not have an answer. Neither did Shaul.

Chapter Forty-Six

15 Sep 66 CE / 8 Tishrei 3827

It seemed a good maxim to live by. If everyone followed that rule the world would be more peaceful and just, a better place in which to live. Did the rule apply to everyone and all interactions? Between master and slave? Noble and commoner? Rabbi and illiterate? Husband and wife?

Metilius wished he could ask Rabbi Aaron. That was no longer possible. Reuven told him that his father was forbidden to see him. Reuven did not know why; he surmised the people now running the City were afraid his father would influence Metilius with his political views. Metilius then might not give the advice needed to help the Jews achieve a military victory; instead he'd try to convince them victory was impossible and surrender the only option.

Since his father was not available, Reuven had offered to teach Metilius himself, promising that for things he did not know, or could not answer, he would consult his father or another rabbi. Reuven also brought the two books which were on the table before Metilius. They were written by rabbis to instruct those who wanted to become Jews. One, in Greek, was in the form of a volumen, a scroll ten inches wide and thirty feet long with the text in columns down its width. The volumen was held horizontally and wound off the right-hand roller onto the left as it was read. The other book, in Latin, was in the newer form of a codex, sheets pasted together at one edge and inside a cover thicker than the sheets with writing on it.

Metilius read aloud from the open volumen the words he was contemplating:

"What is hateful to thee, do not unto thy fellow man: this is the whole Law; the rest is mere commentary."

This dictum of Rabbi Hillel was an echo of the story Rabbi Aaron had told when they first met.

Did the Jews themselves live by it? The Romans certainly did not. Did any of the other nations of the world?

Rabbi Aaron himself seemed to. On the other hand, the revolutionaries, including Reuven, did not. These other Jews, more numerous than Rabbi Aaron's single example, were not so different from the Romans who occupied their land.

Metilius sighed so loudly that Drusilla entered the room.

"Can I get you something, sir?"

"No," Metilius replied. He pointed to the two books. "Something for you to read. Impress your new friend." Drusilla blushed. Metilius pointed to the codex. "This is easier to handle than the scroll."

"It's the new form of book, isn't it, sir?"

"Yes."

"I'd guess it's probably in Latin," she said wistfully.

Metilius nodded.

"I can't read Latin, sir," she said. She looked away as if ashamed.

"Yes, I forgot. You'll learn one day. You're a clever girl. Take the scroll then," he replied. "It's in Greek. Surprise Reuven with your knowledge of his religion. Here, let me read something to you."

Metilius read Hillel's saying. Drusilla listened carefully, a thoughtful expression on her face.

"What a wonderful world if everyone followed that rabbi's words." Then she laughed. "You Romans never would have conquered this world if you had." She snorted with derision. "Men are alike in all places, in all nations. They pursue their own ends as best they can, and then come up with complicated reasons to justify what they do."

"Even the Jews?" Metilius asked.

"I don't know any, sir."

"You know Reuven."

"I hardly know him, sir. He's such a strange boy. You said he's a brave warrior who's experienced battle. Yet I've seen him cry. Roman soldiers don't cry, do they, sir?"

"Is it such a weakness for a man to cry?" Metilius asked.

"The gods themselves would cry," Drusilla replied bitterly, "if there were any, if they looked down at this world."

"I wonder if the God of Israel cries," Metilius said. "I will have to ask Reuven."

"I would first wonder if there is a God of Israel," Drusilla responded quickly. "If there were, why would he let the Romans rule his land? If you just look at the world as it is, the Roman gods, as absurd as they are, seem more real than the invisible God of the Jews."

"Take the scroll," Metilius said. "I want to hear you argue with that young Jew, Reuven."

"He's so strange," Drusilla said softly. "I suppose he's already a man in some ways; in others he's like a child..." Her voice fell almost to a whisper and she gazed at the floor.

You're still a child yourself, Drusilla, Metilius thought.

Drusilla looked up at him and smiled.

"I'll take it!" she said brightly. "And read it when I have time from my duties."

"I will make sure you have the time," Metilius said.

"Thank you, sir, thank you!" Drusilla said as she carefully rolled up the scroll and took it with her as she left the room.

Metilius stared at the remaining book on the table and shook his head sadly.

Poor Drusilla. She has such promise. What does she have to look forward to? If she had been born Roman…

A chill went through Metilius as another thought came to him.

What if his daughter had been given Drusilla's fate?

For a moment Metilius could not breathe.

The world is good if you have power. It's not if you don't. It's good if you're Roman, bad if you're Jew…

These abstract thoughts became too much for Metilius; he replaced them with the smiling images of his wife and children.

How I miss them! I would gladly give up empire to see them one more time.

His body sagged as if a great weight was bearing down on him. Metilius laid his head on the table and tears flowed from his eyes.

Chapter Forty-Seven

26 Sep 66 CE / 19 Tishrei 3827

What was he doing here among all these men of war? He was a simple man, a metalsmith, a rabbi it was true, but no great scholar.

Rabbi Hania ben Avel-Mayim looked around and grew even more uncomfortable. Next to him sat his nemesis, Judah ben Ezra. Judah looked down at him, smiled, and clapped him on the shoulder.

"I'm glad you're with us," Judah said amiably. "We need you, Rabbi Hania."

All Rabbi Hania could think of was that terrible smile.

He should keep his mouth closed, Hania thought.

Reuven's voice was droning on. Hania was having trouble concentrating.

The Romans should have arrived days ago, Rabbi Hania thought, trembling. Where are they?

"Listen carefully," Reuven said, "as to how they set up camp." The nine others sitting at the table were clearly paying attention. Hania struggled to focus on Reuven's words and push away the conversation he had with his wife earlier that day.

"If the ground where they want to set up camp is uneven the Romans completely level it," Reuven explained. "The shape of the camp is rectangular. They have many building engineers with all the tools they need. The camp itself is like an orderly small town, with streets clearly marked out. At the center is the commander's headquarters. Around this are the officers' huts. Why, there's even a marketplace and workmen's quarters!

"The outside perimeter is a wall," Reuven continued. "There are towers evenly spaced. Between the towers the Romans have their war engines, all ready to be fired. There are catapults, spear-throwers, stone-throwers…" Reuven fell silent before resuming. "Each of the four walls has a gate, wide enough for armed sorties and the entrance of their baggage animals. Sometimes they build a trench all around, six feet deep and wide."

These last sounds from Reuven entered Hania's mind and were gradually replaced by the worried voice of his wife.

"Why are you doing this?" Naomi asked. "You said it was hopeless."

"I have no choice now, Naomi. The war has started. My duty is to my people and my country, to help them as best as I can."

"Can we win?" Naomi asked plaintively.

Hania could feel the look of hopelessness on his face as he shook his head.

"I don't know, Naomi," he muttered. "I don't know."

"Are you paying attention, Rabbi Hania?" Reuven asked sharply.

Hania was brought roughly back to the present. He was aware of the eyes of the men in the room upon him, aware that he had just shook his head.

"Yes, yes," he stammered. "I'm sorry…"

The room burst into laughter. Once again Judah clapped him on the shoulder.

"His job is to make the weapons," Judah said. "Not use them!"

Reuven smiled and nodded.

Hania could feel his face turning red. Then he noticed something about the men in the room around him. Only Ananus ben Ananus had not laughed or smiled.

Reuven resumed speaking. At once Hania realized that he had missed an important thread of the lecture, but was too embarrassed to ask Reuven to repeat himself.

"Sleep, guard duty, reveille; all begin with trumpet calls. At dawn the soldiers report by units to their centurions, then the centurions to their tribunes, and then the tribunes with their superior officers go to head-quarters. There they get the password and other orders to be given to their subordinates," Reuven said, and then added, with emphasis, "There is strict discipline throughout. Nothing is done without orders!"

"The Romans can't think for themselves!" cried Judah. "They'll be flummoxed by unorthodox tactics!"

"I wouldn't be so sure about that, Judah," Reuven warned.

"Bah! What do you know, boy?" demanded Simon ben Gioras loud-ly.

"I agree with Reuven," Ananus ben Ananus said gravely.

"Bah!" spat Simon ben Gioras. "A boy and a priest. What do they know about battle? Tell us the news, Ananus. We've heard enough from Reuven!"

There were shouts of agreement from others at the table. Reuven shrugged and sat down. Hania saw resignation on his face.

Ananus ben Ananus rose and walked to the front.

"The Roman host is upon us. Cestius has marched from Caesarea to Antipatris and from there to Lydda. He burned Lydda and killed fifty of the inhabitants. Cestius is now six miles from Jerusalem; he has just arrived at Gibeon, and is setting up camp there."

"Let us go out and greet him!" whooped Simon ben Gioras with glee. "Tomorrow, at dawn!"

"Tomorrow is the Sabbath!" Reuven protested from his seat.

"Then the Romans will not be expecting us!" roared Eleazar ben Simon.

Ananus ben Ananus raised his right hand.

"Wait!" he counseled. "We are prepared for defense. Our walls will protect us. We are not yet organized for attack."

Simon ben Gioras laughed.

"We will fall upon them like lions upon sheep!"

There was excited chattering in the room. Reuven and Ananus ben Ananus looked crestfallen.

"This will end in disaster," Rabbi Hania whispered, to no one in particular.

Chapter Forty-Eight

26 Sep 66 CE / 19 Tishrei 3827

He walked as a stranger through the streets of the City of his birth. He recognized all the landmarks; none looked familiar to Rabbi Aaron ben Avraham.

Did Reuven know? Before it happened? Or after, when it was too late?

Rabbi Aaron did not want to believe that his son had sunk so low that he would countenance such a foul deed. To break an oath to commit murder! And on the Sabbath! But Reuven had changed so much. Perhaps he had imbibed all the poison of the revolutionaries.

And what of Metilius? Did he know of the slaughter of his men after the promise of safe passage was given?

Rabbi Aaron stopped walking. He trembled where he stood.

People flowed by him, ghosts they seemed. Their looks of surprise at the tall man with the ashen face barely registered with him.

"I fear the wrath of God," he murmured.

It was getting late. Soon it would be evening and the beginning of the Sabbath. Rabbi Aaron found himself outside the house where Metilius lived. Reuven was supposed to be staying there, too.

It was not his son that he wanted to see.

The guards outside the gate eyed him suspiciously.

"I want to see the Roman commander!" Rabbi Aaron demanded.

"You're not allowed in," one of the guards said, stepping in front of the rabbi and blocking his way.

Rabbi Aaron pushed. The man stumbled backwards, a look of surprise on his face. He drew his sword and growled:

"Careful, Rabbi!"

"How dare you threaten me!" Rabbi Aaron exclaimed, stepping forward, closer to the gate.

The flat of another sword struck his right shoulder. The blunt end of a club was thrust into his back. Two pairs of hands pulled him away from the gate. The man in front of him brandished his sword.

Rabbi Aaron began shouting.

"Metilius, Commander Metilius!"

Rabbi Aaron's voice filled the air with its anguish and rage.

A hand clamped over his mouth, silencing him. Rabbi Aaron tried to bite the hand but could not. He was dragged backward so that his feet were no longer supporting him as they trailed helplessly after the rest of his body.

Has anyone heard me? he wondered. Would it matter?

Rabbi Aaron struggled to free himself. Against one man he might have succeeded, there were too many now. Weary, physically and emotionally, he finally gave up and allowed himself to be taken further and further away.

"Release my father immediately!"

It was Reuven, in a tone of command he had never heard his son use.

As he struggled to his feet and regained his balance one of his captors said:

"He tried to see the Roman."

Reuven frowned and Rabbi Aaron could not tell if the frown was for him or his captors.

"They won't let you, Father," Reuven said gently.

"Did you know, Reuven? Did you know?" Rabbi Aaron's voice quivered. "Did you have anything to do with that abomination?"

Reuven took a deep breath before answering.

"No. I only found out after."

"Yet these are the kind of men you associate with!"

"My friends tried to stop it." Reuven sighed. "It was Eleazar ben Ananias's doing."

"The leader of your revolution!"

"Not anymore."

"Who is then?" Rabbi Aaron asked, puzzled.

"No one. Everyone." Reuven shrugged with resignation.

"As in the time of the judges, when every man did what was right in his own eyes," replied Rabbi Aaron.

"Until we get a king who gets his hand around our throat," responded Reuven bitterly. "I do not know what it will come to."

Rabbi Aaron scowled.

"Or until the Romans return to Jerusalem and take vengeance for this atrocity," he said.

"Pray for us, Father. Tomorrow we go out to meet the Romans in Gibeon."

Rabbi Aaron stared at his son. For a moment he could not speak.

"I will pray that God does not punish us for our sins," he said at last.

"But he always does."

Chapter Forty-Nine

27 Sep 66 CE / 20 Tishrei 3827

The smell of the rich earth tickled his nostrils. Stretched out on the ground, Shaul peered through the pre-dawn twilight. He could barely make out the Roman camp ahead in the distance; the soldier striding down the road in his direction was much clearer. Shaul had jumped off to the side of the road and assumed a prone position at first sight of him so that he himself would not be seen.

A few miles behind Shaul, marching from Jerusalem, were tens of thousands of armed Jews. The City was stuffed with pilgrims for the Festival of Tabernacles, thousands of thousands of them, from whom could be drawn additional men to create a force large enough to face the Romans that threatened the Holy City.

The Holy City! It was also a holy day, the Sabbath, and Shaul felt more than a tinge of guilt. What would Rabbi Zechariah say? Would he have given his approval? But Zechariah had fallen silent of late, retreating into a small circle of students. He no longer spoke out on matters of war and peace, or even on matters of law.

Why? What happened to him?

Shaul brought his mind back to the matter at hand; the Roman scout—in breastplate and helmet, shield in left hand, javelin in right—was now about twenty yards away. His purposeful pace convinced Shaul that this heavily-armed enemy was heading straight for him.

Shaul went into a low crouch. The Roman barked something at him. Shaul recognized it as Latin but did not understand the words. He continued to crouch silently. Again a command was barked. Shaul knitted his brows, threw up his hands, raised his head, and cried "Nero! Nero!"

The Roman looked puzzled.

"Nero! Nero!" shouted Shaul wildly.

The Roman's expression changed. Shaul guessed he thought he was dealing with a madman. He motioned with his javelin for Shaul to rise and then pointed down the road toward the Roman camp.

Shaul did not move. He did not repeat his cry. He waited, almost patiently, a mix of fear and excitement coursing through him. The wrong move and he would die, the right move and his enemy would.

The soldier, scowling, came closer. He was slightly more than an arm's length away. He pointed the javelin at Shaul threateningly.

Shaul began to jabber gibberish. He pointed off to the side. The Roman followed the direction with his eyes. In that moment of distraction Shaul leaped at him, brushing aside the javelin. The force of Shaul's jump against the Roman's breast-plated chest sent both of them tumbling to the ground, the Roman on his back, Shaul on top of him. Shaul's knife was out before the Roman could recover from the assault; Shaul drove the point of the blade downward into the exposed section of the soldier's neck. Shaul pulled the knife out and thrust it down again, over and over, as he found more exposed flesh, all the while keeping his mouth tightly closed so that none of the spurting blood would enter it.

When the Roman soldier stopped struggling and lay still Shaul stood up and looked down at the dead man. Shaul waited for his heart and breath to slow before deciding what to do next.

The Roman was taller than most Jews but shorter than Shaul. He wondered if the helmet and breastplate could fit.

Shaul pulled them off the dead man. They did fit him, barely. Then he went through the soldier's belongings to see what might be useful. There was the sword, the long knife, the shield, the javelin, and even a stretch of rope. Thus accoutered, and after dragging the body further away from the road so it would not be seen, Shaul resumed his journey toward the Roman camp, once again walking upright. He was no longer afraid of being spotted as an enemy Jew.

From a distance they'll think I'm just another one of their soldiers, he thought.

Shaul moved quickly. The light grew stronger. Shaul could see what Reuven had told them to expect: a wall with watchtowers protecting the camp. There was no moat.

He stopped, debating what to do next: Return to Niger the Peraean with what he saw or press on to gain more intelligence?

The tower facing the road beckoned to him.

Don't take foolish chances, he told himself. Get back to your own side.

Shaul ignored his own advice. He resolutely stepped forward, quickening his pace to almost a run but avoiding that last burst of speed so as not to draw attention to himself if someone saw him.

The wall, made of sharpened wooden posts, was not much taller than he was. If he looped the rope around the top he could pull himself up, reach into the platform of the tower, and, if he were quick enough, propel himself inside and overpower the guard. Then he could get a good view inside the camp.

Or, the guard could see him enter and, while he was still scrambling, kill him.

Should he really take the chance?

Shaul laid down the shield and javelin. His heart beating wildly, Shaul looped the rope around the top of the fence, pulled himself up so that his feet were on the top of the fence, and with his long reach grabbed the side of the tower. Then he swung himself around and jumped inside.

The guard was half-asleep! He looked at Shaul with confusion and then horror but before he could raise an alarm or draw a weapon Shaul was upon him.

It was an easier kill than the Roman scout. That done, Shaul went to the entrance of the tower and peered out over the Roman camp. The dawn was brightening and Shaul could see clearly.

The camp was just as Reuven had described.

There was already activity inside the walls. It did not appear to Shaul that Cestius was getting ready to march on Jerusalem yet. He went back inside the tower.

Should he go down from the tower, into the camp, and see what else he could find out?

A voice called out from the ground below. Shaul froze. Again Latin, again words that were not understood.

The voice called out once more. The person below would expect a response from the guard, now dead.

I can't take on the whole Twelfth Legion single-handed, Shaul thought. I better get out of here, quick!

Exiting was not as easy as entering had been. He had to watch his feet as he swung out of the tower and landed of the top of the fence. Then, instead of using the rope, which was still there, he bent down and carefully held onto one of the fence posts, sliding down before letting go and jumping free. Once on the ground, he took off running, leaving the shield and javelin behind.

Shaul ran and ran. A mile or two, maybe three, and Shaul saw a clump of men. His own people! Shouting and waving his arms, Shaul ran toward them.

Shaul was about fifty yards away when one of the men raised a bow and drew an arrow. Astonished, Shaul halted and threw himself to the ground as an arrow whizzed overhead.

What's going on? he wondered.

Then Shaul broke out laughing. He forgot that he was wearing Roman gear. They thought he was an enemy.

Shaul flung off his helmet, stood up, and shouted: "I am one of you, brothers!"

The men approached, their weapons drawn, but the bowman did not notch another arrow. Their looks of suspicion turned to surprise and then amusement.

"Have you gone over to the Romans, Shaul?" one of them called out.

"Cestius has made me his deputy!" Shaul cried, out of breath, as he ran up to them. When the laughter died down he said, his tone serious, "Take me to Niger."

Niger the Peraean had red hair and red beard. Like King David, Shaul thought. Judah was with the other men clustered around Niger. In the morning light Shaul could see masses of armed Jews arriving from Jerusalem, marching haphazardly toward them.

Shaul related what he found out and what he had done.

Judah, frowning, was the first to speak.

"Once they find the dead guard in the tower, the whole camp will go on alert. They will send out units in all directions to find the men who did it. The element of surprise may be lost."

Niger nodded in assent. Shaul looked crestfallen.

"It's all right, Shaul," Niger said reassuringly. "You did well. We know how the camp was set up and we know the walls will be easy to bring down. We were not counting that much on surprise anyway."

"Do you hear it?" one of the men asked excitedly.

The question was greeted with silence as they all listened and then shook their heads.

"The beat of galloping horses," the man who asked the question explained.

"So soon?" asked another.

"Perhaps not so soon," Shaul replied. "Their camp is a couple of miles down the road and I was on foot."

Judah dropped to the ground and placed his ear against it.

"Horses," he confirmed. "Many."

Niger swept his arms in a great half circle.

"We too have many," he said gravely.

And indeed, Shaul saw more and more of their men arriving from the southeast. Then he turned and looked down the road from whence he came.

There were at least one hundred Roman auxiliaries on horseback riding toward them.

A thrill went through Shaul.

Now, he thought, we will see the power of the God of Israel.

Chapter Fifty

27 Sep 66 CE / 20 Tishrei 3827

Reuven awoke to the singing of birds. Aghast, he sat bolt upright in bed. It was too late now, he realized that immediately. Somewhere not far from Jerusalem a great battle was taking place and he missed it because he was asleep. A restless night; not sleep disturbed by troubling dreams but sleep postponed by troubling thoughts. It kept him up for hours, maybe the whole night, until he finally drifted off to the sound of voices and words in his head: his father, Shaul, Judah, Eleazar ben Ananias, Simon ben Gioras, Metilius, Drusilla, and even his murdered uncle, Moshe.

Reuven started to panic; he did not know why. There was a tightening in his chest and his breath came heavily. He swung his feet over the bed.

He could not stand up. It was as if he were rooted to the bed.

Was it fear of what the future would bring? Shame at not being with his comrades when they were fighting the Romans?

Reuven did not know.

He struck his forehead with his open palm and cried: "Stand up, l-Azazel!"

At this he got to his feet, unsteady at first, and then, as he paced about the room his stride grew firmer.

Reuven thought of going outside and asking the guards if they had any news of the battle. After his confrontation with Eleazar ben Ananias, Reuven had insisted on changing the guards back to Judah's men. With the announcement of an upcoming battle with the Romans no one in Judah's band wanted to be relegated to watching the compound that housed the Roman commander, so two men, obviously unfit for battle, were chosen for the task. One was tall and fat, the other was short and thin. Both were merchants, one of wine and the other of oil. Each had attached themselves to Judah. Reuven thought they looked funny together when they were stationed outside the compound.

Reuven stopped at the threshold of the room. He did not want to see them now. There was someone else he wanted to see.

He walked through the halls. As he approached the section that held Metilius' quarters he began peering through the doorways.

He stopped when he saw her.

Drusilla was so busy with her work that she did not notice him. He watched her silently. The agitation that was squeezing his insides gradually loosened its grip. He felt calm and at peace.

She was doing washing. On a long, broad table were three large tubs. On the floor was an even bigger one. Drusilla stood in it, moving her legs up and down rhythmically as she stamped on the clothes in the tub.

At last she noticed Reuven standing in the doorway. She smiled.

"You should not be working," he said. "It's the Sabbath."

"So if I were your servant I would not have to work today?" She looked amused, with the slightest hint of mockery in her voice.

Reuven blinked away the beginning of tears.

"Drusilla, you would not be my servant. You would be celebrating the Sabbath with me."

Her face became serious, filled with longing. And though Reuven saw she was about to say something he spoke first:

"I wish I could go away with you, Drusilla. Flee to some warm, sunny place where I could grow olives and dates and raise sheep and goats. Live peacefully and forget about Rome and war."

He looked down at the floor, covered his face with his hands and sighed.

"Why did you join the rebels, Reuven?" Drusilla asked. "Your uncle was for peace and so is your father."

Reuven removed his hands and raised his head. She had stopped moving her legs up and down in the washing.

"I have your Commander Metilius to thank for that," he answered. "He came to our house to talk to my father about the murder of my uncle and the murder of another rabbi during a rabbinical assembly. I followed him outside one of those times and told him that I wanted to be like him, to carry a sword and a knife and to walk down the street unafraid, to not bow down before anyone. He asked me if I wanted to become a soldier of Rome. I did not answer. I did not tell him that I wanted to become a soldier of Israel and free the Land from Rome."

"Will you free your land?" Drusilla asked earnestly. "Can you?"

Reuven shook his head.

"I do not know, Drusilla."

"Commander Metilius gave me a book in Greek about your religion," Drusilla began. "In it I read what your Rabbi Hillel said. 'What is hateful to thee, do not unto thy fellow man: this is the whole Law;

the rest is mere commentary.' It's a beautiful sentiment, Reuven, but the Romans do not worry about their fellow man. That is why they rule the world, including your own country."

Reuven was silent, full of wonder for this strange servant girl so far from her own home, in her own way a stranger in a strange land as much as his own ancestors were in the land of Egypt. She's not only beautiful, he thought; she's intelligent and wise.

"Tell me, Reuven, do the Jews themselves follow Rabbi Hillel's dictum?"

Reuven laughed bitterly.

"If we did we wouldn't be killing each other."

"In the end you may do Rome's work for her," Drusilla said.

"I fear that, Drusilla. I fear that."

Drusilla resumed the up and down motion of her feet as she stamped on the washing.

"For now," Reuven said, "we are here, and still alive. I will ask Commander Metilius to free you of all duties on the Sabbath, and if you wish, I will find you more works in Greek. And if you have questions I will try to answer them." Then he added, with a broad smile on his face, "If I can!"

Reuven turned and walked down the hall. He found Metilius in another room sitting at a broad table reading a codex. When Reuven entered Metilius looked up and asked:

"Do you read Latin, Reuven?"

Reuven shook his head.

"Ah, then your education is wanting! Take Horace here," Metilius said, pointing to the book in front of him. "Happy is the man to whom God has given with a sparing hand what is sufficient for his wants."

"Not too much, not too little," said Reuven. "Wise words, I guess."

"So, you do not scorn the wisdom of others," said Metilius. "That is good."

"I do not scorn the wisdom of your servant girl, Drusilla, who is more likely to best me in an argument than even my own father."

Metilius laughed.

"So, you see that I was right about her."

"I have a request, Commander. Free her from all duties on our Sabbath."

"Granted."

"Thank you." Reuven bowed his head. He could not bring himself to look at Metilius now. The thought of what Eleazar ben Ananias had done made Reuven's cheeks burn with shame. He quickly left Metilius' presence.

Reuven walked slowly back to his room. His body felt as heavy as his spirit. He lay down on the bed and closed his eyes.

He remembered a Greek legend about Waters of Forgetfulness.

He wanted to drink from its spring.

Hours later the sound of laughter woke Reuven. Shaul stood in the center of the room, smelling of sweat and covered with grime and blood. An air of triumph flowed in with him.

"Asleep, kid?" Shaul jibed. "You missed all the action."

Reuven got out of bed and shrugged sheepishly.

"I had trouble falling asleep," he said. "When I finally did I didn't wake up until it was too late."

"That's alright, kid, you've already proved yourself. Anyway, you won't have to fight anymore. We won. We defeated the Twelfth Legion. We're free!" Shaul shouted his final words.

"What?"

"Yes! You heard me right!"

"That's impossible!" Reuven felt dizzy and steadied himself against the bed. It was too soon, too easy. Shaul had to be wrong.

"Listen, kid. Let me tell you what happened. I scouted their camp, killed two of their men. They sent a whole troop of cavalry after me. Those men on horses ran right into our own fighters. We slaughtered every last one of them. Then their infantry came marching down the road toward us. Thousands of them. We attacked so fiercely we broke through their ranks. We would have finished Cestius and his whole host if fresh cavalry and infantry hadn't come to their rescue. We retreated back toward the City but they abandoned their camp and headed toward the pass of Beth Horon. As they fled, Simon ben Gioras attacked their rear and captured their baggage animals!

"Reuven," Shaul continued excitedly, "the Romans lost more than 500 men. We lost only twenty-two. We smashed the might of Rome. We've won! We're free!"

Reuven stared hard at Shaul.

"Is this true? Does it make sense?" he muttered under his breath.

It took only a moment for Reuven to come to a conclusion.

His friend was telling the truth. The Jews had won a big battle. But Shaul's understanding of what it meant was all wrong.

The struggle was not over.
It had only just begun.
Rome would not give up so easily.

Chapter Fifty-One

1 Oct 66 CE / 24 Tishrei 3827

Reuven examined the man across the table with curiosity. Ananus ben Ananus, who sat next to the man, said his name was Shmuel ben Moshe.

Reuven did not think he looked like a Shmuel ben Moshe. Reuven didn't think he looked like a Jew at all. Not Roman, either. Something about him—Reuven could not say exactly what—made Reuven think of a Greek Syrian.

The man called Shmuel looked back at Reuven with equal curiosity. Reuven was sure he knew what the man was thinking: Why am I talking to a boy?

Why, indeed! Reuven had no idea why Ananus was taking him into his confidence. Why had he been summoned to a meeting with Shmuel ben Moshe and Ananus ben Ananus with no one else present?

Ananus let the silence lengthen. The three sat in a small room that was adjacent to the one where Reuven had delivered his lectures.

Reuven wondered if it was his connection to the Roman commander Metilius. Is that why Ananus ben Ananus had asked him here? Metilius still did not know about the Jewish victory at Gibeon. Reuven could not bring himself to tell the Roman; the massacre of Metilius' men at the north gate still weighed heavily on Reuven's conscience. He would have to tell him about Gibeon, though, and soon. Metilius had the right to know, and Reuven wanted Metilius' advice on what he thought the rebels should do next.

Cestius was still a threat. Shaul had been wrong. Cestius had changed direction after initially fleeing and returned to occupy his camp at Gibeon.

It should have been burned to the ground! Reuven thought.

For three days following the battle at Gibeon Reuven accompanied Shaul on scouting missions. There had been no engagements with the enemy; they had been careful to avoid any contact. Reuven was grateful that his friend did not complain about being slowed down because Reuven was tagging along; no one could travel as fast as Shaul.

During those three days Cestius made no move to march on Jerusalem.

Sooner or later, Reuven thought, that would have to change.

Ananus ben Ananus broke the silence.

"Shmuel ben Moshe is one of King Agrippa's subjects," Ananus said. "He has been sent to Jerusalem to spy on us."

Reuven's eyes widened. He leaned back in his chair.

"Agrippa has sent many spies into Jerusalem," Shmuel ben Moshe said.

Reuven smacked his lips, leaned forward, and punched his left palm with his right fist.

"I guess that makes sense," he said, nodding his head slowly. "But why are you telling us this?"

"Because I am on the side of the Jews," he answered softly.

"You're not one, are you?" Reuven asked.

"No. My wife is." Then he added, in response to Reuven's look of surprise, "She's a convert."

"That doesn't make you one," Reuven said.

The man called Shmuel ben Moshe smiled.

"How old are you?" he asked.

"Almost fifteen."

"One day you'll get married," Shmuel ben Moshe explained. "If you're a good man, have any sense, and want to be happy, you'll try to make your wife happy."

Reuven smiled, too.

"One day," he said sighing, "I'd like your wife to talk to someone I know."

"The Roman's servant girl?" Ananus asked sharply.

Reuven glared at him.

"Do you have spies watching me?" he asked angrily.

"Who else could it be?" retorted Ananus. "It's of no concern of mine."

"Why did you want me here?" Reuven asked, still annoyed.

Ananus tugged his beard once or twice, folded his hands, and regarded Reuven silently. Then he said, obviously choosing his words carefully:

"I think you realize the hopelessness of our situation. If there is going to be an all-out war we have to do everything we can to win. But if we can avoid that war…" Ananus' voice trailed off.

"What makes you think I can do anything to help you avoid an all-out war? Or that I want to?"

"You're Rabbi Aaron's son. You're Rabbi Moshe's nephew. You've learned a lot from that Roman commander and have enough sense to realize that we cannot win. And I see how you present what the Roman taught you. You know we cannot win."

Reuven clenched his right fist. His eyes narrowed.

"And so you consort with spies of Agrippa, that toady of the Romans?" Reuven said with some heat. "Are you one of the leaders of the revolt or are you trying to sap our morale and have us surrender to the Romans?" Reuven looked from one to the other. Suspicion began to prick at Reuven; was Ananus ben Ananus only pretending to support the fight for freedom?

"Come now, boy, you know the real situation as well as I do. I'm sure your Roman has explained it to you. That battle at Gibeon was a great victory for us but a trifle loss to Rome. They will be back."

"Who are the other spies?" asked Reuven, looking directly at Shmuel ben Moshe.

"In truth, I don't know."

"Were they sent to gather intelligence or to cause division and sap morale?"

"I don't know that, either."

"You?" Reuven asked.

"To gather intelligence," Shmuel ben Moshe replied. "To report on the state of the City, its defenses, and any internal conflicts that can be exploited."

"How did you know to go to Ananus?"

"He is a leader of the revolutionaries."

"There are others," insisted Reuven.

"When I got here and spoke to people he was the one with the most stature," Shmuel ben Moshe responded simply.

Reuven looked at Ananus.

"What are you doing about the spies?" Reuven asked.

"What can I do?"

"What can you do?" Reuven exploded. "You can search for them. Warn others."

"Yes, you're right about that. I will. I haven't had time to think about that. Shmuel ben Moshe just came to me. Here's what I want you to know that's important."

Shmuel ben Moshe began speaking.

"Agrippa has convinced Cestius to offer a pardon if the rebels lay down their arms and surrender the City. You must also knock down a section of the north wall that defends Jerusalem. He promises to replace the corrupt Florus with an honest man."

"Very nice of Agrippa and Cestius," Reuven responded sarcastically. "What do you want me to do?"

"Convince your friends to give Agrippa's emissaries a chance to speak," Ananus said. "Don't attack them. Don't intimidate anyone who agrees with them. Listen to what the people want and accept their decision."

"What makes you think I have influence with anyone?" Reuven asked angrily. "I'm just a kid who joined a small band of outlaws. Even our leader has no control over the men who are running things now."

Reuven stared at Ananus ben Ananus.

Is he a traitor or a man who sees clearly what our real situation is?

Reuven shook his head. He didn't know.

He got up, gave one last look at the two men sitting across from him, and left.

Once outside the Temple complex Reuven walked to the Xystus Plaza, the place where his Uncle Moshe was murdered while giving a speech arguing for peace. He stood there, thinking.

The plaza's vast open area after the Temple room's small dimensions was not liberating; Reuven felt as if his mind would explode into the newly-open space available to him.

Was Ananus ben Ananus, like his Uncle Moshe and his father, a patriot who saw the futility of war? Or was he traitor waiting to turn the City over to the Romans?

And even more pressing: Was he, Reuven, a brave patriot willing to die for his country, or a fool seduced by the sight of an armed Roman officer into thinking that by aping him he could help free his country?

It was time to speak to Metilius.

Reuven began walking purposefully toward the house he shared with Metilius and Drusilla. He hadn't seen either of them for more than two days. Two days ago he had given Drusilla two codices in Greek: one, the five books of the Torah, the other, a collection of writings such as Tehilim, Proverbs, Esther, and Ruth.

Did she try to read either one? He hoped she did. She was smart, she would have questions, he could explain things to her! After he spoke to Metilius he would ask her!

Reuven walked more quickly.

He once again found Metilius seated at a table, this time with two open codices.

Drusilla sat next to him, very close, peering into the same books.

A fit of jealousy overcame Reuven; the reason for his visit was forgotten. It must have shown on his face because Drusilla looked at him with a puzzled expression and Metilius relaxed into an easy smile.

"Don't be concerned, Reuven, she's like a daughter to me."

Reuven flushed with embarrassment. He nodded. With a sigh he sat down across from them. He looked at Metilius and then at Drusilla. He frowned.

"You look tired," he said to her.

"Don't blame me!" Metilius said jocularly. "She stays up all night reading. Reads most of the day, too. I've relieved her of some of her duties."

Reuven leaned across the table. They were the two books he had given Drusilla.

"There's something she didn't understand," Metilius went on. "She asked me to take a look. I don't understand, either."

Drusilla pointed to one of the codices.

"I'm confused, Reuven," she began. "Here in Deuteronomion the Torah says that a Moabite is forbidden to enter into the congregation of the Lord to the tenth generation. But here, in Ruth, she is a Moabite and your King David is descended from her. Doesn't one contradict the other?"

Reuven chuckled.

"I gave you these books two days ago and already you're asking me hard questions?" He beamed at her. "Well, let me see if I can explain it to you.

"We have commentaries on the Scriptures. One of them, about Ruth, says that the prohibition against Moabites only applies to men, not women, because in Scripture the Hebrew uses the masculine form of the word for a person from Moab."

"Could I see that commentary?" she asked. "Is it in Greek?"

"Unlike Scripture," he explained, "most of those commentaries are oral, not written."

Drusilla's eyes were fixed on Reuven as she said:

"Then I can't fully appreciate your answer until I can read the text in the original Hebrew."

Reuven nodded.

"You're right, but to be honest, I find the explanation somewhat weak. I've had more than one argument with my father and brother about it. The funny thing is, there's another commentary that says that that interpretation was discovered the day before Boaz met Ruth."

Reuven laughed and then sighed deeply.

"What's wrong, Reuven," Drusilla asked. "It can't be just the question of King David's ancestry. He's been dead a long time."

Reuven sighed even more deeply.

"I wish I could send Metilius back to his family. I wish you and I could leave this place, go somewhere peaceful where I could grow olives and dates and raise sheep and goats."

"You told me that before, Reuven," Drusilla said. "Have you ever grown olives and dates or raised sheep and goats?"

Reuven shook his head.

"No," he said. "There's a small plot of land outside of Jerusalem that's been in our family for generations. We've never worked it. We rent it out; it brings in a small income. My father also has students. I was supposed to follow in his footsteps and become a scholar. Now..," he shrugged. "I don't know what I am."

Reuven looked down at the table.

"Commander Metilius," he said, still looking down, "I came to speak to you about something important." Reuven looked up just in time to see Drusilla getting ready to leave. "You can stay, Drusilla. I don't mind if you hear what I have to say."

Drusilla sat down.

"Four days ago thousands of Jewish fighters attacked the Roman camp at Gibeon," Reuven began. Before he could go further Metilius interrupted.

"Wasn't that the Sabbath? Isn't that forbidden?"

Reuven shuddered, not at the fighting at Gibeon on the Sabbath, but at the slaughter of Metilius' men on that holy day. Reuven looked away.

"It is not rabbis who are in charge of the fighting," Reuven said, his voice trembling. He went on, more firmly. "The Jews won a big victory. Roman forces lost over 500 men, infantry and cavalry. Jewish losses were twenty-two. The Romans eventually blunted the attack, but as they retreated one of the Jewish bands attacked their rear and captured their baggage animals."

Before Reuven could go on Metilius interrupted again.

"Now is the time to sue for peace," he insisted. "Send emissaries to

Cestius saying that you have no desire to rebel from Rome, that you are willing to submit to her. All you ask is that the corrupt procurator Florus be replaced by an honest man."

"Why should we do that if we won?"

Metilius slapped the table.

"Precisely because you won. It would have been better if you had followed my original advice but it is too late now. If you sue for peace after a victory you demonstrate that you accept Roman rule, that it was not Rome you were fighting but a corrupt procurator. It is possible that Cestius will accept that."

Reuven looked down again.

"I have been told," he said, in a soft voice, "that Agrippa convinced Cestius to offer a pardon if we lay down our arms and surrender. He promises to replace the corrupt Florus with an honest man."

"Accept it, unless you are mad!" shouted Metilius.

Reuven looked toward Drusilla, as if seeking... what? Advice? Comfort?

Drusilla's face was blank; he could not read it.

"Reuven, you must convince your people to accept Cestius' pardon!" Metilius insisted.

Unbidden, the thought came to Reuven: Like we convinced you to accept safe passage for your men?

Instead, he said:

"I have no power to convince anyone of anything. I am helpless in this matter."

Reuven stood up. He needed fresh air, and the space to think. Without saying a word he turned and left the room.

Once outside he went into the courtyard and sat on the bench under the trees. His head fell into his hands as he fought back tears, wondering if he should have stayed in his father's house and never joined the rebels, the initial impulse to join the fight for freedom struggling with the growing realization that Metilius and Ananus were right.

He didn't know if he had done the right thing, he truly didn't know, but as regret began to seep through him one thought saved him from utter confusion and despair: Drusilla. He would never have met her if he hadn't joined the revolution.

That thought eased his mind and he began to weigh the words of Ananus and Metilius against the actual victory at Gibeon. Yes, the odds were not good but there had been that victory in battle against the

Twelfth Legion and its allies. Perhaps that was a sign from God to continue the struggle, that He would be behind His people and bring them victory over their powerful enemy! It had happened before, many times, from Pharaoh to Antiochus!

He felt a hand briefly touch his shoulder. He looked up into Drusilla's blue eyes.

"Well?" she asked.

Reuven shrugged.

"I don't know, Drusilla, I don't know."

"You know Commander Metilius is right."

"Perhaps. Probably. From his perspective, yes. Still, how do we know we can trust the Romans to keep their word and not send another corrupt man to rule over us? And there was the victory at Gibeon, perhaps a sign of future ones, telling us not to give up the fight."

"A sign, Reuven? A sign from whom?"

"From God."

"From God? How do you know that?"

"I don't," he admitted.

"Is that what you call faith?" she asked.

He shook his head as he looked at her.

"I don't know, Drusilla. I'd be more inclined to say yes if the majority of the rabbis were behind us, but they're not. So maybe it's just baseless hope. At any rate, I have no influence with anyone to change the course of events."

"You say that, Reuven, but is it really true? That is not what I heard about you."

Reuven's breath came heavy as he remained silent, thinking.

"No, it's not true," he answered at last. "I have influenced the course of events. Not completely, but some, maybe even in important ways. It was my idea to have Rabbi Hania ben Avel-Mayim put in charge of making weapons, it was my idea to have Metilius remain in Jerusalem when his garrison left. I even defied the leader of the revolution and got away with it. No, I guess I really do have influence, some, anyway," he ended weakly.

"Then use it, Reuven! For all our sakes!"

He didn't answer. He bowed his head as she walked away.

He sat thinking for a long time, random thoughts interspersed with focused thinking, unable to come to any conclusions. The uncertainty was what dug at him; a wrong decision, either way, would be catastrophic.

The decision could not be his alone, it could not be any single person's. If only the leaders of the revolt, the rabbis, and even the priests, would get together and discuss what they faced and what options they had, if they would do it calmly, with each side truly listening to the other, while there was still time, the correct course of action could be arrived at. If only…

Reuven heard footsteps approaching. He looked up and saw Judah and Shaul walking towards him. Judah had a stern expression. Shaul looked nervous.

Judah glared down at Reuven.

"Is there anything you need to tell us?" Judah demanded.

"Huh? What?" Reuven responded.

Judah repeated the question.

"I don't understand what you're getting at," Reuven said, confused. "I don't know, maybe that you and all the other leaders of the revolt should get together with the rabbis and discuss the best course of action to take." He shrugged.

"We already know the best course of action," Judah said harshly. "Fight the Romans, drive them from our land, and make sure they never come back." He paused, and added:

"What did you talk to Ananus ben Ananus about?"

"What?" asked Reuven, surprised. He stood and faced Judah. "I was just there. How did you know? Do you have spies watching me?"

"Just answer the question!" Judah demanded.

"Not much," Reuven replied. "He introduced me to a man named Shmuel ben Moshe. Said that he was a spy for Agrippa but was really on our side. Shmuel said his wife was a Jew and that's why he was helping us. He told us there were a lot of spies in Jerusalem."

"And you didn't see fit to warn us?" Judah exclaimed.

"What was there to warn? There are no spies in our group; Agrippa's people have recently come from the outside. Besides, I just found out earlier today."

"Get your sling," Judah ordered.

"Why?"

"Get it," Judah repeated fiercely.

Reuven shrugged and went into the house. He returned with his sling and ammunition.

"Let's go," Judah said.

"Where?"

Judah did not answer.

"I have a right to know where you're taking me," Reuven complained.

"To the north wall," Shaul said.

"Why?"

"You'll see soon enough," Shaul replied.

They passed through the gate where the three walls met, near Phasael Tower, and went from the Upper City into Bezetha and then to the north wall. As they neared the wall Reuven saw clumps of armed men.

On top of the section of the gate was a rampart, on either side was a rectangular tower. Reuven saw men on the rampart and towers. From the other side of the gate, outside the City, he heard the voices of men calling out.

"Where should we take him?" Judah asked.

"It doesn't really matter," Shaul answered. "One of the towers will give him more height."

Shaul pointed to the tower on the left. They went through a small entrance and climbed the stairs. They stepped out onto the tower and Reuven walked to the wall and looked down. He saw two men. They looked up, saw him, and stopped shouting.

"Who are they?" Reuven asked stepping away from the wall and turning to Judah and Shaul.

"Emissaries from Agrippa," answered Judah. "They have been asking to enter the City to present surrender terms from Cestius. *You* are going to kill them with your sling."

"Everyone has been waiting for you!" Shaul said enthusiastically. "They waited for you to send the message to Agrippa!"

"What? Why should we kill them?" exclaimed Reuven. "Wouldn't it be better to let them in to hear what they have to say?"

"No," said Judah firmly. "It has been decided not to let them enter; that is not just my decision but the decision of all the leaders. If we let them in, between them, Agrippa's spies and agents, and the now-quiet members of the Peace Party, they will turn the people against us and convince them to surrender."

Reuven rubbed his forehead.

"If their argument makes no sense it will only strengthen the people's will to fight," he argued.

"No," Judah said. "They will just present lies and fool the people."

"Why me?" Reuven protested.

"You were not there for the battle at Gibeon. You met secretly with Ananus ben Ananus, whom we do not trust. And I suspect you really have sympathies for the Peace Party position."

It was clear that Reuven was hesitating, that he was trying to decide what to do.

"You can always go home to your father's house," Judah sneered.

Reuven looked at Judah with contempt.

"I've already taken part in the revolution. I've advised it and killed for it. I do not need you tell me what my role should be."

Reuven took the sling from his pocket. He took out a stone. Then he walked to the wall and looked down again.

The two men were almost directly below him.

Reuven began to swing the sling in an almost vertical loop. At the right moment he let the stone fly.

His missile entered the top of one of the head of the man he aimed at. The man collapsed to the ground.

The other man began running. Reuven put another stone in his sling and flung it at the fleeing man. It struck him, too, and he went down.

There were cheers from the men on the towers and the wall.

The first man outside the wall lay without moving. The second man got up hesitantly, stumbled, and began running again, more slowly now, his upper body swaying from side to side. Reuven took aim with a third shot but missed. None of the men on the rampart or towers called out to the men below to go after Agrippa's wounded, fleeing emissary. He was allowed to make his tortuous way back to his master.

Reuven put the sling back in in his pocket.

He saw the looks of approval in the faces on the men around him on the tower, especially Shaul and Judah. Reuven said nothing. He turned away from them and left.

Chapter Fifty-Two

12 Oct 66 CE / 5 Cheshvan 3827

Ignoring the hail of arrows raining from the sky, standing alone on the roof of the north colonnade of the Temple, Judah looked down with apprehension at the mass of overlapping Roman long shields, each emblazoned with a bright white lightning bolt against a red background. There, at the base of the wall that protected the Temple complex, ten rows of Roman soldiers were arrayed, fifteen to a row, each soldier under a shield held horizontal. The first row of shields rested against the wall, the second row overlapped the first, with each subsequent row overlapping the one in front of it until all ten rows looked from above like a giant tortoise.

Two weeks ago we won a great battle, Judah thought. We had the Romans on the run. We should have burned their camp to the ground at Gibeon when we had the chance. And when they came to Jerusalem to attack the City we could have fought to keep them out of Bezetha. Now they're threatening the Temple.

The day after Judah had ordered Reuven to kill the two emissaries from Cestius and Agrippa, Cestius marched from his camp at Gibeon to Mount Scopus. Mount Scopus was only three-quarters of a mile from Jerusalem and had an excellent view of the City. Cestius remained on Mount Scopus for three more full days and then entered Jerusalem from the north meeting only token resistance. He set fires in Bezetha; spectacular flames leapt high from the Timber Market producing thick smoke that drifted over the entire City, smoke so thick Judah coughed for hours. Then for five days Cestius attacked the City in all directions from Bezetha. Judah split up his band to join the fighters in three sections of the City; the areas near Phasael Tower, the Markets, and Antonia and the Temple.

The walls protecting Jerusalem south of Bezetha proved so strong and the Jewish resistance so determined that Cestius decided to change his tactics.

He concentrated a large force of infantry backed by several units of bowmen in an assault on the Temple from the north. From the heights of the colonnade the Jews repeatedly drove back the attackers who tried to approach the wall. Eventually, the mass of arrows from the archers forced the Jews off the roof and allowed the Roman soldiers to reach the wall below Judah.

Judah was sure he knew what that first row of soldiers was doing: Trying to undermine the Temple wall. It would not be easy, but with enough time they might succeed in at least weakening the wall, readying it for a battering ram. The Romans had to be stopped, but the tortoise-shell of shields protected them from the missiles that the Jews—those who braved the arrows—threw down on them.

One of these arrows flew uncomfortably close to Judah.

I better get out of here, he thought. He bent down, slid over the edge of the roof while holding on, and then allowed himself to drop to the floor.

Judah frowned at Reuven and Shaul, who were waiting for him.

"We have no leadership," Judah complained. "It's every man for himself," he added, making a sour face. He then explained the situation on the ground at the foot of the wall, concluding with, "We must stop them!"

Shaul and Reuven said nothing.

"Maybe if that third wall had been finished to its full height everywhere along its length the resistance wouldn't have abandoned Bezetha." Judah sighed with disgust.

"The first Agrippa built that wall," Reuven said. "He didn't complete it because he was afraid that the Roman emperor at the time, Claudius, would think he was planning a revolt when he saw how massive the ramparts were on the finished parts." Reuven paused, and added, "That first Agrippa was a good Jew, unlike his son, the present Agrippa."

"And not like his grandfather, that vile Herod," added Shaul.

"A worthy descendent of the Maccabees," concluded Judah, stroking his beard as he calculated what had to be done next.

Antonia, at the northwest corner of the Temple, had a small door that opened east and faced the area where the Romans were working to undermine the Temple's north wall. A raiding party sent out to disrupt their work would take the Romans, with their shields raised to the sky, by total surprise.

Judah described his plan to Shaul and Reuven, and looking at Shaul, said, "Get as many of our boys as you can find, and anyone else you can gather, and quickly organize a group of men to stop the Romans."

"Judah!" Reuven cried. "Their shields will only protect them from spears or arrows or rocks. Something really heavy will crush them. There must be enough large blocks of stone in the Temple complex that can be safely pried away. The priests are familiar with the complex, they will know where to find such blocks. Teams of two or three men can carry the blocks up through the Basilica to its second floor and then along the roof of the colonnades. They can bring them there," here he pointed upward, "and drop them on the Romans below."

Judah gave a slow smile and then spoke rapidly.

"Brilliant idea, Reuven. Now go organize it, and quickly!"

As the two went off on their separate tasks, Shaul to gather fighters and Reuven to find priests who could get blocks of stone and organize men to bring them to the roof of the north colonnade, Judah made his way to the Basilica on the south end of the Temple plaza, up to the second level, and then back along the roof of the colonnade so he could follow the action at the foot of the wall.

The rain of arrows had ceased. To make sure that he was not plainly visible to the archers in the distance Judah did not stand but knelt on the upward slanted edge of the roof and peered over the short wall down into the scene below.

Judah waited and waited, anxious as the Romans continued their infernal work undisturbed.

And then the small door to Antonia flew open and a stream of Jews rushed out with spears, javelins, and swords. The Romans were taken completely by surprise. The orderly rows of men with their shields forming the tortoise jostled against each other as they struggled to bring down their shields to defend themselves. Soldiers stumbled, some against the wall, some falling to the ground as the disorder in their ranks spread like a wave. The thrust of spear, javelin, and sword against shield was fierce as the Jews tried to force an opening in their ranks.

Judah noted with satisfaction that the Jews kept the advantage as they pressed against the scrambled formation of Roman infantrymen, but when reinforcements arrived the Jews withdrew back into Antonia, closing the heavy door behind them.

The Romans made no attempt to force their way into Antonia.

Judah was relieved that he did not see any Jewish casualties on the ground.

After removing their dead and wounded, the Romans reorganized their troops and resumed their work on the wall. They sent an additional unit of men to guard the door to Antonia to prevent another attack.

Judah tapped his fingers lightly on the short wall of the roof's colonnade as he pondered his next move.

I need a way to communicate with Shaul to direct further action, he thought, nodding his head.

Judah stood for a moment and looked at the Temple court. It was empty; Shaul had managed to enlist all the men waiting there. Judah let himself down directly from the roof and began searching for someone to be a conduit of orders to Shaul and information back from him.

At the south end of the complex, in the Basilica, Judah thought he saw what he needed. A man was leaning against a column. But as Judah got closer he wasn't sure if the man would be useful for anything. He didn't look like he was leaning against the column either to rest or because he was idle; he was clutching it as if he would fall if he let go. The man was of medium height, with streaks of white in his hair and beard and blood on his ragged clothes. Judah noticed a wound on his neck but to Judah's eyes it seemed little more than a deep scratch.

"What's wrong, brother?" Judah asked as he came up to him.

The man was trembling.

"All is lost!" The man's lower lip quivered as he spoke.

"Nonsense!" insisted Judah. "We can drive them out and you can help!"

The man looked at Judah unbelievingly.

"What's your name, brother?"

"Adlai ben Binyamin."

"Well, Adlai ben Binyamin, are you going to help me or not?"

The man's eyes grew wide.

"How can I help you?" Adlai asked.

"Do you know your way from here to Antonia?" Judah asked.

Adlai nodded.

"Well, there's a very tall young fellow leading a bunch of my boys down there. His name is Shaul. I want you to relay orders from me to him and bring back information from him to me. Think you can do that?"

Judah saw hope in the man's face.

Adlai ben Binyamin nodded vigorously. He let go of the column.

"Well, follow me now," Judah said. "And when we get up there," he pointed to the roof at the north end, "keep low. I don't want any more blood coming from you!" Judah clapped Adlai ben Binyamin on the back and laughed.

The man who had seemed to Judah like a beaten cur only a moment ago now laughed with him. Adlai ben Binyamin was transformed.

Once back on the roof, with Adlai beside him, Judah leaned over the short wall, pointed downward and said:

"The Romans have joined their shields to protect themselves from spears and arrows from above. They are working to undermine the wall. We are going to stop them. I sent another young fellow to collect large stones, huge stones, actually. Once we drop the stones on the Romans below, we will smash them for good."

Judah stood up, heedless of Adlai's look of caution, and turned toward the Basilica.

"L-Azazel," he muttered, "where are you Reuven?"

Then he dropped to his knees, knit his brows, and considered whether to order another attack by Shaul or wait for Reuven to arrive.

The Roman unit guarding the door to Antonia will blunt an attack, he thought. I have to wait for Reuven. Then one-two! Drop the stones, crushing the first few rows. While the guards at the door are distracted, tell Shaul and his men rush out. But how to coordinate the two?

Judah rubbed his forehead as he tried to figure out the puzzle.

"I have it!" he cried, snapping his fingers, startling Adlai. "A shofar! We need someone who can blow a shofar loudly. There must be someone in the Temple who can do that."

The excitement of having found a workable strategy began to be eaten away by doubt.

What if Reuven doesn't come back soon? How long could I wait before taking a chance and ordering Shaul to mount another attack?

Judah looked down at the Romans. He took several deep breaths.

Steady, he thought, steady. Don't make the wrong decision.

He turned to Adlai ben Binyamin.

"I want you to go to Antonia, find Shaul, and tell him to attack again. But warn him that the Romans are now guarding the door. Here, I'll help you down from the roof."

Holding onto Judah's hands, Adlai slipped over the edge. He dropped to the court below as he let go of Judah. Adlai was about to take off running, when Judah, out of the corner of his eye, caught movement from the Basilica.

Reuven was leading a procession of men carrying large blocks of stone; the men were in groups of two and three.

"Wait!" Judah called to Adlai.

Adlai halted.

"Reuven," Judah said, as Reuven, smiling, came up to him,

"find someone who can blow a shofar loudly. And hurry, hurry."

"I can do that," Reuven said proudly. "I'll be right back with one."

Judah positioned the men with the blocks along the colonnade. They laid their burdens down. Then Judah spoke to Adlai.

"Tell Shaul to attack only when he hears the blast of the shofar! Go!"

Judah did not have to wait long for Reuven to return with a shofar. To the men waiting with the blocks of stone he said: "At my signal lift and drop them on the Romans below." Then Judah positioned himself so he could look down over the edge.

"Now!" he cried. "Drop them!"

The men lifted and heaved. The blocks of stone plummeted down, crashing into the upturned Roman shields, smashing the men underneath them into the ground. There were cries of pain and anguish. The men guarding the door to Antonia rushed to help their fallen comrades.

"Blow the shofar!" commanded Judah.

Reuven raised the shofar to his lips, puffed out his cheeks with new air, and let out a long blast. And then another, and another.

The door to Antonia opened. Armed Jews emerged thrusting spears and javelins and slashing swords. The Romans, overcome by the double blow, were filled with confusion and offered a only feeble defense. They no longer kept their positions; they retreated, dragging their dead with them. Shaul's men pursued them relentlessly.

Out in the open, away from Temple wall and the side of Antonia, fresh Roman troops came to the rescue of those fleeing the partisans led by Shaul, but soon these Romans were countered by waves and waves of Jewish fighters flowing into Bezetha, stirred by the sounds of the shofar.

The Roman host began a disorganized march northward, valiantly fighting off the frenzied assaults of the Jews who were determined to inflict as much damage as possible.

Judah heard cheering and the blasts of other shofars resounding through the City as the last of the Romans exited Bezetha and Jerusalem.

"Well, we live to fight another day," he muttered, to no one in particular.

Chapter Fifty-Three

15 Oct 66 CE / 8 Cheshvan 3827

A strong gust of wind took Shaul's breath away, heightening his exhilaration. He could have been standing at the top of the world; the vast vista held mountains, cliffs, and valleys. The ridge under his feet sloped down to the narrow road that was the pass of Beth Horon. The mountains were filled with Jewish fighters. The road was covered by Roman soldiers marching in formation four abreast. On the other side of the road, just past its edge, were steep cliffs that dropped to bottomless canyons.

"This is the end of the Twelfth Legion and its Syrian allies!" Shaul cried exultantly.

Reuven looked up at him.

"Now we fight the real enemy," Shaul said. "Now you're killing Romans with your sling, not Jews."

Reuven nodded as he placed another stone in his sling.

Shaul patted Reuven on the shoulder.

"We have you to thank for this victory, kid."

"What are you talking about?"

Shaul laughed at the puzzled look on his friend's face.

"It was your idea to use huge stones to crush the Romans at the foot of the Temple wall," explained Shaul. "That started the Romans on their retreat. We harried them all the way to Mount Scopus, destroying their rearguard. They camped the night on Mount Scopus and then retreated to Gibeon. We inflicted more casualties in hit and run attacks on their flanks as they marched. They were afraid to turn and meet us, afraid that if they broke formation we'd force our way through their ranks. And now, after they waited two days in Gibeon, they march through the pass. This will be their grave."

Shaul stopped. His eyes went from Reuven's face to the enemy soldiers below upon whom fell a steady rain of rocks, slung stones, spears and arrows. The missiles took a terrible toll on the Romans and their allies but they could not respond to the onslaught; the heavy infantry could not run up the slopes to confront the Jews on the heights and the cavalry was even more restricted.

Shaul was eager for the real battle to start, to race down with his comrades and overwhelm the weakened enemy in hand-to-hand combat. That would have to wait until the head of the Roman column was further down the road; a large force of Jewish partisans was preparing to block the pass at its narrowest point, effectively trapping the entire Roman host.

Shaul looked at Reuven and grew somber. He rarely thought about the death—he called it death, not assassination anymore—of Rabbi Moshe. The memory returned, though, at odd times.

Like this moment, when he was taking part in the victory over the Romans.

Eliminating Rabbi Moshe was necessary, but however necessary it was, that death now left a bad taste in his mouth because of Reuven.

How would his friend react if he ever found out that it was he, Shaul, who killed his uncle? Would Reuven hate him? Want revenge? Or would Reuven understand?

No matter, Shaul thought. Reuven must never find out who killed his Uncle Moshe.

The progress of the Roman column slowed as row upon row jammed into those in front of them.

"They're bottled up," Shaul said, laying a hand on Reuven's shoulder. "Cease your slinging." Shaul picked up the spear that lay on the ground by his side.

The Roman column came to a halt.

"They're trapped!" Shaul cried triumphantly.

Then he, along with thousands of others waiting on the heights, let out deafening shouts and yells and charged down the slopes to storm the now disorganized Roman lines.

The infantrymen turned their lightning emblazoned shields to face the waves of attacking Jews armed with spears and swords. The Romans, hemmed in by their fellow soldiers, could not counterattack. They tried to stand behind their shields and hold their ground. Gradually, the Roman lines were pushed back toward the edge of the road.

Those closest to the cliff stumbled and pitched over the precipice. Their screams of terror as they fell to their deaths stiffened the resolve of those who remained; they fought back fiercely, driving the Jews up the slope.

Shaul called out to his fellow fighters.

"Follow me!" he cried. "I will break through their ranks!"

Shaul charged, coming face to face with a shorter Roman standing behind his shield. Their eyes locked. Shaul saw fear in the Roman's light eyes. Shaul grinned and shouted and the Roman flinched. Shaul pushed the point of his spear against the other's shield, forcing the Roman backward. He stumbled and fell, his shield on top of him. Shaul stomped on the shield as he stepped over the Roman to force a break in the line and go after his next quarry.

Two enemy soldiers stood by the edge of the cliff. The one on the left had dropped his shield and unsheathed his sword. The one on the right swayed on unsteady feet behind an upright shield.

Shaul jammed his spear against the shield of the man on the right and stepped inside the swing of the other man's sword, shoving him with his shoulder. The man with the shield tumbled over the edge, his screams filling Shaul's ears. The man with the sword also went over the cliff, but not before dropping his sword and grabbing Shaul by the head, bringing Shaul with him down into the bottomless abyss.

Chapter Fifty-Four

17 Oct 66 CE / 10 Cheshvan 3827

"You are mad!" Rabbi Aaron shouted, at no one and everyone, as he walked down a street filled with joyous people celebrating wildly. A man standing on a short improvised podium on one corner loudly declaimed biblical verses praising God to the cheers of those listening. On another corner a woman tapped on a timbrel and a man played a flute as others danced and sang.

"You are all mad!" Rabbi Aaron shouted even more loudly. "All of Jerusalem has gone mad! It is a city filled with madmen!"

The objects of his rebuke looked back at him with amusement. There was no anger on their faces.

"We won a great victory, Rabbi," one them called out calmly. "We are happy. We defeated the Twelfth Legion and the might of Rome!"

"It is only a prelude to our destruction!" Rabbi Aaron cried. He shuddered and quickened his pace. He had to see Reuven.

What especially frightened Rabbi Aaron was that many of those who had opposed war with Rome were now resigned to it. Some of these were even convinced that the victory over Cestius was a sign from God that Rome would be defeated and switched to actively supporting the war party.

They, too, are mad, Rabbi Aaron thought.

Two men were on guard duty outside the house where Reuven lived. They appeared drunk.

"I've come to see my son," he said, expecting an argument in return.

To his surprise, the tall one waved him through the gate saying:

"Bah! Go ahead. What harm can you do now?"

There was no need for Rabbi Aaron to enter the house. He saw his son sitting on a bench under a tree. Reuven's posture signified dejection, not the exhilaration of victory.

"Well," Rabbi Aaron said to his son as he came up to him, "why aren't you celebrating?"

"They let you in without asking for permission?" Reuven shook his head in disgust. "No discipline," he said and then added, "There is much to celebrate, Father. The forces of Cestius suffered a major defeat as they fled from Jerusalem. They lost many men as they went through the pass at Beth Horon. We would have destroyed their whole army if they hadn't tricked us. As darkness fell they camped at the town of Lower Beth Horon. All night long they kept calling out the password so we assumed they were waiting for first light to flee. At dawn we attacked. There were only 400 of them; all the others had run away in the darkness. We killed those who stayed in the camp and went after the rest but they were too far ahead for us to catch them. They left behind their war engines; battering rams and spear throwers. Their equipment and supplies, too. We seized it all. They suffered terrible losses; 5,300 infantrymen and 480 cavalrymen killed. We hardly lost anyone."

"You don't seem very happy," Rabbi Aaron said to his son.

Reuven buried his head in his hands to hide his tears.

"My best friend was killed during the battle at the pass of Beth Horon," he said, stifling sobs. "He was like a brother."

"I lost a real brother," Rabbi Aaron shot back. "To some murderer, and for all I know someone connected with one of your revolutionary gangs."

Reuven looked up.

"Moshe was my uncle, I mourn his loss, too," responded Reuven softly. "And I will find his murderer and avenge his death. But I am also sad that Shaul ben Yitzchak, my friend and my teacher, was killed."

Rabbi Aaron glared down at his son.

"I know your Shaul ben Yitzchak," he said harshly. "He was a thug, one of the robbers who invaded the rabbinical assembly and forced the passage of those cursed Eighteen Decrees. I saw him beat Rabbi Tarfon ben Zadok with a stick."

"Shaul was a patriot! He died for his country and his people!" Reuven protested. He let his head fall back into his hands.

Rabbi Aaron put a hand on Reuven's shoulder. His son did not move.

"That is what happens in war," Rabbi Aaron said gently. "That is what happens when violence is unleashed. The innocent and the guilty are killed. The bad die but so do the good."

Reuven did not raise his head. He did not respond.

Rabbi Aaron looked in the direction of the house. There was nothing stopping him now, nothing stopping him from going inside and telling Metilius what he deserved to know, that his men had been slaughtered even after having been promised safe passage.

Rabbi Aaron gave one last glance at his son and then strode purposefully toward the house.

Chapter Fifty-Five

17 Oct 66 CE / 10 Cheshvan 3827

Fresh blood dripped from Metilius' sword. He marched toward Antonia arrayed in full battle gear. Jerusalem residents, standing alone or in twos and threes, scattered when they saw him striding down the street, his bloody sword unsheathed and held aloft. There were frightened cries of "The Romans have returned!"

Metilius approached a large cross-street. On one corner a man on a short podium was speaking to a cheering crowd. On another, two musicians, a man playing a flute and a woman tapping a small drum, were accompanying dancers moving about in wild, jerky motions.

So preoccupied was everyone that no one noticed him.

Metilius let out a roar and charged. His sword sliced through the air and into unprotected bodies. Men and women fell, dead and wounded, blood gushing from newly-opened flesh. The cheers that had accompanied the speaker's words turned into shrieks of horror as men and women fled from the enraged Roman officer. Metilius pursued them.

"Stop!" he heard a voice cry.

Metilius recognized that voice. It was Reuven.

Metilius turned around. Reuven was walking slowly toward him. Rabbi Aaron was by his son's side.

When Rabbi Aaron had told him of the massacre Metilius was incredulous at first.

"What, on the Sabbath?" he demanded of the rabbi, the full import of what he was hearing not sinking in. Once the reality of the massacre sunk in, Metilius slammed his fist on the table and glared at Rabbi Aaron.

"I knew nothing about it," Rabbi Aaron protested. "Neither did Reuven."

What did it matter who knew what? His men were dead, slaughtered like sheep, and he was ultimately responsible. What a fool he was for trusting their word!

"Get out!" he had shouted at Rabbi Aaron. "Get out! Now!"

"We had nothing to do with it. They were madmen, all of them, and they will destroy Jerusalem."

"Get out before I kill you!" Metilius warned.

He saw the terror in Rabbi Aaron's face before the rabbi ran from the room.

Metilius arrayed himself for battle. The guards outside stared at him with open mouths as he left the house where he had been effectively held captive. They made no attempt to stop him; they saw the expression on his face and started running away.

Metilius was quicker; in a few steps he reached them. He grunted and plunged his sword into their backs, first the tall one and then the short one.

Metilius continued his bloody march to Antonia, his head filled with an agonized series of thoughts: I never should have left the fortress. I should have stayed at my post with my men and defended Antonia, dying there if necessary.

"Commander Metilius, did you hear me?" Reuven called. "These people had nothing to do with the massacre. It was all Eleazar ben Ananias' doing. He no longer leads the revolution."

Reuven's voice brought Metilius back to the present moment.

Reuven had not moved while he spoke but when he finished he resumed his slow approach, never taking his eyes off Metilius. Rabbi Aaron stayed behind.

Reuven stopped when he was about an arm's length away.

Metilius wanted to tell him to take care of Drusilla, to protect her when he was gone. Then he thought of his own children.

Who will protect them?

Metilius said nothing.

"Please, Commander, listen to me." Reuven knelt to the ground and swept his hand over it.

"Are you begging me?" Metilius asked.

Reuven stood up and looked at him calmly.

"No, Commander, I'm appealing to your reason."

In truth, Metilius saw neither fear nor supplication in Reuven's face.

"What good will killing these civilians do?" Reuven asked. "And what will your death accomplish?"

Metilius let out another roar. He began to swing his sword at the boy. Reuven's hand flicked forward and dust and dirt flew into Metilius' eyes, blinding him. He swung his sword wildly back and forth, hoping to fend off the expected attack from Reuven.

None came. When Metilius' eyes cleared Reuven had stepped back several paces, and still regarded Metilius calmly.

"Go back home, boy. Take care of Drusilla." He looked at Rabbi

Aaron. "Who will take care of my children?"

Metilius turned on his heels and quickened his pace toward Antonia. He passed several streets unmolested; people ran at the sight of him. There was grim satisfaction that a lone Roman soldier on a rampage raised fear in the hearts of the Jews of Jerusalem, but he wanted more blood before his own death came.

He soon had his chance. Two armed Jews headed straight toward him. The one on the left held a spear, the one on the right carried a sword. They were very close to each other and stayed close as they approached.

Metilius deflected the thrust of the spear with the round shield in his left hand; with his right he slashed the sword arm of the other man. Then he swung his sword around against the spearman's neck, practically severing the head from the body. Metilius whirled to the man with the useless arm from whose hand the sword had fallen. Metilius kicked him to the ground and plunged his own sword into the fallen man's chest. Then he extracted his weapon and continued his march.

Word of his rampage must have spread because the closer Metilius got to the Temple the more resistance he encountered. There were never more than three men at a time, and each close combat left Metilius without a scratch and his opponents dead. Metilius lost count of his victims. He knew, though, with absolute certainty, that before long enough men would go up against him to seal his own death.

Metilius entered the Temple complex and made his way to the Basilica. From there he went to the roof of the colonnade and walked north along the east section of the roof. He reached the corner and turned west. Halfway he stopped.

There would be no making his last stand in Antonia. In his despair and rage he had forgotten that the section of the colonnade that joined the Temple complex with Antonia had been cut and never repaired.

I will die here, he thought.

A crowd had gathered, a crowd that grew with every passing moment. Some were armed, others not. The crowd fell silent as Metilius looked down on them.

Metilius caught motion coming from the Basilica, three figures making their way along the roof of the colonnade.

Drusilla was in the lead, running. Behind her was Reuven, and behind him was that revolutionary Judah ben Ezra whom he had questioned in Antonia.

Drusilla rounded the northeast corner, clearly out of breath. Reuven was a few steps behind her.

"Take me with you, Commander!" pleaded Drusilla. "Take me with you!"

Reuven grabbed Drusilla, wrapping his arms around her, holding her back. She struggled to free herself; Reuven held tighter. She bent her head and bit fiercely into his arm. He wrestled her to the ground. Judah ben Ezra came up to them. Metilius did not see a weapon in his hands.

Metilius turned to the crowd in the court below.

"I lay a curse upon Jerusalem and all its inhabitants!" he cried. "May Rome and your God burn it to the ground and kill all its inhabitants."

Metilius looked for a moment to the left. Drusilla had ceased struggling in Reuven's arms. Judah ben Ezra stared at him calmly. Metilius thought he saw understanding and even respect on Judah's face.

Judah slowly raised his right arm from his side. He held it straight forward, palm down, fingers touching. Metilius nodded in reply to the salute. Judah let his hand fall back to his side.

Metilius looked back down at the crowd.

"See how a true Roman dies!" he shouted. His voice echoed through the gathered assembly.

Metilius rotated his right hand so that his sword pointed downward. He grasped its blade a few inches below the hilt with his left hand. He took his right hand from the hilt and clutched it over his left hand. Then he threw his head back, opened his mouth, and plunged the entire length of the blade down his exposed throat.

The gasps of horror from the crowd joined the dying echoes of Metilius' curse. Then his body pitched forward and fell to the Temple court below.

Book II: The Eagle Returns

"…these curses shall come upon thee…The LORD will cause thee to be smitten before thine enemies; thou shalt go out one way against them, and shalt flee seven ways before them; and thou shalt be a horror unto all the kingdoms of the earth… The LORD will smite thee with madness…The LORD will bring a nation against thee from far, from the end of the earth, as the vulture swoopeth down; a nation whose tongue thou shalt not understand; a nation of fierce countenance, that shall not regard the person of the old, nor show favour to the young…And he shall besiege thee in all thy gates, until thy high and fortified walls come down, wherein thou didst trust…And thou shalt eat the fruit of thine own body, the flesh of thy sons and of thy daughters…And the LORD shall scatter thee among all peoples, from the one end of the earth even unto the other end of the earth…In the morning thou shalt say: 'Would it were even!' and at even thou shalt say: 'Would it were morning!'"
Devarim #28

"Whom Fortune wishes to destroy she first makes mad."
Publilius Syrus, Maxim 911

Part Three: A Corpse Leads to Romance
November 66 CE – October 67 CE

Chapter Fifty-Six
17 Oct 66 CE / 10 Cheshvan 3827

Reuven glanced down at Drusilla, shivering in his arms, her eyes closed tight, and then over at Judah, whose gaze was riveted on the Temple court below.

"I've never seen anything like what that Roman just did." Judah's voice was full of wonder. He shuddered and shook his head in disbelief. "Never!" he added with finality.

Reuven, who did not loosen his hold on Drusilla, responded:

"What would we have done in his place?"

"I don't know," Judah answered. He laughed bitterly. "Never trust a foreigner." Then he sighed. "There's a crowd gathering around the body. I'm going down to make sure he gets an honorable burial. He deserves it."

"You're right," Reuven agreed. "He does."

"In the meantime," Judah said, "I suggest you get your barbarian girlfriend out of here and take her home."

Reuven hugged Drusilla more tightly as he glared sharply at Judah.

"Please don't call Drusilla a barbarian!"

Judah shrugged.

"No offense meant," he apologized. "These are dangerous times for anyone connected to Rome. And you be careful yourself. The last woman I slept with tried to kill me, and she was a Jew."

"What?" Reuven was so taken aback both by what Judah said about himself and the implication that he, Reuven, was sleeping with Drusilla, that it took him a moment to come up with a response. By that time Judah had swung over the roof of the colonnade and dropped into the Temple court.

Reuven looked down at Drusilla. She was staring up at him with reddened eyes. Her cheeks were stained by tears. He knew she had been listening, trying to follow the strange language of Israel that she did not understand.

Sleep with her? So often he dreamed about it. Not now. He just wanted her to be safe.

"If I let you go, do you promise not to hurt yourself?" Reuven asked gently.

Drusilla did not answer.

"I won't let go then," he said firmly.

A weak smile crossed her lips.

"I feel safe in your arms," she said softly. "Even though I know I shouldn't."

"Don't say that, Drusilla. I will keep you safe."

"Like you kept Commander Metilius' men safe? He trusted you, Reuven." She paused. Reuven shifted uncomfortably. "In the end, Metilius couldn't live with himself knowing that his men died because they trusted him."

Reuven's grasp on Drusilla loosened slightly. Her last sentence, was she implying...

"Does that mean I'm supposed to kill myself in atonement?"

"Oh no, oh no!" she cried in horror.

Reuven sighed in relief.

"Drusilla, I had no idea his men were going to be disarmed and slaughtered. I only learned about it much later. I was devastated; that's when you found me on my bed with tears in my eyes and you comforted me." Reuven's words came out with the rhythm of his gasps of breath.

"What could I have done at that point?" he continued, his voice earnest. "And my friends, Shaul and Judah, they tried to stop the massacre. They were physically prevented from doing anything. All I can tell you is that the man who was responsible for the killing of Commander Metilius' men no longer leads us, in part because I defied him."

Drusilla tried to wriggle free from his arms. His heart pounding, on alert to grab her if she tried to leap off the roof to the ground at the foot of the Temple wall outside, Reuven allowed her to free herself. She got to her knees and looked into his eyes.

"How can I trust you, Reuven? You gave your word to the Commander. You say you will keep me safe now. Perhaps tomorrow or next month, deliberately or by accident, you will allow someone to hurt me."

Reuven shook his head.

"I love you, Drusilla," he said, choking on his words. "I would never let anything happen to you."

She nodded. Tears filled her eyes.

"I love you, too, Reuven. Please understand, Metilius was like a father to me. I'm all alone in the world now."

"You're not alone, Drusilla. You have me."

"And when you're away, as you will be, and I'm alone in that big house?" she asked.

"You're safe there. Guards protect it."

"What guards?" Drusilla retorted. "They're dead now."

"Judah will assign new ones."

"The guards were there for Metilius," Drusilla persisted. "To keep him locked up and keep others, like your father, away from him. Everything has changed now. Metilius is dead."

"I can make sure Judah assigns new ones," Reuven insisted.

"And if you can't?"

Reuven stared down at his hands thoughtfully.

"I'll bring you to my parents' house. You'll be safe there."

"Your parents will accept me, a barbarian girl who was a servant to a Roman commander?"

"My mother is a good woman," Reuven replied quickly. "She'll have pity on a girl who is all alone in this world. And my father, well, my father knows how Metilius was betrayed and knows you've done no wrong. He owes you shelter and protection, and if he doesn't realize that, I'll remind him." Reuven's face became hard and determined. "They'll accept you, all right, I'll make sure of that."

"Do they know what we mean to each other?" she asked.

"Of course not!" His reply was immediate.

"You're still a little boy, Reuven. There's so much you don't know about this world. All your parents have to do is see us together and they'll know."

"Stop calling me a little boy, Drusilla," Reuven protested, obviously peeved. "I ceased being a little boy during my first battle, when I dropped stones on men's heads, when I gouged the eyes of a man trying to kill me… And if not then, when I slit the throat of a man trying to kill my friend Shaul, my friend Shaul who died in the battle at Beth Horon." He closed his eyes and rubbed his forehead. "Sometimes I wish I was a little boy again." He looked at her. "Except that I wouldn't be with you now if I was." He inclined his head closer to her. "If they do see that I love you, so be it. I don't care. They will still give you sanctuary and not throw you out. I promise you that. You will be safe in my father's house. He's a respected rabbi, no one will touch anyone in his household."

Reuven stood up. He extended his hand to help her.

"Come," he said. "For now, let us return to the house in the Upper City."

She took Reuven's hand and stood up. Then she stepped to the edge of the roof and looked down at the Temple court on the body of the man who had been her protector.

"What will happen to his body?" she asked.

"My friend Judah will see that he gets a proper burial," Reuven assured her.

"I must be there for it," Drusilla said with conviction.

"You can't," Reuven replied curtly. "It's not the place for you, not here, not now, not with the current state of Jerusalem. I want you back safe at the house."

Drusilla stamped her foot, tossed her head, and flashed him a determined look.

Chapter Fifty-Seven

20 Oct 66 CE / 13 Cheshvan 3827

It's hopeless, Judah thought. We'll never find Shaul's body.

Reuven walked beside him along the path trod by the Roman soldiers when they were defeated five days ago. Behind them walked Drusilla, leading a donkey that followed stubbornly behind her.

What's going on between Reuven and that girl, Judah wondered, shaking his head. You see Reuven, you see her. It's like she hasn't left his side since Metilius plunged a sword down his throat. She was with Reuven when he helped bury the Roman and now she's with us while we're searching for Shaul's remains.

Reuven was right to insist on looking for Shaul's body—Judah completely agreed—but that didn't make it any less hopeless. There was a huge area to cover, with many dead bodies lying around, almost all Roman. Five days was a long time for a corpse to be out in the open, and there had been a heavy rain since Shaul was killed. Even if they found the body who knew what shape it would be in?

They managed to bury Metilius the same day he committed suicide. When they finished it was too late to search for Shaul. The next day was the Sabbath. The day after, Yom Rishon, the first day of the week, had heavy rain, an unusually early start for the rainy season. Today, Yom Shani, the second day of the week, the downpour had stopped, so they could begin the search.

Early rain, Judah thought. An omen? If so, bad or good?

The road was cleared of the few Jews who had died on it. The Romans had been pushed over the cliff or carted away in those places where the road went between hills on both sides.

Judah glanced back at the girl and the donkey.

She's a tough one, he thought. Reuven better be careful.

"What's going on between you and the girl?" he asked Reuven.

"What do you mean?"

"Looks like she hasn't left your side since her master killed himself."

Reuven frowned.

"I'm her protector," he explained. "She's all alone in this world and afraid to stay by herself. I want her safe. Judah, can we get new guards for the house?"

Judah considered Reuven's request.

"I can assign some men," Judah said at last. "We don't control the house, though. With Metilius gone we have no idea what the new government will do with it but it doesn't seem likely that they will assign the house to just the two of you. The truth is, she'd be better off, and safer, somewhere else."

"My father's house?" Reuven asked.

Judah nodded.

"Yes," he agreed. "He's a respected rabbi. No one will bother him or anyone in his household. Tell me, are you sleeping with her?"

"Oh no!" shot back Reuven immediately. "Of course not!"

Judah laughed.

"Why of course not?" he asked. "Don't tell me, are you still—"

He saw Reuven's face turn red and stopped his question mid-sentence.

"What do you plan to do with her?" Judah asked.

"I want to marry her."

Judah laughed again.

"I'm sure that will make your father very happy."

"Not as unhappy as my joining your band," Reuven replied.

"Is she a virgin, too?" Judah asked, throwing delicacy aside in a sudden burst.

"I don't know, Judah. Or care. I love her."

"Good luck, then," Judah offered.

"Judah, why did that woman try to kill you?"

Judah was surprised by the question and chagrined that he had opened himself up to it by a comment he had carelessly thrown out three days ago on the roof of the Temple colonnade. He thought for a moment before answering.

"I told her I wasn't going to marry her."

"Did you promise her you would?" Reuven asked.

"I made it very clear from the beginning that I was not about to marry anyone," Judah answered. "I guess she thought she could change my mind."

"Was she a virgin?"

"Oh no, Reuven. She was the Whore of Babylon."

They walked in silence until Reuven suddenly stopped.

"Here! Here!" he cried. "Shaul fell here."

Judah walked to the edge and looked down. He could see several bodies but was not able to make out any details.

"There's a path not far ahead that leads down into the canyon," he said. "It's a difficult descent. Do you think the girl can make it?"

"We'll find out," Reuven replied.

The path was steep and twisting, often skirting the edge of a long, straight drop to the bottom. In places the ground and rocks on the path were wet and slippery, in others thick mud made the going difficult. Judah was amused to see that the girl and the donkey had no trouble but that it was Reuven who often struggled to keep his footing, once almost tripping and plunging into the abyss were it not for Drusilla grabbing his arm and steadying him.

As they neared the bottom Judah started seeing the bodies of Roman soldiers. There was no sign of Shaul. A few more steps they would be in in the canyon and Judah wondered if--

Drusilla gave a sharp yell and pointed. Judah and Reuven halted.

The barbarian girl was the first to spot Shaul's body.

They approached slowly.

Judah heard Reuven gag.

"Never saw a body that's been left out for a few days, have you?" Judah asked.

Flies were buzzing around the corpse. Flesh from his arms and legs had been torn away by marauding animals. The skin that was furthest from the ground was waxy and gray. The body was bloated, especially around the midsection. The smell almost made Judah gag.

"Well, let's get him on the donkey and bring him back," Judah said.

The barbarian girl spoke something, slowly and seriously, as if she were uttering a prayer, or a curse.

"What did she say?" Judah asked Reuven. "I don't understand Greek."

Reuven repeated her words with the same intonation and a chill went through Judah.

"This is the end that comes to all living things."

Chapter Fifty-Eight

20 Oct 66 CE / 13 Cheshvan 3827

Rabbi Aaron stared back at his inquisitor.

"The Committee for Public Safety," Rabbi Aaron sneered. "You're only a bunch of robbers and highwaymen."

"Please, Rabbi Aaron, just answer my questions."

His interrogator, who refused to identify himself, smiled. It was a genial smile, not a threatening one, Rabbi Aaron noted.

"Why should I?" he retorted.

It was late morning, Yom Shani. Rabbi Aaron was in a small room in a simple house in the Lower City, a few streets away from his own home. He sat at a table across from his interrogator. Standing along the wall facing him were three armed men. One of them he recognized as the killer who murdered Rabbi Shlomo ben Uzziel at the rabbinical assembly that had passed the Eighteen Decrees.

"Because, Rabbi Aaron," the man in front of him went on, his patience still not exhausted, "your answers will determine if we let you go home or lock you up."

"What right do you have to even question me, much less lock me up?"

"We've been through that already, Rabbi."

And indeed, they had. It was just five days since the stunning victory at the pass of Beth Horon and the revolutionaries lost no time in trying to organize some semblance of an independent government. Committees were formed of prominent and not-so prominent men. And it was not only trusted revolutionaries who were heading the committees: Rabbi Hania ben Avel-Mayim was in charge of collecting and producing weapons; the priest Ananus ben Ananus, whom Rabbi Aaron suspected of not being wholly behind the war with Rome, was put in charge of strengthening the City walls. Commanders were chosen for the rest of the country: the Galilee and Gamla, Idumaea, Peraea, Jericho, Gophna and Acrabata, and the toparchy of Thamna which included Lydda, Joppa, and Emmaus. There was even a committee whose task was to mint coins of the newly free country, a committee composed of business men who had stayed completely out of the political fight.

Bah! thought Rabbi Aaron. Free! We're only free until Rome sends a decent general to destroy us.

He glared at his interrogator.

The Committee for Public Safety was composed of and run by only the most dedicated and extreme revolutionaries, and the enemies they were supposed to combat were not Romans but fellow Jews who were suspected Roman sympathizers and spies. And this man who was questioning him was not even a Jerusalemite! From his accent Rabbi Aaron guessed he was from Idumaea.

"You're not even from Jerusalem," Rabbi Aaron said. "What business do you have here?"

"You're right, I'm not from Jerusalem," the man across the table from him agreed. "I'm from Idumaea. Like Herod, that lackey of the Romans. But I'm no lackey of the Romans. Are you, Rabbi Aaron?"

"I'm no one's lackey, not Rome's nor yours!" Rabbi Aaron responded angrily. "I bend my knee to no one but the Master of the Universe."

"Then you can assure us that you are not a spy for Rome and that you are not trying to contact Agrippa or his Roman overlords to arrange for a surrender?"

Rabbi Aaron laughed.

"Do you take me for a fool? Why would Rome accept a surrender now, after we defeated their Twelfth Legion? No, Rome is not interested in surrender. Their goal will be to punish us."

The interrogator turned to look at the men standing along the wall.

"No!" Rabbi Aaron shouted. "It is not to Rome that I will appeal. It is to the Holy One, Blessed be He, to destroy all you madmen!"

The interrogator turned back to Rabbi Aaron. His voice now harsh, he said:

"You are under suspicion because of your brother's views, because of your views, and because of your son's involvement with the dead Roman commander of Antonia. Your son is also suspected of having a relationship with the servant girl of the dead Roman commander."

"My son?" Rabbi Aaron screamed, unnerved. "My son? I am told that my son is responsible for the victory against Cestius when the Roman governor attacked the Temple north wall. They are saying it is because of my son that the Twelfth Legion was ultimately defeated. How ashamed I am that he has joined himself with you robbers and murderers!" His hand shaking, Rabbi Aaron pointed at one of the men standing against the wall. "You! You! I saw you murder Rabbi Shlomo ben Uzziel. You probably had something to do with the murder of my brother. You defile the Land when you walk free and unpunished!"

John Dorcas smiled slowly.

"Rabbi Shlomo ben Uzziel and your brother both deserved to die. And you will be locked up, tried, and executed to serve as an example to all traitors!"

Chapter Fifty-Nine

20 Oct 66 CE / 13 Cheshvan 3827

When he was sure no one could see, Reuven took Drusilla's hand and squeezed it gently.

Was it for her reassurance or his?

He did not know.

They were walking back together to the house in the Upper City after burying Shaul in the hills outside Jerusalem. A family was walking toward them down the street; a father, mother, and two small children. Behind them a man was driving a donkey laden with a burden wrapped in a leather covering.

People just going about their business, Reuven thought. Do they know what's in store for them? Do any of us? Only the Holy One, Blessed be He, knows what awaits the City and the nation.

Drusilla's voice broke into his thoughts.

"You lost two people who were close to you," she said gently. "And buried them both." She squeezed his hand in return and then released it. After a moment she asked: "What happens now?"

"Tomorrow I bring you to my father's house."

"Why?" she demanded.

"It's safer that way," Reuven insisted. "Even Judah agrees. No one will touch you there. My father is a respected rabbi; all in his household are safe."

"Why can't we stay where we are?" she persisted.

"Even if Judah were to post new guards," Reuven explained, "we have no claim on the house itself. It can be taken away any time. Besides, you told me that you don't want to be alone there when I have to be away."

"I can follow you wherever you go."

Drusilla sounded very determined.

"No you can't," he said firmly, trying to tamp down any expectations she had.

"I was there when you prepared Commander Metilius' body and buried it," she replied heatedly, her pale face reddening. "I was with you when you searched for Shaul. I even stopped you from tripping and falling into the canyon."

Reuven frowned.

"I was there when you prepared Shaul's body, too" she went on. "And when you buried him. I can go anywhere you can go. I want to stay by your side."

"Those were all different, Drusilla," Reuven said. "It didn't matter whether you were there or not. But if I'm called to meetings where secret things are discussed, as has happened many times before, you can't be with me."

"What difference would it make?" she countered. "I won't understand what's being said. I don't speak their language."

Drusilla stopped walking and turned to him. Tears were streaming down her face.

"I can help you, Reuven!" she said earnestly. "I can help you! When you were arguing with your father over Commander Metilius' body I asked you what was happening. You explained that your father wanted to treat Commander Metilius as a suicide. Who convinced Rabbi Aaron that Commander Metilius had gone out of his mind when he learned of the massacre of his men, and could not be considered a suicide because he was not responsible for what he did? Who convinced him, Reuven? You? Judah? No, it was me. I did!" She stamped her foot angrily. "Keep me by your side, Reuven; you need me!"

Reuven gasped at her outburst. But however much she moved him, he could not give in.

"Be reasonable, Drusilla," he pleaded. "You know I can't take you everywhere with me."

"Humph!" she uttered in exasperation, turned from him, and resumed walking.

"You're angry," he called, as he rushed to catch up to her.

Drusilla did not respond.

They passed through the unguarded gate to the house. Drusilla went to her quarters without saying a word but not before giving him a long, sidewise glance, her eyes narrow and her jaw set tight.

Reuven went to his room, physically and spiritually exhausted from the long day. He wanted to rest, to sleep, but felt obligated to first immerse himself in the ritual bath after having handled a corpse. He took off his clothes, wrapped a towel around his naked torso, and walked out of his room. He made his way down the stairs to the basement where he carefully laid his towel on a ledge and slowly walked down the stone steps leading to the bath.

The cool water caressed his body. He closed his eyes.

He breathed deeply and allowed his wandering thoughts to enter and exit his conscious mind, a never-ending, always-changing parade of unconnected images, voices, and words.

"Reuven!"

Drusilla woke him from his reverie. She was wrapped in a towel.

"What are you doing here?" he asked in alarm.

She smiled, as if to say: *What do you think?*

"You shouldn't be here now!" he insisted.

"Make me go away," she challenged, beckoning with her hand for Reuven to emerge from the water. She made a motion as if she were going to remove the towel.

"No!" Reuven shouted. "Don't do that!" In a lower voice, he went on: "I'm unclean because I touched a corpse. I have to bathe in the mikveh and will not be purified until the evening."

Drusilla laughed derisively.

"Aren't you forgetting about the ashes of the red heifer?" she asked.

"What?" Reuven asked, amazed. "How do you know—"

"Your book of Arithmoi," she replied. "You gave me a copy in Greek. It also says you're unclean for seven days."

Reuven rubbed his hand over his face several times and shook his head. He looked down and said:

"From the time of Moses there have been only eight or nine red heifers sacrificed. The rules determining whether a cow qualifies are very stringent, almost impossible to fulfill… We try to make do…" He looked up at her. "Regardless, you should not be here with me, Drusilla."

She allowed the towel to fall to the floor.

Reuven gasped. He had never seen a naked woman before. Reuven's heart beat wildly as he stared at Drusilla standing at the head of the stairs leading to the bath.

She must be the most beautiful woman who ever existed, he thought, overwhelmed.

"What difference do any of your rules make now, Reuven?" she asked, as she slowly descended into the pool of water. "In the end it does not matter. Rome will burn this city and kill us all."

Chapter Sixty

21 Oct 66 CE / 14 Cheshvan 3827

Reuven looked across the table at Drusilla and smiled. He pointed to the breakfast he had spread out before them—bread, olive oil, figs, dates, olives, and dried fish—and said, "Our first meal together. Eat!" Then he smiled again, a dreamy, contented smile.

Drusilla cocked her head to the side and raised an eyebrow.

"Aren't you forgetting something?" she asked.

"What?"

Without saying a word Drusilla rose and left the table. She returned carrying a bowl of water and two towels.

"I read it in one of the books you gave me," she explained, to his look of surprise.

Reuven laughed. He took the bowl and a towel, washed his hands, dried them, and handed the bowl to Drusilla. She, too, washed and dried her hands. Reuven took a piece of bread and was about to take a bite when she interrupted him with a question.

"Aren't you supposed to say a prayer?"

Reuven shrugged and bit into the bread.

"What, are you becoming a rabbi?" he asked, chewing slowly.

"I'm leading you astray, Reuven," Drusilla said, frowning.

"Well, are you becoming a rabbi?" he asked, laughing, trying to swallow the food in his mouth at the same time. "Too bad you're not a man, Drusilla. You would have made an excellent scholar. Probably better than me, I suppose."

"Would you prefer me to be a man?" There was mockery in her voice.

"Oh no! Oh no, Drusilla. Heaven forbid. Though I hear that the Romans do such things."

"The Romans do many things of which you Jews do not approve," she said, nodding her head.

"And do you approve of the things the Romans do?"

Drusilla spread out her hands in a gesture of helplessness.

"The strong do what they like, Reuven. The weak suffer. Their judgment does not matter."

Reuven gave her a sharp look and said:

"The judgment of the Holy One, Blessed be He, does matter. Before Him even the strongest are as thin twigs that break from the trees in the wind."

"I see what I see in the world," Drusilla responded.

"You don't believe the God of Israel exists, do you?"

Drusilla brought the fingertips of each hand together. She stared down at them pensively. It took several moments before she responded to his question.

"I do not know, Reuven. The God of your books makes more sense than the gods of Rome. One God to create everything. Perhaps there is such a God. I do not know. But, Reuven, if that God does exist He is not the God of Israel. If He were, you Jews would not be under the heel of Rome."

"We are free now."

"For how long?"

"Drusilla, you are sure that Rome will burn Jerusalem and kill us all. If you get out of this alive will you believe that He is the God of Israel?"

Reuven could see Drusilla considering the question.

"Yes," she conceded at last. "I will take that as a sign that God is your God."

"Very good, very good!" Reuven exclaimed, rubbing his hands together.

"If you are alive with me," she added.

"No, no, no! Too late for that! You already said yes before you added that condition. You can't go back on your word!" Reuven's eye's twinkled as he spoke.

Drusilla tilted her head and winked at him.

"I will accept your God if I get out of this alive. But if you are not with me I will demand to know why He didn't spare you, too."

Reuven nodded.

"That is acceptable. The prophets often argued with God."

Reuven's face grew thoughtful.

"You know, Drusilla, there's a long passage in Deuteronomion that lists the curses that will fall upon us if we do not follow the Law. If we are destroyed by Rome perhaps it will be because we sinned."

Drusilla rested her elbows on the table and her chin on her hands as she looked deep into his eyes.

"Have I caused you to sin, Reuven? I fear I'm leading you astray."

"I went astray well before I met you," he responded.

"No," she replied. "It's not right. I do not need to add to it. I don't want to do that to you." She paused, lifted her head, and asked, her voice trembling, "Do you consider me wicked because of what we did?"

"What?" Reuven's face scrunched up in confusion. When he grasped her question he retorted: "Do you consider *me* wicked because of what we did?"

"Oh, Reuven, it's not the same!"

"Why is that?" Reuven popped an olive in his mouth while he waited for an answer. It did not come. Instead, after a moment Drusilla turned scarlet.

"Reuven, does it bother you that—"

He did not let her finish.

"Drusilla, I don't care," he said, spitting out the olive pit. "I don't care about the past. I only care about now, and the future." He stood up, reached across the table and caressed her hand. "In my whole life I've never been as happy as I am now. I love you, Drusilla."

She kissed his hand.

"Are you taking me to your father's house today?"

Reuven grinned.

"Let's stay here together for another day," he said.

Drusilla smiled broadly.

"Why not longer?" she asked.

"The truth is," Reuven replied, "we're going to run out of food in a few days. With Metilius gone they're no longer sending supplies." He bounced an olive up and down his plate. "Judah has some income from rich supporters in Jerusalem and the Galilee; he spreads it around to his men. It wouldn't be right for me to ask for any support, though; technically I still belong to my father's household." He sighed. "I am part of the revolution now, so maybe I could get..." His voice dropped; he did not finish.

They ate their meal without speaking further. Reuven grabbed his food and chewed without taking his eyes off Drusilla. He finished eating and then waited patiently for her. When she had consumed the last bite of the fig she was eating he stood up.

"Drusilla, take me to the Garden of Eden again."

Drusilla trembled. She stood, also. Reuven came around the table and took her hand. He was about to lead her away when they heard the clatter of footsteps in the hallway. Startled, they turned toward the doorway.

Benjamin entered the room, breathing heavily. The look of astonishment on his brother's face upon seeing the two hand-in-hand made Reuven burst out laughing.

"It's fine, brother," Reuven said jocularly, "I want to marry her."

The astonishment on Benjamin's face changed to fear.

"Reuven, this is no laughing matter. We haven't seen Father since yesterday morning."

Reuven dropped Drusilla's hand.

"What? Why? Where is he? What happened to him?" Reuven's questions flew out in a rush.

"We don't know," Benjamin answered. "Mother says that in the morning he abruptly left the house. She thinks someone came to the door, but she's not sure. In the afternoon I went looking for him. No one had seen him, no one knew where he was, but there's a rumor that he defected to the Romans."

"That's ridiculous!" Reuven cried. "He'd never do anything like that! He'd certainly never abandon Mother or you."

"I know that, Reuven, I know that." Tears started streaming down Benjamin's eyes.

"When he didn't come home last night," Benjamin continued, his voice breaking into sobs, "we were terrified. We stayed up all night. We fell asleep before dawn and woke up a few hours later. Mother and I agreed that I should get you to help find him."

Reuven stroked the scraggly hairs of his beard as he struggled to determine what steps to take to find his father. He heard Drusilla ask him what was going on; he heard his brother answer for him, explaining in Greek what had just been said.

Reuven worked feverishly to organize the thoughts cropping up in his head.

What if no one came to the door and Mother was mistaken? Where would Father go if he went off on his own? The rumor that he went over to the Romans is absurd. So if not to the Romans, where?

Reuven shivered as his thoughts began to follow their own path.

What if Father has lost his mind from the stress of recent events? He may have gone into the wilderness to pray to God to save the nation. Yes, I can see him doing that! We must search for him! He may not be safe out there.

Then another possibility occurred to Reuven.

What if someone did come to the door and took Father away? To be killed.

Reuven began to shake. He stared wild-eyed at his older brother but said nothing of his fear. He decided to keep that to himself.

Chapter Sixty-One

23 Oct 66 CE / 16 Cheshvan 3827

Three days of torment building to this: Reuven glaring at an Idumaean with no name.

It was late afternoon, Yom Khamishi, the fifth day of the week.

Reuven, flanked on his right by Judah and on his left by Ananus ben Ananus, faced his father's interrogator in the house where Rabbi Aaron had first been brought for questioning. Reuven could not make up his mind whether to be calm and diplomatic or aggressive and threatening, or even whether to leave the negotiations to the more experienced man on his left.

After Benjamin ended Reuven's plan for a leisurely day with Drusilla, he, Benjamin, and Drusilla went to see Ananus ben Ananus. Reuven didn't want Drusilla to come along, but she simply refused to leave his side and be deposited at his parents' house.

At that time, Ananus ben Ananus had no information about Reuven's father; he simply repeated the rumor that the rabbi had defected to the Romans. Reuven, almost at wits end at hearing this again, assured Ananus that his father would never have done such a thing. Ananus shrugged, as if to say it was none of his affair.

The three then went to his mother. As Reuven listened to her recount the events of the morning that his father disappeared, Reuven doubted that someone actually came to the door before his father left. It was a relief to conclude that no one took his father away but that did not stop the worry. It now seemed likely that his father had suffered some kind of emotional or spiritual breakdown and had gone off into the hills around Jerusalem to pray for the City's deliverance. His father alone in the wilderness was not a comforting thought for Reuven.

"Had he ever done this before?" Drusilla asked when hearing Reuven's conclusion.

Reuven looked into Drusilla's clear blue eyes and shook his head.

"But I can see him doing it now," Reuven mumbled.

From the skeptical look on Drusilla's face Reuven knew she thought he was going down the wrong path. Reuven ignored her.

With Benjamin and Drusilla in tow, Reuven went to Judah to ask for help searching for his father.

"Yeah," Judah half-agreed, "he may have gone off by himself the way you say; even if he did, he'll probably just come back on his own."

"He's not safe out there, Judah. My father doesn't know how to survive in the wilderness."

Judah raised his eyebrows.

"Come on, Reuven. What, do you think he's going to starve in a few days? When he's hungry he'll come back. Do you think he tried to climb some steep rock and broke his leg? You're father's not a fool. He won't do anything dangerous. Besides, he could be anywhere outside Jerusalem. It will be almost impossible to find him."

"We found Shaul's body," Reuven responded, his voice determined.

"You saw where he fell," Judah countered. Nevertheless, Judah agreed to help and ordered most of his band to join in the search.

They spent the rest of that day and the next searching the hills and valleys around Jerusalem, starting at the burial cave of his uncle. When no sign of his father was found, Reuven agreed to call off the search.

Back in the house in the Upper City, Reuven had sat with his head in his hands at the table where he had spoken to Metilius.

What do we do tomorrow? he asked himself.

Drusilla came into the room and sat down opposite him.

"Are you ready to listen to me now?" she asked patiently.

"Yes," Reuven said, sighing. He raised his head and looked at her.

"From the very beginning you Jews have been disorganized," Drusilla began. "You still haven't figured out the Roman way of doing things. Jews were fighting Jews; not just those supporting war against those wanting peace; there was fighting within the war party. And you tell me that now there are several committees running Jerusalem, yet there is no central authority in charge. It's very possible that one of the factions took your father, or even one of the official committees."

"In that case he may already be dead," Reuven said glumly.

"No, Reuven," Drusilla replied quickly. "It would make no sense to kill your father. They may be holding him hostage, or trying to force him to support whatever goal they are working towards."

Reuven weighed her words.

"My best move is to go back to Ananus and Judah," he concluded. He smiled, for the first time since the frightening news of his father's disappearance. "You're a smart girl," he said.

"Then keep me with you!" she exclaimed.

Reuven shook his head.

"I can't, Drusilla. Tomorrow I will bring you to my mother. I can't have you following me around anymore. I promise to let you know everything that is happening, and to seek your counsel."

Early next morning when he brought Drusilla to his parents' home she did not protest. It was somewhat awkward since his mother spoke very little Greek. Despite this, Reuven's mother welcomed her new charge warmly.

"Goodbye, Mother," Reuven said. "Please take good care of her. She's all alone in the world." He gave Drusilla a reassuring smile as he left with Benjamin to see Ananus.

Benjamin went with Ananus to the heads of the committees. Reuven went to see Judah, and accompanied him as he spoke to the chiefs of the different groups of fighters.

Judah's efforts bore no fruit. Ananus ben Ananus' did; by midafternoon he found out that a branch of the Committee for Public Safety was holding Reuven's father.

Now, face to face with his father's interrogator, Reuven chose the aggressive path.

"Why are you holding my father?" he demanded.

"We think he's a security risk," came the answer.

Reuven stared at the man. Reuven guessed he was in his late twenties or early thirties. His curly black hair and beard were streaked with white, he was short and powerfully built.

"Why do you think my father is a security risk?" Reuven asked, glowering at the man standing arm's length away from him.

The recipient of Reuven's scowl gave an amused smile.

"Why am I being questioned by a mere boy?"

"Because," growled Judah, "if you get this boy angry enough he's liable to pull a knife and cut your throat."

"Let him try," came the unconcerned response.

"And I will help him," Judah added, smiling menacingly.

"Who are you?" the interrogator asked, clearly agitated now. "You're a nothing, a nobody, the head of some outlaw band. I'm an official of the City administration!"

"Gentlemen, gentlemen, this is getting us nowhere," interrupted Ananus ben Ananus. "What is your name, sir?"

"Yoseph ben Micah."

"Yoseph ben Micah," asked Ananus ben Ananus, "why do you think Rabbi Aaron ben Avraham is a security risk?"

"He refused to assure me that he wasn't a spy for Rome and that he would not try to contact Agrippa or his Roman overlords to arrange for a surrender."

"What?" cried Reuven. "I can't believe my father would be so stupid. Let me talk to him."

"If you wish," Yoseph ben Micah said amiably. "He's being held in the house next door. Come, I'll take you to him."

Reuven followed Yoseph ben Micah out of the house. A burly man, armed with a club, was standing guard outside the house next door. Reuven's father was in a small room with a bed, a table, and a chair.

"Reuven," Rabbi Aaron called. "Reuven, get me out of here!" He embraced his son and did not let go.

"Leave me alone with him!" Reuven demanded, pulling away from his father.

Yoseph ben Micah shrugged.

"No harm in that," he said, and left the room.

"Are they mistreating you, Father?" Reuven asked anxiously.

"Apart from holding me prisoner? No one laid a hand on me, they give me enough to eat and drink, and let me go to the privy when I need to."

"Good," Reuven said. "I'll get you out of here. Tell me, Father, why do you refuse to say that you won't spy for the Romans or contact them for a surrender?"

"Is that what that robber told you?"

"Yes."

"He's lying."

"What did you tell him?"

"I said I wasn't a fool to believe that the Romans would accept a surrender from us after what we've done. And I said I prayed that the Master of the Universe would destroy them, the robbers, the evil ones who are bringing destruction on our people."

Reuven laughed.

"Father, what's the matter with you? Couldn't you just tell them that you have no intention of contacting the Romans or their lackeys?"

"What? I should give in to those thieves and murderers?"

"Did you have to curse them, too?" Reuven laughed again. He shook his head at his father's angry stare.

"I'll get you out of here, Father!"

"How?"

"Don't worry. You'll be coming home with me soon." Reuven

sighed. "This is ridiculous," he added, and was headed to the doorway when his father stopped him.

"Reuven, there's something important I have to tell you," Rabbi Aaron said, his voice so low it was almost a whisper. "Come close to me." Rabbi Aaron waited until Reuven was standing right next to hm. "I know who killed Uncle Moshe."

"Are you sure?"

Rabbi Aaron gripped his son's arm.

"Reuven," Rabbi Aaron said excitedly, "the same criminal who murdered Rabbi Shlomo ben Uzziel at the rabbinical assembly was with the Idumaean interrogator when he questioned me." He paused and added, "That murderer who was brought by your friend Judah ben Ezra."

Reuven sighed with exasperation.

"Father, Judah and John ben Dorcas had a very severe quarrel because of that murder. They're practically enemies now."

"Humph!" went Reuven's father. "Well, listen to me, son. I accused Dorcas of killing not only Rabbi Shlomo but also of killing my brother Moshe. He did not deny it! He said both Rabbi Shlomo ben Uzziel and my brother deserved to die. He as much as admitted it!"

Reuven nodded.

"Yes," he said. "I can believe he did it. I will take vengeance, Father."

"No! He must be brought before a court!" insisted Rabbi Aaron.

Reuven frowned.

"We'll see," he said. "We'll see." To himself he thought: I don't need a court. I will find a way to take my own vengeance.

And then something occurred to Reuven.

"Father, what about that witness? The tall woman?"

"We don't need a witness! Dorcas has confessed."

Reuven nodded.

"As you say, Father," he said. "Let me get you out of here."

Still frowning, Reuven left. In the next house, with Ananus ben Ananus and Judah by his side, he addressed Yoseph ben Micah.

"You weren't completely honest with me. My father did say he had no intention of going to the Romans. He did, however, curse you, which under the circumstances was not the most intelligent thing to do. However, I understand the position of the Committee for Public Safety. I know my father is being difficult, but I can assure you he is no threat. Let me take responsibility for him. I will act as his bond. If he does go to Agrippa or the Romans, I will accept his guilt and you can punish me in his place."

Yoseph ben Micah looked surprised. He gave it a moment's thought and then said:

"All right, take him home. He's probably harmless. Remember, you are responsible for his behavior."

Judah clapped Reuven on the shoulder.

"Good work, Reuven," he whispered in Reuven's ear.

"Don't forget, boy," Yoseph ben Micah warned again, "you are—"

Someone stepped into the room. All heads turned toward him.

It was John ben Dorcas. As soon as he saw Judah he scurried away.

"You will be held responsible for your father's behavior," Yoseph ben Micah repeated, "and suffer his punishment."

Reuven didn't hear these last words. He was listening instead to the voice inside his head saying: I will kill you, John ben Dorcas.

Chapter Sixty-Two

23 Oct 66 CE / 16 Cheshvan 3827

The look on Rabbi Aaron's face was not reassuring Drusilla. Would he let her stay in his home?

Rabbi Aaron had just returned with his son from the house where he was held prisoner. He sat across the table from her. Reuven was by her side. In the background were Reuven's brother and mother. Rabbi Aaron was saying something to them.

Reuven interrupted him.

"Father, please speak Greek so Drusilla understands you. She does not know Hebrew. Yet."

Rabbi Aaron gave his son an annoyed look; nevertheless, he switched to Greek.

"Leave us be!" he said to the room.

Benjamin led his mother away.

"You, too," he said, turning to Reuven.

Drusilla trembled.

Reuven held his father's determined stare. At last the older man lowered his eyes.

"She's frightened and alone," Reuven explained gently. "I'm her protector."

"Her protector? Is that all?" Rabbi Aaron sounded dubious. He turned back to Drusilla.

"Have you slept with my son?"

Don't lie, she told herself, still trembling. Don't lie. He'll know. My best hope is to be honest.

"Yes."

Reuven gasped.

"Did he force himself on you?" Rabbi Aaron asked, glancing at his son.

"Of course not!" Drusilla answered.

"Did he seduce you?" Rabbi Aaron continued.

Drusilla looked straight into Rabbi Aaron's eyes.

"I seduced him," she said slowly.

Drusilla saw the shock on Rabbi Aaron's face.

"Why?" he asked.

Drusilla took a deep breath.

"The Romans are going to burn Jerusalem and kill us all." She spoke slowly and emphatically. "I love Reuven. I wanted to find some happiness before I die."

She saw Rabbi Aaron shudder. When he composed himself he asked:

"Were you a virgin?"

"No."

Rabbi Aaron turned pale. He shouted something at Reuven. Reuven shouted back even louder and pounded the table with his fist. Drusilla silenced them with her next words.

"Rabbi, I hope you have the understanding to realize that a girl in my position did not have a choice in certain matters."

The look on the rabbi's face changed. Sympathy, even pity, showed in his eyes.

"Were you Metilius' mistress?"

"No. He was like a father to me. He protected me from the men in the garrison."

Tears sprung into Rabbi Aaron's eyes.

"He was a good man," Rabbi Aaron said.

"Yes, a very good man," Drusilla agreed.

"We did an evil thing," Rabbi Aaron said. "We drove him to suicide."

"The world is a harsh place," Drusilla said softly.

Rabbi Aaron nodded. He turned to his son.

"What do you plan to do with her? Keep her as a concubine?" There was anger and disappointment in the father's voice.

"I want to marry her, Father."

Rabbi Aaron turned back to Drusilla.

"He cannot marry you unless you accept the God of Israel and His laws," Rabbi Aaron said with finality.

"Father, that's not fair," Reuven protested. "The Herod men married gentile women without making them convert. Only the gentile men who wanted to marry Herod women had to."

Rabbi Aaron turned back to Reuven and shouted something.

"Please, Father," Reuven entreated, "speak in a language Drusilla understands."

Rabbi Aaron looked at Drusilla.

"I'm sorry," he said. "I asked my son if he now holds that vile Herod family as an example."

Drusilla stayed silent. She wanted to ask if the first King Agrippa, grandson of Herod and Mariamme, a descendent of the Maccabees, was also vile, but she held her tongue.

"Do you believe in the gods of the Romans?" Rabbi Aaron asked.

She cocked her head to one side and raised her eyebrows.

"I may be a simple barbarian girl," she replied, "but I'm not a fool."

Rabbi Aaron smiled.

"She's not simple, either!" Reuven exclaimed. "Who convinced you that Metilius was not responsible for his own death?"

Rabbi Aaron, still smiling, said:

"Reuven sees you through the eyes of love, but I agree, you're not simple."

"Rabbi Aaron," Drusilla began earnestly, "if Reuven asks me, I will follow all the laws of his people."

"That would be more than he does," Rabbi Aaron said, casting a disparaging glance at his son. "Tell me, from your answer, it seems that our laws are one thing, our God another."

Drusilla sighed.

"I've read a little of the Greek philosophers," she said. "A few of the Socratic dialogues. And I've read the books Reuven gave me, and will read more. And I'm familiar with the stories of the gods of Rome, and have seen how the Romans, and others, worship those gods, and how these pagans behave.

"Rabbi, I'm no philosopher. Still, I can see that a single God that created everything there is makes more sense than the gods of Rome. I suppose I could accept that such a God exists. But how can I believe that this God is the God of your people? Look how you have suffered under Roman rule."

Rabbi Aaron sucked in a large gulp of air through his nose and let it out of his mouth in a sigh.

"Drusilla, God sometimes punishes His people for their sins. And we *have* sinned."

"You, Rabbi Aaron? You, a sinful man? I find that hard to believe."

Rabbi Aaron looked over at his son and then back at Drusilla.

"God makes an accounting of all His people. The righteous suffer along with the wicked, the innocent along with the guilty."

"Punished for the sins of another? That does not seem fair, Rabbi Aaron."

"The ways of God are beyond the understanding of man. Has Reuven given you the book of Job?"

Drusilla shook her head.

"I will find a copy for you in Greek," he said.

"I will read it," she replied.

Rabbi Aaron nodded.

"I'm sure you will, I'm sure you will. And after you do, please explain it to my son."

Reuven snorted with derision. Rabbi Aaron and Drusilla both turned toward him, Rabbi Aaron with a look of disapproval and Drusilla with an amused smile.

Rabbi Aaron's face relaxed for the first time. He gave Drusilla a warm smile.

"You will have shelter under my roof," he said, "but there must be no immorality in my home."

Drusilla nodded.

"I promise," she said.

Drusilla looked over at Reuven.

On his face she read annoyance and disappointment.

Chapter Sixty-Three

6 Nov 66 CE / 30 Cheshvan 3827

Ananus ben Ananus pointed toward his right. Reuven followed the motion with his eyes. They were standing outside the north wall of the City.

"You see," Ananus said, "how the wall is built to its full height there, while in front of us the wall is considerably lower."

Reuven nodded and mumbled yes.

Why is he showing me this? Reuven wondered.

Ananus turned to face Reuven.

"In every section where the good King Agrippa, fearing the wrath of the Roman emperor, did not raise the wall to its planned height, it is now our job to complete the task. Do you understand, Reuven?"

Reuven nodded again.

"You're probably asking yourself why I'm showing you this," Ananus said.

"I was," Reuven agreed, not bothering to hide the puzzled expression on his face.

"I want you to follow the work as it is being done and report its progress to me," said Ananus.

Reuven's look of surprise needed no words.

"I want you to join the administration of the City, Reuven," Ananus explained. "You will work under me. I can arrange a small salary for you. It won't be much, but should be enough to take care of your personal needs, and perhaps..." Ananus did not finish the thought.

"I'm as confused as I was when you first brought me here," Reuven said. "Why me? I know nothing about the construction of defensive walls."

"I realize that," Ananus replied. "You will be assigned men who know how to build a wall. They will accompany you."

"Why not have them report directly to you? This makes no sense."

"I want someone I can trust, on many levels. You've already shown brilliance, tactically and strategically."

Reuven laughed.

"Are you kidding me, Ananus? What's going on here? Are you trying to buy my loyalty? I can assure you, I have no influence with the rebel chiefs."

Ananus put his hand on Reuven's shoulder.

"What was done to Metilius' men while under truce, on the Sabbath, was a terrible thing. I know how you feel about it. I am no less horrified. I think we see things the same way, even though you won't admit it now. Oh, I know that you killed one of Agrippa's emissaries, and wounded the other. I also know that you tried to convince Judah ben Ezra to allow them to present their offer. It was only after he insisted that you kill them immediately that you carried out his order. But you were not happy about it. No, you were not. I need you as an ally, Reuven."

"What good can I possibly do you, Ananus? I told you, I have no influence with anyone. I'm just a peace rabbi's son who happened to join a small band of rebels. You yourself have seen that Judah ben Ezra pays me no heed."

Ananus grasped Reuven's shoulder more firmly and shook it.

"You're wrong about yourself, Reuven. You are held in esteem by many of the partisan leaders and their men. You are regarded as one of the heroes of our victory; the others are admired for their courage and fighting skills, you for your brains."

Reuven laughed again.

"Come now, Reuven. This false modesty of yours is foolish." Ananus removed his hand from Reuven's shoulder.

"It's not false modesty. It's realism."

"Realism, eh?" Ananus regarded Reuven thoughtfully. "How is Metilius' servant girl? I understand your family took her in."

"Yes. We did. It's the least my family could do after what we Jews did to Metilius." Reuven paused, to let what he said sink in, and then, removing the righteous indignation from his tone, along with any other emotion, he added, "She's doing fine, poor girl."

Indeed she is, Reuven thought. She helps my mother; the two seem to be getting along despite the language barrier. And Drusilla is starting to pick up some Hebrew. In her spare time she's reading the books my father gave her. As for me, she practically ignores me! But why did Ananus ask about her?

"They say that she does everything you tell her to do, that she follows you like a lamb follows the shepherd," Ananus went on.

I wish she did! Reuven thought. Since I brought her to my father's house two weeks ago she has not let me touch her. She behaves toward me the same as she behaves toward my father and brother. My mother is the only one she touches; I have seen them embracing more than once.

"Well, is it true what they say?" Ananus asked sharply.

"What? Oh," Reuven responded, Ananus' question bringing him back to the moment. "I'm nobody's shepherd," he said firmly, "nobody follows me like a lamb."

Bah, Ananus mouthed wordlessly.

And then, despite the fact that he knew he should not ask, despite the fear that Ananus might divine the reason for his question, Reuven did ask:

"What's being done with the house I shared with Metilius in the Upper City?"

"Nothing, for now. I'll let you know if we have to take it back. Until then you can use it as you see fit."

Ananus gave Reuven a sly smile.

Reuven could not stop his cheeks from reddening.

"Tell me, Ananus, do you have spies everywhere?"

Ananus ben Ananus looked Reuven straight in the eye and held his glance for longer than Reuven felt necessary, without bothering to answer.

"What about Agrippa's spies?" Reuven asked. "Did you search for them as you promised?"

Ananus frowned and sighed.

"Shmuel ben Moshe tried to help us find them. He was not able to detect any."

"What happened to him?" Reuven asked, his suspicion aroused.

"He brought his wife and child to Jerusalem. He will suffer our fate," Ananus replied, as if sensing Reuven's suspicion.

"Well, that makes him enough of a Jew for me," Reuven said, his doubts about the convert's husband allayed. "A loyal one, at that."

Ananus folded his arms.

"Will you accept the position I'm offering you?" he asked.

Without hesitating, Reuven responded.

"Yes," he said. "Yes, I will."

"Good," Ananus said, reaching out with his right hand and taking Reuven's arm. "Come, let us return."

They walked together silently. Just before they reached the north gate Ananus stopped, a worried look on his face.

"Reuven," he asked, "did Metilius ever mention a general called Vespasian?"

Reuven stopped mid-step.

"Why?" he asked, his eyes fixed on Ananus, his breath held tightly.

"We have received word that Nero has appointed him commander of the armies of Syria. It is he who will lead the war against us."

Reuven shivered.

"That is not good, Ananus," Reuven said. "Metilius told me about Vespasian. He said that even if we managed to defeat Cestius, which we did, it would only be a temporary victory. Rome will never let us go; Nero will simply replace Cestius with a better general like Vespasian. Metilius assured me that we will never be able to defeat him. And not long ago I asked Drusilla, his servant girl, if Metilius had ever spoken of Vespasian. She said yes, Metilius told her that Vespasian had put down the German revolt and conquered Britain. He was loved and respected by his men; Metilius even thought Vespasian might be emperor one day. Ananus, this is very bad news indeed."

Ananus bowed his head.

"I feared it would be so," he said.

Chapter Sixty-Four

6 Nov 66 CE / 30 Cheshvan 3827

He found her walking on the street toward his house carrying a large jug of water. It seemed almost as tall as she was.

Reuven marched resolutely toward Drusilla and blocked her way. She put the jug down.

"I'll carry it for you," Reuven said. It was a command, not an offer.

He lifted the jug and immediately returned it to the ground.

"Heavy, isn't it?" she smirked.

Her golden hair was hidden under a light gray shawl. Reuven wanted to pull the shawl off so he could see the sunshine that crowned her head.

"No burden is too heavy to bear for you," Reuven said solemnly.

"We'll see about that," she replied.

A wrinkled old woman carrying something on her back passed them, stopped to stare, and moved on.

"Why are you avoiding me?" Reuven demanded.

"I'm not avoiding you, Reuven."

"You treat me the way you treat everyone else in my house."

"No, Reuven. I act toward you the way I act toward your father and brother. It is your mother that I touch and hug. She told me that I'm like a daughter to her." A puzzled look appeared on her face. "At least, that's what I think she meant. Anyway, what do you want from me, Reuven? To lure you onto a bed? In your parents' house? I made a promise to your father and I intend to keep it." Her voice was firm, determined. She added, more gently, "Our time will come, Reuven. Be patient."

Reuven smiled broadly.

"Ananus ben Ananus made me a member of the City administration today," he said. "I'm supposed to inspect the work on the north wall and report back to him."

Drusilla beamed at him.

"I'm very proud of you, Reuven," she said. "Does your father know?"

"You're the first person I told," he answered. "There's something else that comes with that position. The house in the Upper City. Ananus ben Ananus told me that until it is needed by the City, I could use it as I see fit."

"Are you moving out of your father's house?"

It was Reuven's turn to look puzzled. He had never even thought of that. Perhaps he should?

"Because if you are, Reuven," she went on, "I'm not coming with you!"

The vehemence of her response surprised him.

"Your father, and even more, your mother, have offered me a home. It's your home, too, Reuven."

"I wasn't thinking of moving there. I was thinking that we could use it to be alone, that's all."

"A secret trysting place to take your concubine?" she asked indignantly.

"You're not my concubine! I want to marry you!" Reuven responded, with equal indignation. "Is it my fault if you still have questions about the God of Israel?"

"Is it my fault if no one can answer them?" she retorted.

"You don't want to be with me anymore, do you, Drusilla?" Reuven asked, alarmed now.

"Oh, Reuven, Reuven, you silly boy," she said sadly, shaking her head, "of course I do. But as long as we're living under your father's roof we are going to obey the rules he laid down, and to live by the laws of your people."

"The house in the Upper City is a separate dwelling," Reuven countered quickly.

"But we are part of his household," Drusilla responded, just as quickly.

"In my father's house I obey him," Reuven said slowly. "When I am outside of his house I am outside of his jurisdiction. Otherwise, I would have to leave Judah's group; otherwise I might not even be allowed to work for Ananus ben Ananus." He paused, before ending his argument with finality, "The house in the Upper City is outside of my father's jurisdiction."

Reuven stared at Drusilla's furrowed brow; he could see she was trying to come up with a reply. He did not give her the chance.

"Drusilla, I told you that no burden is too heavy to bear for you. I will wait until you are willing, even though it is hard for me, even though every night I dream of you and wake up longing to be alone with you…"

Drusilla took a deep breath. It seemed to Reuven that her eyes glowed with love as she looked at him.

Drusilla flung the scarf from her head and shook her golden hair free.

"I will go with you to the house in the Upper City," she said.

Reuven wanted to sing with joy.

"When I am free from my chores and you from your work," she added.

Drusilla pointed to the jug filled with water. She raised an eyebrow and cocked her head.

Reuven dutifully lifted the jug and followed her to the house of his father.

Chapter Sixty-Five

18 Nov 66 CE / 12 Kislev 3827

One month ago the Jews defeated Cestius at Beth Horon; now Judah was looking forward to another victory against enemies of the Jews. And here was Reuven raising questions and doubts. Judah wanted to slap the boy and tell him to shut up.

Judah hadn't wanted Reuven tagging along on this expedition. He tried to tell Reuven that his sling would do no good in the assault on Ascalon, a three day march south and west of Jerusalem. Reuven insisted on coming, claiming that Ananus ben Ananus wanted him there to report on the battle being led by John the Essene, Silas the Babylonian, and Niger the Peraean. Judah wondered if it was Ananus' orders or Reuven's own desire to take part in the coming fight that caused Reuven to insist on marching with the army to Ascalon.

"Well!" Judah exclaimed, his voice full of enthusiasm, deliberately ignoring what Reuven had just said. "Maybe we'll both get a chance to see the Middle Sea for the first time in our lives. I can almost smell the salt in the air!"

"Judah," Reuven replied, ignoring Judah in return, "Ascalon is walled. There are reports it's protected by a cohort of Roman soldiers and a troop of horse. Now I see that the whole area is flat and open, giving the Romans the advantage. This isn't a narrow mountain pass or a defense behind sturdy walls."

"We've taken Ascalon in the past; we can take it again," Judah countered. He was so exasperated that he raised his hand to strike Reuven and then thought better of it.

"Ascalon was not defended by Roman troops then," Reuven said. "It may be now."

"It may be now, it may be now," Judah mimicked Reuven, mocking him. "Look, it doesn't matter. Romans or not, we have so many men that they're vastly outnumbered."

Reuven said nothing. Judah knew he was not convinced.

"You can always go home if you're afraid," Judah sneered.

Reuven remained silent.

They continued marching, two among tens of thousands.

When he was an outlaw in the Galilee, Judah and his men survived by raiding enemy villages. In Jerusalem he found rich patrons that gave support, but it always helped to find other sources of needed food and equipment. A victory in Ascalon would provide such pickings for his men.

Judah nodded with satisfaction.

It will be good, he thought.

They could see the walls of Ascalon now. Reuven pointed to a small grassy knoll forward and to the right.

"I'm going there," Reuven said. "To observe and use my sling." He broke away from Judah and started running. Judah followed him with his eyes for a short distance and then turned his attention to the wall and the gate of Ascalon that were getting closer and closer with each step he took.

Suddenly the gate flew open. Armed men on horseback streamed out. Their appearance was met by piercing shouts and howls from tens of thousands of throats.

The cavalry charged toward the oncoming mass of Jews. Judah drew his sword.

And then, to Judah's amazement, the lead horseman fell off his mount, as if knocked from the saddle by an unseen force. Judah turned to look at the knoll Reuven had pointed to, and there stood the boy with his sling circling around him.

Another cavalryman, further back, fell from his saddle, but that did not stop the forward charge of the men on horseback. They sliced through the disorganized mass of Jews. The men on foot fell to the flashing javelins of the men on horse. The Jewish forces were split in two as the cavalry rode unopposed through their ranks leaving behind a trail of dead and wounded men in the middle of the Jewish army.

When the cavalry passed completely through, they brought their horses to a halt, wheeled them around and charged again, just as a cohort of infantry poured out of the gate in their direction. The two wings of the Jewish attackers were now under assault from the front and the rear. Jews fell helter-skelter under the double blow of javelins from cavalry-men and swords from infantrymen. They were unable to bring down the men on horseback or break the solid, disciplined ranks of foot soldiers swinging and thrusting their weapons from behind the safety of upraised shields. The hoped-for victory was turning into a defeat.

Judah turned to face the charging horsemen and moved to the left to get out of their way. It was just in time to see one of them coming straight at him. Judah stood there, waiting, as the horse and rider with javelin in hand were almost upon him. At the last moment Judah leaped to the side. He saw the look of surprise on the horseman's face at the speed at which he executed the maneuver. Judah gave him no time to respond. He slashed the cavalryman's exposed side and back with his sword. The man shrieked with pain and fell off the horse. Judah grabbed the reins.

For the first time in the battle, Judah was terrified. It had been years since he had ridden a horse.

He lifted himself onto the saddle and froze.

Don't show fear, don't show fear, he told himself. The horse will sense it. You can do it, you can do it!

Judah gently touched the horse's flanks with his feet. He guided it out of the scrum of fighting men and looked back.

The Jewish forces were fleeing now. It was not a mere retreat; it was a disorganized rout.

Time to leave, Judah thought.

Then he looked toward the knoll where Reuven stood.

Riding toward the boy was a lone cavalryman from Ascalon. He must have spotted Reuven slinging stones from the knoll.

Judah watched, fascinated. Reuven did not move. He held his ground as the enemy rider drew near. And then, when man and horse were about one hundred feet from Reuven, the boy raised his sling and hurled a stone.

The horse stopped and stumbled, lost its footing, and rolled over on its side, pinning the rider.

Reuven had aimed for the horse's head! Judah thought in amazement. Not the rider!

And then something happened that Judah found even more amazing. Reuven took off running toward the fallen horse and rider, his knife held high and flashing in the sun.

Reuven stood above the struggling cavalryman trying to free himself from the horse on top of him.

Reuven calmly put his knife away and withdrew the cavalryman's long sword from its scabbard. Then he raised the sword above the screaming man's head and brought it down sharply on the man's neck.

The sword sliced into flesh. Blood spurted free. The cavalryman ceased struggling. But Reuven was not done. He raised the sword again. His first blow had not severed the man's head and it looked as if Reuven

was attempting to cut the head off completely. As Reuven swung repeated blows Judah struck his horse's flanks sharply and galloped toward
Reuven.

He reached the blood-spattered boy and pulled him onto the horse
as the sword fell from Reuven's hand.

Reuven's eye's gleamed fiercely with the lust of battle. Judah had
seen it in other men before, he must have had it himself many times,
but he had never seen it in one so young. Judah shivered. As he galloped
off toward Jerusalem with Reuven slung across the saddle, Reuven cried:

"Wait, Judah. I want his head as a trophy!"

You're mad, Judah thought. And then, in a fit of despair, he called
out:

"We're all mad."

Chapter Sixty-Six

28 Nov 66 CE / 22 Kislev 3827

The small room in the Temple complex was dimly lit. Reuven had been summoned by Ananus ben Ananus to meet with him and Niger the Peraean. Reuven sat down at the table, facing the two men.

It had been ten days since the disastrous attack on Ascalon. John the Essene and Silas the Babylonian, along with 10,000 men, were lost in that battle. Almost immediately after that defeat Niger led an even larger force against Ascalon and suffered another defeat, this time losing over 8,000 men. Niger himself was trapped in a fort in a village called Belzedek. The Roman commander of Ascalon, rather than attack the fort, set it ablaze. All, Romans and Jews, assumed Niger was killed, but he miraculously escaped the fire to the joy of those Jews still hoping to free the Land of Israel from the Romans.

Niger spoke first.

"You're the boy who lectured us on what you learned from the Roman commander of Antonia."

Reuven nodded. He was in awe of Niger, whose reputation had grown even larger since Reuven first met him.

"And you're the one who stopped Cestius from undermining the north wall," Niger added.

Reuven gulped. Even in the dim light he could see the red of Niger's hair and beard.

"I didn't do it alone, sir," Reuven said.

"Modest, too," Niger said approvingly, nodding his head. "Well, young man, you supplied the idea to stop them, so you deserve the credit." He paused, obviously contemplating something, and continued:

"The victory at the wall propelled our push of the Romans away from Jerusalem, so you deserve a lot of credit for that, also. Now, tell me about your exploits at Ascalon."

Reuven looked at Ananus.

"Go ahead," Ananus encouraged.

Reuven hesitated.

Niger slapped the table.

"Come, boy, no false modesty here. I want to hear the story from your lips so I can judge what else you have to tell us afterwards."

Reuven shrugged.

"I wouldn't call them exploits, sir, especially compared to what you and the others accomplished. I brought down the horseman who led the attack with my sling, and then another one behind him. That's all, sir."

"I heard there's more than that," Niger said.

Reuven shrugged again.

"A cavalryman was charging toward me. I brought down his horse with my sling and then cut off his head."

Niger chuckled.

"Did you take his head as a trophy, like David with Goliath?"

"I wanted to, sir," Reuven said eagerly, "but Judah ben Ezra, who came by on a horse he took from another Roman, wouldn't let me. Judah brought me back to Jerusalem."

Niger chuckled again.

"What a fierce warrior for a scholarly son of a rabbi," he said.

"I'm no scholar," Reuven said quickly, embarrassed.

"I don't know enough to judge you on that," Niger countered. "But you are fierce. I know Judah, he's a good man. By the way, the cavalry aren't usually Romans. The legions draw the horsemen from the local population."

"Yes," Reuven admitted. "I knew that."

"I figured you did," Niger said. "Well, Reuven, let me tell you the reason we called you here. Ananus wanted you to give me an assessment of what you saw at Ascalon."

Reuven looked Niger straight in the eye.

"As soon as I saw the layout of the land outside Ascalon I knew an assault would end in disaster. If there were cavalry and infantry inside Ascalon, as had been reported, the flat, open ground would have given them an advantage over our numerical superiority. I would have called off the attack."

"So you are questioning my judgment as a commander?" Niger asked harshly.

Reuven did not flinch.

"I am telling what I believed and events proved me correct," Reuven said firmly.

Niger tapped the table with his fingers. He turned to Ananus.

"Very good," he said. "You were right, the boy is without a doubt an asset. He sees clearly and speaks honestly. We should include him in our councils."

Niger turned to Reuven. Before Niger could speak Reuven said:

"We should avoid attacks in open spaces in the future. We should fight only from behind solid walls or from heights or in narrow places, as we did in Jerusalem or at the pass at Beth Horon. And we need organization and discipline, the way the Romans do." Reuven paused and trembled. "Above all, we need unity!" he said, his voice breaking.

Reuven looked down at the table.

Will my words make any difference, he wondered.

"Thank you, Reuven," Ananus said. "We will be calling on you again for your point of view on important matters. You may go now."

Reuven nodded at both men and left. Outside, he noticed that he had been sweating despite the coolness of the room.

All he wanted was to go home, take Drusilla to the house in the Upper City, and forget himself in the beautiful maiden from beyond the Middle Sea.

Chapter Sixty-Seven

16 Sep 67 CE / 19 Elul 3827

He caressed her naked body, gently with his hands and then more firmly with his lips. Her eyes half-closed, she basked in his love with soft sighs and delicate trembling.

It would be their last time together until…

Reuven did not know until when.

Perhaps never, he thought sadly. He was beyond fear now.

It was almost eleven months since Drusilla had given him that wonderful gift in this very house, the day he had buried his friend Shaul.

Reuven was nearing sixteen, and in the last few months had shot up in height. He was taller than his older brother and almost as tall as his father. His voice had deepened. Even his beard had filled in. No one took his presence in meetings and councils as unusual anymore. No one referred to him as a boy anymore.

Except Drusilla, when she teased him.

Reuven got up off his knees and looked down at Drusilla. She opened her eyes and looked back at him.

"Do you have to go tomorrow?" she asked plaintively.

He nodded dumbly and then sighed.

"Talk to me," she said.

They had their own secret language now, an idiosyncratic melding of Greek and Hebrew, words and grammar switching from one language to another in rhythms only they could follow.

"I can't turn down this mission," Reuven explained heavily. "Almost all of the Galilee has fallen to Vespasian. Gamla, in the Golan, is the last free city left in the north, and it may be the one place that can hold out against the Romans. Ananus says he needs to know the situation in Gamla; we might have to send men and supplies."

"Why you, Reuven?"

Reuven shrugged and raised his hands in a gesture of helplessness.

"Ananus says he trusts me to give an accurate, clear, and honest accounting. I think it's also because he sees me as his only reliable ally among the revolutionaries."

Drusilla rolled over, pushed herself up, and stood naked before him. Reuven's eyes moved up and down her body.

"Please keep yourself safe, Reuven."

"I will. I promise." He hesitated, then added, "I'll try."

"It's a dangerous mission, Reuven. What if the Romans catch you when you cross the Galilee? What if you're trapped in Gamla when they start the siege?"

"I'll be safe, Drusilla. The Holy One, Blessed be He, will protect me."

"If you return," she cried, her breath coming heavily and her eyes widening, "I will know the God of Israel is real!" Her last words were a shout of affirmation.

"And I will marry you, even without my father's consent!" came his immediate response.

Reuven then shuddered.

"You're the only happiness I have, Drusilla. The only joy in my life. I want to live, because of you." He shook his head and fought back tears. She stepped close and embraced him.

"Talk to me," she whispered in his ear.

He sighed and placed his head on her shoulder.

"Only you, Drusilla, only you," he murmured. He raised his head.

"I look at the City," he said thoughtfully. "It is quiet and peaceful now, but I see faction bubbling under the surface, waiting to boil over. Beyond Jerusalem the Land is ravaged by Vespasian. It is only a matter of time before the City is isolated and Vespasian comes knocking at our gates. Sometimes I feel like I'm dying inside. What can I possibly do to prevent the inevitable?

"And even what is within my power," he went on, his voice now rasping, "I have been unable to accomplish. The death of my uncle is still unavenged. Dorcas is a free man. I asked Ananus about bringing charges against him; he said it is not the time. It would cause too much trouble with Dorcas' allies. I should take my own vengeance! And I will!"

Reuven stopped, squeezed Drusilla tightly, and added:

"Don't Metilius and his men deserve justice, too? Eleazar ben Ananias, though diminished, has gotten away with his crime. Oh, Drusilla, my mind's in a torment!"

Drusilla tilted her head upward, pulled his down, and gently kissed his forehead.

"Come," she said, drawing him to the bed, "we still have the rest of the night before us. Let me help you forget your troubles."

Chapter Sixty-Eight

21 Sep 67 CE / 23 Elul 3827

The smell of the dough was making her nauseous. This had never happened before.

Drusilla's fingers kneaded the dough on the table in front of her. In a corner of the kitchen, Ruth, Reuven's mother, was bending over a pot suspended above a small fire. Occasionally Ruth wiped sweat away from her forehead. The two women worked in silence, as they had every morning since Reuven left for Gamla four days ago. Before that, the two had chatted gaily as they worked.

Ruth was kind to her, kinder in her own way than even Reuven was. Ruth, as a woman, understood things that Reuven could not. Ruth made her feel that even if Reuven were to leave the house, she would be warmly welcomed to stay. For the first time in her adult life, Drusilla felt as if she had a home.

The nausea was starting to return, even more strongly. Yesterday morning she had to flee the house to vomit in the street.

I can control it, she thought. It is just worry about Reuven.

It was three days before their last night together that Ananus ben Ananus had charged Reuven with the mission to Gamla. When Reuven told her about it Drusilla was gripped by terror.

"You could be killed!" she had cried, upon hearing the news. "There are Roman patrols, hostile Syrian towns, even gentile bandits!" She tried, unsuccessfully, to talk him out of it. He assured her he would be safe, that there was no real danger, but she knew, and he knew that she knew, that those were simply brave words spoken to reassure her.

Things have been so happy until now, she thought, as she reminisced about the last eleven months. She and Reuven had gone many, many times to the house in the Upper City.

They managed to go even though they were both very busy, Reuven even more than she. In addition to his work for Ananus ben Ananus, Reuven took part in the military training given to the young men. He also went into the hills to practice with his sling. Once, he took her along. She watched as he swung the sling wide, letting go of the string at the precise point to ensure that the stone would hit the mark he had called out. In the middle of his practice session Reuven had broken into tears as he recalled the friend who had taught him to use the sling.

They always returned home from their outings before dark, except for that last night together before he left for Gamla. At that point, they were beyond caring what his parents thought.

Rabbi Aaron had said nothing about their trysts. He pretended not to notice when they went off together. Perhaps he really did not notice, perhaps he did not want to. But Ruth knew. The first time they went Reuven wanted them to go out from the house separately, but Drusilla insisted that they always leave together. She did not want his mother forming suspicions about her going out alone.

The smell of the dough was overpowering. She almost left to run outside.

Something's been happening to me, she thought.

Drusilla tried to remember when it began, the tiredness, the sensitivity to smells, the nausea.

She stopped kneading the dough and wiped her forehead.

As her mind went back over the preceding days she searched for the slightest signs that something was different, that something had changed.

She stood straight up, away from the table, when she realized that the changes had started before she learned of Reuven's mission. It was not fear for Reuven that was causing whatever was wrong.

Am I really sick?

Drusilla had always seen herself as hardy and strong, and indeed had proved it throughout her difficult life. And now that she had a home and had experienced happiness she was starting to fall apart!

What a weakling, she thought with disgust.

At that moment a wave of nausea overcame her, a wave so strong she could not fight it, a wave so strong it was all she could do to turn her head and vomit on the floor instead of on the table.

Ruth came over to her. There was a strange look on her face; her brow was furrowed with concern but her mouth was smiling.

"I'm sorry, Mother," Drusilla said. "I could not help it. I've been feeling strange lately."

"Does Reuven know?" Ruth asked.

"Know what, Mother?"

Ruth looked puzzled as she stared at Drusilla.

"Don't you know, child?"

Drusilla shook her head. What was Ruth talking about?

The frown disappeared from Ruth's face. So did the smile.

Ruth took a deep breath before speaking.

"So you really don't know, do you?"

Ruth paused once more, before intoning to the astonished younger woman:

"Drusilla, you are pregnant."

Part Four: A Little Town Defiant
October – November 67 CE

Chapter Sixty-Nine
21 Sep 67 CE / 24 Elul 3827

The fire crackled and danced, sending billows of white smoke skyward. Framed by the night of the Golan, his hard features illuminated by the flames, the centurion spoke, and with each word Albus thrilled to the mission that he and the legions of Rome had been given.

"Soldiers of Rome!" cried the centurion, "It is not only for the glory of Rome that you fight. We bring peace to the world. We bring Pax Romana to the barbarians who would otherwise kill each other and themselves. We are saving the Jews from the terrorists and revolutionaries among them. We are saving their Syrian neighbors from these same criminals. We are bringing peace and freedom to the East!"

Albus nodded vigorously. He avoided looking to his right, where his comrade Gnaeus stood, for Albus knew what he would see on Gnaeus' face.

"What could be more noble?" exclaimed the centurion, and he was answered by the shouts of the eighty men listening. All except Gnaeus, who emitted a low growl of anger.

As the shouts died down a strong wind roared through the Roman camp, flattening the flames and making the men shiver.

The centurion dismissed his soldiers. They went off, some to guard duty, others to their tents. Albus walked quickly beside Gnaeus.

"What did you think of the centurion's speech?" asked Albus as they approached their own tent.

Gnaeus spat.

"I suppose you believe his garbage," was the reply.

"He spoke the truth!" responded Albus.

Gnaeus laughed bitterly.

"He spoke lies! Noble! What *merda*! We don't bring peace to anyone! We kill old men and children, rape women, burn towns. That's peace? Tell me, what have these Jews done to us?"

They entered the tent. It belonged to four men, was big enough for two and their equipment, and was used in shifts of two soldiers each.

"The bad ones have rebelled against Rome," Albus said, removing his clothing and squatting down. He lit the small lamp next to him, keeping its light low. He wrapped himself in a blanket and looked over at Gnaeus.

Gnaeus was on his back, naked, seemingly immune to the chill night air that was still making Albus shiver. Gnaeus was staring up at the ceiling as if contemplating something. The harsh wind made fierce whipping sounds against the outside of the tent.

"Tell me, Albus," Gnaeus asked, as if posing a philosophical question. "What are we doing in the country of the Jews?"

Albus did not know what to say. It seemed the most natural thing in the world for Rome to rule.

"We're not doing the locals any good," Gnaeus went on. "Look how many we killed and how many towns we destroyed taking the Galilee. That's bringing peace?"

Gnaeus laughed again, a laugh that was almost a growl. Albus shuddered.

Gnaeus sat up.

"You know who benefits, Albus? Not the Jews. Not even the Syrians. Certainly not us. We work like mules, and for what? To be whipped by the centurions when we break some rule? For 225 denarii a year? After they deduct for food and equipment and everything else, what are we left with? One hundred and fifteen denarii?"

"You're forgetting the three year bonus of seventy-five denarii," Albus said brightly, "plus the discharge bonus of 3,000 denarii."

Once more Gnaeus laughed.

"You won't be getting that bonus, Albus. Neither will I. We're going to die in the town on that opposite slope."

Gnaeus pointed to where Gamla stood on its own peak. He lay down again and resumed staring at the ceiling.

"We're not going to die there, Gnaeus," Albus insisted. "You saw it in the daylight. Gamla is a tiny little place with only a few thousand people in it."

Gnaeus spoke calmly now.

"It's not going to be fighting in the open, Albus. It will be house-to-house where the Jews know the narrow streets the way we know the hair on our balls."

"We have more than 300 artillery pieces," Albus said, trying to reassure himself as much as Gnaeus, "and 7,000 archers."

"Albus," Gnaeus replied, his voice still calm, "that won't be enough to force the Jews to surrender. We still have to enter Gamla on foot to subdue it."

Gnaeus sighed.

"I'm not even sure why we're bothering with Gamla," he went on. "It's not near anything else. It's no threat to anyone. Why don't we just march straight on to Jerusalem? I'd hate to die taking some small, unimportant town. What a waste!"

"Are you afraid, Gnaeus?"

Gnaeus shot straight up and glared at Albus.

"I'm afraid of nothing!" growled Gnaeus.

Albus shuddered again. He knew that was true.

"I'm not afraid to die, Albus. You are, I know that. You never should have joined the service." Gnaeus snorted. "I shouldn't have, either. Most of the time we're not even fighting, but working like slaves."

"Why did you join?" Albus asked, though he had heard the answer many times before.

Gnaeus' voice grew soft.

"I wanted to be a farmer like my father," he said. "I wanted to grow up, be a farmer, take a wife, and have children, just like he did."

Gnaeus' voice became harsh and filled with anger again.

"A rich man stole my father's farm. That's why I joined the army. I thought it was an opportunity. Was I wrong! Some opportunity it turned out to be. An opportunity to die young. You know, Albus, Rome's conquest does nothing for the conquered, nothing for its troops, nothing for its poor or common citizens. We fight and die for the rich and powerful, for the patricians, the senators, the equestrians. I tell you what. Here's what we should be doing. Instead of killing these poor Jews, we should be slitting the throats of our masters!" Gnaeus grinned, and in the dim light his eyes seemed to glow with satisfaction. "Yes, I'd rather slit the throat of a general or a senator any day." Gnaeus chuckled with growl-free mirth.

"That's treason," Albus said. "I should report you."

"Go ahead," Gnaeus said, without any rancor, as he lay down again and closed his eyes. "I don't give a damn."

But Albus knew he would not report Gnaeus. His tent-mate was one of the best soldiers in the legion, and one of the most fearless. Besides, Gnaeus had saved his life more than once. Gnaeus had already fallen into a deep sleep, his heavy snores filling the tent; he would bother Albus no more with pessimistic speech.

Albus turned off the light and lay down.

But he could not sleep. Unlike the peacefully snoring Gnaeus, Albus was afraid.

Chapter Seventy

22 Sep 67 CE / 24 Elul 3827

Reuven caught his breath as he gazed at the sight before him: a magical city, suspended among the clouds. He forgot his exhaustion, and even his aching backside. Early morning mist rose from the ravines and valleys that surrounded Gamla, exposing parts of the house-crowded slopes and obscuring others as the mist moved skyward.

Reuven made an awkward dismount from his donkey. He wanted to pray, to thank the Master of the Universe for such a gift, but no words came.

"Beautiful, eh?" cackled the wizened man on the other donkey.

Reuven nodded, still unable to speak.

The wizened man pointed to the higher slope opposite the city in the sky.

"We better get moving," he said, frowning. "The Romans have already arrived."

Reuven adjusted his dark leather cloak and reluctantly got back on the pale gray, almost white, equine that waited patiently where it had stopped.

Reuven and his guide, Amram ben Gedalyahu, had pulled out of their last campsite before dawn. Amram awoke Reuven from a deep sleep, a sleep full of dreams forgotten at the moment of awakening. Amram had been tasked with leading Reuven safely from Jerusalem to Gamla, and when Reuven's mission was complete, leading him safely back again.

Reuven sighed heavily.

How will I be sure when I have enough information to bring back to Ananus? he wondered.

"Don't worry," Amram reassured him, hearing the sigh. "I know Gamla and its hills and valleys like a mother knows her infant's cry. I'll get you past the Romans." He chuckled. "They won't stay long either; you'll be home soon."

"Agrippa spent seven months besieging Gamla," Reuven replied. Gamla, in the Golan on the other side of the Sea of Galilee from the Galilee region, was in the territory assigned to Agrippa.

"And he gave up!" Amram declared.

"Vespasian is not Agrippa," Reuven responded. "The three Roman legions here, and their auxiliaries and allies, are vastly superior to what Agrippa had available."

"We'll see about that, my young friend, we'll see about that."

The two continued moving north on their donkeys. The sun rose higher on their right, burning away the moving shroud of mist that covered one part and then another of the peak on which Gamla sat.

As Reuven bounced up and down on his slow-moving mount the view of Gamla from the south became sharper.

A sheer cliff stood out in the distance. From the rocky outcropping at the top to the base of the mountain far below was an almost vertical drop. The mountain sloped sharply down on the east and west, with the western slope sharper than the east. The slopes were thick with houses that seemed suspended in the air, looking as if at any moment they could tumble off the slope and into the valley. A wall snaked around the mountain, enclosing the town.

"Gamla seems impregnable from the south, east, and west," Reuven remarked.

"That it is, young fellow, that it is," Amram agreed cheerfully.

"The Romans will never get up that south face, and the east and the west are almost as steep," Reuven added.

He squinted into the distance. There was a mountain north of Gamla on which Reuven thought he could see Roman encampments.

"Amram," Reuven asked, "that rise beyond Gamla, to its north, are the two connected?"

"Yes," Amram said. "Gamla is a spur coming off of the larger mountain."

"So the Romans could attack Gamla from the north," Reuven concluded.

"They can try," Amram replied. "They can try. Gamla may not be impregnable, as you put it, from the north, but the Romans have to ascend a path that's narrow and treacherous from the base of the spur just to get to the north wall and if they make it we have trenches and mines everywhere to trip them up."

"I want to see, Amram."

"You will, you will, soon enough."

They continued plodding forward without speaking, Amram leading the way. When they neared the south face of the cliff Amram veered right, toward the east, skirting the vertical drop. As they passed the eastern slope Reuven looked up and to his left at the jumble of houses that went from the crest to the wall three-quarters of the way down the slope.

Amram stopped and waited for Reuven to come alongside him.

"We'll go up here," Amram said. He gently nudged his donkey to turn to the left and urged it up the mountain. Reuven took a deep breath and followed. The angle of ascent was so sharp that he had to lean forward with his head almost touching the donkey's neck to ensure he would not pitch backward and fall off his mount.

They reached the wall, a variety of stones, some large, some small, piled on top of each other in an almost haphazard manner.

Not like the well-constructed walls of massive stones protecting Jerusalem, Reuven thought.

He guessed that this wall was about the height of a two-story house.

Amram whistled rhythmically. He whistled the same pattern several times and then waited.

A narrow section of the wall moved slowly inward on hinges. Amram laughed at the surprised expression on Reuven's face.

The gate opened onto a small street that went up the slope. Both sides of the street, all the way up to the crest of the hill, were dense with two-story houses.

Reuven passed through the gate and saw that the outside wall of haphazard stones was set against the solid walls of the houses at the edge of Gamla. The bulwark against possible invaders was stronger than appeared from the outside.

What about the north, he wondered.

Reuven got off the donkey. From here on he would walk.

"I suppose you want to see the town on your own," Amram said, as the gate was closed by a stout man with a heavy black beard flecked with white.

"Yes," Reuven replied, handing the reins of his donkey to Amram, who had already dismounted.

"It's still early," Amram said. "Around midday come to the north tower. There's a large plaza in the front. I'll have some of the town leaders there to meet with you."

"Thank you, Amram. Thank you for getting me here safely."

"And I'll get you back safely, whenever you want to leave," Amram assured him.

Reuven removed the two saddle bags that had been on his donkey and slung them over his own shoulders. He followed the street up to the crest of the hill.

A wider street ran along the crest in a north-south direction. To the left Gamla rose to a high rocky outcropping. To the right the street sloped downward in a northerly direction, ending at a round tower. Reuven walked higher up the hill to get a better view of the northern edge of the town. In front of the tower was a large, open plaza. Just north of the tower was the city wall. From the wall the ridge of Gamla slanted down to a neck where it was joined to the larger mountain. On that mountain Reuven saw Roman camps. Soldiers were moving up and down between the camps and the neck.

Reuven walked further up the street, to its end at the rocky outcropping. It was large, large enough to hold perhaps one or two hundred men. In the distance, past the hills and valleys of the lower Golan, he could see the Sea of Galilee. Reuven went right up to the edge and looked down.

He turned his head and stepped back. The vertical drop and its distance to the ravine below made him dizzy.

Reuven sighed. He had several hours in which to tour Gamla before he met its leaders.

Reuven walked and walked. He did not stop to speak to any of the people that he saw. Men, women, children; the young and the elderly, rich and poor; all seemed to go about their business without a care in the world, as if the Roman host on the opposite peak had nothing to do with them.

Yes, there were rich and poor in Gamla, though none as rich as the rich in Jerusalem. There was a section of Gamla where the well-to-do clearly lived, though their homes were in no way as luxurious as the luxurious homes in Jerusalem. There were also sections of more modest homes, and on some of the open areas of both slopes Reuven even saw tents. During the journey Amram had told him that normally Gamla had a population of about 20,000, but that refugees fleeing Roman depredations in the north, as well as revolutionaries from defeated cities, had swelled the population. Reuven assumed that the tents were occupied by the refugees.

The Gamla streets that ran parallel to the ridge were straight and leveled-out. They were connected by steep alleys and stairs; some were wide, others were narrow; some were straight and others were twisted and turned back on themselves. The open areas of Gamla, in addition to the tents of refugees, held grazing cattle.

On the eastern slope not far from the ridge Reuven stopped to gaze at a flour mill where a workman was busy at the heavy round stones of the mill. A series of steps led down to another level where through a double archway Reuven saw an olive oil press.

It was almost noon when Reuven reached the northern end of Gamla. The plaza in front of the tower held a market area, with stalls selling everything from food to cloth, an inn with tables set under a wooden canopy, a public latrine in a closed building and a fountain outside it to wash. Reuven used the latrine which he found to be fairly clean. He stepped out and washed his hands in the fountain and then sat down at a table in the inn. He lifted the bags from his shoulders and placed them beside him.

A boy several years younger approached to take Reuven's order. He had freckles and straight hair that refused to stay flat on his head. The boy laid a pitcher of water down on the table.

"Fresh from our spring," he said.

Reuven was hungry. He asked for bread, rice, soup with lentils, chickpeas, and onions, goat cheese, and grapes and figs. Then he reached into one of the bags and pulled out two coins, a silver denarius and a newly-minted half-shekel from Jerusalem.

The boy's smile grew wider and wider as he stared at the Jerusalem coin.

"A coin of freedom!" he declared.

Reuven flipped the coin to him. The boy snapped it out of the air and left to bring Reuven his order.

When Reuven finished eating he sauntered around the market area. Then he examined the wall. It, too, was constructed of a variety of stones fitted together in an almost random manner.

The wall was strong enough to support the five men standing on the rampart gazing north, but one or two blows from a Roman battering ram would be enough to break a huge opening in it.

Reuven shook his head with disappointment.

He climbed the spiral staircase on the outside of the round tower. Two watchmen were on top, staring north. They gave Reuven a brief glance and returned to their watch.

The way to Gamla from the north was treacherous; the steep snake path, the ditches, and the mines whose presence would not be noticed by troops on a run toward the city.

It would stop the forces of Agrippa, Reuven thought, but not the Romans, with their engineers and war machines.

And indeed, the Romans had made progress since the morning.

Reuven was amazed how quickly they had brought up their rams and catapults and ballistae. Platforms were being constructed, platforms that had not been started when Reuven had earlier looked down from that high point in the south.

Reuven pulled at his beard and frowned.

The men of Gamla are not trying to hinder their work, he thought anxiously. Are they so sure of their defenses?

Reuven made his way down from the tower. Amram ben Gedalyahu was in the square. Seven men were with him.

Reuven walked over to them. He did not wait for Amram to introduce him.

"I am Reuven ben Aaron. Ananus ben Ananus, the head of the government in the capital of Jerusalem sent me." Not quite true, Reuven thought, as soon as he finished speaking. There is no head of a government in Jerusalem.

The men around him nodded.

"I am to report back on the situation in Gamla," Reuven continued, "and also find out what your needs are."

"We have enough fighting men," one said. "And water from a spring inside the city walls. They only thing we may need is food, if our supply from the countryside is cut off."

It will be, Reuven thought, as the others around the man who spoke nodded in agreement.

"What do you think of our situation?" another called out.

How do I tell them it's hopeless? Reuven wondered. He remained silent, trying to think of what to say that would force them to face reality but would not at the same time totally destroy their morale.

A trumpet blast sounded outside the city's wall. A man on the rampart shouted, his voice full of sarcasm:

"It is our king, Agrippa II! And he is surrounded by his retinue!"

A voice from beyond the wall called out:

"King Agrippa wishes to discuss the terms of your surrender!"

The men around Amram laughed. Amram did not. His eyes were fixed on Reuven, looking for his reaction.

"You should find out what the terms are," Reuven said, in a low voice, looking down at the ground. "If they are acceptable, agree. If not, bargain for better terms. The Romans would prefer a bloodless victory."

Reuven silently cursed Eleazar ben Ananias; Vespasian had Agrippa, the Jews could have had Metilius advising them if not for the mad

Temple captain.

"Why should we surrender?" one of the men asked. "They'll never take Gamla! We're like Jerusalem; impassable ravines on three sides and a strong wall on the other."

"You are not like Jerusalem," Reuven explained, trying to be patient. "Jerusalem's walls are solid stone with a strong foundation. Your wall will collapse under their battering rams. Jerusalem has thousands of thousands of people, Gamla has only thousands."

"What do you know, coward?" one of the men taunted. "Why should we listen to you?"

Reuven gave a quick glance at Amram and was about look down again and reply when he noticed Amram was very fidgety, barely standing in one place as his arms and body jerked from side to side.

Reuven stared at each man in turn.

"I fought in three battles against the Romans. The first was at the north wall of the Temple. They worked for hours trying to undermine that wall and accomplished nothing. I am the one who got the stones to drop down on them. That drove them away, that started their retreat from Jerusalem. And I was at the battle of Beth Horon, where once again we were victorious. But I was also there at Ascalon, where we were de—"

Reuven did not get the chance to finish. A wild whooping came from the rampart.

"I got him! I got him with my sling! I hit Agrippa on the elbow. They're all running away like scared rabbits!"

The whoops of others joined in.

Reuven's face fell.

Amram sidled up to him and whispered in his ear.

"Do you want to leave now?" he asked, his voice trembling. "I can take you back."

"Wait," Reuven said.

"How long will your supply of food last without replenishment?" Reuven asked the men around him.

"A month or two," was the answer.

Reuven nodded.

He knew all he needed to know. Gamla did not stand a chance and would be occupied in a month. It was time for him to leave and report back to Ananus.

Reuven turned to Amram.

Amram ben Gedalyahu was nowhere to be found.

Chapter Seventy-One

23 Sep 67 CE / 25 Elul 3827

Fierce Jewish resistance from the wall of Gamla—a barrage of spears, arrows, and rocks—forced Albus, sweating heavily, to retreat. Along with the rest of his comrades he ran back down to the saddle joining the hill of Gamla to the larger mountain to its north. The jeers of the Jewish defenders rang in his ears.

The day after the centurion's speech Albus had worked furiously all day and into the night to prepare for the invasion of Gamla. He was part of the huge enterprise carried out by the three legions under Vespasian's command: Gamla's defensive ditches were filled and her artfully hidden mines discovered and plugged. An earthen ramp was built up to the wall. The three battering rams plus the platforms to hold the bowmen, slingers, and light artillery were mule-dragged to the foot of the ramp.

But now, this morning, they could go no further. The platforms and the rams remained where they were; the hail of Jewish missiles prevented the troops from bringing their war machines up to the wall.

Albus wiped the sweat off his brow. From his vantage point the southern edge of Gamla with its high outcropping looked like a hump; Gamla's hill reminded him of a camel.

I'd like to chop off its head, Albus thought, licking his lips.

Gnaeus stood next to him. Albus noticed that Gnaeus was not sweating; he was looking calmly at Gamla.

"Our heavy artillery will get them off the wall," Gnaeus said confidently. "It's a good thing it's not the rainy season yet; with wet cords the ballistae might not work properly."

Gnaeus walked over to a nearby ballista. Albus followed.

The artillerymen who worked the ballista, and in particular the man in charge, were specially trained. Albus suspected that they were paid more than a regular infantryman. Each legion had ten ballistae.

To Albus, the ballista was a complicated machine. He saw a wood and metal frame that consisted of two parts. The first part, a long and narrow wooden box parallel to the ground, contained a movable track. The rear of the track had a rope that was wrapped around a cylinder. A large lever on the cylinder could be pulled to tighten the rope, making the track move backward.

A wire looped around a metal safety-latch on the track connected the first part of the ballista assembly to the second part. This second part was composed of two identical upright sections: Wooden housing holding a twisted cord of skins through which passed a long wooden stake that was horizontal to the ground. The stake was attached to an end of the wire.

When the ballista operator pulled the lever, causing the track to move backward, the wire tightened, increasing the twisting, and hence tension, in the cords. It was the tension in the cords that provided the ballista's power to shoot missiles.

The safety-latch had a trigger mechanism. A stone placed on the track inside the wire loop was ready for launching. Pulling the trigger freed the wire and released the tension in the cords, firing the missile.

The ballistae shot stones that ranged in diameter from four to eighteen inches and weighed from one and a half pounds to 100 pounds. They had a maximum range of 1200 feet. They were highly accurate; Albus had seen skilled artillerymen pick off individual defenders during sieges.

Other artillery pieces were catapults that shot lances. While the artillerymen worked to get their weapons ready, the infantry and their allied forces waited.

"It won't be long," Gnaeus said.

Gnaeus was right.

The artillery units reported ready shortly after he spoke. Vespasian gave the order to begin firing.

All at once the sky was filled with stones and arrows flying toward the defenders on Gamla's wall. Albus watched as many hit their mark and felled men perched bravely on the wall. Another volley followed, and more men fell. By the time a third was launched the Jewish fighters had retreated into the town.

Shouts of victory came from Roman and Syrian throats. The platforms and rams were brought up to the wall, along with the infantry.

The battering ram was a huge log with a lump of iron, shaped like a ram's head, at its end. This log was suspended by ropes from another stout log supported by a metal frame. Albus helped pull the log with the ram's head backward before releasing it to crash against the wall, which shook at the pounding. At the next blow, the wall shuddered and some of its stones knocked off, leaving a large gaping hole. With the blaring of trumpets and cries of war Roman infantry poured through the breach in Gamla's wall.

As he passed through, Albus saw that the other two rams had achieved the same effect.

At first the Jews put up stiff resistance to the Roman incursion, but gradually, it seemed, the defenders were overwhelmed by the onslaught and forced to retreat deeper into Gamla. Albus and Gnaeus moved along with their advancing columns. Suddenly Gnaeus stopped.

Albus stopped, too.

"What's wrong?" he asked.

Gnaeus looked wary, not frightened.

"I smell a rat," he said. "Something's wrong. The Jews are retreating too easily. It's a trap. We'll be caught in the narrow streets." Gnaeus paused. "We should be securing the initial area first. Where are the commanders? We shouldn't be rushing in helter-skelter!"

Albus looked around at the nearby houses. Then he licked his lips. Albus had caught sight of a female form.

He rushed toward the house. A wounded Jewish fighter lay at the doorway just outside, moaning in pain. Albus stepped over the wounded man, his eyes fixed on the girl who had been ministering to him. At Albus' approach she backed away, into the house. The girl, of perhaps fifteen, was dirty and covered with blood.

Albus entered. He grinned and moved toward the girl. She was trapped against the wall with no way to escape.

Albus' grin became broader.

"I won't hurt you," he said, "no, it won't hurt, as long as you don't struggle."

"Leave her alone!"

Albus recognized the growl.

"I won't be long, Gnaeus."

"I'm not telling you twice!" Gnaeus said threateningly.

Albus turned from the girl, whispering, "I'll be back, darling." He looked at Gnaeus as he stepped over the wounded Jew. There was a look of contempt on Gnaeus' face. Albus shrugged.

Gnaeus walked over to the Jew on the ground, who was moaning and writhing with pain.

"Poor devil. It would be a kindness to put him out of his misery," he muttered. Gnaeus stepped over the man on the ground and drove his sword deep into the man's chest. There was a spurting of blood, more writhing, then stillness, broken by the girl's scream of horror.

Gnaeus removed his sword.

"Come on," he said to Albus, shaking his head with resignation, his voice rich with dry irony. "I guess we have no choice but to follow our comrades into the trap."

"Perhaps we can stay here and see how things develop," Albus offered.

"You want to go back inside to rape the girl?" Gnaeus sneered. "No, Albus, we're soldiers of Rome in the middle of a battle. Follow me, into the fray!"

Albus dutifully followed Gnaeus. Along with the rest of the invasion force, they chased the retreating Jews, moving south, up the main street that ran along the ridge of Gamla. With each passing step they went deeper into the town. As the pursuit grew hotter the Jewish fighters began to melt into the alleys and stairways of the east and west slopes.

Albus, Gnaeus, and two dozen others barreled down a steep stairway after a group of armed, fleeing Jewish fighters. The hill was so steep that the houses on both sides seemed piled on top of those further down the slope; so steep that a man could leap from the stairway to the roof of a house on a lower level.

Albus heard Gnaeus curse and mutter something about their forces being scattered now. Was Gnaeus' prediction of disaster correct? How could that be? The Jews were totally on the run without even the pretense of resistance.

Albus soon had his answer.

Gnaeus shouted, "Here it comes!" just as the most terrifying screams came from right and left. Jews streamed from the buildings on both sides of the stairway. They were armed with swords, spears, and clubs, wielding them with deadly efficiency. In response, the outnumbered Romans turned their backs to each other to face the Jewish fighters on either side. At that moment the Jews who had been chased by the Romans turned around and charged up the hill. Now the Romans were assaulted on three sides.

Gnaeus pointed to a roof and shouted, "There!"

Besieged Romans leaped onto the roof and formed a protective circle.

Albus tensed for the leap. His foot slipped and he rolled down several steps, his sword escaping from his hand.

A tall, bearded Jew jumped to his side and grabbed the fallen sword. Albus thought that the Jew looked less like a local and more like a young rabbi, except that his face gleamed with hatred and his eyes glowed with the lust for battle, as if he were a Roman. Albus raised his shield to protect himself from the inevitable downward thrust.

The blow bounced off his shield. Albus' relief vanished when a kick wrenched the shield from his hands. The Jew raised the sword again, and Albus saw that the Jew was preparing to lop off his head.

Filled with terror, Albus tried to wriggle away.

He heard a loud growl and now saw fear in the Jew's eyes.

Gnaeus was coming to the rescue, shield and sword raised.

The Jew swung his sword around his head in a circle and flung it at Gnaeus, stopping the latter's advance. In that moment, the Jew retreated and disappeared. Gnaeus, easily fighting off the men trying to attack him, pulled Albus to his feet. Albus quickly grabbed his sword and shield. Together they leaped to the roof. The remaining Romans joined them. Albus could feel the roof starting to give way. For a moment he froze, not sure what to do. As the roof fell in, he jumped back onto the stairway. Only a few Romans were able to follow.

Not Gnaeus. Not most of the other Romans.

The collapsing roof brought down the rest of the house. Its ruins tumbled down the slope, flattening the house below.

The screams of the dying men filled Albus' ears. Chills ran up and down his body as he heard Gnaeus' deep voice among them.

The collapse of the houses left the Jews open-mouthed. It was enough time for the Romans who had leapt free to collect their wits and link shields to fight their way through the mass of Jews who had been besieging them. The Romans ran up the stairs and turned left, fleeing northward along the ridge of Gamla to the safety of the breach in its walls and the Roman camp beyond.

Albus caught sight of other groups of soldiers running north to safety.

Even without a count, Albus knew that the incursion deep into Gamla had been a disaster.

Chapter Seventy-Two

24 Sep 67 CE / 26 Elul 3827

The disorder in his own mind contrasted sharply with the orderly arrangement of the Roman camp on the opposite hill. He stood in the circular tower at the north end of Gamla and looked around. Questions were coming at him one after the other.

What would the Romans do next?

What should he do next?

What was happening to him?

This last question vexed Reuven more than the other two, but it would have to be dealt with later.

It was the morning after the Roman attempt to take Gamla, Reuven's second day in the city. Jewish fighters manned the wall and the gaps in the wall. Just outside the city stood the burned hulks of the war machines that the Romans had been unable to drag away. For the Jews the results of yesterday's battle were the three breaches in the town's walls, many collapsed houses, and some Jewish dead and wounded. For the Romans it was many, many dead, as well as the destroyed platforms and rams. The scene Reuven had witnessed was repeated all over Gamla. Roman soldiers, drawn into the warren of houses deep in the city, were overwhelmed by the Jewish defenders who knew the town. It was a humiliating defeat for the Roman legions, reminiscent of the battle at the pass of Beth Horon.

The differences between the positions of Jerusalem and Gamla were stark, but their similarities were intriguing.

What would the next Roman move be? Offer terms once more, giving the town another chance to surrender? Or would they gather their forces and conduct another assault, this one better planned and more likely to succeed? The Roman response to the initial defeat in Gamla might reveal what they would do if they suffered initial reverses at Jerusalem.

This led to his next question: What should he do?

Reuven had wanted to leave the day he arrived. Amram's disappearance postponed that. A search of the town and thorough inquiries led to the same result: Amram had simply vanished. No one had seen him. The tiny house where he lived alone was empty. His two donkeys were gone. It was now assumed that he fled Gamla before yesterday's battle.

Would he return?

Reuven was hesitant about going back to Jerusalem by himself. He had a general idea of its direction, and remembered some of the landmarks on the way. It could be done, but would not be easy.

Amram was not the only one leaving Gamla. Others were fleeing, stealthily. They did not want to arouse the suspicions of their neighbors and be accused of being traitors or cowards.

Where were they going? Jerusalem? Could he travel with a group heading there? Would the risk of being caught by the Romans be greater with others not as adept as Amram? Would he be safer alone?

The questions around leaving Gamla, however, did not involve him alone. There was another important factor to consider. The Roman response at Gamla would be vital information for Ananus ben Ananus and the other leaders. It would enable them to make the right decisions when the Romans finally arrived at the gates of Jerusalem.

It's decided, Reuven thought. I stay, for now.

Reuven sighed and climbed down from the tower. He walked aimlessly around a town that had almost returned to normalcy now that the Roman threat had receded.

The change that had come over him in the last year disturbed Reuven deeply. He was still terrified by combat but at the same time exhilarated by it. Reuven experienced thrilling waves of hate, and the overwhelming desire to kill his Roman and Syrian enemies. Worse yet, a kind of barbarity had entered his soul. Yesterday he was about to cut off a Roman's head. All that stopped him was another Roman who rescued his fallen comrade. At Ascalon, he wanted to cut off the head of the cavalryman he had brought down. He would have taken his head home as a trophy if Judah had not stopped him!

Were his father and uncle right all along, that violence consumed those who embraced it?

Reuven stopped in the middle of the street.

He did not know the answer.

Perhaps I do not want to know, he thought.

The growl and the face of the Roman soldier who saved his fallen comrade remained with Reuven. Though everything external in appearance was different, that Roman soldier reminded Reuven of Judah. Was he as sure of the cause for which he fought as Judah was of his? Was he basically a good man caught up in circumstances that he could not control?

Reuven sighed again and shook his head.

He noticed a tall, willowy girl with long brown hair standing not far away.

The girl was staring at him.

She's very tall, he thought.

And then he remembered the tall woman who was a witness at his uncle's murder.

Could that be her? he wondered.

He caught himself.

"That's an insane idea," he muttered.

The girl came up to him boldly.

"I hear you're from Jerusalem," she said eagerly. She did not smile.

"Yes," he replied.

The girl nodded.

"I know Jerusalem is a big city," she said hesitantly, "a very big city. Perhaps…" She paused. To Reuven it seemed she was unable to continue.

"My name is Reuven," he said, hoping to coax out of her whatever she wanted to ask. "I was sent here by Ananus ben Ananus, the leader of the revolution, to gather information and report back to him. What's your name?"

"Dvorah."

Reuven turned pale.

"Perhaps, perhaps…" she began, and hesitated again. "There is a boy from around here that I was supposed to marry. He joined the freedom fighters who went to Jerusalem."

Reuven trembled.

"His name is Shaul ben Yitzchak," Dvorah continued. "I know how big Jerusalem is, but he's easy to notice. He's very tall and handsome."

Reuven was crying now, openly. He could not control his tears.

Should he tell her the truth? Should he lie and say he did not know Shaul?

"Why are you crying?" Dvorah asked sharply. "Oh no, oh no!" she wailed. "My Shaul, what happened to my Shaul?"

Reuven tried to stop the tears and stifle his sobs.

"He was like my brother," Reuven said. "He was my best friend. He taught me how to use the sling, how to become a fighter. He saved my life."

Dvorah straightened her posture. Her face was composed, dignified.

"Tell me how he died," she said softly.

"At the battle of Beth Horon," Reuven said somberly. "I was with him. He killed several Romans. One of them pulled Shaul over a cliff with him." Reuven took a deep breath. "We found his body and buried him. Dvorah, your Shaul died a hero."

Dvorah nodded gravely, her face and eyes hard as stone.

"Thus will I die," she said solemnly.

Chapter Seventy-Three

19 Oct 67 CE / 22 Tishrei 3828

The thirst for revenge scorched his insides. Albus' mouth remained dry no matter how much water he drank.

Soon that thirst would be slaked. Rome would repay those perfidious Jews for the humiliating defeat they inflicted twenty-six days ago.

Albus worked silently as he painstakingly dug away the earth from underneath one of the stones that formed the base of Gamla's tower. The tower had no foundation; once enough stones were removed it would come crashing down. Two men worked beside him on their own stones. It was still dark; they had been working since the heart of night. Albus gripped the long handle of his tool with such force that his fingers hurt.

We will have our revenge, he thought. And I will have mine for the death of Gnaeus. We will kill every man, woman, and child once we take the town.

Albus knew Gnaeus would not approve. Gnaeus would say that they lost in a fair fight. The Jews simply outsmarted them.

But Gnaeus, the honorable man, was dead.

He, Albus, was alive.

The dead did nothing. It was the living who decided and acted.

Albus had grown impatient during the intervening twenty-five days. The Jews had been allowed to carry on life in the town undisturbed. Oh, there was one other attempt, half-hearted, to attack Gamla, but when the defenders displayed unexpectedly strong resistance the attack was called off. The strength of that resistance surprised the leadership, who thought the town had been weakened by hunger and defections.

Jews, the wise ones, Albus thought, had started abandoning Gamla the day after the Roman defeat. The Romans were unable to put an unbroken ring around the town because of its geography. They posted sentries wherever they could and occupied the hill that overlooked Gamla. Jews who made the difficult trek down the steepest ravines where no sentries were posted were able to flee unmolested. Those who came directly to the Roman camp to surrender were, after questioning, allowed to go on their way.

Jews who fled Gamla while trying to evade the Romans but who did not take the most difficult route met a different fate. All captured males above military age were put to death. The rest were imprisoned, later to be sold as slaves.

All who remained in Gamla, thought Albus, will fall to the sword.

Something bit his neck and Albus slapped loudly at the unseen insect. Then he winced at the sound he made, and sensed the anger of the other two men whose position he may have given away by breaking the silence.

The three stopped working and waited. Anxiety rose in Albus; his carelessness may have caused the mission to fail.

No sign of alarm was given by the watchmen; the defenders on the tower and the wall must have heard nothing. Perhaps all the sentries had fallen asleep!

The men resumed their work.

Another insect landed on his cheek. Albus gently brushed it away. As dirt from his hand fell onto his lips the insect returned to his cheek.

Albus shook with suppressed rage. He blamed the Jews for his discomfort but took solace from the knowledge that the time of Roman dithering was about to end.

After the second feeble attempt on Gamla was rebuffed, Vespasian decided to wait a little longer, and let more defections and hunger further weaken the town. He sent some of his forces to deal with a Jewish garrison on Mount Tabor. These troops had just returned from their successful mission; the three legions were at full strength, Roman patience was wearing thin, and now there was a palpable sense of excitement throughout the Roman camp as all knew that a final assault was imminent.

Albus was proud that his efforts, along with that of his two comrades, would be the beginning of the end for Gamla.

With barely audible whispers the three men determined that a sufficient amount of dirt had been dug away from beneath five of the stones. With two men to a stone, they started tugging away the stones one by one, with the free man contributing to the final pull.

When the last stone was removed Albus and the two men ran down the slope and waited.

They did not have to wait long.

In the now faint pre-dawn light they watched as the tower trembled, gently at first, then violently, finally collapsing with a loud crash.

But the crash was not so loud that it masked the cries of terror of the men who went down with the tower or the screams of surprise of the men on the walls who saw the tower mysteriously fall.

Victory! Albus thought jubilantly.
I shall have my revenge soon.

Chapter Seventy-Four

19 Oct 67 CE / 22 Tishrei 3828

Reuven groaned with dismay. The tower's collapse was bad enough; the reaction of the populace was worse. Panic seized fighters and civilians alike. People were fleeing the lower part of the city. Some were shouting that God himself had brought down the tower.

Reuven shook his head with disgust.

Not God, he thought, but some clever Roman who realized that the tower had no foundation and could be brought down by digging out the base stones.

Were the watchmen sleeping?

Reuven stood at the post he had taken up in the last few weeks. Every day, just before dawn, he went to a vantage point on the ridge where he could see the Roman camp, the city's wall and tower, and the saddle where the two hills joined.

When a week went by after that initial Roman defeat and there was no offer of terms for Gamla to surrender, Reuven realized that such an offer was never going to come. The Romans would accept nothing less than unconditional surrender; perhaps they were planning on destroying the town and everyone in it.

Reuven wanted to leave Gamla once he understood Roman intentions.

One thing was keeping him there.

Dvorah.

He owed it to his friend Shaul to make sure that Dvorah got to Jerusalem safely. Until now, Dvorah had refused to leave Gamla.

Dvorah lived alone with her father. Her mother died years ago giving birth to Dvorah's younger sister, who also did not survive. Dvorah invited Reuven to stay with her and her father, who was eager for news of Jerusalem. He listened closely to all the stories Reuven told of the City, its politics, defenses, and the battles between the Jews and with the Romans.

When Reuven first met Dvorah's father, Shmuel, he was a heavy-set man with a jolly face. After almost a month of the siege both his face and body had shrunk. He was thin now and his eyes peered out of bony sockets. The smile was gone from his face.

This transformation was not caused by the hunger that stalked

Gamla as the siege lengthened. There was enough food in Shmuel's household. Dvorah's father had started eating less and less, his appetite sucked away by his growing conviction that Gamla was doomed.

Dvorah asked Reuven to tell her stories about Shaul, which Reuven did with relish. Often Dvorah would demand that he repeat the same story over and over again, as if she were a child. She especially liked to hear the exchange between the two friends when Shaul said that if Dvorah were a man she would be fighting alongside him. She laughed at Reuven's response: "If she were a man, then she wouldn't be your girl."

As she listened to these stories of Shaul, Dvorah's face glowed with happiness.

Reuven sighed. The journey to Jerusalem would be hard enough with Dvorah alone. Taking her father would not make things easier.

Reuven heard approaching footsteps behind him. Dvorah was trudging down the hill, ignoring panicked people moving in the opposite direction.

"What's happening?" she asked with alarm.

"The beginning of the end," Reuven responded. "The Romans will soon master all of Gamla. We must find a place to hide and stock it with food. There isn't much time."

Chapter Seventy-Five

20 Oct 67 CE / 23 Tishrei 3828

The din of battle was sweeter than the music of the flute and cithara, the smell of death more fragrant than a courtesan's perfume, as long as the battle was going Albus' way and the dead were those who fell by Roman hands.

Today was the day that the gods had given such gifts to Albus.

Dead bodies littered the ridge road and the streets that led down from it. Fresh blood washed the stone stairways that descended the slopes. Roman trumpets blared, barely drowning out the shouts of the Romans and the screams of the Jews.

The collapse of Gamla's tower yesterday also collapsed the cunning that the Jews had previously displayed. Panic seized both fighters and civilians.

Now, as the Roman forces moved higher into Gamla, Albus encountered only token resistance. Occasionally small groups of Jews challenged the marching Romans. Albus and his comrades dispatched them without suffering any casualties of their own. The bulk of the Jewish fighters were fleeing further south. To that high rocky outcropping, Albus thought, to make their last stand.

Civilians—whether standing on the doorsteps of their homes or running north to the now-open gate of the city—were pleading for mercy.

None was given by the soldiers still enraged by the death of their comrades in that first battle a month ago. Old men, women, and children were killed as they begged for their lives.

After the tower fell the Romans methodically took control of the lower ground of Gamla before proceeding further. They did not make the same mistake of rushing headlong into the town as they had done when they breached the walls last month.

Gnaeus' spirit is guiding us, thought Albus.

As the troops marched along Gamla's ridge men were assigned to go down the narrow, steep streets, searching for survivors to slaughter.

About halfway up the main road an officer signaled to Albus' unit. The officer pointed to a steep stairway. Albus' unit descended.

The first houses were empty. The entrance of four soldiers into a house three levels lower was followed by screams of terror and pain.

Albus smiled.

The screams brought out an old man and woman from the house across the one which the four soldiers were exiting, their swords dripping with blood. The old woman held an infant in her arms.

The old couple were crying out to Albus in words he did not understand.

Begging for their lives, no doubt, he thought.

Albus raised his sword high, pointing it straight upward. The old man just stared at him, wide-eyed. Albus snarled and swung the sword with all his strength, the blade splitting the man's skull. Bits of brain and blood clung to the already stained sword as he pulled it out of the dead man. Albus turned to the old woman. Her screaming stopped. She trembled and seemed about to drop the baby.

Albus took it from her.

Then he snarled again and smashed the baby's head against the side of the house.

The old woman shrieked so loudly his ears hurt. He kicked her to the ground and drove his sword into her chest.

The soldiers did not go all the way to the bottom of the hill. They were called back to search another street.

Albus remained for a moment.

There must be others down this street, he thought.

Albus' caligae clattered on the stone steps as he descended the slope. He peered into several houses but saw nothing. He was about to go back to rejoin his comrades when he spotted a woman leaving a house further down the slope. Her hands were full with several bundles. She turned right, went down several steps, and then turned left at the next north-south alley.

Albus ran as fast as he could after her.

He reached the alley in time to see her go left up the next stairway. Still running at the same speed he arrived at that stairway only to find that she had disappeared.

Unwilling to admit failure, Albus made a guess as to where she could have gone.

He went into several houses.

No sign of her.

One more try and that's it, he thought.

"Help me, Mars!" he cried, about to enter a house on the right side of the street.

Albus smiled with satisfaction. The god had answered his prayer.

The woman turned to face him. She dropped her bundles and took several paces backward until she was against the wall. She jerked her hands behind her. As she did, her dress, already in disarray, fell off her left shoulder, exposing her breast. She made no move to cover it again.

Albus placed his sword and shield on the floor. He removed his helmet and breastplate.

He stood looking at her for several moments.

She was tall and willowy, with long brown hair. Albus found her attractive, for a Jewish girl.

Her eyes were fixed on his. The look in them was strange; Albus could not decipher it.

She knows what to expect, he thought.

She trembled, then held herself rigid. This cycle repeated more than once.

There were no screams, no attempt to run away, just the steady gaze into his eyes.

Albus lifted his tunic and pulled aside his subligacula.

Her eyes fell to his exposed erect organ. She looked into his eyes again with that same strange expression on her face.

He took a step forward, and then another.

The girl's gaze moved from his eyes to the part of him revealed by the lifted tunic and then returned to his eyes. These up and down glances continued; the closer he got the longer she looked down, as if fascinated by what she saw. Albus felt he was engaged in a secret dance or mysterious ritual with her.

He drew within arm's length.

She took her left hand from behind her back and hesitantly moved it toward him. He came closer and thrust his hips forward. She touched what he offered, gently closing her fingers around it.

Albus' breath came in sharply. His heart pounded.

This was better than if he had to force himself on her. Who knows what delights she was offering? Perhaps she was one of the public women of Gamla.

Albus resolved at that moment, as her fingers tightened slowly around him, that he would not kill her when it was over. He would keep her, as his slave.

He barely saw the flashing of her right hand as it came out from behind her, the left hand now grasping his penis so hard that it hurt.

Albus howled in agony as something sharp slashed into it. The knife went from his penis to his right eye, then down his check, and then slashing the side of his neck.

Through his howls Albus heard footsteps behind him. Strong hands pulled him down to the floor.

Through his uninjured eye Albus saw a bearded Jew standing above him.

It was the young rabbi who had tried to chop off his head in the first battle of Gamla!

"Kill me!" Albus cried, in Latin.

The Jew was staring down at Albus' midsection, a look of amazement on his face. The Jew started to laugh.

"Well," the Jew said in Greek. "I tried and failed to cut off your big head. I guess your friend wasn't here to save you when this girl cut off the little one."

The Jew laughed again.

"Kill me!" Albus cried, this time in Greek.

"Oh, you'll die soon enough," came the reply.

Albus began shouting for help in Latin. The Jew bent down, knife in hand, and cut away a large section of Albus' tunic. He then stuffed it into Albus' mouth, stifling his screams.

"How dare you come to our country and try to rape one of our women!" the Jew said, straightening up, staring down at Albus with hatred in his eyes.

Albus struggled to move his hand, hoping to take out the gag.

The Jew bent down again and calmly slashed both of Albus' upper arms so deeply that the knife penetrated the muscle, rendering his arms useless.

As the Jew turned away, leaving him writhing on the floor in agony, Albus prayed to Mars to end his life quickly. This time, Mars did not answer his prayer.

Chapter Seventy-Six

20 Oct 67 CE / 23 Tishrei 3828

Reuven, his brow furrowed, stared down at the floor. Deep in thought, he tugged his beard. The wounded Roman soldier continued writhing and moaning through the gag in his mouth.

"We can't leave him here," Reuven said at last to Dvorah. "And wherever I dump him, I want to make sure the Romans don't find a mutilated dead soldier. There's no telling how they'll take it out on any Jews they capture, never mind that this Roman had it coming."

Reuven nodded; his own words pleased him.

"Go across the road, three houses down," Dvorah replied. "You can put him there." Her voice quavered. Reuven barely noticed; he didn't bother looking up at her. "The house was abandoned," she went on. "The family fled Gamla yesterday."

Reuven slowly shook his head.

"Not good enough," he responded. "A few streets north is one of the places where houses collapsed. I'll put him under the rubble. They'll never find him." Reuven paused, still staring at the floor. "While I do that, take what you found and what I just brought," he said, pointing to the bundles behind him. "That was our last supply run. We should have enough now for two or three weeks. When I come back we'll go into hiding."

Reuven glanced up at her. "How's your father doing?" he asked.

Dvorah was trembling, her body making small jerking motions.

She's still shaken up, Reuven thought.

"He's fine. Sleeping," she answered.

"Well, with all this noise, he probably woke up." He gazed into her eyes. "Was that your first time? In combat, I mean, because that's what it was."

She nodded. Reuven could tell she was unable to get out the words she was mouthing.

He smiled at her reassuringly.

"Listen, Dvorah," he said, "the first time I knifed a man in close combat—killed him, too—I cried and threw up afterwards." Reuven chuckled. "What a baby I was! You're braver than I was. A Jewish warrior! Shaul was right about you."

He noticed her exposed breast.

"Cover yourself," Reuven said, looking away. He bent down and grabbed the Roman by his ankles. "Get hold of yourself, Dvorah. We don't have a lot of time. I'll return soon."

Without looking back at her, or waiting for an answer, Reuven dragged the Roman outside. He pulled him across the street and then down the stairway. As he passed the house Dvorah mentioned, he thought about saving time and depositing his prisoner there, but decided against it. He continued down the stairway to the accompaniment of louder groans. He reached the alley where he was about to turn right when he heard discordant sounds in the distance. There was the blaring of trumpets and the shouts of men.

Reuven froze. He swallowed hard.

"L-Azazel," he spat. "There's no time."

Though all the houses around him seemed deserted, he went through the trouble of hauling the half-dead body back up the stairway and to the house that he knew for sure had been abandoned.

Reuven pushed the door open and yanked the Roman inside. The house did have an abandoned look; clothes, urns, and sacks were scattered about, as if the occupants had fled in a hurry. A large table stood at an unsymmetrical angle to the walls of the room; near the entrance to the kitchen two low benches were lying on their sides.

Reuven haled the slowly-dying man, whose moans had grown feebler, into the kitchen and left him in a corner by the stove. He was about to go back to get the table when he caught the Roman soldier's eyes.

The look in them was pleading.

Reuven hesitated for a moment.

He bent over the man, whose belt still held the shorter blade that infantrymen carried. Reuven pulled it out, looked the Roman in the eyes, nodded solemnly, and plunged the knife into the Roman's heart.

Reuven turned, leaving the knife in its owner, and moved the table into the kitchen. He turned it on its side and adjusted each pair of legs so they were touching the walls that formed the corner. The top of the table hid the man who had been sped on his way to death; someone casually entering the house without inspecting it further would not see the corpse.

The job done, Reuven went out of the house. The distant noise was no closer or further than when he had first heard it. He ran up the stairway to Dvorah's house.

She was waiting for him, the bloody knife in her hand, a determined look on her face. She was not trembling; she had gotten hold of herself as he had demanded.

"I'm going to join the fighters in the citadel," she said.

"No, you're not," Reuven said firmly. He had no intention of allowing her to join a hopeless last stand on the rocky outcropping at the south end of Gamla.

"You can't stop me," she insisted.

Reuven shrugged.

"Maybe not," he said, "but I tell you this, if you're not here when I leave here for Jerusalem I'm not taking your father with me."

Dvorah stamped her foot and glared at him.

"You'd abandon an old man?"

Reuven heard the fury in her voice. He pointed at the floor.

"Get down there!" he said harshly. "You're wasting time. I still have to prepare the rug and the table."

Dvorah's hesitation lasted only a moment. She turned, took three steps, and went down on her haunches. She took hold of a small knob coming out of the floor; as she pulled on it a square section of the floor came free. Dvorah laid the panel, roughly two and a half feet on each side, next to the opening.

Dvorah meekly climbed down the ladder that led into the empty space below.

Reuven looked around. Dvorah had brought all the supplies into the hidden storeroom. She had even taken the dead man's equipment; his sword, shield, helmet and breastplate.

Shmuel, Dvorah's father, had a house that was modest by Jerusalem standards but on the well-to-do side for Gamla. Shmuel, close to being prosperous, was a trader buying olives, grain, and fruit from the surrounding farmlands. He had them processed in town to make olive oil, various breads and cakes, and wines from fruits in season. Shmuel sold these finished products to townspeople and rural folk alike. During his stay with Dvorah and her father Reuven had eaten well, despite the starvation that was beginning to strangle the town as the food supply dwindled.

The house had three levels. The top floor held bedrooms reached by a wooden ladder permanently in place. The ground floor had a large living room and kitchen. Stone steps on one side of the living room led to a bath in the basement.

The living room had a beautiful mosaic tile on the floor, rich with geometrical shapes in blue, red, and green. Until yesterday, a table of dark, polished wood stood close to the edge of the mosaic. Under the table had been a dark blue rug.

Now table and rug had been moved away to allow entry to the underground room. Dvorah's father had never accessed it when Reuven was in the house; Reuven only learned about it after he told Dvorah that they needed a place to hide until the Romans left Gamla.

The room was large, its area about half that of the living room. It was already well-stocked with olive oil, jugs of water, dried fruit, and dried, unleavened flat squares of bread. Reuven and Dvorah, with furious foraging in abandoned houses over the last day, had added to the supplies.

Reuven was certain of what he told Dvorah; they had enough food and water for the three of them to last several weeks.

Reuven moved the rug back to its original place; the opening and the trapdoor were no longer visible. Then he moved the table over the rug. Anyone entering the living room would have no idea that there was a room underneath,

Now came the hard part. Reuven would have to lift the rug just enough so that he could crawl under it, slither to the ladder and climb down head first. He would then climb back up the ladder, pull the bulge in the rug down, and slide the trap door back into place. With luck the rug would almost flatten out so that no bulge remained for any uninvited visitor to see.

Reuven took a deep breath. He looked around the room one more time and almost choked.

Blood on the floor near the far wall. Blood staining the mosaic tile and the rest of the floor where he had dragged the wounded Roman. And without doubt blood all along the stairway between Dvorah's house and the abandoned one where he had left the dead Roman.

There was nothing he could do about the blood outside. Again, luck would have to take the place of certainty; rain would have to come before the Romans searched the street, strong rain to wash away the bloody trail. The blood inside was a different matter. Reuven quickly climbed the stairs to the bedroom, found some of Dvorah's clothes, and rushed back down. He tried as best he could to wipe the drying blood. Then he climbed back up and stuffed the clothes he had turned into rags under a bed.

On the main level again, Reuven went flat against the floor next to the rug. He gently lifted its edge and crawled under it.

Slowly, he slithered to the opening. Reaching it he thought:

Now comes another hard task, going down the ladder head first. I can use Dvorah's help.

Reuven called to her. There was no answer. All he heard were sobs that only grew louder.

Reuven grasped one of the rungs of the ladder and pulled himself along it. He reached a point where he was bent at the waist, his legs still on the floor above. As he moved further down, his hands were almost at the bottom of the ladder. Unable to control the motion of his vertical body, he flopped over onto the dirt floor of the storeroom.

"Ugh!" he cried as he landed with a thud.

The fall hurt.

An oil lamp threw light and shadows over the room with its walls of stone. At one end Dvorah's father lay asleep.

At the other end Dvorah was on her knees, crying loudly. The oil lamp was on the floor next to her.

"What's wrong?" he asked, alarmed.

"He's dead, Father's dead!" she shrieked.

"What? How? Are you sure?"

"He's dead! He's dead!" she shrieked.

Reuven went over to check. There was no breath, no pulse, no heartbeat that he could feel.

"His heart must have given out," Reuven said heavily. "The screams upstairs from the Roman must have frightened him."

"What do we do now?" she asked plaintively.

"Do you have something to cover him with?"

Dvorah pointed at one of the walls. There was a pile of blankets. Reuven walked over and took one. He covered Dvorah's father with it.

"Are we just going to stay here with him?" she asked.

"We have no choice, Dvorah. It's too dangerous to go back out now. The battle is still raging."

"How long will we be here?"

"Until it's safe to go out again."

"How long will that be?"

To Reuven her question sounded like whining. He sighed and replied:

"I don't know, Dvorah. When there is quiet for several days…"

"How will we know the passage of time without going outside?"

That's a good question, Reuven thought.

He had no idea.

Reuven climbed up the ladder. He carefully pulled the rug flat and slid the trapdoor back into place. After climbing down, he removed the ladder and laid it against a wall. Then he went over to Dvorah and sat beside her.

"I'm frightened, Reuven," she said, shivering. "More frightened than when that Roman soldier tried to attack me."

Reuven put his arms around Dvorah.

"You're safe now, Dvorah."

She snuggled tightly against him.

"I'm so weary, Reuven."

Reuven turned off the lamp. They were entombed in utter darkness. It might as well be night, he thought.

"Sleep, Dvorah," he urged.

Soon he heard her regular breathing.

Reuven could feel himself drifting into sleep.

His last waking thought was that this would be the longest night of his life.

Chapter Seventy-Seven

4 Nov 67 CE / 8 Cheshvan 3828

The heavy sounds of caligae pounding on the floor above as Roman soldiers stomped around the house shook Reuven from his reverie. He could not determine how many there were from the footsteps or the indistinct voices that filtered through the floor.

No matter. He knew that one heavily-armed Roman soldier would be enough to kill Dvorah and him.

The pleasant remembrances of Drusilla that had danced through his mind were swiftly replaced by the fear of discovery.

It would almost be a relief, Reuven thought. These past days, weeks—he did not know how long—had been filled with unbearable tension.

Reuven had planned for many things, but the need for a privy had not occurred to him. The stench of his and Dvorah's bodily wastes was becoming overpowering. There was another smell, even more overwhelming, that had grown with the passing of time.

Shmuel's corpse?

Reuven shuddered.

Dvorah stirred from sleep. She had not taken well to the confinement in the basement. She complained often, accusing Reuven of keeping her captive. She demanded the right to go outside. Reuven steadfastly refused. She declared she would have been better off joining the fighters at the citadel; her father was already dead, she didn't need Reuven anymore to take him to Jerusalem. She kept imploring Reuven to go out and check if it was safe for them to leave Gamla.

Their self-imposed imprisonment was made worse by not knowing how long they had been in hiding. Without the sun, without the sky, there was no way to know. Even a rough estimate based on how much food and water they had already used—Reuven guessed a week's worth—could very well be far off the mark.

The darkness did not help, either. Dvorah wanted the lamp lit constantly. Reuven insisted on turning off the lamp for long periods of time to conserve the fuel and the wick.

More than once Dvorah had cried out in despair that she was going mad. Reuven tried to distract her by retelling stories of Shaul. He even lectured her on religious texts and repeated lessons learned from Metilius. None of it worked. Dvorah only listened with one ear.

It's true, he thought, she is going mad.

So am I.

Dvorah stirred again. Reuven grew alert, ready to place his hand over her mouth in case she made any noise on waking. In the utter darkness he could not see her eyes and did not know if she were still sleeping.

He soon found out.

Dvorah pulled his head close to hers.

"If they find us I want you to kill me," she whispered fiercely in his ear.

She thrust her knife into his hand.

Reuven swallowed hard. He did not close his hand around the knife.

"Take it," she insisted.

Reuven's hand remained limp.

"Take it and promise you will kill me if they open the trapdoor or I swear, Reuven, I will start screaming right now!"

Her voice had gotten louder.

She is losing her mind, Reuven thought.

He grasped the knife, pulled it away slightly, dropped it softly on the ground and then clamped his right hand over Dvorah's mouth. With his left he held her tightly.

She did not struggle.

Her body trembled as they waited.

Reuven was afraid to breathe.

The rough steps above continued. There were the sounds of overturned furniture and smashing pottery.

A new fear gripped Reuven.

Would they set fire to the house?

Reuven heard the table above them being dragged aside. He imagined he saw them pulling the rug away.

He prayed that the Romans would not find them.

Then Reuven actually saw something.

Light.

The trapdoor had been lifted.

Immediately he heard excited chattering from above.

It was followed by the sounds of disgust from several voices.

Reuven could not make out the Latin, except for one word.

"Stinks!"

Reuven allowed himself a smile.

There was more chattering, louder and more forceful, as if an argument was going on.

Reuven waited. He could feel Dvorah's body stiffen.

Someone spoke, his head leaning into the void of the basement. Then Reuven heard the sound of retching, and the falling of something wet and slimy down onto the ground.

Reuven struggled to control his own stomach.

The trapdoor was slammed back into place.

Once again he and Dvorah were plunged into darkness.

The sound of footsteps resumed. Dvorah began shivering in his arms.

They won't come down, Reuven thought. I'm certain. Will they fire the place after they leave?

Reuven closed his eyes so hard the muscles in the upper part of his face started to ache.

If a fire were set upstairs would it move to the basement? Would the house collapse on them? And if the fire did leave the basement intact, would smoke enter and overwhelm them?

Reuven was at a total loss as to what to do next.

Would it be better to slit Dvorah's throat and plunge a knife into her heart and then race upstairs to be killed by the Romans rather than wait to see what fate had in store for them?

Did he have any good choices?

The sounds above them faded.

Were the Romans about to toss flaming torches into the house?

Reuven prayed to The Master of the Universe to change their hearts if that was their plan.

He removed his hand from Dvorah's mouth. He released her from his other hand. He felt for the lamp and lit it. As he opened his eyes the new light made him blink.

"I have to get out of here!" Dvorah said, her voice low and raspy. "I don't care what happens. I can't stay down here anymore."

Reuven nodded.

"Just wait a little longer," he pleaded, "and then I'll go up and look around. Dvorah, we've survived so much it makes no sense to put our lives in jeopardy now."

She doesn't know what's worrying me, he thought. Good! I don't know what we should do if they do decide to set the place on fire.

Dvorah did not reply.

They waited. And waited. The Romans did not set fire to the house. God had again answered his prayers. Reuven stood.

"I'll go up and look around," he said.

"I want to go with you."

She had grabbed hold of his hand with such force that Reuven knew that if he did not agree she would not let go.

"I agree," he said reluctantly. She released his hand.

Reuven got the ladder and put it back into place. He noticed that Dvorah, who had stood up, did not move her eyes from the covered form of her father.

Reuven started to climb, studiously trying to ignore the filth that had fallen under the ladder from the mouth of the Roman who had peered down into the basement. He did not want to add to the disgusting slime.

He reached the top and pushed the trapdoor off. As he stepped out to the floor Dvorah climbed up the ladder.

The room was in a shambles. Broken furniture, broken pottery, things left behind scattered around the room; even the beautiful mosaic had been defaced.

Dvorah saw the look on his face and squeezed his hand.

"It was lost to us when the Romans began their siege," she said.

Reuven smiled grimly.

"You are comforting me about the loss of your home," he said.

Reuven walked to the far side of the living room and then descended the steps that led to the bath. He bent down and examined the water.

"It's clean," he said with surprise, straightening up. "The Romans left it alone." He walked back up the steps. "You can bathe, and then I will. If your father's clothes don't fit me—and they probably won't—I'll wash mine. If you can't find ones for yourself—I used some of them to clean the blood in here before we went into hiding—you can wash what you're wearing now. It wouldn't do to travel with blood on us; never know who we'll run into."

Reuven went back and stood near Dvorah.

"What about my father?" she asked.

Reuven waited before answering.

"I'll put the rug and table back before we leave," he said solemnly. "The basement will be like a tomb. When the war is over you can come back and collect his bones. I'm sorry, Dvorah; that's the best we can do in the circumstances."

"I understand," she replied, in a voice that was almost a whisper.

Reuven touched her shoulder and squeezed it gently.

"It will be all right, Dvorah, I'll get you safely to Jerusalem. In a while I'll go outside, to the ridge road and see as best I can what's happening in the Roman camp."

Reuven walked to the opening of their basement cell. He started down the ladder. When he came up he had the Roman's helmet on his head and was carrying the breastplate. He tried on the breastplate; though short and snug, it nevertheless fit. He took off the breastplate and put it on the floor. He took off the helmet, placing it next to the breastplate. Two more trips brought up the shield and sword.

"With these, from a distance, I may be taken for a Roman," he explained. "Close up is another matter." He shrugged. "Guess I'm taking a chance."

"You have to," Dvorah said. "We both have to take chances, unless we want to rot down there."

"Maybe I'll be lucky," Reuven said. "No one will see me. Even better; there won't be any Romans remaining in Gamla to see me when I go out."

"When will we leave the city?"

"I don't know yet. It depends on what I see in the Roman camp. We may have to stay here a few more days, but we can start sleeping upstairs tonight. I don't think they'll be back here anytime soon."

"Good," she said quickly. "I don't think I could stay down there again."

Reuven nodded.

"I don't want to, either," he said. "Here's the plan, Dvorah. We bring food up from the storeroom for the journey, and all the money your father had. It took Amram five days to get me here from Jerusalem. It should take us about the same, maybe a bit longer, if we don't get lost. Amram often rested the donkeys, and my backside, and he mostly refused to travel in the dark.

"Ah, how I wish we had his donkeys to carry our supplies! Because we don't, we can't haul everything we need for the entire trip. We'll have to stop along the way to purchase new stocks."

"I can fashion some bags so we can carry things on our back," Dvorah said. "This way your hands will be free to carry the sword."

Reuven sighed.

"I should have taken the Roman's belt so I'd have a place to hold it," he said. "Maybe I'll go back and get the belt." He screwed up his face at the thought. Then he laughed.

"You know, Dvorah, I received training in Jerusalem on how to use a sword. The truth? I'm not very good with one. I'm much better with a sling and a knife. I've killed with those. Your Shaul taught me." Reuven picked up the sword, hefted it in his hand, and swung it through the air.

"No," he said, laying it down. "Not good at all. Against someone with a knife or a club maybe, but I wouldn't stand a chance against a legionnaire." Reuven shook his head. "With a sling, that's another matter," he concluded confidently.

"Take the sword," Dvorah insisted. "If you don't want it, I do."

Reuven looked at her. She was serious. She picked up the sword and held it in both hands, a determined look on her face.

Reuven took the sword from her. He hoped they would not need it.

Or her courage.

Chapter Seventy-Eight

4 Nov 67 CE / 9 Cheshvan 3828

It was strange lying in the bed of a man whose corpse was rotting two floors below.

He was wearing the dead man's ill-fitting clothes, too.

Reuven's thoughts went to the Book of Kohelet.

Does it matter if we make it to Jerusalem? he wondered. Or win our fight for freedom? In the end we are all dead. Everything passes away.

Reuven sat up in the bed, pondering when they should pick up and leave on their journey.

Clad in the Roman's helmet and breastplate, carrying his sword and shield, Reuven had cautiously made his way to the ridge road in late afternoon. From that vantage point he examined the activity on the opposite mountain. The legions were busy dismantling their camp; already its size had shrunk by half. Would it be gone in another day? Would they leave a token force, or decide to garrison what remained of Gamla?

Reuven had seen no movement within the town itself, except for scattered plumes of smoke. There had been places set on fire; it seemed less a deliberate effort to burn Gamla to the ground than spontaneous acts of arson committed by troops following no orders but their own.

We were lucky, he had thought, watching the smoke drifting to the sky. They spared our house.

Then Reuven laughed, a laugh that sounded insane even to his own ears.

In Gamla, the Romans burn down Jewish buildings. In Jerusalem, the Jews burn down their own.

With a heavy heart Reuven had returned to Dvorah's house.

Shmuel's clothes were uncomfortably tight; Reuven removed them and sat naked on the bed. Dvorah was surely asleep by this time in the other room. By tomorrow his own clothes would be dry.

Leave tomorrow? he asked himself. No, came the answer. We'll wait one more day.

Reuven heard stirring in the next room, followed by the faint sound of footsteps. He quickly covered himself as Dvorah entered carrying an oil lamp. She set it down on a table in a corner of the small room.

Dvorah looked at him, hiding his nakedness.

"I couldn't sleep," she said.

"Are you frightened?" he asked.

She sat down next to him.

"You kept me alive!" she said.

He looked back at her, wondering where this was leading.

"You kept me alive," she repeated, taking his head in her hands. "But I'm going to die anyway." She pulled his head to hers and kissed him passionately on the lips.

Startled, he moved slightly back.

She took hold of the clothes hiding his nakedness and yanked them away. She stared as if she had never seen an unclothed man before.

Reuven became aroused. His reaction shocked him as much as her actions.

"What are you doing?" he exclaimed. "You're Shaul's girl!"

"Shaul is dead," Dvorah retorted heatedly. "I'm alive, now, but not for long. I'm going to die soon." She looked up at his face. "I don't want to die a virgin. I want to know what it's like to be loved by a man!"

"What?"

She put her arms around him and drew him close. He pulled away again.

"Dvorah, you're not going to die. I will get you safely to Jerusalem. I promise."

She laughed bitterly.

"You promise! What do your words mean?" She looked at him slyly. "Perhaps you will get me safely to Jerusalem. You can marry me there! Maybe you will even give me a child tonight. We will call him Herut, for Liberty!" And she laughed again, insanely, tore off her clothes and clutched his body to hers as she pulled them both prone onto the bed.

Overwhelmed, Reuven felt as if he himself were going mad, as if all boundaries were dissolving, all rules collapsing. There was only this moment, its immediacy compelling him to give in to his desire.

He responded to her passion. His hands moved softly over her back, his lips caressed her cheeks and neck and shoulders...

And then he stopped himself. He gently separated their bodies.

"Dvorah, I can't, I can't." He was shaking with suppressed desire and with guilt. "I'm engaged to a girl in Jerusalem. We're supposed to be married when I return. It's not right, not to you, not to her!" Yet even as he spoke these words his mind screamed:

She's right! We're both going to die. This may be my last night alive, seize it and enjoy the embrace of a woman who desperately wants you!

Dvorah gasped. She quickly covered Reuven with the clothes she had pulled away and got dressed herself.

"Oh, Reuven, I'm so sorry! I'm so ashamed! You must think I'm a whore!"

His heartbeat slowed slightly, his breathing became normal, his thoughts calmer. He wanted to reach out and touch her shoulder, but thought better of it.

"Dvorah, it's all right," he consoled her. "I understand. There's no reason to be ashamed. These are times to drive us mad. Dvorah, in the battle of Ascalon I brought a cavalryman down with my sling. I wanted to cut off his head and take it for a trophy! Me! A rabbi's son. That is much worse than what you wanted to do. Oh, Dvorah, we are caught in circumstances that strip away the veneer of our civilized selves! Please, please, do not blame yourself."

She nodded. He could see tears flowing down her face. She left the room hurriedly.

The lamp still burned on the table. Reuven rose, turned off the light, and went back to bed.

It was a long time before he slept.

Chapter Seventy-Nine

5 Nov 67 CE / 9 Cheshvan 3828

His deep sleep rudely came to an end with rough shaking. At first Reuven didn't know where he was or recognize the face above him.

"Get up, get up! Time to get out of here!"

"Huh?" Reuven rubbed his eyes and stared at Dvorah. He sat up, forgetting he had no clothes on. She ignored his nakedness and focused her eyes on his face. "What happened?" he asked.

"Time to get up, lazybones!"

"Why? It's early morning," he protested.

"It's not morning anymore," Dvorah retorted. "It's past noon by now. I've already packed up everything. Come on, let's go. The Romans are almost all gone."

"How do you know?" Reuven demanded.

"I went out and looked," she replied. "I was scouting around most of the night and early this morning. They've taken down the camp. There are very few soldiers moving about on the hill." Dvorah sighed and frowned. "Gamla's empty of the living. It's full of dead bodies, Jewish ones. Many of the houses were burned. We were lucky." She paused, then added: "I went to the citadel. The ravine below was full of bodies. Either the Romans pushed them off or they jumped to their deaths."

There was an awkward silence as Reuven took in the news. They both looked down at the floor.

"One day," he said, "we will have to return to bury the bodies, even the Roman ones."

She raised her head and allowed her gaze to fall over Reuven.

"Let's go, Reuven," she said. "And if you don't mind," here she gave a brief smile, "please get dressed." With that she left the room.

Reuven yawned, stretched, and put on Dvorah's father's clothes. Then he went downstairs and changed into his own dry ones.

Dvorah already had a pack on her back, one that was almost as big as she was. Its weight made her bend slightly forward. There was a large pack for him. He slung it on his back.

"You have the money?" he asked.

"Yes."

"Let's go, then," he said.

"Take the sword, Reuven."

He sighed deeply, picked it up, and followed her out of the house.

"I can get us to the Kinneret," she said, using the local name for the Sea of Galilee. She called it out over her shoulder to a chagrined Reuven, who was nonplussed that she took no precaution to make sure it was safe to leave the house. "After that, it's up to you."

Reuven hurried after her.

"From there we go south and a little west," he shouted, trying to catch his breath.

Dvorah walks fast for a woman, he thought.

"We can stop and resupply in Scythopolis," Reuven said, as he caught up to her.

"Beit She'an," she corrected.

"It's not called that anymore," he said. "Hasn't been since the days of King Shlomo."

"It will be again," Dvorah asserted. "When we free ourselves from Rome."

The pace she kept, between a walk and a run, caused Reuven to lose his footing on one of the stairs.

"I'm glad to hear how positive you are," he said, as he righted himself.

They reached the east gate where Reuven had entered Gamla a month ago. It was already open. She passed through and without waiting for him started down the slope.

Reuven followed, stopping just outside the wall.

"Wait!" he called.

Dvorah turned.

"What is it?" she asked impatiently.

"What if we're seen? There are still Roman troops in the area. Maybe we should wait until night to leave."

"They won't see us," she insisted, resuming her downward march.

Against his better judgment, Reuven followed without protesting. There was no regular stairway now to moderate the steepness of the slope; the rough ground caused him to stumble several times as he tried to catch up with her.

"I wish I had a donkey," he murmured.

Dvorah slowed to wait for him.

"You're from Jerusalem," she said. "This should be nothing for you."

Reuven smiled.

"I wasn't raised to be a farmer or a shepherd," he replied. "I was supposed to be a scholar."

Dvorah didn't reply. She increased her pace.

"I bet she's the daughter of a famous rabbi," Dvorah said, as Reuven caught up to her.

"Who?"

"The girl you're going to marry," came Dvorah's wistful answer. "I'm just the daughter of a trader from a small town in the north."

"My best friend was in love with you," Reuven responded. "That makes you special no matter who your father is."

"Thank you," she replied. Reuven could hear the gratitude in her voice.

"Never feel that you're less than anyone else," he added. "You're as courageous as any of the heroines of our people!"

Dvorah smiled shyly.

"Do you love her?" she asked.

Reuven stopped walking.

"More than anything else," he said. He started walking again, trying to keep his balance as he negotiated the descent. For a moment he had a puzzled look on his face; it disappeared when he began using the sword as a staff to ease the way.

"More than your country?"

The question took Reuven by surprise. He stopped once more.

"I don't know, Dvorah. I'm not sure what I would do if I could go with her to a warm, sunny place where I could grow olives and dates and raise sheep and goats. To live peacefully and forget about Rome and war would tempt me greatly."

"What do you know about growing crops or raising livestock?" Dvorah asked sharply.

"Nothing," he admitted.

"Humph!" she uttered. "Is she pretty?"

"The most beautiful woman I've ever seen," he answered quickly.

"My!" Dvorah responded. "A beauty, then. You're lucky, Reuven, and a rabbi's daughter to boot!"

Reuven laughed.

"She's not a rabbi's daughter," he responded, amused.

"A priest, then?"

"No," Reuven said. "Not a priest either."

"So you're marrying the daughter of a common man! How do your parents feel about that?"

Reuven wanted to laugh again.

"I'm marrying the daughter of a barbarian from somewhere far north of Rome and Italy!"

It was Dvorah's turn to stop.

"A gentile woman?" Dvorah asked, amazed.

"She already accepts our laws and customs. She said if I return safely she will know that the God of the Jews is God. She promised to become one of us. She won't be a gentile when I marry her."

They resumed their descent. Reuven envied how easily Dvorah made her steps, not struggling the way he was.

"How do you know her?" Dvorah asked, her curiosity still not satisfied.

"She was the servant of the Roman commander Metilius I told you about."

They were walking side by side now. Reuven looked at her face; he could tell she wanted to say something but was hesitating.

"Well?" he asked. "What is it?"

"Have you slept with her?" The words tumbled out of Dvorah.

"Yes."

Dvorah said nothing as they continued down the hill.

They reached the bottom. Dvorah turned right, following the same path Amram had taken, in reverse.

Again there was silence, and again Reuven was sure something was on her mind. He waited.

"Was she a virgin?" Dvorah asked at last.

"No."

Dvorah stopped.

"You don't care?"

"No."

"Was she a prostitute?"

The question seemed to come out of nowhere. Reuven could feel his face redden.

"Dvorah, if you were a man I would cut your throat."

Dvorah laughed and resumed walking.

"Have you really ever cut someone's throat?" she asked. "In battle, I mean, not after some girl seriously wounded him for you."

Reuven smiled. The tension dissipated. He wanted to tell her about Drusilla, to tell her that just as Shaul had said that she, Dvorah, would have been a great warrior if she had been a man, he, Reuven, knows that Drusilla would have been a great scholar if she were not a woman.

Instead he responded to her question.

"Did you forget what I told you, how I cried and threw up after the first time? What I didn't tell you was that by killing the man I saved Shaul's life, as he had already saved mine."

"Yes," Dvorah replied, "so you claimed. To be honest, I find it a little hard to believe. Most of the time you seem more like the son of a rabbi than a fighter." She paused. "Did you really want to cut off a Roman's head and take it as a trophy?"

"Well," Reuven explained, "to be precise, that cavalryman probably wasn't a Roman; they're usually foreign auxiliaries."

"What did you do with the head?"

"I wasn't able to finish chopping it off."

"What stopped you?" Dvorah asked.

"Not what, who. Judah ben Ezra came along on a horse and pulled me away."

"I know of him," Dvorah said softly. Then, louder, she added: "Shaul joined his band. He took Shaul away from me, took him to Jerusalem. Now Shaul is dead."

Dvorah's face fell. Reuven wanted to say something to shine light into the darkness, to lift her spirits.

"How did you meet Shaul?" he asked.

Instantly Dvorah's mood brightened. She smiled.

"Shaul's father had a small farm," she began. "My father did business with him. He'd buy his grapes, olives, and figs. The two men liked each other. They both shared the same views. They were both widowers who never remarried. I used to accompany my father on some of his business trips. I remember the first time I saw Shaul. I thought he was the handsomest boy I had ever seen!" There was excitement in her voice.

"Of course, he ignored me," she went on. "Nevertheless, I used to find excuses to go with my father when he went to their farm. As the years went by Shaul began to notice me."

Dvorah smiled. Reuven could see that the last month had disappeared; it was as if it had never happened. What he heard now was a young woman in love reminiscing about the past.

"We found ways to meet each other," she continued. "We'd talk, plan our future. Eventually our fathers found out about us. His father was thrilled; compared to them we were rich. But I think he genuinely liked me. He often said that the two of us would live on his farm; not in Gamla. And my father liked Shaul, even after the troubles started and he joined Judah's band, even after Shaul left for Jerusalem…"

Dvorah's voice dropped. Reuven could feel her slipping back into sadness.

"What was it like growing up in Gamla?" Reuven asked.

Dvorah began to tell stories of her childhood, and her mood lifted. Except for the death of her mother, which she remembered very clearly, it was a happy childhood. Her father showered her with love, and without spoiling her, indulged her every whim. All of Gamla and its surroundings was her playground, and while she didn't have many friends she had a rich imagination that filled her life.

As Reuven listened he thought that if he hadn't met Drusilla he could have easily fallen in love with this charming girl from the north. He understood why Shaul loved her, and the conflict Shaul had felt between joining the revolution and staying with Dvorah.

Reuven was not sure he would have made the same choice that Shaul did.

They marched between hills that were covered with brown grass and occasional clumps of green trees. The height of the hills decreased and the number of trees increased as the road from Gamla descended southwest from the Golan plateau toward the Sea of Galilee. The water shone blue in the sun that moved steadily toward the west.

Reuven pointed with the sword.

"The first time I saw the Kinneret was when Amram brought me here. The first time I saw the Galilee, too. The north is beautiful!"

She gave him a nod of assent as she looked at him and not the Kinneret; something in her eyes made him believe she was saying: Oh, if we could only stay here together…

I'm imagining it, he told himself.

"I've never seen Jerusalem," she said, breaking into his thoughts.

"You will, in a few days."

Once in a while a traveler passed them going in the opposite direction, usually a man leading a donkey laden with bags.

The time between such sightings was long; after the second Dvorah said:

"There used to be more traffic on this road, before the troubles…"

It was getting late. The sun was low in the sky.

"We should stop soon," Reuven said.

"I'll find a good place for us, city boy," came the reply.

They continued walking, getting closer to the sea, until Dvorah left the road and headed to a stand of trees. When she returned she said:

"Follow me. I found a place with shelter and soft ground."

It was an open spot in the center of four trees whose spreading branches provided a canopy. Underneath the earth was soft.

Dvorah took off her pack. Reuven took off his, after carefully laying down the sword. Dvorah took a blanket from the pack and spread it out on the ground. Then she sat down and took out some dried fruit and flat squares of unleavened bread. She stood a jug of water on the blanket.

Reuven sat facing her.

They ate and drank. When they finished they talked, mostly Dvorah with her tales of growing up in the north.

Reuven felt at peace. He was almost happy.

It was growing dark.

"We should sleep soon," he said. "Tomorrow at dawn we'll resume our journey."

"May I sleep next to you?" Dvorah asked shyly. "I'll feel safer."

"Of course."

He lay down on the blanket. She covered him with another one and lay down next to him, back to back.

"What's her name?"

"Drusilla," Reuven replied.

"She's a lucky girl," Dvorah said. "You're a good man, Reuven. A very good man." After a moment of awkward silence during which Reuven did not know what to say, she added, "Thank you for keeping me alive." Again Reuven did not know what to say.

Soon he heard her regular breathing and knew she was asleep.

Not long after so was he.

They awoke to the sounds of birds. It was a beautiful sound.

Deciding to eat after they had gone further, they packed up and resumed their journey on the road. The Kinneret was closer now; Reuven could see it sparkling in the morning sun.

"Can you swim?" he asked.

"Yes," Dvorah replied.

"I can't," came his sad reply.

"I'll teach you!" she said.

Reuven laughed.

They continued walking.

A vague, disturbing sound entered Reuven's ears from somewhere far behind him.

The drumbeat of horses' hooves?

Reuven whirled around.

In the distance he made out several horses and their riders, cavalry-men, galloping toward them. One of the riders raised a trumpet to his mouth. A thunderous blast followed. Reuven was sure it was aimed at him.

Dvorah also turned.

Alternatives raced through Reuven's mind:

Use the sling to bring them down?

No, there were at least six of them, too many for that.

Flee and hide?

No, the horses could outrun them.

"What should we do, Reuven?" a terrified Dvorah asked.

"Stay calm," came his immediate answer. "Let me do the talking."

There were seven horses and riders in the unit. The officer in charge rode right up to Reuven and stopped his horse. A satisfied grin spread over his shaved face.

"Found you," he said, in Greek.

Reuven could tell from his looks that he was a Syrian serving Rome.

He wouldn't have bothered to address me if he was sent to kill me, Reuven thought, trying to stay calm himself.

"Where are you going?" the officer demanded.

"Jerusalem," Reuven replied.

"To join the rebels?"

"No. To go home. I want nothing to do with the rebellion. I'm the son of a famous peace rabbi who was arrested by the rebels. I want to let everyone know what happens when they defy Rome."

Can he smell my fear? Reuven wondered. Can he hear the beating of my heart?

"Humph!" declared the officer. "Who is she?"

"A distant cousin," Reuven answered. "I came to Gamla to bring her to Jerusalem. We're to be married."

Reuven could see the officer weighing his words.

"Why didn't you surrender?"

"I've done nothing wrong, sir. I just want to get home with my bride-to-be after being trapped in Gamla by the same maniacs who arrested my father and murdered my uncle."

"Where did you get that Roman sword?"

"It's a Jewish sword, sir. I found it on the street as we were leaving Gamla."

"It's a Roman sword."

"I apologize, sir. How would I know the difference?"

"Then you don't know how to use a sword?"

"I'm a rabbinical student, sir," Reuven explained. "How would I have learned to use one?"

"Why would you carry one then?" the officer demanded.

"There are brigands about, sir, brigands who rob people. I thought that the sword would scare them off. Can you blame me, sir?"

The officer leaned forward and examined Reuven's face.

"You don't look like the son of a rabbi at all," he said. "You have the eyes of a killer." The officer straightened up in the saddle as he announced:

"You're under arrest for fleeing Gamla, both of you."

Part Five: The Autóphagos Lamb

November 67 CE – May 68 CE

Chapter Eighty

15 Nov 67 CE / 19 Cheshvan 3828

The sight of the food on the table in front of her made Drusilla nauseous. It was not the nausea of early pregnancy; that had passed. What Drusilla experienced now was not a queasiness that came from the wonder of a new life to-be; it was a sickness in her stomach that came from the knowledge that an existing life had ended.

Her Reuven was dead.

Drusilla no longer wanted to live.

Gamla had fallen. Everyone left in the city had been slaughtered. There was no doubt. Reuven was dead. Eating seemed pointless. Her child would be born into a world at war, without a father. She herself was a stranger in a strange land, and so her child would be.

Better to end it now, she thought. Slowly fade away…

She glanced up at the presence by her side, a presence that rarely left her since that morning when her pregnancy revealed itself.

"You've got to eat, dear," Ruth, Reuven's mother, insisted, putting a gentle hand on her shoulder. "For the baby."

"What does it matter? Reuven's dead."

"You don't know that," Ruth admonished.

"What else can it be? Why isn't he home? Gamla fell almost a month ago. If he made it out alive he had more than enough time to get back to Jerusalem,"

"I don't know," Ruth said, shaking her head, the grip on Drusilla's shoulder tightening. "He's in God's hands. He will return safely. I know it."

Drusilla did not have the heart to argue with Ruth.

She also did not have the heart to eat.

"Eat," Ruth insisted again. "The baby needs it. Even if our Reuven is dead—God forbid—at least we will have his child to carry on his name. Eat, Drusilla, if not for yourself then for Reuven and his unborn son."

Drusilla lifted the bread soaked with olive oil and covered with goat cheese to her mouth. She ate, taking several reluctant bites. She kept eating, watching Ruth out of the corner of her eye, until she saw the older woman nod with approval.

Drusilla closed her eyes and sighed.

I will keep myself alive, she thought, for the sake of Reuven and his son. Ruth will help me.

Drusilla gave Ruth a weak smile. She stood and embraced the woman she had once thought would be her mother-in-law.

"Thank you," Drusilla muttered.

She walked on unsteady legs toward the outside door.

Rabbi Aaron was just coming in. He looked haggard, withdrawn into himself.

He, too, knows that his son is dead.

Drusilla said nothing him. He said nothing to her.

Since Reuven left for Gamla fifty-nine days ago—Drusilla had marked each day of his absence as it passed—Rabbi Aaron had been cold; he barely spoke to her during that whole time. Even after being told she was carrying his grandson, he kept his distance.

It does not matter, Drusilla thought. I will never become his daughter-in-law, and the Romans will probably come and slaughter us before the child is born.

She stepped into the street. There were people walking, absorbed in their business. Some walked alone, deep in thought, others in groups of two, three or more, talking casually or animatedly with each other.

Drusilla wanted to scream at them: How can you go about as if nothing has happened? Don't you know that your world is about to come to an end? Don't you know that my Reuven has been killed?

She kept silent and turned back into the house.

Soon we will all be dead, she thought, and none of this will matter.

Chapter Eighty-One

15 Nov 67 CE / 19 Cheshvan 3828

Once again her eyes filled with terror; once again she asked the same question.

"What are they going to do to us?"

Reuven looked at Dvorah and then at the two oxen pulling the four-wheeled wooden cart they sat in.

"This ride from Gamla is more uncomfortable than the donkey ride to Gamla," he said off-handedly, almost as if he were speaking to himself. "Every time we hit a bump, one of those bags of grain the Romans are transporting hits me in the back or side. Bah! Those five, no six, days atop Amram's donkey were better than these five in this bouncing cart."

Then he laughed.

"Reuven," Dvorah said heatedly, "don't play with me. I'm frightened. What are they going to do with us?"

"Look, Dvorah," he began, with some exasperation, though he did understand her fear, "they haven't killed us. They haven't touched you. They haven't taken our food or money. We've been treated well so far, considering the circumstances. How many times do I have to say the same thing?

"I've been in worse jams, Dvorah," Reuven continued. "All I have to do now is keep my head. I'll talk our way out of this."

"How can you be so sure?"

"I'm sure," Reuven explained, "because after my dealings with those two officers, I feel fully confident of my ability to talk my way out of our current predicament."

Only partially true, Reuven thought. Not fully confident; partially confident. So far, I've done all right. The cavalry officer who captured us may have said I had the eyes of a killer, but telling him that the revolutionaries had murdered my uncle and imprisoned my father had an influence on him. He didn't treat us badly. Though we had to walk back to Gamla, he let us walk at a reasonable pace. At what remained of the Roman camp opposite Gamla, I handled myself pretty well with the cavalry officer's superior. After questioning me, that superior said:

"Well, I'm not quite sure what to do with you. I could kill the two of you, or sell the both of you into slavery. On the other hand, if your story is true, you could be useful to our effort to put down the rebellion.

You saw what we did in Gamla. You can warn the people in Jerusalem that resistance is futile. Commander Vespasian has gone to Caesarea. I'll send you there and let the general himself decide your fate."

I've done all right, so far…

"Those were low-ranking officers," Dvorah said, breaking into his thoughts. "What if you're brought before Vespasian?"

"I hope I will be. I know exactly what I will say to him."

Dvorah shook her head.

"You should have let me join the fighters at the citadel," she muttered. "You should have slit my throat when that Roman opened the trapdoor to the basement. Who knows what awaits me now?"

"When I get you safely to Jerusalem you'll thank me," Reuven retorted.

"If you get me to Jerusalem…"

"I will," asserted Reuven.

Dvorah's face grew pensive.

"I did not give my father a proper burial," she said.

This was not the first time Dvorah said this. Reuven gave her the same answer he had before.

"We said the prayers for the dead. There was no more we could do."

They rode on in silence.

Reuven began to catch glimpses of the great Middle Sea. He could hardly contain his excitement.

"Look!" he cried to Dvorah.

Dvorah had no response when he pointed to the blue expanse shining in the distance.

"Well," he said, "at least it means we're getting closer to Caesarea."

The quality of the road had changed, going from a flat dirt road to a paved one with a bulge down the center. Reuven was certain that this new road was built by the Romans. He wondered about the bulge until he finally realized its purpose.

"These Romans are clever!" he exclaimed. "They think of everything when they build their roads. See how it's higher in the middle? That's so rain will flow off to the sides and not collect on the road itself." He turned to Dvorah. "Say what you want, but the Romans are wonderful engineers!"

Dvorah shrugged in response.

"They're just a bunch of murdering pagans as far as I'm concerned," she replied. "I don't share your admiration for them."

Reuven stretched his legs as far as they could go. He leaned back against one of the bags. He yawned and closed his eyes.

The next thing he knew Dvorah was tugging at him anxiously.

"I think we're there," she whispered.

The cart was still moving.

Reuven looked around. They were traveling through a huge Roman military camp.

Reuven sat up and examined his surroundings carefully. Metilius had done a good job describing what it would look like. Rather than surprise, Reuven felt awe at its orderliness; huts laid out neatly, streets running parallel and perpendicular, as if this were a city built by a master designer.

He did not share this response with Dvorah. Instead, he said:

"Stay calm, Dvorah. I promise I'll get us out of this. Remember, let me speak. Be silent, even if someone questions you in Hebrew or Aramaic. Turn to me instead. But if you have to answer questions, remember the story I concocted, and stick to it."

The cart came to a halt. A soldier on horseback rode up to them.

"Get out!" he said.

"We get out here," Reuven said to Dvorah.

They got out of the cart, collected their bags of supplies, and followed the soldier.

After several steps the horse released a string of dung. Startled, both Reuven and Dvorah stopped, then walked around the pile on the ground. Reuven wondered if the Romans had someone who went around cleaning up after the horses, or if they let the dung sit there to be baked by the sun or washed away in the rain.

The man on horseback pointed to a small shed. It had a door that was swung open against the side of the shed. Reuven entered, Dvorah two steps behind him.

The shed was high enough for Reuven to stand comfortably. It was rectangular, its walls made of untreated wood, its ceiling made of thickly-woven thatch. A window on one side opened inward. The shed was empty except for a long, low bench.

Reuven smiled and sat down. He motioned for Dvorah to do the same. She stared at him uncomprehendingly.

"I'm hungry," Reuven said, opening one of the packs. "I'm going to eat something."

"How can you eat at a time like this?" Dvorah exploded. "How can you be so calm?"

"Shh!" Reuven reproved. "Not so loud!" Then he shrugged, and went on:

"If we're going to get out of this I need to keep my head. So if I'm hungry, I'll eat!"

He pulled out a few squares of unleavened bread and dried figs. He chomped on them noisily, glancing at Dvorah as he did so, and when he finished he took a long drink of water from a jug.

"You might want to eat, also," he suggested. "Won't be long before our food runs out and we'll have to eat Roman slop."

The senior officer in the Roman camp opposite Gamla had allowed them to keep their packs of supplies.

"Use your own food as long as it lasts," he had told them. "I have no idea what you Jews are permitted or forbidden to eat."

That was not all Reuven was able to keep.

The Romans did not search his person. He still had his sling and knife.

They spent four days in the Roman camp before leaving for Caesarea. They were kept in a tent large enough for two people. Only one guard stood outside.

On the second day Dvorah suggested in hushed tones that they plan an escape.

Reuven would have none of it.

"Even if we manage to get away from the camp," Reuven explained to Dvorah, "the cavalry would just hunt us down, and when they found us they'd surely kill us. Be patient, Dvorah. It will turn out all right, I promise."

Reuven looked from Dvorah to the door.

I doubt she'll suggest an escape from here, he thought.

"Really, you should eat something," he said to her.

Dvorah glared at him angrily, sat down on the bench, and deliberately turned away from him.

Reuven put the water jug bag into the pack. He stood up and went to the opening. A guard stood at attention outside the door. He gave Reuven a curious glance, and straightened up so that he seemed taller. He was still shorter than Reuven.

Reuven went back to the bench.

"How long will we be here?" Dvorah asked anxiously.

Reuven sighed.

I don't know what to do to calm her down, he thought. I don't know what to say to take away her fear. She was so brave when she was free, whether in Gamla or that brief period of freedom on the road. But hiding in the storeroom of her house, or as a Roman captive, she seems to be falling apart.

"I don't know, Dvorah," he replied. "We just have to be patient and wait."

They waited, and waited.

Four times Reuven had to ask the guard for permission to use a privy for himself or Dvorah. Each time Reuven walked back from the foul-smelling building, with the guard accompanying him, Reuven looked around eagerly, filled with curiosity.

The things I've seen since I left Jerusalem! he thought.

They were still waiting when the sun went down. The guard outside had changed for the evening watch.

When darkness fell Dvorah lay down on the bench. Reuven stretched out on the floor of the hut.

"Yes," Dvorah said, her voice dripping with sarcasm, "they really are treating us well."

Reuven did not respond.

He was starting to worry.

How long will they keep us here? he wondered.

How long have I been away from Jerusalem? was his next question.

Reuven got up, went to the door, and stepped outside.

The guard, who had been sitting on the ground, his back against the hut, half asleep, jumped up to attention and glared at Reuven angrily.

"What do you want?" he snapped.

Not Roman, Reuven thought. Syrian.

"Excuse me, sir? What day is it?"

"You don't know what day it is?"

"No, sir."

"Why do you care, Jew? You'll be dead soon."

"What? How do you know that?" Reuven asked in alarm.

"Everyone knows that," the guard responded. "Not soon enough for me. I have better things to do than guard you. Maybe they'll let me slit your throat and take the girl. Then I can sell her." He chuckled. "I'd like that very much."

Reuven started to tremble and fought to control it.

I came out here for a reason, he thought.

"Well, sir, if I really am going to die tomorrow the least you can do is tell a condemned man what day it is."

"The fifteenth of November," the man spat.

"Thank you, sir."

Reuven went back into the tent. He was still trembling.

How could it be? he wondered. Why would they go through the trouble of bringing us here just to kill us? They could have done that back in Gamla. They have to give me a hearing first!

Reuven lay down, his thoughts cycling through possible scenarios that might confront them.

Then he remembered why he asked the guard in the first place.

Reuven did some calculating in his head.

If it's the fifteenth of November then that should be the nineteenth of Cheshvan. No, wait, it's after sunset. So it's the twentieth of Cheshvan.

Reuven shivered.

We were in that basement for more than two weeks! And two months since I left home!

Will I see it again?

Reuven stared up at the sleeping form above him, surprised and envious of her sound sleep. He attempted sleep, but constantly woke from troubling thoughts. He tried changing his position, though he knew the source of his restlessness was not physical.

Reuven shut his eyes and ignored all thoughts of the present and future. He went back to the past, replaying Drusilla's voice singing her lullaby to him, as she did that day long ago in the house in the Upper City.

Soon, Reuven slept.

Chapter Eighty-Two

27 November 67 CE / 2 Kislev 3828

Daylight streamed through the open window, waking Reuven. He yawned and stretched. It was the twelfth night they had spent in the hut.

They had not been executed. Or questioned. It was as if they had been forgotten, except for the guard outside and the food that was brought to them once a day after their own ran out.

Food, Reuven thought, that Dvorah refused to eat, fearful there was something forbidden in the cold stew, fearful of committing a transgression, until I convinced her it was permitted to violate such laws in order to save a life. "If you don't eat, Dvorah, you will die, a greater transgression."

Reuven rubbed his beard and grunted. He sat up. Dvorah was staring at him.

"Why are they just making us sit here?" she asked. "What's going to happen to us?"

These were questions that Dvorah kept asking him. He was growing tired of giving the same answer.

"Vespasian and his staff have more important things to deal with," Reuven replied, sighing. "We just have to wait, Dvorah."

Her response was a sigh louder than his own.

"It's still better than the basement," he added, trying to console her.

Morning dragged on. During their captivity Reuven had tried to stay alert and keep Dvorah's mind occupied by giving her lessons on Torah and commentary. Sometimes she would pay attention and engage him with sharp questions, other times he could see her thoughts wandering.

When the sun had just crossed the meridian a soldier in full battle dress appeared at their hut.

"Come with me," he ordered.

Reuven and Dvorah followed him toward the center of the camp.

The camp was full of activity; men moving about, oxen pulling carts, mules with bags on their backs.

Their escort stopped in front of a tent whose size seemed to Reuven to be closer to that of a small building rather than a tent. Reuven guessed it was large enough to hold several dozen people and that it was Vespasian's general headquarters.

Two guards, also in full battle dress, stood at the entrance. Reuven's escort spoke briefly to them and then motioned Reuven and Dvorah forward.

The guard on the right began to search Reuven.

A relieved Reuven was glad that he had stashed his knife and sling at the bottom of his pack. There was nothing for the guard to find. Reuven assumed that because he was not armed they decided not to search Dvorah.

"Follow me," their escort said as he entered the tent. They followed; he then stepped off to the side.

Sitting at a wide and sturdy table was a man with a broad face, thin lips, a prominent nose, and large ears. He had close-set eyes and a high forehead with a receding hairline. Reuven guessed that he was in his mid-fifties. Clustered around him stood three men to his right and two to his left. The men were looking down at a large map spread out on the table. The man sitting was staring straight at Reuven.

A stab of fear went through Reuven.

That must be Vespasian, he thought. And I can see he's no fool.

"What's your name?" Vespasian asked curtly.

"Reuven ben Aaron, sir." He glanced briefly at the general and then down at the floor.

"Where are you from?"

"Jerusalem, sir."

"Why were you in Gamla?"

"To bring Dvorah, my cousin, to Jerusalem, sir. We are supposed to be married."

He must have already known my answers, Reuven thought. He must have been briefed about me. Why else would I be appearing before him?

Reuven kept his eyes on the ground.

"How do I know you didn't go to Gamla to fight with the rebels?"

Reuven took a deep breath. He could feel himself relaxing. His feet moved into a wider stance. He looked Vespasian directly in the eyes and did not lower his glance.

"Sir, my uncle, my father's twin brother, Moshe ben Avraham, was murdered by the rebels while addressing a public meeting," Reuven answered with heat. He saw the men around Vespasian staring at him. He sensed Dvorah was, too, though she would only understand the names he spoke. "My uncle was arguing for peace and submission to Rome. For that he was murdered. Everyone in Jerusalem knows this." Reuven paused, as if to catch his breath. "His wife, my aunt, vanished soon after, probably murdered by those same rebels to silence her voice that was demanding justice for my uncle. Later, my father, Aaron ben Avraham, was imprisoned by the rebels. Why would I attach myself to men who so grievously injured my family? I also would not join the rebels because I'm not a fool, sir. Rome is the mightiest empire the world has ever seen. Rome has the strongest military. And the rebels are facing Rome's greatest general."

Vespasian smiled.

"Do you know who I am?" he asked.

Without hesitating, his eyes still locked on Vespasian's, Reuven replied:

"Today you are General Vespasian, commander of Rome's forces to put down the rebellion in Judea, the general who put down the German revolt and who conquered Britain."

"*Today* I'm General Vespasian?"

His tone indicated anger, his face amusement.

Reuven was unflappable as he continued.

"Today you are a general, one day you will be emperor."

Vespasian laughed.

"You are the second Jew to tell me that," he said. "What, are you also a prophet or a seer?" And he laughed again.

"No, sir," Reuven responded. "If I were a prophet or a seer I would have come to Gamla before the siege started and gotten my future wife and her father out before the city fell. No, I'm no prophet. One doesn't need prophecy to know that sooner or later, and sooner rather than later, you will rule Rome. Rome is a great empire. It did not get that way by having weak or foolish leaders, but by having men like the great Augustus. We hear stories about the current emperor, even in Judea. He will not last long. And who else could possibly replace him but Rome's greatest general?"

There was a stir among the men around Vespasian. A few of them smiled. One nodded his head in agreement.

"How old are you?" Vespasian asked sharply.

"Sixteen." And then, because he decided that the fewer lies he told the better, he added, sheepishly, "Almost sixteen."

"Almost sixteen? You're a bold fellow for one so young. You're very confident."

"I am not bold, sir," Reuven insisted. "I am not confident in myself. My confidence is in you. One does not become a great general simply by being a brave and superb fighter. It takes strategic and tactical brilliance. It also takes the ability to inspire men, and that requires the ability to see into men's souls. Those are the reasons you are a great general and will be a great emperor. It is why I am not afraid to speak openly to you. I have nothing to fear from a just and rational man."

Reuven did not flinch from Vespasian, who had a look of amazement on his face.

"I don't know whether to slap your face for impudence or congratulate you on your wisdom," Vespasian said laughing. "You really aren't afraid, are you?"

Reuven shrugged and threw up his hands.

"I know I'm taking a chance by speaking openly. Perhaps I should be trembling and pleading for my life. But the truth is, I have done nothing to offend you or Rome. If you are not a just man you will kill me no matter what I say. If you are just I have nothing to fear. It's in God's hands, and I can't believe that a just God would have delivered so many victories to an unjust man."

Vespasian regarded Reuven silently for several moments. Finally he nodded.

"Young man," he said, "if you are telling the truth you will be free to go back to Jerusalem with your bride-to-be, who I get the feeling is not someone you are in love with. Tell me, what do you plan to do when you get back to Jerusalem?"

"Tell them what I saw in Gamla. Tell them that resistance to Rome is futile."

"And if you don't succeed?"

"Get my family out before it is too late."

Vespasian nodded.

"I will help you return to Jerusalem. I will send you with a detachment to make sure you get there safely. And in case you do not succeed convincing the people of Jerusalem to surrender I will give you a letter with my seal promising you and your family safe passage through Roman lines. This all on condition that you are telling me the truth."

Reuven bowed his head.

"Thank you, sir," he said. "Your offer is very generous. If I may, I'd like to make one suggestion. It would be better if our escort left us about a day's journey from Jerusalem. If I'm seen in the company of a Roman detachment they will say I counsel surrender because I've turned traitor, and not because I saw the futility of opposing Rome. I want them to listen to me when I tell them what I saw in Gamla, a city with the same formidable defensive geography as Jerusalem."

Vespasian smiled.

"Very clever of you, young man. Good strategy!"

I'm as good a speaker as my uncle, Reuven thought, exhilarated at the outcome.

"Now I have to warn you," Vespasian began. "I don't know if you're telling the truth or you're just another crafty Jew who thinks he can trick a Roman. I have someone from Jerusalem who can question you and let me know if your story is true."

A chill descended on Reuven.

"Perhaps you've heard of him," Vespasian went on. "Yosef ben Matityahu. He was a prominent man in Jerusalem. I captured him when we took Jotapata."

Reuven nodded. He knew who Yosef ben Matityahu was. He had been appointed one of the commanders to defend the Galilee. After losing Yodfat, he went over to the Roman side.

He will know about my uncle, and my father. He will corroborate that part of my story. But will he know that I was a rebellious son who joined the revolutionaries?

"Yosef ben Matityahu will question you," Vespasian said. "If he believes you are telling the truth, I will do what I promised. If he says you are lying…" Vespasian's eyes narrowed. His face became hard. He drew his right index finger across his throat.

A traitor, Reuven thought with anger, struggling to stay calm. A traitor will now determine whether we live or die.

"I will have him come tomorrow. For now both of you are dismissed."

Reuven suppressed a shudder. He couldn't get out of there quickly enough.

Chapter Eighty-Three

27 November 67 CE / 2 Kislev 3828

Reuven was unnerved. When they returned to the hut he could barely attend to Dvorah's questions about what had transpired with Vespasian. He brushed off her concerns with general assertions that it went well and that everything would be fine. He did not want to share his fear with her.

Reuven had convinced himself that Yosef ben Matityahu knew he had joined the rebels.

He has to know, Reuven thought.

Reuven was terrified. Unlike the fear he experienced in combat or when the Romans entered Dvorah's house, this was not something that would last a few moments; what clutched at his insides threatened to stay with him until final judgment was passed. It clouded his ability to think clearly.

This was the worst part of it; by preventing him from thinking straight he was unable to plan responses to the questions that the traitor Yosef ben Matityahu might throw at him.

There was nothing Reuven could do about it.

He barely ate for the rest of the day. He spoke only a few words to Dvorah after responding to her initial questions. Reuven suspected that his mood was affecting Dvorah, filling her with the same terror he was experiencing, but there was nothing he could do about it.

At sundown, the Sabbath began. Reuven felt no joy in it. When night fell, even thoughts of Drusilla and her lullaby did not bring him sleep. He tossed and turned the whole night on the hard floor.

Reuven was no better the next morning. He passed the slow-moving time in the same state. In midafternoon another Roman soldier came to escort him back to the headquarters tent.

He and Dvorah started to leave the hut.

"Just you," the soldier said, pointing to Reuven. "She stays."

Reuven relayed his words to Dvorah.

"No!" she begged, clutching his arm. "Don't leave me here alone."

Reuven nodded and patted her hand.

"It will be all right," he said.

She tightened her grip.

"No," she hissed furiously. "Don't leave me."

"You don't understand," Reuven said, trying to make his tone calm and reassuring. "I won't."

He looked at the escort soldier's face. He may not have understood Dvorah's words but Reuven was sure he sensed their meaning.

"I'm not going without her," Reuven said firmly.

"Orders are just you!"

"I'm not leaving her," Reuven said. "Unless you kill us both, if I go, she goes."

The soldier stood there for a moment, saying nothing, doing nothing.

Reuven knew he was considering his options.

"All right," he said at last. "Take her along. I'll let the higher-ups decide. I have no authority to kill either one of you."

The soldier abruptly turned and started marching toward headquarters, Reuven and Dvorah in tow.

In the large tent, Reuven recognized the men he saw yesterday, but there was one new person.

That addition was clearly a Jew. He was about medium height, with a prominent nose, dark eyes, and a dark beard. Reuven guessed he was about thirty years old.

That must be Yosef ben Matityahu, Reuven thought bitterly. Should I wish him Shabbat Shalom and ask if this is what we should be doing on the Sabbath?

The soldier who had brought them spoke quickly and in a low voice to Vespasian.

An amused smile appeared on Vespasian's face when the soldier finished.

"Well," Vespasian said, "I guess I was wrong about you, young fellow. I thought you were entering a loveless marriage, but apparently you were willing to die rather than abandon her, so you must really love her. Either that, or you're a remarkably honorable and noble fellow."

Reuven was tempted to say: *Didn't I tell you that you were able to see into the hearts of men? It's the latter case for me, though it's less that I'm honorable and more that it was the right thing to do not to leave her behind.*

Instead, Reuven held his tongue.

"This is Yosef ben Matityahu," Vespasian went on. "He has some questions to ask you. I've asked him to speak Greek and not your own language, so I will understand."

Reuven looked toward Yosef ben Matityahu.

"What's your name?" he asked Reuven.

"Reuven ben Aaron."

"What was your uncle's name?"

"Moshe ben Avraham."

"You have two brothers and a sister. What are their names?"

Reuven gave him a look that said: *Are you really trying to trip me up?*

Reuven eyes went from Yosef ben Matityahu to Vespasian and back to Yosef ben Matityahu. He furrowed his brow.

"Hmm…I didn't know I had such a big family," Reuven said sarcastically. "I know I have a brother two years older than me named Benjamin, but I'll have to ask my parents about the other two." Yosef ben Matityahu smiled. "If I get home…" Reuven added.

Yosef ben Matityahu turned to Vespasian.

"Reuven is who he says he is."

Vespasian nodded.

"Continue, Yosef," he said.

"Where was your uncle killed?"

"Xystus Plaza."

"Do you know who did it?" asked Yosef ben Matityahu.

"One of the revolutionaries, John ben Dorcas," answered Reuven.

Yosef ben Matityahu stroked his beard.

"I've heard of him," he said. "A very bad man. I can believe it. But how do you know for sure?"

"He told my father, when my father was arrested."

"What are you going to do about it?" Vespasian asked, breaking into the interrogation.

Reuven pivoted to the Roman general. For a moment he forgot his own perilous circumstances and said, his voice quivering with anger:

"Kill him."

Vespasian nodded in approval.

Yosef ben Matityahu again turned to Vespasian.

"So far, General, his story holds together and is believable." He resumed questioning Reuven. "Why was your father released?"

"I went to the Committee for Public Safety and told them that I would be responsible for my father. If he did anything wrong they could punish me."

"Ah," interrupted Vespasian, "you *are* a noble young man."

Reuven bowed toward Vespasian.

"Thank you, sir," he said.

"Did you go alone?" Yosef ben Matityahu asked.

"I went with Ananus ben Ananus."

Yosef ben Matityahu nodded.

"I heard you were very close to him."

Reuven shrugged.

"Ananus ben Ananus," Yosef ben Matityahu explained to Vespasian, "is one of the leaders of the government in Jerusalem. This boy was close to him." He paused. "Reuven seems to be well-connected. He had a quarrel with the captain of the Temple ministers, Eleazar ben Ananias. Eleazar was about to slap him in the face. Reuven threatened to kill him. The boy suffered no consequences for the threat."

"Oho! A most modest young man also," exclaimed Vespasian. "You didn't tell me that about yourself, that you were someone of importance."

Reuven caught his breath, fearful that he was about to be tripped up.

"I'm not modest, sir," he said quickly. "I have a sense of proportion and the ridiculous. It would be absurd for me to claim that I'm someone of importance. I'm a nobody. Ananus ben Ananus is a priest, as is Yosef ben Matityahu. I come from a prominent rabbinical family. I'm a kind of connection between the two groups, that is all."

"Did Ananus send you to Gamla?" Vespasian's question was accompanied by a hard, penetrating stare.

"He asked me to let him know about the state of the town, sir," answered Reuven.

"Young man," Vespasian said, his voice as cutting as a double-edged Roman sword, "I think you're hiding things from me. I don't think you're quite what you make yourself out to be. For the moment only, I'll ignore that. For the moment." There was menace in Vespasian's tone. "Tell me, do you think the Jews can win the war against Rome?"

"We haven't so far," Reuven replied quickly.

"Jerusalem is a big city. It is well-protected by stout walls and deep ravines," countered Vespasian.

It took Reuven a moment before he answered.

"I don't know sir, I truly don't know. Before you conquered the north I might have thought it was possible. Now, I would not wager my next meal on it. Rome has a large, well-disciplined army, powerful weaponry, and excellent leaders. We," here Reuven shrugged, 'have none of that." He paused. "I should add, sir, that though Ananus ben Ananus is one of the leaders of the government, he is aware of the futility of the struggle. He has told me so."

Vespasian looked from Reuven to Yosef ben Matityahu. The latter continued his questioning.

"You told General Vespasian that you were supposed to bring your future wife's father out of Gamla. What happened to him? What about her mother?"

"Her father died during the siege. Her mother died a long time ago, giving birth to her sister, who also died."

"Was her father killed during the fighting?"

"No. He started declining during the siege. In the end his heart gave out."

Yosef ben Matityahu nodded and made a sympathetic face directed at Dvorah. Then he continued.

"There's something I don't understand. You described your future wife as a cousin, but your family is from Jerusalem while she is from Gamla."

"She's a distant cousin, through my mother's family," Reuven responded. "Or so I'm told."

"One last question," Yosef ben Matityahu said.

Reuven stifled a sigh of relief.

"Was there anyone else with you besides Ananus ben Ananus when you went to get your father released?"

Reuven felt panic overtake him.

When did Yosef ben Matityahu leave Jerusalem for the Galilee? Before or after my father's release? Does he know Judah ben Ezra was with us? If he does, I'm done for. Everyone knows Judah ben Ezra was a revolutionary.

"Yes," Reuven said, gambling that the truth was safer than a lie. "Judah ben Ezra."

Yosef ben Matityahu scowled.

"He was one of the revolutionaries," he said. "Why would Judah ben Ezra work for the release of your father?"

Reuven shrugged and suppressed a need to swallow deeply.

"Perhaps he thought it made no sense to arrest a prominent rabbi who was not a threat. Maybe he thought arresting such a person would harm the revolution." Reuven shrugged again.

"No personal connection between the two of you?" Yosef ben Matityahu pressed.

"I thanked him. I was grateful for what he did." Reuven threw up his hands in a gesture of helplessness.

Yosef ben Matityahu's eyes narrowed.

He knows, Reuven thought, he knows.

"Tell me, Reuven. Am I a traitor?" Yosef ben Matityahu asked sharply.

"Am I?" retorted Reuven. "I, too, am a prisoner of Rome. I, too, see the futility of war with Rome."

Yosef ben Matityahu turned to Vespasian.

"I have no further questions, General."

"Good," replied Vespasian. To Reuven, he said:

"You will know my decision on your fate tomorrow. I must discuss this with Yosef ben Matityahu. You are dismissed."

As Reuven left the tent of Vespasian's general headquarters, a chill danced down his spine; even the warm sweat dripping down his back could not stop it.

Chapter Eighty-Four

29 November 67 CE / 4 Kislev 3828

Amram ben Gedalyahu couldn't leave Caesarea fast enough. He felt the contempt in the eyes and voices of the Romans who paid him. He knew what they were thinking:

Traitor to his country, spying on his own people, all for money, the lowest kind of scum.

It didn't bother him. Why should he care as long as they paid him?

Amram's foot dug into the flank of the donkey he was riding while his right hand gripped the rope tied to the bridle of the donkey behind him.

It was a good business, spying for the Romans. In addition to the pay, he was granted certain concessions and privileges for his other business, the small-scale buying and selling of a variety of goods that he transported on his donkeys. No taxes were levied by the Romans, a monopoly was granted for a few small regions, and he was allowed to deal in minor contraband.

The Romans paid better than his own people did. This was to be expected; the Romans paid him to be a traitor while the Jews paid him to carry out his patriotic duty. The money the Jews gave him was simply to keep him and his donkeys fed as he reported on the doings of the occupier.

Neither side knew that he worked for the other.

Amram liked it that way.

If he had to choose—and he was glad he didn't—Amram would have chosen to work only for the Jews. As it was, the information he gave them was more valuable than what he told the Romans, at least as far as he could tell.

Amram was anxious to get to Jerusalem as quickly as possible. If he alternated short bursts of speed with periods of walking, switched his own weight and supply bag between donkeys, and continued a bit through the night, he could reach Jerusalem in less than two days.

The Committee for Public Safety would be very interested in his information, rewarding him with money and gratitude. Ananus ben Ananus would also be interested. Unlike the committee, who would eagerly gobble up what Amram had to tell them, Ananus ben Ananus would find the news about his protégé very disconcerting.

Amram wondered who would pay him more: The Committee for information damaging to Ananus or Ananus for keeping that information from coming to light.

Amram was surprised the first time he saw Reuven in the Roman camp. The boy was heading toward the privy with a Roman guard and hadn't spotted him.

He almost couldn't believe his eyes. If Reuven hadn't made it back to Jerusalem on his own how did he escape the slaughter in Gamla? What was he doing in the Roman camp at Caesarea? Had he been captured or did he surrender voluntarily?

Amram briefly considered informing the Romans that Reuven had connections to both the government in Jerusalem and the rebels, with whom Reuven had fought the Romans. The Romans would certainly pay him for that information.

He decided to wait so he could spy on Reuven to get a better fix on what the boy was doing there. A few days later he got an even bigger surprise. Reuven entered Vespasian's tent and emerged unscathed.

On the Sabbath there was another surprise. Reuven entered Vespasian's tent a second time, this time with Yosef ben Matityahu, a real traitor, also inside. Reuven came out from that meeting once again a free man.

It could only mean one thing.

There was no point in giving the Romans his information about Reuven. They probably knew already. Even if they didn't, they wouldn't care.

No, better to warn The Committee for Public Safety, and Ananus, as well.

They all should know, and beware, if Reuven were sent back to Jerusalem by the Romans.

The boy, like Yosef ben Matityahu, had turned traitor and spy.

Chapter Eighty-Five

1 December 67 CE / 6 Kislev 3828

He gazed out at the Middle Sea with awe. The wind took his breath away. The sound of the surf filled his ears. Waves driven by some unseen power crashed onto the shore.

Reuven had never seen anything like it.

"Blessed be the Lord, Master of the Universe, who created such wonders," he murmured.

The sea led to the wider world beyond, to lands and peoples unknown.

Oh, Reuven lamented, why must I be captive to this small portion of the earth?

It's beautiful here, he thought. The sky and sea are brilliant blue. But not as brilliant blue as Drusilla's eyes! She must have crossed this sea. She must have seen much of the world. Oh, when I get home I must ask her about it!

Oh, Drusilla, how I long for you!

Reuven turned and started walking north, toward the waiting Dvorah.

Three days ago, on the Sabbath, after Reuven had been questioned by Yosef ben Matityahu, he and Dvorah did not have long to wait for Vespasian to come to a decision. It was late afternoon when they were called back to the general's headquarters. Yosef ben Matityahu was no longer there. Vespasian greeted them with a warm smile. The smile was a catalyst that caused relief to flood through Reuven.

"I shall do as I promised," Vespasian said. "A detachment will make sure you get to Jerusalem safely. One will be put together in the next few days. They will leave you at dawn within a half day's march of Jerusalem. A half day, not a full day. I want to lessen the chance something evil befalls you. In addition to the document that guarantees you safe passage through Roman lines, should you need to leave Jerusalem with your family, I will give you another document, granting an audience with me in Rome, if, as you say, I do become emperor. I will reward you handsomely for your foresight."

Reuven bowed and said in a clear, calm voice:

"Thank you, sir. May God grant you good fortune and a smooth path to leading the great Roman Empire."

"Is there anything else I can do for you in the meantime?" Vespasian inquired.

Reuven had looked down at the ground. His feet had shifted uncomfortably. He took a deep breath.

"Sir, I know this sounds foolish, but before we leave may I see the Mare Nostrum?" he asked, using the Roman term for the Middle Sea. "I've hardly seen anything in my life."

Vespasian laughed.

"Of course!" he said jovially, and then began to expound on the amazing harbor and city Herod had constructed and named in honor of Caesar Augustus. When Vespasian had finished Reuven could hardly wait to see the city and its harbor as well as the sea.

And now he had seen it! As he approached Dvorah she gave him a puzzled look.

"So?" she asked.

"All things reveal the Glory of God," he answered. "You should have come with me."

"If I could only go back to Gamla," Dvorah responded sadly. "Go back home, the way it used to be. I have no use for the sea, or the world beyond. Or even the great city of Jerusalem."

Reuven sighed with weariness. How could he make her understand?

The surf was calmer where he stood now, the sea was tamed. What had once been an unprotected shoreline—such as where he had stared at the unbroken sea—was a magnificent artificial harbor enclosed in two jetties. There were hundreds of ships, docking and undocking, loading and unloading, entering and leaving the broad harbor.

Vespasian had said it was bigger than the port at Piraeus in Greece.

Bigger than the one in Greece! Here, in his own country!

The southern jetty was just to his left. It was 1600 feet long and 200 feet wide. Its base went down 120 feet into the sea. The outer edge of the jetty served as a breakwater, protecting the harbor from the waves to the south. Massive towers, buildings, and a broad walkway topped the jetty. Docks ran along the entire inner edge. The other jetty further north was 900 feet long.

Vespasian was right, Reuven thought, when he said the harbor of Caesarea was magnificent!

The complexity of life weighed on Reuven; the strange tension between good and evil whipsawed his mind, spawning conflicting currents coursing through his head.

Before they left Vespasian's headquarters, the general had said:

"May your God go with you and protect you, always."

Here was a man who might very well crush Jewish freedom forever wishing him well in the name of the God of the Jews.

There were more conundrums. When he looked around at the harbor, and back at the city of Caesarea, he saw wonders. But unlike the sea, which was the work of the Holy One, Blessed be He, what Reuven gazed at now was created by a wicked human, King Herod, cursed be his name.

The world's contradictions overwhelmed Reuven. He felt dizzy and stared down at the ground beneath his feet to gain some kind of stability.

How could he reconcile any of this?

He felt Dvorah's impatience as she shifted on the sand next to him.

"These Gentiles are amazing," he said, as much to himself as to Dvorah. "Herod was simply aping Roman and Greek civilization. He added his own brilliance and ability to organize. But it's theirs, not ours, and I'm envious."

"You're envious?" Dvorah retorted. "Civilization? Brilliance?" she sneered. "We passed the stadium. There they stage fights to the death between humans and animals, and humans and humans. That is civilization? You saw all the idols to their imaginary gods. That is brilliance? You yourself told me about the slaughter of 20,000 Jews in Caesarea. How can you possibly admire them? What's wrong with you, Reuven?"

Reuven took a deep breath before answering.

"You know, Dvorah, it was admiration for a Roman officer that inspired me to join the revolution. I saw him walking the streets of Jerusalem unbowed and unafraid. I wanted to be like him, to be a fighter, for our people. My father was horrified.

"Have I become like them? Did that admiration lead to accepting some of their values? I don't know, Dvorah, I don't know. Come, they are waiting to take us to Jerusalem. Let's go."

They had gone only a few steps when Dvorah asked:

"What will you advise Ananus when you see him? Will you advise cowardly surrender to your new-found living, breathing golden calves, or will you tell him we should fight on bravely for our freedom?"

Reuven gave a mirthless chuckle.

"I like the way you phrase that, Dvorah," he said. "What I will do is tell him what I saw. I don't know what course the nation should take. Perhaps when I talk to my father, to Judah, and to Ananus, I will know. Perhaps not."

Reuven kicked at the dirt.

No, he thought, I don't know, and they probably don't either. Only God knows, and no one speaks to God anymore; prophecy died long ago.

Then someone whose advice might be worthwhile, even above all the others, occurred to him: The barbarian girl with golden hair and blue eyes that he was going to marry. Perhaps she had more wisdom than the lot of them.

The very idea made him laugh.

Dvorah turned to him with a questioning look but Reuven said nothing.

Chapter Eighty-Six

2 December 67 CE / 7 Kislev 3828

A deep and troubled sleep was shattered by the loud banging that echoed throughout the house. Drusilla's disturbing dream fled; she could not grasp or recall it.

The banging continued.

Someone was at the front door of Rabbi Aaron's house.

At this hour? It was after midnight, well before dawn.

Drusilla shivered and pulled the blanket tighter around herself.

The fog of sleep dissipated. She stood up, the blanket still covering her, and shivered even more violently.

It must be about Reuven, she thought. They found his body!

The light in the main room was dim; its single lamp's wick trimmed. Drusilla, waiting in the back so as not to be seen, watched as Rabbi Aaron, still in his night clothes, went to the door.

When he opened it, the small flame of the oil lamp danced, sending spectral shadows scurrying along the wall.

Three men burst into the house. Even through the gloom Drusilla could see the hardness and anger on their faces.

This was not about Reuven, she realized. This was no condolence call.

"What do you want?" Rabbi Aaron demanded.

"You are under arrest," the man in front of the other two answered. His face made Drusilla think of a monstrous toad.

Monstrous Toad carried a tablet bound in a leather strap. The other two men carried weapons; one a sword, the other a javelin.

"By whose order? For what crime?"

Drusilla heard no fear in the rabbi's voice, only outrage. It was so strong that it caused Monstrous Toad to take an involuntary step backward. He removed the leather strap and opened the two-leaved wax tablet.

Benjamin came and stood in the middle of the room. Ruth hung back, standing an arm's length away from Drusilla.

Rabbi Aaron squinted through the darkness as he read what was inscribed in the wax.

"He's not just a murderer," Rabbi Aaron spat out with contempt. "He's an ignoramus, too."

"You better come with us," Monstrous Toad said, taking the tablet back and binding it again.

"The Committee for Public Safety," Rabbi Aaron sneered. "An arrest warrant signed by John ben Dorcas. Bah, you're nothing but a bunch of robbers and murderers."

Monstrous Toad grabbed Rabbi Aaron's arm and began pulling him toward the open door.

"There's no charge listed here!" Rabbi Aaron exclaimed.

A gust of wind entered the house, its air heavy with the promise of rain.

"It listed treason," was the response.

"But there are no particulars given!" retorted Rabbi Aaron.

"You'll learn the details soon enough," and with that Monstrous Toad tugged harder at Rabbi Aaron.

"Keep your hands off my father!" Benjamin shouted.

"Shut up or we'll arrest you, too!" came the harsh reply.

"Quiet, Benjamin," Rabbi Aaron said gently. "You're needed at home, to watch over the family." Rabbi Aaron shook off the grasping hand as if it were no more than a child's appendage. "All right, I'll go with you." Then he shouted: "Isn't it enough that my son died fighting for you madmen?"

Ruth appeared at his side, holding his cloak and sandals. He slipped his head through the cloak so that it covered his night clothes and then placed his feet in his sandals.

The wind howled as the three men escorted Rabbi Aaron from his home. The door stood open.

Drusilla rushed to close it.

"What shall we do?" wailed Ruth.

Benjamin stood rooted in the center of the room. His body was trembling. Drusilla made out tears trickling down his cheeks.

"Listen," she said. "You have to go to Ananus ben Ananus. He will free your father."

Benjamin nodded dumbly.

"Now!" Drusilla insisted.

"Now? At this hour?"

"Yes! These men mean business. They are dangerous. Ananus sent your brother to Gamla, he is responsible for the safety of Reuven's family."

She could see Benjamin hesitating.

"I'll go with you if you wish," Drusilla said softly.
Benjamin looked at her helplessly.

Chapter Eighty-Seven

2 December 67 CE / 7 Kislev 3828

Like a caged animal, Rabbi Aaron paced his prison cell; though aware in some back corner of his mind that his life was in danger his overwhelming emotion was outrage.

"How dare they! By what right?"

He muttered these sentences over and over again, sometimes softly, under his breath, sometimes so loudly that the guards and functionaries in the other part of the home that was serving as a makeshift prison could hear him.

"Shut up!" they yelled in response. "Shut up or we'll come and beat you until you stop shouting."

Rabbi Aaron was undeterred.

No one came to silence him.

At last he grew weary. Rabbi Aaron sat down on a bench in the corner and ceased his cries and murmurings.

A small lamp on a stand gave feeble light to the bare room.

It didn't seem possible for him to be arrested for something he did not do, but here he was. Perhaps the revolutionaries were arresting all the rabbis who had argued for peace?

How could they do such a thing? The people will rise in protest!

Rabbi Aaron remained lost in thought when he heard the sound of many footsteps approaching. He rose from his seat.

The door flew open.

There, at the head of the three men who had come to his home and arrested him, was Judah ben Ezra!

"Have you come to torture me?" he shouted at Judah, not in fear, but with a mixture of anger and contempt.

And then, to Rabbi Aaron's amazement, Judah ben Ezra was shoved roughly into the room. The door closed and was locked harshly behind him.

"What, what?" Rabbi Aaron sputtered.

Even in the dim light he could see Judah's gap-toothed grin.

"Have you come to spy on me?" Rabbi Aaron asked incredulously.

Judah laughed.

"I'm a prisoner, just like you, rabbi."

"Why?"

"They charged me with treason, just like they did you," Judah explained. "For the same reason. Because of Reuven."

"That makes no sense. My son was killed in Gamla."

"No, Rabbi, he was not. Somehow he survived. He was seen at the Roman camp in Caesarea, twice in Vespasian's tent."

"He's alive, he alive!" cried Rabbi Aaron. "My son Reuven lives! Praised be the Master of the Universe!"

Tears filled Rabbi Aaron's eyes.

Then he shook his head.

"But why were we arrested?" he asked, confused.

"They say he went over to the Romans and is now supporting them!"

"Oh! Praised be the Master of the Universe!" Rabbi Aaron shouted again. "At last my son has got some sense and opposes this disastrous war!"

Judah ben Ezra was on him in an instant, one hand on his throat and one hand clamped firmly on his mouth, silencing him.

"Shut up, you old fool!" Judah hissed. "Are you trying to give them a reason to execute you?"

Judah released him; Rabbi Aaron could see that Judah was ready to resume his grasp at the first outburst.

"Listen, you," Judah continued, "maybe you don't care if you live or die, but I don't want to see the revolution execute you, for Reuven's sake, if nothing else."

Rabbi Aaron took several deep breaths.

"So I was arrested because they think I'm connected to Reuven's defection," he whispered. "Why did they arrest you?"

"They demanded that I denounce Reuven. I refused."

"Why?"

"Because Reuven is not a traitor," Judah said with conviction. "I don't know what he was doing in that camp—I suppose he was taken prisoner—but I am positive that he will not betray his country. He's a brave cub, and very clever, and the revolution already owes much to him."

Rabbi Aaron's body shook. He covered his face with his hands.

Judah gently laid his palms and fingers on Rabbi Aaron's shoulders.

"Listen, Rabbi Aaron, it will turn out all right. We'll get out of this; our fellow Jews will not execute us. And your son Reuven will find a way to return to Jerusalem and rejoin the fight for freedom."

Judah's hands increased their grip, gently embracing Rabbi Aaron's shoulders, as if trying to reassure him.

But Rabbi Aaron did not remove his own hands from hiding his face.

He did not believe Judah's optimistic prediction.

Chapter Eighty-Eight

2 December 67 CE / 7 Kislev 3828

Ananus ben Ananus gazed sympathetically at Benjamin, while studiously avoiding looking at Drusilla, whose body was draped in a shapeless cloak and whose hair and face were covered. Only her forehead, eyes, and cheekbones were exposed. They both stood before Ananus, dripping wet.

For her part, Drusilla was glad Ananus was ignoring her; her eyes did not leave his face as she stared intently, searching for clues as to how he might be induced to use his power to free Rabbi Aaron.

Drusilla and Benjamin had made their way in the rain through the darkened streets of Jerusalem to Ananus' magnificent house in the Upper City without speaking a word to each other. The sleeping watchman outside the home's gate, obviously derelict in his duty, was unhappy with being disturbed. Benjamin had ordered him to bring them to Ananus immediately. But the high priest was deep in sleep, and it took a while before they were finally brought into his presence.

Benjamin began to apologize. Ananus waved him off.

"I know why you're here," Ananus said. "No doubt they arrested your father. They came at night." He paused and sighed. "I'm afraid I can't help you. John ben Dorcas is now head of the Committee for Public Safety. I have no power over him or the committee." He sighed again. "One day they may come to arrest me."

"But why?" Benjamin asked. "The charge sheet said treason. What treason has my father committed?"

Ananus nodded.

"There's a small-time trader from the Golan, Gamla, in fact. He does some business with the Romans. He saw Reuven in Caesarea, going into Vespasian's tent. Twice, the second time with Yosef ben Matityahu."

"My brother is alive?" shouted Benjamin.

Drusilla's heart pounded.

"The God of Israel lives!" she cried.

Ananus looked at her with a mixture of surprise and annoyance.

"What's she doing here?" he asked.

Benjamin ignored the question. Drusilla became silent again.

"My father is arrested because my brother is a prisoner of the Romans?" asked Benjamin in disbelief.

"Reuven is accused of going over to the Romans, the way Yosef ben Matityahu did."

"He would never do such a thing!" Benjamin insisted. "My brother would never turn traitor."

Ananus shrugged.

"You're probably right," he agreed. Drusilla did not understand the tone of dejection in his voice. "And it's too bad," Ananus went on. "It would help to have someone I trust over the lines if we do have to surrender."

"What?" asked Benjamin. "What do you mean by that?"

Drusilla heard the amazement in Benjamin's voice. She, too, was surprised at Ananus' statement. Wasn't he responsible for the defense of Jerusalem?

Was he right? Would it be better if Reuven had gone over to the Romans?

Ananus did not answer Benjamin.

Benjamin did not pursue that line of questioning. Instead, he asked:

"Why arrest my father? What does he have to do with this?"

"They believe that his son is a traitor, and that Rabbi Aaron may have influenced him to go over to the Romans." Ananus shook his head. "These radicals are becoming more oppressive and dangerous than the Romans."

"Is there nothing you can do for Rabbi Aaron?" Drusilla quickly asked.

"What are you doing here?" Ananus retorted sharply.

Drusilla could feel her face flushing. She hesitated between answering and keeping silent.

"When Reuven returns we are to be married."

Ananus snorted with contempt.

"Perhaps, perhaps not," he responded. "He was reported to have been accompanied by a Jewish woman. They were said to be very close."

Drusilla felt the floor rushing up towards her. Only Benjamin's strong grasp stopped her from hitting its hard surface.

Chapter Eighty-Nine

3 December 67 CE / 8 Kislev 3828

A dazzling snow-white mountain blazed with golden fire.

Reuven gasped.

"Is there anything like it in all the world?" he exclaimed.

In the distance stood the Temple, the heart of Jerusalem, its gold plates reflecting the brilliance of the sun, its stones so pure white they seemed not to be of this earth.

"It is beautiful," agreed Dvorah.

"And you've never been here, even during the pilgrimage festivals!"

"My father told me how crowded the city was at those times," Dvorah replied. "I wanted to stay home; he went alone. Gamla and the north were all I needed. The Kinneret was far enough from home for me." She added, softly, "God is everywhere, not just in the Holy of Holies."

"Yes, that's true," Reuven replied, nodding his head slowly.

They continued their climb toward the holy city, without their Roman escort since dawn. The road to Jerusalem was filled with travelers in both directions. If he hadn't seen the devastation himself, he would not know that Roman legions were occupying the north and were preparing to descend on the rest of the country.

Reuven glanced over at Dvorah, whose eyes were fixed on the road in front of her and who walked with determined steps.

He wished he had her certainty. Reuven could see the walls of the City, knew their strengths, knew their weak points. He knew, too, the people inside, some of whom wanted to fight, others who wanted peace at any cost.

Most of them probably just want to be left alone, he thought. Left alone to live their lives in peace.

But Florus and the legions of Rome would not let them.

Neither would the Jewish revolutionaries whose cause he himself had joined.

Reuven felt a sudden rush of revulsion for the world he lived in. He shuddered violently.

"What's wrong?" Dvorah asked.

"Nothing," he replied, his eyes cast downward.

Reuven was certain that Dvorah knew, that she was aware of the doubts that had been creeping into his mind, of the pull he felt for the outside world of the Gentiles, and that she sensed it more strongly the closer they got to Jerusalem.

The City's north wall loomed larger and larger.

Off to the side of the road a woman rose from the rock upon which she had been sitting. The woman was shrouded in a cloak that covered her body and a scarf that covered her head completely except for an opening for her eyes. Reuven watched as the woman seemed to walk directly towards them.

And then Reuven saw the eyes, bluer than the sky, bluer than the sea at Caesarea.

"Drusilla!" Reuven cried with joy.

"The God of Israel lives!" responded Drusilla, in a voice just as loud as his.

They ran to each other. Drusilla removed the scarf, freeing her long hair. Reuven embraced her fiercely, lifted her in his arms, and swung her around joyfully, not caring that the passersby saw.

Dvorah came up to them and looked at both dourly.

"Why, Drusilla, are you getting fat?" Reuven exclaimed, laughing. "Doesn't my mother make you work, or does she let you sit like a queen all day and do nothing?"

"She's pregnant, you fool!" hissed Dvorah. "With someone's child."

Reuven ignored Dvorah's implication.

"Is it true? Am I to be a father?" Reuven cried.

Drusilla nodded.

Though Reuven shook his head, his face shone with delight. "I'm happy, and scared, too. Why, I'm barely a child myself!" And he laughed again.

"I'm carrying your son," Drusilla said proudly.

"My son?" Reuven asked. "How do you know it's a son? Maybe it's a daughter." He grinned mischievously. "I hope it's a girl, and I hope she looks just like you so I can see what you were like as a little girl." He clapped his hands. "And so you waited out here to tell me, instead of at home? How did you know I would arrive today?"

"I was going to wait every day until you came back, or until the baby was born," she said softly.

"Is it his?" Dvorah asked harshly.

Reuven turned to Dvorah.

"How dare you!" he snarled, his voice breaking with rage.

"Wait, Reuven," Drusilla said. "Is this the woman you were seen with in Caesarea?"

Her question astonished him. How did she know? She saw the expression on his face and quickly added:

"I heard about it yesterday, after midnight, before dawn, from Ananus ben Ananus. I will tell you more later."

Reuven caught his breath, even more surprised. He looked at Dvorah and then back at Drusilla.

"Yes, she is, her name is Dvorah—"

"Ah, Shaul's girl," Drusilla interrupted. "Do not be angry with her, Reuven. I thought you were dead when we didn't hear from you after the fall of Gamla. I was broken; I did not want to live. Have pity on her; be kind, Reuven, and forgive her harsh words." She turned to Dvorah. The hardness had drained from Dvorah's face.

"Yes. I am carrying Reuven's child." Drusilla spoke without rancor. She looked at Reuven.

"You've changed, Reuven," Drusilla said. "Something is different about you." Her eyes immediately went to Dvorah's face.

"I have much to tell you," Reuven replied. "About Gamla and Caesarea. Come, let's go home."

Drusilla did not move. Her gaze remained fixed on Dvorah.

"Did you have a pleasant journey from Caesarea?" Drusilla asked, abruptly switching to Greek.

The bland tone and innocuous question, as well as the change in language, momentarily surprised Reuven. Then he understood.

He replied in Greek.

"She doesn't understand anything but Hebrew and Aramaic," he said.

"Good," she responded. "Reuven, you can't go home now. You'll be arrested."

"What?" He gaped at her in shock, unable to believe what he was hearing. "Why?"

"You were seen in Caesarea going into Vespasian's tent. Twice. You're accused of treason. The Committee for Public Safety will have you arrested if you're found in Jerusalem. They've already arrested your father."

"This is madness!" Reuven exclaimed. "Come. Ananus will straighten this out."

Reuven started to stride away, motioning for Dvorah to follow.

Drusilla grabbed his arm, stopping him. He turned to Drusilla.

"Ananus cannot," she said. "He told us so. Ananus has no power over the Committee for Public Safety, which is now run by John ben Dorcas. Even Ananus himself is afraid of getting arrested."

Reuven took several deep breaths.

"I have to get back in the City, Drusilla. I have to get my father out of jail. I have to clear my name. And I have to kill Dorcas. Judah and his men will help me."

"I will get you back into Jerusalem, Reuven. Just be a little patient. But first, can you trust her?"

"Of course. Shaul was like my brother."

"I'm not sure, Reuven. There is something hard about her. In her face I see a willingness to fight to the death. I do not see that in yours anymore. She might betray you to the radicals."

Reuven's brow furrowed.

"I really don't think she would do that, Drusilla."

"I hope you're right, Reuven. For now, be careful. Don't tell her why I have to sneak you into the City. Tell her that you have enemies in the Peace Party, if she asks."

"How will you get me in?"

Drusilla smiled.

"I used to call you my little boy," she said, her voice gay. "Now I will call you my old man."

She winked at him and pointed to the satchel she had left next to the rock where she sat waiting for him to return.

Chapter Ninety

3 December 67 CE / 8 Kislev 3828

An open door, immediate recognition, joy, then confusion and fear over the aged appearance; Drusilla watched the changing expressions on Ruth's face with an amused smile on her own lips.

The confusion and fear disappeared when Ruth looked at Drusilla and saw the smile; Ruth quickly pulled the two travelers and Drusilla into the house and closed the door before embracing her son.

Benjamin came home from his father's synagogue soon after. He stared at the bent man sitting in the corner, his beard and hair white, his face lined and wrinkled. The man looked up at him and Benjamin burst out laughing.

"Now you're the older brother!" Benjamin cried.

Reuven winked at him.

"I think it will work," Drusilla said. "The guards at the north gate believed me when I told them they were father and daughter refugees from the slaughter in Gamla."

"We have work to do," Reuven said heavily. "We have to get father out of prison." He paused. "And I want to clear my own name," adding, heatedly, "I'm no traitor!"

Drusilla glared at Reuven sharply. Her face tightened with annoyance.

"Don't worry," Reuven said to her, in Greek. "We have to trust Dvorah. Anyway, we won't be able to keep the truth from her forever."

Drusilla's eyes remained narrow; she wanted to call out his indiscretion but remained silent.

"We'll need Judah ben Ezra's help," Reuven said to his brother.

"We won't get it," Benjamin replied.

"Why not?"

Yes, Drusilla wondered, Why not?

"He was arrested, too," Benjamin said.

Reuven and Drusilla looked at each other in surprise.

"What?" Reuven stammered. "Why?" he asked plaintively.

"He refused to denounce you."

Reuven's eyes grew wide. Drusilla could see that he was trying to come to grips with this new information.

"*Elohim Gadol,*" he muttered. "Lord Almighty!"

"That's not all," Benjamin went on. "They're both being held in the same cell, Father and Judah ben Ezra."

"Oh no!" exclaimed Reuven. "It would almost be funny, but it's not. Are they getting along all right? I know Father hates him."

"I don't know, Reuven. They're not being allowed visitors."

Reuven's chin sunk into his hands. He sighed.

"We'll have to fix that," he said. "Somehow."

Dvorah stood silently in a corner, watching, listening.

There was a long silence as Reuven sat thinking.

Dvorah walked over to Drusilla, took her gently by the arm, and led her into the kitchen. The two women, away from the others, stared at each other.

"You started speaking to Reuven in some other language outside Jerusalem," Dvorah began. "Just now, you gave Reuven a look and he spoke to you in that language. I heard my name mentioned." Dvorah's eyes narrowed. "You don't trust me, do you?"

"Should I?" Drusilla replied coldly.

"Drusilla," Dvorah began, "Reuven truly loves you." Dvorah paused, and began to tremble violently. Drusilla stared in wonder at the change in Dvorah.

"After days spent days in a basement with the body of my dead father," Dvorah said, her voice breaking, "after almost being discovered by Roman soldiers, when it seemed that for a moment we were safe, in a fit of madness, I offered myself to him. I did not know if we would really make it alive to Jerusalem, and I did not want to die a virgin."

Drusilla paled.

"No, Drusilla, he turned me down. He was tempted, but he stopped himself. He told me he was supposed to marry a girl in Jerusalem." Again Dvorah paused. When she regained her composure she continued.

"You are very lucky, Drusilla. Reuven is a good man. A brave one, too. And cunning, oh so cunning. His cunning kept the both of us alive. He never lost his head, even when the danger seemed insurmountable. I owe him my life, Drusilla. I would never do anything to betray him. Or you."

Tears started forming in Dvorah's eyes. Drusilla could feel them in her own.

"Drusilla," Dvorah continued, "I know Reuven's heart is no longer in the struggle. I know it, even if he doesn't realize it yet. Perhaps you see it, also. And even though I will fight on until freedom or death, I do not judge Reuven for wavering. He is a good and honorable man; perhaps his doubts are truer than my faith. It does not matter; I owe Reuven my life. You and Reuven have nothing to fear from me."

Tears were streaming down both women's cheeks. Drusilla took Dvorah in her arms and kissed her forehead.

"Sister," Drusilla said to her, "will you stay at least until the baby is born?"

Dvorah nodded, unable to speak.

"If it is a boy," Drusilla said, "we will name him after your Shaul."

Dvorah's tears became open sobs and she hugged Drusilla tightly.

Chapter Ninety-One

3 December 67 CE / 8 Kislev 3828

Reuven lifted his head as Drusilla and Dvorah emerged from the kitchen arm-in-arm. Still-wet tears dappled their cheeks; the tension between them was clearly gone. Reuven experienced a moment of relief, then reality returned; he still did not see a clear way forward.

Across from him Benjamin had pulled up a chair.

"You came from Caesarea?" Benjamin asked, breaking into Reuven's thoughts.

Reuven nodded.

"I want to hear all about Gamla and Caesarea," Benjamin said, "but first—"

"We have to free Father," Reuven finished for him.

"Yes," said Benjamin. "And there are things you should know, things that have been happening in Jerusalem during the time you've been gone."

"Go ahead," Reuven responded. "I'm listening."

"The situation in the City has become unstable," Benjamin began. "Few are now openly calling for peace with Rome, or what you might term surrender, but there is a split between those who take a moderate tone and those who are more radical."

"Brother," Reuven interrupted, sighing, "after what I saw in Gamla don't assume anything about what I believe."

Benjamin leaned forward, put his hand on Reuven's shoulder, squeezed it gently, sighed himself, and then leaned back, letting his hand fall to his side where he sat.

"The moderates are led by Ananus ben Ananus," Benjamin continued, "but the radicals are not united, and seemed to be composed of more than one faction. For example, Eleazar ben Simon has become the head of a group that calls themselves the Kannaim. They have taken over the Temple area. Shortly after Gush Halav in the north fell, John ben Levi arrived with followers who escaped before its fall. There are other groups, too. John ben Dorcas, who managed to become the head of the Committee for Public Safety, leads one of the smaller ones.

"The split hasn't turned violent. Yet." Benjamin paused. "I fear it will. Soon."

"Then we have to get Father out as quickly as possible," Reuven interjected.

"Yes," Benjamin responded. "And your friend, Judah, too. The violence may not just be between the moderates and the radicals, but among the radicals themselves. Besides, there's no need to tell you of the bad blood between Judah and Dorcas; you've already told me about that in the past."

Reuven scowled. After a moment's silence he asked:

"Benjamin, does the House of Shammai still have influence over the revolutionaries?"

"I don't know," Benjamin answered. "From what I see, the only man with broad influence is Ananus, and that is only over the moderates and many of the common people."

"Well, Benjamin, we have to find out. I want you to go see Rabbi Zechariah. He and Judah were once close. You must ask him to help release Father and Judah."

Benjamin immediately rose from his chair.

"I go now," he said.

Benjamin looked his brother in the eyes, held his gaze for a moment, and glanced over at the women who had been sitting quietly, listening to the conversation. Without saying anything further, he left the house.

Reuven again lowered his head, chin in hands. He desperately wanted to get up, embrace Drusilla, and tell her everything that happened in Gamla and Caesarea. But the need to free his father and Judah pressed on him. He struggled to come up with a course of action that would save them. There were several possible options, but none guaranteed success and some were fraught with danger.

Reuven lost track of time as his thoughts went round and round in circles. He was vaguely aware of the three women moving around the house. The smell of food cooking on the fire in the kitchen entered his nostrils. Despite not having eaten, he felt no hunger.

The door flew open. Reuven looked up. Benjamin entered, a dejected expression on his face. Reuven knew his brother's mission had not gone well.

"Rabbi Zechariah was a lost cause," Benjamin began, barely moving from the entrance. "His study hall was empty. He sat at a desk and did not even look up when I entered. Reuven, when he finally raised his head I barely recognized him. He had hollow eyes and sunken cheeks. I remember him as powerful and dynamic; the man I saw today was a lifeless shell, a passive soul waiting for death. When I asked him for help he said: 'I am able to help no one. Not even myself.'

"I told him Father's arrest was unjust. His reply? 'That is none of my business.' He did not even raise his head to look at me when he said this. I reminded him he had influence over the revolutionaries if he wanted to use it. He said he had influence over no one. I pleaded for his help with Judah, saying that Judah had been a student of his. 'He was no student of mine,' was his reply. His voice was filled with contempt. I realized there was no point in continuing, so I left."

Benjamin shrugged.

"You were gone a long time, brother," Reuven said.

"Yes. I made one stop before coming home. To see Ananus ben Ananus. There were certain things we should have asked that night when we visited him." Benjamin shrugged again. "I guess Drusilla and I were not thinking as clearly as we could have. There is an arrest warrant for you, Reuven. It was also signed by Dorcas. And the man who denounced you, to both Ananus and the Committee for Public Safety, was Amram ben Gedalyahu, which we should have realized from Ananus' initial description. Ananus was reluctant to give his name. I guessed it. Ananus merely nodded. By the way, Amram is still in the City."

"These things are good to know, Benjamin," Reuven said. "Thank you, brother."

"Wait, there's more," Benjamin went on. "Ananus told me that the revolutionaries have started a rumor that some of the moderates are planning to send a delegation to Vespasian to offer surrender, and to open the gates of the City to him. And because of that rumor, which they started, Eleazar ben Simon's men and the Committee for Public Safety have begun arresting prominent moderates, threatening trials and executions."

Reuven rose from where he sat.

"We don't have much time," Reuven said heavily.

"No, we don't, Reuven."

Reuven turned toward Drusilla.

"Drusilla, if you remove the white from my hair and beard, and the makeup from my face, will you be able to put them on again?"

"Yes," she answered.

"Good. Then remove them now."

"Why?" she asked.

"I must go to Rabbi Yoel ben Jotham. I studied under him. I even stayed with him when I left Father's house. He is truly one of the revolutionaries. He will help."

"Why remove the disguise?" Drusilla asked.

"I must go to him honestly, as I am, so he will know that I am no traitor."

"No, Reuven," Drusilla insisted. "You must not. He may turn you over to the Committee for Public Safety. You must not go."

"Drusilla is right!" cried his mother, who had come in from the kitchen.

"I agree with her," Dvorah said. "It is too dangerous. You can't risk it."

Reuven looked at his brother.

Benjamin remained silent.

Reuven smiled sardonically. Then he turned to Drusilla, his face set hard, his eyes narrowed. He beckoned to her.

Chapter Ninety-Two

3 December 67 CE / 8 Kislev 3828

Two of Rabbi Yoel ben Jotham's students stood guard outside Rabbi Yoel's synagogue and study hall. One carried a sword, the other carried a javelin.

Reuven looked at them skeptically.

I've seen worse, he thought.

What worried Reuven was not that Rabbi Yoel would betray him, but that Rabbi Yoel would be unable to help.

"What do you want?" the student with the javelin demanded.

"To see Rabbi Yoel," Reuven replied.

"Is he expecting you?" challenged the one with the sword.

"No."

"Who are you?" the first barked, raising his javelin threateningly.

"I'm a friend of Shaul ben Yitzchak. I was in Gamla."

"You don't sound like someone from the north. You sound like a Jerusalemite."

"Are you here to give language lessons?" Reuven asked sarcastically.

"What's your name?" The javelin remained raised.

"Ain-shem ben Klum," Reuven responded, his tone still sarcastic.

"That's not a name," came the retort. The javelin was drawn back, as if to be thrust. The sword in the hands of the other student was raised.

"It's all right," came a voice from inside.

Rabbi Yoel ben Jotham stepped outside into the fading light of late afternoon.

"Well, Adoni No-Name son of Nothing, what do you—"

Rabbi Yoel stopped. He stared at Reuven.

"Don't I know you?" he asked.

Reuven grinned.

"Of course you do," he replied.

"Oh my!" cried Rabbi Yoel with delight. "Reuven, Reuven, come in!"

Rabbi Yoel's study hall was large. Five students, their backs to the entrance, were sitting at a long table. They turned to look at the visitor.

Rabbi Yoel pointed to Reuven.

"This was one of my students. He came to live here when he first joined the revolution. Welcome, Reuven ben Aaron! When did you get back to Jerusalem?"

"Today."

"I am honored that you have come to visit me so soon. My, how you've changed. It's been at least a year since I last saw you. You've gone from being a boy to a man!"

"Do you think I've also gone from being a patriot to a traitor?"

Rabbi Yoel chuckled.

"If that is so and you've come to me, then you're a fool, and from everything I know personally about you, and from everything I've heard since you left my school, you're no fool."

"Did you know that there is an arrest warrant for me?" Reuven asked.

"Not exactly," Rabbi Yoel answered. "There was talk of you having turned traitor in Caesarea, so I'm not surprised. Was it true you were in Vespasian's tent?"

"Three times. We were taken prisoner after we escaped from Gamla after its fall."

"We?"

"I brought Dvorah bat Shmuel to Jerusalem. She was Shaul's girl."

Rabbi Yoel nodded gravely.

"Did you escape from Vespasian's camp?"

"No. He let us go freely to Jerusalem."

"Why?"

"I told him that I would relate what I saw happen in Gamla."

"Did you also tell him that you had killed Roman soldiers, and that you had spurred the retreat of Cestius from Jerusalem?" Rabbi Yoel asked.

"As you said, Rabbi Yoel, I'm no fool."

"Reuven, have you come to Jerusalem to counsel surrender?"

Reuven sensed the suspicion that was growing in Rabbi Yoel.

"Rabbi Yoel, the walls of Gamla were weak, the walls of Jerusalem are strong. There were not many men of fighting age in Gamla; there are many in Jerusalem. They did not have enough food stored to withstand a long siege; we have plenty. But, Rabbi Yoel, we have something else. Internal strife. It will destroy us."

Rabbi Yoel sighed.

"You are right. It is a serious problem, Reuven. Our internal strife is far more dangerous than the Roman legions."

"Did you know my arrest warrant was signed by John ben Dorcas?"

"He's a bad one," Rabbi Yoel said, shaking his head.

"Tell me, why did they arrest my father?"

"They did? I had no idea. It makes no sense. When did this happen?"

"Yesterday. Before dawn. Yom Revi'i. They also arrested Judah ben Ezra."

"What?" The question exploded from Rabbi Yoel's mouth. "Why?"

"Because he refused to denounce me."

Rabbi Yoel's breath came out sharply. He glared at the floor.

"This is insane!" he shouted.

"Can you do something about it?" Reuven asked.

Rabbi Yoel nodded. The rabbi was momentarily speechless. Reuven let the moment pass and waited anxiously for an answer.

"I will do what I can," Rabbi Yoel finally said. "I will do everything I can to get Judah, and your father, released." He paused. The ebullient mood with which Rabbi Yoel had greeted Reuven was completely gone. Rabbi Yoel was obviously shaken. "Give me a few days, Reuven. I will have to work at building allies for this." He fell silent before saying, in a voice so low Reuven could barely hear him, "I have no control over Dorcas or his men. No rabbi does. At the very least I must ensure that there is a fair trial."

Darkness had almost fallen by the time Reuven left Rabbi Yoel's study hall. Reuven knew what had to be done. It was something he should have done long ago.

Chapter Ninety-Three

4 December 67 CE / 9 Kislev 3828

It was a different kind of fear. She had never done anything like this before.

Dvorah did not ask Reuven why he was offering to give himself up to John Dorcas. Had Reuven wanted to tell her he would have; but she knew, and said nothing.

A shawl covered her hair and head, leaving only a circle of her face exposed. She was carrying a bag with food and water with both arms. She shifted the weight to free her right arm and felt for the knife she had hidden in her dress. It gave her a feeling of security. Then she shifted the bag again so that both arms embraced it.

I have nothing to fear, she thought.

For now.

She shivered, knowing that many things could go wrong.

Dvorah approached the two-story building that housed the Committee for Public Safety's headquarters. A single guard stood outside, scanning the street, his eyes watchful. There was a short sword in his belt and a javelin in his hands.

"State your business," he said.

"I want to see John ben Dorcas," she replied.

"Why?"

"It is a matter of great importance. I must speak to him alone."

"What's your name?"

"I am Dvorah bat Shmuel. I escaped from Gamla after it fell."

"Wait here," the guard ordered. He ducked inside and emerged a few moments later. He said nothing to Dvorah, ignoring her as his eyes resumed their hunt for potential enemies.

Dvorah continued to wait, impatiently.

A man came out of the building. He was of medium height, slightly shorter than her, with a broad face and close-set eyes.

John ben Dorcas looked exactly as Reuven had described him.

"Yes?" he asked, looking at her with curiosity and suspicion.

"I wish to speak to you alone," she said.

"Why?" he asked.

"I have something important to tell you."

"What's in the sack?"

"Food and water for someone you are looking for."

Dorcas nodded at the guard. Dvorah opened the bag. The guard stepped toward Dvorah, looked inside and stepped back.

"That's what she's got," the guard said.

"Go inside," Dorcas said to the guard. "I'll speak to the young lady alone." After the guard left, Dorcas gave Dvorah a sharp look and said: "Well? What is it?"

"I escaped from Gamla," Dvorah began. "After it fell. Reuven ben Aaron saved my life. He got me to Jerusalem. He's here, in the City." Dvorah paused, watching his face for a reaction. There was none.

"Go on," said Dorcas.

"He knows there's an arrest warrant out for him. He's willing to give himself up on two conditions: You release his father from prison and you promise him a fair trial."

"Tell him," Dorcas said, "that I accept his conditions."

"He wants to hear it from you personally."

Dorcas gave a sly smile. He pointed to the sack she was carrying.

"That's for him?" Dorcas asked.

"Yes."

"And you're to bring me to him so I can give him my assurance personally? And I'm to come alone?" The slyness was now in Dorcas' voice; the expression on his face was suspicion followed by amusement.

Dvorah nodded. She couldn't get the word "yes" out, it remained stuck in her throat.

"And how do I know he is alone?" Dorcas' smile went from sly to beaming.

Dvorah didn't know what to say. What proof could she give? Reuven had not coached her on this.

"He is alone," Dvorah said, shrugging helplessly. "He is hidden. I bring him food and water. I don't know how to convince you except to say that it is the truth."

"I'll tell you how you'll convince me," Dorcas said harshly. "I will have you arrested now and held until I return. If I don't come back because he is not alone then you will be executed!"

Dvorah's breath came out in a hiss of surprise. Reuven had not prepared her for this. Her back stiffened. She glared at Dorcas.

"Then I will not be able to take you to him."

"Tell me where he is!" Dorcas ordered.

"I can't. I won't!" Dvorah cried defiantly. Then, in a softer tone, she added, "The truth is, even if I were willing, I couldn't describe it. I don't know Jerusalem. I can only retrace my steps to get there."

"Bah!" exclaimed Dorcas. "I believe you," he added with disgust, nodding his head.

"Malachi!" he called out. "Come outside and resume your guard duties. I'm going with the girl." To Dvorah, he said, "Lead the way!"

Dvorah nervously began walking south and slightly east. Cardinal directions were no problem for her; from the position of the sun, time of day, and time of year, she could always figure out which direction was north, east, south, or west, but there were too many landmarks in this strange city; she was worried she would not be able to retrace the path that Reuven had shown her only once.

Dvorah, with Dorcas only a few steps behind her, reached the eastern edge of the jumble of humble houses that Reuven had called the Lower City. A depression, almost like a small valley, separated these houses from a rise across that valley, on which was a section of the City Reuven referred to as the Ophel. South of the Ophel stood splendid palaces. Reuven explained that these palaces had been built by foreign kings who converted to Judaism. An occasional arched footbridge spanned the east and west slopes.

Dvorah crossed over the first footbridge to the eastern slope. Irregularly spaced tunnels drained from the bottom of the opposite side. She started counting as she passed the tunnels.

One, two, three, four…

Dvorah climbed down the short steep slope and walked to the mouth of the tunnel. Dorcas waited on top of the western embankment.

"Reuven, Reuven!" she called.

There was no answer.

Sweat formed on Dvorah's forehead.

Had she counted wrong and picked the wrong tunnel?

Dvorah called again. There was no reply. She could hear Dorcas impatiently stamp his feet above her.

"I've only been here a few times," she explained. "I'll find him," she insisted.

Dvorah walked further south and stopped at the next tunnel. She called Reuven's name loudly, as loudly as she could. No answer came from that tunnel but from further south she heard the faint sound of a cry. She turned and ran, stopping where she heard the call. More softly now, she called out Reuven's name. She heard Reuven call back.

Dvorah turned to the north, where Dorcas was waiting.

"He's here," she shouted.

Dorcas scrambled down and trotted to her. He looked at the entrance to the tunnel and then at her.

He smiled at her, an evil smile that made her shudder.

Then he strode confidently into the tunnel.

Chapter Ninety-Four

4 December 67 CE / 9 Kislev 3828

Steel struck flint, sparks flew, a lamp blazed. Reuven had prepared the wick so that even the joints between the stones in the walls of the tunnel were illuminated.

He had waited patiently in the darkness for Dvorah to arrive. Reuven was calm. Everything had been carefully planned. There was minimal danger to Dvorah. If Dorcas ignored her warning to come alone Reuven would know when Dvorah called out to him. To be prepared for that possibility Reuven had already familiarized himself with the tunnel network and had waited before lighting the lamp. It would be easy to disappear if others came with Dorcas. Dorcas entered the tunnel, stepping over refuse and around large stones as he approached Reuven. Dorcas stopped three lengths away.

"I heard," he began contemptuously to Reuven, "that you impregnated some barbarian whore and promised to marry her. What did you promise this Jewish whore to get her to do your bidding?"

Reuven's right hand rested down at his side, his fist holding the knife in a reverse grip. His left hand was inside a pouch tied to his belt. Reuven ignored Dorcas' taunts.

"It does not matter what you promised, traitor," Dorcas went on. "You shall not live to keep any of them. And when I'm done with you, I'll see your father executed, and your friend, Judah, too."

Reuven saw the knife in Dorcas' hand, held in a forward grip.

"This has been a long time coming, Dorcas." Reuven spoke slowly. "I will have vengeance for my uncle's death, and I will free my father and my friend from prison."

"Prepare to die, traitor," Dorcas spat. "I am going to send you to the same place I sent your uncle."

The knife in Dorcas' hand flashed in the lamplight as he seemed to glide toward Reuven.

Reuven held his breath expectantly, waiting until the last moment. His left hand, balled up in a fist, flew from the pouch. Reuven thrust that hand forward, almost to Dorcas' face, opening his fist before jumping backward. Dorcas' knife sliced his beard and reached his chin.

Dorcas screamed as sand entered his eyes.

Reuven leaped forward, seized Dorcas' knife hand in his own left, and with his right hand drove his knife deep into Dorcas' right arm.

Dorcas screamed again.

Reuven pulled the knife out and drove it into Dorcas' arm once more. Dorcas blinked furiously, rubbing his eyes with his free hand, trying to get the sand out.

Reuven raised his knife and slashed Dorcas' neck, severing tendons.

A shudder went through Dorcas' body. Reuven released the hand and let Dorcas fall to the ground. Reuven stepped back and watched the body writhe.

"That's for my uncle," Reuven said with satisfaction.

"I'll spit on him in Gehinom and wait for you there!"

Dorcas feebly tried to raise the hand that still held the knife. Reuven kicked the knife out of it.

He's not dead yet, Reuven thought. If I leave now, and he manages to crawl out, or…

Dvorah came running into the tunnel, her own knife in her hands.

Reuven looked at her, a puzzled expression on his face.

"I was worried, I thought you might need help, I…" Dvorah stammered.

"I'm all right, Dvorah, thank you."

"You're hurt," she said, pointing to his chin. For the first time Reuven realized he was bleeding.

"I'm all right," he insisted. "Did you know what I had planned?"

"Yes," she answered. "Is he dead?"

"Not yet," Reuven replied. "Soon."

Reuven put his knife away. He picked up the one on the ground. Then Reuven bent over the fallen form and slit Dorcas' throat with Dorcas' own knife. Blood spurted from Dorcas, staining Reuven's cloak and mixing with his own.

Reuven waited until the body at his feet stopped moving. He bent down once again and felt for a pulse. There was none.

Reuven straightened up.

"Take the lamp, Dvorah. Further into the tunnel is a place where I can drag the body. It will not be easily discovered there."

He grabbed both of Dorcas' legs and began pulling.

Then he stopped and took a deep breath.

"I've avenged my Uncle Moshe," he intoned. "This is the last Jew I will ever kill."

Chapter Ninety-Five

5 December 67 CE / 11 Kislev 3828

As he paced the small rented room, Amram suddenly felt the urge to flee the City and return to the north. His business in Jerusalem was almost done; nothing was keeping him here.

The Sabbath had just ended. Tomorrow he would go to the market for his last purchase before heading to the Galilee. A rich Gentile customer in Sepphoris had asked for a hand-sized sculpture made of porphyry from the workshops of Egypt.

An object of idolatry, no doubt, thought Amram. No Jew would ask for such a thing. And he trusts my artistic judgment, so he says. Bah, what do I know? Still, I will find something beautiful for him.

Amram stopped pacing.

Why am I so nervous?

He sighed.

The situation in Jerusalem was precarious. No question about it!

A harsh knocking came from the door.

Who could that be? Amram wondered.

He went to the door and opened it cautiously.

Amram was thrust roughly backward by two men who stormed inside. Both were wearing masks. One held a knife.

Amram was so petrified that he was unable to scream. With wide eyes he stared at the knife as the man who held it pushed him against the wall and placed the knife against his neck. The other man spoke in a low, unnatural voice, the voice of a demon.

"Scream and you die!" it warned.

Amram could barely breathe.

"Where is John ben Dorcas?" it demanded to know.

Amram's body began to shake.

"I don't know," he replied, his voice trembling.

Who are they? his mind screamed.

"Now listen, Amram," the voice without a face began, its tone menacing, "you'd better not lie to me. I'm going to ask you a few questions, and if you lie, my friend here will finish you off. Is that understood?"

Amram nodded, afraid to say anything.

"Did you denounce John ben Dorcas to the revolution?" the man facing him asked.

"What? Denounce him? Why?"

Amram was confused. How could he denounce Dorcas? For what?

The man with the knife shook him fiercely.

The man who spoke, said, in a voice just above a whisper, made more menacing by its softness:

"Don't lie to me!"

"I'm, I'm not—" stammered Amram.

"Where is he then?"

"I don't know. I don't know!"

"He's disappeared, Amram. Where is he?"

Amram wanted to shake his head but the knife now was pressing so hard against his neck that he could not.

"I-don't-know." Amram could hardly get the words out.

The man across from him said something. It sounded like Latin, which he did not know, but whose sounds and rhythms he recognized. However, it wasn't exactly Latin, of that Amram was certain.

The man with the knife answered in the same language.

"I'm going to find out now if you're lying," his interrogator said. "Have you denounced anyone to the revolution?"

Amram froze. He did not know what to answer. His life depended on giving the correct response, but what that was depended on who was asking.

"Who are you?" Amram asked, in a quaking voice.

The man holding the knife slapped him across the face. Amram almost collapsed to the floor.

"I ask the questions!" the man facing him snarled.

Amram hesitated. They couldn't be from the revolution, he thought. They know I did. They couldn't be from Ananus. He knows I did. It couldn't be from the peace party, they would never behave like this.

They must be Roman agents! That's clear. I should have known from the beginning.

"Our arm is long," the interrogator said, interrupting Amram's thoughts. "It reaches from Rome to Antioch to Caesarea to Jerusalem. We have eyes and ears everywhere. It will be better for you to tell the truth rather than lie."

"Yes," Amram answered.

"Who?" came the demand.

"Reuven ben Aaron," Amram answered.

"Who?"

It sounded as if his interrogator did not believe him.

"Who?" the man repeated.

"Reuven ben Aaron," Amram said again.

Gales of laughter broke out from the two men. When they stopped laughing they again spoke in that strange Latin-like language.

The man with the knife struck Amram in the solar plexus with his free arm, at the same moment pulling the knife away. Amram slumped to the ground.

The two men abruptly left without saying a word.

There will be no statue for that buyer in Sepphoris, Amram thought. I'm getting out of Jerusalem.

But first there is someone I have to see.

Chapter Ninety-Six

5 December 67 CE / 11 Kislev 3828

They sat in the darkness, their bodies hunched, facing each other. They spoke in low voices. The three women had just gone to bed and it was their first chance to speak alone.

"Why did you strike him at the end, brother?" Benjamin asked. "There was no need for that."

"I was angry," Reuven answered. "Because of him Father was arrested. Judah, too."

"It was wrong, Reuven. There was no need for it."

Reuven shrugged.

"Perhaps. Anyway, you were great," Reuven said. "Very convincing."

Benjamin beamed.

"Did you see his face when we spoke that Latinized gibberish?" Benjamin asked.

Both brothers laughed.

"Yes, you were very convincing," Reuven said again. "Tomorrow your task will be more difficult. We won't be dealing with the likes of Amram, but harder, more dangerous men."

"How do you know Amram will go to Ananus and the others?" Benjamin asked.

"I don't know for certain. We have to try everything we can, Benjamin. Tomorrow I will ask Judah, once you get me in to see him, how we can organize his men to break him out of prison. As for Amram, I'm convinced he's a double agent, but I believe his real loyalties lie with us, the Jews, and that—"

A loud knocking at the door interrupted Reuven.

"At this time of night?" he asked, looking at his brother quizzically.

The loud knocking repeated.

Reuven stood and drew his knife. Benjamin got up and answered the door.

Ananus ben Ananus stood at the threshold.

"Come in," Benjamin said.

Reuven went to the lamp and lit it.

"Why am I not surprised to see you here, Reuven?" Ananus said.

"Why am I surprised that you were unable to help my brother,"

Reuven countered.

Ananus entered the house. Benjamin closed the door.

"There have been some new developments," Ananus said. "Favorable developments from your point of view." His eyes went from Reuven to Benjamin, who had gone to stand next to his brother. "I suspect that the two of you are involved in this change of circumstances."

"What new developments?" Benjamin asked.

Ananus smiled knowingly.

"Amram came to me this evening with an amazing story. Just after the Sabbath ended two men broke into his room. They made it clear that they worked for the Roman secret police. He was not sure if the two were Jews or not. He said they spoke with a strange accent and spoke to each other in something that sounded like Latin."

Again Ananus smiled knowingly.

"Go on," Reuven urged.

"He said that they asked him about John ben Dorcas. Where Dorcas was, and if he had denounced Dorcas to the revolution. Amram is convinced that Dorcas is a Roman agent. He's also convinced that you, Reuven, are innocent. They demanded to know if there was anyone he had denounced to the revolution. Amram, fearful of lying, told the truth. When he said he had denounced you they laughed. Very clever."

Ananus paused.

"Are you, Reuven? Innocent of making any deals with Vespasian?"

"Yes," Reuven replied.

"What a shame. I was hoping you could be an emissary to Rome when we finally have to surrender. That you could get us good terms before the Roman legions utterly destroy us. Why did Vespasian let you leave?"

"I promised him that I would tell everyone in Jerusalem what I saw in Gamla."

"And did what you saw in Gamla convince you that resistance is futile?"

"When my father and Judah are freed I want to meet with the three of you. I want my brother and Drusilla there, too."

"Ah, that bold barbarian girl. And what of that woman who was with you in Caesarea."

"She was Shaul ben Yitzchak's girl. I got her out of Gamla after it fell. I owed it to him. He was my friend."

"I see," said Ananus stroking his beard. "Well, it will be interesting to see how Dorcas defends himself against Amram's story once I spread it around. I just hope Amram will be there to back up what I say. He seemed very nervous and I'm afraid he will flee Jerusalem. Perhaps I should have him arrested and held until he gives evidence."

"Perhaps," Reuven said.

"As for Dorcas…" Ananus began.

Reuven smiled despite himself. Benjamin, too, smiled.

Ananus continued:

"I have the feeling that he, too, will be unavailable to defend himself against Amram's story. I suspect that you have something to do with that, also."

Benjamin's smile disappeared. Reuven's remained.

"Ah, gentlemen," Ananus continued, "every defeat for the extremists is a victory for the moderates. We need victories, for every day the extremists grow bolder. Soon I will have to move against them. I hope that the sons of Rabbi Aaron and nephews of Rabbi Moshe will stand with me at that time."

Reuven folded his arms and gazed at Ananus across the dimly lit room before responding.

"I do not know the proper course of action, Ananus. I hope to have some idea when I speak to you, my father, Judah, my brother, and my future wife. In the meantime, I ask that you go to Rabbi Yoel ben Jotham with what you told us tonight. Perhaps the two of you working together can help secure the release of my father and Judah."

"Perhaps," replied Ananus. "For now, it is late, and I will take my leave of you."

Ananus bowed and left the house, closing the door behind him.

Reuven turned to Benjamin.

"Ananus is right," Reuven said. "It's late. Let's go to bed, brother. A dangerous day awaits us."

Chapter Ninety-Seven

6 December 67 CE / 11 Kislev 3828

Benjamin took a deep breath as he faced the guard in front of the building that housed the Committee for Public Safety.

He was getting used to this, almost enjoying the missions with his brother.

He glared at the guard.

"I demand to see my father. He has a right to have his tefillin."

The guard glared back at him.

"I'll give the tefillin to your father. No need for you to see him. Dorcas ordered no one to see him."

"Then I demand to see John ben Dorcas! Immediately!" Benjamin spoke with authority.

The guard looked uncomfortable. He glanced down at the ground and then looked at Benjamin.

"Who are they?" he asked, pointing to the two standing behind Benjamin.

"That is Dvorah bat Shmuel and her father. They escaped from Gamla. They knew Judah. She was Shaul ben Yitzchak's girlfriend. He died in the battle at the pass of Beth Horon."

The guard stared at Dvorah.

"Malachi!" he called. "Come here!"

Despite the late autumn chill Benjamin started to sweat. He could feel the tension rising in the two standing behind him. Perhaps Reuven's impatience was a mistake; perhaps they should have waited for Rabbi Yoel and Ananus to work things out.

Malachi came out of the building.

"Malachi, is this the girl who last saw Dorcas?"

"Yes," Malachi answered. "What happened to him?" he asked Dvorah.

She stepped next to Benjamin.

"I don't know," she answered.

"Why did you want to see him?" Malachi demanded.

"He told me not to tell anyone," Dvorah responded.

"You better answer me! Dorcas has gone missing and you're the last person to see him."

"He warned me not to say anything! He said bad things would happen to me if I did."

"Dvorah," shouted Benjamin. "You went to see Dorcas? You did not tell me. Speak, girl, now!"

Dvorah shook her head.

"Speak, I say!" shouted Benjamin, even more loudly.

Dvorah trembled.

"In Caesarea," Dvorah began, "a Jewish trader came up to me. He said that when I got to Jerusalem there were two things I had to give John ben Dorcas. I said I didn't know if I would make it to Jerusalem and that I didn't know who John ben Dorcas was. He said that I shouldn't worry, that I would be allowed to go to Jerusalem. He said Dorcas was with the Committee for Public Safety, and told me that their headquarters would be easy to find."

"What did he give you for Dorcas?" asked Malachi.

Dvorah took a deep breath and sighed.

"I wasn't sure what to do. I didn't want to take anything from him. I was afraid to refuse. He gave me money and a small scroll. They were in a pouch."

"How much money? What was in the scroll?"

"I don't know," answered Dvorah. "I didn't count it, barely looked at it. They were gold coins. I never opened the scroll."

Malachi's eyes narrowed. Benjamin could see the suspicion on his face.

"There was no such pouch when I examined your sack!" Malachi said.

"It was hidden in my dress."

"Could it be?" asked the guard on duty to Malachi. "Is the rumor true about—"

"Shut up!" Malachi cried.

He stared angrily at the three people in front of them.

Benjamin waited for Malachi to say something, anything. He could hear Reuven, in disguise, shifting his body, and imagined his brother reaching for his knife.

The guard gave a questioning look toward Malachi.

"All right," Malachi said at last. "Let them in."

Chapter Ninety-Eight

6 December 67 CE / 11 Kislev 3828

Judah had wanted to strangle Rabbi Aaron. Yesterday, the Sabbath, was worst of all. Rabbi Aaron had spent the entire day praying, chanting, in a sing-song voice that drove Judah crazy. Today was slightly better; the rabbi seemed less infused with religious fervor.

Lucky for him, Judah thought. If that kept up I would have strangled him.

Judah heard footsteps. The guard who opened the door stepped aside and ushered three people into the cell. Judah saw a young man, a young woman, and an old, bent, man. He stared at the three, puzzled.

Rabbi Aaron immediately recognized the youth.

"Benjamin!" he cried. "Benjamin! It is so good to see you!"

Ah, Judah thought. The rabbi's eldest son. Yes, I remember now. I have seen him before. And the other two?

The girl was tall and pretty. The old man, whose appearance struck Judah as exceedingly odd, stared down at the floor.

As if reading his thoughts, the old man looked up at Judah and winked.

Judah furrowed his brow. There was something strangely familiar about him.

Rabbi Aaron released his son and stepped up to the old man. With tears in his eyes the rabbi embraced the bent figure, murmuring profuse thanks to the Master of the Universe.

Judah was totally confused now, and unprepared for more surprises.

The young woman stepped up to him.

"I am Dvorah bat Shmuel," she said.

Judah turned pale. His legs grew weak. An old memory flashed through his mind: Shaul with a knife trying to kill him.

She looks nothing like Bruria! Why did Shaul think it was Dvorah?

"Ah," Dvorah said. "So I see Shaul's death weighs on your conscience. We would have married if you had not taken him away from me."

Judah quickly recovered.

"Your Shaul was a brave man who died fighting for his people."

"Thus I want to die, Judah ben Ezra," Dvorah responded.

"Why talk of death?" the old man cackled. He shuffled over to

Judah. He stood up straight, looked Judah in the eyes, and winked again.

Judah's mouth fell open in amazement. A fierce laugh erupted; he quickly suppressed it. Judah clapped Reuven on the shoulder.

"Who turned you into an old man?" he asked.

"Drusilla," Reuven answered proudly. "It got me into the City, and it got me into here."

"Dorcas ordered no visitors," Judah said.

"Dorcas is no longer a problem," Reuven replied. "He is accused of being a Roman agent."

"What?" Judah's question came out as a laugh.

"Yes," answered Reuven. "And unfortunately for him, he's not around to answer the charge!"

"Where is he?"

"He?" responded Reuven in a low voice. "In Gehinom, I would guess, if there is any justice in the universe. His body is in one of the tunnels that come out from the Lower City."

"His body?" asked Judah, also speaking softly despite his surprise. "How did he die?"

Reuven smiled.

"I killed him."

Another loud laugh burst from Judah. He took Reuven's face between his hands and shook Reuven's head from side to side.

"Look at you!" Judah cried with delight. "A rabbi's son. You should have been my son. You are a worthy brother to Shaul ben Ezra!"

Reuven gave quick glances toward his father and brother.

"I avenged my uncle's death," he said. "And made it easier to free you and my father without Dorcas around. I went to Rabbi Yoel ben Jotham. He is working for your release, and my father's. I think Ananus ben Ananus will help also. Judah, I don't want to wait to see what they can accomplish. Why can't I organize some of your men and break you out of jail?"

Judah, whose hands had fallen to Reuven's shoulders, now let them drop to his sides. He grimaced.

"I have no men," he said sadly. "They're gone. Most joined John ben Levi from Gush Halav. Some joined Eleazar ben Simon; a few others left Jerusalem to join Simon ben Gioras in Masada. Simon went there after getting kicked out of Acrabata by Ananus. All this happened just before I was arrested."

"Why did your men desert you?"

"No money," Judah answered, shrugging helplessly. "My patrons all deserted me, two in particular, both very rich. One, wisely, fled Jerusalem with the rise of Eleazar ben Simon and the Committee for Public Safety. The other was not so lucky. Elimelech ben Baruch. He stayed in Jerusalem and was arrested by Dorcas who then had him executed. Dorcas took over his house. And his wealth. My, was Elimelech rich! I once saw a chest he had hidden in his house. It was filled with gold coins! All that money and no family. What I could have done with it! Now Dorcas has it."

"Had," Reuven corrected. "Dorcas is no more. If you saw so much money why didn't you ever steal it?"

"I am no thief," Judah protested.

Reuven smiled broadly.

"Perhaps you're not," he said. "But I am."

Chapter Ninety-Nine

6 December 67 CE / 12 Kislev 3828

It was late afternoon, growing dark, shadows lurked everywhere. In front of the gate a single guard stood sentry. As Benjamin walked past him on the opposite side of the street he casually glanced at the guard.

Alert, Benjamin thought. Possibly formidable. But only one.

He had told himself that he didn't want to do it, that his brother had pressured him. But deep down, Benjamin reluctantly admitted that he found the mission exciting.

It had nothing to do with politics. For that, he was closer to his father. Besides, he wasn't sure what Reuven believed anymore; Gamla, and Caesarea, seemed to have changed him, to have taken off the revolutionary edge.

No, the cause was secondary; his younger brother was leading him on an adventure, and who knew where it would lead? He felt alive, more alive than when he spent hours in the study hall listening to the lectures of his father and the other rabbis.

Judah had given Reuven the location of the house of Elimelech ben Baruch: one street east of the Upper Market, on the east side of that street, the second house from its south end. The house was grand, but modest compared to its neighbors.

There was a short stairway at the end of the street that led to an unpaved road. Further south was the palace of Yoseph ben Caipha. Further south and west, at the very corner of the City, was the Dyers' Quarter.

All that wealth, Benjamin thought, and they are still not spared some of the worst smells of the City.

Benjamin descended the stairs and looked around.

A good escape route, he thought. Go all the way south and then east into the Lower City.

Benjamin had taken note that there were not many people on the street at this time.

He turned back to look at the house. He waited before going up the stairs, this time to the same side of the street on which Elimelech's house stood.

He was going to test the measure of the guard.

Benjamin approached the guard, who eyed him suspiciously.

"I want to see John ben Dorcas!" Benjamin demanded.

The guard was shorter than Reuven, wiry, probably in his twenties. He looked like he could put up a fight, and might be quick enough to draw a weapon before being subject to a surprise attack. The question was: Did he have reinforcements nearby?

The guard just stared at him.

Benjamin waited and then repeated his demand, more firmly.

"You can't," the guard replied at last.

"Why?"

"You can't!"

Benjamin glared back at the guard, refusing to be intimidated.

"He arrested my uncle!" Benjamin shouted. "I demand to see him and know why!"

The guard took a step toward Benjamin, who stood his ground.

A short sword hung at the guard's side.

He hasn't reached for his weapon yet, Benjamin thought.

The guard took another step. This time Benjamin stepped away.

He glanced around him. There were even fewer people on the street. None was taking notice of the confrontation.

"I'll be back tomorrow, with all of my uncle's students, and you'll have to let us see him then!" Benjamin warned.

"Good luck with that," the guard said contemptuously, quickly adding, "I'll get a club and beat the lot of you."

Benjamin backed away, his eyes on the guard.

Benjamin grinned, and thought, I'll see you tomorrow! Then he turned, walked south to the stairs, and began the escape route he planned for Reuven.

But despite that silent pledge to the guard, there was still something unresolved for Benjamin. Had he become so involved with his brother's schemes that he would actually help Reuven steal Elimelech's treasure?

Chapter One Hundred

7 December 67 CE / 12 Kislev 3828

How much longer will I be stuck here? Judah wondered.

He stared at Rabbi Aaron, who swayed in the corner, praying, his tefillin wrapped around his forehead and upper arm.

It was a day since Reuven had come with his brother and Dvorah. They were still locked up.

Judah began pacing his cell. He passed close to the praying rabbi; Judah had to fight the urge to deliberately bump into him.

The door to the cell opened. It was not the jailer bringing food; it was a man Judah had never seen before. He was of medium height, a broad face, and light brown eyes. He seemed to be in his mid-thirties. He carried a sword at his side.

The man gave a quick glance around the room. Rabbi Aaron did not look up from his prayers. The stranger's gaze went from the rabbi to Judah, and as his eyes fixed on Judah his face broke into a broad smile.

"You must be Judah ben Ezra," the man said. "John ben Levi heard much about you when we were all still in the north." The man sighed as he looked up and down at Judah, who had a puzzled look on his face. "My name is Yehoshua ben Betuel," the man said. "John sent me here to have you released. You never should have been arrested."

Judah clapped his hands and grinned.

"It's about time," he said. "Soon I would have gone mad." He turned to Rabbi Aaron. "Rabbi!" Judah shouted. "Your prayers have been answered. It's time to go."

Rabbi Aaron continued swaying and praying, as if he hadn't heard Judah.

Judah shouted again.

No response from Rabbi Aaron.

Judah strode over to the rabbi and shook him.

"Come on!" he said. "Time to go. We're being freed!"

Rabbi Aaron looked at him with surprise. He did not move.

Judah seized him by the arm and started toward the open door.

Yehoshua ben Betuel raised his hand.

"Wait!" he said. "Only you are to be freed. Nothing was said about him."

Judah let go of the rabbi's arm. Rabbi Aaron, a blank expression on his face, went back to his corner and resumed his prayers.

"Come," Yehoshua ben Betuel said, beckoning with his right hand.

Judah ben Ezra remained where he stood, his brow furrowed.

"No," he said finally. "I will not leave without him." He pointed to Rabbi Aaron.

The look of surprise on Yehoshua ben Betuel's face lightened the weight of the decision he had just made; Judah broke into a broad smile.

"Is he a friend?" Yehoshua ben Betuel asked.

Judah laughed.

"Heavens no!" Judah exclaimed. "I can't stand the man!" And Judah laughed again.

"Then why are you giving up freedom for his sake?"

"He is the father of my comrade," Judah said solemnly.

"Are you sure?" Yehoshua ben Betuel asked.

Judah nodded.

In truth, he was not sure. It just seemed the decent thing to do.

"All right," Yehoshua ben Betuel said. "I'll let John know."

And with that he turned and left the room. The cell door closed behind him.

The reality of that door slamming shut struck Judah.

What have I done? he thought in panic.

He wanted to run to the door, pound on it, and cry out that he changed his mind.

Judah did not move.

Rabbi Aaron ceased praying. He looked at Judah and said, wonder in his voice:

"What kind of man are you, Judah ben Ezra?"

Judah sighed wearily.

"I don't know," he said. "I truly don't know."

Chapter One Hundred & One

7 December 67 CE / 13 Kislev 3828

A thick hide hid the burden in Reuven's arms. Benjamin could not bear to look at it as he walked with his brother to the house of Elimelech.

Is it cowardice? he wondered. Or conscience?

When Reuven had gone into the tunnel to commit the terrible act that procured the unclean thing, Benjamin had been unable to follow. He had waited outside, trembling.

"Was that really necessary?" Benjamin had asked afterward.

"Yes," Reuven asserted. "Especially if I am going to carry out the robbery by myself."

"Why is it necessary to steal Elimelech's money? Can't we wait to see if Rabbi Yoel and Ananus get Father and Judah released?"

"How long will that take, Benjamin?" Reuven countered. "And if they cannot? With the money we can free them!"

"How?"

Reuven had paused. Benjamin realized that his brother was searching for an answer.

"I can't say exactly how," Reuven admitted, at last, "but Judah will know how to spread the money around. Perhaps by bribing the guards."

Benjamin tightly gripped the handle of the torch he held. There was no question of turning back despite his doubts.

It's wrong, he thought. Robbery is forbidden, as is mutilating a corpse. Is there anything that can justify these unseemly acts?

A light and cold rain fell, light enough so that the torch was not extinguished but cold enough so that it stung the exposed parts of their faces, which except for their eyes and upper cheeks were covered by a thick layer of leather. The torch's dancing light threw shadows on the street and the buildings around them as they walked silently through the dark City under a sky giving illumination only with the utmost stinginess. Yom Shlishi was only a few hours old.

They were now in the neighborhood of Elimelech's house. Benjamin stepped ahead of his brother to lead the way. He broke the silence.

"Brother, are you calm and unafraid?"

"Of course not," Reuven replied. "I am as nervous and frightened as you are. Much can go wrong. But it is something we must do. And thank you for deciding to join me."

Benjamin was afraid that he would not be able to carry out his part of the mission. He had never struck someone before. And with a torch! What if he killed the guard?

Ananus had said that every defeat of the extremists was a victory for the moderates. Is that true? What does Ananus know? He's a priest, not a rabbi. Father is the man to go to for guidance, and I know what he would say.

The pack on Benjamin's back felt heavy, even though it only contained empty sacks and lengths of rope.

They reached the gate of the house that had once belonged to Elimelech. It was shut and locked. Benjamin began banging on it with his free hand and shouting loudly.

"Open the gate, open the gate!" he cried.

He was making so much noise he worried that people in the neighboring houses would hear.

The sound of solid, steady footsteps approached. Benjamin ceased the shouting and banging.

"Who is it?" came the voice behind the gate. "What do you want?"

Benjamin recognized the voice.

"Hurry!" Reuven cried. "Dorcas needs help! Open the gate!"

"Dorcas?" Benjamin heard the guard's confusion.

"Yes!" replied Reuven. "Dorcas needs help. Badly. I have something of his to show you."

The gate was unlocked and swung open. The two brothers pushed their way inside. Benjamin closed the gate behind him. Reuven stepped a few feet away from the guard and laid the sack in his arms on the ground.

"Here, this is from Dorcas."

The guard had been looking suspiciously from Benjamin to Reuven, all the while with his hand on the hilt of his sword. Reuven bent to the ground and began to untie the hide. More and more of the guard's attention was directed toward the mysterious object.

The hide covering fell away, revealing its contents.

The guard shrieked in horror, his eyes fixed on the severed head of Dorcas. The rain had briefly increased; the water dripping down from the matted hair made the effect more gruesome.

Now! thought Benjamin, and swung the torch at the guard. The flame whipped behind the torch and went out. Benjamin had aimed at the man's head, but the blow merely glanced off his shoulder. It was still strong enough to stagger the guard.

Reuven, knife in hand, leapt. They came crashing to the ground with Reuven on top, the guard face down. Reuven's knife flew to the guard's throat.

"This is what happens to traitors like Dorcas!" Reuven hissed. "Make any sound and you, too, will suffer the same fate."

The guard stammered.

"I had no idea that Dorcas was a traitor. None of us did."

Reuven signaled to his brother. Benjamin laid the extinguished torch down and took the pack off his back. He removed several lengths of rope.

"So you say," Reuven said harshly. "We shall see." Then more gently: "It seems that none of us knew for sure, until we found the Roman money and letter. We now know that Dorcas was even working for that thief Florus."

Benjamin bent down, pulled the guard's arms back and tried to tie his wrists with the rope. Even in the darkness relieved only by a sheltered torch near the house Benjamin could see Reuven smiling and imagined he could hear his brother repeating the words that he had told him earlier: "Benjamin, you should have taken the military training when it was offered."

Reuven spoke to the guard in a voice of authority.

"Remember, the Revolution has eyes that see everywhere and hands that reach far." He sheathed his knife and took the rope from Benjamin.

Benjamin's face flushed with the embarrassment of failure. Reuven finished binding the prisoner, removed his sword, and handed it to Benjamin. He pointed to the house.

The rain was still falling. Benjamin looked with pity at the prisoner tied and lying on the ground. He pointed to the sky.

Reuven frowned. He nodded. He reached into Benjamin's pack and took out a sack. He pulled the prisoner to his feet and slipped the sack over the prisoner's head. Benjamin put the pack onto his back. He and Reuven guided the prisoner into the house. Once inside Reuven moved the tied and hooded man down to the floor.

"Remember what I told you about the reach of the Revolution," Reuven warned. "Remain quiet while we search the house for more evidence of conspiracy against the nation. When we are done you will be freed." He pulled Benjamin off to the side and whispered:

"I don't think he'll give us any trouble. Let's go!"

A lamp burned in the corner of the grand room where they stood. Benjamin went to get it. With the lamp in hand and the sword in the other he led the way; Reuven followed. After a few steps Reuven complained: "You're going the wrong way. It's to the right, not the left."

"No," Benjamin insisted. "I remember clearly what Judah said. We go through the narrower doorway. You're mixing up directions because of the way we turned."

"We'll see," Reuven said doubtfully.

Benjamin was pleased that his brother was listening to him. He led him down a long corridor with doorways that opened to rooms on the right.

The sound of slow, shuffling footsteps ahead reached them.

"Oh, no!" Benjamin groaned.

An old man was making his way toward them. He held a lamp in his hands.

Reuven stepped in front of his brother. He raised his knife threateningly.

"Halt!" Reuven cried. "Face the wall and do not look at us."

The old man stood against the wall and trembled.

"Please don't hurt me," he pleaded.

"No one will hurt you," Reuven said gently, "if you do what you're told. We are secret operatives of the Revolution looking for evidence of others involved in Dorcas' treason."

"Dorcas a traitor!" the old man cried, delight in his voice. "He was a bad man! I'm not surprised. He killed Elimelech ben Baruch."

"Elimelech was your master?" Benjamin asked.

"Yes. He was good man. I served him many years."

"What is your name?" Reuven asked.

"Phineas ben Amos."

"Well, Phineas ben Amos, you just wait here quietly until we come back." Reuven sheathed his knife and took the lamp from Phineas. "Lead the way," he said to Benjamin.

Benjamin walked to the end of the corridor and turned right. At the second door to the left he stopped.

"It's here, brother," he said. He opened the door and stepped inside. Reuven followed.

To the left of the entrance was a large table with two chairs that faced each other. Against the opposite wall was a cabinet about chest high.

"Well, brother," Reuven said, "you were right and I was wrong. I'll have to remember that in the future! This *is* the room!"

Reuven placed the lamp on the table and walked over to the cabinet. He opened its door. At the bottom were two large pots made of thick metal. On top of these were layers of raw wool sheets. Above the wool sheets rested folded papyrus and broken pottery shards. At the very peak of this disparate pile lay writing implements. Most of the cabinet was empty space.

Reuven closed the door.

Benjamin crossed the room and held up his lamp. Reuven wrestled the bulky cabinet away from the wall.

The wall behind the chest was made of rough-faced stones that were one and a half feet on each side. They were smoothly fitted into place. Reuven ran his fingers over the stone on the right that was second to the top, searching for a place that his fingers could grasp.

He grunted with satisfaction when he found what he was looking for. Reuven pulled out the stone, which was only a narrow slab in thickness. He placed it on top of the cabinet. Through the opening Reuven had just created Benjamin saw a hidden chamber. Reuven carefully removed the other three stones blocking the niche.

A wooden coffer with an intricately carved top was revealed.

Reuven put his arms around the coffer and staggered to the table.

"It's heavy," he muttered. "It must weigh more than a talent."

Benjamin held up the lamp as Reuven removed the unlocked top.

The brothers gasped as one. Benjamin dropped the sword and almost lost his grip on the lamp.

Gold coins filled the chest and glinted in the dual lamplight.

"Oh my!" exclaimed Reuven.

He ran his fingers through them. The small Roman coins were aurei. Reuven had never held one in his hand before. The heads of different Roman emperors shined back at him from the obverse faces of the coins.

"There's a fortune here," Benjamin said in awe. "The average worker gets one denarius a day. Each one of these is worth twenty-five denarii!"

"There must be hundreds of them," Reuven exclaimed.

"Thousands," Benjamin corrected. "How can we take them all now? How can we carry all these coins? Where will we hide so much gold?"

"We can't," Reuven agreed. "Judah will figure out how to get the rest and where to keep it. But we can take enough in our sacks to get him and Father released."

"Do you think Dorcas knew about this?" Benjamin asked.

"I don't know," Reuven replied. He sighed. "We may never know."

"What about Phineas?"

"That won't be hard to find out," Reuven answered.

Benjamin put the lamp down. He removed the pack from his back and took out two sacks. He handed one to his brother. They filled the sacks and closed the drawstrings. The majority of the coins remained in the coffer. They returned it to its niche in the wall, put back the stones, and moved the cabinet back to its original position.

"No one would ever know what's inside that wall," Benjamin said in wonder.

Back in the hallway where Phineas waited Reuven approached with deliberately heavy steps, his sandals clattering on the floor.

"Phineas," Reuven called out, in a tone of command, "no, no, don't turn around. Where does Elimelech keep his money?"

Phineas took several deep breaths.

"Dorcas stole it all," he said bitterly. "He hardly pays me anything to care for the house."

"Where did Elimelech keep it?"

Phineas pointed down the hall, in the opposite direction to where they had found the treasure.

"There's an office down there," Phineas said. "There's a table with three chairs. There's an open cabinet with shelves. Elimelech used to keep his strongbox with money and his accounts on those shelves. The money in the strongbox is gone."

Reuven looked at Benjamin and smiled. He placed his lamp on the floor.

"All right," Reuven said. "Phineas, listen carefully. We are leaving now. When you hear me shout from the entrance you are free. The guard is tied; release him. Do you understand?"

"Yes."

Benjamin now followed Reuven. Before stepping out into the night Reuven shouted to Phineas that he was free.

The rain had abated. The clouds had cleared. There was some light from the sky. Benjamin laid the lamp down. When the brothers reached the gate, Benjamin said to Reuven: "What about the head of Dorcas?"

Chapter One Hundred & Two

10 December 67 CE / 15 Kislev 3828

Judah paced the cell like a caged beast. Rabbi Aaron sat on the bench in the corner, silent, his tefillin put away.

It was Yom Rishon, four days ago, that Reuven had visited. Since the discovery of Dorcas' severed head inside the gate of Elimelech's house no prisoner had been allowed visitors.

One of the guards, named Gershom, who had befriended Judah, related the turmoil occurring in the ranks of the rebels.

"They say it was a secret arm of the Revolution that carried out the execution," Gershom told Judah. "There were charges pending against Dorcas, but they were never formalized before he was executed. No one admits to being a member of this shadowy arm, and now everyone is afraid. None of the factions trust each other."

Judah chuckled as he recalled these words. Reuven had created anarchy among the insurgents, which was bad, but the cleverness of it all amazed Judah. He stopped pacing and stared at Rabbi Aaron.

How is it possible, Judah wondered, that such a son came from such a father?

Rabbi Aaron looked up at him.

"You and Reuven had been whispering but I could hear you. My son has become a thief and a desecrator of corpses."

Judah frowned at Rabbi Aaron.

"There has been no theft reported from Elimelech's house," Judah said.

"Humph! Do you take me for a fool? I heard you describe where he kept his fortune. No one would know if every last gold coin disappeared."

"Rabbi, I advised Reuven against it."

"Then why did you give him all the information needed to carry it out?" demanded Rabbi Aaron.

"What else could I do?" protested Judah. "He was resolved. There was no changing his mind. Besides, he did it for us."

"And how has it helped?" Rabbi Aaron countered.

Judah sighed.

"I was waiting to be sure that Reuven actually had the money. Then I would have spoken to Gershom. He is sympathetic to me."

Rabbi Aaron glared at Judah.

"Dorcas may have killed my brother," Rabbi Aaron hissed, through clenched teeth, "and Rabbi Shlomo, but Dorcas was your responsibility and those crimes are on your head."

Surprised by the charge, Judah took an involuntary step backward.

"I am no more responsible for Dorcas than you are," Judah protested. "I never had control over him. See, I was locked up because of him, and if he had lived he would have done everything in his power to have me executed."

"Ach, Judah ben Ezra! You are a moral coward who refuses to take responsibility for your actions. You create monsters and when they commit monstrous acts you walk away and claim you had nothing to do with it."

Judah could feel the color draining from his face.

"I did not create Dorcas," he said. "There was evil in his soul." Judah trembled. "I have always done what I thought was right, and if, perhaps, I made mistakes, they were mistakes, not evil acts with bad intentions."

"Believe what you will," Rabbi Aaron said with contempt. Turning away from Judah, he swayed back and forth in prayer. Judah resumed his pacing.

Hours passed in silence.

There was a thud as the door flew open and banged against the wall. Judah stopped pacing. Rabbi Aaron stopped praying.

Yehoshua ben Betuel stood at the threshold with a big smile on his face.

"Good news!" he exclaimed. "For both of you! John ben Levi has met with Eleazar ben Simon, who now controls the Committee for Public safety. Because the charges were signed by the treasonous Dorcas, Eleazar has agreed to the unconditional release of both of you."

Judah gave a deep sigh of relief.

Rabbi Aaron rose quickly from the bench.

"What about my son, Reuven?" he asked sharply.

"The charges against him have been dropped," Yehoshua ben Betuel said. "Come, both of you are free to leave."

Judah began to follow Yehoshua ben Betuel. When he reached the doorway, Rabbi Aaron, just behind him, touched his shoulder. Judah turned to face him.

Rabbi Aaron's face was stern.

"Tell me, Judah, do you have a place to stay?"

"No," replied Judah, with resignation. "Not anymore. Not since my arrest. I'll have to find something new."

"Then you can stay at my home until you do."

"What?" Judah was stunned. He would have thought Rabbi Aaron was joking, or even mocking him, but there was no humor in the rabbi's voice, just straight-forward matter-of-factness.

"It's the least I can do," the rabbi said. "You stayed locked-up until I was freed; I can, no, I should, offer shelter to you now."

Judah bowed his head.

"Thank you, Rabbi Aaron," he said. Flooded with emotions he could not sort out, Judah ben Ezra quickly turned and wiped his eyes.

Chapter One Hundred & Three

14 December 67 CE / 19 Kislev 3828

Reuven's impatience annoyed Judah. The boy had insisted that he come outside Rabbi Aaron's house just as Judah was finishing a meal. Reuven said he wanted to talk without anyone else hearing.

"When are we going to get the rest of the money?" Reuven repeated.

"It's safer where it is now," Judah replied with exasperation. He leaned against the outside wall of the house and regarded Reuven with curiosity. "If the Romans conquered the City and burned it to the ground *they* would never find it. Who are *you* worried about, Reuven?"

Reuven did not answer.

"What do you need the rest of it for?" Judah asked.

"I took it to help you and my father get out of jail."

"We're out," Judah replied. "Without the money's help. Anyway, what's the rush? You planning to set yourself up in some fancy house in the Upper City?"

Reuven laughed.

"I already had that," he said. "It was nice. However, I'm not stupid enough to start spending money wildly. People will ask too many questions. Anyway, the money's not for me."

"Don't be too sure," Judah replied quickly. "You're expecting a child. Conditions are going to get very hard when the Romans come. Food will become scarce and expensive. You'll need that money to feed your family." Now he laughed. "Feeling guilty about possessing stolen money, Reuven? I thought you said you were a thief!"

Reuven smiled. The smile disappeared when he said:

"I'm not worried about someone else finding it. I'm worried about how we'll get to it again."

Judah nodded. He gestured with his hand. The two began walking down the street.

"I've been thinking about that," Judah said. "I have an idea how we can access it whenever we want, and," here Judah paused, "also how you can live in a fancy house in the Upper City again," he concluded with a flourish.

"That I want to hear, Judah."

"I told you I had two rich patrons," Judah began. "One was Elimelech. We know what happened to him. The other fled Jerusalem. His name was Mattan ben Ehud, and he went to Yavne. I told John ben Levi that Mattan had sent me a message. He heard of my arrest and was willing to help by sending me money." Judah paused speaking and walking. Reuven looked at him expectantly. "I offered to give John most of it if he could get me a place to stay," Judah continued. "I indicated that I wanted Elimelech's house, arguing it was only right after what its previous but temporary occupant had done to me. I added that other people would share the house: Dvorah, you, your future wife, and your brother."

"Benjamin?" Reuven asked in surprise.

Judah started walking again.

"There were stories going around," he said. "Two Roman agents paid a visit to Amram. Two members of a secret arm of the Revolution overpowered Dorcas' guard and searched Elimelech's house. Two men, Reuven. I have no doubt you were one of the two in both cases. As for your accomplice, who else could he be but your brother?" Judah threw his head back and laughed. "You're corrupting your older brother, Reuven!"

Reuven did not respond. He didn't have to. Judah knew he had guessed correctly.

"What did John ben Levi say?" Reuven asked.

"He said he'd speak to Eleazar ben Simon; the Kannaim now control the house. John ben Levi has good relations with Eleazar. Perhaps my subterfuge will work with John, and perhaps he will be able to convince Eleazar to let me use the house." Judah stopped walking and sighed. "John also has good relations with Ananus. Perhaps he will be able to bring about some unity. We need that."

"More immediately," Reuven asked, "how much money do you need, Judah?"

Judah placed his arm on Reuven's shoulder and nodded.

"I'll let you know. By the way, Reuven, where did you hide the loot?"

"In the house. Upstairs, in the sleeping quarters."

"Is it safely hidden?"

"Yes," Reuven answered, "I believe so. I took an aureus to a money changer at the Temple and exchanged it for denarii." Reuven's face curled in disgust. "He cheated me. Only gave me back twenty-four denarii and one sestertius." Reuven shook his head. "He said it was his commission, how he made his money. Said he was giving me a good deal." Reuven shrugged. "I didn't want to go to the Upper Market with something worth as much as an aureus and have the shop owner ask how I had a coin of such large value." Reuven sighed at the loss of the three sestertii. "After I changed the money I went to the Upper Market and bought some pillows, you know, soft ones like the Romans and the rich Jews have. I brought them home, opened them up, put the coins on the bottom. Drusilla sewed each pillow perfectly back together. Now Benjamin, Drusilla, and I go to sleep at night with our heads on a fortune!"

Reuven's eyes now seemed to twinkle as he spoke. Judah was not amused.

"Let's hope someone doesn't go into your bedrooms and lift those pillows. They'll feel the weight and hear the clinking of coins. I'm not sure you chose the safest way, Reuven."

"No one goes up there except for us," Reuven reassured Judah, "and my father and mother, and they don't touch our bedding."

But Judah barely heard him. He had stopped walking. He tried to stop his knees from buckling. He stared down at the ground, his heart beating furiously.

Is Reuven's hiding place any worse than the wooden box where I hid the bloodstained dress from Rabbi Moshe ben Avraham's assassination? Did Bruria, when she was alone in my room, find that dress? Is that what convinced her to try to kill me?

"What's wrong, Judah?"

Judah heard the alarm in the boy's voice. He looked at Reuven but said nothing. In his mind questions raged.

Will I ever tell him the truth about the death of his uncle: Who was responsible and who wielded the knife?

Chapter One Hundred & Four

20 December 67 CE / 25 Kislev 3828

Reuven could not take his eyes off Dvorah. In this room in the Temple complex, fifteen months ago, Shaul ben Yitzchak had sat in the very same seat where Dvorah now sat.

Reuven shivered.

Three of those who were there to hear Reuven lecture on what he learned from Metilius were now present for his report on what he saw in Gamla and Caesarea: Judah ben Ezra, Ananus ben Ananus, and Niger the Peraean. Rabbi Yoel ben Jotham had been asked to join. In addition, his brother and father sat facing him.

There were two women at the table, as well: Dvorah and Drusilla. The thought of Metilius made Reuven's eyes shift from Dvorah to Drusilla. Then he stared down at the floor for several moments before beginning.

"I'm here to tell you about the siege and fall of Gamla. And of my meetings with Vespasian in Caesarea. Dvorah is here to correct me if I left out anything, or if she disagrees with something I said. Afterwards, gentlemen, you can decide on our best course of action. Such a decision is beyond my knowledge and experience."

All eyes were on Reuven, all ears were attentive. He spoke for a long time.

Dvorah had nothing to add or correct.

When Reuven finished Judah was the first to speak.

"The fall of Gamla says nothing about our situation here in Jerusalem!" The certainty in Judah's voice filled the room.

"It says everything!" countered Ananus, with equal certainty.

Judah stood up.

"Reuven himself informed us that the walls of Gamla were not well-constructed like the walls of Jerusalem," Judah said evenly. "They had far fewer fighting men than we have." He raised his large hands, fingers outward, then closed them into a fist. "The walls of Jerusalem are mighty; they will withstand the Roman siege engines. We have thousands and thousands of men to defend the City, more than the Romans and their allies can bring against us. We have stored enough food to outlast any siege the Romans want to lay upon us. Did we not defeat Cestius and the Twelfth Legion and drive them out of the land, as we defeated

Antiochus? Is not this the first day of the Festival of Dedication?"

Ananus banged the table with the flat of his palm.

"We have something else, too!" he cried. "Internal division, which will destroy us before Vespasian even reaches our walls."

Judah slumped down into his seat, his eyes downcast, muttering something beneath his breath. Reuven thought of a goat bladder, puffed up with air, suddenly deflated by the prick of a pin. He almost laughed.

"Well, Judah, is Ananus wrong about that?" Reuven asked. "Am I?"

Judah shrugged and shook his head.

"No," he admitted dejectedly.

"Does anyone here think we can defeat the Roman legions if we are not united?" Reuven asked, looking around the room. He saw Drusilla, staring at him, the corner of her lips raised in the hint of a smile.

Am I just trying to get at the truth, he asked himself, or am I performing for *her?*

Reuven felt his cheeks flush.

Niger the Peraean stood up. He looked in the faces of all the other men in the room.

"If we are not to eat our own flesh and leave the bones for the Romans, we must stop this internal bloodshed."

"I agree," said Rabbi Yoel ben Jotham.

"And how do you propose to do that when your side is arresting moderates?" Ananus asked heatedly.

"Our side?" retorted Rabbi Yoel. "I've arrested no one."

"Why didn't you invite John ben Levi and Eleazar ben Simon?" Niger asked, looking straight at Reuven.

Reuven held Niger's gaze as he answered:

"I invited people I know and trust. I don't know John ben Levi and I don't trust Eleazar ben Simon; he was connected with the organization that imprisoned my father."

Rabbi Aaron stood up.

"You are all mad! Mad!" he shouted, flinging his arms about. "We are all doomed. God has abandoned us!"

He stormed out of the room without looking back.

Reuven raised his eyebrows and smiled ironically.

"Let us pray that my father is wrong," he said.

Niger sat down. Rabbi Yoel let out a long sigh and said:

"We must work to end all our divisions."

"Yes," Niger agreed. "All sides must be brought together and a way found to resolve our differences peacefully."

Ananus stood up and shook his fist in the air.

"You can start by having the revolutionaries release all their prisoners!" Ananus demanded.

"That is a reasonable request," Rabbi Yoel agreed. "And if there are to be arrests, we have to follow an open, orderly procedure when someone is charged."

"I'll believe it when I see it," Ananus responded.

"Ananus, why don't you give the other side a chance?" Reuven asked gently.

"I do not need to be schooled by a mere boy!" Ananus shot back angrily.

"I didn't know that's what you thought of me." Reuven spoke the words calmly.

Ananus sighed.

"No, Reuven, it's not. I want to talk to you, alone, when you're done here."

Reuven nodded and folded his arms across his chest.

"Well, gentlemen," he concluded. "I've said everything I have to say. For now. You can think about what I've told you and come to your own conclusions. Those of you who have influence with others can try to work for unity, and for whatever course the people and their leaders decide. As for me, I am confused and await wiser counsel."

Reuven watched as everyone except Ananus filed out of the room. He waited for Ananus to approach.

"You know I respect you, Reuven, but the time has come when you're going to have to choose sides. It's either Judah and his revolutionary friends or me."

"What do you mean, Ananus?" It was not merely the high priest's words that sounded ominous, it was the way he spoke them, with a threat lurking in his tone.

"The outrages committed by the Kannaim have gone too far. They not only pollute the Temple, they have been arresting more and more of the young nobles and those they perceive as enemies. Last night they came to my house and took my nephew. I am going to put a stop to it. I am going to organize the people and drive the extremists from their seat of power."

"Ananus," Reuven pleaded, "can't you wait to see if the efforts of Niger and Rabbi Yoel yield results?"

Ananus snorted with contempt and left the room without answering.

I fear, Reuven thought, that my father may be right.

We have gone mad, and we are doomed.

Chapter One Hundred & Five

27 December 67 CE / 3 Tevet 3828

Reuven anxiously scanned the room in Rabbi Lemuel ben Talmai's study hall. On one side of a large table were Rabbi Lemuel, Rabbi Aaron ben Avraham, and Rabbi Yiftach ben Neriah. Across the table sat Drusilla.

Reuven, with his brother Benjamin on his right and his mother Ruth at his left, sat at the end of the table. In a corner of the room, on a bench, sat Dvorah and Judah.

The three rabbis were questioning Drusilla.

She seems calm, Reuven thought. Calmer than I am.

"Do you still believe in the gods of the Romans and Greeks?" asked Rabbi Lemuel.

Reuven saw a smile cross his beloved's lips.

"Their gods are nothing but human beings with great powers and no consciences. I never believed in them," Drusilla replied.

"And the gods of the land where you were born?" inquired Rabbi Yiftach.

"I was too young when I was taken away. I never learned anything about them. I don't suppose they're much different in essence than the gods of Rome and Greece. Why should they be? God revealed himself to Avraham, he gave Moshe the Torah. It is your people who have the truth. That is why I want to become one of you."

The other two rabbis nodded their approval. His father remained stone-faced.

"Tell me, rabbis," Drusilla went on, "what statement in all of Greek philosophy is more noble than Hillel's dictum?"

This time even his father smiled.

Very clever, Reuven thought. They are all members of the House of Hillel. No, wait, she means what she says!

"Are you taking this step because you want to marry Reuven?" Rabbi Yiftach asked.

Drusilla looked all three rabbis in the eye before she spoke.

"That is part of the reason, but only part. I have seen the life of the Romans. They think they are civilized. They think they are cultured, with their art and poetry and philosophy. They have beautiful banquets where they solemnly discuss these things, and then conclude their festivities with drunkenness and orgies. They do not even know that what they do is vile. They are like the people of Nineveh; without Jonah to admonish them. The Children of Israel have the Law; they know right from wrong. Even when they transgress, the Law pulls them to the right path. The Jewish world has light to guide it; the Gentile world dwells in darkness. I want the light. I want to become one of you."

Rabbi Lemuel clapped his hands and exclaimed:

"Ah, Rabbi Aaron, this girl is too good for that robber son of yours! You should give her to your older son, Benjamin! He's a good boy."

The two brothers laughed out loud. Benjamin slapped Reuven on the back. Reuven leaned over and whispered in Benjamin's ear, "If they only knew you're almost as bad as I am!"

The three rabbis glared at them.

"Silence!" Rabbi Aaron ordered.

Both brothers bowed their heads in submission.

"Are you prepared to follow all the laws of the Torah?" Rabbi Lemuel asked.

"As best as I understand them, with my limited knowledge. Ruth, Rabbi Aaron's wife, is instructing me in the proper behavior and duties of a Jewish woman and a wife."

Reuven's mother nodded.

"I must say, gentlemen," Rabbi Aaron began, turning to the right and left to look directly at his colleague on either side, "she is already knowledgeable. She has the sharp mind and memory of a scholar. I am truly amazed by what I've heard from her."

Rabbi Yiftach grunted. He asked:

"Are you pregnant?"

"Yes."

"Who is the father?"

"Reuven ben Aaron."

"Are you sure the child is his?"

"It couldn't possibly be anyone else's."

"Did he take you by force?" Rabbi Yiftach asked.

"No, I seduced him," Drusilla answered, without hesitation.

Rabbi Lemuel and Rabbi Yiftach stirred. Rabbi Aaron was motionless.

"Why?"

"I fell in love with him the first time I saw him. He is noble and good." Drusilla took a deep breath.

I'm neither, Reuven thought, a sly smile on his lips. I'm a killer and a thief.

"I thought we were all going to die," she continued. "I wanted to find some happiness before that happened."

"Do you still think you are going to die, Drusilla?" Rabbi Lemuel asked.

"That is not in my hands, Rabbi Lemuel. It is in the hands of the Master of the Universe."

"All things are in His hands," Rabbi Aaron said.

"Were you a virgin when Reuven took you?" Rabbi Yiftach asked sharply.

"No."

Rabbi Yiftach shot a glance at Reuven. Reuven glared back at him.

"Were you a whore?"

Rabbi Yiftach's question was like a slap in the face for Reuven. His body tensed with anger and he reached for his knife. Almost immediately Benjamin's hand grasped his wrist so tightly the skin felt hot. Reuven relaxed his body. Benjamin removed his hand.

"Whatever happened to me before I met Reuven was not by choice," Drusilla answered calmly, her cheeks turning red. "Can you understand what it's like to be powerless, Rabbi Yiftach?"

"I'm afraid we may all find out soon enough," Rabbi Aaron interrupted softly. "Perhaps all the indignities you suffered brought you to us," he added, wiping a tear from his eye.

"Thank you," Drusilla said. She bowed her head and started weeping.

From the corner Dvorah stamped her feet and shouted:

"Stop tormenting the poor girl!"

Reuven rose to his feet. Benjamin tried to hold him back but Reuven broke free and rushed to Drusilla to comfort her.

"Sit down, son," Rabbi Aaron gently admonished. "Rabbi Yiftach is only doing what he is supposed to." As Reuven returned to his seat, without having touched Drusilla, Rabbi Aaron turned to Dvorah.

"Dvorah, if you are not silent, I will have to send you out of here."

Rabbi Aaron stood.

"I vote to accept you as a Jew."

"I agree," said Rabbi Lemuel.

There was a moment of silence.

Rabbi Yiftach smiled.

"I, too, agree," he said.

Drusilla lifted her head. She smiled through her tears.

"We will write you a certificate of conversion," Rabbi Aaron said. "My wife will take you to the mikveh and I will take you to the Temple to purchase two pigeons to sacrifice. And you will have a new name to go with your new identity. You have no parents—" Rabbi Aaron's voice broke. It took him a moment to compose himself. "You are a daughter of God, The Most High. Therefore, you shall henceforth be known as Batya."

She'll always be Drusilla to me, Reuven thought angrily.

His father smiled and said:

"Welcome to the Jewish people, Batya bat Avraham and Sarah."

Chapter One Hundred & Six

3 January 68 CE / 10 Tevet 3828

Reuven stood, alone, on the rampart of the western wall of the Temple complex, now a spectator, not a participant. He had been back in Jerusalem for a month, thirty-one days to be exact. A week ago on Yom Rishon, Drusilla had faced the panel headed by his father that declared her fit for conversion.

"Welcome to the Jewish people, Drusilla," Reuven muttered. "What nonsense," he said louder. "We're no better than the Gentiles. Worse, maybe."

A week from now he and Drusilla were to be married. Today, he was about to witness Jew slaughter Jew.

We will celebrate with war raging around us, a war between brothers. A present for my wedding, he thought. At least at Gamla we were fighting the enemy.

Reuven sighed. He imagined that the bitter taste in his mouth came from something real he had swallowed.

Below him, on the Temple courts, armed men who belonged to the Kannaim were preparing for battle. Some were already leaving to confront their enemies.

Reuven switched his gaze to the City outside the Temple. Masses of men were streaming toward it. Partisans were rushing out to meet them. This time the action would take place not on the bridge to the Upper City but in the streets of Jerusalem.

Ananus succeeded in rousing the people against the Kannaim who took over the Temple, thought Reuven. Will he succeed in bringing peace to the City? In keeping it safe?

A man further north on the ramparts came toward Reuven. He was in his twenties, slender, with angular features. He was shorter than Reuven.

"What are you doing here?" he challenged Reuven.

"Observing the insanity of the Jews," Reuven replied.

"Are you a spy for Ananus?"

"I'm a spy for God."

"I should hurl you off the ramparts into the City below."

"You should, but you won't," Reuven responded calmly. His hand went inside his cloak and lightly grasped the knife hidden there.

"No one's throwing anyone anywhere!" a familiar voice behind him said.

Reuven whirled in surprise. Judah was sauntering towards them along the rampart from the south.

"I think you've got a fight to join," Judah said, his voice menacing, "and it's not here." The man who had challenged Reuven scurried away.

"I think I saved that fellow from getting his throat cut," Judah observed.

"I'm done killing fellow Jews," Reuven said.

"Didn't stop you from killing Dorcas," Judah retorted.

"That was different. He killed my uncle."

Judah didn't reply. Reuven assumed that he understood the difference. Then Judah said:

"We should be down there, fighting, not up here, watching."

"Perhaps, but on which side, Judah?"

Judah took out a gold coin, flipping it with his right hand into his left palm. He did this several times.

"There's a picture of some Roman on this coin," he said, a puzzled look on his face.

Reuven took the coin out of Judah's palm and examined it.

The obverse side depicted a man's head in profile. There was a crown of curly and wavy hair that flowed down to the nape of the neck. A large nose ended in a bulb that pointed toward lips curled in a sneer. A flabby chin joined the front of the neck without any discernible boundary.

"That's our emperor," Reuven said, laughing, pointing to the Latin lettering circling around the golden coin. "See, it says: NERO CAESAR AUGUSTUS'." He handed the coin back to Judah. "The great Nero!" Reuven exclaimed. "They say he is a madman. If so, then it is fit that he should be our emperor also, for we Jews are certainly madmen, too." Reuven pointed to the City below. "I've spoken to Vespasian three times. He's no madman. He's not even a Cestius. He's a cunning general who inspires the loyalty of his men. Let me tell you what he's going to do. He's going to take the rest of the country, isolate Jerusalem, and then wait. Wait for us to kill each other off. Look down and you will see, the fighting between brothers has already begun."

Groups of better armed partisans faced larger groups of ordinary citizens in more than one theater of battle in exchanges of stones and spears. Occasionally a partisan or a citizen fell from the long-range struggle.

That will change, Reuven thought, when they meet hand-to-hand and more blood is spilled.

"The day is coming," Reuven spoke aloud, "when we'll be eating our own flesh and leave nothing for the Romans, just as Niger said."

"That's not what Niger said," Judah corrected. "What he said was: 'If we are not to eat our own flesh and leave the bones for the Romans, we must stop this internal bloodshed.' What kind of scholar are you, rabbi's son, with a memory like that?"

Reuven grinned sardonically.

"I'm neither scholar nor soldier," he said. "It appears you are both! And, apparently a diviner of signs! What did your coin toss tell you? Ananus or Eleazar?"

"I am no diviner of signs!" Judah responded quickly. "That is an abomination! And I do not need a coin to decide. I would choose Eleazar ben Simon over Ananus. I know which you would choose."

"Do you, really?" Reuven asked, amused.

"Yes," Judah replied. "You would choose neither. You've lost your stomach for the coming fight, but you don't have confidence in Ananus' leadership anymore."

Judah's perspicacity surprised him. Rather than compliment him, Reuven asked:

"What of you, Judah? Why haven't you joined the fight?"

"I've attached myself to John," came the reply. "For now, he is currying favor with both sides."

"Ah," Reuven said, "you northern boys stick together."

"Yes, we do. And we are stronger and tougher than you Jerusalem fellows. We will save the country. Even Eleazar ben Simon, from a priestly family, is no match for John ben Levi."

"What about the boys down south? I hear they're pretty tough."

"Yes, the Idumaeans are," Judah agreed. "As tough as we are, maybe."

"Perhaps we should call on them for help defending the City," Reuven said. "Before the Romans come. No," he added, laughing, "well before they arrive, to boost our morale in case there is a mood for surrender."

Judah looked thoughtful. He nodded after a moment.

"I'll tell you something, Reuven," he said. "If they were here now, on the side of the Kannaim, the citizens under Ananus wouldn't stand a chance."

Reuven shrugged.

"Are any of us a match for the Romans?" he asked.

"We shall see," Judah answered.

Reuven and Judah had been facing each other. Reuven again pointed to the City below, where the long-range combat had been replaced by hand-to-hand fighting with swords and javelins. Many more men had fallen now.

"Look, Judah," Reuven said. "Even from here we can see the blood flowing in the streets. Is that not a true abomination, when the People of the Torah slaughter each other?"

Judah sighed. "Yes," he said sadly, "it is a true abomination."

Chapter One Hundred & Seven

10 January 68 CE / 17 Tevet 3828

Morning light came through the high window of the grand room of Elimelech's house. Reuven slowly swung the necklace of tiny silver links back and forth. At its end, in its gold setting, the clear purple stone shone and sparkled in the rays of the sun.

"It's beautiful!" exclaimed Dvorah. "It takes my breath away. Batya will love it."

"Who?" Reuven asked.

"Batya. Your bride."

"Ah." Reuven made a sour face. "She'll always be Drusilla to me."

Dvorah and Judah were living in Elimelech's house now. Reuven had spent the night there. In the afternoon, they would accompany him to the wedding venue.

There's still time, Reuven thought.

"Yes," Reuven agreed. "Batya will love it. I will also love to see it around her neck. And so I shall give it to her." He passed the necklace to Dvorah, who handled it with awe. "But I know," he said, "what would make Drusilla truly happy!"

"What?"

"A book."

"A book?" Dvorah asked incredulously. "A book?"

"A book. That is what would make my Drusilla truly happy. Don't worry, Dvorah, I will be back in time to prepare for the wedding."

Judah came into the room.

"Where are you going, young man?"

"To the Upper Market. To buy a book of philosophy for my Drusil-la."

The object of his trip didn't seem to faze Judah. Something else did.

"It's not safe going alone. Let me accompany you," Judah insisted. "Bands of citizens and Kannaim are still fighting in the streets. There are even men out there belonging to neither side who are bent on doing mischief."

"Judah, I've handled myself well in battle. You've seen that. I'm not afraid."

"Battle or man-to-man combat is one thing. Three men bursting from an alley to ambush you is another."

"I'll be fine, Judah. Don't worry. Anyway, the Upper Market is close by."

Reuven pointed to the necklace.

"Guard it well, Dvorah," he said laughing.

Reuven walked out the door, and then the gate, singing, a broad smile on his face. Fighting or no fighting, the world seemed a happy place.

He noted the curious looks other people on the street gave him. He wanted to shout "I'm getting married this afternoon!" but knew that in dangerous times the wisest course was to be unobtrusive and keep one's head down.

Still, a smile on his lips and a song in his mouth would do no harm.

He walked north up the street gazing at the fine houses around him.

Could I afford to buy such a house? he wondered.

It's really not my money. I took it to release my father and Judah. But now, there's no one else to claim it. Judah says it's really mine. Well, mine and Benjamin's. He helped me take it from the house of Elimelech.

Reuven stopped walking and singing and watched a bird fly in the direction of the Temple.

If I hadn't killed Dorcas I wouldn't have the money. I did kill him to avenge my uncle, but does the money color the motive, turning an act of justice into the crime of murder and robbery?

Reuven resumed walking, his mood turned somber.

The Upper Market's building consisted of three adjoining two-story sections at right angles to each other, a north wing, an east wing, and a south wing. The wings enclosed the large central plaza of the Upper Market.

The market faced Herod's Palace. The tower that had been toppled in the beginning of the revolt had never been rebuilt. The part of the wall that was destroyed with the tower had been replaced by a much shorter and less sturdy wall.

Reuven shivered. Not restoring the tower and wall to its previous glory always seemed a bad omen to Reuven, a harbinger of things to come.

As usual, the market's central plaza was filled with people, coming and going to the established shops in the surrounding structure. Unauthorized stalls and carts were scattered throughout the plaza, any one of which could be shut down by the authorities, such as they were, unless the unauthorized merchant was willing to pay a bribe to the officer putting the squeeze on him.

It was Reuven's second recent visit to the market. He had purchased the necklace at one of the established shops, at the cost of seventy-five denarii, which he had heedlessly paid with three gold aurei. That shop had been on the ground level, in the central wing. Now Reuven climbed to the second level, on the north wing, and walked down the corridor, past shops selling expensive pottery, household items, tools, and fine clothing. Some of the shop owners stood in the corridor, trying to entice customers to enter with the promise of good deals, made especially for them.

Reuven ignored their entreaties.

Three-quarters of the way down the corridor, before reaching the east wing, was the shop Reuven wanted. Its owner was not in the corridor trying to hawk customers; he was deep inside the store.

The walls were lined with shelves that contained scrolls and codices. Two long tables stood in the center, a gap between them. Each had a large lamp that burned brightly, giving the interior of the store strong illumination.

Between the tables stood the proprietor. He came around the near table to greet Reuven.

"Good morning, young man. Can I help you?"

The owner was elderly, with a white beard flecked with black. He had deep-set eyes that seemed oddly far apart. The eyes were set under a high forehead. He wore no cloak but a clean tunic that was nonetheless threadbare.

The store itself had a musty smell.

"Sir," Reuven began, "do you have a book on philosophy in Greek by a Jewish writer? Something that discusses religious topics from—" Reuven paused, trying to find the right words "an intellectual or rational point of view, that is, dare I say, from a Greek point of view?"

"Ah," the bookseller responded, "I have just the author for you. Philo of Alexandria. An observant Jew who also has studied the thinking of the Greek philosophers."

"That sounds perfect!" Reuven could not keep the excitement out of his voice.

The proprietor walked deeper into the store, turned to a shelf on his right, and removed a thick codex.

"This, my young scholar, is a multi-volume work. One deals with sections of Breshit. Another discusses the nature of God and how much we can know about Him. I must warn you, however, that this book is not cheap. It will cost you one hundred denarii. But if you can raise the money, you will find it very enlightening."

Reuven was so excited about the find that he would have paid double the price.

"It's not for me," Reuven said. "It's a wedding present."

"What a wonderful present that will be!" exclaimed the bookseller. "For a good friend, or your brother?"

"For my bride!" Reuven replied proudly.

The bookseller looked shocked. He raised his thick white eyebrows in surprise.

"Your bride?" It took him a moment to recover. "All credit to you, young man, to look beyond physical beauty and to choose a woman for her intellect, even though she may be homely, no offense to you or her intended."

Reuven laughed.

"None taken, sir. I deserve no credit at all, for without doubt, she is the most beautiful woman God ever created, with hair as golden as the sun and eyes as blue as the sky."

Once again, surprise showed on the elderly man's face.

"Is she one of our own?"

Reuven grinned.

"She converted two weeks ago. She was born beyond the Middle Sea, far, far to the north of Rome and Italy."

"My!" gasped the bookseller. "Well," he paused, thinking, "I am willing to sell it to you for seventy-five denarii. I know it will be put to good use."

Reuven reached into his cloak and pulled out a purse. He opened the drawstring and took out three gold aurei. The bookseller's eyes widened at the large denomination coins. He was even more surprised when Reuven pulled out an additional thirteen denarii and handed all the coins totaling eighty-eight denarii over to him.

"Because you were so kind I wanted to meet you halfway, sir," Reuven explained.

The bookseller ran the coins between his fingers.

"What is your name, young man?"

"Does it matter?"

The man put the coins down on the table and threw up his hands.

"I am no gossip," he said. "But no, it does not matter. My name is

Yechezkel ben Elkanah."

Reuven nodded, looked the man in the eyes and said:

"My name is Reuven ben Aaron. I thank you for finding this book for me. It will make my wife very, very happy."

"I would like to meet your wife one day," Yechezkel said.

"You shall."

"And if she enjoyed and understood what was in the book you purchased," Yechezkel continued, "then I will find other books for her to buy or even borrow."

"Thank you, sir. That is very kind of you."

As Reuven was leaving, clutching the book to his chest, Yechezkel called out:

"May you and your wife be blessed with health, happiness, and long life, Reuven ben Aaron, and may you have many children."

Reuven stepped to the railing of the balcony and looked down. The crowd in the plaza milled around as if the only concerns in the world were private ones.

Reuven remembered Drusilla's reference to Jonah and Nineveh at the rabbinical court.

Were the people below like the people of Nineveh, who could not discern between their right hand and their left hand? Was he?

Would God spare Jerusalem and its people as he did for the people of Nineveh, or would he allow it to be destroyed?

Reuven swayed back and forth and began to pray.

"Oh, Master of the Universe, grant to me and Drusilla, whom You have brought to me, Yechezkel ben Elkanah's blessing, and grant it to all the people of Israel."

Then he turned away from the railing and made his way to the house of Elimelech, his heart heavy.

Chapter One Hundred & Eight

10 January 68 CE / 17 Tevet 3828

The flute, lyre, and timbrel fell silent. The musicians put down their instruments and joined the others standing around the canopy. Now there were ten male witnesses to the ceremony and it could proceed after the blessing had been given by Rabbi Aaron.

Drusilla's dress was magnificent. It flowed around her; white with purple and crimson threads running through it. Reuven couldn't understand how his mother had managed to create such a dress in so short a time. On Drusilla's head was a crown of flowers. A veil covered her face.

Benjamin stepped under the canopy and handed Reuven a goblet of wine.

Reuven lifted the veil from Drusilla's face. His hand trembled and he almost spilled the wine. He raised the cup to her lips and she drank. Then he drank.

Reuven gave the cup back to his brother. A moment later his brother handed him the necklace he had bought for Drusilla. Reuven gave it two small swings. Drusilla gasped and went "Ah" as he put it around her neck.

"Wait," he whispered, "there's more."

Benjamin then passed Reuven the codex he had bought in the morning.

"The necklace was for me to see you in," Reuven whispered. "This book is for *you*."

"Oh Reuven!" she cried with delight. Drusilla could not contain herself. She opened the book to see what it was. "Oh Reuven!" she cried again and looked at him with such love and wonder that he wanted to grab her then and there, without waiting to finish the ceremony.

Drusilla had not allowed Reuven to touch her from the day his father told them that he would set up a religious court for Drusilla's conversion. The day after the conversion, Reuven had given Drusilla a marriage agreement, in Hebrew and Greek, along with ten gold aurei coins. In the agreement he promised to marry her and to take care of her and protect her once they were married. He signed the agreement, and Benjamin and Judah also signed it as witnesses.

Thus started the betrothal period. Though Reuven knew that it was ridiculously short—a betrothal could last months or even a year—the two weeks from the betrothal ceremony until the wedding were too long for him.

But soon, but soon…

Reuven licked his lips.

"Reuven!" his father admonished.

Reuven cleared his throat.

"Behold!" he intoned solemnly, "You are consecrated to me with these gifts according to the law of Moses and the people of Israel!"

Then he kissed her, gently, on the lips.

The crowd cheered. The musicians returned to their instruments. One by one the guests came up to congratulate the married couple.

Niger the Peraean was the first to come up.

"Well, lad, you were already a warrior, and now you've become a husband." He smiled as his gaze went from husband to wife. "I've never seen a husband give a wife a book as a wedding present, or seen a wife so happy to receive a present, book or otherwise. May the Lord in Heaven bless the both of you."

Rabbi Yiftach ben Neriah and Rabbi Lemuel ben Talmai, the inquisitors at Drusilla's rabbinical court, both stepped under the canopy to wish them well. Both remarked on the present of the book and how Batya reacted to it. Rabbi Lemuel added, looking at Reuven and then at Batya: "May your son become a scholar like his grandfather and grand uncle, and," here his eyes seemed to twinkle mischievously, "like his mother would have become if she had been a man."

Rabbi Yoel ben Jotham came up to congratulate them also.

"Well, Reuven," he said, "remember that Scripture allows a married man to stay out of the host for a year to remain home to cheer his new wife. So, unless the Romans come knocking before that, let all the political strife in Jerusalem blow by you like the scorching sharav of summer."

Judah walked over, clapped Reuven on the shoulder, and declared:

"Well, it seems that the barbarian Drusilla has become the Jewish Batya. Congratulations to you, Reuven. You made a fine catch, beautiful, intelligent, and loyal."

Reuven balled his fist in mock anger.

"Judah," he said, "if you weren't tougher than me I'd punch you in the nose. Barbarian or Jew, she's Drusilla, not Batya."

"I'll decide what my name is," Drusilla said firmly.

"Ho, ho, ho!" Judah cried, "she's already taken the reins." Judah's face grew serious. "Where's Ananus? Why didn't he come?"

"I didn't invite him, Judah. He's a busy man."

"Ah, I see." Judah squeezed Reuven's shoulder so hard that he winced in pain. "I heard what Rabbi Yoel said to you. He's right. Stay out of everything and make your wife happy." He released his grip. "Just one favor I ask. If the two of you, and your brother, could spend some time at our house, it will reduce the risk of them demanding it back because only two people are using it."

"I will do that, Judah," Reuven said.

Dvorah came and hugged Drusilla.

"Take good care of her, Reuven!"

"I will, Dvorah." He sighed. "I wish Shaul were here. And my Uncle Moshe and his wife Bruria. Those are three people I miss at this celebration."

As Dvorah stepped away Reuven's mother replaced her and hugged her son and new daughter-in-law.

"I hope you are always as happy as I am right now," she said to them. Once more she hugged them, now first Drusilla and then her son.

"Mother," he asked, "how did you make this beautiful dress so quickly?"

"Reuven, my boy," Ruth replied, "I started the day you left for Gamla. And even after news of Gamla's fall reached us, and you didn't come home and we feared you might be dead, I continued working on it to make sure you did return to marry Batya."

A single tear trickled down her cheek. Reuven brushed it away with a finger.

Benjamin approached.

"Well done, brother," Benjamin said. "I'm happy for you."

Reuven grinned so broadly that even his ears moved.

"I promised Judah," Reuven said, "that the three of us would spend some days and nights in the house he and Dvorah now occupy, so that those who have ultimate control of it won't take it away when they see a crowded house instead of an empty one."

"I won't complain about a little luxury," Benjamin replied, laughing and walking away with his mother.

Reuven and Drusilla remained alone under the canopy as Rabbi Aaron approached with a serious mien.

"I don't mind telling you, Batya, that when Reuven first brought you to our house you were not what I imagined I would want as a daughter-in-law. Now I can honestly say that you are too good for my son."

"I whole-heartedly agree!" chimed in Reuven.

"Don't be flippant with me, Reuven!" Rabbi Aaron's cheeks turned red with anger. "My son has turned into someone that causes me great pain. I am counting on you, Batya, to tame him and bring him back to the right path. And to make sure his son grows into a good Jewish man."

"I will do my best, Rabbi Aaron," Drusilla said.

"You may call me Father, now, Batya," Rabbi Aaron said gently.

"All right, Father," she said.

When his father walked away Reuven said:

"Wow! He hates me, doesn't he?"

"No, Reuven," Drusilla explained, "he's just disappointed in you. Try to understand him and not be angry or hurt. He sees things very differently than you do."

Reuven took her hands in his.

"How lucky I am to have such a wise wife." He sighed as he looked into her eyes. "Did the midwife say it was all right to…"

Drusilla smiled.

"Yes, she said it was all right. But you must be gentle, Reuven."

"Aren't I always?"

She playfully shook her index finger at him.

"Sometimes, no."

Reuven looked crestfallen.

"I'll try from now on. Come, let me show you. Let's leave now!"

Drusilla laughed gaily.

"Can't I even enjoy my own wedding?"

The guests were sitting down at the two tables laden with food and drink. There was bread and cheese and fish and meat. Soups in bowls. Wine and water to drink. The musicians had resumed playing, their work sometimes drowned out by the chatter of those at the tables.

"I should have given you a grand wedding," Reuven said with regret. "The way every other bride in the Land of Israel gets. We should have celebrated for days. Not something simple and plain like this."

They were in a small pavilion in the southern part of Bezetha. In the center of the pavilion was an inn where travelers stayed and ate. On the outer circle of the pavilion stood tables where patrons could dine and celebrate. Reuven had rented part of the space for the afternoon, along with the musicians the inn had recommended.

"This is a wonderful wedding," Drusilla said. "I'm very happy with it. Besides, we agreed, these are dangerous times and it's best not to be too conspicuous. I hope we haven't overdone it as it is. Besides, I don't want you to spend too much money."

Reuven clapped his hands with delight.

"Truly, I am the luckiest man in the world!" he cried. "I married not only the most beautiful woman in the world, but the wisest, too!" He shouted these last words, so loudly that all conversation ceased, as did the musicians.

And then, in a clear voice so pure the hair stood up on Reuven's arms, Drusilla began to recite, in Hebrew, from Shir ha-Shirim:

"I am a rose of Sharon, a lily of the valleys.

As an apple-tree among the trees of the wood, so is my beloved among the sons.

Under its shadow I delighted to sit, and its fruit was sweet to my taste.

He hath brought me to the banqueting-house, and his banner over me is love."

Reuven was beside himself. Drusilla's recitation was unexpected. He had to answer. And Reuven, who never felt shy about addressing people, felt it now, and fought to overcome it with three deeply-drawn breaths, answering her from the same biblical poem:

"Rise up, my love, my fair one, and come away.
For, lo, the winter is past, the rain is over and gone."

Here Reuven stopped and smiled despite himself, for it was still winter in Jerusalem and rain could come at any time. Then he continued:

"The flowers appear on the earth; the time of singing is come, and the voice of the turtle
is heard in our land;
The fig-tree putteth forth her green figs, and the vines in blossom give forth their fragrance.
Arise, my love, my fair one, and come away."

The guests, even the waiters, were mesmerized by the couple's performance. They continued staring at the new husband and wife even after they finished their recitation.

At one table sat the four rabbis. At the other sat Benjamin, Judah, and Niger. Across from them sat Ruth and Dvorah. Reuven and Drusilla joined this latter table, she sitting with the women, he with the men.

Judah slapped Reuven on the back as he sat down.

"Drink some wine, Reuven! It's your wedding day."

Reuven did not want to drink wine. He wanted a clear head. He stared fixedly across the table at Drusilla, who seemed perfectly happy chatting away with his mother and Dvorah.

Reuven had one thing on his mind, and he felt he had waited long enough for it.

I'll just have to wait longer, he thought. Until she's ready to leave.

Reluctantly, he put a piece of fish in his mouth, drank some water, and took an apple slice.

The conversations buzzing around him, the music of the flute, lyre, and timbrel, the food in his mouth; none of these distracted him from the images that played in his mind, images willfully fed and given energy.

I don't want to be a soldier, he thought. I don't want to be a scholar. I just want to be alone with Drusilla, forever.

The waiting was interminable. Finally Drusilla stood. She thanked all the guests for their blessings and their gifts, gifts of money discreetly put in the hands of the groom's brother. Then she motioned toward Reuven. He jumped up from his seat eagerly.

The guests laughed.

"It is time to take our leave," Drusilla said.

Reuven walked around to her side of the table.

Judah stood up.

"You're not going back alone."

Niger stood also, followed by Benjamin. Even Dvorah got up from her seat. At the other table Rabbi Yoel rose from his seat.

"Judah is right," Rabbi Yoel said. "The new bride and groom should not travel through the streets alone. There is danger about. We will follow at a discreet distance so that you can have your privacy but we will make sure you get to your destination safely."

Reuven shrugged. There was no point in arguing.

He and Drusilla walked at a stately pace down the main street that passed Antonia, and then the Temple, on their left. Their escort of four men and one woman was visible but out of earshot.

If Reuven had married a daughter of the Land of Israel she would have spent the night before the wedding with her parents, as he would have with his. Then, after the wedding, the couple would have gone off on their own. But Drusilla had no parents; Ruth was acting as her mother, so she stayed at Rabbi Aaron's house and Reuven stayed at the house of Elimelech, which is where they would spend their wedding night.

Reuven was glad he had not married a daughter of the Land of Israel, a woman or girl picked for him by his father. He had won a prize beyond reckoning.

He leaned toward Drusilla and sang in her ear the opening lines of Mishlei thirty-one:

"A woman of valor who can find? For her price is far above rubies."

Drusilla gasped with delight.

Then Reuven whispered fiercely:

"I can't wait until we are finally alone so I can touch you and taste you."

Reuven sensed Drusilla's body tremble and felt the passion flowing from her.

He took her arm in his.

They walked without speaking. They passed under the bridge that led from the Temple to the Upper City. They passed the Xystus, where his uncle had been murdered. They were walking along the shallow depression that separated the Upper from the Lower City when they began to hear sounds from ahead.

They quickened their pace.

From an alley on their left in the Lower City they heard the groans of someone calling for help.

A man lay in the alley, blood seeping through his cloak from somewhere in his rib cage.

The newly-married couple stared in horror.

"Water, water," the man pleaded.

"We must get help!" cried Drusilla. She ran wildly to the nearest house and banged on the door. From further back, Reuven saw his escort rushing forward.

Reuven looked down at the man whose life was bleeding out from him. The man looked back in terror.

A political assassination? Reuven asked himself. A murder carried out by criminals for robbery, something which had only just begun to appear in the City?

Did it matter?

Reuven shook his head.

No, he said to himself. Just as it doesn't matter when Drusilla gets back with water. He will be dead.

Reuven bent down toward the man.

"I'm sorry," Reuven said. "I'm sorry this happened to you. May you find peace in the world to come."

The terror went from the man's eyes.

"*Sh'ma Yisra'eil Adonai Eloheinu Adonai echad,*" the dying man gasped.

Reuven was the only witness to the stranger's passing.

Chapter One Hundred & Nine

10 February 68 CE / 19 Shevat 3828

Reuven gently caressed Drusilla's belly.

"Do you feel the baby?" she asked.

"Yes," Reuven answered, smiling happily. He placed his cheek softly on her stomach, barely touching it.

"I can still feel her kicking," he said.

"Him kicking," Drusilla corrected.

"We shall see," Reuven said, sitting up in the bed, winking mischievously at her.

They had been married for a month and for that month had moved into the grand bedroom in the house of Elimelech with its luxurious bed that rested on a frame with raised legs, a bed that had a soft mattress, smooth sheets, and warm red and purple covers to keep out the winter's chill. Reuven spent his days and nights in the presence of Drusilla, talking, reading, and making love.

Have I been gentle? he wondered. I have tried. I have really tried!

Reuven stood up. He threw his hands into the air.

"I don't want to be a soldier! I don't want to be a scholar!" he declared. "I just want to be your servant for the rest of my life and attend to you!" He bowed deeply and concluded: "Forever!"

Drusilla laughed.

"For the world of men there is no forever," she said, "and for us even this one month is enough. I want to return to your father's house and resume helping your mother, and learning from her. What of you, Reuven, what will you do, with all your knowledge and experience?"

Reuven laughed. It was a hard laugh, not the bright laugh he had heard from his wife.

"What knowledge? What experience?" He tried to keep the bitterness out of his voice; he did not want to ruin this magical time. "No one listens to me."

"I saw you speaking to Judah yesterday. For a long time. What did you discuss?"

Reuven sighed. He sat down at the edge of the bed.

"Judah related the goings-on in the City," Reuven began. "Ananus' forces have won the first round. The Kannaim, vastly outnumbered, have withdrawn to the inner court of the Temple, where they are surrounded. Ananus has posted 6,000 men to guard the colonnades. He's unwilling to invade the sacred grounds, so there's a standoff for now. John ben Levi is acting as a go-between trying to arrange a truce so that normal Temple activities can go on without the threat of further conflict." Reuven sighed. "I wish that was all, but it's not. Judah suggested something to John: Tell Eleazar ben Simon, the head of the Kannaim, to ask for help from the Idumaeans in their struggle with Ananus. Eleazar took the suggestion; several days ago he sent a request for help to the Idumaeans." Reuven shook his head wearily. "I may have inadvertently given Judah that idea about the Idumaeans."

"Does Ananus know about the Idumaeans?" Drusilla asked sharply.

"No." Reuven smothered a laugh. "He'll find out, though, when they arrive." He gave Drusilla a look that said, "Yes, I know the whole situation is crazy."

"Reuven," Drusilla said anxiously, "you must warn Ananus!"

"Why?"

"If the Idumaeans come without warning there will be even more bloodshed. There must be compromise and peace in the City before the Idumaeans arrive. And, and, well," Drusilla's words came out quickly here, "it sounds as if John ben Levi is doing something underhanded here, pretending to act as a go-between to achieve a truce but recommending that the Kannaim get outside help in their struggle. You should be the go-between!"

Once again Reuven laughed.

"You have too much faith in me, my dear wife." He stroked her golden hair and leaned in toward her. She roughly pushed him away.

"This is not funny, Reuven!" she insisted, more than a hint of anger in her voice. "You should warn Ananus and offer yourself as a mediator. Look what you achieved with Vespasian!"

Reuven got to his feet.

"You know what I achieved with Vespasian!" he shouted with heat. "Two documents. One guaranteeing me and my family safe passage through Roman lines. The other promising to reward me if he becomes emperor, as I predicted. And what should I do? I should use that first document to get all of us out of this accursed city to somewhere safe and then wait for Vespasian to become emperor and go to Rome where we can live a life free of the madness that grips us here!"

The shock on Drusilla's face made Reuven gag.

"How can you think of deserting your people and your country at a time like this?" she cried in dismay. "Go at once to Ananus!"

"You're mad, too, woman!" Reuven screamed. "You're as mad as the rest of them!"

With a sweeping motion he grabbed his cloak and his sandals and stormed out of the room.

Chapter One Hundred & Ten

10 February 68 CE / 19 Shevat 3828

Reuven sat across the table from Ananus.

He was no longer sure what he wanted to say.

The walk through the City had calmed Reuven, while at the same time raising uncomfortable questions in his head. His outburst about leaving Jerusalem and eventually going to Rome had come out of nowhere, but a stew of disquiet had been cooking in his head for a very long time. It started with his feelings toward Drusilla, telling her that he wished they could go somewhere peaceful where he could grow olives and dates and raise sheep and goats. It grew stronger as their relationship developed; the experience of love received and given made him long to be free of the strife around him. But it was the fall of Gamla, especially after its initial victory, followed by what he saw in the pagan city of Caesarea, which shook his moorings. It wasn't just that he saw the hopelessness of the fight against Rome given the lack of unity among the Jews; it was also the admiration he felt for what he saw in Caesarea, stoking in him the desire to see the world beyond the one corner occupied by the Land of Israel.

Should he take the family, leave Jerusalem, and eventually go to Rome?

Would that make him a traitor, like Yosef ben Matityahu?

Reuven shook his head. He did not know.

He stared at the man across the table. Reuven couldn't decide if the expression on Ananus' face indicated amusement or determination.

Did it matter? Why involve himself in the City's twisted politics? He had a wife and baby on the way. Better to keep his head low.

No, Reuven was no longer sure what he wanted to say to Ananus, despite what his wife told him to say. Reuven was no longer sure what he wanted at all.

He became aware of the long silence. His cheeks flushed with embarrassment.

"Well," Ananus said drily, "since you seem to be at a loss for words I'll begin. It really is time for you to choose sides. Six thousand men from the citizen's army guard the inner court of the Temple. Their task is to keep the Kannaim inside; we do not want them getting out and causing more havoc. I want you in that army!"

Reuven said nothing.

"Of course, I've allowed the option for a rich man to hire a poor man to take his place guarding the Kannaim," Ananus said, adding slyly, "I have heard that you've been flashing some large denomination coins in the market."

Reuven's eyes narrowed.

"I'm not rich," he retorted. "Before escaping Gamla I scavenged money, that is all. My wedding was a very modest one. And by right I have a year to stay home to cheer my wife."

"You've had a month already!" snapped Ananus. "None of us have the luxury you claim." Ananus drummed the table with his fingers. "I must say, Reuven, I was offended that you didn't invite me to your wedding."

Reuven took a deep breath.

"It was small and modest," he said, "as I just told you." Then, heedless of the consequences, he went on:

"I'll be truthful with you, Ananus. I'm sick of all this strife! Jew fighting Jew. Jew fighting Romans. Do we stand a chance against Rome? No, not as long as we are not united. But I no longer trust your judgment, Ananus. There was no need to start hostilities with the Kannaim. You should have waited for Niger and the others to—"

"No need?" shouted Ananus, pounding the table. "They were polluting the Temple, making mockery of our rituals, even using lots to choose the high priest." Ananus was breathing heavily. It took him several moments to calm down. Reuven waited.

"Reuven, I've seen this coming with you. I'm not surprised at what you're telling me. Listen, I respect you and appreciate what you've already done for the nation. Not only fighting the Romans, but going to Gamla and reporting back. Your testimony is powerful evidence of the futility of this struggle. Heed my advice now. Leave Jerusalem. Go somewhere and find peace, for you, your wife, and the child to come. I give you this advice in all sincerity."

Reuven nodded.

"Thank you, Ananus," he said. "I think you are right."

"Why did you come to see me in the first place?" Ananus asked.

Reuven stood up.

"It does not matter anymore," he replied.

Outside, in the streets of Jerusalem, a light rain had started to fall. To Reuven, unprepared though he was, it seemed a minor annoyance. He was about to come to a major decision; wet clothing was unimportant.

Ananus was right with his advice. Reuven knew it, he was already coming to that conclusion himself.

It was time to get out of Jerusalem. Not just Drusilla and himself, but Benjamin, mother, and father. And Judah and Dvorah, if he could convince them

Drusilla was only about halfway through her pregnancy; she was still strong enough to travel.

Reuven began running through the streets. He wanted to tell Drusilla, and then the others, of his decision.

He charged through the gate of Elimelech's house and burst through the door. He must have made a lot of noise because as he entered Dvorah came before him, her face ashen. She stared at Reuven dumbly.

At last, barely able to get the words out, Dvorah spoke.

"Drusilla, she, she, got up to leave to go to your parents' house. Before she got to the door she collapsed and could not get up."

Chapter One Hundred & Eleven

10 February 68 CE / 19 Shevat 3828

A little rain never bothered Judah. He walked quickly through Bezetha toward the gate in the north wall. The Idumaeans were on their way and should arrive in the next day or two, possibly sooner. Twenty thousand fighting men would quickly change the balance of power in Jerusalem, Judah thought with satisfaction. The Kannaim, outnumbered three to one, were locked up in the inner court of the Temple by a guard of 6,000 members of the citizen army formed by Ananus. Once freed by the Idumaeans, the Kannaim would join them, along with John ben Levi's growing forces, and effect a bloodless takeover of the City. Jerusalem would be as it was after the victory at the pass of Beth Horon; even those who think defeat is inevitable and believe surrender the only option would participate in preparing for the coming fight against Rome. In this effort Ananus would be an excellent asset; despite the high priest's doubts about the struggle, Ananus was, Judah thought, an excellent administrator.

Judah grunted as he almost slipped on a wet stone.

I'm optimistic, he thought with excitement. For the first time, truly optimistic. There will be unity!

Judah approached the vicinity of the gate.

It was closed, barred. A force of armed men stood behind it. On the tower, on the ramparts, were other armed men.

Ananus' citizen army! How did Ananus know the Idumaeans were coming? Now there would be no peaceful entry of the Idumaeans, no easy, blood-free rescue of the Kannaim by the overwhelming numbers of Idumaeans. The realization dismayed Judah.

Ananus had been given warning and had shut the gates of the City. He was going to keep the Idumaeans out.

Judah rushed to the wall. He wanted to see what was going on. As he climbed the steps to the rampart he remembered what happened before he left the house of Elimelech. He heard Reuven shouting at Drusilla in their room, and then heard Reuven leaving the house. Judah went to the room to find Drusilla sitting on the bed crying. "What's wrong?" he asked. Drusilla did not answer. "Where did Reuven go?" "To Ananus, I hope," she replied. "Why?" Drusilla gave no response; she continued weeping.

Had Reuven betrayed his confidence and told Ananus about the coming of the Idumaeans? How else would Ananus have known? No! Reuven would never do that!

Judah was breathing heavily when he reached the top of the wall, less from physical exertion than from anxiety.

The Idumaeans must have mobilized and marched with incredible speed. The first of their troops were already outside the wall. Their general stood at the head of the column. Behind him more and more men, thousands and thousands, were arranging themselves in disorderly rows in front of the City wall.

"Open the gates to your fellow Jews!" the general demanded. He was tall, broad-shouldered, with a wild beard that seemed to stick out at all angles from his face.

Standing on the wall, Jeshua ben Gamaliel, senior priest after Ananus, called out:

"Why do our brothers come armed for battle?"

"To protect the holy City!" came the immediate reply.

"From whom?" Jeshua retorted.

You know from whom, you clever devil, thought Judah.

"From the traitors who would surrender Jerusalem to the foreigners," responded the Idumaean general.

"And who would those traitors be?" Jeshua asked, his voice dripping with sarcasm. "The criminals who took over the Temple, whom we have now confined to its inner court? Are you here to protect us from those who have arrested innocent men and caused more widows to wail and left more orphans than that thief Gessius Florus ever did?"

"I see," cried the general. "Just as you bar the gates of the City to lock honest Jews out, you bar the gates of the Temple to lock honest Jews in. We demand entrance!"

"Lay down your arms!" cried Jeshua in return. "Then I will open the gates."

"Never!" shouted the Idumaean general. "We will remain out here until the Romans come, or until you allow us enter!"

A standoff, Judah thought, looking around at the armed men on the wall. I've got to let John ben Levi know.

Judah went down from the wall as quickly as he had ascended. He started running, through the streets of Bezetha, through the open gate of the City's second wall, past the pavilions and storehouses north of Antonia, past Antonia itself, and into the Temple complex. As he ran he noticed that all the people he passed on the street looked at him with curiosity, as if they could not understand why someone would be rushing through Jerusalem with an expression of alarm on his face.

Judah found John ben Levi, surrounded by several followers, in the outer court of the Temple.

"The Idumaeans have arrived," Judah gasped, as he tried to catch his breath. "Ananus somehow got wind of it. His forces are not letting them in. Jeshua is demanding that they lay down their arms first." Judah took a few breaths before continuing. "The gates will have to be forced open for them to enter."

John ben Levi's narrow, foxlike face showed concern.

"We must inform Eleazar ben Simon," he said. "The Kannaim will have to break out of their confinement to let the Idumaeans in. We are not yet strong enough to do that ourselves. Unfortunately, the guards just stopped letting me in." He pointed toward the gate of the inner court, guarded by the men of Ananus' citizen army. On top of the wall of the inner court were a few fighters of the Kannaim. "You go, Judah, and warn them. Perhaps the guards will let *you* in."

Judah's breath was still labored when he hurried to the gate. He immediately realized his mistake; if men guarding it had seen him talking to John ben Levi, someone already forbidden entrance, they would most likely not allow him to enter, either.

The guards glared at him as he ambled slowly to the gate.

No point in asking, he thought.

Judah contemplated what to do next. He was not about to give up.

Cupping his hands, Judah shouted as loudly as he could.

"The Idumaeans arrived! Ananus is not letting them in. They are waiting outside the north wall!"

Judah repeated the cry a second time before some of the guards came at him with raised swords. As Judah quickly backed away, he saw the fighters stationed on the wall raise their right arms in reply.

It's up to them now, Judah thought.

Judah walked over to John ben Levi.

"There is something I have to find out," he said. "A very important personal matter."

John ben Levi nodded.

"Go," he said.

Judah was grateful John didn't ask what that matter was. Judah would not have told him, and he didn't have enough mental energy to come up with a convincing lie. He would have just walked away if John ben Levi had asked.

He left the Temple complex and made his way to the house of Elimelech. It was growing dark now; Judah was not sure how much was from the late hour and how much from the thickening clouds overhead. The rain was growing stronger; large, cold drops soaked Judah, making him shiver.

Had Reuven betrayed his confidence? Had he warned Ananus of the coming of the Idumaeans? If Reuven had, could he ever trust Reuven again?

Judah had to know.

The rain intensified. A flash of lightning lit up the sky followed by a peal of thunder that made Judah's eardrums tingle.

A terrible storm is brewing, he thought.

By the time Judah entered the house of Elimelech he was drenched. He shook off his wet cloak and dropped it by the entrance.

Phineas, whom Reuven had insisted on keeping employed as caretaker, came over to greet him.

"Have you seen Reuven?" Judah snapped.

Phineas' head bobbed up and down.

"He's in his room with Drusilla and Dvorah, sir."

Judah strode out of the entrance room and down the hall. Halfway to Reuven's room Dvorah met him. She looked anxious and worried, but instead asked him:

"What's wrong, Judah?"

Judah smiled grimly.

"Maybe I should be asking you that?" he responded. "Where's Reuven? I must talk to him."

"He's with Drusilla now. He's stroking her hair and apologizing for yelling at her." Dvorah sighed. "She collapsed not long after he left. She couldn't get up. I had to carry her to bed. I wanted to get help, but she didn't want me to leave. When Reuven returned, she wouldn't let either of us go for help. She wanted us around. Judah, you must go and find a physician for her."

Dvorah's words were emphasized by a double clap of thunder from the world outside.

"How is she now?" Judah asked, worried.

"Better, she's awake and alert, but she's still weak."

"And the baby?"

"Drusilla can still feel him moving."

Judah sighed and nodded.

"I don't know any doctors," he said. "Or midwives. Ruth would know."

"Then go to her," Dvorah insisted. "She'll bring someone to see Drusilla."

Judah watched the lamplight play across the angles of Dvorah's face.

"Come with me," he said gently. "I want to show you something."

He led Dvorah to the outside door. He opened it slowly.

Gusts of howling wind swept into the room. Drops as thick as ripe grapes and as cold as ice slanted in from the sky. At that moment there were two flashes of lightning followed almost immediately by rolling thunder that made the door tremble.

Judah quickly shut the door.

"No physician, not even a midwife, would venture out now," Judah said. "It's not just a storm, it's a raging tempest. I've never seen anything like it. No one will come until it abates."

Dvorah leaned against the door for support.

"Here's what I'll do, Dvorah," Judah said, trying to make his voice sound comforting, despite another crash of thunder. "I'll go to the house of Rabbi Aaron and inform them of what happened. When the storm slows, they will find a doctor or midwife to take care of Drusilla."

He gently nudged Dvorah away from the door.

"And then," he added, "I have some business of the City to attend to!"

Judah put on the cloak he had discarded on the floor, opened the door, and stepped out into the storm.

Does the violence of the heavens presage violence in the streets? he wondered, before slamming the door shut behind him.

Chapter One Hundred & Twelve

11 February 68 CE / 20 Shevat 3828

Reuven stood by the bed, holding Drusilla's hand. Last night's fierce storm had passed. Dvorah had assured him that a physician would be there once the rain stopped and the morning came. But it was already late morning, almost noon, and Reuven was worried, though Drusilla insisted that she was fine and did not need to stay in bed.

Reuven stroked her hand and her hair.

"Can you still feel the baby?" he asked anxiously.

"*You* can feel the baby if you want to," Drusilla replied.

Reuven sighed.

"I'm so sorry I yelled at you, Drusilla."

"It's all right, Reuven. Did you go to Ananus?"

"Yes."

"Did you warn him about the Idumaeans? Did he agree to make you a mediator?"

Reuven sighed again. Before he could answer, the sound of visitors made its way into the room.

Dvorah, Ruth, Rabbi Aaron, and Benjamin entered, accompanied by a man with a neatly trimmed black beard and a fine cloak of dark gray. Except for Dvorah, they all had gloomy faces.

"This is the physician," Ruth said, "Hoshea ben Asa."

"I'm sorry I'm late," the physician said. "On our way over I came upon a gravely wounded man. I was unable to save him. He joined many others who were dead."

It was then that Reuven noticed the spatters of blood on the doctor's fine cloak.

Hoshea ben Asa walked over to the bed and looked down at Drusilla.

"You must be Batya," he said, smiling. "How are you feeling?"

"I feel fine now, Doctor," Drusilla replied.

"Why don't you tell me what happened?" Hoshea ben Asa asked.

"I was walking in the house when I suddenly fell down, collapsed. I don't know why. There was no warning."

"Were you aware the whole time?" queried the physician.

"Yes."

"Was your heart racing?"

Drusilla paused to think.

"I don't know. It might have been."

Hoshea ben Asa nodded.

"Can you get up?" he asked.

Drusilla immediately sat up in the bed, her feet on the floor.

"Can you stand and take a few steps?"

Drusilla did so.

"Walk across the room," he ordered.

She walked to Ruth and then back to the bed.

"Good, good," Hoshea ben Asa said. "Sit down, Batya. I want to examine you."

The physician looked into her eyes. He held up his right index finger.

"Follow my finger," he said, watching as Drusilla's eyes matched the movement of his finger.

"Good, good."

Out of the corner of his eye Reuven caught the arrival of Judah, who remained in the doorway. None of the others noticed Judah. Reuven glanced at him for a moment. Judah's cloak, usually clean though threadbare, now had mud stains.

Hoshea ben Asa felt Drusilla's forehead and temples. He held her wrist and placed a finger lightly on her pulse. He asked her to open her mouth and peered inside.

Holding up his right hand he said:

"Batya, touch my palm with your right hand."

Drusilla's right palm rested against his. The physician began to push, saying, "Resist!" Drusilla pushed back, stopping the backward movement of her hand.

"Good, good," Hoshea ben Asa said. "Now with your left."

"Excellent," the physician said, when he saw the same results with Drusilla's left hand.

"Out of delicacy, I will not feel your belly if you tell me that you still feel the baby."

"I do," Drusilla said. "He is kicking as strongly as ever."

Hoshea ben Asa took a step backward and sighed.

"I don't know why you fell, Batya," he said. "You seem in good health, but you must be careful for the rest of your pregnancy. Do nothing strenuous. I'm prescribing barley soaked in curdled milk once a day for two weeks for the heart palpitations. And you might try rubbing fresh olive oil on your temples every night before you go to sleep."

"Should she be confined to bed?" Reuven asked.

"No, no!" the physician quickly replied. "She can move about, take short walks, do light chores, but nothing strenuous. No hard work. She must rest often and eat well," Hoshea ben Asa concluded, and then added, "As I told your parents, my fee is twenty-five denarii. They said you would pay."

Wow! Reuven thought. That's a lot of money!

He walked over to a small table on the other side of the bed. Beneath the table's flat surface that held the lamp was a drawer. Reuven opened it and pulled out a purse. He extracted a gold aureus.

He handed it to the physician, who seemed surprised at the large denomination coin.

"That should take care of your fee," Reuven said.

Reuven looked over at his father, who held his glance.

He knows where I got the money, Reuven thought. I wonder what he thinks now.

"Thank you," Hoshea ben Asa said. "Your wife should be fine if she follows my advice for the rest of the pregnancy. Rest, don't overexert herself, eat well, barley soaked in curdled milk once a day for two weeks, fresh olive oil on the temples before sleeping… If there are any other problems, you can send for me, otherwise, the midwife should do just fine. Good luck."

"One question, doctor," Reuven began. "Is she well enough to take a long journey?"

Drusilla gave him a puzzled look. The physician gave him an ironic one, as if he understood.

"No," Hoshea ben Asa said, his voice sympathetic. "You're stuck here like the rest of us, at least for the rest of the pregnancy." Reuven was crushed at the doctor's reply. Hoshea ben Asa gave a brief, bitter laugh. "Otherwise, I'd ask you to take me along. I'd even return my fee!" His laugh was hearty now. "Don't worry, Batya. You and the baby will be fine. Well, good day to you all."

Reuven followed him out of the room. He tugged at the physician's cloak.

"Doctor, one more question, please."

Hoshea ben Asa stopped walking.

"Yes?" he responded.

"How long can we continue… to…"

Reuven turned red. The physician smiled.

"Almost to the end, until the last month, if she is willing, and you are gentle."

"Thank you."

Phineas was waiting at the end of the hallway to show Hoshea ben Asa out. Reuven returned to the room.

He smiled at Drusilla.

"Why did you ask the doctor about taking a long journey?" she asked.

Reuven shrugged.

"I'll explain later," he replied. He turned to his parents.

"Why still the gloomy faces? My wife will be fine."

"We have seen death in the streets," his father growled. "Everywhere!"

"What? What do you mean?"

Judah tapped him on the shoulder.

"Come," he said. "I want to talk to you."

Reuven followed Judah out of the room. They stopped in the hallway.

"What is going on, Judah?"

"First, answer some questions of mine," Judah responded. "Did you go to Ananus yesterday?"

"Yes," Reuven answered. "Why do you ask?"

"Why did you go?"

"Drusilla asked me to."

"Why?" Judah persisted.

"She wanted me to warn Ananus about the Idumaeans. And she wanted me to tell him to make me a mediator between the moderates and the revolutionaries."

"What?" Judah laughed.

Reuven threw up his hands in a gesture of helplessness.

"That's what happens when you get married," Reuven said. "Your wife thinks you can do anything."

"Did you tell Ananus about the Idumaeans?" Judah asked sharply.

"Of course not! I assumed you told me that in confidence. How could you even ask?"

Judah laid a hand on Reuven's shoulder.

"I never really doubted you, Reuven. Tell me, what did you talk about?"

"Ananus did most of the talking," Reuven replied. "He wants me to join the citizen army. When he finished I told him what I thought about the revolution and about him. To be honest, though, Ananus isn't a bad man. We do need him. Anyway, there is one thing he convinced me of, or more precisely, strengthened my conviction about a decision I already— Wait a minute!" Reuven exclaimed, interrupting himself. "It's your turn to tell me what's going on, Judah!"

Judah removed his hand from Reuven's shoulder. He took a step backward.

"The Idumaeans arrived yesterday. Jeshua ben Gamaliel refused to let them in unless they laid down their arms. That they refused to do; their general said they would remain outside the gate until the Romans came or until they were let in. Last night, during the storm, the Kannaim took the Temple saws and cut through the bars of the gates. Thunder from the storm covered the noise they made. Some of the Kannaim stole past the guards, who were either asleep or wrapped up against the downpour. The Kannaim made their way to the north gate, where they used the same saws to get the gate open. The Idumaeans poured into the City."

Judah paused and stared down at the floor. Without lifting his eyes he continued.

"The Idumaeans didn't just free the Kannaim from their imprisonment in the inner court of the Temple. The Idumaeans, and the Kannaim, attacked anyone who was connected with Ananus and the citizen army. There was a terrible slaughter, Reuven. Hundreds, maybe thousands, were killed. The streets of Jerusalem are littered with the slain."

Judah paused again and took a deep breath. He raised his head and looked at Reuven.

"And among the killed, Reuven, was Ananus ben Ananus."

Reuven's body swayed. The floor rushed up to meet to him. Too late Judah reached out to grab Reuven before his knees buckled. There was just enough time for Reuven to spread his palms to break his fall.

He remained on the floor, hands and knees supporting him. His mind was empty.

Reuven did not want to think.

Chapter One Hundred & Thirteen

25 February 68 CE / 4 Adar I 3828

Rabbi Aaron paced back and forth, casting furtive glances at the outside door of his house, as if he were expecting an unexpected visitor.

A stranger would knock on the door, perhaps dressed in rags. Rabbi Aaron would offer him food and shelter, despite his ragged and unwholesome appearance.

The stranger would turn out to be an angel in disguise whose mission was to save Jerusalem from the destruction threatened by the revolutionaries and the Romans. Or, if that was too much to hope for from The Master of the Universe, who may have already decreed the destruction of the City, then the angel's task would be to lead to safety all those who had not yet lost their minds.

Rabbi Aaron laughed bitterly.

Clearly I have lost mine! I have already gone mad! The general distemper of the City has infected me, too.

A week ago Rabbi Aaron had gone to the family tomb in the Kidron Valley and stood over the ossuary that held the bones of his brother Moshe. Rabbi Aaron spoke to his brother, telling him once again that his murderer had been found and punished.

This time, his brother answered.

"But I did not understand his answer!" Rabbi Aaron called out to the empty room. "It was in a strange language!"

Rabbi Aaron laughed again.

Yes, clearly I am mad!

He continued pacing but stopped glancing at the door.

It had been two weeks since Batya had taken ill. Ruth had insisted on staying in that large house in the Upper City to care for Batya. Rabbi Aaron, who himself worried about the girl, agreed to stay in that house also. So now the whole family, father, mother, two sons, a daughter-in-law, and the refugee from Gamla, Dvorah, with that robber from the north country, Judah, all lived in the house near the Upper Market. But every few days, and sometimes every day, Rabbi Aaron returned to his own house to think, to pray, to study.

Yes, it was two weeks since Batya had gotten sick but it was also two weeks since the robbers had killed the one man who might have been able to guide the City to safety.

Was the murder of Ananus a prelude to Jerusalem's destruction?

"No!" Rabbi Aaron shouted, answering his own question.

It was the murder of my brother that began the madness.

Rabbi Aaron allowed himself one more glance at the door before turning away.

Oh, he prayed silently, come, angel, come!

A moment later there was a knock at the door.

His heart racing, Rabbi Aaron practically leaped to open it.

Two men stood there. One had a sword at his hip and a javelin in his hand. The other held a wax tablet.

These were clearly not angels.

"What do you want?" snapped Rabbi Aaron.

"You are called to jury duty," the man holding the tablet said in a stentorian voice. He handed the tablet to Rabbi Aaron.

Rabbi Aaron squinted as he read the almost illegible writing scratched into the wax of the tablet.

"This is ridiculous!!" he cried. "Niger the Peraean? On trial for treason? Have you all lost your minds? This is absurd!"

"That is something you and sixty-nine other distinguished citizens will decide at the trial."

"I'm not taking part in this farce!" Rabbi Aaron declared.

The man who had been silent raised the javelin and put his free hand on the hilt of his sword.

"Seventy distinguished men, rabbis, priests, nobles, and businessmen will judge the traitor Niger's guilt or innocence," the man who had given Rabbi Aaron the tablet said, taking it back from him.

Rabbi Aaron looked at the man with the sword, whose weapon was slowly being drawn out from its scabbard.

"I guess I have no choice," Rabbi Aaron grumbled. "Do I have to go now?"

"Yes."

Rabbi Aaron stepped out of his house and shut the door. He followed the two as they led him in the direction of the Temple.

They brought him to the court in front of the Bronze Gate. Along one side were rows of wooden benches. There were already many men there, also jurors Rabbi Aaron supposed, some of whom he recognized. They all had the same puzzled expression he had. The man with the tablet motioned for Rabbi Aaron to take his place among them. As Rabbi Aaron walked to the benches, still more jurors began arriving.

Across the court stood armed men with cold, angry looks on their faces. Rabbi Aaron guessed that there were about fifty of them. One in particular stood out. He was tall and broad, with huge muscular arms that were exposed. In his hands he carried a large ax. His head was hooded with only slits for his eyes.

Where did they get that *golyat*? Rabbi Aaron wondered.

At the foot of the fourteen curved steps that led up to the Bronze Gate, sitting in a chair, flanked by two armed guards, was Niger the Peraean. He sat with his head held high, no sign of fear on his face.

Out of the gate room came two men, one slender with a light brown beard and pockmarked cheeks, the other heavyset and dressed like a member of the priestly class, though the state of his clothes told Rabbi Aaron that he probably came from one of the poorer classes of priests.

The two men walked to the center of the top of the stairs that led down from the Bronze Gate. The heavy-set one, older, stood with his eyes downcast. The slender one, younger, with a sword by his side and a sneer on his face, swept the crowd of jurors with his eyes.

"My name is Kayin ben Kelev," he said in a voice that was heard throughout the court of the Bronze Gate. "I am from the Committee for Public Safety. I will be the prosecutor. By my side is Machli ben Peleg, a priest from a distinguished family in Chorazin, who will be a judge in the trial of the traitor Niger the Peraean."

There are no distinguished families in Chorazin, thought Rabbi Aaron.

"Is this a trial, or a sham?" he shouted. "What kind of procedure is this, where you have already judged the man guilty?"

Kayin ben Kelev slowly descended the fourteen steps. He stopped in front of the jurors' section.

"The juror will be silent," Kayin ben Kelev declared, "until the time of deliberation." He motioned toward the top of the stairs. A large chair was brought out. Machli ben Peleg sat down.

The jury benches were filled. Spectators had gathered in the court. Among the spectators Rabbi Aaron spied his two sons with Judah ben Ezra.

A man carrying a large tablet walked up to the seated judge, who nodded and took the tablet.

This is a farce, Rabbi Aaron thought.

The judge, without getting up, lifted the tablet in the air and said, in a gravelly voice:

"All the jurors are here! Be seated! Let the trial of the traitor Niger the Peraean begin!"

This *is* a farce, thought Rabbi Aaron again.

Kayin ben Kelev walked back and forth in front of the seated jury.

"I will prove," he announced, "that the prisoner, Niger the Peraean, is a traitor, that he is a tool of the Romans, a trickster who used his reputation as a hero to undermine the morale of our City, a spy who has conspired with others to contact Vespasian, and a criminal who has plotted with others to kill Eleazar ben Simon, leader of the Kannaim."

Rabbi Aaron laughed out loud.

"Will you also prove that white is black and heaven is earth?" he shouted.

The other jurors also laughed. So did spectators.

"Silence!" the prosecutor snarled. "You will not think it funny once I present the evidence. The prisoner will stand!" he ordered, pointing at Niger.

Niger remained sitting.

The guard to Niger's right pulled Niger roughly to his feet. It was then that Rabbi Aaron noticed that Niger's wrists and ankles were shackled.

"How do you plead?" Kayin ben Kelev demanded.

"I do not recognize your right to try me!" Niger retorted. "This is not a court of justice, this is a travesty. A drunken Nero could not have come up with a better farce!"

"How do you plead, traitor?" shouted the prosecutor.

"There is a prosecutor," stated Niger, "but no defense lawyer. What kind of trial is this?"

"No one was willing to come forward to defend you, traitor!"

A buzz filled the court of the Bronze Gate.

"I will defend Niger the Peraean!" Reuven roared, stepping forward.

Silence in the court; for a moment no one spoke, or even whispered.

"Stay out of this, boy!" yelled Niger. For the first time Rabbi Aaron saw alarm on Niger's face. Niger's outburst was followed by Judah grabbing Reuven, pulling him backward, and clamping a hand over his mouth. Judah moved his head close to Reuven's ear and whispered something. Reuven ceased struggling.

"I plead not guilty," Niger said. He sat down.

The prosecutor smiled.

"I will now prove my case," he said to the jury. He turned to Niger.

"Is it not true," Kayin ben Kelev asked, "that after the entrance of our Idumaean brothers, you went around Jerusalem denouncing them and the Kannaim, saying that we behaved like criminals?"

"You *are* criminals!" Niger responded. "You slaughtered innocent civilians, Jews, not Romans! You killed common men and leaders alike. Why, you even killed Ananus ben Ananus, who had been an able administrator in preparing the defenses of the City."

"We did not kill any of the common people!" Kayin ben Kelev shot back hotly. "We only killed the supporters of Ananus who opposed us, and they were not of the common folk!" The prosecutor continued, more calmly now, "Ah, but it is interesting that you mention Ananus ben Ananus, a well-known traitor who all here know wanted Jerusalem to surrender to Rome. You seem to think his death was a loss. So you admit before this court that you admired Ananus ben Ananus, and that you denounced the freedom fighters to anyone in the City who would listen?"

"I do not admit it," shouted Niger. "I proclaim it loudly!" He raised his shackled arms toward the jury. "Freedom fighters," he sneered. "They are no freedom fighters! They are criminals, the scum of the earth! They fought Jews. I fought Romans! You all know me!"

Some of the spectators cheered and shouted Niger's name.

Kayin ben Kelev raised his hand.

"No one denies your heroic past," he said. "That only makes your present treachery more reprehensible. Jurors, you see that he has undermined the morale of the City by condemning those who are steadfast in their resistance to Rome."

"Is there no longer freedom of speech in God's holy City?"

Niger's question rang out over the assembled crowd.

"Yes," responded the prosecutor, "there is freedom of speech, but not if that speech undermines morale!" Kayin ben Kelev walked back and forth in front of the jury benches, pulling at his beard, seeming deep in thought. "Gentlemen of the jury," he began, "it is now clear that the condemned man himself has proven my first two points in the charges against him, with his own words! He has been a tool of Rome who tried to undermine the morale of Jerusalem. Indeed, in doing so he has proven my third point, that he has conspired with others to contact Vespasian. You see, he defended Ananus ben Ananus, and it is well-known that Ananus wanted to contact the Roman general Vespasian to discuss terms of surrender."

Niger stood up.

"'Justice, justice thou shall pursue,' demands Scripture!" Niger cried. "You desecrate God's holy Name with this mockery of a trial."

Kayin ben Kelev pointed in turn to each guard at Niger's side. One punched him hard in the stomach, the other punched him hard on the side of his head. Then they both shoved him back down into the seat.

Rabbi Aaron saw no fear in Niger's face; only pain and rage.

"There are more points I could prove, more points I could make," the prosecutor said breezily, "but I will rest my case here." He pointed toward the judge.

"Arguments have concluded," the judge declared, still sitting. "The jury will now deliberate to convict the traitor."

Rabbi Aaron stood up.

"Is this a joke?" he demanded. "The accused was not even given a chance to defend himself."

"There is no need," announced Judge Machli ben Peleg, to a smirk on Kayin ben Kelev's face. "The prosecutor has proven his case. It is time for you to deliberate and find the accused guilty."

Rabbi Aaron turned to his fellow jurors. The look of amazement on his face matched the looks on theirs.

"The prosecutor, the judge, and all their lackeys are the ones who should be on trial, not Niger the Peraean," said Rabbi Aaron. "Is there anyone here that thinks that Niger is a traitor?"

No one raised a hand.

"Then how do we vote?" Rabbi Aaron asked.

All the other jurors rose.

"Not guilty!" they shouted in unison.

The prosecutor smiled.

"All have heard the judgment of the jury!" Kayin ben Kelev declared. "Now see the judgment of the Revolution!" He pointed to the giant with the large ax.

The hooded man walked slowly toward the shackled Niger. He stood in front of the just-exonerated accused. He raised the ax high above Niger's head.

With a speed that seemed surprising in one so big and strong the executioner brought the ax down and split Niger's skull in two.

Gasps of horror filled the court of the Bronze Gate.

Kayin ben Kelev laughed as he called out:

"Now you have heard *our* judgment and your trials are over!"

Chapter One Hundred & Fourteen

25 February 68 CE / 4 Adar I 3828

Judah didn't even give Reuven time to react.

"Get your father out of here!" Judah barked. He grabbed Reuven and Benjamin, pulling them toward the jury section. The three reached Rabbi Aaron just in time; the armed men lined up on the other side of the court, along with an influx of more Kannaim, began beating members of the jury and spectators alike with the flat of their swords and with staves.

With each brother grabbing an arm of their father, they hustled him out of the court of the Bronze Gate, Judah bringing up the rear, growling and brandishing his knife at any of the Kannaim who dared approach. The cries of pain of those being beaten filled the four men's ears as they retreated.

Once out of the Temple complex and on the street Reuven and Benjamin released their father from their grasp. The four slowed to a brisk walk.

"I can't believe what I just saw!" Reuven exclaimed.

"I can," Judah said, his voice low. "I was half-expecting this."

Rabbi Aaron stopped walking. He turned toward Judah.

"It was your madness that began all this!"

"Me? I fought under Niger. He was a strong leader; I was proud to serve under him. I never would have wished for a great patriot like Niger to be killed, especially by his own people. Even Ananus, whose ideas I opposed," here Judah gasped for air, "even Ananus; his killing horrified me."

Rabbi Aaron shook his head sadly.

"You still do not understand, do you, Judah? You revolutionaries, by grasping the fate of the nation in your own hands, unleashed forces that even you could not control."

They were at a crossroads where one direction led to the house of Elimelech and one led to Rabbi Aaron's home.

Rabbi Aaron started walking in the direction of his own house.

"Come with us to the house of Elimelech now," Benjamin pleaded.

Rabbi Aaron stopped walking.

"All right," he said softly, bowing his head.

The four made the rest of their way in silence.

Reuven went straight to Drusilla, wrestling with the question of whether he should tell her what happened. He still hadn't decided when he entered the room and she looked up at him from their bed and asked:

"Was Niger acquitted?"

"Yes," Reuven replied, in a hoarse whisper.

"Good," Drusilla responded, with a tone of satisfaction.

Reuven sighed. Before he could say anything, Judah and Dvorah came into the room.

"I'd like to speak to you," Judah said heavily.

Reuven followed the two into the hallway.

"Reuven," Judah began. "We've decided to leave Jerusalem."

Reuven swallowed his gasp of shock. He had seen too much already today.

"I swore that if they executed Niger I would leave Jerusalem," Judah said with finality.

"Where will you go?" Reuven asked.

"I will join Simon ben Gioras in the south. He is a good man. He has freed slaves and forgiven debts in the areas where he has influence. His strength grows every day. I am certain that in the near future he will return to Jerusalem and restore sanity and order here."

Reuven nodded.

"Dvorah is coming with me."

Another shock. Reuven turned to her.

"Is that true, Dvorah?'

"Yes, Reuven, it is," she answered. She reached out and touched his arm for a moment. "You and your family will be all right. They will not harm you. And when we return with Simon…"

Reuven gasped for air twice.

"We won't be safe here, without you, Judah," he said. "We will have to go back to my father's house in the Lower City."

"That is probably best," agreed Judah. "They are leaving the poor alone."

Reuven stared down at the floor for several moments. When he looked up, he asked, his voice pleading:

"Will you help me move the money from here, Judah? Help me find a safe place for it? Half of it is yours, by right."

"I will help you with that, Reuven," Judah reassured him. "And all of it is yours. You will need it; we will not."

"Thank you," Reuven sighed. He turned away and went back into the bedroom. He slumped onto the bed, leaning forward, his eyes unfocused downward.

"What's wrong, dear?" Drusilla asked, alarmed.

Reuven did not reply. He did not know how long he continued sitting silently. He heard people entering the room. He looked up to see Dvorah and Judah.

"We've changed our minds," Dvorah said. "We're not going to abandon you. We've become like family."

"Yes," Judah agreed. He nodded gravely. "We are staying in Jerusalem for now, until all of us are able to leave."

Reuven wanted to tell them that though he desperately wanted them to stay, they should leave because that's what they decided; they should not make change their minds on his and Drusilla's account.

But Reuven said nothing. He did not have the strength or will to argue.

Chapter One Hundred & Fifteen

1 May 68 CE / 11 Iyar 3828

Each time Drusilla screamed Reuven felt as if a knife were being thrust down his throat. His own body shook violently.

Rabbi Aaron put a hand on his son's shoulder.

"Thus it is when women give birth," he said.

"Why can't I be with her?" Reuven asked.

"It is not allowed," came his father's stern reply. "That is the way it has always been, that is the way it is now, that is the way it will always be."

Inside the room with Drusilla were his mother, Dvorah, and the midwife. Waiting outside, further down the hall, were Benjamin and Judah.

The screams seemed to go on forever.

Are these the screams of childbirth, Reuven wondered, or the screams of a dying city?

A cloak of fear had descended on Jerusalem since the murder of Niger the Peraean. Men were afraid to discuss anything remotely political; it was said that the walls had ears. If even a patriot like Niger could be charged with treason and executed by the revolutionaries, who else could possibly be safe?

A slow upheaval had begun. Many Idumaeans, disgusted by the excesses of the Kannaim, left Jerusalem and returned home. John ben Levi, who in a short time gained many new followers, first joined and then split from the Kannaim, who continued to arrest and execute those they branded as traitors.

People began fleeing the City in droves, not an easy thing to do because the radicals kept watch on the gates, stopping those trying to run away. If someone did manage to evade these men, there were the Roman legions to worry about; after resting his forces at Caesarea and Scythopolis for the winter, Vespasian went on the march again, subjugating most of Judea, Idumaea, and Peraea, isolating Jerusalem from rest of the country. The great Torah scholar, Rabbi Johanan ben Zakkai, was able to flee, to Yavne, only, it was said, because his followers had smuggled him out of the City in a coffin, thereby escaping detection by the radicals whose job was to keep the population locked into its large prison cell.

The festival of Passover had come and gone. What was normally a joyous week had turned somber this year in Jerusalem.

Drusilla's screams grew sharper, piercing Reuven's ears. Just when he felt he could take no more, the house fell silent.

Reuven shivered, the worst of thoughts passing through his mind.

And then he heard the cry of an infant, loud, lusty, demanding.

Dvorah came to the doorway, a huge smile on her face.

"Come," she said to Reuven, beckoning with her arm, "see your new child."

Reuven rushed into the room.

Drusilla was leaning back in bed, tears streaming down her face, looking exhausted. She held up a baby in her arms.

"Come say hello to your new daughter," she said.

Reuven felt as if his heart would burst from joy.

Reuven had never seen a newborn baby before. He had heard that they came out of their mothers looking like wrinkled monkeys. But this daughter of his was beautiful, with smooth skin and perfect features.

"A daughter," he said, thrilled. "She's so beautiful. She's going to look just like you!"

This is the happiest day of my life, Reuven thought. Even happier than my wedding.

Then a sobering thought came to him.

"Drusilla," he asked, "what kind of world have we brought our daughter into?"

Drusilla took a deep breath, looked at Reuven as if her heart was pouring through her blue eyes, and said fiercely:

"We will name her Tikva! That shall be her name, Hope, for that is what she shall give us!"

Part Six: A Little Town Quiet

December 68 CE – September 69 CE

Chapter One Hundred & Sixteen

14 December 68 CE / 2 Tevet 3829

Eight small oil lamps, simple cups of rough gray pottery, burned brightly, taking pride of place in the grand room in the house of Elimelech. The lamps sat on the dark, polished wood table in the center of the elegant room. An elaborate mosaic composed of sparkling stones the color of rubies, sapphires, and emeralds decorated the wall facing the door. Against the other walls rested low, soft couches with luxurious embroidery holding threads the color of gold and silver. On the tops of high shelves larger and stronger lamps lit even the furthest corners of the spacious room.

But it was those eight unpretentious lamps celebrating the start of the eighth day of the Festival of Dedication that were the focus of everyone's attention as they stood and listened to Rabbi Aaron chanting prayers of thanksgiving and deliverance.

Reuven's extended family was with him: daughter, wife, brother, mother, father, Dvorah. Even Phineas had joined the celebration. Only Judah was missing, claiming to be ill and hiding in his bed. Reuven was certain that Judah was faking, but Judah had refused to answer any of Reuven's questions in the matter.

Tikva, seven months old, squirmed in Reuven's arms. He bent his head and kissed the top of hers. Everyone had wanted and expected a boy, everyone except him, and Reuven had gotten his wish for a daughter.

But Reuven had wanted a girl who looked exactly like her mother, and Tikva resembled Drusilla not at all. The infant had the brown curly hair, dark eyes, and olive skin of her father.

Nevertheless, Reuven could not have loved his child more.

This house where he lived, thanks to Judah's connections, was a place of sanctuary and peace in a City that was outwardly calm but seethed underneath. Jerusalem was ruled by two factions, one headed by John ben Levi from Gush Halav, the other by the Kannaim led by Eleazar ben Simon. They had divided the City between them and ruled with an iron fist, but studiously avoided bloodshed between them. The population that they ruled suffered in silence out of fear.

At least there is order in Jerusalem, Reuven thought, his mind straying from his father's prayers. And the Romans are occupied elsewhere and do not threaten us at the moment.

A month after Tikva's birth Nero was overthrown and had killed himself. A fight for succession ensued, and a man named Galba became emperor. This instability in Rome and change in ruler left Vespasian's commission in doubt; the new emperor could easily replace him. In the meantime, Vespasian was refraining from further activities in the conquest of Jerusalem. His grip on the immediate area around the City and on Idumaea in the south loosened; bandits and revolutionaries reappeared.

Reuven was disappointed his prediction did not come to pass; had Vespasian become emperor Reuven would surely have left Jerusalem; Drusilla was well enough and Tikva old enough to travel. This turn of events in Rome left Reuven feeling stuck in the City of his birth. It might be too dangerous now to travel to Caesarea; as for eventually making his way to Rome, Vespasian's letter promising rewards was worthless.

But while the Roman army was quiet, and factional fighting had been quelled in Jerusalem itself, the City's rulers saw a different threat on the horizon.

Simon ben Gioras was rising in the south. After Ananus had kicked him out of the toparchy of Acrabata, Simon went to Masada. Upon learning of Ananus' death, Simon left Masada and withdrew to the hill country, collecting followers by proclaiming liberty for slaves and rewards for the free. He overran villages in the hill country. He began attracting many men of good position so that his army consisted not only of slaves and bandits but included many respectable citizens.

Simon ben Gioras was able to retake the toparchy of Acrabata and the whole area as far as Great Idumaea.

Reuven did not regard Simon ben Gioras as a threat, mainly because Judah did not. Reuven's friend thought of Simon as some kind of savior who would bring true unity. However, John ben Levi and Eleazar ben Simon did see Simon ben Gioras as a threat, and that, from Reuven's perspective, meant trouble would soon disrupt a temporary peace brought about by the upheaval in Rome.

Reuven sighed and returned attention to his father's chanting.

The family was now supported by the money Elimelech had accumulated and that had fallen into Reuven's hands after he killed Dorcas. The small amount his father used to receive from the land owned outside of Jerusalem was no longer sent, and the students he still had hardly paid him anything.

How does he feel, Reuven wondered, living off the money I have gotten in a way he calls robbery?

Reuven sighed again.

What a twisted world this is, he thought.

The sound of knocking on the outside door reached them.

Rabbi Aaron fell silent.

The gate was locked, Reuven thought in dismay. Who could have gotten to the door?

As Phineas went to answer the knocking, Reuven handed Tikva to his father.

Rabbi Aaron sighed gently and took his granddaughter into his arms. He smiled broadly as Tikva squealed with delight and pulled at his beard.

Father loves her almost as much as I do, Reuven thought with satisfaction.

Then he hurried after Phineas to see who had come to disturb them.

Phineas had already opened the door.

Five men, all armed, stood there.

"How did you get through the gate?" Reuven demanded.

A skinny youth named Arieh who Reuven knew to be associated with John ben Levi answered.

"I climbed over the wall and opened it."

"Well," Reuven said, "a happy holiday to you all." His heart was pounding. One of the other men belonged to John ben Levi's group, the other three were Kannaim. "What do you want? It must be something important if men from both factions have come to see me."

"Not you, Reuven," a burly man, one of the Kannaim, replied. His name was Yair. "We know what you would say: 'My year is not up yet!'" Yair spoke these last words in a mocking tone. "And so it is not, but will be soon enough, and we'll be back for you then. You've proved your worth as a fighter many times in the past. No, for now, we're here for Judah. We need him. There's an important mission coming up; that's why both parties are together in this."

Reuven shrugged, puzzled.

"Vespasian's nowhere near Jerusalem. There aren't any Roman legions nearby," Reuven said.

"We've been watching Simon ben Gioras," came Yair's reply. "It's clear what he's up to. Jerusalem is his next target. We're going to nip his plans in the bud. Go get Judah."

"Well, that is certainly news," Reuven responded. "I'm sure Judah would welcome some action. But not now, the fellow's pretty sick."

"What's wrong with him?" Yair asked. Reuven could not tell if Yair was concerned or suspicious.

"I don't know," Reuven answered, "but he looks terrible. Must be a flux of some kind. He refuses to have a doctor come. It must be something bad because," here Reuven curled his lips with disgust and shook his head, "he's thrown up a couple of times. It stinks something awful!"

The men all stepped back.

"Tell Judah that we came," Yair said gruffly.

"I will do that," replied Reuven, adding, "and if you don't mind, Arieh, after the others walk through the gate would you mind locking it and climbing back out?"

Reuven watched them turn and walk away. He didn't wait for them to exit; he ducked back into the house, pushed Phineas to the side, and shut the door, leaning heavily against it as he did so. His breath came in short gasps; his heart still pounded.

"What's wrong, sir?" Phineas asked.

"Trouble, Phineas, trouble."

The old man nodded gravely.

"Shall I inform Judah?" he asked.

"No, I will," Reuven said. A moment later he was running down the hall and burst into Judah's room.

Judah sat up in bed, a look of understanding on his face.

"Well, Judah," Reuven said, as he caught his breath and forced himself to calm down, "you appear as healthy as you did the last time I saw you, though that is not what I told your visitors."

"Are they gone?"

"Yes."

"Good."

Judah stood up and flexed his arms.

"What's going on?" Reuven demanded.

"I think you know," Judah replied. "Trouble. Big trouble. John and Eleazar are teaming up to stop Simon ben Gioras by going to meet him in battle. They don't stand a chance. They'll get their noses bloodied. I want no part of it." Judah grinned, and for a moment Reuven thought that Judah was going to stick his tongue out through the gap in his teeth.

"Reuven, the truth is, I am sick! I have Reuven's disease."

"What's that?" Reuven asked, starting to laugh.

"I don't want to kill fellow Jews anymore." Judah sat down, his face serious.

Reuven let him think. At last Judah spoke again.

"Once we were all united in Torah. Then we split, fighting each other over honest differences of opinion. Now, now, we fight because of clashing personalities. This isn't the peace party against the war party; it's the rough country boy John ben Levi against the aristocratic Eleazar ben Simon. Neither can bear to take orders from the other so they go their separate ways. But when a third claimant to power shows up, then the two decide to unite, temporarily.

"It's madness, Reuven. We should be uniting, all of us, preparing for the coming of the Roman legions, who will certainly return. This war of liberation is not over by any means."

Judah stood up again. His voice full of despair, he cried:

"Once we were filled with the spirit of God, then we became men who thought for ourselves; now we are nothing but a shrieking mob heading for the destruction that we are bringing upon ourselves."

Then he added, calmly:

"Your father is right. We are doomed."

Chapter One Hundred & Seventeen

21 December 68 CE / 8 Tevet 3829

Judah paced the corridors and hallways, occasionally peering into one of the lavish rooms still kept up by Phineas.

"Well," he muttered sardonically, "it may be a prison, but it's certainly a fancy one."

It had been a week since the men from John ben Levi and Eleazar ben Simon had come calling, and more than a week since Judah had been afraid to step outside, even just to stroll the grounds of Elimelech's house. He did not want to be spotted somehow, and have an end put to the fiction that he was too ill to take part in any planned military action against Simon ben Gioras.

Judah did not want to get drafted into a foolhardy exercise in futility.

Down a dimly lit cross-corridor Judah saw Dvorah, her back to him, bent at the waist, beckoning to Tikva, who was determinedly crawling toward her. Further down the hall from Tikva stood Drusilla, watching her daughter crawl toward her friend. Both women were uttering cries of encouragement.

Well, he thought, at least they are enjoying themselves.

Judah went to the outside door and opened it. The smell of rain reached his nostrils and he breathed in deeply. It gave him a moment of satisfaction.

He was getting quite bored, and he did not like that. He couldn't wait for Reuven to come with the news that the hopeless mission to attack Simon ben Gioras was over.

Judah shut the door and resumed his aimless pacing.

He was walking head down, his mind deep in random thoughts, when he bumped into someone in the hallway.

It was Reuven, smiling broadly.

"The deed is done!" Reuven announced. "The forces of John and Eleazar met Simon on the field of battle." Reuven paused for dramatic effect.

"Well?" Judah asked impatiently.

"You were right. Simon bloodied their noses. Actually, their defeat was worse than that. They lost a lot of men and had to run back to the City and shut the gates."

"I knew it!" spat out Judah. "The fools!"

"Simon did not pursue them, however," Reuven went on, "so maybe they did forestall an attempted takeover of Jerusalem by him. I don't know. We'll see. There were no reports of Simon's casualties, and the Kannaim are being tight-lipped about the magnitude of their own forces. But you can't hide the number of bodies that come back, or the wails of mothers and widows…"

Reuven shook his head. His face puckered as if he had just bit into an especially sour lemon.

"Reuven," Judah said, "I don't know if Simon had been planning on taking Jerusalem by force, but he will be now, after he was attacked without provocation. He won't take this lying down. Simon ben Gioras will be back. Ach, the fools!"

Reuven nodded in agreement

"There seems to be another effect of all this, Judah," he said. "John ben Levi has joined forces with Eleazar ben Simon again. There's one unified rule in Jerusalem again."

Judah snorted with contempt.

"John's been influenced by those Kannaim lunatics," he said with disgust.

"Or he's got some trick up his sleeve," offered Reuven.

Judah shrugged helplessly.

"Either way it's no good," he sighed. "Ah, what can we do?" Judah put his hand on Reuven's shoulder. "I need some fresh air. I can't hide forever. Come, my friend, and take a walk with me."

Chapter One Hundred & Eighteen

2 April 69 CE / 22 Nisan 3829

Judah carried a big stick as he patrolled the Upper Market. Reuven was by his side, also carrying a big stick. Reuven was not prepared to use that stick.

Judah was.

"I don't like this anymore than you do, kid," he said to Reuven. "It's a job we must do. For two important reasons. Help keep the City safe, calm and free of disturbances, and maybe more important, keep your family safe and in that nice house of ours."

Fourteen weeks and three days ago Judah had experienced that miraculous cure from the flux that had kept him cooped up in the house for more than a week. The very next day after walking outside with Reuven, Judah had been drafted into the Civil Guard. His assignment was to patrol the Upper Market and the streets in the area of the house of Elimelech.

Reuven was drafted almost three weeks after Judah was. They grabbed Reuven the day after the year of cheering his wife was over. Judah managed to use his influence to get Reuven assigned to him. The boy who had brought down a Roman cavalryman with his sling and then had tried to chop off his head had grown into a more subdued man.

Did he get some sense, or did he lose his fire? Judah wondered.

Could I ask the same question about myself?

The Upper Market was busy today. Yesterday was the last day of Passover and the Sabbath; pent-up demand made the market burst at the seams. A crowded market was a great opportunity for agitators to cause trouble.

Judah understood that his most important task, even more important than stopping criminal activity, was, from his superiors' point of view, to ensure that anything that threatened the rule of the Kannaim was throttled before it could do any damage.

And indeed, one person was already taking advantage of the opportunity.

Rafael ben Terach stood on a wooden crate, haranguing an audience that had gathered around him. At his side, on the ground, stood a large muscular man, Aran ben Eitan.

Judah was familiar with both of them. Rafael, who owned one of the shops on the second level, was a half-way decent speaker obviously dissatisfied with the state of things in Jerusalem. He was complaining about the Kannaim administration of the City, the taxes they levied, and their heavy-handed rule. He was urging his listeners to unite and protest. Aran was an Idumaean who seemed to be acting as Rafael's bodyguard. Aran had entered Jerusalem along with the mass of other Idumaean fighters almost fourteen months ago. He was one of those Idumaeans who did not return home after the murder of Niger the Peraean.

"Rafael," Judah said genially but authoritatively, "time to move on. Go open your shop and make some money."

"So you thieves can tax me and take it away?" Rafael retorted hotly.

"Listen, Rafael, we've always been taxed. The money now goes to the defense of Jerusalem instead of the pockets of Florus. But I'm not here to debate you. Get moving or—"

"Or what, Judah?"

Rafael's question was a direct challenge to Judah.

Judah glared angrily at him and raised the thick wooden stick in his hand.

"Why don't you arrest me, Judah?" Rafael sneered. "Maybe you can put me in the same cell the Kannaim put you. Or have you forgotten already?"

Judah laughed.

"Rafael, I don't want to lock you up. You're not a bad guy. I just want you to shut up and open your store, like you're supposed to."

"I have every right to speak my mind!" declared Rafael.

Judah stroked his beard with his left hand. He could feel the growing discomfort of Reuven, who was standing beside him. He didn't feel so comfortable himself. On the other hand, the growing crowd of onlookers seemed to be enjoying the spectacle.

"Theoretically speaking," Judah began, "you are correct. But not today, not in these dangerous times. When we are free—"

"Until then we are slaves?" demanded Rafael. "Romans, Jews, does it really matter who our masters are?"

Before Judah could answer Rafael posed another question.

"Do you enjoy being a censor for John ben Levi?"

No, Judah thought, I do not. Citizens should have a right to speak their mind freely.

But didn't I order a man killed to silence him, the uncle of the boy standing next to me?

That was different!

How?

I don't know! I'm certain it was.

"Hello, Judah?" exclaimed Rafael, laughing, breaking into Judah's thoughts. Members of the crowd laughed, too. "Are you still here? Have you fallen asleep? Or are you unable or unwilling to answer?"

Judah took a deep breath.

"I don't want to arrest you, Rafael. But I can't let you go on like this. So I have a proposition. It looks like that big Idumaean next to you, Aran ben Eitan, is serving as your bodyguard. Here's the proposition: He and I fight. Just fists. No weapons. If he wins, you're free to continue haranguing the crowd. If I win, you shut up and go to your store. That seems like a fair and civilized way to resolve our dispute. Do you agree?"

Before Rafael could reply, Aran spoke.

"I'll take you up on that, Judah."

Aran strode toward Judah.

Judah dropped his stick and waited calmly, both arms relaxed along his sides.

The bigger Aran came less than an arm's length away.

Judah's right fist rose in a straight line toward Aran's face. Judah saw the look of astonishment in Aran's eyes as the fist came closer. Aran did not have time to dodge or block the blow, did not have time to stop his own forward motion. Judah's fist slammed into his nose.

Aran was rocked on his feet. Blood spurted from his nose. Stunned, he collapsed to his knees.

Judah spread out his arms.

"Do you want more, Aran?"

Rafael answered.

"We'll leave, Judah," he said, crestfallen.

"Good," Judah replied. He bent down and grabbed Aran's left arm. "Up you go, big boy," Judah said, as he helped Aran to his feet.

"I've never seen anyone hit so hard or so fast," Aran muttered, as he followed his master away. The crowd started dispersing.

"You handled that perfectly," Reuven said with admiration. "No arrests, no bloodshed."

Judah laughed.

"There was plenty of blood," he said. "Did you see his nose? Say, let's take a break and go back to the house for a while."

They left the Upper Market.

"Do you think there will be a popular uprising?" Reuven asked.

"I'll tell you what I think, Reuven," Judah said. "Simon ben Gioras has conquered Idumaea. He's now got an army of heavy infantry and 40,000 men. John ben Levi and the Kannaim won't stand a chance against him when he comes to Jerusalem. And he will come. If that failed expedition against him a few months ago wasn't enough, the hit-and-run attacks that are still going on will bring him here to take on the Kannaim. They won't lose power from a popular uprising; the dissatisfied citizens will call in Simon to throw out the Kannaim. And the Idumaeans in the City will help in that effort; they've grown tired of taking orders from John, and many of their fellow Idumaeans joined Simon after he conquered Idumaea. Don't be fooled by what you just saw, Reuven. Those Idumaeans are tough soldiers."

"Where does that leave us, Judah? We're on the losing side."

"I know, Reuven, I know. It does not leave us in a good position."

"What do we do?" Reuven asked.

"Damned if I know," Judah answered.

"I know," Reuven replied with certainty. "We should get out of Jerusalem."

"Humph!" was Judah's response.

At the house they were greeted by Benjamin with a worried look on his face.

"What's wrong, brother?" asked Reuven with alarm.

"John's forces captured Simon's wife, along with all her servants," Benjamin said.

Judah groaned.

"Simon will be coming sooner than I expected," he said.

"Let's go inside and talk," Reuven said.

The three went to the grand room and sat at the polished table in its center. They were soon joined by Rabbi Aaron, Ruth, Dvorah, and Drusilla holding a sleeping Tikva. The four had also heard about the kidnapping of Simon's wife.

"Why did they do it?" Reuven asked.

"I'm guessing they want to come to terms with Simon," Judah answered. "They release his wife in return for a promise not to take over Jerusalem."

"Will it work?" Benjamin asked.

"No," Judah said. "It will just speed his march on Jerusalem, and woe to anyone who falls into his hands. And if she's harmed…"

He shook his head.

"This is insanity!" cried Rabbi Aaron.

"We agree on something at last," Judah said heavily.

"What are we going to do about it?" demanded Drusilla. "Taking women hostages is wrong!" She banged on the table.

Tikva stirred and started crying. Drusilla moved the baby under her *simla* and allowed her to suckle. After a few moments Tikva went back to sleep and the conversation resumed.

"What can we do, Drusilla?" Judah asked.

"We can organize the women of Jerusalem to protest," Drusilla replied, more softly. "We can force the Kannaim to release her."

Judah furrowed his brow. Reuven laughed.

"Don't be ridiculous, Drusilla," Reuven began. "The men of the Kannaim don't care what a bunch of women—"

"Batya, your role is to stay home and raise Tikva," Rabbi Aaron interrupted. "Not to engage in political organizing. You're not Dvorah the Prophetess!"

"*I'm* Dvorah of Gamla!" exclaimed Dvorah. "And I think it's a great idea!"

"I can help," offered Ruth. "I know women who will be as outraged as I am!"

It was Judah's turn to laugh. He slapped Reuven on the back.

"Well, young man, you certainly did a good job picking a wife. If I may make a suggestion, ladies?" The three women nodded. "Go to Naomi, the wife of Rabbi Hania ben Avel-Mayim," Judah continued. "She's a real spitfire! I once tried to intimidate her into giving me information about her husband. Didn't work. She wasn't afraid of me at all, stood up to me face-to-face and didn't budge." Judah laughed again, this time at the memory. "She'll definitely help, and she'll be very useful because she must know a lot of women. Her husband is in charge of making weapons."

Judah leaned back into his chair. He looked at Reuven.

"You're losing your cunning, kid," Judah said. Ignoring Reuven's puzzled expression, he turned to the women.

"Well, ladies," he exclaimed with enthusiasm, "it seems you have a plan. Let's see where it takes us!"

Judah smiled with satisfaction. Reuven wanted to know what they should do now that it appeared they were on the losing side.

Reuven's wife had just come up with the solution.

Chapter One Hundred & Nineteen

6 April 69 CE / 26 Nisan 3829

They wouldn't dare hurt a woman with a baby, Drusilla thought.

Of that she was certain, otherwise she would have followed Rabbi Aaron's advice and stayed home with Tikva.

Walking next to Drusilla were Dvorah, Ruth, and Naomi, Rabbi Hania's wife. Behind them marched at least 300 women. It had taken four days to organize the march that was approaching the house in Bezetha where Anat bat Yoseph, the wife of Simon ben Gioras, and her servants, were being held. Ruth enlisted several women, Naomi even more, and each of these women brought their own relatives and friends in an ever-growing chain. As they marched, more women joined.

The four armed men guarding the house were taken by surprise by the mass of women descending on it. The women began chanting a demand to free Anat. Their raised voices filled the street and the neighborhood of expensive houses beyond.

Drusilla saw that the guards did not know how to respond. All they did was draw their weapons and scowl.

She knew there was no way for the guards to call for reinforcements; the overwhelming bulk of the Kannaim, now under the control of John ben Levi, were manning the ramparts and the gates of the City in case of assault by Simon ben Gioras, who had camped beyond the walls with his vast military. Simon, enraged that his wife was taken, was threatening to kill anyone he caught outside unless his wife was returned. It was also clear that Simon was preparing to force an entry into Jerusalem.

Tikva was strapped tightly to her mother. She stirred. She craned her neck and looked around, babbling.

Drusilla walked up to the guards.

"I demand to see Anat!" she said.

One of the guards, an older man with a white beard, replied:

"Go back home with your baby! Does your husband know you are here? He'll give you a good beating when he finds out." He sneered, then shouted, "The same goes for all of you!"

"What are you going to do?" Drusilla asked calmly. "Kill all of us? Let me see her!"

The guard who had taunted her remained silent. Drusilla sensed his confusion.

Just in front of the gate, standing behind the other three, was a tall, thin man with small eyes, a hooked nose, and pockmarked upper cheeks.

"Let her in," he said, with the voice of authority. "It won't do any harm." To Drusilla, he added, "Just you."

He opened the gate and she entered. The chanting stopped.

The grounds and the building were as fine as Elimelech's. She was told that it had been confiscated from a young man of a noble family who was arrested and later executed.

Drusilla shuddered as her eyes swept the property.

She entered the house and followed the voices she heard into a large room with several couches, luxurious rugs on the floor, and a beautiful mosaic of red, blue, and green geometrical shapes on the wall. Four women occupied the room. Their chatter stopped as soon as she entered.

It was obvious who was the mistress and who were the servants.

Anat bat Yoseph was leaning back on the couch. Her long black hair was free. She glided gracefully off the couch and rose to her full height.

"Who are you?" she demanded imperiously. "What do you want?"

A peasant woman who has achieved a high position, Drusilla thought. Not born to it, like the ladies of Rome. Tall, handsome, intelligent, sure of herself. Tough, cunning.

"My name is Batya," Drusilla answered in a tone of deference, looking down at the floor. "My husband is Reuven ben Aaron. His father, Rabbi Aaron ben Avraham, is a respected Torah scholar."

"What do you want?" Anat snapped.

"My lady, have you heard the shouts of the women outside?" asked Drusilla, looking up.

"Yes, it stopped just before you entered."

"They are calling for your freedom, my lady. After we are here we will march to the headquarters of the ruler of the City and demand your release. I have come to make sure you are being treated as befits a woman of your station."

Anat's hard features softened. She smiled.

"It is not bad," Anat answered. "But I'm still a prisoner held against my will."

"We women will end that," Drusilla said firmly, "and see that you are free to return to your husband."

"My husband will free me, by force of arms, if necessary."

"I hope it does not come to that, my lady. Brothers shedding blood would be a terrible thing."

Anat regarded Drusilla silently for a moment.

"Come here," she said. "I want to see your baby."

Drusilla stepped forward and held out Tikva.

"Ba, ba, ba," said Tikva. She smiled at Anat.

"She's lovely," Anat said smiling back. She brushed the covering from Drusilla's head, freeing her golden hair. "So are you." She gazed silently at mother and child for a moment. "She looks nothing like you."

"She takes after my husband."

Anat nodded.

"You are not from this land," she said.

"No," Drusilla answered.

"Nor from anywhere near here," Anat added.

Drusilla smiled.

"You are correct."

"But you are a Jew," Anat went on.

Drusilla smiled again.

"I am now," she replied. "Since just before I married my husband. I suspect that I always was, in my soul."

The hint of a smile crossed and stayed on Anat's features.

"Tell me, Batya, was it you who organized these women?"

"Yes."

The smile on Anat's face disappeared. In the tone of a solemn promise she said:

"I will never forget what you have done for me, Batya, wife of Reuven ben Aaron."

Chapter One Hundred & Twenty

9 April 69 CE / 29 Nisan 3829

Drusilla stamped her feet. She made an angry face.

"Absolutely not!" she declared. "I want our children growing up in Jerusalem, God's holy City."

Reuven slapped his forehead in dismay.

"I should have never let you convert!" he cried.

"I didn't do it for you," Drusilla immediately corrected. "I promised God that if He delivered you from Gamla I would become a Jew. God kept his part of the bargain, I'm keeping mine!"

Reuven shook his head in disbelief. He paced back and forth in the bedroom.

"I can't believe this," he said. "You've turned into a fanatic, like my father!"

"Your father is not a fanatic, Reuven. He's a good man. You could learn a lot from him."

"Drusilla, we have to leave Jerusalem. I am no longer safe here."

"Nonsense!" Drusilla asserted.

Reuven stopped pacing and buried his head in his hands.

The day after Drusilla led the demonstration, Simon ben Gioras' wife was returned to him. The day following the release, on the Sabbath, the Idumaeans in Jerusalem, joined by many regular citizens, turned on the Kannaim and attacked them in force. This desecration of a holy day bewildered Reuven. To attack on a Sabbath? And why did they wait until Simon's wife was released? The dissatisfaction stoked by the Kannaim's rule was long-standing. Did their opponents see the release as a sign of weakness?

The Kannaim, driven out of the City, managed to regroup and take refuge in the Temple, where they promptly locked the gates.

"Drusilla," Reuven cried, letting his hands fall to his sides and straightening up, "Judah and I are seen as part of the old regime! We *are not* safe anymore!"

"Is that why you've been afraid to go outside today?" Drusilla asked.

Reuven sighed. It was the afternoon of Yom Rishon, the day after the Sabbath, and his wife was right. The two of them were afraid, and had sent Benjamin out to get information about what was going on in the City.

"You have nothing to be afraid of," insisted Drusilla. "Anat, Simon's wife, will protect us. She knows I helped get her released from captivity."

"Oh, Drusilla, please, you're not thinking clearly!" exclaimed Reuven. "Simon's not in the City. Yet. And even if he does come in, which I admit will probably happen sooner rather than later, what makes you think he will listen to his wife? You don't know if John ben Levi released her because of what you women did or because of Simon's frightening threats." Then he added, his voice thoughtful and calm, "Only John ben Levi knows that."

"You're being silly, Reuven."

"Drusilla, you're not listening to what I'm telling you!"

"Maybe, Reuven, it's time for you to start calling me by my name. Batya!"

"Ugh!" was Reuven's disgusted response.

"Where do you want to go, Reuven?" Drusilla snapped.

"Caesarea," he replied. "I'd say Rome, if Vespasian had become emperor."

The instability in Rome continued. About a month after the Festival of Dedication, Galba, after a reign of seven months, was overthrown and killed. Now a man named Otho ruled Rome. He had been on the throne for almost three months. So far. How long would his rule last?

"You want to go to that pagan city where they slaughtered 20,000 Jews? You think we'll be safe there?" Drusilla asked.

"We have money," replied Reuven. "I can set us up in a secure neighborhood. We'll keep our heads down, live quietly, no one will bother us."

"You're the one not thinking clearly, my dear husband."

"Drusilla, listen to me," Reuven implored. "Our children will not have a chance to grow up if we stay here. Before the Romans come, we'll have destroyed ourselves."

"I won't go to Caesarea. I won't go to Rome," Drusilla insisted. "I would rather die in Jerusalem than raise our children in a pagan city!"

"You have become a fanatic!" shouted Reuven.

Benjamin entered the room. They both turned to him.

"News, brother?" Reuven asked.

"Much," replied Benjamin. "The leaders of the Idumaeans in Jerusalem have been meeting with the chief priests. A decision has been made to open the gates of Jerusalem to Simon ben Gioras and invite him and his army to enter."

"See!" cried Drusilla. "You have nothing to worry about, Reuven."

Reuven shrugged.

"We'll see," he said drily. He put his hand on Benjamin's arm. "I want to talk to you, Benjamin," he said, and led his brother out of the room.

As soon as they were in the hallway Reuven whispered:

"My wife lives in the land of dreams, not in the real world."

Further down the hall Reuven's voice grew louder.

"Benjamin, we have to get out of Jerusalem. A storm is about to hit, fiercer than the one that struck the night the Idumaeans came and murdered Ananus."

"Yes, you're right," Benjamin agreed, "but where can we go?"

"Caesarea."

Benjamin frowned.

"How will we get out of Jerusalem?" Benjamin queried. "Simon is no more likely to let people leave than John was. And how will we make the journey safely?"

"Listen, Benjamin, I know this sounds crazy, but if we can get hold of Amram—"

"Amram?" Benjamin interrupted. "It is crazy. After what we did to him?"

"He doesn't know it was us."

Benjamin sighed and rubbed his beard. He looked at Reuven quizzically.

"Do we even know where he is?" Benjamin asked.

Reuven shook his head.

"But he must come to Jerusalem once in a while," Reuven said hopefully. "And even if he doesn't, he has to be somewhere in Judea or the Galilee. There must be people here, in the City, who can get hold of him. He'll know how to get us out of Jerusalem and the best route to Caesarea. He'll do it for money."

"How will we find Amram?"

Reuven smiled.

"Not we, Benjamin. You!"

Chapter One Hundred & Twenty-One
11 April 69 CE / 1 Iyyar 3829

Reuven sat on the bed next to Drusilla, who was suckling Tikva. He softly stroked Drusilla's leg.

"You see," she said reassuringly. "Simon's in the City, everything is peaceful, and nothing has happened to you or Judah."

Reuven gave her a wry grin.

"It's only been two days, Drusilla. The Kannaim still control the Temple."

"There has been no bloodshed since Simon entered. As for the standoff with the Kannaim, that will be settled peacefully. Perhaps you, Reuven, will help forge a compromise. Yes, I think I will go to Anat and suggest that."

Reuven laughed bitterly.

"I think you lost your wisdom when you took on the burden of the Law," Reuven said. "You should have stayed a free-thinker, your mind was clearer then."

"That is *hilul ha-Shem*," Drusilla said angrily. "You are desecrating God's Holy Name by saying that."

"On the next Day of Atonement I will request forgiveness for that transgression, Rabbi Drusilla," Reuven retorted sarcastically.

"It's Rabbi Batya!" she shot back.

There was a moment of tense silence.

Then they looked at each other and laughed.

Judah came into the room.

"We have a visitor," he said.

"Who?" Reuven asked.

"Rafael ben Terach, you know, that agitator I had to shut up by busting the nose of his Idumaean bodyguard. He's acting awfully cocky. Says he wants to speak to the both of us."

Reuven patted Drusilla's leg, gently kissed Tikva on the top of her head, and followed Judah out of the room. Rafael ben Terach was waiting for them at the entrance.

"Nice place you have here," Rafael greeted them. He looked around and smiled. "I'm sure Simon, our new master, will be pleased to learn that one of the Kannaim is still living well in the Upper City."

"Who's going to tell him?" Reuven asked.

"I will," Rafael replied, standing a bit taller. To Judah, he said, "No doubt you now regret not letting me speak freely in the Upper Market." He snickered.

"Who's going to tell him?" Reuven repeated.

"I will!" Rafael said again.

"I don't think so," Reuven said.

In one motion Reuven stepped forward and raised his knee into Rafael's groin. He punched the doubled-over Rafael in the jaw. Rafael shrieked in pain. As he fell to the floor Reuven jumped on top of him.

"Get a rope!" Reuven called to a surprised Judah.

"What?"

"Get a rope!"

"What are we going to do with him?" Judah asked, shaking his head.

"I haven't figured that out yet, but we can't let him go to Simon."

Drusilla and Dvorah came into the room. Drusilla handed the crying, squirming Tikva to Dvorah.

"Let him go, Reuven," Drusilla said softly.

"What?" Reuven asked, astonished at his wife's interference.

"I said, let him go!" Drusilla repeated, this time in a voice of authority.

"Why?"

"Listen, Reuven," she explained calmly, as if she was talking to a child, "you may have the cunning to stop the Romans from undermining the wall of the Temple, you may have the courage and the skill to bring down a cavalryman with a stone and the wildness to try to cut off his head, but it takes a woman to know how to deal with a person one-on-one. Now let him go!"

Reuven stood up. He helped Rafael to his feet. The latter brushed off his cloak in an exaggerated manner and tried to resume an air of dignity.

"I apologize for my husband's rudeness," Drusilla said. She smiled warmly. "Wait here for a moment, please."

The three men looked at each other in amazement when she left the room.

A few moments later Drusilla returned, her right hand closed in a fist.

"I hear you have the finest dress shop in the Upper Market, indeed, in all of Jerusalem."

Rafael ben Terach drew himself up even further.

"So it is said," he announced proudly.

"Tell me, Rafael ben Terach," Drusilla went on, "were you aware that I am a friend of Anat bat Yoseph, the wife of Simon ben Gioras, and that I helped gain her release from the captivity by the Kannaim? What do you think will happen to you if you try to denounce my husband to Simon?"

Rafael's face fell. He looked chagrined. He started to stutter his apologies.

Drusilla stepped forward and opened her fist. A gold aureus gleamed in her palm.

"I'd like to buy a fine dress from your shop," she said. "Something appropriate. I trust your judgment. But nothing too fancy, nothing too expensive."

Rafael gasped. He opened his hand palm up. Drusilla dropped the coin into it.

"We're your customers now," she said. "That's almost like friends, and friends never say bad things about each other."

"No, they don't." Rafael said, looking down at the floor. His hand, which had closed over the aureus, trembled. "Thank you, my lady." His voice quivered.

Then he looked up at Reuven.

"Your wife has more sense in her little finger than you have in your entire head," he spat angrily.

Reuven's face turned red. Drusilla laughed.

She was still laughing when Rafael ben Terach went out the door.

Chapter One Hundred & Twenty-Two
20 June 69 CE / 12 Tammuz 3829

Drusilla lifted her head from the bucket. She stared at the contents and wanted to throw up again. She closed her eyes and took a few deep breaths. After a while her stomach calmed down.

She rinsed her mouth and spat into the bucket.

This time she did not need Ruth to tell her that she was pregnant.

Tikva was almost fourteen months old. If the second pregnancy was like the first, she had about seven months to go before the child was born. Now it was late spring, almost summer. The baby would be born in winter.

Drusilla was certain she knew what Reuven's reaction would be when she told him they were expecting another child: Joy.

But there was something else she had to tell Reuven, and she knew what his reaction would be to that: I told you so.

Almost two months and two weeks ago Simon ben Gioras had been invited into Jerusalem. For several weeks, the City was quiet. The Kannaim had continued to occupy the Temple, allowing worshippers who were not armed to enter. Simon's forces controlled the rest of the City. There was no fighting between the two sides.

Then Simon's army and the citizens tried to storm the Temple. Despite being outnumbered, the Kannaim were able to hold onto their position; the height of the Temple's colonnades and battlements gave them a decided advantage when they threw spears and slung stones. Many of Simon's men were killed and many carried away wounded.

Simon did not give up. He tried again and again to take the Temple. His losses mounted.

And then the Kannaim came up with a tactic that truly gave them an advantage. They constructed four immense towers on which they placed archers and slingers and on which they mounted spear-throwers and stone-throwers.

They were able to rain destruction not only on Simon's forces directly attacking the Temple but on those held in readiness in nearby parts of the City.

It was not only the fighting men who fell from the missiles hurled from these towers. Ordinary citizens going about their daily business were also killed.

The carnage was frightening.

Drusilla would have to go to Reuven and admit that he had been correct: Jerusalem was going to tear itself apart before the Romans came; it was not a safe place to raise their children.

There was something else to take into consideration. If this pregnancy was to follow the same course the first one did she would have to leave Jerusalem before she was unfit to travel. That meant she would have to leave before the middle of her pregnancy.

But where to go? She still did not want her children to be raised in a pagan city like Caesarea.

Rabbi Aaron would know.

Tikva was peacefully asleep on her small mattress next to her and Reuven's bed.

Drusilla found Rabbi Aaron in a room that he used for study. It was bare except for a large table and four chairs. Rabbi Aaron sat at the table reading a codex.

"Am I disturbing you, Father?" she asked hesitantly.

"Not at all, Batya," he said, looking up from the book. "What can I do for you?"

She sat down opposite him.

Smiling, she said:

"I see you're reading the book Reuven bought me as a wedding present." Smiling again, she added, "It made my head spin."

"So you read it?" Rabbi Aaron asked.

"Yes," she answered.

"It makes my head spin, too," he admitted. "I think at heart he's a heretic, though I'd be hard pressed to prove it." Rabbi Aaron sighed. "I don't think you came to discuss philosophy with me, Batya."

"No, I didn't, but I would like to one day."

Rabbi Aaron did not answer.

Drusilla frowned.

"Rabbi Aaron, do you consider me a bad wife or mother?"

"No, not all, Batya!" he answered immediately. "Not at all! Why would you even think such a thing?"

"Does it bother you that I read books on philosophy?" she asked.

Again Rabbi Aaron did not answer.

"Is it because I'm a woman?"

Drusilla could see he was taken aback.

"No, no." He looked down at the table and then back up at her. He shrugged, raised his eyebrows, and sighed. Then he laughed.

"A stupid prejudice, perhaps," he said sheepishly. "I have more evidence to call Philo a heretic than to say your intellectual pursuits are wrong. You are as quick as my two sons, and they lack nothing in strength of mind, even if the younger one lacks in morality." Rabbi Aaron made a face of disgust. "No, you certainly lack nothing as a mother, and as a wife, I hope you will turn my younger son back into the path of Torah." He took a deep breath. "So, Batya, my precious daughter-in-law, why did you come to see me?"

"Months ago, Reuven told me that he wanted to leave Jerusalem. He said the City would tear itself apart before the Romans got here. That it was not safe."

"Any fool can see that! Where did he want to go?"

"Caesarea, Rome."

"Ach! What did you say?"

"I said that I did not want to raise my children in a pagan city."

Rabbi Aaron smiled with satisfaction.

"Batya, if it were not for you, I might refuse to acknowledge him as my son."

"Father, he was right," Drusilla said earnestly. "After the Kannaim raised their towers and ordinary citizens started to be killed I realized that we should leave. But not to a pagan city. Father, can you recommend a place for all of us to go?"

Rabbi Aaron thought for a moment.

"Rabbi Johanan ben Zakkai left Jerusalem for Yavne. He has founded an academy for Torah there, so learning is not lost if Jerusalem is destroyed." He looked down at his hands. "When it is destroyed," he added sadly. In a stronger voice, he went on, "The Romans are not interfering with it, and they are keeping order and not allowing any sedition to rear its head, so it is a safe place with a Jewish atmosphere."

"Good," Drusilla replied. "Thank you." She stood. "I have to start making plans." She nodded at the book. "Perhaps when we are in Yavne we can discuss philosophy."

She had almost left the room when Rabbi Aaron called out to her in a firm voice:

"I'm not leaving Jerusalem, Batya."

She turned back and smiled.

"We'll see about that, Rabbi Aaron."

As Drusilla raced through the house her mind kept pace.

Before I tell Reuven I must make sure we will be able to get out of Jerusalem, she thought.

She entered Dvorah's room.

Dvorah looked at her with surprise.

"What's wrong, Batya?"

"Dvorah, would you mind taking care of Tikva for a while? I have an important errand to run."

"I'd love to," Dvorah replied. She hurried after Drusilla as she followed Drusilla to her room. Watching Drusilla dress, Dvorah asked:

"Where are you going, sister?"

"To Anat bat Yoseph," Drusilla replied, when she almost finished.

"Good luck with your mission, whatever it is."

"I will let you know," Drusilla promised.

She left the house and walked quickly through the streets of Jerusalem. The people, the shops, the buildings, even the Temple, barely registered on her consciousness as she headed to Bezetha. Anat bat Yoseph had set herself up in the same house where she had been held captive.

Drusilla had no difficulty entering the guarded compound, or being admitted to the house.

She found Anat sitting on a couch with her husband, Simon ben Gioras. Drusilla knew it was him from the descriptions she had heard: tall, broad, powerfully built and very handsome. There was a foot or two distance between husband and wife.

Anat bat Yoseph introduced Drusilla to Simon.

"My dear, this is Batya, the young woman who organized all those women to free me."

Simon grunted.

"You were freed because they feared my wrath if you were not," he grumbled. Despite the tone, he had a rich and fluid voice, a voice that was persuasive.

Simon smiled at Drusilla.

"Where is your adorable child, Batya?" Anat asked.

"A friend is watching her. I came to ask for a favor, my lady."

"Batya's rather beautiful, my dear," Anat remarked to Simon, as if she hadn't heard what Drusilla just said. "Come here," she ordered Drusilla, beckoning with her right index finger. Drusilla approached.

Anat pulled away the shawl from Drusilla's head, freeing her golden hair, as she had done the first time they met.

"You are right," Simon agreed enthusiastically. "Come Batya, sit between us." He patted the empty space on the couch next to him.

Drusilla stepped back, the shawl in her hands. Her heart was pounding.

"Lady, it is a serious request."

"Go ahead, my dear. How can I deny you anything?"

"My husband, his brother, and their father wish to go to Yavne to study with Rabbi Johanan ben Zakkai. I am asking for permission for our whole extended family to go there." Seeing the dubious look on Simon's face she added:

"Once the land is free of the Roman oppressor it will be important to have as many Torah scholars as possible in Jerusalem."

"They cannot study here?" Simon asked.

"Oh please, Simon, grant her wish!" It was less a request than a demand by Anat. "Don't worry dear, you will get permission for you and your household to leave Jerusalem for Yavne. And I shall look forward to your return."

"Thank you, my lady," Drusilla said breathlessly. She took her leave and hurried out of the house of Simon and Anat.

Her heart was still pounding as she started her journey home.

"Thank you, Master of the Universe, for taking me out of the lion's den," she murmured.

When Drusilla got back home she found that Reuven had also returned. He and Judah were on their hands and knees in a well-lit hallway. Tikva, also on all fours, shrieked with laughter as the three of them crawled around in a circle, the two men barking like dogs and growling like lions.

Dvorah stood at the other end of the hallway, laughing.

Reuven stood up when he saw Drusilla. Judah remained on the floor. Tikva looked up at her mother and babbled. She reached up with her arms. When Drusilla made no move toward her, she started to cry and crawled toward her mother.

Judah started barking wildly. Tikva turned back to him and resumed their play.

"Greetings, wife," Reuven said.

"Greetings, husband. I have to talk to you."

Judah called out:

"You can leave Tikva with me while you talk. We're having fun."

Reuven and Drusilla went to their bedroom. Once inside she turned to him.

"Why the serious face, Drusilla?"

"I have things to tell you," she answered. She paused and smiled.

"We're having another child, Reuven."

His whole expression changed. His face beamed with joy. He let out a whoop of delight.

When he had calmed down a bit he said:

"This time, I hope it's a boy." Then, a moment later, "Are you sure?"

"Yes, I've been having the same signs as I did with Tikva. It's just the very beginning."

Reuven hugged and kissed Drusilla on both cheeks.

"There's something else, isn't there," he said.

"Yes." Drusilla sighed. "You were right. We have to leave Jerusalem. It is no longer safe here. The factional fighting has gotten out of hand and threatens to consume us all."

"I told you so," he responded.

"Yes, you did," Drusilla admitted, more than a little annoyed.

"Admit that you're not the only one with brains in this family," Reuven pressed.

"I'm not the only one with brains in this family," Drusilla said, and then added, her voice teasing, "Your father and brother are also very intelligent."

They both laughed.

"Well," Reuven said, "the truth is, things aren't too stable in Rome, either. After only three months on the throne Otho was overthrown. For the last two months Vitellius has been emperor. I wouldn't be surprised if soon Vespasian makes his own bid." Then, anticipating what she wanted to say next, he added:

"We have to leave before you're too far into the pregnancy," Reuven said. "Otherwise it may be too late for you to travel."

"I was just going to say that," Drusilla responded. "I've taken the first step. I went to Anat, wife of Simon, and asked her for permission for our household to leave Jerusalem. Her husband was there when I asked. She agreed."

"You told them we're going to Caesarea?" he asked.

"No," Drusilla replied, "because we're not. We're going to Yavne."

Reuven nodded.

"It is safe there," he said. "The Romans are leaving the Jews alone, and they have allowed Rabbi Johanan ben Zakkai to open an academy.

He's no radical nationalist."

"I told Anat that your father, your brother, and *you* want to study there."

"Hah!" responded Reuven. "We'll see about that."

He cleared his throat.

"I, too, have taken the first step," he said. "After our last discussion about leaving Jerusalem I told Benjamin to find Amram. He can lead us out of Jerusalem to safety." Reuven's face fell. "It's been more than two months. If word doesn't come soon, I'll have to come up with something else pretty quickly. Let's tell Dvorah and Judah the news, and then my parents."

He hugged Drusilla again and held her for a long time.

Benjamin came into the room. Reuven released Drusilla. They both turned to Benjamin.

"News about Amram," he said. "I've been told by more than one merchant that he is expected next month, on the ninth of Av."

"That's good," Reuven responded. Looking at Drusilla, he said, "That's not too late."

Benjamin took several deep breaths.

"There's more news, Reuven," Benjamin said somberly. "Frightening news."

"Tell us, Benjamin," Drusilla urged, seeing Benjamin hesitate.

"There are reports," Benjamin said, "that in Caesarea Vespasian has begun preparing his troops for another campaign. In a few days he will be on the march."

Benjamin paused and looked down at the floor as if he could not face them for what he had to say next.

"Vespasian, at the head of three legions, is headed for Jerusalem."

Chapter One Hundred & Twenty-Three

14 July 69 CE / 7 Av 3829

Judah surveyed the road that led from Jerusalem, watching people go back and forth. He stood atop the left rectangular tower that flanked the north gate.

They're gathering herbs or firewood from the surrounding hills, he thought. It seems peaceful enough at the moment.

As if answering his thoughts Dvorah said:

"There's no sign of Vespasian."

Judah nodded.

"No, we won't see him anytime soon. Benjamin's information was wrong; Vespasian isn't coming to Jerusalem yet. He *did* march from Caesarea two months ago. And he reconquered territory he let slip from his grasp: Gophna, Acrabata, Ephraim. Bethel, Hebron, Idumaea." Judah sighed. "Only Herodium, Masada, and Macherus are free," he concluded.

"And Jerusalem," Dvorah added.

"And Jerusalem," Judah agreed. "We're safe, for the moment. Vespasian will hold off attacking us. Here's why, as Reuven explained it: Vespasian's challenging the current emperor, Vitellius, for the throne. Two weeks ago Vespasian's troops declared him emperor. Reuven also explained it's not that simple; the Roman senate has to confirm. Reuven thinks there will be fighting between Vespasian's and Vitellius' forces. The strongest and wiliest man will win, and Reuven's betting on Vespasian." Judah chuckled. "Dvorah, it was here, on this very tower, at the beginning of the revolution, that I ordered Reuven to kill the emissaries sent by Agrippa. Reuven was reluctant, but he followed my orders."

Judah felt Dvorah's gaze and turned to her.

"Reuven leaves for Yavne in a few days," she said.

"Yes," Judah responded. "It is a wise move on his part."

"Judah, we must go with him."

"Why?" Judah asked, throwing her a puzzled look.

"Without us Rabbi Aaron won't go with the rest of his family."

"He's an old fool," Judah shot back angrily. "I don't know why he wants to stay. He opposed our war of liberation from the very beginning. He still opposes it. What makes you think my leaving will change his mind?"

"Not just you, but me also," Dvorah explained. "If everyone else in the household says they are going, it will be harder for him to resist."

"Humph!"

"I agree, he's a stubborn man," said Dvorah. "But he won't stay here alone."

"Let Reuven convince his father to go," Judah countered. "He's a good talker. Like his uncle…"

Judah shuddered. He ran his hands over his face and pushed the memory out of his mind.

"Judah, let's not break up Reuven's family," Dvorah pleaded. "We can always return after they are settled. Sneak away before dawn."

"I'm not part of his family!" Judah protested. "And Rabbi Aaron doesn't make his decisions based on what I do. *That*, I can tell you for sure!"

"You and I have become part of the family," Dvorah insisted. "You know that's true. And Batya said she thinks Rabbi Aaron will change his mind and leave if, indeed, you and I join them."

"Ah, Batya, Drusilla, whatever her name is, *she's* the real head of the family!" Judah grunted, annoyed at Dvorah's prodding. "I don't care. I like Jerusalem," he said at last. "My place is here."

"You're not even from Jerusalem!" Dvorah exclaimed. "We're both from the north. This isn't our home."

"Jerusalem belongs to every Jew," Judah said solemnly. "It doesn't matter where he was born. It's the capital of our people."

"Oh, Judah, we only have to leave for a while!" Then she added, her voice hopeful, "We'll avoid the faction fighting that's going on now. We can get back here before Vespasian arrives and take part in the fight against Rome. You just said that won't be for a while."

Judah did not respond. He turned away and stared into the distance, into the land beyond Jerusalem.

Dvorah waited.

"Will you come with us, Judah?" Dvorah's voice was plaintive; Judah was moved by it. "I won't ask again, Judah, even if you say no."

"I don't know, Dvorah," Judah said heavily, after a long silence.

I really don't, he thought.

Chapter One Hundred & Twenty-Four

17 July 69 CE / 10 Av 3829

It was real now. Though he had pushed for it, knowing without a doubt it was the right thing to do, Reuven felt uneasy leaving the City of his birth.

Am I having second thoughts? he asked himself. Is regret rearing its ugly face inside my soul?

It was early morning, the tenth of Av. Amram was busy arranging the order of the ten donkeys that would carry fifteen people, including Amram himself, plus all the baggage.

Amram had arrived in Jerusalem several days earlier than planned. Reuven was informed that Amram was shocked at the request for a meeting.

"I'm so sorry I accused you," Amram stammered, when they met for what he thought was the first time since Gamla. "I saw you enter Vespasian's tent in Caesarea—"

"Think nothing of it," Reuven had reassured Amram, "it was an honest mistake."

Reuven saw that Amram was willing to make amends; thus he was able to persuade Amram to lead him and his family to Yavne, despite the travelling trader's obvious reluctance.

It was no longer just the family; the group Amram was to lead had grown into a caravan.

Judah at first said he would remain in Jerusalem. Reuven half-expected that. His father's insistence on staying surprised Reuven. He did not understand why his father wanted to stay in a City that he had long proclaimed was doomed. No amount of arguing changed Rabbi Aaron's mind.

When Judah finally agreed to go with the group, everyone else in the household successfully pressured Rabbi Aaron to join the exodus.

Phineas begged to be taken along. Reuven did not have the heart to refuse the old man. Then the midwife who had been with Drusilla during Tikva's birth requested to join them. Finally, the doctor, who was informed of the trip by the midwife, asked to come along with his wife and two children.

Reuven hesitated at the doctor and his family.

When the good doctor offered to finance half the expedition if he and his family were allowed to join, Reuven happily agreed to bring him along. It was a great opportunity to extract an extra condition: the promise of free medical care for his family in Yavne.

The people and animals milling about outside the house of Elimelech drew curious stares from passersby. No one dared ask any questions.

"Will you miss it?" Reuven asked Drusilla.

She shrugged.

"We will get something much more modest in Yavne," Drusilla said.

"Of course," Reuven agreed. "We don't want to call attention to ourselves. Besides, we may have a large supply of aurei, but it's not inexhaustible. Yes, something small and modest." He smiled. "But comfortable!" he added enthusiastically.

"Take your positions!" shouted Amram, already atop his donkey.

It was Reuven's job to assemble the ten donkeys and the fifteen people in the order Amram had decreed.

Amram already owned two donkeys. Once it became clear how many people were actually going, Amram realized he needed eight more.

"It will cost me forty aurei to buy eight donkeys," Amram had informed Reuven. "I must have the money before I do anything else."

"Well," Reuven said, sighing. "I guess I have no choice. But I should get some of that back if you're going to keep them."

"Reuven," Amram replied, "I can sell them in Yavne and you will get some of that returned to you."

The doctor, when informed of the extra cost, objected to paying for half; he insisted that he only needed three, not four donkeys.

Reuven had stared at him without saying a word.

The doctor got the message and paid.

The doctor did only need three donkeys. He, his wife, and their two children would take turns riding two of the donkeys. The third was to carry their belongings.

Phineas and the midwife were to alternate on the donkey assigned to them. Reuven had worried that the old man would not be able to walk half the distance to Yavne. When Reuven expressed his concerns, Phineas assured Reuven that he was up to the journey.

"Sir!" Phineas exclaimed forcefully, "if need be, I can walk the whole way!"

Judah, Dvorah, Reuven, Benjamin, and Aaron, would take turns riding one of the donkeys. Ruth would have her own, as would Drusilla, with Tikva strapped to her body. The last two donkeys carried the possessions of Reuven's family, with the entire treasure of gold aurei carefully secreted away in the sacks containing clothing, blankets, pots and pottery, and the books that Rabbi Aaron, and Drusilla, had insisted on bringing. Reuven had made sure that the packing of his family's possessions was done out of Amram's sight.

Swords and spears for the men and Dvorah were brought along in case they would be needed. The weapons were not only to defend their lives, but also the precious gold cargo. Reuven had his sling, with a pouch full of stones collected especially for the trip.

Reuven began getting everyone in order.

Behind Amram on the lead donkey was the pack animal with the doctor's belongings. The third position was taken by the doctor's wife, her husband on foot beside her, followed by their two children sharing a donkey in the fourth position. Behind them sat the midwife, with Phineas on his feet beside her. Next came the two donkeys with Reuven's family's possessions. At their side walked Benjamin, Reuven, Dvorah, and Judah. Drusilla had the eighth position, followed by Ruth, and finally Rabbi Aaron on the tenth donkey, bringing up the rear.

Once everyone was in position, Amram raised his arm and shouted "Go!"

What began as a straight line gradually became more disorganized. Once in a while Amram stopped and reorganized the train of donkeys and walkers. When the travelers learned to maintain position the donkeys marched slowly and stately through the City. Curious stares accompanied their progress. No one tried to stop them; even the armed men of Simon ben Gioras did not question their passage. The trip to the north gate was uneventful, except for a moment of fear Reuven felt as they neared the Temple.

Would the Kannaim loose another barrage just as they were passing by?

Fear, Reuven thought. The others are afraid of encountering Roman troops; I'm afraid of the brigands, whether Jew or gentile.

At the north gate Amram showed the guards the scroll with Simon ben Gioras' signature granting permission to the household of Reuven and Batya to exit Jerusalem for Yavne.

One of the guards began questioning Amram about the size of the group.

"This is a very big household," Reuven heard the one in charge objecting.

Amram just sat on his mount, saying nothing. It was clear that he was unprepared for the challenge. Reuven ran up to them.

"I am Reuven ben Aaron," he said. "Yes, this does seem large, but my wife, Batya, is pregnant, and we are taking our doctor and his family, as well as the midwife, because my wife had complications with her first pregnancy."

The four men guarding the gate conferred with each other. Reuven began to grow impatient. The four men stepped back to their previous positions.

"You're all free to go," said the one who had questioned the party's size.

The gate swung open and they marched out.

Reuven felt a flash of panic.

Will I ever see my home again?

For the briefest instant he wished he could go back in time and not have insisted on leaving Jerusalem. Then the reality of his situation, and the state of the City, sank in, and he moved resolutely forward.

Drusilla suddenly stopped her donkey. She dismounted.

"I'm walking," she announced.

"Drusilla, dear, it's a two day trip!" Reuven responded.

"Reuven, if I stay on this bouncy beast for another mile, I'll lose the baby inside me!"

Reuven shrugged.

"I guess you know best," he said. He ran up to Amram to tell him that one of the donkeys was free.

"Well," Amram replied, "someone else can ride."

"Not me," smiled Reuven. "If my pregnant wife can walk, so can I."

Phineas refused to get on the donkey.

"You don't have to prove anything," Reuven said to him.

Phineas clenched his jaw.

"I'm not a doddering old man," he insisted.

"You're not," responded Reuven, and walked back to his wife.

The doctor took Drusilla's donkey, moving it up in front of the one his wife was riding.

There was silence along the line as it descended from the heights of Jerusalem, except for the doctor and his wife who chatted as if they were out for a country picnic.

Reuven felt alone with his thoughts, unwilling to share them with his wife.

Would he ever see his home again? He was afraid to look around for one last glimpse.

On the side of the road stood two trees, their boughs and branches intertwined.

Like lovers, he thought.

"Look!" he cried to Drusilla.

She turned to see and squeezed his hand, smiling.

Reuven's heart was pounding; he had been wanting to sneak a look back at the City.

Now's the time! he thought. I'll look now, where those trees are a marker, and when I do return to Jerusalem, I will stop here and look again!

Reuven paused in his march and turned back to the City.

Jerusalem bid him farewell with the same view it had greeted him with a year and a half ago, when he returned from Gamla and Caesarea: A dazzling snow-white mountain blazing with golden fire; the Temple, the heart of Jerusalem, its gold plates reflecting the brilliance of the sun, its stones so pure white they seemed not to be of this earth.

For several moments Reuven stood transfixed. The column passed him by. He could not move.

Then he spun around and ran after the human and donkey procession.

I will not look back, he promised. I will not see Jerusalem and the Temple until I return.

They marched through the morning. At the beginning of their trek they saw a scattering of travelers along the road. The further away they got from the City the fewer they saw, until they were completely alone.

Tikva stirred. Reuven took her from his wife and let the child sit on his shoulders.

At midday they came to a halt under Amram's command. He guided them off the road a short distance until they reached a small stream. Those who had been riding dismounted. Amram removed the packs from the donkeys to rest them. The donkeys drank from the stream, then Amram fed them. The people sat and rested. They ate their midday meal and drank the water they had carried with them.

All too soon Amram clapped his hands and reloaded the donkeys.

Tikva had fallen asleep again and was strapped to her mother.

My wife is starting to look tired, Reuven thought.

The march resumed.

They had not gone very far when one of the donkeys carrying the Reuven family goods stopped. It refused to move despite prodding. Reuven ran up to Amram.

As both men walked back to the donkey, the caravan came to a halt.

"Is he stubborn?" asked Reuven. "Or just lazy?"

Amram shook a crooked index finger at Reuven.

"Young man," he admonished, "if a donkey stops and refuses to go on it has a good reason."

Amram carefully inspected the load on the donkey's back.

He shook his head.

"I have to readjust everything," he said. "I wish you would have let me pack for you, Reuven."

Reuven remained silent.

It took Amram several minutes to readjust the cargo on the donkey. When he finished, he walked back to his own mount and the journey continued.

The sun was dipping west, starting to shine in their eyes. Reuven wondered where and when Amram would decide to stop for the evening.

Ahead, in the distance, a cloud of dust rose. Tension flowed along the line of marchers. Everyone realized that riders were heading up the road in their direction.

"Romans!" the doctor's wife shrieked. "They must be Roman soldiers! We are doomed."

"There's no way she knows who those riders are," Reuven muttered, barely under his breath, "but I hope she's right."

Amram halted. The line behind him did so, too.

Reuven ran up to Amram. Reuven could see the terror in Amram's face.

Reuven shook his head with disgust.

The others were also afraid, except for Judah, who looked like he was ready for a fight, and Benjamin, who realized there was no danger.

Drusilla, too, was unafraid. She had the beginnings of a smile on her weary face.

"There's nothing to be afraid of, Amram," Reuven said calmly. "I will deal with them." Then he shouted: "Do not fear. It will be better if they are Romans."

Reuven's words had no effect on Amram, who sat shivering in his saddle.

"You of all people have nothing to fear from Rome," Reuven said knowingly, "unless someone has betrayed you."

Amram stared at him wide-eyed.

"How am I to know?" he gasped. "My last dealings with them were in Caesarea."

Reuven patted Amram on the back.

"Wait here, then," Reuven said.

Reuven started down the road. He was already some distance from his companions when the riders came clearly into view.

There were seven, and one of them held the standard of a Roman unit.

Fifty yards away the riders halted.

Reuven walked slowly toward them.

As Reuven approached, the lead rider looked at Reuven with suspicion. He drew his sword.

"*Salve, domine!*" cried Reuven. Then, switching to Greek, he proclaimed:

"Greetings, in the name of General Titus Flavius Caesar Vespasianus Augustus, the new emperor of Rome and of all the civilized world!"

Reuven suppressed a smile at the look of surprise on the cavalryman's face.

Then he reached into his cloak and pulled out Vespasian's letter of safe passage.

Chapter One Hundred & Twenty-Five

15 Sep 69 CE / 11 Tishrei 3830

Reuven, munching on a piece of bread, sat on a wooden bench by the side of one of the main streets of Yavne watching the residents of the town go about their business. Though the fast for the Day of Atonement, the tenth day of the month of Tishrei, had ended the previous evening, Reuven was still hungry. He should have been in Rabbi Johanan ben Zakkai's Academy studying, as his brother was doing.

Reuven just could not bring himself to go today.

Their caravan had arrived in Yavne two months ago. Reuven found Yavne very disappointing. The only thing of distinction about it was Rabbi Johanan's Academy.

"A nothing of a place," Reuven had complained to Drusilla not long after settling in. "Caesarea would have been much more exciting."

Drusilla showed little sympathy for him.

"You should be ashamed for thinking such a thing," she admonished. "From this nothing of a town the light of Torah will shine forth after…"

Drusilla could not complete the sentence.

Reuven did not finish it for her; its conclusion remained in his own thoughts:

After Jerusalem is destroyed.

His only response was an emphatic: "Ugh!"

By agreement they chose a modest house, but one that was bigger than his father's home in Jerusalem. The kitchen was larger, and it had a small garden. There were five sleeping quarters: four on the second story and one on the first. The second floor had a bedroom for his father and mother, one for him, Drusilla, and Tikva, one for his brother, and one for Dvorah. Judah slept in the bedroom downstairs. As for Phineas, the doctor took him on as a servant. Reuven was glad the old man found a place where he could be useful; the simple house they now lived in had no need for one.

The Yavne house was nothing compared to that of Elimelech, or the first one in which Reuven lived in the Upper City with Metilius. Reuven was disappointed in himself for having gotten used to those more luxurious homes, and for missing them.

Reuven took another bite of bread and chewed it thoughtfully.

There was one thing he did appreciate about Yavne: its closeness to the Middle Sea. Less than three miles, not that long of a walk, and he could stand on the beach and dream of the sea and the world beyond.

Reuven quickly swallowed the chunk in his mouth, deciding that's where he would go now. He sighed and was about to get up when a distinctly odd fellow sat down next to him.

Reuven guessed him to be in his late twenties. He had a scraggly beard, a chubby face, and small, sharp eyes. The strangest cloak covered his protruding belly. It was composed of squares of different bright colors: red, blue, green, gold, and silver. The material seemed smooth, smoother than anything Reuven had ever seen. He was tempted to touch it and see.

"Greetings, Reuven ben Aaron," the fellow said, to Reuven's surprise. "My name is Hiram ben Koresh."

"How do you know my name?"

"Ah, I know everything that goes on in this town," Hiram replied. "And you are famous, for having stopped Cestius at the north wall of the Temple in Jerusalem."

Reuven's eyes narrowed.

"Are you a spy for the Roman secret police?"

Hiram laughed. It was a jolly laugh that did not seem to be hiding anything.

"Do I look like a spy?" He leaned forward, and added, winking confidentially, "but I can tell you who the spies are."

Hiram leaned back.

Reuven was intrigued but cautious.

"I don't want to be famous," he said. "I came to Yavne to live a quiet life and study at the Academy." He took another bite of bread.

Hiram chuckled.

"I can see how much you like to study, Reuven ben Aaron."

Reuven smiled and shrugged.

"No," Hiram went on, "you're not one for the books. You're a man of action! You'll soon cry from boredom in Yavne."

Reuven hurriedly swallowed the half-chewed bread in his mouth.

"There are worse things than boredom for a man to cry about," Reuven retorted. "Besides, I love books, especially the ones discussing philosophy that my wife reads, books that *I* gave her."

"Your wife reads books on philosophy!" Hiram exclaimed with surprise. "Well, I would have thought you married a beautiful woman. They don't need to read books on philosophy to attract a man."

"See," Reuven replied, keeping the smile from his face, "you don't know me at all. My wife is rather plain, almost homely. You might even call her ugly. So what? I love her just the same."

Hiram quickly recovered. His face once again assumed a mask of studied geniality.

"Well, if you ever want to spice up your life and have a beautiful woman on the side," Hiram said, winking again, "stick with me and you can have the best of both worlds."

"Are you a pimp as well as a Roman spy?"

Hiram turned more toward Reuven and leaned back. He ignored Reuven's question. Instead he studied Reuven's face for several moments.

"You jest with me," he said at last. "Your wife is not ugly at all. She's probably very beautiful."

Reuven's eyes narrowed.

"I hope you didn't start this conversation to discuss my wife."

"You brought her up," Hiram said quickly.

"True enough," Reuven agreed. "What do you want from me?"

Hiram leaned forward.

"You have the eyes of a killer, Reuven ben Aaron," he said.

Reuven did not respond. He continued looking into Hiram's eyes, waiting for what would come next.

"I've seen you looking at my cloak," Hiram said, his voice serious, the false jocularity gone. "Go on, touch it."

This sudden change in approach threw Reuven off-balance. It was true, he had kept eyeing the cloak while talking to Hiram. Reuven reached out and ran his hand lightly over the multi-colored garment. He had never felt material so soft and smooth. Reuven marveled at it. The only thing he could think of was Drusilla's skin.

"Do you know what the material is, Reuven?"

"No."

"It is called silk," explained Hiram. "The Romans love it, though some call its use decadent. No matter, they, and the Greeks and Syrians and Egyptians, pay dearly for it. Silk comes from Thinai, a land far, far to the east, the farthest east civilized men have ever travelled. It is a land of men with yellow skin and slanted eyes who play flutes and harps that entice magic worms to spin from their own bodies threads of silk." Hiram's eyes gleamed. His voice, strong and clear, filled Reuven with wonder, transforming the simple bench on a nondescript street in Yavne into the stage of his imagination upon which danced images of an exotic land with even more exotic doings. "Reuven, Thinai is beyond Parthia, beyond Skythia, beyond Ariake, beyond even Khruse and the Ganges River."

Reuven had only heard of Parthia and Skythia. The other names were unknown to him.

Oh, how I want to see the world! he thought.

Reuven could not keep the excitement from his face and eyes, and he caught Hiram taking note of that.

"You make your living selling silk," Reuven said.

"Very good, Reuven ben Aaron. And not just silk. You see, even if I were a pimp and a spy, which I am not, those two activities together would not bring me enough money to have this cloak made."

"What do you want with me, Hiram ben Koresh?"

"I will tell you, Reuven ben Aaron," Hiram began. "Until now I have travelled overland to the eastern end of the Roman Empire to buy the finished silk from Parthian traders. Reuven, every step from producer to consumer requires a middle man, and every middle man takes his cut. The more middle men I eliminate the more profit I make. In the month of Tammuz I will sail from the port of Berenike, in the south of Egypt, along the coasts of Arabia, Karmania, Gedrosia, and Indo-Skythia, until I reach the port of Barugaza. From there I will sail north to the trading seaport of Barbarikon, by the mouth of the Sinthos River, on the coast of Skythia. But first, in the month of Iyar, I will travel to Alexandria. There I will arrange passage and buy the goods I take with me. When I get to Barbarikon, I will trade the flowered cottons, the frankincense, the glass vessels and silver plates, and my gold aurei, for silk thread, emeralds, and sapphires. For every aureus I invest I expect to make at least twenty or thirty! I will be richer than I ever dreamed!"

What an exciting life this fellow leads, Reuven thought. I envy him.

"What do I have to do with this?" Reuven asked.

"I am a coward, Reuven," Hiram said, shrugging. "I am afraid to make such a journey alone. I need a bodyguard. I am willing to pay you and your friend Judah ben Ezra three denarii a day to accompany me."

Reuven laughed.

"If you are even thinking of such a journey, Hiram, you are no coward. But I am no bodyguard."

"I know your reputation, Reuven. And your friend's."

"Hiram, if I deserve any credit for driving Cestius away from the Temple wall it was only due to my cunning, not my prowess in battle or my courage. And if I have taken part in battles, it is through the use of the sling, a long range weapon, not one used by a bodyguard. And if I have used a knife in close combat," and here Reuven drew the knife he always kept with him, "and I am still here to tell you about it, it's because I used guile to succeed."

"You are just the man I need, Reuven!" Hiram cried enthusiastically, clapping his hands with delight. "And so is your friend, Judah ben Ezra. They say his smile is enough to strike terror in a man's heart."

Reuven put the knife away.

"I can't answer you now, Hiram. I have to think about it. The offer is tempting, and not just because of the money." It's not the money at all, Reuven thought.

"I see your eyes, Reuven. The prospect of this voyage excites you." Hiram rose from the bench. "It seems you are a lover of books after all. Wait here for me; I will return shortly with a book for you to read. It is very precious; I want it back when you've finished. *The Periplus of the Erythraean Sea* will whet your appetite for the voyage! It was written by a Greek trader; he describes all the trading routes around the Erythraean Sea. I will show you the one I plan to take." He smiled. "Reuven, instead of three I will pay five denarii! And a share of the profits!" Hiram concluded with a flourish. "Think, Reuven, a chance to make money and to see a world you would never see but for me!"

Reuven watched Hiram walk away. Then he stared down at the bread in his hand.

Reuven was no longer hungry. He was too excited to eat.

Chapter One Hundred & Twenty-Six

15 Sep 69 CE / 11 Tishrei 3830

Reuven was unable to pull himself away from the book Hiram gave him. He sat at the small table in his bedroom, an oil lamp burning on a stand nearby. The book, in the form of a codex, consisted of sixty-six short chapters, filled with wonderful descriptions of sea routes, strange places, and the goods that were traded over those routes between those places.

Hiram was right. It did whet his appetite. Reuven, now more than ever, wanted to be free of the confines of his own country and see the vast world beyond. He might even find a place where he could peacefully raise a family with Drusilla!

First, he would have to get permission from Drusilla to go on the journey with Hiram, and then convince Judah to join him.

Perhaps Hiram will let me invest some of my own money, Reuven thought, and then I can truly share in the profits. A twenty or thirty times increase! That will provide security for my family into the next generation!

Drusilla was asleep with Tikva at her side. They lay upon the low bed of soft straw enclosed in rough cotton.

No luxurious bed in this house, Reuven thought.

Reuven closed *The Periplus of the Erythraean Sea*. He got up and left the room. He climbed down the ladder, his mind fevered with excitement.

Dvorah was at the bottom, waiting to ascend.

She gave Reuven a long, intense look.

"I'm going to try again," she said fiercely, her voice barely above a whisper. "Perhaps I will succeed this time."

"What?" Reuven asked, thoroughly confused.

Dvorah did not answer. She went up the ladder.

Reuven walked out of the house.

Benjamin was approaching the front door.

"Brother," Reuven asked, still puzzled about Dvorah's last words to him, "do you have a few moments?"

The two brothers began walking together.

"Once again," Benjamin began reprovingly, "you did not go to the Academy."

"There are many ways to learn, Benjamin," Reuven replied. "Let me tell you whom I met today."

When Reuven finished telling Benjamin about his encounter with Hiram, the contents of *The Periplus of the Erythraean Sea*, and of his own plans to join Hiram's expedition, Benjamin broke into laughter.

"Little brother," he said, "you are a hopeless dreamer!"

"Benjamin, you can join us!"

Benjamin laughed again.

"Have you told Drusilla about any of this?" he asked. "I doubt whether your wife will allow you to go."

Reuven stopped walking. His face fell.

"You are probably right, older brother. How can I convince her?"

"You can't."

"Ah," Reuven said, sighing, resuming the walk, "having a wife is such a bother. It's like having a mother and father rolled into one." Reuven's voice rose into a childlike whine. "Mother, may I do this? Father, may I do that?"

Benjamin laughed.

"Say, brother, why aren't you married?" Reuven asked. "Why should I suffer alone?"

Benjamin chuckled.

"Seriously," Reuven continued, no longer joking, "Dvorah is a nice girl. Pretty, too. She's practically part of the family already."

Now it was Benjamin's turn to stop walking. He put his hand on Reuven's shoulder and gazed into his brother's eyes.

"The biggest mistake a man can make is to marry a woman who is in love with someone else," Benjamin said solemnly.

Reuven looked down at the ground.

"Shaul is dead," Reuven responded softly.

"Shaul ben Yitzchak lives in her memory," Benjamin replied, dropping his hand. "And if there is someone living in her heart, it is not me."

"Who then?" Reuven asked.

"At first it was you, Reuven. Now, I think it is Judah."

"Judah? Oh no, Benjamin, I don't think Judah would be interested in any woman. He told me long ago that the last woman he slept with tried to kill him."

"Why?"

"Because he told her he didn't want to marry her," Reuven answered.

"How disappointing," Benjamin said. "Judah didn't seem like the kind of man that would seduce a nice girl and then abandon her."

"She wasn't a nice girl. Judah said she was the Whore of Babylon."

"Oh my! Well, I suppose I'll marry some girl Father picks out for me. Another rabbi's daughter, no doubt."

"Will you be happy with a rabbi's daughter?" Reuven asked.

Benjamin smiled broadly before replying:

"Aren't you happy with Rabbi Batya?"

Both brothers burst out laughing at the same time.

They turned and started back home, walking arm-in-arm.

Rabbi Aaron was waiting for them, a troubled look on his face.

"I want to speak to both of you," he said and led them to the big table in the family room. The two brothers sat side-by-side facing their father.

"I want you to listen carefully," Rabbi Aaron began. "I'm giving my blessing to you, Benjamin, to be the head of the family. You are the elder brother." He gave Reuven a sharp look. "Do you accept that, Reuven?"

"Of course, Father," Reuven said. "Benjamin is my big brother."

"No," said Benjamin firmly. "We are equals."

"Benjamin, don't *you* argue with me," Rabbi Aaron began. He was interrupted by Dvorah coming down the ladder, followed by Drusilla with Tikva in her arms.

"Would you watch Tikva?" she asked Reuven. "I have some business to attend with Dvorah."

"Batya, I have important things to discuss with my sons," Rabbi Aaron said, clearly annoyed, his voice rising. "It will have to wait until later."

Ruth came out of the kitchen.

"I'll watch her, dear," she said.

Tikva jumped happily into her grandmother's arms. Drusilla and Dvorah disappeared in the direction of the bath.

"Father," Benjamin said, laughing, "the truth is, Batya will be running things here, unless you find me a wife, or I find one myself."

Both brothers grinned at their father, obviously suppressing more laughter.

Rabbi Aaron slapped the table angrily.

"This is not a subject for jokes!" he said sternly.

"Why do you speak as if you are about to die?" Benjamin asked.

"That is what it sounds like," Reuven added.

Rabbi Aaron took a deep breath. He looked down at the table, then at the elder son, and finally at the younger.

"Last night I had a dream," Rabbi Aaron began. "An angel, a messenger of God, came to me. He wore a cloak of many colors, much as the young Joseph wore."

Reuven felt the hair on his arms rise. His brother shuddered.

"The angel told me," Rabbi Aaron said, "that yesterday was my last Day of Atonement; before the first of Tishrei comes again, I will be dead."

Chapter One Hundred & Twenty-Seven

15 Sep 69 CE (evening) / 12 Tishrei 3830

Dvorah held the small mirror Drusilla gave her and moved it around so she could see herself better.

"You are even more beautiful than you were before!" Drusilla exclaimed.

"Thank you," Dvorah said, trembling. "Thank you for helping me."

Earlier in the day she had gone to Drusilla with an embarrassing request.

"Make me beautiful," Dvorah asked.

"You're already a very pretty girl, dear," Drusilla replied.

"Make me beautiful, like a bride."

Drusilla had gasped.

"For Benjamin?"

Dvorah did not answer, but she could see that Drusilla understood her reaction and knew the answer was no. Dvorah was grateful that Drusilla did not probe further.

So Drusilla had helped her bathe, anointed her with oil and perfume, and even given her the exquisite dress, brand-new and never worn, that Drusilla had purchased as a peace offering from Rafael ben Terach, the store owner who had threatened to denounce Reuven and Judah to Simon ben Gioras.

Dvorah handed the mirror back to Drusilla.

Tears started forming in Dvorah's eyes.

"Don't cry, dear," Drusilla said gently, "it will spoil the makeup I worked so hard to put on you."

Dvorah nodded and fought back the tears.

"I won't see you again, sister," she said.

"You don't know that," Drusilla said.

"We both know that," Dvorah said with finality.

"Here," Drusilla said, handing her a small pouch. From the weight and the jingling of its contents Dvorah knew it was money.

"Gold aurei," Drusilla explained. "I took them from Reuven."

"You don't have to do that," Dvorah said, her breath rushing from her.

"Yes I do," Drusilla insisted. "You will need it."

"Thank you."

They embraced for a long time. Dvorah's repressed tears appeared on Drusilla's cheeks instead and she gently wiped them away.

Then Dvorah left Drusilla's room before her own tears could burst through their restraining dam.

Judah looked up in surprise when Dvorah entered his room. He had been sitting in a chair, staring down at his hands.

What is he thinking? Dvorah wondered.

Judah's eyes widened with amazement as he took in Dvorah's appearance. He looked at her questioningly.

"Judah," she said, her voice solemn, "the time has come. Reuven's family is settled, and as each day passes it will become harder and harder to get through the Roman lines."

Judah nodded.

"I have been contemplating the same thing," he said. "It is time to leave." His voice was heavy. He looked down at his hands again.

"Judah!" Dvorah called, her heart pounding. "Look at me!"

Judah looked up at her.

"You are truly beautiful, Dvorah!" he exclaimed.

Dvorah could hardly breathe, afraid to speak the next words, afraid Judah would refuse her offer. She gathered her courage.

"Judah, I need to know happiness before I die. You are the only one who…" Her voice trailed off.

Judah took a deep breath. He rose from his seat and came toward Dvorah.

Then he took her into his arms, gently.

Chapter One Hundred & Twenty-Eight

16 Sep 69 CE / 12 Tishrei 3830

They were as quiet as assassins as they moved stealthily through the house. Judah heaved a sigh of relief once he and Dvorah made it outside without being discovered.

Judah wanted to say goodbye to Reuven but feared the boy would insist on joining them.

Reuven's place was in Yavne, with his wife and child, not in Jerusalem.

The holy City will be our tomb, Judah thought. Not theirs.

Judah and Dvorah walked silently through the empty streets of Yavne in the faint pre-dawn light. When they reached the outskirts of the town and entered the road to Jerusalem Judah took Dvorah's hand.

"I will marry you before we die," he promised.

Dvorah squeezed his hand.

When they passed the last street and house of Yavne and stepped onto the road to Jerusalem, the sun was beginning to peek over the horizon.

We'll have to be careful to avoid Roman troops, Judah thought. He did not repeat this to Dvorah; she was well aware of the danger. There was no sense emphasizing it.

Judah gradually became aware of someone following them. He stiffened, and Dvorah noticed the motion of his hand.

"What's wrong?" she asked.

Judah released Dvorah's hand and pulled out his knife. He whirled around to face the path behind them. Dvorah turned also.

A solitary figure took a step and then stopped.

Judah waited.

The tall figure began moving toward them. It came faster and faster. Judah detected nothing threatening about the motion, but he remained alert.

"Ho there!" cried Rabbi Aaron.

"What are you doing?" Judah demanded as the rabbi reached them.

"Why, the same thing you are," Rabbi Aaron said. "Going to Jerusalem for the Festival of Tabernacles."

"Go back to the house in Yavne," Judah demanded. "It's the Sabbath. You have no business travelling."

"That is true," Rabbi Aaron admitted. "I considered that, gave it much thought. But if I let you leave without following you I would never be able to get to Jerusalem by myself, and I have as much right to make the pilgrimage as you do."

"Go back!" Judah repeated. "Go back to your family. There is no reason for you to die in a war you opposed from the beginning."

"Put the knife away, Judah. Or do you plan to use it on me?" He smiled as Judah put the knife away. "Tell me, you two, what will you say to a Roman patrol if they stop you?"

Neither Judah nor Dvorah answered him.

"You see," Rabbi Aaron said with satisfaction, "you need me. I will simply tell any Roman officer that I'm going to Jerusalem to make the Festival of Tabernacles pilgrimage. That I plan to bring other rabbis out of the City and also try to convince anyone who will listen that the war is hopeless. So, who do you think has a better chance of getting through Roman lines, the two of you by yourselves or the three of us together, with me speaking Greek and convincing the Romans that our going to Jerusalem poses no threat to them?"

Again, there was no answer.

"You can share my house in the Lower City with me," Rabbi Aaron added.

Judah looked at Dvorah. He saw helpless uncertainty on her face. He looked back at Rabbi Aaron.

"I know full well," said Rabbi Aaron, "that you only agreed to leave Jerusalem for Yavne to pressure me to go with my family, and that all along you were planning to return to Jerusalem. Well, so was I." He waited for his words to sink in before adding:

"If the two of you have joined my family in life, let *me* join you in death."

Chapter One Hundred & Twenty-Nine

16 Sep 69 CE / 12 Tishrei 3830

Reuven stared glumly at the living room floor. He sat on a chair turned away from its table. In front of him stood Drusilla. From the kitchen he could hear his mother crying and his brother trying to comfort her.

"You knew?" Reuven asked.

"Not about your father," Drusilla replied. "Are you surprised about any of them?"

Reuven looked up and shook his head.

"No," he admitted. "From the very beginning neither Judah nor Father wanted to leave Jerusalem. I think they only came here because of us, and left as soon as they saw us settled. But why Dvorah?"

"She is with Judah now."

"Ah." Reuven did not need his wife to explain. "But why couldn't Judah have said goodbye to me? Father, I understand. We would have stopped him."

"Perhaps Judah was afraid you would follow him."

"Oh." Reuven shrugged. I guess there's no way I could have convinced Judah to go with Hiram and me, Reuven thought.

"Would you have?" Drusilla asked.

"What?"

"Would you have followed them to Jerusalem if you had known?" Reuven smiled.

"No," he said.

"Good."

"Jerusalem is not my destination anymore. Barbarikon is."

"What?" Drusilla asked, sounding annoyed. "What are you talking about?"

"The book I was reading, Drusilla. *The Periplus of the Erythraean Sea.* You never asked me about it."

Reuven told her about his meeting with Hiram, and about his desire to join him on the voyage.

"Reuven," Drusilla said, with exasperation, "we're expecting another child."

"The baby is due in Shevat. Hiram's not leaving until Tammuz. Our child will be at least three months old by then."

"And how long will this voyage take?" Drusilla asked skeptically.

"I-I don't know," Reuven replied. "I should have asked him. I didn't," he admitted sheepishly. Then he added, his voice bright and cheerful:

"It's a chance for me to find a place for us to live that's not wracked by war and conflict!"

"Humph!" was Drusilla's response.

"It's also a chance for me to make a lot of money and secure our future!" Reuven gave his wife a hopeful look.

"We have enough money for a long time if we live modestly and frugally," Drusilla insisted. "This idea of yours is crazy. You belong in Rabbi Johanan's Academy, not on some ship sailing to Barbarikon." She spat the place-name out as if it were something vile. "It sounds like Greek for Land of the Barbarians."

Reuven laughed.

"It's not funny, Reuven."

He shrugged.

"Your place is in the Academy with your brother." Drusilla spoke as if her words would brook no opposition.

"The Academy is boring," Reuven countered. "Men droning on all day about nothing. I once listened to a lecture about the hairs of the red heifer; how you can be sure if its hair is straight and that a particular hair of very dark red color is not really black. I fell asleep! More interesting is to read books in Greek on philosophy, and discuss their ideas with you! Like they did in ancient Athens!"

"I'm sure they didn't discuss philosophy with their wives!" Drusilla said.

Reuven sighed.

"Their loss, then. To be honest, Drusilla, our talks were more fun before we got married. You would ask such deep questions and come up with such interesting ideas. Since you've found faith your mind has narrowed. You even sound like my father!"

"Thank you!" Drusilla exclaimed. "That is a great compliment. Your father is a great scholar!"

"Ugh!"

"And my faith has made me a better person," she added.

"Well, mine is rather shaky at the moment," Reuven responded. "And that's thanks in part to the woman who opened my mind during all our discussions, before she married me!"

Drusilla stamped her feet.

"Don't blame me, Reuven, for your loss of faith. As for your voyage with your new friend Hiram, well, I can't force you to study at the Academy, but I can stop you from going with Hiram to Barbarikon."

Reuven frowned.

We'll see about that, he thought.

Chapter One Hundred & Thirty

17 Sep 69 CE / 13 Tishrei 3830

Rabbi Aaron laughed maniacally. Blood dripped from the cut on his forehead, staining his beard and his cloak.

Judah wanted to slap Rabbi Aaron to shut him up.

If the large stone propelled by Kannaim artillery that struck the wall behind them had been just a few inches lower it would have taken off both their heads. As it was, the stone bounced off the wall, loosening a fragment that only grazed the rabbi's forehead as it fell.

Dvorah, a few feet away and crouched lower, had not been in danger.

They had entered the City via the gate in the north wall. Bezetha was peaceful. Inside the second wall the market area was stuffed with locals and pilgrims for the Festival of Tabernacles, pilgrims from other regions of the Land and from as far away as Egypt and Parthia. Locals and visitors went about their business as if there was no faction fighting to worry about. Judah and Dvorah expressed relief. Rabbi Aaron remained skeptical.

Then the first missile fell. There were screams of terror as people ran in all directions. A man lay on the ground, his chest crushed by a rock, the life bleeding out of him.

As people ran, another stone plunged from the sky.

Rabbi Aaron led the way to the gate in the inner wall. They passed Antonia, and slowed their pace to a brisk walk as they crossed the Xystus.

A huge stone landed a few yards away. Instinctively they fled the open area, running to a wall bordering the Xystus. That was when the stone that almost killed Judah and the rabbi struck.

Rabbi Aaron touched his head and looked at the blood on his hand with detached curiosity.

"You're not afraid to die, are you, Rabbi Aaron?" Judah asked.

Rabbi Aaron stared at him, his eyes gleaming fiercely.

"Today is as good a day to die as any," he said.

"You would have made a good fighter," Judah muttered, shaking his head.

How ironic, he thought. Here I am with the man whose brother I ordered killed, in the very place of assassination, barely escaping death myself by the same forces I unleashed!

Judah felt the overpowering urge to tell Rabbi Aaron the truth about his brother's death.

He stopped himself.

Not now, Judah thought. This is not the time.

"Let's get out of here," Dvorah urged, keeping her crouched position. "It's just random firing; they're not aiming at us."

Rabbi Aaron stood up.

"Yes, now is as good a time as any to leave!" he announced with a lopsided grin on his face.

"Get down, old man," Judah growled, dragging Rabbi Aaron to the ground.

The rabbi resumed his maniacal laughter.

"How long are we going to stay here, Judah?" Dvorah asked.

"I don't know," Judah answered. "Until they stop firing."

Another missile was launched high into the air. It came down on the other side of the Xystus, nearer the Temple complex.

"We're still exposed in this position," Dvorah argued. "You saw what just happened."

Judah pulled at his beard.

"You're correct," he agreed, adding, his voice bitter, "What a nice greeting for our return to Jerusalem."

Judah got to his feet but kept his body bent. He gave a hand to Rabbi Aaron, who stood up straight. Dvorah rose unaided.

"Follow me!" cried Rabbi Aaron, beginning to run. Judah waited for Dvorah to start running before he joined her.

They were alone on the street, and Judah thought that if John's Kannaim were on the lookout for targets, the three of them made convenient ones.

An archer appeared on the rampart. Judah, out of the corner of his eye, saw him fit an arrow to his bow. Judah watched as the arrow flew in the air and lodged in Dvorah's pack. As she ran it fell out, clattering onto the stone street.

Once they made it to the warren of houses in the Lower City, they stopped running. Rabbi Aaron was out of breath and had to stop for a moment. Dvorah was unfazed, neither frightened nor breathing heavily.

"You're quite a girl," he said to her admiringly.

When they got to Rabbi Aaron's house they were in for another surprise.

His home was occupied by three scruffy young men. The house

stank from the occupation.

"Squatters," said Rabbi Aaron with contempt.

The three young men formed a line facing Judah and his companions. The two men at each end held knives in their hands. The man in the middle, his hands empty, had a scraggly reddish beard.

Judah took out his own larger knife. Dvorah took out hers.

"What do you want?" red beard asked.

"Get out!" Rabbi Aaron snarled. "This is my house."

The rabbi's threatening tone caused the three facing him to take a step backward.

Then red beard sneered and pulled out his knife.

"We're not going anywhere," he said. "This house was empty when we took it. It was yours and now it's ours!"

Rabbi Aaron raised his fist above his head. He took a step forward.

"I'm back," Rabbi Aaron said. "If you know what's good for you you'll get out now!" He shouted the last word.

Judah and Dvorah, their knives raised, stepped forward, standing on either side of him.

"If you want trouble," red beard warned, "we'll give it to you. And then, if anything is left of you, you'll have to answer to Simon ben Gioras. He gave us permission to occupy this house."

Rabbi Aaron sneered in return.

"Unless you want more trouble than you can handle you'll get out of here immediately. My daughter-in-law is a good friend of Simon's wife."

There was a moment of silence. Judah could see that the man in the middle was trying to decide what to do. Before Judah could say or do anything to make the fellow leave, the squatter said:

"All right, we'll go. Just let us get our things."

The three didn't have much. They were gone quickly, and when they were out the door, Judah said:

"Well, Rabbi, I know where Reuven gets his balls!"

Rabbi Aaron shot him an angry glance, and in just as angry a voice said:

"This place stinks. We have to clean it up."

Judah leaned against the now-closed door.

"Why did you come back, Rabbi Aaron?"

Rabbi Aaron did not answer. His face softened as he looked down at the floor.

"To witness a miracle?" Dvorah asked, her voice barely above a whisper.

Rabbi Aaron nodded.

"The Master of the Universe parted the Sea of Reeds for Moshe," he said. "He made the sun stand still for Joshua."

"Are you a prophet of the Land of Israel?" asked Judah.

"Aren't we a nation of prophets?" Dvorah retorted.

"Yes, you are right, Dvorah" Rabbi Aaron said. "The miracle is not for me. At Sinai, 600,000 people witnessed the miracle of Moshe and the Tablets of the Law. I wait for a miracle to be witnessed by the thousands of thousands in Judea, the Galilee, the Golan, Idumaea: Our deliverance from the hand of Rome!"

Judah trembled.

Am I hearing the voice of a prophet now?

Rabbi Aaron raised his hands, palms upward.

"An angel of the Lord came to me in a dream. I will die before the next coming of Tishrei." The rabbi's breath came hard, he shook his head back and forth. "Will I die sanctifying the Name of the Lord, with the Shema on my lips?"

Rabbi Aaron's fierce gaze went from Judah to Dvorah.

"'Hear O Israel, the Lord is God, the Lord is One!'" he chanted, his voice filling the once abandoned room.

The rabbi's voice lowered.

"Or will I die cursing the Holy One, Blessed be He?"

A silence just as powerful enveloped the room.

"I do not know. I wait for an answer. That is why I returned to Jerusalem."

Part Seven: Of Orange Flames and White Hair

January – August 70 CE

Chapter One Hundred & Thirty-One

21 Jan 70 CE / 21 Shevat 3830

Judah laughed. He laughed so hard his sides hurt. He laughed so hard tears came to his eyes. He bounced the thick club he was carrying up and down on the stone of the street, bounced it to the rhythm of his laughter.

If only Rabbi Aaron or Reuven were with me now to share this moment, he thought. They would appreciate it. Perhaps they could even answer my question: Is God playing a cosmic joke on us?

Judah stopped laughing. He wiped away the tears.

Seventy-five yards down the road from where he stood the City's grain storehouse was in flames, sending huge clouds of smoke billowing straight up into the winter sky. The grain, enough to last many years, was the newest casualty of the faction fighting.

It could have kept us through a long siege, Judah thought. Now it's gone! In a burst of flame and a puff of smoke!

Judah started laughing again.

The loss could not be made up until the next spring harvest; the previous year had been a sabbatical year when the land was required to lie fallow.

When Judah left Jerusalem, back in the summer, and when he returned four months ago, in the autumn, the City had been divided between two warring factions. John ben Levi, at the head of his own forces and Eleazar ben Simon's Kannaim, held the Temple, its immediate environs, and part of the Lower City. Simon ben Gioras held the Upper City and most of the Lower.

Since Judah's return, the internal fighting had gotten worse. Eleazar ben Simon and many of his Kannaim split from John ben Levi and seized control of the inner court of the Temple. The split had nothing to do with ideology and everything to do with personality.

Thus, what had been a two-way struggle turned into a three-cornered fight, with a subsequent increase in bloodshed.

Eleazar's men took up positions over the Holy Gates. They had almost unlimited supplies of sacred commodities from the Temple. The heights they commanded allowed them to rain missiles down on John's positions in the rest of the Temple complex.

John was able to respond to any attack from Eleazar with his artillery, for he had plenty of stone-throwers, catapults, and spear-throwers.

Despite the on-and-off fighting around the Temple, the sacrifices went on. But not infrequently, innocent priests and those making offerings became victims of the long-range fighting.

John, while assailed from above, also attacked Simon below, over whom he had a height advantage. This positional disadvantage did not stop Simon, often with the help of Jerusalem's population, from trying to take the Temple. Sometimes John's forces would stream out of the Temple complex to attack Simon's men directly.

The result of this fighting, in addition to the death and wounding of combatants, was the destruction, by torching, of the buildings near the Temple.

But the torching of the granary was the worst, Judah thought. We have done Rome's work for her.

Judah had returned to Jerusalem to fight against the Roman legions in defense of the capital. He had not come to kill fellow Jews. Despite this, he was forced to take sides in the fratricidal struggle.

Because Rabbi Aaron's house was in Simon's territory, Judah was drafted into Simon's forces. Once again, this time for a different master, Judah's job was to patrol the streets in the neighborhood where he lived and make sure order was kept. He became a disheartened observer of the organized fighting that broke out at random intervals, fighting which

Judah tried to avoid.

The wind shifted direction. Smoke burned his eyes and nose.

He struck the ground one more time with his stick and sighed. His laughter had dissipated.

Judah faced the Temple. To his right was the City's first and oldest wall. Beyond the wall, ahead and to the right, stood the magnificent palace of the Hashmonaim, where Agrippa and his sister Berenice stayed when they used to visit Jerusalem, in more peaceful times. So far, that palace had not been burnt to the ground.

The buildings in the area where Judah stood were storehouses. Some had already been set aflame in past fighting, others still stood.

Time to go back to Rabbi Aaron's house, he thought. He turned his back to the flames and started quickly down the street. Further west would be a gate that would let him pass through the wall and continue through the Upper City and then the Lower until he reached Rabbi Aaron's house.

Running footsteps sounded behind him. Three men, he guessed.

Are they pursuing me or escaping the fire?

Judah did not want to wait for them and ask. He quickened his pace.

Judah heard his name called. In anger. He recognized the voice of Barak ben Banoch, a fellow fighter from the Galilee with whom Judah had gone on raids when both were outlaws in the north. Barak was a follower of John ben Levi.

Judah whirled to face his pursuers.

"Traitor!" shouted Barak.

A long knife was in his left hand. The man on his left carried a javelin; the man on his right carried a sword.

Have I returned to Jerusalem only to be killed by fellow Jews?

As the three approached Judah moved backward. If he could get far enough west he would be firmly in Simon's territory. There, his hunters would become the hunted.

"Barak!" Judah called. "The word traitor has lost its meaning. When we were fighting Syrians and Romans the word had fierce sting when it referred to real traitors, the toadies of Rome. Now, it simply means someone who fights under a different commander. And why is this? Because our leaders don't get along, each one wanting to be the supreme commander."

"You left John to join that pig, Simon ben Gioras," Barak sneered. "Simon wants the Temple so he can make a deal with Rome. To become the next procurator. But that's not going to happen. We'll kill all you traitors first."

Judah had heard that before. Each side said these exact words about the other.

"Barak, that is insane!" Judah cried, still moving backwards as the three men moved toward him. "Barak, if you kill me there will be one less fighter in the coming—"

Judah stumbled and pitched over onto his back. He fell in a gutter leading to an alley that ended at the wall. He scrambled to his feet, the club still in his hands, and reached the wall just as the three came up to him.

His back to the stone, Judah faced them. Its rough surface dug into his shoulders.

I'm trapped, he thought. Outnumbered, out-armed. I can't run. No way to talk reason to them.

Judah smiled.

In that brief moment of his would-be killers' confusion, Judah leaped forward, his club high in the air. It came down with vicious force on the top of Barak's head. Before Barak crumpled to the ground the club swung a second time, into the stomach of the man to Barak's right.

Judah ran, ran as fast as he could, ran faster than he had ever run before, out of the alley and west down the street.

He was gasping for air when he reached the safety of a patrol from Simon's army. They looked askance at him but he said nothing. He leaned against a building to catch his breath.

Something was happening to him. He had never been as scared as he had been when facing those three. He had come to Jerusalem to die, but not at the hands of other Jews. Would that be his fate? Had he been mad to return?

Judah's breathing gradually slowed to its normal rhythm. He went through the gate in the first wall, through the Upper City, and finally the Lower City, with its jumbled warren of small, cramped houses.

As he arrived at the house of Rabbi Aaron, Judah came to a realization: He had to marry Dvorah, and do it as soon as possible, before he was killed, by Roman or Jew.

Rabbi Aaron greeted him with a grunt, Dvorah with concern.

"What's wrong, Judah?" she asked.

"Three of John's men tried to kill me," he answered.

"Oh no!" Dvorah cried.

"Maybe it's too bad they didn't succeed," Judah responded. "They say starvation is one of the worst ways to die."

"What are you talking about?" Rabbi Aaron asked sharply.

And then Judah started laughing again.

"We burned all the grain!" he said. "If there is a siege before the next harvest Jerusalem will starve."

"Who burned the grain?" Dvorah asked, shocked.

"Does it matter?" Rabbi Aaron asked.

And he, too, started to laugh.

Chapter One Hundred & Thirty-Two
30 Jan 70 CE / 30 Shevat 3830

Judah, the guests, the musicians, even the food servers, all wore expressions of rejoicing and excitement on their faces. Only Rabbi Aaron looked mournful, but then, he rarely smiled anymore.

Dvorah gazed around somberly.

This is definitely not what she wanted.

"We have to be frugal with our money," she had told Judah emphatically. "Hard times are coming. After the fire, the price of bread will rise. It should be a modest wedding, Judah, even more modest than Drusilla's. And for the same reasons. No, even more so. These are dangerous times, Judah."

Judah had scowled.

"You have the right to have as beautiful a wedding as any bride in the Land of Israel," he insisted.

"Not when there is war within the City and war approaching from without," she had countered.

The argument, almost a fight, ended with Judah's silence. Dvorah assumed she had won.

She was wrong.

Two days later a servant of Anat, wife of Simon ben Gioras, came calling on Dvorah.

"Mistress wants to see you!" she announced peremptorily to Dvorah.

Dvorah had no idea what Simon's wife could possibly want and the servant wouldn't say. Dvorah didn't like having to answer such a summons, but since Simon was the ruler of most of the City Dvorah felt she had no choice.

"Dear," Anat declared when Dvorah entered her presence, "your husband-to-be, Judah ben Ezra, told me of your coming wedding. It is to be a simple one. No, I cannot allow that! Not after what Batya has done for me! Why, you were part of her household. I hear you were practically sisters! What would she think of me if I, wife of the ruler of Jerusalem, did not make sure you had the wedding you deserve?"

Dvorah had tried, gently, to argue with her, but only got Anat to agree on skipping the customary period of betrothal and have the wedding as soon as possible.

Earlier today, in the morning, Anat's servants had bathed Dvorah, anointed her with oil, and put makeup on her face. Anat herself had given Dvorah a dress fit for a queen.

Dvorah was uncomfortable with the spectacle her wedding had become. She would have walked away from it all if she hadn't desperately wanted to sanctify her relationship with Judah.

To sanctify it before the both of them died defending Jerusalem.

It was now ten days after the burning of the granary. Dvorah stood under the canopy. Rabbi Aaron had just finished giving the blessing.

Through the veil covering her face, Dvorah looked around the room thinking:

I have more musicians than Drusilla had, and more guests. Even the self-styled ruler of Jerusalem and his wife are in attendance. But, oh, how I miss Drusilla. I have less hope than she had when she married Reuven. What future can Judah and I possibly have?

Judah lifted her veil and gave her the wine, he handed her the gold aureus as a gift and recited the words "Behold, you are consecrated to me with these gifts according to the law of Moses and the people of Israel!" Dvorah's mind drifted far away.

Has Drusilla given birth yet? If Drusilla has a boy will she name him after my Shaul, whom I loved when there was still hope in my life?

And then Dvorah began to cry.

Judah, and others in attendance, smiled at her display of emotion. A few cheered.

They don't understand, Dvorah thought. These are not tears of joy; they are tears of desperation.

My marriage will be barren. It will bear no fruit. I will die before I have the chance to raise a family.

Oh Drusilla! Tell your children about Judah and me, and about my first love Shaul, and his great friendship with their father. Speak of us, so that we shall not be forgotten.

Chapter One Hundred & Thirty-Three

30 Jan 70 CE / 30 Shevat 3830

Reuven was certain that if he had one hundred children with Drusilla he would never get used to the screams.

She sounds worse now, he thought. Are her screams actually louder than the first time?

Reuven wished his father were with him as he waited outside the room where Drusilla was giving birth, with the midwife and his mother in attendance. Though Benjamin stood beside him, and tried to keep him calm, his brother's efforts were not succeeding. With each cry of pain Reuven grew more nervous.

Tikva, twenty months old, shivered in her father's arms every time her mother howled in agony.

"It's all right, it's all right," he tried to reassure her. "Mommy will be fine soon."

Reuven was not sure of that himself.

In the long intervals of silence, Tikva babbled "Baby, baby," with excitement and grabbed at her father's beard.

Reuven had worked to prepare his daughter for a new sibling. Both he and Drusilla told Tikva over and over again that the baby in Mommy's belly was *her* little brother or sister. Benjamin would stand next to him, put his arm around Reuven, and proclaim in a loud voice, with a big smile on his face, "Your Daddy is *my* little brother!"

Reuven bought a doll with a red dress and a yellow kerchief around her black hair, to give Tikva when the baby came, a doll from her new sibling.

For Reuven, there were too many stories among the Jewish people, as far back as Scripture itself, of sibling rivalry gone horribly wrong. Reuven wanted to avoid this at all costs. True, these warning object lessons were always about brothers, but one could never be too careful. Perhaps, if the proper groundwork were laid, things could be harmonious between his children.

Reuven wanted peace not only within his family.

He wanted peace outside it, as well.

This motivated his decision to go with his new friend Hiram on the voyage to Barbarikon. Not only for adventure, not only to increase his fortune, but also to find, as he had once told Drusilla: "some warm, sunny place where I could grow olives and dates and raise sheep and goats. Live peacefully and forget about Rome and war."

No matter that he did not know how to grow olives and dates, or how to raise sheep and goats. He could always learn, or, better yet, hire workers and live like a patrician, like the Roman upper class! Yes, like the Roman upper class.

He hadn't told Drusilla about his plans yet. She would be furious! But she could not stop him, once he was gone. And she would have to forgive him when he—

Another scream, louder than all the rest, broke his reverie. There was silence, and then the sound of a baby crying.

Reuven's heart beat with anticipation. He wanted to run into the room.

Benjamin restrained him.

"You must wait for the midwife!" Benjamin admonished.

The wait seemed forever.

The midwife stepped out. She looked exhausted as she wiped her brow. Taking a deep breath she said:

"Come, see your new son."

Reuven rushed past her and burst into the room.

Drusilla smiled weakly as she held up their new child.

Reuven could hardly believe it; despite the screams, all seemed well.

"Mommy, mommy!" cried Tikva, trying to wriggle out of her father's arms. As he held her tightly she began to cry, the sound mingling with the newborn's own occasional wails.

The married couple tried to speak above the cacophony.

"You have a son and daughter now," Drusilla said happily.

Reuven smiled. He felt as he if could explode from joy.

"Oh, Reuven," his mother cried, "if only your father could see his grandson!" Tears fell from her eyes.

"Father will see him one day," Reuven said with forced certainty.

Ruth looked at her son and Reuven knew that she did not believe him. His mother's look made Reuven doubt it himself.

Drusilla clutched the baby to her body.

"What shall we name him?" Drusilla asked. "I gave our first child her name. Perhaps you should decide on our son's name."

Reuven handed Tikva to his mother. His face grew grave as he considered what to call his new child.

"There were two people close to me who are now dead," he said after a moment's thought. "My friend Shaul and my Uncle Moshe. We shall give our son both names and call him Shaul Moshe."

Drusilla nodded.

"So it shall be," she said.

Reuven smiled, pleased with his choice.

Chapter One Hundred & Thirty-Four

10 Apr 70 CE / 11 Nisan 3830

With a shield in his left hand, a javelin in his right, the height of Jerusalem's eastern wall behind him, and the ground beneath his feet sloping down to the deep Kidron ravine, Judah ben Ezra stared across the abyss at the Tenth Legion constructing its camp on the Mount of Olives.

By the end of the day, will Dvorah, my wife of ten weeks, become a widow?

Or will Roman wives and mothers weep instead?

Will Rabbi Aaron have his miracle, or is this the beginning of the end?

Only God knows.

The Roman legions had come at last, with their infantry, cavalry, and engines of war, headed not by Vespasian, officially emperor and far away in Rome, but by his son, Titus, who had already fought beside his father in Vespasian's Galilee and Judea campaigns and had shown himself to be an able soldier and commander.

North of the City, on Mount Scopus, the Romans were building two camps for their other three legions.

If the Romans were allowed to continue unmolested Jerusalem would truly be surrounded and cut-off. This clear and present danger was like a bucket of cold water flung on a pack of fighting dogs; the factions made a temporary truce and agreed to work together.

Simon ben Gioras, as leader of the largest faction, was put in charge of the operation. He decided the target would be the camp in-progress on the Mount of Olives; the Romans would not be suspecting an attack across the Kidron.

Almost 10,000 men had gathered in the pre-dawn light. Just inside the City wall 10,000 more were held in reserve.

Simon raised his hand and the mass of men followed him down the slope in silence.

Judah descended the steep western flank of the Kidron carefully, anxious not to lose his footing. The smell of the rich earth tickled his nostrils. A cool breeze briefly sprung up to brush the sweat from his forehead.

The armed host of partisans crossed the stream at the bottom and marched up the opposite hill, still silent. When they reached the top thousands of throats erupted in panic-inducing screams. Judah's own throat hurt from shouting; his ears rang from the cries of his comrades.

The Romans were taken completely by surprise. Unarmed, without their protective breastplates and helmets, still in the midst of their dawn chores, they began to flee the Jewish onslaught.

Low laughter came from Judah.

"They thought we're still fighting among ourselves!" he cried to those around him.

The front rank of the partisans caught up with some of the fleeing legionnaires and struck them down with swords and spears. Others were killed by Jewish archers.

Judah saw unfinished huts, sections of palisades already set-up, and even a catapult and stone-thrower.

We need torch-bearers, he thought, to burn their whole camp down.

A fleeing Roman stopped and turned to face Judah. All he had in his hand was a stout digging tool.

"Brave fellow," Judah hissed in Hebrew, to the Roman who he knew did not understand, "what a shame I have to kill you."

The soldier came at Judah swinging the tool. Judah blocked it easily with his shield and then dug his own javelin into the legionnaire's upper stomach. There was a shriek of pain, a spurt of blood, and the writhing body fell to the ground. Judah extricated his javelin and stood over the fallen man, who looked up at Judah, sneered, and uttered a curse in Latin.

"You should have stayed home with your wife and children," Judah responded as he raised his javelin and plunged it into the legionnaire's chest.

A warning cry came from behind Judah.

"Look out!" the voice cried.

Another Roman, this one with a sword in his hand was upon Judah before he had a chance to raise his shield and free the javelin.

The enemy's sword, raised high in the air, came straight down toward Judah's head.

In an instant Judah saw the end of his life.

The sword never reached him. A foot from Judah's head, the man wielding the weapon staggered backwards and collapsed to the ground, an arrow buried deep in his upper left chest.

Judah turned and saw that the archer who had saved his life had notched another arrow to his bow. Before Judah could catch his breath and give thanks for still being alive, another fleeing Roman fell with an arrow in his back.

I'll have to thank that fellow one day, Judah thought.

Javelin again in hand, Judah moved deeper into a Roman camp that was littered with bodies. None were Jewish.

So far, Judah thought. That can't possibly last.

There was a blast of trumpets and a detachment of Roman troops, fully armed, with breastplates and helmets, marched against the flanks of the disorganized Jewish ranks.

The Jews turned, and with yells that were just as chilling as those let loose in the initial assault, charged the Romans like a herd of wild animals.

The Romans fell back.

They're only trained to fight by the book, Judah thought with glee. They don't know how to handle irregulars.

A Roman in full battle gear strode resolutely toward Judah. The first blow of his sword was blocked by Judah's shield. Judah thrust with his javelin; a second blow from the sword deflected the javelin, forcing its tip to the ground and snapping Judah's weapon in two.

The Roman soldier raised his sword in the air. As he brought it down Judah raised his shield with his left hand and pulled out his knife with his right.

The sword crashed down on Judah's shield as it was held high and horizontal. Giving the enemy soldier no time to attack again Judah leaped, knocking the man to the ground. Judah's knife sliced through the short space between his hand and the exposed neck of the legionnaire, cutting deep into the flesh. Before the blade struck Judah saw the look of astonishment in the man's eyes.

Judah got to his feet as the life slowly flowed from the fallen soldier. His lance now useless, Judah picked up the Roman's sword.

What would Reuven do? Judah thought sardonically.

Judah raised the sword high in the air. With one blow he lopped off the head of the man on the ground.

The partisans from the city now had control of the entire camp. They paused in their attack, not sure what to do next. Even Simon ben Gioras, who had been in the thick of the action, did not seem to know what to do.

The blare of trumpets woke them from their stupor. Fresh Roman troops appeared, more and more of them rushing to challenge the invaders who had seized their camp.

The tide of battle turned. The new legionnaires pushed the Jews out of their camp. Pressing their attack, they chased the Jews down the steep western slope. Their higher position gave the Romans an advantage. Now it was Jewish fighters who fell. But when the partisans from Jerusalem reached the bottom and crossed the stream, they turned and put up a determined resistance.

The fighting went on all morning, with neither side giving in, as spears, stones, and arrows flew back and forth. Whenever a Roman spear crashed against his shield and fell to the ground, Judah picked it up and hurled it back.

At noon, Titus, the Roman commander, appeared on the ridge with more reinforcements. Some of these stood guard with him, others resumed work on the fortifications. Titus called back those in the ravine. The weary Roman soldiers, who had just fought a long engagement against the Jewish irregulars, trudged up the steep eastern slope in orderly ranks, their eyes on the enemy at the bottom.

"We've won!" screamed Judah.

But the fighting was not over and the battle not yet won. As the Romans retreated fresh fighters emerged from the City, thousands and thousands of them. Passing by their own tired comrades, they charged up the hill after the Romans, whooping and shouting as they ran.

Judah watched with admiration as Simon ben Gioras, who had been resting by the stream with the first wave of fighters, joined the second wave in their upward charge.

The Romans broke ranks and ran pell-mell up the slope, trying to get away from the Jewish onslaught. The Roman soldiers above, working on the camp, hearing the cries and seeing their fleeing comrades, were overcome with terror. Fearful that the Jewish attack was unstoppable and thinking that Titus himself had fled, they abandoned their positions and took flight.

The partisans would have captured the camp a second time if Titus and the men around him had not stood firm. Titus rallied more Roman troops and auxiliaries, including archers whose fusillades stopped the Jews from advancing further. The partisans were slowly driven from the Mount of Olives, off the hillside, and into the valley, where they joined those who had remained at the bottom. The Romans did not pursue them.

Simon, taking up the rear of his retreating men, shook his fist at

Titus who stood looking down.

"Victory, the first of many!" he cried, in Hebrew and then in Latin.

Titus only smiled, a smile of supreme confidence and certainty.

We'll wipe that smile off his face the next time he meets us, Judah thought. Let him look at his ruined camp and the bloody corpses of his men.

Simon signaled to the men to return to Jerusalem. There had been enough fighting for one day.

The partisans went up the western slope and through the eastern gate. As Judah filed back with the other fighters he shouted, "Rejoice!" startling the grimy, dust-covered men around him.

They soon recovered.

"Rejoice!" shouted hundreds of men, "Rejoice!" shouted thousands more joining their fellow Jews in unity.

Praised be the Master of the Universe, thought Judah. Rabbi Aaron has his miracle!

Chapter One Hundred & Thirty-Five

11 Apr 70 CE / 12 Nisan 3830

Small gray-black sparrows circled lazily under a blue sky free of clouds. Across the Kidron the shining mass of the Temple blazed white and gold. Amram, standing at the edge of the Roman camp on the Mount of Olives, nervously wiped the sweat from his forehead.

It was not the temperature making him perspire.

Amram was terrified.

The harsh gaze of Rufus was on him. Amram could not bear to turn to the right and face the Roman staring at him.

What does he want of me now?

It was the day after the Jewish attack on the Tenth Legion's camp. Order had already been restored there. Anger and desire for revenge seethed among the Romans. Amram could feel it in the man who now controlled him: Rufus, the Roman intelligence officer.

Rufus was tall, as tall as a German, with a shock of red hair and blue eyes. Amram knew little about him, except that he was Roman through and through. Amram suspected that before his current position Rufus had been a centurion.

Rufus was smooth and aristocratic. In addition to Latin and Greek, he spoke perfect Aramaic and could even converse in Hebrew.

Amram was one of his spies. All of Amram's dealings with Rufus had been in Caesarea. When Rufus showed up in Yavne looking for him Amram almost fainted.

Amram had been busy negotiating a price for his eight surplus donkeys. Unable to find anyone in Yavne willing to buy the animals for a fair and reasonable amount, Amram was thrilled to have a traveling trader approach him with a request to purchase the donkeys. Just as Amram was about to clinch a satisfying deal, Rufus appeared as if by magic. The trader then disappeared just as quickly.

Amram could not control his trembling.

"What are you so afraid of?" Rufus had asked, the sly smile slowly fading from his face. "You are loyal to Rome, aren't you?"

Amram nodded, unable to speak.

How did he know I was here? Amram asked himself. What does he want with me?

Rufus had laughed at his confusion.

"So sorry to have ruined your sale," Rufus said, his voice brimming with mock concern, "but Rome can always use eight good donkeys." Then, he added, sharply, "And I can use you."

"H-How?" Amram's voice shook.

"Rome is about to crush Jerusalem," responded Rufus. " I need you inside the City to inform me of its goings-on."

"Me? Why me?" Amram asked quickly.

"Come, Amram. You're smarter than that. We leave tomorrow."

Amram had no choice. He left for Jerusalem, riding on one donkey and leading another, while Rufus rode with a detachment of cavalry. Amram, as he made the ascent to the Holy City, comforted himself with the thought that Rufus paid him what the eight donkeys originally cost, forty aurei, and because he was forced to leave Yavne so quickly he avoided having to share any of the proceeds with Reuven and the doctor.

Amram's gaze went from the Temple and the free-flying sparrows to the ground at his feet. He kicked at a pebble.

"It's time, Amram," Rufus said, at last breaking the silence between them.

Amram sighed heavily and turned to look at Rufus.

"I'm afraid," Amram said. "If I go now, they'll know I'm a spy."

"Then it's up to you to make sure that they don't," Rufus said harshly. "I'm sure you're capable of that."

Amram stared back down at the ground. There was no way he could get out of it.

"Camillus the quartermaster has prepared your supplies," Rufus said. "You can sell the grain and keep the money. I want intelligence: the strength of their forces, the morale of the fighters and the people, and conditions in Jerusalem itself."

Amram nodded.

Perhaps I should remain in Jerusalem once I get there, he thought. After yesterday's victory the City may hold out against Rome. In truth, I'm more afraid of Rufus and the Romans when I'm with them than I am of the partisans. There's much information I can give the defenders of the City.

"Amram," Rufus said, breaking into his thoughts, "do not think of defecting to the rebels, because if you do, when we take Jerusalem—and we will, make no mistake about that—I will find you and before I'm through with you, you will curse your mother for having brought you into this world."

Amram looked up at the Roman.
Amram barely managed to hide the defiance in his eyes.

Chapter One Hundred & Thirty-Six

13 Apr 70 CE / 14 Nisan 3830

Rabbi Aaron's eyes, ears, and nose were filled with the sights, sounds, and smells of the inner court of the Temple: Men, rich and poor, well-dressed and threadbare, from Jerusalem itself, the north, the south, and even Jews from beyond the Land, milling about in preparation for the festival of Passover to start this evening. Sheep, cows, birds; bleating, mooing, beating wings, cacophonously competing with the buzz of random human conversation. The smells of the animals, and even the people, mixing with the odors of blood and incense and sharp smoke wafting in from the sacrifices at the altar.

The rhythms and rituals of life go on, Rabbi Aaron thought, in spite of the presence of four Roman legions outside Jerusalem.

He stood against the south wall of the enclosure. Ahead and to the left loomed the Temple; to his right was the Court of the Women.

If the Romans destroy this, will Torah and the Jewish people survive? he asked himself.

Rabbi Aaron shook his head and fought back tears.

There is Yavne, and Rabbi Johanan and his Academy, and my sons, he answered. They will continue even if we are doomed here. But why the gloom? Wasn't there a great victory yesterday? Perhaps Jerusalem will escape destruction and I *will* have my miracle.

Rabbi Aaron scanned the crowd. Eleazar ben Simon's Kannaim, who controlled this area of the Temple complex, had opened the gates and allowed worshippers to enter. Rabbi Aaron had asked Judah to join him, but the gap-toothed rebel had simply grinned sardonically and responded by saying Eleazar's men might let him in, but he would never get out again.

Rabbi Aaron sighed, shook his head, and stared down at his feet.

He couldn't figure out how he felt about Judah. On the one hand, he was clearly one of the robbers who had started Jerusalem's plunge into the abyss. On the other hand, he seemed to be a man who had principles and lived by them, and compared to those who came after him during the revolt, Judah was almost a righteous man.

Rabbi Aaron sighed again and looked around.

Across the court, sometimes hidden by the crowd that moved back and forth, Rabbi Aaron thought he saw a familiar form.

Yes, that's him! Amram, the trader who took us to Yavne! What is he doing here? Perhaps he has some news of my family!

Rabbi Aaron was about to move away from his station by the wall when a whirlwind of disruption struck the inner court of the Temple. Scattered throughout the crowd, groups of men, as if by prearranged signal, began whipping out weapons hidden in their clothes and attacking those around them. Moments later Kannaim came rushing out of the court chambers to confront the attackers. Knives, swords, and javelins flashed as men who had been temporary allies now sought to kill each other.

Screams and wails from the innocent bystanders echoed throughout the court, accompanied by the shouts and curses of the fighting men.

Rabbi Aaron stood rooted to his spot.

Am I afraid to die? Rabbi Aaron wondered.

Despite the chaos around him, Rabbi Aaron's cool analysis brought him to the conclusion that he was not.

If the Master of the Universe has decided it is time for me to die, then I will die.

Rabbi Aaron stayed to watch the fighting instead of fleeing with the other non-combatants.

The struggle now was between two groups of fighters. The newcomers who had snuck in their weapons began to gain the upper hand. Some of Eleazar's men fled with the common citizens and priests, others locked themselves in the court's chambers.

To Rabbi Aaron the conflict seemed to last forever, but from the positions of the shadows and the sun in the sky he knew that the struggle had been brief.

Quiet reigned in the holy court littered with bodies.

John ben Levi entered to the cheers of the men who had driven out the Kannaim.

"The Temple is ours!" he cried triumphantly.

Rabbi Aaron stifled a shriek of dismay.

God is indeed playing a joke on us, Rabbi Aaron thought, wringing his hands. First unity, then defeating the Romans, and now back to killing each other.

"Why, Oh Lord, why?" he cried out in anguish. "Why do you permit this?"

Rabbi Aaron saw a man lying on the ground stagger to his feet. The look of fear on the man's face was as clear as the sky above his head.

It was Amram.

He took a step backward and then forward, and stood as if he did not know what to do next.

John ben Levi noticed Amram. He pointed at him and shouted something.

Two armed men walked quickly toward Amram. As Amram screamed in protest the men grabbed each arm and dragged him away.

Chapter One Hundred & Thirty-Seven
1 May 70 CE / 2 Iyyar 3830

The wind blew in from the sea. Reuven tasted the salt in his nostrils. He looked at Hiram. Envy, like the distant waves, washed over him.

"Good journey, my friend," Reuven said. "I wish I could go with you."

"It's not too late to join me!" Hiram responded hopefully. "I can wait for you."

Hiram was about to mount the donkey that would take him to Caesarea. From there he was to sail to Alexandria in Egypt, and then to the East over the Erythraean Sea.

"I can't, you know that," Reuven replied mournfully.

"I understand," Hiram responded, nodding his head sympathetically.

"Instead of sneaking off with you I may have to sneak off to Jerusalem," Reuven began. "The siege has started. I can't go on this great adventure with you to the mysterious East. My father is in the City. If things get bad, I may have to go to him."

Hiram nodded again and held out his arms. Reuven embraced him. Hiram mounted his donkey. As Reuven looked up at him, Hiram glanced back down fiercely.

"That 500 aurei you invested with me will come back to you as 10,000, no, 15,000!" Hiram's eyes gleamed as he announced the figures for Reuven's gain.

Reuven believed him.

"Till we meet again," Reuven said.

"Till we meet again," replied Hiram and spurred his donkey to a brisk trot.

Reuven stood there, watching, as man and mount traveled down the road. It was not until Hiram went left and disappeared from view that Reuven turned away and began a dejected walk home. A path he had longed to take closed to him, by his own choice.

Drusilla was in the garden, singing, Shaul Moshe in her arms. Tikva was dancing with uneasy steps around the fig tree, moving her body in time to the rhythm of her mother's song. It was one that Reuven had heard her sing many times before; that song was one of the few things

Drusilla remembered from her childhood, in a language she could barely recall. The cheerful melody and rhythm nevertheless always filled Reuven with melancholy the way Drusilla rendered it.

Tikva spotted her father.

"Daddy, Daddy!" she cried with delight, and toddled over to him. Reuven scooped his daughter into his arms and kissed her.

Drusilla gave her husband a warm smile.

"Did you say goodbye to your friend?" she asked.

"Yes."

"Good. I'm glad you're not going with him. And I'm glad you didn't invest any of your money with him. It would have just been throwing it away."

Reuven said nothing.

"You don't look very happy about not going," Drusilla said, anger in her voice.

"I'm not."

"Are you really so anxious to leave your children and your wife for how long even you cannot say?"

Reuven pulled his face away from Tikva's little hands that had been grasping his beard.

"The Erythraean Sea and Barbarikon would have been better than Jerusalem," he said heavily.

"What does Jerusalem have to do with it?" Drusilla asked sharply.

Reuven put Tikva down. He sighed.

"If things get bad in Jerusalem, I may have to get Father out," he said.

"No!" Drusilla cried. Her voice was edged with hysteria. "I forbid it! Your father made his decision, he knew the consequences, he left without saying a word to anyone. Your responsibility to him is over; your responsibility is to your children's father now!"

Reuven gave his wife a long look. Once again he did not reply to her. His head bowed and his heart heavy, he walked into the house without saying a word.

Chapter One Hundred & Thirty-Eight

1 May 70 CE / 2 Iyyar 3830

Judah's eardrums throbbed. The balls and heels of his feet hummed. The Roman battering ram crashed into the City wall, metal head butting against solid stone.

The battle for Jerusalem has begun in earnest, Judah thought. Everything before? Mere skirmishes. We won most of those. Now victory is less certain. The wall holds; how much longer?

Judah stood on the rampart of the Third Wall, not far from Hippicus Tower. Four hundred yards away the Romans had set up a fortification.

A large stone rested in his hands. A few feet to his left a fighter with a flaming brand also waited. The Romans below operating the battering ram were protected by a stout screen held by uprights attached to the war machine's housing.

The Third Wall, the last to be built, enclosed Bezetha. It ran from the northeast corner of the Temple complex, enclosed Bezetha, and ended on the east side of the City, at the juncture with the other two walls, not far from the three towers that Herod built to honor his brother, his wife, and his friend, Hippicus. It was this wall that was under attack from the Roman battering rams.

The Jews had done everything to stop them from bringing up the rams. They fought from the wall and from the ground. The Romans paid a heavy price as they built their platforms, set up their engines, and finally moved the rams into positions.

If they are not stopped here, Judah thought, and the wall falls, it is only a matter of time until the City itself falls.

Judah gripped the stone impatiently.

Shouts came from below as the Romans operating the ram pulled it back and began to propel it forward.

They did not finish the motion. Screams that made Judah's hair stand on end interrupted the Roman assault as Jews who poured out of a secret gate near Hippicus Tower overwhelmed the war machine's crew. They tore off the protective screens, attacked the legionnaires, and then withdrew. At that moment the men on the walls let loose with their weapons. Judah threw his stone down as hard as he could. The man to his left flung his firebrand.

Simultaneous attacks by Jews on all the rams stopped the battering.

The engines abandoned, hordes of partisans streamed from the gate armed with swords, spears, and flaming torches. Judah joined them, sword in right hand, shield in left.

A first wave of legionnaires rushed out to save the engines. They were overwhelmed by Jewish numbers and ferocity. A second wave swept out, trying to overcome the partisan resistance and stop the Jews with torches from firing the rams.

A Roman soldier strode toward Judah. He was in full battle gear, with a larger shield and stronger sword. From the first clash of swords and shields Judah knew he was outmatched in weapons and training.

Am I to die here? he wondered, blinking the sweat from his eyes, stepping backwards, desperately trying to ward off the sword strikes that seemed to come from every direction.

Judah saw confidence in enemy eyes; he knew fear showed in his own.

And then it happened. Perhaps the Roman grew careless, perhaps he tripped over one of the stones that had been hurled from above. No matter, he fell forward.

Judah had to leap out of the way.

Judah stood over the Roman. Now fear was in the Roman's eyes, triumph in his own. Judah slashed the legionnaire's sword arm and took his sword.

Judah looked down, and said, in a language that he knew the fallen warrior did not understand:

"Was it what you pagans call fate, or the hand of the Holy One, Blessed be He?"

And with that Judah drove the Roman's own sword deep into the struggling man's throat.

Judah's triumph was short-lived.

A cavalry charge dispersed the partisans, driving them back into the City. The Romans extinguished the flames that threatened their battering rams and replaced the protective screens over them. They deployed forces opposite the wall to prevent Jewish sorties: three rows of infantry, a line of archers, and three rows of cavalry. For the moment, they left off battering the wall.

Judah, back on the rampart, looked down at the battering rams sitting quietly.

It's not over, he thought.

Chapter One Hundred & Thirty-Nine

2 May 70 CE / 3 Iyyar 3830

Judah wanted to stop up his ears so he wouldn't hear the screams.

It wasn't just dead fighters left behind when the partisans were driven back. The Romans had captured a live fighter and crucified him before the City walls.

The crucified man was screaming in agony. Judah forced himself to listen because he owed it to his brother warrior.

The partisan's arms were tied and nailed to the crossbar, his legs to the upright. A stake had been driven into his seat. He had not been there very long; it could take days before death would end his agony.

Judah, from the rampart, looked away, first down, and then around.

He cries for the ravaged Land, Judah thought.

The suburbs of Jerusalem, once bright green from trees and parkland, were now a dark desert of denuded hills, its trees cut down to build the Roman platforms and towers.

Anyone who had seen Jerusalem before the siege would not recognize it now, Judah thought.

Another scream made Judah shudder.

An archer walked up to the rampart. He stared across the space that separated him from the fighter writhing on the upright and crossbeam.

The archer gave a quick glance at Judah and resumed staring into the distance, his brow furrowed.

"You don't remember me, do you?" he said to Judah, almost out of the side of his mouth.

"Do I know you?" Judah asked, puzzled.

"I saved your life on the Mount of Olives."

"It was you!" Judah exclaimed. "I owe you my life."

The archer nodded.

"I saved one Jewish life," he said. "I'm now about to take another. I'm going to put this fellow out of his misery."

The archer fitted an arrow to his bow, his brow still furrowed.

"You can hit him from here?" Judah asked, amazed.

"I think so." A pause. "I know so." Another pause. "I hope so, with God's help," he added.

He took several deep breaths.

What a skill, Judah thought. He must be gauging how to point the arrow.

The archer took one more breath and held it. He raised the bow and arrow, holding it steady for the briefest moment before letting the arrow fly.

It arced high in the air. Judah watched its trajectory, fascinated.

The arrow came down one or two feet to the right of the struggling captive.

The archer seemed unfazed. He fitted another arrow to his bow and once again took aim.

The arrow flew high into the air, this time coming down one or two feet to the left of its intended mark.

The archer grunted.

"I've got it now," he said, more to himself than to Judah.

The archer took several deep breaths. He fitted the third arrow to his bow. He mumbled some words.

A prayer, no doubt, Judah thought.

Judah watched as the arrow took off on its flight.

Its motion is beautiful, Judah marveled.

His eyes fixed on the arrow and his brother warrior still writhing in agony on the upright and crossbeam, Judah now held his own breath as he waited for the arrow to descend.

Chapter One Hundred & Forty

2 May 70 CE / 3 Iyyar 3830

The screams of the crucified Jewish prisoner were unnerving Amram. He couldn't concentrate on what Rufus was saying.

"I asked you, why did it take you so long to get back?" Rufus' voice was harsh, and his question was accompanied by a slap to Amram's face.

Amram trembled and shook.

"I almost didn't make it back at all!" he shouted.

"Explain," Rufus said, in a low, threatening voice.

"They arrested me for being a spy," Amram said.

"Who arrested you?"

"The partisans. They said the Romans must have sent me with the grain to spy on them. They confiscated the grain and my donkeys. They took all the money I had. They held me in prison and said they might even execute me without bothering to try me." Amram shivered at the memory.

"How did you get out?"

"I told them if they let me go and returned my donkeys and my money I could go back to Yavne and get more grain for them."

"They believed you?"

Amram heard suspicion in the question.

"I'm here, aren't I?"

Rufus rubbed his smooth cheeks and continued to look at Amram suspiciously.

"Tell me about conditions in Jerusalem," he ordered. "Remember, you're not the only spy we have there. If you lie to me I'll have you crucified also!"

Amram swallowed hard.

"Food is getting scarce and expensive," he began. "The common people are hungry and frightened. They want peace and are willing to surrender."

"And the revolutionaries?" Rufus interrupted.

"They will never surrender!" Amram replied fiercely, trying to stifle the pride in his voice. "They will fight to the death."

"What is the status of their forces?"

Amram swallowed hard again. He wanted to lie, but feared that Rufus might already know the answer and was simply testing him.

"John ben Levi, through a trick, took over the inner court of the Temple, driving out the Kannaim. But now they have joined forces under his command again. Simon ben Gioras controls the rest of the City."

"Numbers!" Rufus demanded, snapping his fingers. "I want numbers!"

Amram sighed. Was this a test? It might very well be.

"John has 6,000 of his own men," Amram began reluctantly. "The Kannaim who have joined him number 2,400. Simon commands 10,000 men plus an additional 5,000 Idumaeans."

"Are they still fighting among themselves?"

Amram's eyes narrowed as he looked at Rufus and suppressed his anger.

"When you threaten, they unite."

Rufus laughed.

"In the end it won't matter," he chuckled. "Well, we'll wait a decent amount of time and send you back there."

Amram was about to protest when another scream made him jump. Tears sprang to his eyes and he sniffled.

Rufus laughed again.

"Stop sniveling, Amram. Be glad that's not you up there."

Amram stared at the ground.

Yes, he thought. Coward that I am I'm glad it's not me.

A cry from the prisoner ended with a loud gurgling sound.

Rufus, looking puzzled, ran to the upright and crossbar that held the prisoner. Amram followed close behind.

And then Amram saw what he could only describe as a miracle.

The prisoner was dead, freed from his suffering, an arrow through his neck.

Chapter One Hundred & Forty-One

4 May 70 CE / 5 Iyyar 3830

Judah and Dvorah stood alone on the rampart. It was early afternoon. A strong wind blew across their cheeks in more of a slap than a caress. Below, unmolested, the Roman battering ram crashed over and over again into an unyielding wall.

Sooner or later the wall will collapse, Judah thought. It was a mistake to abandon its defense.

From the very beginning of Titus' attempt to breach the wall the Jews had fought stubbornly to stop the Romans, making them pay a heavy price for continuing the assault. There were strikes from the wall and ground sorties. They had begun using the artillery that Simon had captured from Cestius. At first Simon's forces did not use these war engines effectively, lacking experience, but as days went by they learned to turn Roman artillery against its former owners.

Dvorah had joined one of the ballista units. Despite being the daughter of a Gamla trader, she showed mechanical ability, and helped the men figure out how to make the device work the way they wanted it to. She also served as part of the crew during battles, sometimes pulling the trigger, sometimes moving the lever to put tension in the cords. She helped carry the stones that served as the ballista's ammunition.

Judah was proud of her.

Unfortunately the tactical situation changed when the Romans placed towers on top of the platforms they had succeeded in building. Seventy-five feet high, the towers held the lighter engines, and spearmen, bowmen, and stone throwers. These successfully bombarded the defenders on the wall, forcing them off, while they themselves were out of reach of Jewish weapons. Sorties sent out to eliminate the towers failed; they were too heavy to overturn and fireproof because they were encased in iron.

The decision was made to abandon active defense of the wall. Judah had tried to argue against that decision, but he could not come up with a plan to counter the towers.

"There's nothing to be done anymore," he said, sighing and turning to look at Dvorah.

"Come, Judah," she said. "You alone cannot stop them."

Judah shook his head sadly in agreement.

As they walked through Bezetha, now almost abandoned, a troubling thought that had nothing to do with Jerusalem's peril came to Judah.

"Dvorah," he began almost hesitantly, "it's been almost two months since—"

"Yes, I know," she interrupted, reading his thoughts. "I cannot say, Judah. It is possible."

"Maybe, maybe, because we haven't been eating so well?" he offered.

She sighed and stopped walking.

"I do not think so," she said. "We must be honest with ourselves, Judah. Surely you must have noticed that my breasts have become firmer."

Judah, who had also stopped walking, gasped for air.

"Yes," he whispered. "I have. I wondered about that."

"It's a sign, Judah, a sign."

Judah trembled and then slammed a fist into his thigh.

"I should never have brought you back to this accursed City," he said angrily. "We should have stayed in Yavne." He shook with rage now. "I should have gone with Reuven and that fop Hiram on their voyage." Judah took several deep breaths. Calmly, now, he continued, "I'm getting you out of here. I'm taking you back to Yavne."

"There's a siege, Judah," Dvorah replied, smiling. "How will you get me through the Roman lines?"

Judah smashed his right fist into his left palm.

"I will find a way!" he insisted.

"No you won't," Dvorah said gently. "Because I refuse to go. I do not want our child to be a slave to Rome. I will die in this City you call accursed, unless the Holy One, Blessed be He, decides to give us a miracle and save Jerusalem."

"Then I forbid you to risk your life and take part in any combat!" Judah shouted.

"You forbid me?" Dvorah asked, her eyes twinkling and her voice mocking.

Dvorah's defiance both angered and aroused Judah.

"Yes, I forbid you!"

"You cannot stop me, Judah," Dvorah said simply.

We'll see about that, Judah thought.

Chapter One Hundred & Forty-Two

10 May 70 CE / 11 Iyyar 3830

There will be no more miracles, Amram thought.

He stood in Bezetha, inside what had once been the third wall, under the watchful gaze of Rufus, not far from the ruins of what had been a pavilion where the people of Jerusalem, and beyond, held wedding celebrations and festive meals for family and friends.

Four days ago, on the fifteenth day of the siege, the third wall had finally been breached under the incessant pounding of the battering rams. Titus demolished a large part of it, along with the northern suburbs of the City. He occupied an area from the ancient Camp of the Assyrians to the Kidron Valley, staying out of bowshot from the second wall, which the Jews defended fiercely. John's forces, from Antonia and the northern colonnade of the Temple, and Simon's, from the approach near the Tomb of John Hyrcanus and as far as the gate by which water was brought to Hippicus Tower, fought the Romans from dawn to dusk, attacking from the wall and sallying out in company strength to meet them in hand-to-hand-combat.

It had taken a while, but the battering ram Titus brought against the middle tower of the north section of the second wall finally succeeded in making a narrow opening. Roman troops began lining up to enter the breach.

Rufus looked down at Amram.

"One wall remaining now," Rufus said with satisfaction. "Then Jerusalem is ours. Come with me, the General wants you with us."

Amram shivered with fear.

"No, I don't want to go," he said.

"You're always sniveling," Rufus retorted. "Be glad I never sent you back into Jerusalem again. There is nothing to fear at this point. The General is entering with 1,000 heavy infantry and his special bodyguard. He wants you to address the people."

Amram's eyes grew wide.

Oh no, he thought. They will know I'm a traitor.

"Sir," Amram said hurriedly, "it's a mistake to enter with only 1,000 men. They'll be trapped inside the wall by the partisans."

Rufus laughed with amusement.

"So now Amram the petty trader has become a great military tactician, greater even than General Titus himself!"

Am I more afraid of Rufus or of what happens if I go with them? Amram wondered.

"Amram, you slimy worm, you really have no choice. Either you come with me now and address your people or I kill you on the spot."

It took Amram several moments to gather his wits about him.

He followed Rufus toward the breach.

Rufus walked up to a man in full battle dress who stood at the head of a large formation of infantrymen. He looked about thirty years old, with a broad face, thin lips, a prominent nose, large ears, and close-set eyes.

Rufus greeted General Titus as if they were old comrades.

General Titus looked Amram in the eye.

Amram looked away, down at the ground.

"Do you speak Greek?" Titus asked.

Amram nodded.

"I want you to tell your people the following: If the partisans wish to fight without harming the citizens they are free to march out and fight us elsewhere. Rome has no desire to destroy Jerusalem or harm its civilians."

Amram nodded again. He wanted to tell Titus that something was wrong, that the fact that there was quiet after the breach was made, and fighting had ceased, most likely meant that they would be walking into a trap.

Amram remained silent, not knowing whether it was fear of offering tactical advice to a Roman general or the desire to actually see Titus and his infantrymen bloodied by partisan cunning.

Titus, Rufus, and Amram, along with the Roman host of 1,000 heavy infantry and Titus' special bodyguard, passed through the breach in the second wall and entered the area where the wool shops, forges, and cloth market stood.

Amram began his task of proclaiming to the people Titus' message, expecting, at any moment, to be killed by a Jewish arrow, spear, or stone.

Chapter One Hundred & Forty-Three

10 May 70 CE / 11 Iyyar 3830

The smell of metal was so strong that Judah could taste it on his tongue. He grimaced as he listened with disbelief to Amram announce Titus' offer.

Of course, Judah thought. The Romans want us out of here. We know the streets, we know the houses. It's our territory; they will pay a heavy price trying to take Jerusalem if we continue to resist.

Judah stood half-hidden in the open doorway of the metal forge. Across the opening, also half-hidden, was another fighter whom Judah did not know. In the back, as if there was no threat of a Roman incursion, Rabbi Hania supervised workers who were repairing or fabricating new weapons in the metal forge.

Judah regretted the contempt he had for Rabbi Hania back in the days just before the revolution started.

Hania's a good man, he thought.

Judah felt no such admiration for Amram.

"That traitorous rat!" exclaimed Judah. The fighter a few feet to his right gave him a curious glance. "I know him," explained Judah. "He's working for the Romans now."

The fighter smiled.

"Here's your chance to make this his last day working for them," he said jovially.

There was enough time from the forced opening in the second wall until the entry of the Roman troops for the partisans to gather their own forces, position them, and wait until the Romans were deep into Jewish territory. Once trapped inside the area between the first wall and the second, almost all of which was still standing, they would be unable to escape through the narrow breach the ram made.

The clatter of the metal workshop went on as Judah waited to hear the war-cry that signaled the start of the assault on the Romans. Judah wasn't sure if it would come from John or Simon. Unlike the disciplined Romans, there was no organized chain of command for the coming battle.

A strength and a weakness, Judah thought.

A piercing shout broke the quotidian noise around him. It was followed immediately by hundreds of war-whoops as thousands of partisans poured out of their hiding places in the buildings and on the rooftops and set upon the surprised Romans.

Some legionnaires, marching alone, were cut down at once by the onslaught. Others gathered in groups of threes, their backs to each other, as they tried to defend themselves against a greater number of attackers on the ground. From the assaults above, they were defenseless.

Judah, along with six others, surrounded such a triad. The Romans fought bravely, Judah noted with admiration, but their struggle was doomed to fail. As Judah clashed sword and shield with one of the legionnaires, another partisan slashed the infantryman's arm. The wounded man, his arm useless and bleeding severely, quickly succumbed to his two attackers. The two men remaining in the triad were then killed as quickly.

There was a large core of several hundred expeditionary soldiers who remained together. In their center Judah saw Amram, a tall red-haired man, and someone who looked as if he were issuing orders to those around him.

Titus? Judah wondered.

This core was subjected to wave after wave of ferocious attacks by thousands of partisans. But the legionnaires locked shields, forming a solid defensive phalanx that the Jews could not break through.

Their discipline saves them, Judah thought.

Slowly the Romans withdrew, marching steadily backward to the wall's opening. It was only when they began filing through the breach that the partisans were able to kill some of those in the tail end of the retreat.

The Romans had been expelled from the area between the walls. A shout of triumph went up from the Jewish fighters. Immediately many went to fill the breach to prevent the Romans from returning.

Judah, exhausted, gasped for breath and leaned against the liberated wall. He was thirsty and hungry. The constant fighting was draining him. His fellow fighters, too.

Aren't the Romans sick of this, also? he wondered.

This latest clash is a victory for us, he thought, regardless of what the ultimate outcome will be. I have to tell Dvorah about the battle.

Judah was glad he had forbidden Dvorah to take part in the fighting and that he had ordered her to remain at Rabbi Aaron's house. The battlefield was no place for a pregnant woman.

Judah sighed.

The second wall is ours again, he thought. I am tired, thirsty, and hungry. I'm going back to see my wife before returning to battle.

Judah left the wall and began walking to Rabbi Aaron's house, passing the Temple, passing Xystus, looking curiously at the common people he saw going about their business in the war-torn City.

They were different than they had been even a month ago; then talkative and ebullient, now subdued and downcast. Some were hollow-eyed as they glanced around; the scarcity of food was starting to produce hungry bellies and anxious faces.

When Judah reached Rabbi Aaron's house he found the Torah scholar sitting at the table staring down at a closed scroll.

"Rabbi, we won another victory!"

Rabbi Aaron responded with a weak smile.

"Where's Dvorah?" Judah asked. "I want to tell her about the battle."

Rabbi Aaron shrugged.

"Dvorah!" Judah called in a loud voice.

There was no answer.

"Where is she?" Judah demanded. "Did she go out seeking food?"

Again Rabbi Judah shrugged. Then he said:

"She left, Judah. She left. And she told me that she is *not* coming back."

Chapter One Hundred & Forty-Four

28 May 70 CE / 29 Iyyar 3830

Fire danced at the end of the torch. Dvorah held it carefully as she walked down the tunnel, making sure not to let the flames kiss the upright wooden pillars that supported the ceiling of the newly constructed mine.

Embrace of wood and flame would come soon enough.

Dvorah had begged John ben Levi and his lieutenants to let her lead the way into one of the tunnels once all was ready. She reassured them that after spending days in total darkness in a basement next to her dead father, with Roman soldiers roaming through the defeated Gamla above, nothing scared her anymore.

Hadn't she helped with the underground digging?

And so they had given her permission to lead the way with her torch into this tunnel.

It had been eighteen days since she left Rabbi Aaron's house. She held no anger towards Judah; she understood why he had forbidden her to join the fight against the Romans again.

There was new life inside her; she had no doubt about that now. But what could she give her child? Slavery to Rome?

No. Better never to be born.

The fragrance of freshly dug earth filled Dvorah's nostrils. The ground was hard and uneven under her feet. Eerie shadows cast by the torchlight on the uprights played along the barely-lit walls and ceilings.

The tunnel opened up into a large man-made cavern, whose roof was wooden beams supported by wooden uprights, the beams themselves supporting the land above them. Dvorah thought she heard the movement of men and equipment above her.

Or was it just her imagination?

Her torch was daubed with pitch and bitumen. It burned hot.

Dvorah murmured a prayer, asking God to grant her success and His people victory. She walked to the upright at the furthest left corner. She touched her torch to it. As soon as a flame leaped onto the upright, she went to the next one, and then to the one after that, until row after row of the uprights supporting the ceiling were ablaze.

As she stood where the tunnel opened to the cavern, she watched the flames as they curled from the uprights.

Then she turned, torch still in hand, and began running through the tunnel.

Her right sandal caught on a clump of dirt and stone. Losing her balance she fell to the ground. Her torch flew from her hand and bounced off one of the uprights, landing on her back.

Dvorah screamed as she felt the heat and the flame begin to consume her dress. She rolled over to smother the flames but only succeeded in rolling onto the torch itself.

More flames embraced her as the fire in the cavern sucked air from her lungs. Struggling to breathe, she staggered to her feet, only to collide with the upright she had accidentally set aflame. As she slipped to the ground, she automatically clung to the post, scorching her arms.

Screaming in pain as she fell to the ground, she cried out, just before the flames completely consumed her:

"Shaul, I come to you!"

Chapter One Hundred & Forty-Five
28 May 70 CE / 29 Iyyar 3830

Rabbi Aaron stood on the rampart of the northeast tower of Antonia staring at the newest threat to the City: two enormous Roman platforms facing Antonia. Hard by the Tomb of John Hyrcanus were two other platforms of the same size. All four platforms had been built in seventeen days.

For three days the Jews had resisted Roman attempts to recapture the area inside the second wall. On the fourth day Titus succeeded. He threw down the northern stretch of the wall from end to end and placed garrisons on the towers of the portions toward the south. Now his target was the first wall, the last remaining wall protecting Jerusalem.

Jerusalem's misfortunes had increased. As food stocks decreased, hunger and famine stalked the City. More people deserted, the rich selling their property, swallowing their gold pieces to take with them in exile, swallowing them so they would not be robbed by the partisans if caught or by bandits once on the road. Titus let deserters go through his lines unmolested. The partisans tried to stop them, often succeeding. Others were not so lucky. Jews who were not deserting and were caught outside the City searching for food in the valleys were crucified in sight of the City. Some days hundreds fell into Titus' hands and were scourged and crucified. Sometimes the soldiers who nailed their victims to the crossbar placed them in various upright positions as a grim joke.

It was not easy time for the Romans, either. They paid a heavy price in toil and blood to raise those platforms. Because the area around Jerusalem had been stripped of trees, the Romans had to go miles to collect the timber. Because of Jewish missiles aimed at them, the Romans suffered many casualties at the hands of the Jewish defenders who had finally learned to use all the war engines they had in their possession, including 300 spear-throwers and forty stone-throwers. The men working at Antonia were hindered by John ben Levi's men and the Kannaim; the men at the Tomb of John Hyrcanus by Simon ben Gioras' men and the Idumaeans.

But just as the partisans refused to give up the struggle despite the screams of the Jews being crucified outside the City walls, the Romans persisted in the building of their platforms made of earth and timber.

And now, with their war engines moved atop the platforms facing Antonia, Rabbi Aaron wondered if this were the beginning of the end for Jerusalem

"I better get out of here," he muttered, "before the Romans begin their bombardment."

There was no one to hear him. He was alone on the rampart. Indeed, there were no defenders on the wall of Antonia or the north wall of the Temple complex.

It's strange, he thought. All the defenders have disappeared. There's no one to oppose the Roman invaders.

Rabbi Aaron sighed. He knew he should get moving but he tapped his feet impatiently, not knowing why.

Let them hit me with one of their stones, or spears, or arrows, he thought. God has abandoned Jerusalem and I am ready to die.

Rabbi Aaron thrust out his chest. His eyes blazed with fury.

And then the most amazing thing happened. The platform nearest Antonia collapsed. A dense cloud of smoke and dust billowed from the newly created cavity. A brilliant flame broke through the smoke and dust.

A few moments later the same thing happened to the other tower.

Rabbi Aaron raised his arms and face toward the heavens. His face glowing with joy, he cried:

"Praised be the Almighty! Praised be the Master of the Universe, Who delivers miracles to His people!"

Chapter One Hundred & Forty-Six

29 May 70 CE / 1 Sivan 3830

Judah was hungry but had no appetite. He picked with his spoon at the bowl of barley he had prepared.

Rabbi Aaron ate his bowl of barley, which Judah had also prepared, with relish. He was in an ebullient mood, every once in a while chattering that God had delivered a miracle yesterday when the Roman platforms outside Antonia collapsed.

Judah's explanation of why the collapse occurred—John's men building a tunnel from Antonia to the ground underneath the platforms, supporting the roof of the mines with wooden posts that were then burned away once the war engines were moved to the platforms—did nothing to dampen the rabbi's enthusiasm.

"John's stratagem was God's instrument to deliver us from the Romans!" Rabbi Aaron exclaimed.

There was still the problem of the two platforms by the Tomb of John Hyrcanus.

Tomorrow Judah would be joining Simon's expeditionary force in the attempt to destroy them.

Judah stared down at his barley with disgust. Despite having sweetened it with the last drops of date honey, his stomach revolted at the prospect of eating it.

"We haven't had meat, fish, or cheese in weeks," he grumbled.

Rabbi Aaron smiled.

"The Children of Israel complained that they had no fish after they were freed from slavery in Egypt. They cried for the fleshpots of Pharaoh," he said.

The old man is crazy, Judah thought.

"What's really bothering you, Judah," Rabbi Aaron began, his tone now matter-of-fact but sympathetic, "is that Dvorah left you."

The words struck Judah like a slap in the face.

It's true, he thought. The crazy old man is right. I miss Dvorah. In truth, I'm heartbroken.

Judah's fingers drummed the table. He followed their motion as he took several deep breaths.

As soon as Judah had been told that Dvorah left he began searching for her, abandoning the battles around the second wall. It took a few days, but he learned that she had joined John's fighters. He went to the Temple complex to see her.

The guards at the entrance, recognizing him, refused entrance. They knew why he had come.

"We can't let you in," one of them said.

"I demand to see my wife!" Judah thundered.

"We don't want to hurt you, Judah," another said apologetically, as it appeared that Judah was about to pull out a knife. "Those are our orders, directly from John himself."

"I demand to see him!" Judah cried, his right hand dropping empty to his side. I'll kill him if he's sleeping with her, Judah thought.

Judah waited as one of the guards went to fetch John.

It was not long before John appeared.

"Hello, old friend," John greeted Judah. Then, seeing the look on Judah's face, he put both palms open and out facing Judah and exclaimed:

"Judah, I swear I have not touched her. Neither has anyone else. She's here because she wants to fight the Romans and you won't let her."

"She's pregnant! She's carrying our child. The battlefield is no place for a pregnant woman!"

John ben Levi sighed.

"In normal times you would be right," he said. "These are not normal times. All of Jerusalem is a battlefield. She wants to die here, Judah, she wants to die before the baby is brought into this world. And if we're to be honest, we're all going to die here before this war is over."

"At least let me see her and talk to her," Judah pleaded.

"She doesn't want to see you, Judah. She made that very clear. We all tried to convince her that it wasn't right, but she wouldn't listen. She said she loves you, but she does not want to see you."

Judah was devastated. He believed John. He bowed his head and returned to the house of Rabbi Aaron. There was nothing Judah could do.

Judah stopped drumming. He looked up at Rabbi Aaron.

"You are right, Rabbi," he said sighing.

Rabbi Aaron clucked sympathetically.

There was a knock at the door.

John ben Levi stepped into the house.

He wore a glum expression on his face.

"Congratulations, John," Judah said immediately. "That was a brilliant move against the Roman platforms. Tomorrow is our turn. It won't be quite as brilliant."

"I have bad news, Judah," John said heavily. "Dvorah was killed when the tunnel collapsed."

An agonized scream erupted from Judah. Tears flooded his eyes. Then he laid his head on the table, sobs wracking his body. He wept for Dvorah, for Shaul, even for Rabbi Aaron's brother, Rabbi Moshe, whom he had ordered Shaul to kill. And he wept for all those who had died in Jerusalem and in the Land beyond.

Judah barely heard John ben Levi as he offered condolences and then took his leave.

Rabbi Aaron rose from his seat and put a hand on Judah's shoulder.

"Judah, her soul is in a better place now."

His words gave Judah some slight comfort as he continued weeping. When at last he stopped he looked up at Rabbi Aaron with reddened eyes.

"Where did we go wrong?"

Rabbi Aaron sighed.

"We, Judah? We?"

"I did what I thought was right!" Judah replied with desperation. "How could we continue to live under tyranny?"

"You started a war the people did not want. You started a war the Torah scholars opposed."

"Not all the scholars!"

"The majority, Judah, the majority. And you perverted the process by which they arrive at their decisions by sending your robbers into the rabbinical assembly. You upended generations of tradition with your violence."

"If a man knows what is right isn't he obligated to do it?" Judah asked, pounding on the table for emphasis.

Rabbi Aaron gazed down at him sadly.

"Does not Scripture say: 'In those days there was no king in Israel; every man did that which was right in his own eyes'? Those times of anarchy, there was much unrighteousness. That is what you have brought upon us, Judah, anarchy and unrighteousness."

"I did not do it for gain, or lust, or glory," exclaimed Judah.

"It does not matter. Your sin was arrogance; not simply holding to your opinion but arrogating to yourself the right to force it on the rest of the community."

"I behaved honorably. I strove not to kill my fellow Jews. I even tried to stop the massacre of Metilius' men."

"In the end it does not matter, Judah. You did more damage than a man like Dorcas, the man who killed my brother."

Judah trembled. His breath failed him and he had to fight for air. Rabbi Aaron continued looking sternly down at him.

"Rabbi Aaron," Judah began, barely able to speak, "I have a confession to make."

Rabbi Aaron looked puzzled.

"I am responsible for your brother's death."

Rabbi Aaron gasped. His eyes widened. He took a step backwards.

"I ordered Shaul ben Yitzchak to carry out the act, but the responsibility is mine. I wanted you to know. Please, never tell your son Reuven…"

Judah, who had been looking up at Rabbi Aaron pleadingly, averted his eyes and stared at the table.

"Why are you telling *me*?" Rabbi Aaron asked incredulously. "Why are you telling me *now*?"

"Tomorrow I go to meet the Romans in battle. To meet my death."

"I cannot grant you absolution, Judah. You must live, and die, with your guilt."

Strange guttural sounds came from Judah's throat. He nodded and rose from the chair. He walked to the door, his eyes downcast, afraid to look Rabbi Aaron in the eye.

Then he left the house of Rabbi Aaron, never to return.

Chapter One Hundred & Forty-Seven

30 May 70 CE / 2 Sivan 3830

I should run away, thought Amram. It's dangerous here. I'll get killed.

Amram could not move. He was rooted to the spot, watching with fascination and awe.

Hard by the Tomb of John Hyrcanus, Roman battering rams were rocking the last wall protecting Jerusalem. A little longer and it certainly would be breached. Then, lo, three Jews ran out with firebrands. They began setting the artillery on fire. Despite being attacked on all sides they did not waiver and only withdrew when the engines were blazing.

Flames shot from the rams. Romans came running from their nearby fortification to save the artillery. Jews rushed from the wall to stop them. The two sides embraced in a ferocious grappling.

Amram looked up at Rufus. The red-haired Roman had a look of utter astonishment on his face.

Amram had already been hearing the rumblings in the Roman camp, among officers and enlisted personnel alike. Stubborn Jewish resistance was sapping Roman morale. With every victory the Jews whooped and crowed; every defeat only increased their willingness to fight on. Roman platforms, war engines, discipline and training still had not overcome the strength of the wall or the inner courage and determination of the Jewish fighting men.

Would more Roman toil and blood be the price of the eventual conquest of Jerusalem?

Yes, answered Amram, with excitement.

Amid the flames the Romans pulled at the battering rams; the Jews pulled the other way. The fires spread to the platforms.

More and more Jews came from the walls, overwhelming the Romans, who began to withdraw toward their camp. Amram, along with Rufus, joined the retreat.

The partisans pressed on, with swords, spears, javelins and burning torches, following the Romans as they fled. The fighting was now taking place at the edge of the Roman fortification.

Fear was gone from Amram's mind. He watched with excitement, praying for Jewish victory.

Rufus had drawn his sword and raised his shield.

He's preparing to enter the fray, Amram thought. Should I try to stop him? How?

Fear once again entered Amram's mind and made him immobile.

Amram's eyes moved back and forth, feverishly scanning the melee. To his surprise, he made out the face and form of one of the men he had taken to Yavne, Judah ben Ezra.

As Judah fought, he came closer to Amram and Rufus.

A pitched battle began between Judah and a Roman. It became clear after a moment that Judah, his back to Amram and Rufus, was gaining the advantage.

Rufus strode quickly toward Judah, his sword raised.

Amram shivered. No, no, he thought. I can't.

And then:

"Judah ben Ezra!" Amram shouted as loudly as he could, "Watch your back!"

Rufus whirled, a look of rage on his face. For a moment he hesitated.

It was enough time for Judah to finish off his opponent, but not enough time to defend himself from Rufus' attack.

Judah fell to the ground, bleeding heavily from his side.

Rufus turned back to Amram and walked slowly toward him.

Amram was too frightened to run.

"You little Jewish worm," he spat. "This is the end of you."

Rufus raised his sword as he glared at Amram.

And then, lo, a second amazing thing happened.

Judah had staggered to his feet. A blazing torch was in his hand.

"Vespasian!" Judah shouted.

Rufus turned. Judah was already upon him. Amram watched Judah's torch move from Rufus' head down the length of his body. The Roman intelligence officer screamed in horror and ran, himself now a flaming human torch.

Judah came up to Amram. He threw the torch away and collapsed at Amram's feet.

"You're a good man, Amram ben Gedalyahu," Judah muttered hoarsely. "You're a good Jew."

Judah stretched out at Amram's feet. Amram watched the life slowly fade from the Jewish partisan.

Amram lifted his voice to the heavens and cried:

"Praise be the Master of the Universe, who grants victory to His people!"

And then an arrow from a Jewish bow pierced Amram ben Gedalyahu's chest and he fell to the ground beside Judah ben Ezra.

Chapter One Hundred & Forty-Eight

28 June 70 CE / 1 Tammuz 3830

"The Lord of Hosts has abandoned His people!"

Rabbi Aaron groaned in despair.

He stood on the rampart of the northeast tower of Antonia watching the Romans complete work on the biggest platforms yet, platforms rising in four sections facing Antonia.

Rabbi Aaron clutched at the parapet.

Soon they will put an end to our misery, he thought, an end to the starvation, an end to the unburied corpses, and an end to the jackals feeding on those unburied Jewish dead in the valleys.

The words of Scripture came back to him:

"…these curses shall come upon thee…The LORD will cause thee to be smitten before thine enemies; … The LORD will smite thee with madness…The LORD will bring a nation against thee from far…And he shall besiege thee in all thy gates, until thy high and fortified walls come down…And thou shalt eat the fruit of thine own body, the flesh of thy sons and of thy daughters… In the morning thou shalt say: 'Would it were evening!' and at evening thou shalt say: 'Would it were morning!'"

Surely this prophecy was coming to pass!

A month ago Jewish fighters had destroyed the two platforms near the Tomb of John Hyrcanus. That was the last Jewish victory.

The Roman response was to cease attacks. They built an earthen siege wall that completely encircled the City, going down even into the valleys. On top of the wall they built a series of forts, thirteen of them. The entire circumvallation was built so quickly it seemed to Rabbi Aaron that Heaven must have speeded its completion.

The Romans scrupulously patrolled the intervals between the forts. Rabbi Aaron was no military man but he understood what Titus' intentions were. Weaken the City through starvation and then resume the attack.

The plan was clearly working.

Jerusalem was completely cut off from the outside world. No longer could any food be brought in. Because the City was invested people could not go out to gather anything edible. The price of grain rose astronomically. A tiny bunch of hay sold for four denarii. People ate leather, searched sewers and dunghills for scraps. As the famine intensified people already weak from hunger died, so many that the bodies were stacked one on the other in the larger houses or else thrown over the City wall into the valleys. The howls of jackals fighting over the human flesh could be heard throughout the dying City.

Rabbi Aaron, though he still had money left, was reduced to eating once a day. When evening came, the rabbi, faint from hunger, would try to sleep until the next morning when he would have a small bowl of barley.

Amidst all this were reports of partisans breaking into houses to steal the people's food so they themselves would have the strength to continue fighting, for the partisans had no intention of surrendering.

The Romans fiendishly added to the suffering by displaying their plentiful supplies of food in front of the wall.

As all this was taking hold, Titus built the platforms now facing Antonia. Rabbi Aaron was convinced these platforms must have been harder to build than the previous ones. The Romans certainly had to go farther to get the timber to build them, because everything had already been stripped away from the immediate surroundings of Jerusalem. The Romans completed the platforms in twenty-one days.

Rabbi Aaron sighed. His eyes grew wide with wonder. For as he watched the Romans finish their work, the partisans, who had made no attempt to stop the construction of the circumvallation nor hinder the building of these newest platforms, were rushing out, torches in hand, to attack.

The fight is still in them, Rabbi Aaron thought with amazement.

It soon became apparent that the fearlessness and tenacity the partisans had exhibited in previous clashes were missing now. The forward line did not plow heedlessly into the enemy, there was no massed charge that followed. There were only small groups of men who fell back against the solid Roman defense without further engaging the enemy. Rather than boldness and the refusal to accept defeat, confusion and hesitation bedeviled the partisans.

This feeble attempt ended in failure. The Romans, while bombarding Antonia from the platforms, began bringing up the battering rams. Though the Jews fought back from Antonia itself using firebrands, rocks, arrows, and spears, they could not stop the Romans from delivering the battering rams and begin the shaking of the wall.

Rabbi Aaron stood tall and resolute on the tower. He did not duck or run for cover from the bombardment.

It is not my day to die, he thought. That will come soon enough. A day or two at most, and the Romans will have everything.

Chapter One Hundred & Forty-Nine

5 Aug 70 CE / 10 Av 3830

Drusilla opened her eyes. Reuven's moaning and thrashing on the other side of the bed had wakened her.

It must be past midnight, she thought. Poor Reuven is having a nightmare.

Drusilla sat up. In the bed between them Shaul Moshe slept peacefully. To her right Tikva was sleeping in her own little bed.

Reuven groaned loudly and muttered something inaudible.

What is he dreaming? Is he reliving battles?

Drusilla sighed. She had no nightmares, instead worries about her father-in-law, her friend Dvorah, and Judah, plagued her during waking moments. Were they faring well?

Were they alive?

Terrible tales were drifting down from Jerusalem. Were they just wild rumors or were they true? There was no way for her to know.

She had heard that the famine was so bad people ate whatever scraps of food they could find, combing through sewers and eating leather. Drusilla could believe this.

There was also a fantastical tale of a woman who slaughtered and roasted her own child, offering it to the partisans who burst into her house demanding a portion of her food.

This Drusilla did not believe.

There were two other stories Drusilla heard, both which she judged to be possible. Those who managed to desert Jerusalem and make their way to Roman lines were allowed to pass through. Some of those who were close to starvation were wise enough to take the unaccustomed food a little at a time; others were foolish and stuffed their empty stomachs non-stop till they burst. There was a different fate for other refugees who thought they were now safe behind forward Roman lines. Many Jews were caught by Syrians soldiers, and even legionaries, who killed them and slit their bellies open searching for gold, all because a Syrian had seen a refugee pick gold coins from his excreta, causing the rumor to go around that all the Jews had swallowed their gold before fleeing Jerusalem.

Drusilla shivered.

Who knew the truth? she asked herself. In this war, the most horrible stories might be true!

Reuven began to cry out loudly. Shaul Moshe started to stir. Tikva remained sleeping.

Reuven shouted in his sleep. Drusilla leaned over and shook him awake.

"What is wrong, my dear? What were you dreaming?"

She ran her hand over his forehead. It was beaded in cold sweat. He was shaking.

For several moments he said nothing. Then his trembling stopped and he seemed calmer. In the dim lamplight a resolute expression appeared on his face.

"I dreamed of Father," he said. "He's in trouble. He needs me. I must go to him and bring him out of Jerusalem. I must leave at first light."

Tears began to drop from Drusilla's eyes.

This time, she knew, there would be no stopping Reuven.

Chapter One Hundred & Fifty
5 Aug 70 CE / 10 Av 3830

Rabbi Aaron huddled in a far dark corner. The sounds of fighting filtered through the heavy doors of his hiding place in the southeast chamber of the inner court of the Temple. Others, too, were in the dim light, trying to escape the bloody mayhem in the Temple courts outside.

The inner court and the Temple were no longer a place of animal slaughter. The daily Temple sacrifice had ceased twenty-two days ago. Now, it was human beings who were slaughtered in its environs.

It was thirty-eight days since Rabbi Aaron stood on the rampart of the northeast tower of Antonia, watching the Romans complete work on their biggest platforms yet and seeing the failed partisan attempt to stop them. That night, after incessant pounding by the rams, the wall collapsed, weakened by the tunnel underneath dug by John ben Levi's men to bring down the earlier platforms.

From then on, the Roman advance was inexorable. Four days later the Romans took possession of Antonia. Fighting still continued—the partisans not having abandoned their stubborn, ferocious resistance— but while the Jews defending the Temple had their minor victories, small successful stratagems, and battles that ended in a draw, the eventual outcome was clear to Romans and Jews alike.

The Romans continued their methodical conquest. Antonia, after a week of work, was laid flat and a wide road built to the Temple. Construction was started on four new platforms: One opposite the northwest corner of the inner court, one near the northern arcade between the two gates, one opposite the western colonnade of the outer court, the other opposite the northern colonnade. Roman advances once again came at a cost in toil and blood extracted by partisan tenacity that only postponed by days the inevitable.

Fighting moved to the colonnades, portions of which were then fired by both sides. Two days ago platforms were completed, rams brought up opposite the western recess of the outer court, and attempts made to scale the outer wall of the Temple with siege ladders. The wall held against the pounding; the initial attempts to scale the wall failed.

Yesterday the Roman troops succeeded in seizing the outer court of the Temple.

That is when Rabbi Aaron, who throughout the conflict had been following the battles at a safe distance, fled to the chamber in the inner court. He had spent the last night slumped against a wall in fitful sleep, tormented by disturbing and terrifying dreams.

Rabbi Aaron was grateful that his sons were safe in Yavne and that they were looking out for Ruth, Drusilla, and Tikva.

That rascal younger son of mine, in the end he saved the family. Even his theft of money from Elimelech, without that who knows what condition they would be in? Ach, what is the meaning of all this? Is there any? Is The Holy One, Blessed be He, simply a trickster, playing with us the way Tikva plays with her rag dolls?

And what was Drusilla's second child? A boy? A girl? I'll never know...If it's a boy I hope she named him after my brother Moshe. The child must be about six months old now.

I hope Benjamin finds a good wife. No, don't think that! Drusilla is wonderful. In truth I'm lucky! Her wisdom will hold the family together.

Did Reuven fall in love with her because of her wisdom? Ach, of course not. It was lust, lust, pure and simple. But he loves her for her wisdom now, I'm sure of it! Lust! Ah, remember what you felt when you looked at Bruria after Moshe's death? Death? No murder!

Judah! Judah! I should hate you but I have no strength for hate anymore. I found out what happened to you after you left my house. You were right, you did meet your death. Was that the price God extracted for your crimes?

But it was a noble death! Or was it? You and your comrades destroyed the Roman platforms.

To what end? It did not stop the pagans from polluting our sanctuary; it only hastened it. Even now they have penetrated the inner court of the Temple!

Bruria! What happened to her? Did Judah kill her, too? Why would he do that? Did he know something about her disappearance? Where is she? Ah, that is another thing I will never know.

There is one thing I do realize now. The very tall and large woman in a gray dress that Reuven said was a possible witness to my brother's murder; that was no woman! That was Reuven's friend Shaul in disguise. Shaul ben Yitzchak! Reuven's friend! Faugh! My son will never learn the truth!

Is it better that way?

And Metilius, why were his men slaughtered on the Sabbath, breaking a solemn agreement? It drove him to suicide. Why, oh why?

So many things, so many things I do not know or understand. I am not afraid to die, at least I think I am not, we shall see, but still, why can't I live long enough to learn the answers?

Ah, if Drusilla only knew! Our discussions, arguments, no debates…She would read Philo to me, and we would argue, little did she know the doubts she planted in me! Doubts that even she does not have! Doubts that have grown…

My Lord, why have you abandoned your people?

Rabbi Aaron smelled smoke. He opened the door to his chamber and stepped out.

The Temple was blazing. Wood aflame, stone blackening, gold and silver melting, running like rivulets.

The heat was intense. Roman soldiers shouted and cursed, Jews screamed with agony as they were slaughtered.

"Is this the end of the Jewish people and Torah?" Rabbi Aaron cried out to the maelstrom.

"No!" he shouted defiantly. "There is still Yavne!"

A Roman soldier came toward him with raised sword. Rabbi Aaron ran to the fourteen steps that led to the Bronze Gate. He ascended to the very edge of the conflagration. He turned to his pursuer, who looked back up at him in amazement.

Rabbi Aaron hesitated only for a moment.

Chanting, as loudly as he could, "Hear, Oh Israel, the Lord is our God, the Lord is One," Rabbi Aaron leaped into the raging inferno.

Chapter One Hundred & Fifty-One

7 Aug 70 CE / 12 Av 3830

Reuven adjusted the pack on his back. It was filled with food for his father. In the folds of his cloak were gold aurei, his knife, his sling and stones, and the all-important documents from Emperor Vespasian.

It was early in the second day of his journey to Jerusalem to rescue his father. He had begun the ascent from the coastal plain to the hill country. There was not much traffic on the road. Occasionally he saw groups of people heading away from Jerusalem. Groups, never solitary travelers. Many looked bedraggled and weary. Reuven saw no one else going toward the capital city. A few times mounted Roman patrols passed him in either direction. No one spoke to him, and he spoke to no one.

Once in a while Reuven stopped and took a deep breath. The air was fresh, the trees green and full, the grass off the road was lush. It would have been a pleasant hike for him if not for the urgency of the mission.

Father will have to come back with me, Reuven thought, whether he wants to or not. If he refuses, I'll take him by force, if necessary. I'm stronger than him now. And I have the money to bribe the revolutionaries so they will allow the both of us to leave, and the letters from the emperor that will get me through Roman lines. Father has to listen to reason and come back with me; just as a son is bound to obey a father, a father is bound to obey a son.

Reuven stopped his hike. He screwed up his face in puzzlement. He idly kicked at a stone.

That last thought makes no sense. I'm not thinking straight. Besides, I never obeyed my father! Oh, if Drusilla were with me, she could convince him. Quote Scripture, or some rabbi. Oh Father, why did you leave Yavne?

Reuven was under no illusion that he could convince Dvorah or Judah to come with him, as much as he wanted to bring them back. They were too committed to the struggle.

Ah, Judah, he thought, you and I could have gone off with Hiram to Barbarikon! And Dvorah, what good friends you and Drusilla became!

Reuven was now about twelve miles from Jerusalem. As he walked he kept his head down, looking only at his immediate surroundings. He did not want to look forward into the distance; he wanted to wait until he came to the two trees, their boughs and branches intertwined like lovers. That would be his sign; he would look up to see once again the dazzling snow-white mountain blazing with golden fire, the Temple, the heart of Jerusalem, his native City!

Reuven plodded onward.

The landscape began to change. Reuven did not understand why.

The larger trees had disappeared. Only their stumps remained.

Who could have chopped so many trees? he wondered. And why? Will my two embracing trees still be there?

Hours later he came to the spot where the two trees should be.

They were there!

Reuven lifted his head for inspiration and began to pray in expectation of the glorious view of the holy Temple of Jerusalem, the center of the Jewish people.

The prayer died in his throat. An agonized gasp emerged instead.

No dazzling snow-white mountain blazing with golden fire greeted his eyes. All he saw in the distance was smoke rising to the sky.

Reuven groaned. He cried out in despair. Then he collapsed to the hard ground at his feet.

Chapter One Hundred & Fifty-Two

9 Aug 70 CE / 14 Av 3830

Drusilla stood at the entrance to Yavne looking down the road that led to Jerusalem. In her arms was Shaul Moshe, suckling contentedly at her breast. At her sides, clutching her skirt, was Tikva.

It was late morning. The sun was already approaching the zenith. Drusilla was starting to sweat.

This was the second day in a row she stood waiting at the entrance to Yavne.

It was too soon for Reuven to come back with Rabbi Aaron, but she couldn't help herself. If there was any chance that Reuven managed to complete the task more quickly than expected she wanted to be there waiting for him.

Drusilla saw a man, head bowed, coming down the road.

"Daddy?" cried Tikva excitedly. "Is that Daddy?"

"No dear," replied Drusilla. "But perhaps this man has some news for us."

I hope so, she thought. This is the first traveler I've seen coming from the direction of Jerusalem. It must be an old man. He's very bent, though he must have been tall as a youth. His beard is white and so is his hair. Why is his head uncovered? That is very strange.

Strange, too, is the way he walks. He does not have the stride of an old man. I hope he has some news of the Holy City.

Drusilla waited. The man came closer. She felt a chill go down her spine as he approached.

The man raised his head. The skin on his upper cheeks and forehead was still youthful and smooth, but the whiteness of his hair and beard matched his hollow, sunken eyes.

It was Reuven.

The End

Epilogue

It took the Romans another month, and much fighting, to conquer all of Jerusalem. The cost of the war was horrific: hundreds of thousands died in the siege of Jerusalem alone.

Both John ben Levi and Simon ben Gioras did not die fighting; they were captured by the Romans. John was sentenced to life imprisonment; Simon was kept for Titus' triumphal procession and ultimate execution. Emperor Vespasian died 24 June 79 at the age of 69. He was succeeded by his son Titus who ruled for two years until his death on 13 September 81 at the age of 41. Shortly after Titus' death, his younger brother, Emperor Domitian, constructed the Arch of Titus, which still stands in Rome today. The arch commemorates Titus's victories, including the Siege of Jerusalem. On the arch is a relief showing spoils from the siege, including the menorah from the Temple.

The loss of the war and the Temple did not spell the end of the Jewish people or their religion. Yavne kept the flame of Jewish learning alive. And, 2,000 years after the defeat, the Jews returned to rebuild their ancestral homeland and capital.

Ruth remained a widow for the rest of her life. Benjamin married the daughter of a rabbi and had many children. Reuven and Drusilla went on to have more children. Among their descendants were famous rabbis, philosophers, scientists, writers, and artists.

As for Reuven himself, that is a subject for another story.

Appendix A: Author's Afterword

Historical novels are strange creatures. They're not quite history and not totally imaginative fiction. The events in a historical novel are supposed to occur in a specific time and place and should exhibit a certain amount of fealty to the actual period of the novel. How much is the question.

I hung my tale on the framework provided by Josephus' *The Jewish War*. While *The Sikarikin* is not history as such, I tried to make the retelling of the lives of my characters—Judah, Reuven, Rabbi Aaron, Drusilla, Shaul, Dvorah, and all the others—fit into a real historical era, and I tried to make the events, descriptions, and atmosphere as realistic as I could.

This required a great deal of research. Often, there was a conflict between the story I wanted to tell and the actual historical truth. I almost always chose the latter.

Every successful historical novelist I've heard speak always said the same thing: They did their research and then ignored it while writing the novel.

I wish I could have done the same thing! I'd have saved myself a lot of agita. In addition to the intensive research I did before beginning the actual writing, I found myself constantly stopping the work to look something up. I had to do this even when writing the last few chapters.

I am not a trained historian. My degrees are in physics and I made my living as a software engineer in the space program. As I dug into topics trying to get information I was amazed to find that historians often disagreed with each other.

Here's the rule I used: If a credible scholar took a position that fit the narrative I wanted, I took it, even if it was a minority position. I'm sure there are rabbis, who for their own reasons, and scholars, for theirs, who will say I got this or that wrong. In general, I found some source that backed up what I wanted. If I couldn't, I did not go in that direction.

Now, there were a few times I broke that rule. The issuing of the "Eighteen Decrees", which is recorded in the Talmud, does not have a date associated with it but was said to have occurred during a different time of year than I put it in the novel. I put it where I did for dramatic reasons.

There are many characters in the novel. Some are in the historical record, some are not. Those who are in the historical record are rarely point-of-view characters, and I tried to treat them as close to the historical record as I could.

There are two exceptions to this. Metilius is given one line in Josephus. I turn him into a full-fledged character. His end is the same as that of one of the people described elsewhere in The Jewish War. I leave it to the reader to decide if they met their fates for the same reason. John Dorcas, while having the same evil nature as the John Dorcas in Josephus, has a much larger role in my book.

A few other points.

With regard to my characters' use of Hebrew instead of Aramaic, I'm aware that most historians claim that Aramaic, not Hebrew, was the language of the Jews of this period. Most, not all.

Once in a while I lifted parts of sentences from the Williamson translation of Josephus' *The Jewish War*. This was deliberate. It made me feel that the tale I was telling was closer to the actual happenings being described. Which brings me to my last point.

There are characters in *The Sikarikin* who, though not in the historical record, are as real as the ones that can be found in written histories. Unfortunately their lives were not recorded anywhere else except in these pages. I truly believe that if Dr. Who were to pay me a visit and offer a trip in the Tardis to the time and place of *The Sikarikin*, I would find the gap-toothed revolutionary Judah, the thoughtful and tormented Rabbi Aaron, and the wily but romantic Reuven. It is out of loyalty to them and all the others who never made it into the history books that I tried to make this novel as true to the real world in which they lived as possible. They deserve no less.

Appendix B: Sources

The main research source for *The Sikarikin* was Josephus's *The Jewish War*. I read and made notes from the G. A. Williamson translation with notes and appendices by E. Mary Smallwood. Ms. Smallwood's comments were very helpful in giving context and more than once I used her insights in the novel. I used the Barnes and Noble NOOK version of the Penguin Books edition. (Occasionally I looked at the William Whiston translation.)

Another important resource was the model of Jerusalem in the Second Temple Period at the Israel Museum in Jerusalem. Over the years I made several visits to the model. At my last visit I took hundreds of photos with a digital camera. The model gave me an actual physical image to use in placing the events in Jerusalem.

One of my earliest sources, in addition to *The Jewish War*, was the Babylonian Talmud's Gitten 55-56, a later rabbinical version of the war.

And, while it was not a research source, the quote given at the beginning of *The Sikarikin* from Walter Laqueur's *The History of Zionism* was one of the two inspirations for this novel.

What follows is a list of the main sources I used for research. (There were many others I used for bits of information.)

- Josephus: *The Jewish War*
- The model of Jerusalem in the Second Temple Period at the Israel Museum
- Babylonian Talmud: Gitten 55-56.
- Jerusalem Talmud: Shabbat 1:4 (3C)
- Henri Daniel-Rops *Daily Life in the Time of Jesus*
- "Periplus of the Erythraean Sea" in *The Commerce and Navigation of the Erythraean Sea* (translated by J. W. McCrindle 1879) Project Gutenberg e-book.
- Haim Shapira "The Schools of Hillel and Shammai"
- Israel Ben-Shalom *The School of Shammai and the Zealots' Struggle against Rome* (In Hebrew)
- The Burnt House in the Wohl Architecture Museum in Jerusalem
- The Israel Museum in Jerusalem
- Jewish Encyclopedia
- The Jewish Virtual Library
- The Flavius Joseph website by J. J. Goldberg.

- Marriage and Divorce in the Herodian Family: A Case Study of Diversity in Late Second Temple Judaism by Ingrid Johanne Moen
- Josephus "Antiquities of the Jews" Book XVIII
- Ruth Rabbah
- Pesikta de Rav Kahana, Nachamu 16.1
- Forum Ancient Coins
- Wikipedia articles
- Google maps

Appendix C: Dates given in The Sikarikin:

In *The Sikarikin*, at the top of each chapter, I give dates in the Julian calendar followed by the corresponding date in the Hebrew calendar. (Note: The Hebrew day begins at sundown on the previous Julian day, so some chapters have the same Julian date but different Hebrew dates.)

To correlate Hebrew dates with Julian dates, I used the website "Rosetta Calendar" by Scott E. Lee. (http://www.rosettacalendar.com/) Mr. Lee even provides the source code in C for his calculations.

Josephus, in *The Jewish War*, reports dates using the Macedonian names for months. There is a historical debate about what those names refer to: The Syro-Macedonian calendar, the Hebrew calendar, or the Roman calendar. (See "Appendix 2: The Calendars of Josephus" in *Eusebian Chronography* by Richard W. Burgess and Witold Witakowsky.)

In some cases, it's clear that Josephus is referring to the Hebrew calendar. For example, the takeover of the inner Temple from Eleazar ben Simon by John ben Levi is reported as happening when "the day of Unleavened Bread arrived (the 14th of Xanthicos.)" Here, Xanthicos clearly means Nisan, as Passover begins on the 15th of Nisan.

However, sometimes it's clear that Josephus is referring to the Syro-Macedonian calendar. The death of Vitellius is reported as occurring on the 3rd of Apellaios. If we use Benedict Niese's calculation of adding 18 days to the corresponding Julian month, we come up with Dec 21, which agrees with the historical record.

For events in the novel that correspond to events in Josephus' *The Jewish War*, I made the simplifying assumption that the month names refer to the Hebrew calendar.

Appendix D: Maps

General Map of Land of Israel First Century
with some of the locations mentioned in the novel

Jerusalem 70 CE

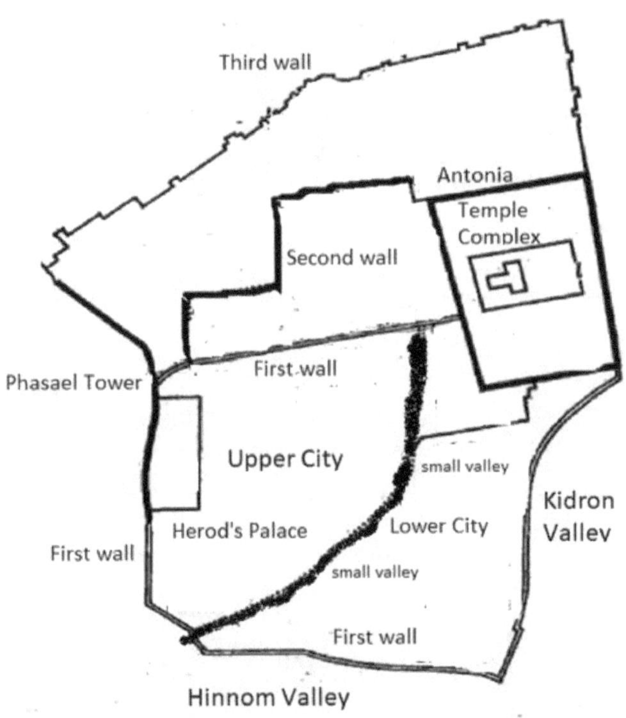

Author Bio

Harry Steven Lazerus was born in Brooklyn in the last century. He's lived in New York, Israel, Texas, Chicago, Thailand, and a work cubicle in California. Harry has degrees in physics and taught physics and astronomy at CCNY, worked as a software engineer in the space program, and picked apples in Kibbutz Tsuba. His op-ed column, "The Contrarian", appeared in Houston's Change Magazine from 2011 to 2015. His short stories have appeared in more than a dozen online and print magazines; "Becky" won Anotherealm's Higney Award for 2009. In 2017, Spuyten Duyvil published a collection of his short stories, *Thirteen Tales from the Hippocampus*.